FEN-WOLF

S. PITT.

'Cattle die; kindred die;
every man is mortal.
But there is one thing that never dies:
the fame he leaves behind.'

Firsthale

Glossary

Balter: fictional term for *bolas*, a hunting weapon of three or more stones or balls of clay connected by lengths of rope, designed to entangle an animal's legs and bring it down.

Byrnie: Anglo-Saxon word for mailcoat, usually of scale armour rather than chain-mail.

Carucate: ploughland (originally the area that could be ploughed by an eight-ox team in a day).

Danegeld: originally the tribute money paid to the Danes by Aethelred II, then an annual tax paid for protection from the Danes; the area of England upon which the tax was imposed.

Demesne: land whose produce is intended for the landlord.

Fyrd: the English levy.

Hauberk: mailcoat, usually 'chain' or ring mail.

Hide: the standard unit for assessment of tax, notionally the amount of land that would support a single household.

Hundred: an administrative division of the Shire with fiscal, judicial and military functions, notionally comprising 100 hides.

Vill: settlement (strictly an administrative area smaller than a Hundred which might contain one or more settlements).

Wapentake: an administrative division equivalent to the Hundred in northern and eastern England.

List of Characters

Acer the Hard: a Fen-wolf, second-in-command to Hereward
Ade the Crone: an aged bondswoman at Bourne.
Aedgifu: 'the Golden,' eldest daughter of Hereward and Turfrida.
Aelfgar: see Hereward.
Aelgytha: Eadgytha's sister, wife of Cole One-Hand.
Athelric: Bishop of Borough Abbey (St. Peter's).
Athelwine: Bishop of Durham. Brother of Athelric, bishop of Borough.
Athelwold: prior of Borough Abbey.
Aldred: Bishop of York. In 1066, one of the most powerful churchmen in
England.
Arnkell: a thegn in the service of Eorl Waltheof
Brand: Lady Godgifu's brother and therefore Hereward's uncle. A monk at
Borough who became abbot after Abbot Leofric's death.
Cole One-Hand: reeve or steward of Laughton.
Eadgytha: Toli's wife (Aelgytha's sister)
Eadric: son of Toli and Eadgytha. Held the estate of Bourne for Morcar.
Eadric the Wild: a rebel leader in the Welsh Borders area.
Edda: matriarch of the reed-cutters. One of the Gyrwas, the Fen-folk.
Edgar Atheling: one of the claimants to the English throne, grandson of
Edmund Ironside, the brother of King Athelred ('the unready').
Edward the Confessor: sometimes known as 'the pious,' King of England
from 1043-1066. He outlawed Hereward therefore Hereward could
only return to England after his death.
Edwin: eldest son of Aelfgar, therefore Morcar's brother and Hereward's
nephew. Eorl of Mercia.
Erik Winter: a refugee from the north along with his mother, Gerd.
De Warenne: Frederick: leader of the raid on Bourne.
De Warenne: William: brother of Frederick, Hereward's sworn enemy. .
Gamal Longbow: a Fen-wolf, a skilled archer.
Gilbert de Ghent: Hereward's godfather, possibly a son of Baldwin, ruler of
Flanders. According to legend, he kept caged wild animals and set
his young knights against them for sport. The 'Fairy Bear', his prize
possession, was killed by the young Hereward after he was outlawed
by Edward the Confessor.
Godgifu: youngest daughter of Hereward and Turfrida.
Gospatrick: a distant member of the English Royalty and Eorl of Bernicia.
Harald Hardrada: King of Norway and claimant to the English throne.
Harold Godwineson: King of England after Edward the Confessor's death.
Son of Godwine, Eorl of Wessex and East Anglia.
Hereward: son of Eorl Leofric of Mercia and Godgifu (Lady Godiva).
Leofric had two sons by his first wife, Aelfgifu: Burgheard and
Aelfgar, father of Edwin and Morcar. There was around a fifteen

year age gap between Aelfgar and Hereward. Leofric had Hereward outlawed and exiled by King's decree when he was about 18 years old.

Ivo Taillebois: a Norman knight, an enemy of Hereward from the war in Scaldemariland.

Leofric: Abbot of Borough (Peterborough) in 1066.

Leofric the Deacon: a monk of Borough who joined the rebellion.

Malcolm: King of Scotland

Marleswein: Sheriff of Lincolnshire

Martin Lightfoot: Hereward's companion and servant.

Morcar: younger son of Aelfgar, therefore Hereward's nephew. Became Eorl of Northumbria after Tostig Godwineson's exile.

Ogier the Breton: a mercenary in the Norman army who was given Bourne estate as a fiefdom.

Osbjorn: Sweyn of Denmark's brother

Outi and Douti: twin brothers, both Fen-wolves.

Rahere 'the Heron': eldest Fen-wolf. One of the Gyrwas (Fen-Folk).

Richard FitzRichard: castellan of York.

Siward Beorn: a Northumbrian thegn of Viking origin with a formidable reputation as a fighter.

Siward the Red: a Fen-wolf, named for his red hair.

Stigand: Archbishop of Canterbury. In 1066 the most powerful churchman in England and a major supporter of the Godwine family though he held his position without papal endorsement.

Sweyn: King of Denmark. Had two sons, Cnut and Harald.

Thorald: a clinchman, son of one of the original Fen-wolves.

Thorfin: one of Morcar's hus-carls from Northumbria

Thurstan: Abbot of Ely (St. Etheldreda's)

Toli: thegn of Laughton and Hereward's unofficial foster-father

Tostig Godwineson: Harold's brother. Eorl of Northumbria until the eorldom was given to Morcar, after Tostig was exiled.

Turfrida: Hereward's wife, a Flemish noblewoman

Turold: a warrior monk from France, appointed Brand's successor as Abbot of Borough by King William.

Ulfkil: abbot of Croyland Abbey (St. Guthlac's).

Waltheof: heir of Eorl Siward of Northumbria, passed over by King Edward in favour of Tostig Godwineson and given lands in Mercia instead.

William Malet: Norman Sheriff of York

William of Normandy: known as 'the Bastard' because he was illegitimate. Also called 'the Usurper' before gaining the title 'Conqueror' after invading and subjugating England.

Wuleric: groom at Bourne.

Ymma: Eadric of Bourne's wife.

FEN-WOLF

Part 1: Besetment

1. Spring, 1066

Soon after the appearance of the long-haired star, I came home.

Clad in the rich trappings and hauberk of a foreign knight, I rode vanguard on my warhorse, Tiw; my servant, Martin Lightfoot, escorted a light wagon. His chestnut palfrey ambled lazily save when the sour-faced wagoner flicked his whip. Then the gelding tossed its head but its pace increased no more than the mules'. Inside the wagon sat my wife, Turfrida, dark-haired and grey-eyed, and our daughter, Aedgifu, whose hair shone like oat-straw in the sun. They had pulled back the covers to see the country and the child smiled and waved to everyone we passed.

Tethered to the back of the wagon was another horse, a roan mare remarkable at first sight only for her ugliness. She was hammer-headed, ewe-necked and so lean her ribs stuck out like the hoops of a barrel. But none could match Swallow for speed.

Lambing was early and the weather mild (a good portent to set against the ill-omens, some said). The air was sweet with the scent of blossom, full of birdsong and the sound of sheep calling their young. After the fortified manors of Flanders and Maine, the open settlements and unguarded halls of Sussex were a welcome sight; woods and tillage appeared prosperous; the road to Mercia was well-tended and we made our way unmolested by cut-throats and beggars.

Nine years had passed since I was outlawed. England seemed a blessed land.

It was after noon, the fifth day from our sea-crossing, when we came within sight of the ancient lightning-blasted oak that marks the edge of Barholm Hundred. Martin pointed it out to Turfrida. She nodded. 'Are we come then to our lands?'

Martin did not reply but looked to me for guidance. He knew (as Turfrida did not), that the lands of my patrimony had been forfeit the day I was outlawed. My father, Leofric of Mercia, and Godgifu, my mother, had forsaken me as one abandons a rogue pup and, from pride, I had waited for fame to be my messenger (it came too late for my father, who died a few months later). With the passing of Aelfgar, my half-brother, five years on, the eorldom of Mercia should have been mine but instead it had gone to my nephew, Edwin. I was an outlaw, a nithing, and the King's death now could not change the past.

Once, I had imagined riding boldly to demand my inheritance but with no men to back me, my claim would have earned scorn rather than respect. Here in Lincolnshire there was but one place I was sure of a welcome. I avoided Turfrida's eyes and said roughly, 'Make for Laughton, I will ride ahead so the hall is ready.'

I urged Tiw forward and he sprang into a gallop. As we sped away, Martin's gaze bored into my back but I did not care.

The track bent, climbing the last ridge before the fens, and at last we left the hawthorn cover and came out into open pasture. With the wagon left far behind, I drew rein, laying one hand against the stallion's sweat-glossed shoulder. He stretched his neck to breathe while I surveyed the landscape spread before me.

The hills of my country are not high but the great expanse of marsh to the east makes them appear so. Looking across their slopes, the tree-filled valleys, I saw buildings of wood and thatch nestled amid the patchwork of fields and pasture; rivers glinted silver until they were lost in the fens. To the east, a dark blue line marked the sea while to the west lay the green mass of the Brunneswald, the great forest which stretches far into Mercia. In nine years all seemed little changed. I breathed deeply and the air was cool and clear, the cloying sweetness of hawthorn and the dust of the road replaced by the cleaner, sharper tang of grass and saltmarsh. My heart exulted at being home. As the mule-driver's voice sounded from the track behind, I dug my heels into the stallion's sides. He leapt forward with a snort and charged headlong into the sloping pasture.

Tiw could not match his dam, Swallow, for speed or endurance but at that time there were few horses in England to equal his power. I bent low over his neck, urging him on, felt my cloak tug in the wind of our going and freed it so that it billowed and was lost far behind. At the thunder of hooves, folk stopped work to stare, at first in alarm then, seeing a lone horseman, curiosity; sheep leapt to their feet and scattered in panic while their shepherds shouted abuse after so reckless a rider. My father's hall at Bourne we passed in a fleeting instant: a glimpse of startled faces and the cackle of geese is all I remember, aye and the shock of seeing a stone church where the stables had been before, then I turned Tiw onto the old Roman road that runs along the edge of the marshland.

Foam flew from the stallion's mouth, spattering his neck and chest and I straightened in the saddle, allowing him to slacken pace. The noise of geese and voices died away and I heard skylarks singing and, far-off, a curlew's call. The horse eased from a canter to the steady gait characteristic of his breed which ate up the miles seemingly without effort.

Laughton lies off the road in a shallow valley sheltered from the wind.

Too small to be called a vill, it comprised a few cottars' huts and the thegn's hall. As the thatched roofs came into view, I saw a man walking slowly across the pasture to my left. I turned Tiw across the ditch between track and field and galloped to intercept him. The man stopped but did not speak when I brought the stallion to a plunging halt less than a spear-length away. I slackened the reins and he held out his hand for the horse to sniff while his gaze travelled slowly upwards.

At first his face betrayed nothing of his thoughts: he had glimpsed only a foreigner, likely enough come to ask the way. But seeing my hair which, contrary to the fashion of the Continent, I wore long (though Turfrida complained it was the mark of a barbarian), and meeting my eyes, which are odd-coloured, one grey, one of greener cast, the blood drained from his face and he staggered as if struck an unexpected blow.

I leapt from the saddle before he could fall and caught hold his shoulders to steady him.

'There's no need to look like that: I am no ghost, Toli.' Leaving the stallion loose to graze, I guided the man to a nearby tree-stump. He seemed bereft of speech and I was glad of the quiet for I remembered my foster-father as a man in his prime, strong and enduring as an oak tree. In nine years he seemed to have aged twenty, his eyes sunken in a face become gaunt and sallow, his muscles shrunk to knotted fibres on sticks of bone. He sat on the stump and stared, taking in every detail of my face and clothes until, to ease his shock, I said, 'Nine years' fighting in a foreign land is enough for any man. Now I have come home.'

'God's grace,' he murmured weakly. 'We had no word of you in all that time: hearing nothing after Aelfgar's death, we thought you lost. At least, I assumed you must be dead: Eadgytha had more faith. "He will return when he is ready, not before," she said. "Likely enough with a woman in tow. So keep the Hall prepared for when he comes it will be at the breaking of a storm."' He hesitated and shook his head disbelievingly. 'Hereward, you were a raw stripling when you rode away.'

'Aye, and I have seen and done things since you would not believe.' I could not wholly conceal my dismay at finding him so altered and added lightly, 'Eadgytha's right though: I have a wife and daughter in train and Martin Lightfoot is still in my service. They'll be here soon: I left them on the road.' I paused and glanced into the sky where a few wisps of cloud were strung out by a high wind. 'But I see no storm. It's just like Eadgytha to temper good news with ill omens. How is she?'

His haggard features tightened. 'She died on Christmas Eve two years ago,' he said bleakly. 'Almost to her last breath she asked what she had done to earn her son's disfavour. Eadric was there all the time: it was you she meant.'

His pale eyes, faded with age, locked with mine and I felt the blood rise to my face.

'Have you forgotten why I left, Toli?'

He clenched his teeth like a man in his death throes but his stare did not waver and I knew he was trying to reconcile the man who stood before him, stern of feature, accoutred as a knight, with the youth he had loved as his own son. His mouth worked a little then he said desperately: 'You could have sent word: Martin was not exiled. Did our care, your home, mean so little? Only now, when you are so minded, you come, expecting all to be as it was. She wanted to see you once more: was that too much to ask?'

'How should I have known?' The pain in the old man's tone and face shamed me. 'You and Eadgytha were as mother and father to me and, truly, I am sorry she is dead. I waited until Harold Godwineson was proclaimed king and I had obligations to fulfil in Flanders. Would you rather I had returned a hunted man? I came as soon as I could.'

He stared at me a moment longer, then gave a great sigh and shook his head slowly from side to side.

'You are here: that is what matters,' he said at last, levering himself to his feet. 'Forget it: I am grown old and fretful as a toothless hound. Tell me all you have seen and done, how you came by this wife of yours. And a child too, did you say?'

His cheerfulness struck false: I sensed he was struggling still with the surprise of my return.

'I'd rather you told me all that has happened here: there will be time enough for the rest.' On impulse, I stepped forward to hug him, the homage of a son to a dearly loved father though we were not blood-kin. 'Toli – it's good to see you!'

He returned my embrace and beneath the stuff of his tunic I felt him all skin and bone, was stunned by his frailty. Seeing my expression as we broke apart, he smiled ruefully.

'You were not twenty when you left.' There was wry amusement in his tone. 'But I was more than twice that age: then, nine years age a man half a lifetime though they pass in a fleeting instant. Still, God has spared me thus far and no doubt to some purpose, if only to keep you from the mercies of the shire-court as before.'

'Those days are long past.' I turned to glance towards the track lest the wagon should have come into view, forgetting how fast I had travelled. Heat-haze shimmered over the marshes; the grazing horse switched his tail and snorted softly. 'And I'd thank you not to mention the Fen-wolves in Turfrida's hearing. She knows nothing of the Terror of the Fens.'

'What?' His worn face spilt in a grin. 'How long do you think you'll keep it from her in these parts? The monks of Borough still travel under armed escort though no ill has befallen them for nigh on nine years. A strange chance, eh?'

'One she need never ponder.' Unbidden, a pang for those heady, reckless days, gripped me. 'How are they, the Wolves?'

'Esbiorn died in a blood-feud not worth his sword; Thorkil of a fever a few summers back.' His smile turned to a grimace: he added seriously, 'The others are all settled down more or less: some even hold forth at the Wapentake. All save Rahere, but he always was a loner. Best forget them, save as old friends. We are blessed with peace here now.'

'Old comrades then,' I remarked and as he looked at me askance, let out a breath of laughter. 'Truly, those days are long gone: I have no quarrel with any man hereabouts. I may yet beat Brain-biter into a ploughshare: is that not what scripture bids us do? I am here to tend my lands and family and with a willing wife to bed, hawking and hunting for other pleasure, who could ask more? I've seen enough fighting for a lifetime. One day a man's luck runs out.'

Toli regarded me steadily, his face grave.

'Then may the pattern of your fate be much as mine,' he said. 'War is for the young. To know the madness of a berserker: that is a kind of joy. But as the body weakens, so fear of death grows and that is no comfort, waiting in a shieldwall. I pray I will die in bed with my children there to bid farewell, no hero's end.'

'God grant it so,' I murmured after a moment's silence, disturbed by the need I detected in his eyes. 'But I would have your counsel for a few years yet. To whom else should I go: Ulf the Simple?'

'Some hold that the simple are the most blessed of God's creatures, being higher than beasts yet free from the cares of ordinary folk,' he replied reflectively then, seeing my expression, gave a self-conscious chuckle. 'Ach, take no notice of an old man's maundering: I am poor company since Eadgytha died. No doubt you are hungry, aye and thirsty too. Come on.'

Tiw followed, seemingly docile as a pack-horse, as we walked across the field.

'We breakfasted on the road,' I said when Toli began to worry where his serving-woman might be and whether there was any food fit for visitors, as is the habit of old men to make large concerns of the trivial. 'Some bread and cheese will serve for now, otherwise I'll wait for Turfrida.'

He glanced at me sidelong, shook his head in gentle mockery.

'What are we coming to: the Leader of the Fen-wolves under a woman's thumb? Still, it's no bad thing if she's knocked sense into your thick skull.'

The Hall and cots which comprised the settlement were surrounded by oak and elm trees planted by Toli's father to protect against the wind. While the cottages were well-tended, the Hall had an unkempt look: the thatch was uneven and blackened with age, the once brightly painted door-posts faded and worm-eaten. Hens scratched in the mud of the yard and midden but the wooden trough was cracked and empty. A pair of deerhounds sprawled in the hall entrance: they raised their heads at our approach and lowered them again. From one of the cottages a woman dressed in a filthy tunic but with neatly braided hair stared at me, then put one hand to her mouth. As she stood transfixed, three children peered round the door and crept shyly forward, blue eyes bright against ruddy faces as they peeped from the shelter of her skirts.

'Gytha, we have guests!' Toli's voice broke the woman's reverie and she brushed the children aside and came towards us in the manner of a sleepwalker, her eyes never leaving my face. I wondered if she were slow-witted and thought it a poor thing if this was the best service Toli could command until she was close enough that I saw the long scar on her cheek. Nine years of child-bearing and labour in the fields had thickened her figure, for she had barely been of marriageable age and worn her hair loose when I saw her last: Aelgytha, Eadgytha's youngest sister. She lifted her right hand absently to her face and I felt a pang of guilt: it was I who put that scar there, flinging a stone to disturb the lovers I had crept upon in the woods. (She had, to my astonishment, borne no ill-feeling for that misdeed, maybe because afterwards her parents no longer objected to her passion for Cole One-Hand, the reeve, who was twice as old as she and newly widowed).

'Hereward!' I think she would have flung her arms around to welcome me: she was artless as a child. But though her mouth spread in a wide grin, she checked herself, daunted maybe by the mail hauberk and the change she perceived in me. 'Are you truly back? I mean' - she looked past me to where the stallion cropped the grass around the disused trough – 'are you alone?'

'His wife and child are but a few miles behind,' Toli said, amused. 'So don't go thinking here's another victim for your match-making.' He glanced helplessly at me. 'Aelgytha's been trying to pair me up this past twelvemonth: thinks her sister won't rest easy in her grave until I've someone to keep me warm at night.'

'No more will she.' It was clear this argument had gone on a long while and would last some time yet. 'What have you gained from your stubbornness, Toli? Miserable as a crow in a rainstorm you've been.' Her eyes met mine. 'Won't even let me cook for him, just sits hungry by a cold hearth all night: no wonder he's turned to skin and bone.' She spread her hands in a gesture of resignation and disgust. 'I suppose you want me to make somewhere decent for these folk to stay from the midden you've made of my sister's home?' As Toli opened his mouth to protest, she added vehemently: 'And no doubt you'd like food and drink while you're waiting? Bide here and I'll bring bread and ale. And don't bother me further!'

'She's a good woman,' Toli said as Aelgytha bustled into her own cottage, herding the children before her. 'Aye and maybe she's right: I should take another wife. There was a widow in Gildenborough but the will failed me. And somehow it seemed like a betrayal.'

Discomfited by his candour, I asked: 'Gildenborough? So they've taken that name in earnest now? I thought it a jest.'

'Oh, it's real enough.' His tone was bitter. He glanced round as if fearful of being overheard, then gestured to a great stone block lying to the right of the hall's entrance. 'Come and sit: she'll bring food out.'

The rough-hewn cube might have dated from Roman times: Toli had had steps cut into it so that it served both as mounting block and seat. As I settled myself beside him, it was as if I had never left: often we had sat here on warm summer evenings, talking of a stranger seen in the marsh, a lame horse, plover chicks almost stepped upon by chance, things as seemed then of great import. But now there was a kind of weary resignation to his tone I had never heard before.

'Things have changed much, these past years,' he said. 'Even here, though you may not see it. Yet you must have noticed the new churches in the villages?'

I nodded.

'Edward the Pious was not a strong king,' he continued, surprising me because he had never much concerned himself with matters beyond his own hundred. 'God knows, this country suffered enough under Harefoot and Harthacnut but there are other ways to destroy a kingdom than by bloodshed. By the end, Edward ruled only in name and I do not think he cared: he was obsessed by the fate of his own immortal soul, or so I've heard. The bishops and Edward's Norman cronies held the power and it is said that the King, being childless, even named William of Normandy heir.

'Until last year, all was quiet. Seeing which way the land was lying, rival eorls and thegns vied to build the biggest abbeys and churches. They were following a precedent set by the King, though no sooner was his West Minster complete than it became his mausoleum.

'Thus it was that Tostig Godwineson built churches in the north and held eorldom of Northumbria while Harold, Eorl of East Anglia, founded Waltham Holy Cross. In return, your parents built an abbey at Coventry and a great church at Stow. The abbots must have smiled as gold poured into their minsters but Borough, standing as it does between East Anglia and Mercia, benefited most because of the enmity between your family and Godwine's. And now Harold is King, Gyrd Godwineson holds East Anglia.'

He paused and sighed. 'I sometimes wonder what Christ would think if he returned to earth and saw what his Church has become. But the clergy are not fools. They grab land as a glutton stuffs meat. No thegn dies childless but an abbey takes custody of his estate and if his widow is poor, she is evicted.'

'I am no lover of the Church,' I said, with more feeling than I had intended.

'And so, under Abbot Leofric, Saint Peter's Minster has become the Place of Gold,' he continued, too engrossed in his own thoughts to heed my comment. 'They've collected treasures there you'd not believe: all to the glory of God and his saints they say. Christ on his crucifix with a golden crown and bejewelled footrest; an altar table sheathed in gold, reliquaries worth a king's ransom. Ach, well, you'll be seeing it for yourself soon enough.'

Some humiliations can never be forgotten, however deeply buried: they are burned into the soul as a pattern may be welded into a fine sword-blade. I sat in the bright sunshine, a fighter in the fullness of his strength, and an icy sweat bathed me as I fought to contain the upwelling of memory unleashed by the old man's artless words. To keep my voice steady took all my willpower: 'What need, Toli?'

'Have you not been listening?' In the manner of the aged, he had forgotten to whom he spoke. His eyes, which had rested on the horse dozing beside the stream, were bright and fierce as he looked at me but seeing my face, he clapped hand to brow in self-recrimination.

'Hereward – fool that I am!' He glanced towards Aelgytha's cottage. 'What's happened to that woman? This news is best swallowed with ale.'

It was well that his sister-in-law came bustling out an instant later. She bore a wooden trencher laden with rye bread, soft cheese and honey-cakes; a small boy followed with two horn cups and a jug of ale. All this was set on the flat surface of the block, then Aelgytha chivvied the child into the Hall, grumbling that with two days to prepare she might have made a place fit for guests, as it was we'd have to make do with a pigsty. . .

We ate and drank in silence, for Toli seemed loth to talk. The ale was like a balm: it was long since I had tasted such. The old man picked at his food, his face troubled then pushed the trencher aside and sat staring at his hands, swollen-jointed, gnarled as tree-roots. I struggled to curb my impatience: when he began, he avoided my gaze.

'It is all gone,' he said simply. 'Morcar holds Bourne but what Leofric and Godgifu did not cede to the abbeys, Aelfgar did. All your birthright they willed to the Church, to ease the passage of their souls maybe. You know an outlaw's land is forfeit to the King: rather than lose it thus, Leofric gave it to Croyland and Borough. Laughton is still your bookland: I held it in both our names to give you somewhere to call home if ever you returned. What Morcar intends with Bourne I do not know. He has been in Northumbria since the rebellion gave him Tostig's eorldom.'

'I must see to my horse.' To hide the anger that pressed like a fist against my throat, I rose and went to where Tiw stood, only his tail moving as he switched flies. Toli's voice, plaintive as a curlew's call followed: 'Hereward – I'm sorry – there was nothing I could do' but I did not trust myself to answer.

It was cool and pleasant in the dappled shade by the stream; the sharp scent of watercress mingled with the smell of the horse. But my hand trembled with suppressed fury as I laid it against the stallion's neck, the stubborn, unreasoning rage of a caged wild beast which refuses to submit to the bars it cannot break. Sensing my agitation, Tiw swung his head round and shifted away but a word from me steadied him and I unfastened girth and bridle, let the harness fall to the ground and stood with bowed head, fighting for calm.

Whilst I understood at eighteen that outlawry meant forfeiture of the lands due to me at my father's death, deep in my heart had lingered a secret hope that he or my half-brother would have somehow safeguarded those estates, forgetting how much they despised and feared me. That hope, which now proved vain, had kept me from admitting the truth to Turfrida, thus she believed I still had a claim on my patrimony. Yet it was not just the reality of my disinheritance which affected me so deeply, though that was bitter enough. This anger had festered since boyhood, rooted in a disgrace I had confessed to no-one.

From that hurt I had seen but one path: revenge. It compelled me to prove myself against my peers and elders; made me leader of the Fen-wolves at fourteen so that some called them 'Hereward's Gang'; turned me into a fighter, my father's disapproval to hatred, and my mother's anxiety to desperation, until they begged the King to outlaw me. Pride had sustained me through the years that followed yet my fame was due less to courage than indifference to misfortune. Until I met Turfrida.

She had calmed the raging fire within, though it had not been extinguished. Possessed of wisdom and self-assurance far beyond her years, her love and steadfastness had all but effaced the anger and shame I had tried vainly to wipe out through bloodshed. Now, standing with one hand on the stallion's shoulder, I longed for her presence. So deep was my introspection, I did not notice the sudden tension of the horse as he raised his head a little and pricked his ears.

'Hereward.' Toli's voice was low, apologetic, yet it startled me. I had lived hard the last years, my life depending on the swiftness of my sword, and I had spun round, weapon drawn, before he finished speaking my name. I shall never forget his shocked expression though it altered to a look of paternal forbearance when I slammed Brain-biter back into the scabbard and begged forgiveness.

'Were you still a boy, I'd dunk your head to cool it,' he said. 'But it's too late for that.' He paused and his glance was suddenly keen and penetrating. 'Truly, you must have seen a lot of fighting. The life of an English thegn may soon pall. If Turfrida has lands in Flanders, why not live there? England is glutted with wealth: neighbours look with envy at the new churches and resent the tithes they have to pay but the last few harvests have been good and the King's gold has kept the Vikings away. Harold Godwineson is too eager to keep his new throne to miss paying geld to his challengers. This is no place for a man of mettle.'

In my bitterness I barely heard the last part of this speech though it was kindly meant.

'I did not leave by choice,' I reminded him. 'And how else could I have lived save by selling my sword to whichever lord would take an untried youth into service? Indeed, it was under another name that I fought at first, till one came who recognized me. Do you think it fitting that I, last son of Eorl Leofric, should crawl back to Flanders like a beaten cur because I have no place in my own country? I would sooner cut off my right hand.'

He stared, then, to my amazement, began to laugh.

'No, no, Hereward. I look upon you as a son; Eadric considers you his brother. Who else would have my trust after drawing sword upon me?' He paused to see how his words were being received and added fervently: 'The wish of my heart is that you settle here at Laughton but I do not want to see you outlawed again. Your nephews betrothed their sister to Harold Godwineson to buy peace between your kindred but you cannot rely on his goodwill.'

From his earnestness, I understood suddenly how, in all those years when my mind had been focused on gaining renown and riches through might of arms, this old man had never ceased caring for me, praying for my safe return, and I was humbled, having spared him never a thought until my feet touched English soil. And so now I did not tell him I had not considered settling on Turfrida's estates because in Flanders I was a marked man, but instead took his right hand between mine and bent my knee before him as if he were my liege-lord, saying, 'As a father you are to me, Toli, and as a father I honour you. If Morcar will not cede Bourne, I shall seek loanland and with that, Turfrida and I will be content. Yet I would have you come and live with us, not stay here alone.'

He withdrew his hand after a decent interval had passed and I sensed he was pleased though he muttered something about only fools heeding the promises of young folk and that those who lived by the sword would die by the sword. But he had no chance to elaborate because the stallion suddenly swung round, head uplifted, then whinnied and trotted across the yard towards the field, crest arched and tail spread like a pennant. Martin appeared a moment later, leading the palfrey with Aedgifu in the saddle, Turfrida walking beside. They had cut across the pasture while the wagon kept to the track.

I admit it was with no little trepidation that I went to meet them. Toli walked at my side, remarking on the Aedgifu's fairness and how Martin Lightfoot looked little different to when he had last seen him, but I heeded his words no more than the cawing of rooks in the elms. As the warhorse pranced around the group, desisting only when Swallow's strident neigh sounded from the track (I knew she would be trying to free herself from the cart), I feared to see disappointment or worse, contempt, in Turfrida's eyes. Even Bourne, with its new stone-built church, great timber hall, granaries, mill, stables, smithy and wood-turner's cot, was a poor outland settlement compared to the castles to which she was accustomed.

(There, the halls where barons entertained were hung with bright tapestries, furnished with finely carved tables and chairs; food was served on fine clay dishes not wooden trenchers, linen tablecloths were common. Separate bedchambers were the norm and there were even stone-built privies, something I had never seen in England where a midden or a pit dug in the ground often served the whole community. And in all my travels in Flanders, I had rarely seen any collection of buildings without a defensive wall: even the monasteries were constructed thus).

'Look!' With a three-year-old's bold carelessness, Aedgifu waved with both hands and almost slid from the saddle. Martin caught her smock to steady her from one side while Turfrida made to lift her down. Then, as the child, proud in her riding, clung stubbornly to the pommel, she gave up and glanced helplessly at me. 'Tell her she can stay there, but only if she holds on!'

Having done so, I put my arm around Turfrida's shoulders and looked anxiously into her face. There was no trace of unhappiness there and she thanked Toli gravely when he welcomed her with stilted, oddly formal words. I think he was taken aback, not by her beauty (which to me, no woman could surpass), but the calm assurance of her demeanour.

'I want to go faster.' Bored with our lack of attention, Aedgifu drummed her heels to urge the horse on. Her legs being so short, she succeeded only in drubbing the wood and leather of the saddle; her face puckered in frustration and Martin caught my eye.

'Go on then.' The two were like blood-kin for I had known Martin since he was adopted into my father's household. He was a little older than I and we had been almost as brothers save for a certain reticence between us which became more marked as I realized the difference between master and servant, something he had been painfully aware of from the first. Now, as he led the palfrey on a wide arc to give the child a longer ride, Turfrida said quietly, 'It's time you gave Martin some land so that he can find a wife and settle down. Now we're home, I doubt he'll be content to stay with us.'

I wondered what Martin had said on the road, for Turfrida never spoke of such things lightly but at least it gave me an opening to tell her of my disinheritance, that I possessed nothing more than my horses and arms, the goods and silver we had brought with us, and a half share of Laughton.

'It may yet prove that I have a claim on Bourne,' I added, keeping my eyes fixed on the dilapidated thatch of Toli's hall, 'but I will negotiate loanland nonetheless.'

She was silent and a cold hand seemed to grasp my heart lest she think I had deliberately deceived her. But instead of blame or recrimination, she put a hand gently on my arm saying, 'Then Martin will have to stay with us a while longer', and it was as if she had known what would happen all along and our new-found poverty was but an inconvenience.

Aelgytha and her brood were waiting in the yard. She ran to hug Martin, who had been her confidant in former times, while the children gaped at Aedgifu sitting high in the saddle. The child returned their stares with her own imperious look yet when Martin, red-faced with embarrassment, lifted her down it took only a few moments for the children to re-appraise each other. Then they were off to see some ducklings behind the Hall, Aedgifu running in their midst.

It was one of Turfrida's gifts to make folk feel at ease, whether high-born noble or the lowest bondsman. Aelgytha's initial circumspection soon gave way to the banter all women seem to indulge in when their menfolk are watching. In response to Aelgytha's apologies for the state of the Hall, Turfrida replied that it was no matter: what else was to be expected from a man for they were all alike, only happy with a sword or ale-horn in their hands, boasting of their prowess on the battlefield or in bed. When the older woman answered, with a swift glance towards me, that a man's hands weren't always the best part of him, nor a sword his most useful tool, Turfrida hesitated, unsure of her meaning. Only when Aelgytha illustrated her point with an unmistakeable and obscene gesture did my wife eye me sidelong then, seeing the helpless forbearance on my face, burst out laughing. The two went into the Hall shaking their heads and chuckling like old friends.

'Women!' Toli grumbled, stumping his way to the mounting block, where he sat down heavily. 'Still, it's a while since such sounds were heard under my roof: long may it last.'

'Can't live with them, can't live without them, is that it, Toli?' While the women talked, Martin had stripped his palfrey of harness and let it loose to graze with the others. He dumped saddle and bridle near the stone block then, seeing the old man's stricken face, cursed softly.

'Don't chide yourself, Martin.' Toli forced aside his grief with a visible effort. 'God knows, it's been more than two years since she died. Take no notice: I wallow in the past like a dotard. Sometimes it seems to me I've lived too long.'

Mercifully, at that moment the wagon came into view.

That night as we lay on a straw pallet in a corner of the Hall, Turfrida said quietly, 'I have been thinking, love. Why don't we take Toli up on his offer and make our home here instead of fighting to gain Bourne? I have estates still in Flanders: they will provide all the income we need. We could be comfortable enough, lead a quiet life far from the strife and politicking of courts, raise our children in peace. Is that not why we came to England?'

I turned onto my back, pulling her against me so that her head nestled in the hollow of my shoulder, my hand spread on the smooth curve of her belly. Her hair smelled of hawthorn flowers from a garland the children had made to welcome her. (I had allowed them to bring it over the threshold because the plant portended no evil in her country but cast it outside and muttered a prayer to ward off ill fortune before barring the door for the night).

'Bourne is my patrimony.' I replied as calmly as I could: something deep within balked at the thought of yielding the last of my inheritance so easily. 'It is mine by right. Even Morcar cannot dispute that.'

'By the same argument, you should be Eorl of Mercia.' She shifted to twine her hand with mine. 'All that is over, Hereward. We could be happy here.'

I thought of the castle she had left, the luxuries she had known since childhood, the sophistication of life on the Continent, and contrasted it with this tumbledown hall of timber and thatch. The only concession to comfort I could remember here was a bearskin spread beside the hearth in winter.

'How can you say that?' I felt her stiffen slightly at my sharpness. 'If your father could see this place, he would have my head for the insult to your blood. Aye, and no blame to him. What am I but a usurper if I can offer no more?'

She was silent and the pulse of blood in my throat marked the moments until almost I spoke to break the suspense.

'After four years, you should know me better,' she said at last, gravely. 'My pride is in you and our child. Is that how you judge my worth: by what I possess rather than what I am?'

The rebuke took me aback: I did not know how to answer. Beneath my encircling arm she was still but tense. At length I stammered, 'Your worth to me would be the same had you been born a beggar or slave' but she snorted at so obvious and trite a remark. Before she could turn away, I added hastily: 'Turfrida, you are my life's love and we can live here if you want. But I must try to regain Bourne. Outlaw I may have been but Edward the Pious is dead and I am still Eorl Leofric's son.'

In the quiet I could just hear Aedgifu's soft breathing where she slept close by; the running of the stream, Toli's slow snoring. Then Turfrida sighed and I realized suddenly that there was more to her request than first appeared.

'I must tell you then, since Toli is afraid,' she said. 'Morcar left Bourne in Eadric's hands, to hold until he returns south. He will not relinquish it to you. Only the King has power to force him and he will not do so until his throne is secure. You know as well as I that Harold Godwineson cannot risk a feud with your nephews. Let it go and be content with Laughton.'

'Eadric?' I stared blankly into the dark, stunned that Toli, whom I had known and trusted all my life, should have deceived me. 'But his lands are the other side of Borough.'

'Some, maybe.' Turfrida's voice was calm and measured. 'Toli did not tell you all at once because he was frightened of your anger, that you would go to Bourne and challenge Eadric directly or else gather men to do him harm. I tried to reassure him that you would never hurt him or his kin but I could see he did not believe me.'

'He said nothing of it!' In my disappointment, I did not perceive the question inherent in her words. 'Eadric and I were like brothers! Toli is right: I shall go to Bourne tomorrow and have this out with him.'

'No, Hereward.' She shifted away a little to prop her head against her hand and I felt her steady gaze though in the dim light from the hearth-embers I could barely make out her face. 'Would you make enemies of those who have loved you since boyhood, who had all but given up hope of seeing you again? When Morcar comes south you could negotiate but if you win Bourne, you will drive your foster-brother from his home. Would you do that for your pride's sake?'

'Turfrida –' I began but in truth I had no words to say, knowing myself trapped. And she must have sensed my frustration turn to a kind of baffled anger because she laid one hand against the side of my face and drew it down in a lingering caress until her fingers pressed against my lips, saying, 'Here there is no need to prove yourself. Do not mistake pride's ambition for need. Take loanland if you wish but leave Eadric in peace. Do not forget: he is Morcar's sokeman, not Lord of Bourne.'

I lifted her hand away.

'Did Toli beg you to plead thus on his son's behalf?' I growled. 'Is it not enough he lied to me that he must go crawling to my wife behind my back?'

In the silence that followed, the fresh straw of Aedgifu's pallet rustled as she turned in her sleep; the old man snored on, oblivious to our argument; from outside came the hoo-wic of a hunting owl over the running of the stream.

'He was afraid you would raise your gang,' she said at last. 'Who are these Fen-wolves?'

Astounded, I lay still for a moment then thrust Turfrida aside and lurched to my feet, snatching my sword from where it was propped against the wall.

'I will have his tongue for this!' Turfrida scrambled after me while from the other side of the hall, Toli gave a rasping snore. I moved forward, borne by my fury as on a mighty wave, my feet tangled in the clothes piled on the floor and I stumbled, the sword descending in a wide arc. The blade hacked into something which, in my confusion, felt like flesh and bone. Aedgifu's scream seemed to rend the night apart.

The horror of that moment haunted me long after though it lasted but the space of a few heartbeats. The child's cry echoed in my ears. I found myself kneeling beside her pallet, feeling in dread along the sword-blade. Though I heard Turfrida comfort the sobbing girl, Toli and Martin calling out in alarm and being told all was well, these sounds meant nothing. When my hand encountered straw and woollen cloth instead of warm, blood-slick flesh, my senses reeled.

I do not know how long I knelt there. When I came to myself, hunched wretchedly on the earthen floor, an unnatural quiet filled the hall. Turfrida's voice was the barest whisper as she rocked Aedgifu to sleep but I knew Toli and Martin must be alert to every sound. Then I heard someone slip from the bed. A rug was draped over my shoulders; next moment Turfrida knelt to put her arms around me.

Other women I have known, before and since, but none with the generosity of spirit and understanding of my helpmeet. Where most would have berated me she said nothing, knowing remorse would be punishment enough. I bent my head into the curve of her shoulder and she held me until my shivering ceased, then whispered, 'Aedgifu is asleep, come' and eased me onto the narrow pallet where the child had been. Somehow she managed to slip under the rug beside me for she had not bothered to cover her nakedness any more than I and the air was chill.

Gradually the night-sounds, which had been shocked into silence (or so it seemed to me), resumed. Turfrida's touch calmed me and I felt sleep begin to wrap me round when she murmured, 'You have still to answer, love. Why did you not tell me of the Fen-wolves?'

I was silent for a while though from her tone I knew she would persist. 'I was ashamed,' I muttered at last. 'It was a long time ago. There are few men who do not regret things done in the rashness of youth. Nor should you believe all Toli's tales: the stories far outstripped the deeds.'

'It was not Toli who told me but Aelgytha,' she replied. 'She said your gang harried priests and monks without mercy, robbing them even of their robes so they had to flee naked to their abbeys. And that you sought to antagonize your father, stealing from his estates and causing trouble with neighbours until he begged the King to outlaw you. She said it was Toli who tried to defend you at manor and shire court but once your parents determined to go higher, he could do nothing.' She paused and my heart was wrenched by the pain in her voice: 'Hereward, you lied! You told me you were exiled for sedition.'

Her body, which had lain as if made to fit against mine, withdrew a little: before she could turn away or leave, I pulled her close and whispered fiercely, 'May the tongue shrivel in my mouth if ever I lie to you, Turfrida. Ten years ago we broke into the tithe-barn at Croyland soon after harvest, stole all the wheat, Church and King's share, and gave it to the Fen-folk: there was rye-blight that year. The bishop was for arresting every young man in the shire, having each cot and byre searched, so I admitted my part though they got no other names from me: the Wolves had a blood-oath on it. With my father's plea to the King, that was enough to have me exiled: putting fealty to my comrades first and, of course, loss of the tithes, for they never recovered them. Did Aelgytha tell you that?'

'No,' she replied simply and ran her hand down my spine with lingering deliberation. 'She said only that you and your father hated one another.'

Her fingers paused, then traced one of the scars that crossed my back, thin silky lines left by my father's belt and his steward's lash, faded now almost to insignificance. But she said nothing more, waiting until I should be ready to reply.

'My mother was my father's second wife: he already had an heir,' I said slowly. 'So when I was born I was an embarrassment. Aye, and a threat to my half-brother's ambition. When I was eight years old, I was sent to Borough to become a monk, as is the doom of unwanted sons. When it became clear my temper was unsuited to the Church, my father's annoyance deepened to anger: as I grew older, I thwarted him until in the end I think he hated me more than Godwine, his rival. When I was held for the tithe-barn raid, he saw a chance to rid himself of an enemy.'

I stopped abruptly because it was on the tip of my tongue to admit that which I had confessed to no man or woman, the shame buried so deep it was embedded at the very core of me. But though I had been but a boy, betrayed by those he was taught to trust and revere, I could not do it. I told myself honour prevented me: some things should remain secret between a man and God, but in truth it was pride and fear. I did not want her to think less of me, nor could I bear pity.

'My childhood was a time of happiness,' Turfrida said, after a long silence. She half-turned to lie on her back and a shaft of moonlight falling through the smoke-hole glossed her eyes, rendering them unreadable as she stared upwards. 'My mother died bearing me so I was twice-beloved by my father: in me I think he hoped she would live again. It was not so of course – I am my own person – yet still there is no doubt of his love. Had it not been so, he would have forced me to honour my betrothal but he bowed to my wish and ceded me to you, withholding nothing though he could have refused my dowry. Instead, he gave us his blessing and for that I will always respect and honour him.'

'He is a noble and generous man.' The sentiment was heartfelt: I owed more to her father than he would ever know, yet I could not wholly conceal my bitterness. 'But have you ever thought, Turfrida, how the pattern of our lives depends on chance? Had my father esteemed me, I would be Lord of Bourne, maybe Eorl of Mercia, one of the most powerful in the land, while you would be wedded to the richest baron in Flanders. Instead we are here, in a poor thegn's hall, all our worldly goods but half a wagon-load and I must beg loanland from those I despise . . .'

My voice trailed into silence for I had not meant to sound self-pitying or regretful. Yet she grasped my meaning straightway. From necessity I learned young to conceal my feelings: she was used to interpreting my clumsy words.

'Every time you go to fight, I think of chance,' she replied quietly. 'I watch and listen for your return, dreading to see Martin come alone with tidings of your death. But the past I do not dwell on: even God cannot change what has already been. For now, is it not enough that we are together, that our daughter is well and happy, that we have a home in a land free from war and famine? Do not brood on the past, love, nor let bitterness taint our lives when the cause is beyond mending.'

To such wisdom I had no answer. I pulled her close and kissed her gently on the forehead and she nestled against me like a child. I held her while her breathing slowed and deepened and her body grew slack and heavy but for me sleep was long in coming.

2. The Storm Gathers

Next day I rode to Croyland by way of Bourne. Turfrida insisted on coming, at least as far as the manor. We did not speak of what had happened in the night (Aedgifu accepted the disturbance as a bad dream and Toli and Martin held their tongues), but to appease Turfrida I put aside my hauberk. While the long tunic I wore was finer than those possessed by many king's thegns (the decorated borders had taken a month on the loom), I felt strangely vulnerable. After winning Turfrida's hand, and the death of my patron in Flanders, wearing mail against an assassin's arrow or knife had become second nature. Nor was my caution ill-founded: three men died attempting to take my life.

Toli watched anxiously as I buckled on my sword-belt but asked only that we tell Eadric he would visit in a few days. For the first time, there was awkwardness between us. Martin Lightfoot, knowing us of old, looked questioningly one to the other then busied himself saddling the chestnut for Turfrida. (It was one of Swallow's quirks that she suffered no-one on her back but me, thus when we three needed to ride together, Martin took Tiw and my wife the palfrey). As Turfrida mounted and Toli lifted Aedgifu to join her, Aelgytha came out. She regarded our small cavalcade with a sardonic eye.

'Are you sure that bag of bones will make it to Bourne?' she asked as the mare gave a groaning sigh and sagged when I swung into the saddle. 'She looks fit for dog-feed.'

It was fair enough comment from one ignorant of Swallow's rare qualities but coming after a broken night, when I was apprehensive of the day ahead, it stung my pride.

'You of all people should know better than to judge by appearance,' I retorted, looking her in the eye and had just time to register her hurt before swinging the mare round and trotting away, the others following closely.

'That was cruel,' Turfrida remarked when we had joined the old road and slowed to an easy walk. 'She and Toli have been kind to us.'

Knowledge that she was right did nothing to improve my mood.

'It was no more than she deserved,' I replied shortly. 'Would you prefer that I bend and scrape like a supplicant? I shall have to do so before the abbots of Croyland and Borough to gain what was my birthright: why not Toli's kin also?'

As soon as the words passed my lips, I regretted them but they could not be unsaid. Turfrida looked searchingly into my face.

'When first we met, courtesy ran deeper in you than bitterness,' she said, then bent to the child who was waving at a herd-boy who stood to watch us pass. Looking away to where boggy pasture was fringed by the blue-green expanse of marsh, I caught Martin's eye. He shook his head slightly but I ignored him and urged Swallow to lengthen her stride, leaving them behind.

I did not slow the mare until we reached the track that leads to Bourne. The others were chatting easily, comparing this countryside to that of Flanders: even the child remarked the lack of a wall around the settlement. We passed a wide pond and entered the yard, bounded on one side by the great timber hall built by my father. It was a busy place: two ox-teams were being harnessed to go to the fields; boys forked soiled straw from the stables; a horse tethered by the smithy shifted restlessly and the farrier cursed at it to be still. None of this activity ceased at our arrival but there was not one person who did not pause to glance at us.

Two lads ran to take the horses and I lifted Aedgifu down while Turfrida dismounted and pulled her skirts into order. The child tried to tug free, then Martin said, 'She spotted a cat carrying a kitten into the barn over there' and took her away to see. Turfrida's hand was on my arm but I did not acknowledge it for the horses had been led away and I was wondering whether anyone had gone to announce us. A voice said 'Hereward?' and I turned to find Eadric there, wiping his hands on a bloody rag.

'Lambing.' He shook his head ruefully. 'Twins snarled like wool in a bramble and the ewe died after all. Still, maybe we'll get another to foster them. The fool of a shepherd tried to yank them out without knowing what was wrong: I'll have to find one who understands his work.' He paused and his grey eyes were suddenly doubtful. 'I'm glad to see you safe. You have often been in our thoughts, especially since mother died.'

'I am glad to be back,' I said. 'It seems there have been many changes hereabouts.'

Turfrida's hand tightened on my arm but I had spoken without acrimony, astounded by the change in Toli's son. A year older than I, he had been a lanky youth growing awkwardly into manhood when I saw him last and while I planned raids or brawled with my comrades of the Fen-wolves, he would be with Siward, my father's clerk, diligently copying script like a monk. Indeed, his quiet and studious nature made him, in a sense, my rival: while we loved one another as brothers, the relationship had sometimes been uneasy. Many were the instances when my parents used him as a model of what I should aspire to and there was no doubt that had circumstances been different, Eadric would willingly have entered the Church. Now it was clear he had inherited his father's mildness along with his mother's sagacity for he did not rise to my comment but simply nodded, saying, 'Come up to the Hall: Ymma is waiting.'

Instead of entering by the great main door, Eadric led us round the side, past the new church. Close to, the stonework looked crude, as if the building had been hastily constructed and seeing my face, Eadric remarked, 'That was your brother's work but if he was thinking to vie with Leofric's church at Stow, he failed miserably. We've had good harvests the last few years so maybe the Almighty is pleased. Our folk complained enough though: Aelfgar raised rents for three years to pay for it.'

Such cynicism would never have passed the lips of the youth I remembered and he grinned. 'I may be no warrior, nor have I travelled beyond Borough, but don't think me a fool, Hereward. I also have learned much since you left.' He hesitated as we came to the back of the Hall where new rooms had been added. 'This is my doing. Morcar wanted to keep the main hall as it was but Ymma's with child and needed her own place. In the end, Morcar thought it an improvement.'

He spoke with quiet pride and for a moment I envied him his peaceful existence. A sprig of green ash was nailed on the lintel to protect against witchcraft; the door was propped open with a smooth river-stone. Eadric leant one hand on the frame and called: a moment later a young woman came out. She was heavily pregnant, fair as Turfrida was dark, her eyes that ice-clear blue which betokens Danish blood. As she welcomed us, Martin and Aedgifu appeared, the latter clutching a mewing kitten to her chest. Ymma shook her head, smiling, then gestured us inside.

After bringing Eadric and I bowls of ale, Ymma took Turfrida into an antechamber, separated from the living room by a heavy hide curtain. By now the kitten had made its escape, pursued by Aedgifu. Martin followed to make sure no harm befell her. I cradled the wooden bowl between my hands and as I looked around the room, a strange yearning grew upon me. An iron pot hung over the raised hearth; brightly coloured hangings lined the walls; the floor was strewn with fresh rushes mingled with herbs to sweeten the stench from the midden outside; skins and rugs were thrown over the benches; cooking pots and stirrers, crocks storing cheese, butter and grain were neatly stacked. Remembering Toli's Hall, neglected since Eadgytha's death, and the silver we had brought, I thought: 'Why not make such a place for ourselves?'

'Morcar is in the north.' Eadric regarded me circumspectly. 'I do not know when he will return. If you wish to dispute lordship of this manor, you must put your case before the Wapentake and they will likely send you to the King. But if you will heed one who considers you his brother, I would ask that you accept things as they are. A storm is brewing and we will not weather it if old feuds are rekindled.'

He spoke with grave deliberation as if he had long considered this speech yet I was taken aback. These were not the words of a country yeoman but those of one who sees far beyond the bounds of his own lands.

'Even in Flanders we heard of the rebellion in the north,' I said. 'But Leofric's kin have never had designs on the throne, even now. There is no-one of royal blood fit to challenge Harold Godwineson: Edgar Atheling is only a boy.'

'Edward the Pious sent Harold Godwineson on a mission to Duke

William of Normandy nigh on two years ago,' he replied. 'Rumour was, Edward named William his heir, aye, and that Harold himself swore fealty, though he has ever denied it. Either way, when William heard of Harold's coronation he swore to be avenged, calling him usurper and oath-breaker, a traitor to his rightful King. But he is no fool to rush into war: he has sent to the Pope for validation of his claim. Yet from what I have heard, this Norman Duke is not a man to sit and wait until England is handed over by papal decree, even if that were likely. I fear what will happen next.'

None of this was new to me yet coldness stroked my bowels as I recalled Eadgytha's warning.

'Likely enough it is gold he wants,' I said, though my dismissiveness was forced. 'The wealth of England is almost legendary, the more so as the Dukes of France are always fighting. All their taxes are spent on petty wars. It will leave a bitter taste in the mouths of Edwin and Morcar if a new geld replaces that once paid to the Danes.'

He sipped his ale and laid his bowl aside, then leant forward, eyes suddenly hard.

'Then why should William go to the Pope? In truth, Harold Godwineson has no more claim than the Norman. The only difference is that he is here. Harald Hardrada of Cnut's line has more right to the kingship than a Godwineson. The Atheling is the only true heir.'

As I considered these words, my foreboding deepened.

'When Tostig was exiled after losing Northumbria to Morcar, he came to Flanders,' I said slowly. 'Baldwin offered him protection. Some of Hardrada's men were there. It would be to both men's advantage to form an alliance against Harold Godwineson. I think Morcar may have his hands full after harvest: no doubt they would strike first in the north.'

'Then he will call on all his men, even this far south.' Eadric's face was deeply troubled. 'I have toyed with the idea of making Bourne more secure, to give folk hereabouts a refuge should trouble come with the fyrd away. This news has made up my mind: I will do so between hay-carting and harvest.' He paused to study his hands, looked up with an anguished expression. 'Curse this fighting. If Edward had had a son, there would be no question of succession. There's not even a bastard hidden somewhere to make a claim: they say he preferred men to women. No doubt he played the boy for them - he was ever weak. Ymma's child is due a month from now. I don't want to leave her alone with a sucking babe while I go to be slaughtered for a Godwineson.' He hesitated then laughed softly, a sound without mirth. 'You chose a dangerous time to return, Hereward.'

I shrugged. 'I was a marked man in Flanders: when Tostig learned of my presence, I thought it best to leave. My death would be small recompense for the humiliation he suffered at the hands of Edwin and Morcar but the head of Leofric's son might have counted for something. Nine years I have lived by the sword and any fighter will tell you that is a matter of chance as much as skill. One day a man's store of luck runs out. I thought to put all that behind, to settle down with Turfrida, make a home much as you have here. Still, war is not certain, Eadric. The Pope may refuse William's claim and Tostig might make peace with Harold if his Eorldom is restored. What you fear may never come to pass.'

'Pigs will fly before Harold and Tostig meet in friendship,' Eadric replied. 'Those brothers hate each other more than your father hated theirs. You know that as well as I. But of Duke William I have heard little. The only Normans I ever saw were those sent with Morcar as part of Edward's treaty last year. Beardless sycophants, yet arrogant nonetheless. Morcar sent them back once he had crossed his own border: no doubt they were spying for the King. Yet I have heard they make good fighters. Have you met any?'

'Yes,' I said shortly. It was not a subject I wished to dwell on: the last Norman I bested in single combat had sent his men to ambush me afterwards and I barely escaped with my life. And I had seen them on the battlefields of Maine, a formidable fighting force, well disciplined and with arms far superior to those of most English thegns.

Eadric did not press me: my reticence must have betrayed my dismay. In the quiet, the voices of the women could be heard, talking no doubt of child-bearing and men.

'Build your defences,' I told him at last. 'Then it is done though I pray they will never be needed. With luck, the ditch will become just another eel-pond.'

'Aye.' He surveyed the contents of his bowl, then raised it a little. 'But let us drink to peace and a strong King.'

We drank, then I got to my feet. 'I must be going: I ride to Croyland to negotiate loanland, if the abbot is willing.' I hesitated, seeing uncertainty in his lean and earnest face. 'When I heard you held Bourne for Morcar I admit I was out for your blood. But if it cannot be mine, there is no other I would see here. I shall not dispute Morcar's claim but live at Laughton maybe. It might do your father good to have someone there to help him.'

He inclined his head briefly in acknowledgement and relief.

'We begged Toli to come and live here after mother died but he refused. Only one person I know can match him for wilful stubbornness and that's you, Hereward. If Aelgytha and Cole One-Hand hadn't been there, he'd have starved himself to death. Mother's buried at Croyland: in the first months he walked there and back to visit her grave every day and it was a bad winter that year. A lesser man would have died on the road, some days he could barely drag himself along. It was pitiful yet I admired him in a way. Such devotion after so many years is a rare thing.'

I wondered how it would be if Turfrida died before me, something I had seldom considered, then pushed the thought aside.

'Toli is a rare man,' I said. 'He had no need to foster me as a boy yet when I begged to stay he defied my father to do so. He and Eadgytha never questioned why, just accepted and even defended me at manor and shire court. It goes to my heart to see him so diminished.'

'If you settle at Laughton, I shall be in your debt.' Eadric rose to his feet. 'And if there is trouble, it will be good to have you as neighbour. Peace has brought comfort and wealth to this part of England but we are ill-prepared for war. Most of the levy have seen nothing more serious than drunken brawls.'

'Long may it remain so.'

We regarded one another steadily then reached out to grasp forearms in a gesture of mutual liking and respect, almost as if a bargain had been agreed between us.

'I dreaded this meeting, remembering your temper,' he admitted. 'But now I'm glad you're back.' He grinned suddenly, teeth white against a skin tanned to leather by wind and sun. 'As brothers we shall be again.'

Such was their delight in each other, Turfrida decided to stay with Ymma for the day, thinking also that the ride to Croyland would tire Aedgifu after the long journey of the days before. Eadric seemed pleased to see his wife so happy, thus Martin and I rode on alone. Heat-haze made the marshes shimmer; larksong sounded clear against the hum of insects and the measured clop of our horses' hooves on the sun-baked mud, a light breeze rustled the grasses and reeds. It was a day such as I had longed for amid the noise and chaos of fighting in Scaldemariland and I tried to push aside my unease and turn my mind to the business ahead. Martin, used to my moods, rode quietly alongside.

'They've put the cattle out early.' We came to the river which forms a natural moat around the abbey. On the other side, steers and heifers, hock-deep in water, raised their heads: dripping weed hung from their mouths. All summer they would graze on the marshes before being brought in before the first winter gales. Then the heifers would be put to the bull for spring calving and the rest slaughtered for their meat and hides.

'Not that early.' I turned in the saddle to look towards Bourne where the fresh greens of spring were already turning to the darker hues of summer. 'Lambing's almost over, then it'll be shearing and hay-making and mid-summer.'

'The year turns,' Martin said reflectively and something in his tone, a kind of wistfulness, made me wonder if he also believed that war was certain. But the walls of Croyland had come into view, grey and tan buildings huddled on a broad mound upstanding from the marsh, which here stretched unbroken to the sea, and so I let the matter rest.

The monks welcomed us courteously, though the novice who took the horses assumed me to be the servant, Swallow appearing a broken nag beside Tiw's magnificence. But the abbot, Ulfkil, knew me; he was a shrewd, practical man whose main concern was the smooth running of his abbey and its lands. When I told him I intended to settle at Laughton, he nodded thoughtfully, then took me into the churchyard to see Eadgytha's grave, a grassy hump surmounted by a wooden cross. From there, the roof of Toli's hall could just be glimpsed and I was strangely moved, guessing that the siting of the grave was his doing.

'Your brother, Aelfgar, ceded us much of the land that was your birthright,' Ulfkil said bluntly, his eyes on the distant buildings. 'And I think your father was trying to buy his way into Heaven by way of Gildenborough. But it is for Toli's sake, not theirs that I will grant you loanland. By chance, the tenancy of our demesne farm at Rippingale is free. Ride out with me tomorrow and we shall discuss terms.'

I bent my head in acknowledgement. 'Come to Toli's Hall and we'll go on from there. He will be glad to see you I think.'

'He was talking of building a church there in Eadgytha's memory.' The abbot turned to look me in the eye, his clear gaze disconcertingly direct. 'I told him to wait: men sometimes do things in the throes of grief which they come to regret, and he is not rich. Yet I would not have him think us ungrateful. I will speak with him tomorrow.'

We walked back towards the abbey. The vast expanse of fen and mere shimmered in the sunlight; a heron flapped overhead with lazy wingbeats while its shadow sped across the ground.

'One more thing.' When we reached the churchyard gate, Ulfkil paused. 'Do not think I have forgotten your past. Our creed urges us to forgive those who wrong us but understand this: one hint that the Fen-wolves are active and our agreement is void. Is that clear?'

His tone was uncompromising: he was not merely arranging tenancy of a farm but ensuring the safety of his abbey.

'The days of the Fen-wolves are over,' I said, 'and I have seen enough fighting to last a lifetime. You need not fear on that account.'

'I'm glad to hear it.' His face lightened in a sudden smile. 'Will you and your man come in for refreshment? I would happily hear news of the outside world. We are apt to become inward-looking in our seclusion: this is not Borough.'

Bread, hot from the oven and a bowl of curds were served in the main hall of the abbey while the abbot himself brought wine, the first I had tasted in England, thin and vinegary after those of France. We talked of Flanders and the Holy Roman Empire then, inevitably, of the threat from Normandy. Coming so soon after my discussion with Eadric, it was disquieting to hear the same fears voiced here.

'I do not think Edward understood the nature of kingship,' Ulfkil confided. 'A king represents his people before God but in the end he cared only for his own soul and disregarded the rest: a childless ruler more than anyone has a duty to make the succession clear. Harold Godwineson is a strong and resolute man but he cannot withstand attack on two fronts. And while the atheling lives, Harold's throne will never be secure.'

'Harald Hardrada and William of Normandy are rivals, not allies,' Martin said uneasily. 'They will never combine forces, even for contingency.'

'Aye, that is one thing.' Ulfkil leaned back and stretched his arms. 'I must bid farewell: I also have duties to perform. I will meet you at Laughton tomorrow.'

Each busy with our thoughts, Martin and I returned to Bourne in silence.

Over-excited by a day in which she had run wild with cottars' children and been spoiled by Ymma and Eadric (culminating in the promise of a kitten in a few weeks time), Aedgifu chattered non-stop between Bourne and the edge of Laughton, finally falling asleep in Turfrida's arms as we turned up the track to the hamlet. Toli was waiting anxiously (though I had forgotten my ill-humour of the morning, he had not), but relaxed when he saw our faces and seemed pleased at Ulfkil's impending visit. It was only later, after we had eaten and left Turfrida to settle the child for the night, that I broached the subject of a church at Laughton.

'It seemed fitting to make some lasting memorial to Eadgytha's goodness,' he said. 'And to thank God for lending her to us.' He sighed heavily and stared with unseeing eyes to the pale shimmer of the twilit marshes (we had gone to check on the horses). 'But when it came to it, I was too tired to go again to Croyland: after the first grief passed, I realized she was truly gone.' He hesitated. 'The past two years I have neglected even the running of the estate: we paid taxes from my store of coin because our harvests were poor though the years were good.' At the sight of my face, which must have expressed incredulity, he added hastily, 'Do not blame Eadric or Cole One-Hand: it was not their fault. I was set on doing things my own way and refused to take heed of the vagaries of the seasons then, when Eadric offered help, I spurned it. Anyway, I am reaping my own harvest from that sowing: I can no longer afford to build here. Thus is Eadgytha's devotion rewarded.'

His bitterness wrenched my heart. I looked across the field thinking how Eadric had compared the old man's obstinacy to mine, wondering what I would have done in his place.

'Then let me atone for my absence by building for you,' I said. 'Turfrida and I have money enough, if we settle here at Laughton. I shall not dispute lordship of Bourne.'

He was silent so long, I feared to have affronted him.

'Were I younger I would likely refuse from pride,' he said at last, speaking with difficulty. 'But I am old and maybe wiser now. Until your return each day was a burden: now life has returned to my hall. Gladly I welcome you and your family and if you wish to build in Eadgytha's memory that is more than I could have hoped for.' He paused and turned his head, tears glistened in the corners of his eyes. 'Forgive my rash words yesterday: you never failed us as a son. Grief, love, hatred: all these may blind a man to what is plain before him.'

'There is nothing to forgive,' I said. 'God knows, I must have caused you and Eadgytha heartache enough in the past. And,' I hesitated, unsure how much he knew or had guessed, 'I shall never forget how you two sheltered me as a boy.'

He smiled faintly in reminiscence. 'Aye, you were a sorry figure when you were brought to us. A shipwrecked stranger lost in the marshes we thought till Martin told us who you were. And look at you now: a warrior of renown with a wife and child that would be a joy to any man, horses and land, returned from foreign wars to set up home here. Truly, God works in mysterious ways.'

Twilight deepened and the first stars appeared. The grazing horses were dark, blocky shapes against the field; the grinding of their teeth and soft snorting filled the air. The old man was still as a tree-stump then, from far across the marshes, came the boom of a bittern.

'If there is war, this is not a bad place to be,' Toli said thoughtfully. 'My grandfather told me that long ago these were the lands of the Iceni whom even the Romans feared. In his day they reckoned the bittern's call was an ill-omen: the ghosts of dead tribesman rallying their host, war-horns sounding from the realm of the dead. The Iceni were defeated in the end of course: Rome never tolerated rebellion, even draining the marshes to deny the tribesmen their refuge. But I have often wondered what compelled those men, aye and women also, to stay and fight on when they must have known they would die. In most folk the will to live outstrips all else. Even Christ begged for water upon the Cross though it would but prolong his agony.'

'It will not come to war,' I insisted, dismayed by his intensity. 'And maybe they did not all die.'

By next evening, I had taken over three carucates of Croyland Abbey's holdings, comprising the farm which supplied all the monk's needs. It was good tillage and had been well-managed: it would give me the chance to prove myself as thegn. Toli was also satisfied by Ulfkil's visit for they had agreed a site for the new church and decided it should be built of stone in lasting memory of Eadgytha and to the glory of God. Before that work started, we would add to the Hall, making rooms for Turfrida and I as Eadric had at Bourne. Because these would be constructed of timber and wattle, we hoped to have them finished before harvest.

The days passed and spring turned into summer. A period of heavy rain delayed the start of hay-making so we used the time to haul timber while the women washed newly-shorn wool in the stream. Eadric fulfilled his promise of a kitten for Aedgifu to the detriment of Toli's hounds whose muzzles soon bore the marks of tiny claws. When there was a break in the wet weather, we sunk the corner-posts of our building and set the children collecting dung for daub. Cole One-Hand announced my return to the Wapentake and it was agreed that my outlawry was annulled on condition that no gang akin to the Fen-wolves raided within Aveland, Barholm and Ness bounds. And it was he brought news of more land for lease, this time from Borough Abbey. Thus it was I went to the place I had vowed never to enter again, save to burn it to the ground.

To Turfrida and Toli's consternation, I insisted on going girt with hauberk and sword though I left behind shield and helm. It made me feel surer of myself to appear as thegn and knight, distanced me from the oblate that had run blindly through the Bolhithe Gate and let the river take him. I had Martin groom Tiw until the stallion's coat shone like polished metal and all his harness gleamed. He took no less trouble with his palfrey (a master's standing is diminished by his servant's slovenliness), and though he left his sword behind, a long dagger hung from his belt. We chatted idly as we rode but he did not ask why we had taken so much trouble with our appearance: of all men, he alone may have understood the reason. (It was he who had found me stranded on a mudflat like a tide-trapped fish, naked and incoherent, and I still do not know what compelled him to take me to Toli and not to my father's steward at Bourne who would have sent me straight back to the monks).

As we approached Borough, the loop of the river shone like silver in the sun and smoke from hearth and forge-fires drifted in the wind to join the brown pall marking the potteries at Stamford to the west. The great stone tower of the minster dominated all the buildings huddled within the burgh walls. We passed unhindered through the North Gate and the stench and bustle of the place enveloped us.

Mind focused on the task ahead, I rode without looking left or right, disdaining the gaze of ignorant folk and the murmur that arose as we made our way through the muddy streets. Had I not been so deep in thought, trying to ignore the clanging bell which summons the monks to prayer, I would have noticed the disquiet of the gathering crowd, which kept a respectful distance yet devoured us with their eyes. It was only when we reached the abbey gates, which unlike those of the burgh were closed, and the stallion, ears quivering with tension, swung round, that I heeded the encroaching mob.

'What's the news?' The shout came from the back of the crowd. 'If you've brought the King's summons, tell us, not the Bishop. We're the ones who'll have to go!'

Tiw was growing restive; my finger on his neck calmed him. Martin, who had dismounted to speak with a door-ward on the other side of a shuttered grille, turned in alarm as an angry murmur arose.

'I am no messenger!' My voice was pitched to carry. I raised my right hand, fingers spread to signal peaceful intent. 'I have business here of my own. What summons do you expect?'

Their mood was turning ugly: someone yelled, 'What kind of business requires a mailcoat save the King's?'

'I am Hereward, son of Eorl Leofric of Mercia, lately returned from Flanders,' I replied. 'Customs differ. And I have been on my own lands these past weeks. Tell me: what has happened?'

I was not sure whether I should feel shame or pride at the townsfolk's reaction. Silence fell and they stared. Then a short, balding man dressed in the leather apron of a tanner stepped forward. He kept his eyes lowered yet I sensed it was not courage which compelled him to speak but ambition. His very pores seemed to ooze sycophancy.

'We did not recognize you, Lord,' he said. 'Forgive our rude welcome to one whose renown' – his eyes moved to take in the stallion's splendour – 'has spread even to this poor burgh, dispelling any ill-wishes stemming from – ahem – past misdemeanours, all long forgiven and forgotten. Only dismay at the news which came last night excuses us.'

My patience was wearing thin. I urged Tiw forward a few paces and the man cringed.

'Peace, lord: I did not mean to offend. A rider came from Norwich: Gyrd Godwineson has summoned the fyrd of East Anglia. The King is mustering land and ship forces such as never seen before. All the southern shires are being raised against Duke William of Normandy. So great a host is already assembled, Tostig the traitor abandoned raids along the south coast from fear.' He raised his eyes to mine and held out an expectant, trembling hand. 'Surely such news is worth a few silver pennies from a great lord to the poorest of men?'

'If you are poor, then I am a Godwineson,' I said, eyeing his paunch and the rolls of fat beneath his poorly-shaven chin. 'What is your name?'

Appreciative chuckles rose from the crowd; the man withdrew his hand, disconcerted.

'I am Oswin, the leather-worker,' he said. 'Any man of merit in the burgh can point you to my house. You will find even his grace Bishop Athelric is a customer of mine.'

'Then someone so well-known must have work to do.' I turned Tiw back towards the gate, ignoring the man's displeasure, his glance of sudden hate as he shouldered his way through the throng.

The crowd dispersed, the abbey gates were opened and we rode into the courtyard beyond. There was no doubting the wealth of the place: the yard was cobbled and many of the timber buildings I remembered had been replaced by stone.

A novice with a thin, ascetic's face came to take the horses; a monk greeted us and said the abbot was awaiting our arrival. Usually Martin would have stayed behind but this time he accompanied me unasked and I was glad of his presence. As we entered the echoing cloisters, each door opening onto a monk's cell, my mouth dried and my guts turned clammily. But we were led through a new archway into a long corridor. I rested my hand on my sword-hilt and the familiar touch of oiled leather and cold iron restored me to myself, banishing memories that the very smell of the place had brought flocking like gore-crows round a corpse.

We halted at a richly carved oaken door. Scenes from the life of St. Peter, the abbey's patron, were depicted there though we did not have long to study them. Our guide knocked and entered, then announced and beckoned us in.

Even in Flanders I had never seen a room so sumptuously appointed. Sunlight falling through glass windows glinted on gold caskets and figures of saints, the walls were adorned with tapestries, rich rugs and cushions padded chairs ornate as thrones. Amid all this splendour the abbot was clad in a simple robe, the only symbol of his status a bejewelled cross which hung at his breast from a heavy gold chain. He was a tall, lean man who must have been in his sixties yet he moved with no sign of stiffness, nor had age bowed him or diminished the keenness of his glance.

'God's grace upon you, Hereward.' He came forward and I bowed my knee before him as custom and propriety demanded. To my astonishment he laid one hand on my shoulder and blessed me before bidding me rise. 'The past we will not speak of,' he said, indicating that I should be seated.

Martin stood unobtrusively by the door as I took my place uneasily on a chair. Leofric had not been in Borough during my time at the abbey but he had presided at the shire-court where I was committed for trial after the tithe-barn raid. Now, it seemed, he had wider concerns.

'Forgive the crowd at the gate: they are much disquieted by the tidings from the east.' He glanced at the sword hanging at my side, and waited for me to state my business. When I had done so, he sighed.

'Men possessed of weapons and skilled in the use of them may soon be of greater worth to this abbey than those who mumble prayers in the hope of God's intervention,' he said heavily. 'In uncertain times the wise man looks to guard his own by whatever means he can. I am prepared to grant you tenancy of Witham-on-the-Hill, Toft and Lound in return for your allegiance. Swear to defend the abbey and its interests with your life and the land is yours.'

His gaze was unrelenting and I looked away, dismayed by his directness, the irony of being asked to protect the place that in the shame and anger of seventeen years before, I had sworn to destroy. To gain time, I said, 'Nine years I have fought in foreign lands. If the fyrd is summoned, I must go with them: my fealty is to the King. But war is not yet certain. Once Duke William realizes the size and strength of the English force, he may think again. Normandy is not a huge province and while his men are renowned fighters, there is a limit to their number.'

He rose from his seat and began to pace back and forth like a caged wolf.

'I tell you this in confidence, though no doubt it will be common knowledge before long,' he said carefully. 'The Pope has endorsed William's claim. Unless Harold Godwineson gives up the throne, war is now inevitable. Rome has ever considered ours a renegade church and, do not forget, Stigand, Archbishop of Canterbury, a man reviled and excommunicated by five popes, gained his position through Godwine's influence. Lanfranc, Abbot of Caen, has persuaded the lords of Brittany and Flanders to uphold William's cause to the greater glory of God and the Holy Roman Church. Mercenaries from all over the Empire are flocking to join in. It is not only the Normans we face.'

He paused and sighed again, swung round to face me.

'Hereward, tell your nephews the kingdom must be united. The men of Northumbria and Mercia are needed in the south. Wessex and East Anglia cannot withstand this threat alone.'

I did not ask how he was so well informed, it was but proof of the Church's influence

'It is more than ten years since I saw Edwin and Morcar,' I replied flatly. 'We got on well enough as boys: since then they have become eorls while I was outlawed. Do not put too much faith in our kinship.'

'I can only work with what is within my reach,' he said impatiently. His glance flicked towards Martin, who stood still and silent by the door, then returned to me. 'I do not presume to come between a man and his fealty to the King: if the fyrd is summoned I shall also go. But I must have your allegiance.'

Pride may be a man's salvation and his downfall. It was Turfrida who, hearing of loanland owned by the abbey, had urged me to take it: for all that she professed contentment with our holdings in Laughton and Rippingale, she was a nobleman's daughter and knew that tenure of land brings power. Without confessing that which I tried to deny even to myself, how could I refuse? Borough was our nearest town, a centre for trade and news along Ermine Street, the great north-south road: had I refused to go there, she would have thought me mad. And now, as Abbot Leofric waited, doubt growing in his eyes with each passing moment, how could I spurn his offer when it was what I had come for, though by pledging loyalty to the abbey I would be foresworn on an oath made not to any man but God? It was of no account that I was a child when I made that pledge: it had been no game but deadly serious. Yet I rose from the chair and knelt before the abbot to swear fealty and I did it so that I would not return empty-handed to my wife.

Success in gaining land was far from my mind as we rode back: the terms by which it had been achieved were bitter as bile. When Bourne came into view, Martin, who had ridden a little behind, leaving me to myself, trotted alongside. 'Should we give Eadric the news?'

I thought of the pair of them in their home, Eadric's quiet pride in Ymma and the child growing in her womb, knew the tidings would shatter the security of that world.

'No,' I said. 'Likely enough he has already heard of the muster in the south; the rest was given in confidence. Even Turfrida will not hear it from me.'

He stared and opened his mouth as if to argue but thought better of it and contented himself with a sardonic shake of the head. Suddenly I wanted to be home. I heeled Tiw into a canter. Workers in the fields looked up and waved in recognition as we passed but to my relief, Eadric was not among them.

News that our land-hold had increased was received with joy by Turfrida. Aedgifu, not to be outdone, asked if she could have another kitten now that we were rich. Martin, though, seemed unusually subdued as he tended the horses and Turfrida watched him thoughtfully before taking my arm and leading me to the back of the hall where the frame of the new building was almost complete.

'What's wrong?' She stared earnestly into my face. 'Something has happened.'

I should have guessed she would sense our foreboding. There was nothing to be gained by concealing news of the muster: she would hear it soon enough from Cole One-Hand, or any of the cottars as the tidings spread. She listened in silence, then asked if we had called in on Eadric and Ymma.

'No.' I could hardly bear her calmness. 'I had no wish to be the bearer of such ill news. To call on the fyrd before hay harvest! When we entered Borough, the townsfolk thought I was a messenger bringing the King's summons.'

She smiled at that and pointed to the stakes we had set for the double walls of wattle. 'It will not be as grand as Bourne but it will serve our needs well enough. Once the roof is on, we'll be treading daub. All the children for miles around are coming: Aelgytha promised honey-cakes in return for a day's labour.'

Her blitheness disquieted me: it was as if she had somehow missed the significance of our tidings. 'Turfrida – '

'No, Hereward.' She turned to take my face between her hands, her gaze fervent, unwavering. 'Let us take each day as it comes and be thankful for those that pass in peace. Why worry about a future that may never be, one we do not want? If there is to be war we cannot prevent it but it need not taint this time we have together. When the call comes, join the fyrd if you must; until then, speak no more of it.'

Against such wisdom I had no argument. Seeing that I was lost for words, she pulled me close and kissed me on the lips. I held her against me and she bent her head into the hollow of my shoulder and it was as if I all I ever wanted from the world was there, the yearning and the fulfilment.

The happiness of that summer was all the more precious because we could never quite forget its fragility. Hundreds of ships had massed in the southern ports; thousands of men were camped between Dover and Portsmouth with watchers and beacons posted along the coast all the way to Exeter. Yet as days turned to weeks and nothing happened, an uneasy calm settled on the country. Folk travelling north spoke of growing dissent amongst the hard-pressed populace of the south who were struggling to harvest crops without most of their men. The threat of hunger replaced that of war in the minds of exhausted women and children, the aged, those too young to bear arms or maimed by the use of them.

Hidden away on the edge of the marshes we seemed immune from such cares. The Wapentake reported that a few young hotheads, eager for renown, had joined Harold's force of their own volition but still no call came. Sheep-shearing was over (the Hall still stank of lanolin from the fleeces); Toli sniffed the air anxiously and went every day to check if the hayfield was ready for cutting; our house grew closer to completion whenever there was a pause in other labour. Busy with the running of our new estates, which meant I was often away from Laughton, it became easy to live day by day and plan according to the turn of the seasons as Turfrida had wished. Indeed, we began to believe that the war might not come after all, though by now it was widely known that William of Normandy's claim had been endorsed by both Pope and Emperor.

The construction of the house gave me a chance to show Turfrida and Aedgifu more of the country which had become their home. We went to the woods with Cole One-Hand to fetch hazel wands to be woven into the walls. While the reeve supervised the woodsmen, I led my wife and child past the coppice into the wilder area of the wood, which stretched westwards to the great Mercian forest. Here, ancient oaks spread gnarled roots like questing hands across the woodland floor: their boles were greater than the three of us could encircle; their branches, green with moss and shaggy with lichen filtered the light into golden shafts. Fine grass grew in the dappled sunlight. We came to a stream and Aedgifu stopped to splash and play while I led Turfrida to a nearly hollow, carpeted with soft leaf litter. We made love in the woodland stillness and afterwards lay listening with a kind of wonder to the self-absorbed chatter of the child, the furtive scratch of a wren's claws against bark, the soft calling of wood-doves over the background hum of insects. Such quiet bliss was there, neither of us moved or spoke for a long while. The shadows slowly lengthened and when Aedgifu came looking, we drew her down between us to point out a spider suspended high above, the strands of its web shining like silver wire; an oak gall like a carbuncle; anything to prolong the spell in which the woodland bound us. At length, when hunger told us it was time to leave, we made our way between the trees in silence. As Aedgifu trotted ahead, (pretending, I think, to be a horse), she seemed almost without substance as she passed from shade into sunlight and back again.

Cole One-Hand was waiting, the mules dozed in the traces; the woodsmen eyed Turfrida and I knowingly and went away laughing. When we set off, the three of us sitting on the back of the wagon, swinging our legs as if we were all children, I wondered what perversity had caused God to mould men's natures towards bloodshed when there was such goodness to be found in the world.

Two weeks of fine weather followed, during which hay was cut and carted. When that was over, all free hands were engaged weaving wattle into the walls of our house, then Turfrida and I went to pick up reed for thatch. Reed-cutting had not yet begun in the marshes but, Toli said, seasoned stems were needed, else the thatch would rot. There had been heavy thunderstorms following hay harvest and the track into the fenland was almost impassable: I had to lead the mules while the wheels slid in the mud. Sedge hemmed us in on either side but above us the sky was a clear rain-washed blue. Only when Turfrida stood on the wagon could she see beyond the reeds: Aedgifu, clinging to her tunic, was not tall enough. The cold, rooty tang of fen mingled with the saltiness of the sea (the wind was from the east), water lapped in the background; close by a warbler unleashed its song, then fell abruptly silent. Then came a faint rippling and Turfrida said quietly, 'I think someone is shadowing us, on the water.'

I pulled the mules to a halt while my hand went instinctively to my dagger (so secure did I feel on my own lands, I no longer always bore my sword). Turfrida sat with Aedgifu in her arms, telling the child to be quiet. We waited, listening for the slightest sound but there was only the water lapping, the gentle clash of reed-stems in a breath of wind, the distant crying of gulls from where a fisherman was pulling in his nets. Then came a faint plop followed by a swirl, unmistakeable to anyone who has ever poled a punt. I looked along the track which here bent away from the waterway and urged Turfrida to take the wagon on a little while I waited to see what kind of threat we faced.

As I loosened the dagger in its sheath, my mind and body slipped into battle-focus, that state of awareness where every sound becomes magnified yet clear, each object sharp-edged: even the grey-greens and browns of the vegetation seemed more brilliant in hue. The plop and swirl came again, then the soft brushing of stems as a boat nosed its way through the reeds. So thick was the growth, I could not see more than an arm's length in.

'Brain-biter!' The words were low and harsh yet so unexpected, I did not respond: they seemed almost an echo of the past, no more than the wind's whisper through the reeds. But when they came again there could be no mistake. I glanced to where Turfrida had halted the wagon, a hundred paces down the track, then hissed: 'Skull-smiter!' and waited with a mixture of anticipation and trepidation, so long was it since I had heard those words or used them.

(It had started as a drunken game one night in a woodland glade, where we of the Fen-wolves were roasting a sheep stolen from my father. Someone (I forget who) suggested we make a battle rhyme in the manner of the Vikings, an ode to our swords. Until then, we had not named our weapons. A sword is a sword when all's said and done: what matters is that it does not break. But we were young and intoxicated by success (though in truth it took no great skill to harry the monks of Borough or rob my father), and thus the rhyme took shape, each member adding a line: their sword was thereafter known by that name. Only next morning, through the fug of an aching head, did I realize the poem's potential: to act as roll-call and inspiration, password and counter, thus I swore my comrades to secrecy and when a new member joined the gang, his contribution to the rhyme became a kind of initiation:

Brain-biter; Skull-smiter;
Rib-raker; Bone-breaker;
Chest-cleaver; Life-reaver;
Blood-flinger; Death-bringer . . . Childish in concept, it yet served a serious purpose. When we chanted it to work up our courage and bring fear to our enemies it was blood-curdling, ending in the wolf's howl with which we launched our attacks.)

'We'd given you up for dead.' One moment I was looking at a dense stand of reeds, the next a man stood there, tall and angular, heron-still, balanced on a slim reed punt I could have spanned with my hands. His sea-grey eyes regarded me steadily from a face of skull-like gauntness; his dark hair and beard hung in matted hanks to his waist. He leant on his pole and his face creased in the grimace which served him as a smile. His teeth glinted white, like a wolf's fangs.

'How goes it with you, Rahere?' He was the oldest of the Fen-wolves though no-one, he included, knew his true age. He had taught us fen-craft: how to move across mire and mere unseen; how to live off the wetlands in winter or summer, yet though his experience far outweighed that of the rest of us who were, for the most part, mere boys, he was content to let others lead. None of us knew where he lived save that it was deep in the marshes, nor had he ever spoken of any kin. He was, in truth, a Wild Man, having sworn fealty to no lord or king, free from Christian notions of guilt and duty. If he believed in any gods they belonged to an older, pagan world and spoke with the voices of water, wind and sea.

'I live.' He jerked his head in the direction of the wagon. 'I see you've not been idle.'

'No.' There was something in his eyes, a kind of barely suppressed excitement that made me uneasy. 'Did you want something of me, Rahere?'

His eyes narrowed slightly, then he answered deliberately, ' 'tis a long time since a wolf's howl was heard in these parts. But it may not be long before it sounds again.'

I was in no mood for riddles, least of all with a man whose nature was unpredictable as the wind.

'What do you mean?'

He looked round furtively and lowered his voice as if fearful of being overheard. 'News sometimes travels fastest by the sea-road. Tostig Godwineson's sail went into Humber Mouth with a ship-force three-score strong not two days ago.'

I glanced to where Turfrida and the child sat on the wagon, playing some kind of word-game but with an eye upon me.

'Who else have you told? The alarm must have sounded all over the North Riding and Yorkshire by now.'

'Ay.' He tilted his head slightly and his gaze was mocking. 'I took a stick of eels to Ulfkil at Croyland yesterday. He bade me warn my friends make ready, for war is certain. And he thanked me for the fish.'

'Then it is a lucky chance you found me here,' I said. 'But what has this to do with the Fen-wolves? They are disbanded.'

'Wherever there is war, there are rich pickings to be had,' he answered and as I stared, he licked his lips. 'A time may soon come when you need us: do not scorn old comrades just because you have a pretty wife and rich lands.'

'"Gore-crow", not heron, we should have named you,' I replied, chilled by his certainty. 'But I thank you for the news. And I have never scorned you or any of the others. You will always find a welcome at my Hall. Only,' I paused to give my words greater emphasis, 'if I hear of any deeds done in the name of the Fen-wolves without my leave, be sure I'll find you Rahere.'

He nodded but the mocking light still danced in his eyes as, without apparent effort, he leaned on the pole and the punt bore him away. So smooth was the movement of the frail craft it seemed almost that it was I who moved, the land slipping backwards while the reeds sprang to screen him from view. And this time no sound marked his passing.

I wanted to consider the implications of his tidings, thus in response to Turfrida's questions, I replied only that one of the Fen-folk, a boyhood acquaintance, had heard of my return. Whether she believed it or not, she accepted this explanation and I forced aside my disquiet for we soon came to the cluster of hovels and stacks which comprised the reed-cutter's settlement.

The huts were built on stilts to protect against spring tides and storm surges and Turfrida and the child looked round in wonder as the Fen-folk came to meet us. They were kindly, especially when they realized I had been the youth who brought them meat and grain (liberated from my father's store), in times of hunger long past. Smoked eels and black rye-bread they gave us and Turfrida promised that in future they would find help and protection at Toli's Hall though their land was not part of our estate. While

I helped load reed-bundles onto the wagon, an old women with gold discs hanging from her ears and a face wizened as a piece of wind-dried driftwood, invited the two inside.

The shadows were lengthening when the loading was finished and a boy scrambled to secure the ropes. I waited beside the wagon, talking idly to the lad, my eyes on the swirl and eddy of the tide for the river ran broad here, treacherous with mudflats and sandbanks. The Fen-folk maintained that the waterways could be negotiated all the way to the great fens around Ely though I had never ventured so far upon them. As the boy left me to go and check his father's pots and traps, I mused upon Rahere's warning and wondered whether even now a summons was being heard in the streets of Borough, calling the levy to march not south but north.

Barely had this thought entered my mind when Turfrida, Aedgifu asleep in her arms, came out of the hovel. She looked pale and tired as she climbed onto the wagon and I wondered if her moon-time was upon her. Having settled Aedgifu next to her and covered the child with a cloak, I went forward to lead the mules. Although Turfrida smiled and waved to the folk gathered to bid farewell, her good-humour seemed forced.

The sun had dried the track enough that we reached the old road without mishap, heavily laden though the wagon was. Yet when we passed the place where Rahere had intercepted us, I felt an odd creeping sensation between my shoulder-blades and kept my hand upon my dagger hilt until we were past the reed beds and into more open country.

I halted the mules at a watering place for they were lathered and panting with the effort of hauling the wagon through the ruts. While I watched lest they guzzle too much, Turfrida slid down to join me. The child was still asleep despite the jolting ride.

'I wish I had not come,' Turfrida said. Her face was drawn as if she were ill or deeply troubled and I felt a touch of fear even as I asked: 'What is it, love? Are you sick?'

'That old woman frightened me.' Her eyes sought mine. 'She told me things I would rather not know.'

'What things?' The dread that had been like an icy finger stroking my spine became a thrill of apprehension. 'Was it about me?'

'No.' She looked at me intently. 'Why: is there more I should know? It was about her own people, whose roots go far back beyond the time of the Romans. The legions, then the Jutes and Angles passed through this land and last the Danes, and still the Fen-folk endured, she said. But then she warned that a tide is coming like no other, which will sweep all before it and change the land forever, an iron heel that will leave its mark even here, crushing all who resist.'

I tugged the mules' heads up and turned them back onto the road.

'Likely enough she's heard the same rumours as everyone else,' I said. 'They are full of old tales, she and her kind. She saw in you a newcomer and sought to impress you so that when winter comes you will not forget them. And she succeeded: did you not promise help when times are hard?'

'Perhaps.' She smiled but did not meet my eyes and I knew then she had not told me all. Yet I could not force from her what she wanted to keep secret. I helped her back onto the wagon and we made our way home talking of small matters. Peace lay across the fields and marshes, all golden in early evening sunlight but it could not wholly dispel my disquiet.

Our roof was soon thatched and we dug a shallow pit in which clay, dung and straw for daub were collected. We waited for a day that was not too hot for the treading and folk came from as far as Bourne and Rippingale to help. Aelgytha had baked enough honey-cakes to feed the whole of Borough while for the adults there was beer, smoked eels and barley bread. An atmosphere of holiday affected us all: naked children, smeared with clay and dung ran round shrieking once the novelty of pushing daub into the walls of woven hazel palled. The women kilted their long tunics through their belts and were soon caked to their knees and elbows no less than the men.

As the day wore on and the walls neared completion, there was much horse-play and some of the younger couples sneaked off to the woods, accompanied by the jeers and raucous advice of their elders. All the while Toli sat like a lord on the stone block outside the Hall, an ale-horn in one hand (which Aelgytha ensured was never empty), and a hazel wand in the other which he waved to emphasize orders and advice no-one heeded. When Aedgifu crept behind to drop a pellet of dung down his back, he rounded on her growling like a bear and she fled, screaming. Since we had settled at Laughton, he had become a different man from the grief-worn ancient we had found on our arrival: he doted on the child as his own kin and she loved him like a grandfather.

It was late afternoon, the shadows stretched long across the yard, when news came that Ymma had gone into labour. A stable-boy brought the message on Eadric's own horse, a dappled grey, small in stature beside Tiw but strong and sturdy. Turfrida washed the mud off at the stream while I ran for Swallow and the palfrey. Turfrida had promised to be there but I guessed that Eadric also might welcome a friend.

The miles to Bourne had never seemed so long but when we arrived, the crone who acted as healer and midwife came out to tell us there was a while yet to go and no need for worry. Turfrida went with her. I heard a woman groan and felt my stomach heave. Pain enough I have dealt out on the battlefield, aye and been wounded many times but that of childbirth, the agony from which we all come writhing and bloody into the world, is something to which women are doomed and men should avoid.

I found Eadric alone in the church but he was not praying. He sat bowed over, his hands clenched before him so that the tendons stood out like cords. Hearing footsteps on the stone floor he looked round, his face pale.

'I do not care what happens, so long as she lives,' he said, then sat rigid as a scream pierced the quiet of the church. 'What if she dies?'

'She will not.' I took his arm and pulled him to his feet. 'Such thoughts do no good. Come on, show me your defences. There is much we must discuss. If you are needed, you will still be within call.'

He came reluctantly and I knew that while we walked the line of ditch and palisade, already marked out with stakes, his whole being was focused on the noises coming from the Hall. It seemed an age before the screams, which had sounded with increasing frequency and anguish, ended in a cry of mingled pain and triumph, followed soon after by a new-born's yowling. Eadric cast me a look of utter relief then sprinted for the hall.

This being a moment to be shared between husband and wife, I wandered to the stables on the pretext of checking the horses. Soon Turfrida came out. She went to the water trough to wash her bloody hands and stood still, her back towards me. As I put my arms around her, she half-turned and raised her face to mine. There was a red-brown smear on her cheek and I wiped it away, wondering what ailed her, for she seemed strangely subdued.

'She was lucky: it was quick,' she said after a moment's silence. 'And it is a boy. But it is early-born and so small, Hereward.' She paused before added fiercely: 'I want more children of our own. Sons to follow after you.'

'If they do not come it will not be for lack of trying,' I retorted. 'You are young: why hurry to be with child again, puking your guts up in the morning, then big so that I can't have you? There is time enough.'

'Men!' She shook her head in exasperation, shrugged free of my embrace and stalked towards the back of the hall. I followed, wondering what I had said wrong, but all such concerns were wiped from my mind when Eadric flung open the door, face split in an inane grin. 'Come and meet my son, Toli the Younger!'

That night we stayed at Bourne, for Turfrida was worried about Ymma and the child while Eadric wanted to celebrate. He and I got very drunk but at least one good thing came of it: we agreed to train our men together, between now and harvest. As our talk turned to the threat of invasion, he confided in me his greatest fear (which was that of most men in those times), that he would be slain far from home, leaving wife and child homeless and without means to support themselves. Under his agreement with Morcar, Ymma had no rights to Bourne should Eadric die.

'Do not march with such thoughts in mind,' I advised, 'else distraction will cause what you most dread. But in any case if ill befalls you, Ymma and the children will find a home with us. I will give my oath on it, if it will ease your mind.'

'There is no need.' He smiled ruefully. 'I cannot believe how much I feared your return. I was a fool: you are not the headstrong youth who left nine years ago.'

I thought of our first night back at Laughton and my hand tightened on my ale-horn. 'He is not so far away as you might think,' I said. 'It was Turfrida guided him to reason. Without her, I might have sold my sword to Duke William.'

He was not listening: befuddled by ale, he began to talk of how he would teach his son all the arts of a nobleman, have him instructed in Latin and French, take him out to learn the ways of the Gyrwas and woodlanders the better to manage his lands.

'Maybe he will become a great man: a King's thegn,' he said excitedly. 'That was what my father wanted for me. I must have been a disappointment to him, preferring study and farming to swordplay.'

'Toli is a man of peace: I do not think he could have wished for a better son.' I drained the last of my ale. 'And think on this: with me as foster-brother, the worst of your misdeeds appeared as nothing.'

'Aye, there is that.' He lurched to his feet, leaning on the table for balance. 'And now I have my own son. I must go and see him.'

Our staggering entry into the rooms behind the hall woke the two women and the babe. Luckily, our drunken state shielded us from the worst of Turfrida's ire: she knew we would rue it in a few hours. But even through the ale-induced haze, I noted the tenderness with which Eadric took wife and child in his arms and I embraced Turfrida in like manner, promising her more children in slurred and voluble tone until she feigned slumber to silence me.

3. Corpse-ring

Weeks passed, marked by the completion of our house and the start of harvest. Before the latter began in earnest, Eadric and I began training the levy though the men grumbled that their time would be better spent elsewhere. They were a mixed bunch, three of whom, Siward the Red, Acer the Hard and Gamal Longbow had been Fen-wolves, but few others had seen conflict more serious than drunken brawls at Yuletide. To mould them into fighters to be reckoned with was my purpose and after a while, as their skills and endurance improved, they began to take pride in themselves which is the difference between ordinary men and warriors.

None of the Fen-wolves mentioned our past within hearing of the others, though they were easily the best marksmen. They told me privately that others of the gang still lived in adjacent wapentakes. Rahere, Esbiorn and Thorkil were already accounted for.

While the men of the fyrd made ready, fashioning weapons as well as becoming practised in the use of them (until the needs of the harvest overtook all other concerns), no news came of war save that Harold Godwineson's force was suffering desertion on a massive scale. It was the sworn duty of every free man in England to pay forty days' service to the King but many of those mustered in the south had spent more waiting. Some discontented thegns now took their men home to gather the harvest and eventually the whole ship and land force was dismissed as hungry men took to pillaging the very people who looked to Harold for protection: months of inactivity had used up all the stores. Meanwhile in the north it appeared that after being routed by my nephew, Edwin, Tostig had fled to Scotland. It was rumoured he had met Harald Hardrada there but this seemed of little account, most of Tostig's shipmen having been bribed to stay behind.

Folk of all ages were involved in bringing in the grain, for a successful harvest meant the difference between hunger and starvation in the spring. But it was not all hard work. To Toli's feigned disapproval Aedgifu persuaded us to decorate the new building. Thus the daub bore the imprints of our hands and Turfrida inscribed our names carefully beneath, then helped the child make patterns of coloured stones and shells around the doorway as was the custom in parts of her country. A knot of ash nailed over the lintel completed our new home and I began to wonder where I could lay my hands on a loom, for Turfrida was a skilled weaver. Yet despite our growing contentment, the shadow of war had not departed. Midsummer had passed, now we all looked to Michaelmas, believing that no ship-force would set sail thereafter for fear of storms. Then we would be safe until the following spring.

It was during the second week in September that tidings came of trouble in the north. I was at Witham checking the apple trees (it promised to be a fine crop), when a boy came running up the hill, red-faced and gasping. He called my name, then blurted his news.

Harald Hardrada and Tostig Godwineson had joined forces and sailed into the Humber with three hundred ships. Borough was like a kicked ant's nest: the messenger had changed horses at the abbey then gone to raise all those with fealty to Eorls Edwin and Morcar. They were to muster at Morcar's manor of Fulford Gate, two days' hard ride away.

I was already in the saddle, turning Tiw's head back towards Bourne, when I thought to ask when the messenger had left Borough.

'At first light, this morning.'

I glanced up: it was close to midday. Cursing, I dug my heels into the stallion's sides and he sprang straight into a gallop. I did not spare him and he went as if he understood the urgency of our errand.

At Bourne, a stable-boy ran to take Tiw. His eyes seemed to start from his head at the sight of us, the horse panting and lathered, my fierceness as I leapt from the saddle and asked for his master. The lad stammered incoherently so that I was tempted to take him between my hands and shake him but something, maybe the unusual quietness of the yard, told me part of the answer. Turning on my heel, I strode towards the house and then the boy found his voice: 'They're all at Laughton. Eadric was going on from there.'

'Going on?' I hurried back and snatched the reins. 'When did the summons come? How many are with him?'

'A messenger came through last night on the way to Borough.' The boy was white and trembling. 'The levy from here's already left: upwards of forty men.'

I caught a last glimpse of his face, open-mouthed and anxious, as I swung into the saddle and heeled the stallion forward. Even going cross-country it was nearly eight miles to Toli's Hall and Tiw's breathing was quick and harsh before we reached the old road. It was no use bewailing the fact I had chosen to ride him instead of Swallow that morning, nor could I afford to founder my war-horse in a pointless race when the likelihood was I would be setting out again that day. Forcing down impatience, I relaxed in the saddle and slackened rein while my mind turned over the implications of the news, considering who should go; how much food and gear to take; whether to use pack-beasts or the wagon, which could carry more but would slow us down.

With such concerns the miles passed yet what should have been foremost in my mind never occurred to me: that while Eadric was Morcar's man, I owed no allegiance to my nephews. Indeed, as Abbot Leofric had made clear, my first duty was towards the King, my second to those from whom I had secured loanland. I pushed Tiw into full gallop when the roofs of Laughton came into view then, on breasting the slope, saw I was too late and let him slacken pace. There was no crowd of men and horses in the yard, only little groups of women and children. Cole One-Hand and Toli sat on the stone block.

At the sound of hooves, all looked round nervously except Ymma who was nursing her babe in the doorway of the Hall. I drew rein in the centre of the yard. 'Where's Eadric?'

The question fell into a well of silence: they stared as if bereft of speech. Then Turfrida came from Aelgytha's cottage. Her face was pale and tense as she went to the stallion's head and laid a hand on his lathered neck.

'He has left for York, to join Morcar at Fulford Gate,' she said. 'He and his men arrived soon after you went. They took the ridge road: that's why you missed them. He wanted to speak with you.'

'Speak?' I was already striding towards the Hall, heedless of the women's frightened glances and Toli's frozen expression. 'Why didn't he wait? You knew where I'd gone.'

We were in the dim interior of the main hall by now. I was wondering whether to take my own javelins or rely on those we had stockpiled for the levy, when Turfrida caught hold my arm and pulled me to a standstill.

'Hereward, listen!'

Almost I jerked free but the urgency of her tone stayed me. Her eyes, wide and anxious, swallowed my gaze. 'What? I must leave now: they already have half a day on me.'

'No!' She seemed close to striking me from fear and exasperation. 'He wants you to stay here until the King's call comes. You have no obligation to Morcar or Edwin.' She paused and glanced all about though there was no-one else in the hall. 'And he told me you pledged to help Ymma and the child. He needs someone to protect their interests and oversee the estate while he is away. You cannot do that by riding with him.'

'But we've been training the men together!' I protested. 'Everything was agreed!' Wrenching my arm free, I continued towards the door to our rooms. 'I shall go nonetheless. Riding Swallow and leading Tiw I can catch up easily enough.'

Inside our main living chamber, which still smelled faintly of damp clay and dung, I crouched and fumbled to free my belt whilst searching for the shirt and leggings I wore beneath my hauberk. Turfrida stood with her back against the door, watching quietly as I destroyed the neatly folded piles in the oaken clothes-chest. When the belt came free at last, she said, 'One last message Eadric left, guessing how it would be. "Tell Hereward this: though not a warrior born, nor am I a child. Between brothers there should be respect as well as love."'

I straightened, considering these words, then reached for the nearest object, a horn cup on the bench, and flung it across the room with such force that it struck the wall and split.

'He would not have spoken thus to my face!' I was breathing hard as if I'd been running: an invisible hand seemed to grasp my throat.

'He meant no insult.' She came and stood close but without touching. 'And he is right: you owe nothing to your nephews. Likely enough he will fight better knowing his family is safe.'

'Ay.' I smiled bitterly at this irony. 'And without me there, who will protect him?'

'Hereward.' There was a warning note to her tone I knew of old: it meant she would brook no argument. 'Eadric will not thank you if you go after like an anxious father chasing an errant son. Your place is here, until a summons comes from those to whom you owe fealty.'

I stared at my hands, scarred and calloused from reins and weapons. 'Are Toli and Ymma so sure?'

'Will you listen to them before me and Eadric?' She shook her head and went to open the back door to let in the afternoon sunlight. 'Come on: with Bourne short-handed there is much to do.'

In the days which followed I began to understand there are different kinds of courage from that required to stand in a shieldwall or fight on the tourney field. My senses pricked to every hoofbeat and each time a cart creaked past I wondered if it bore Eadric wounded or dead though he could only just have reached York. I realized then what Turfrida had meant when we spoke of chance: in some ways the uncertainty faced by those left behind in war is worse than the grim reality of fighting. Yet while an atmosphere of dreadful expectancy hung over Bourne (which had lost its strongest men to Morcar's muster), it was still one of the busiest times of the year, gleaning the harvested fields, fruit-picking, eel-smoking and wood-splitting being but a few of the preparations necessary for the coming winter. Already the days were shortening and in the woods herds of pigs foraged for beech-mast and acorns beneath leaves turning red and gold with autumn.

Although Eadric had taken the levy from Morcar's lands, upwards of fifty men and youths of fighting age remained in Ness and Aveland wapentakes. These I continued training, having them meet at Bourne so that when weapons practice was over, they could help build the palisade. Men of outlying villages complained bitterly at this but I told them they had as much right as Bourne folk to seek protection there and that quietened them. The idea that such defences might be needed was disturbing to men who had lived most of their lives in peace.

An air of unreality seemed to pervade our lives as we waited for news. Ymma had taken the babe back to Bourne but Turfrida was anxious for their welfare. She would ride with me when I went to hammer my band of ploughmen, shepherds and fieldhands into fighters and we rode back together afterwards, talking of light matters. Yet as I had the men form shieldwalls against each other or throw javelins at straw targets, I knew that if it came to real fighting I would be lucky to bring a third of them home alive and unscathed and that was if we had the victory. The English force fought as a single host but the young men of the levy, reckless in their ignorance and expendable, were the main casualties of most battles rather than the better armed and more experienced hus-carls. Remembering some of the fighting in Scaldemariland, I made sure each man had a long knife to hand, a short stabbing blade being of more use than a sword or axe in a locked shieldwall, and told them over and over that no horse will charge into a set spear-hedge but once the line broke, there was only one outcome for those on foot: death.

It was maybe seven nights after Eadric's leaving that Turfrida woke me. So dark was it that the glow of hearth-embers seemed raw and fierce: the smoke-hole was visible only as a paler patch against the blackness of the roof.

'What is it?' I was half-asleep, weary from riding to Witham and back then training hard with the men. 'Turfrida?'

She had raised herself on one elbow: her body seemed taut as a bowstring against mine. 'Shh!' Her breathing was quick and uneven. 'I thought I heard horses galloping, hundreds of them, like thunder.'

I turned over and took her in my arms, one hand cupping a breast, the other laid upon the smooth length of her thigh. 'It was a dream, love: forget it.'

'No, listen!' There was an edge of impatience to her tone that checked the desire that surged through my blood. She shifted abruptly as her nipple hardened under my thumb. 'Hereward, no!'

I grunted to convey my displeasure then, as she did not relax, found myself alert to every sound. Even with a plank door and wattle walls between us, Toli's snoring was clearly audible; mice rustled in the thatch; Aedgifu's breathing could just be heard above the running of the stream outside. There was nothing that sounded like hoofbeats and I had begun to stroke Turfrida's back, all thought of sleep forgotten, when my ears caught something on the very edge of hearing. A low ululation, rising and falling like a paean for the dead, mournful, evocative of loss and grief, of ribcages hacked open to the sky, blood-spattered hair and cloven skulls, red rending death. A wolf's howl.

Like children frightened by the monsters of a gleeman's tale we froze, listening. When the cry was repeated Turfrida jerked, then lay rigid in my arms. For an instant I thought she was in the throes of some kind of fit but her breast rose and fell spasmodically and I realized she was struggling to contain tears. A moment later, whimpering sounded from the other side of the door, then Toli's hounds howled back. And all the dogs in every cot and hall for miles around gave voice, as if lamenting some dire happening of which we knew nothing.

Long after the howling echoed into silence, we lay still, alert to every sound. Neither of us slept again that night, nor did we make love but simply held one another. We sensed somehow that our world was about to change, even as geese grow restless with approaching spring, wing-testing the wind as the days lengthen though they know not what stirs their blood. I rose before dawn and coaxed the embers to life and Turfrida watched mutely from our bed as I readied my weapons, already honed and polished against this day, fastened my leather jerkin over my shirt then pulled the hauberk on. The linked rings of the mail-coat gleamed dully in the firelight as I buckled on my swordbelt and still Turfrida did not move or speak. There was no need to explain why a wolf's howl should compel me to find Eadric. These last days she had seen clearly enough how I yearned to be away.

Tiw and Swallow were stabled in a lean-to we had built next to the house to have them close at hand. Turfrida was helping me tie a bundle of javelins and a leather bag of food to the war-horse's saddle when both horses craned their necks and let out the whinny they use when another is approaching. A moment later the clatter of shod hooves sounded from the yard. I slipped out, hand on dagger-hilt, leaving Turfrida to calm the horses. In the pre-dawn twilight, the bulk of the hall loomed like a black cliff to my right but there was a grey bar of light on the eastern horizon. Against it the figure of a mounted man was clearly defined. He looked about uncertainly, then swung down from the saddle.

'Who's there?' Neither man nor horse had been aware of my approach: both started visibly and the animal backed away. As he regained control, the man said, 'Are you the thegn here? I am sent by the King: he calls on all able men with swift horses to ride north against Tostig the traitor and Hardrada of Norway. The King's force is already on the road: we are mustering as we go. How quickly can you ride, and with how many?'

'I am Hereward, son of Eorl Leofric,' I replied. 'And this summons is not unexpected. There are fifty men of the Wapentake hereabouts but we have few horses. Eadric of Bourne took his men north seven days ago: have you any news? Eorls Edwin and Morcar were mustering at Fulford Gate.'

In the faint light I saw him frown as he led his horse to drink at the stream. 'There has been no news from the north since we heard of the landing. But that the Eorls of Northumbria and Mercia were joining forces is known to the King.'

There was barely time to register the slight hesitancy of his tone before the Hall door opened and Toli came out, Martin at his shoulder. The old man fumbled with his sword-belt but my servant was fully dressed. He glanced reprovingly at me but said nothing as the messenger repeated his tidings.

'Martin, ride with me,' I said, when the man had finished. 'We'll join the King straightway. Toli: see if you can get more horses from Croyland, ask

Gamal and Siward to raise all who can ride well and send them after us. The rest should prepare to march but tell them to wait until you hear from me or Eadric before going north. And have the women and children finish apple-picking: the men should be put to building the defences at Bourne.'

Martin had already gone for his horse when the messenger pulled his mount away from the water and hauled himself wearily into the saddle. 'I must go on,' he said. 'The King left Borough soon after midnight: ride north on Ermine Street and you'll find him. His force numbers hundreds, not thousands but this is no untried levy. He intends reaching York the day after tomorrow. Farewell!'

'God speed you!' Toli called but his face was anguished as the horseman pounded away up the track. A moment later Martin appeared, leading his palfrey at a run.

'Look after Turfrida and Aedgifu for me.' I hugged the old man briefly on my way back to the stable, heard the breath catch in his throat. As I led the horses into the yard, Turfrida came from the house with a thick winter cloak. She watched with a kind of wistful intensity as I tied it behind Tiw's saddle.

'Aedgifu is still asleep,' she said at last.

'Leave her then.' I have never been one for long farewells. Martin was already mounted, his chestnut unusually skittish at the unprecedented pre-dawn activity. I swung into Swallow's saddle and took the stallion's head-rope from Turfrida. Her face, framed by her dark hair, seemed very pale as she looked up. I reached down to touch her head and she leaned against my hand, then stepped away.

'Come back to us,' was all she said.

After a morning's hard riding, Martin and I caught up with the King's force near Grantham. A King's thegn demanded our names and eyed me doubtfully when I told him I was Eorl Leofric's son returned from exile. It was only when I was taken to the King and knelt before him that I realized it was not only the threat from his brother and Harald Hardrada that had compelled this rapid deployment north but also fear of an alliance between Tostig and my nephews in the name of the Atheling, Edgar.

Harold Godwineson I had not met before: he was tall and I guessed many women would find him handsome though his face was grim and he seemed weary. Yet he was courteous enough, welcoming me to his force though his mind was clearly on other matters. Talking with his hus-carls later, I discovered that William's army of battle-hardened mercenaries was waiting for a favourable wind on the other side of the Channel. Far from diminishing, the Norman threat had increased.

Once the horses were breathed and rested, the journey continued. A blustery wind brought clouds scudding from the west and soon we were riding through torrential rain which soaked quickly to the skin and turned parts of the track to a morass. More riders joined us and by mid-afternoon the King's force must have numbered many hundreds. We rode at a steady trot but even so the pace proved too much for some. English horses could not match the *destriers* of the Continent, bred for war and endurance.

We were approaching Lincoln when a lone horseman galloped out of the gloom. Martin and I were in the vanguard, not from choice but because the stamina of our mounts had brought us to the fore. The rider slowed, as if unsure what to make of the mass of mounted warriors filling the road then, as the King's standard billowed in a gust of wind, spurred his lathered and panting horse forward. When he was within a spearthrow, he pushed back his sodden hood and the sight of his face sent a chill through us. It was that of one who has witnessed something dreadful beyond comprehension, exhausted, stunned.

The King's thegns clustered round him and the whole cavalcade halted. The man swayed in his saddle and half-fell from his horse; they raised him and took him before the King. He knelt in the mud, head bowed, trembling.

'We did not know you were coming,' he stammered and the King's men looked at one another, disturbed by his informality. Harold took no notice but waited with a kind of weary patience while the man gained control of himself. When at last he spoke again, it was in the dull tone of someone beyond caring where he is or what will happen to him.

'It was carnage . . . we were trapped in the marshes. Hardrada's men . . . The whole of Morcar and Edwin's forces are gone, slaughtered . . they butchered those that did not drown . . '

The incoherent phrases came clear in the silence which followed his first words: when the man's voice failed, the King asked calmly, 'Is Tostig in York? Were Edwin and Morcar slain?'

The man swayed as if he were about to collapse: two hus-carls bent to steady him.

'I don't know,' he said. 'I heard that Morcar fell. What was left of us withdrew to the city. Waltheof came to our aid but it was too late. The townsfolk watched from the walls while our men died. I saw them trapped to their waists in mire and the Vikings used them as stepping-stones, hacking as they went until the marsh reeked with blood. I got away in the rout.'

Harold Godwineson's face was like something hewn from stone as he straightened and surveyed us, his men, awaiting his command.

'Have this man taken somewhere safe where he can rest,' he said. 'We ride to York with all speed. We will not stop until the heads of Tostig the traitor and Hardrada the usurper are stuck over the city gates. Any man whose horse founders must find another: we wait for no-one. Ride!'

Many leaders I have watched and followed but none so resolute as Harold Godwineson. That afternoon he was like a man possessed yet not for one instant did he lose control: his was a cold, calculating rage. All through the daylight hours we galloped and folk working in the fields stared amazed, hearing the dull thunder of hooves then seeing the host of mailed and helmeted warriors pass like something from a dream or legend of long ago, ghost-like in the sheeting rain. As the afternoon failed and the wind eased, we paused to breathe the horses and to stretch and eat. Martin and I shared bread and smoked eels packed by Turfrida that morning and though we spoke only of the distance yet to go, I saw my own anxiety in his set features, knew he was wondering how long it would take news of the slaughter to reach home, whether Eadric had survived.

When darkness fell we were still riding but, inevitably, our pace slowed: not even Harold's determination could keep weary horses from stumbling, exhausted men from slumping half-asleep in the saddle. It was a black night and still raining: before long most of us went on foot, the horses plodding alongside, the way lit by men with flaring torches. The rain relented before we stopped but for those in the rear the journey must have been like something from a nightmare as they floundered through mud churned knee-deep by the passage of those in front.

It seemed it must be close to dawn but in reality it was before midnight when the King called a halt near Tadcaster. By faint starlight seen through rents in the cloud layer, we found ourselves in a landscape of rolling hills, threads of woodland, broad pasture. We led our mounts into the nearest field and staked them out to graze while we wrapped ourselves in our cloaks and lay on the sodden ground to rest as best as we could. Most sank into the blank sleep of exhaustion while the horses, too tired to forage, stood as if rooted, heads hanging low. I slept fitfully, waking to the sound of horsemen riding away singly. I guessed these were scouts sent to discover the enemy's position and my respect for the King deepened. He was no hothead to lead his men blindly into a trap.

A faint light in the eastern sky presaged dawn when we were roused. Martin groaned when I shook him awake. Men cursed, then came the jangle of harness, the deliberate strokes of whetstone against blade, the neighing of horses. I shared a hunk of dry bread with Martin, dipping it into a bowl of foul-tasting ditchwater to soften it. Though I was never hungry before battle, no-one fights well on an empty belly. He helped me with my gear, strapped the iron-plated greaves over my boots while I loosened my dagger in its sheath lest Tiw should fall and I need to cut myself free. Martin settled his axe in his belt though his role was not to fight but to make sure the horses were safe, ready for pursuit or flight; to aid me if I were wounded or at worst, take Turfrida news of my death.

An atmosphere of tense expectancy hung over the camp: the horses caught the men's nervousness and, despite their weariness, grew skittish. Swallow, perverse as ever, stood quietly amid the chaos, then the preparation was over and we were on the road again.

Whatever news the returning scouts brought, the King did not divulge it. It was full daylight when a boy, galloping down the road on a shaggy pony, brought tidings from York for all to hear. Although thousands had died at Fulford Gate, Morcar and Edwin were among the survivors. Hardrada and Tostig had not entered the city but made terms, amongst which was the giving of five hundred hostages at Stamford Bridge at noon this very day. Hostages from the city had already been taken as surety that the agreement would be honoured. After the battle, the enemy force had withdrawn to where their ships were moored, Riccall on the river Ouse, where they had spent the days and nights since celebrating their victory in time-honoured fashion.

I doubt any of this was news to Harold Godwineson but hearing it he smiled grimly. Riccall lay only a few miles away but it was on the other side of the river and the road kept to the high ground with tall hedges on either side, screening us from watchful eyes. It was still early morning when the city walls came into view. Harold sent three hus-carls ahead to warn the inhabitants of his arrival (it was in part to avoid being mistaken for Vikings that he had waited for daylight).

We entered York with no trouble. Indeed, the King was welcomed with joy and great amazement. To those who had lived in fear that their homes would be sacked after all (the giving of hostages was felt to be no surety against a Viking force), it seemed a miracle that he should have arrived so soon. We discovered then that the populace had pledged to join Tostig and Hardrada on their march south against the King rather than see their city burn and that Morcar and Edwin were among the hostages already handed over.

However, it seemed that Tostig had not forgotten his defeat on the Humber earlier that year when most of his men had deserted him. He had demanded another five hundred hostages, to be taken from the villages around Stamford Bridge which had suffered few casualties in the battle. His hold upon York would thus be strengthened ere he marched south. It was widely believed that whoever held the city controlled Northumbria, (effectively the whole north of England), and knowing that the people of that region bore him no great love (they had rebelled against him the year before), he was taking no chances.

Once the city gates were closed, the King arranged for food and ale to be brought and then he closeted himself with the most trusted of his hus-carls to plan his strategy. It was now, talking to some of those that had been part of the desperate sortie, that we learned Fulford Gate had been no easy victory for the Norsemen. Morcar and Edwin had fought bravely and Hardrada's men were on the verge of a rout when their warrior king rallied them, driving a wedge through the English shieldwall which led to the carnage in the marsh. When Martin and I asked after Eadric of Bourne, none had heard of him: one sokemen among so many dead thegns and hus-carls was of little account.

Refreshed by food and drink, the horses safely stabled and our weapons in battle-readiness, Martin and I went along with many others to the southern wall from which, we had been told, part of the battlefield was visible. Before we saw what lay beyond the wall, the foul stench and great flocks of carrion birds wheeling above betrayed the horror and magnitude of the slaughter. When we looked over, even I, who had seen many battlegrounds, was appalled. The fields were boggy pasture for the most part, merging into marshes through which the river flowed but in places, even after five days, it looked as though the reeds grew from hacked and trampled flesh. Many of the dead had been stripped naked; most were decapitated, some had been horribly mutilated. His face held in that odd tension of one who is fighting the urge to vomit, Martin asked, 'Should I go and look for Eadric?'

Only a small part of the marsh and ditch where most of Morcar and Edwin's men had been trapped was visible from city, yet the bodies must have numbered hundreds.

'If he is there, it is too late,' I said roughly, turning my eyes from the carnage and looking behind to the crowded buildings and narrow streets. 'If he is alive, he will be in the city. Look there first.'

Martin left to begin the search but I waited, with a growing number of fighters and townsfolk, to watch as Tostig and Hardrada's force made their way past the city. They seemed not to care that the gates were closed and wandered in no great order, save for a group gathered round the dread standard of the wing-spread raven, the Land-Waster. I guessed that the King, Tostig and their foremost warriors walked there. While most of the men bore swords, axes or spears, few wore mail or carried shields: they were expecting little resistance and the day promised to be hot.

Coming from the south, they must have deliberately chosen their road to intimidate the city folk for they could have taken a shorter route to Stamford Bridge. Some of the Vikings broke off from the main force to search for plunder but since the field had already been stripped, they turned to the corpses for amusement, dragging them close to the city walls so that those inside could see. The Blood-Eagle had been outlawed in Norway and Denmark long ago, but I saw it done then though the victims were past caring. The laughter of those butchers could be clearly heard: we tightened our grip on our weapons and vowed a swift and bloody revenge.

The sun rose to its zenith and we assembled at the East Gate. Harold wanted to give the enemy time to settle at Stamford Bridge for our main advantage would be surprise: they outnumbered us two to one though, we were told, a third of their force must have stayed with the ships. The horses were restive for it was rare that they were used in fighting and they sensed their riders' nervousness but while he tossed his head, Tiw stood like a rock, awaiting my command. I focused on the fight ahead, pushing Eadric's fate from my mind as the great gates creaked open.

It is upwards of five miles from York to the bridge at Stamford but it was easy going along a broad track: the land was gently undulating and open. We spread out as we rode, forming a line a hundred wide and several deep and while we started at a steady trot, the horses' excitement and our own eagerness to avenge the fallen meant that we were soon cantering and the noise of hooves was like rolling thunder. Our spearpoints and the horses' harness glittered in the sunlight and some of us laughed aloud in the fierce joy of the moment as we breasted a low ridge and saw the northmen, who had been taking their ease on both sides of the bridge, scramble to their feet.

I heard it said afterwards that on seeing our line appear, Tostig urged Harald Hardrada to return to the ships before it was too late, though by then we had already cut off their direct line of retreat. The Norwegian King laughed in his face, calling him a white-livered coward, that they could hold the bridge until reinforcements came from Riccall. In truth, seeing the force arrayed against them, knowing their own men to be lightly armed and unprotected, both must have known it would take a miracle to save them for they had no means to get a message to Harald's sons at the moorings. Yet neither capitulated: Hardrada and his men preferring death in battle to dishonour in defeat; Tostig maybe afraid of what his brother would do to him if he were taken alive. And, in any case, Harold Godwineson was in no mood to parley. He, like the rest of us, was out for revenge.

If blood may be wiped out in blood, then those who died in such desperate straits at Fulford Gate were avenged in full that day. More than a third of the foe was caught on ours, the western side of the flimsy wooden bridge, a structure that could only be crossed in single file. The River Derwent ran so deep, it could not be forded and after the recent rain, the current was swift and deadly.

As we approached, our line must have been an imposing and terrible sight to those who had expected to see only a few mounted men come to escort the hostages. They stared in utter disbelief then ran for the bridge, shouting to their comrades who watched in dismay from the other side. Unable to form a coherent shieldwall or spear-hedge, they could not withstand our charge. We wheeled around and encircled those broken from the main mass, small groups of horsemen surrounding bands of doomed and desperate men, while our main force simply hacked away at those scrambling for the bridge. These shoved and grappled comrades aside in their frenzy to escape but there was none.

There was a pause in the fighting when all who could had got across, for they managed to hold the bridge against us for a while, maybe as long as it takes to strip a corpse. It gave us a chance to rally and breathe the horses, then those upon the bridge fell, pierced by arrows and javelins, and we dismounted and simply pushed our way across.

Despite their unreadiness, their lack of shields, it was a hard fight on the other side although the end was inevitable. Hardrada rallied his men repeatedly and the dead piled up before him. When at last an arrow pierced his throat, a great shout arose and the battle-frenzy of his warriors increased: they threw themselves at us and we slew them without mercy. I saw Tostig hacked down beneath the Land-Waster but the core of Vikings fought on until not one was left alive. A great corpse-ring surrounded the dead King and his standard and an eerie quiet fell, broken only by the cries of the wounded, the cawing of carrion birds wheeling overhead and the screams of a stricken horse.

Whether they had heard of the fighting or they came for some other reason, the remainder of Hardrada's force arrived too late. We turned from the slaughter to see them retreating before they even reached the bridge and those of us with horses still unscathed, went back to harry them. Then they fled for their lives but it was more than fifteen miles to where the ships were moored and they were all on foot.

Harold paused only to have what remained of his brother wrapped in the raven-standard and borne into the city, then came after, mounted on a fresh horse. After the hard slog of battle, a rout comes as reward to those in pursuit: the blood-frenzy kindled from fear can be appeased without great risk, while battle-joy still bears one forward as if on a mounting wave. Until at last the killing becomes a weariness and the cries and stench sicken to the very soul.

We chased them to the banks of the Ouse, slaying all we could reach: even the women and children camped beside the river were not spared. Like cattle penned for slaughter, they were trapped at last on a river-bounded tongue of land and then the King's sons and their bishop threw down their weapons in token of surrender. Of the three hundred ships which had sailed up the Humber, crammed with men who knew no other life than war, only twenty-five returned, bearing all that remained of Hardrada's great host. Of these, many were wounded and all were stunned by the magnitude of the disaster which had followed so quickly upon triumph. They took with them some of their dead, which they were allowed to recover after swearing never to set foot again on English soil save as the King's allies. Thus it was that Harald Hardrada, mighty warrior-king, returned to his own land, though it was not the homecoming he had boasted of.

Once the fighting was over, I dismounted and led Tiw back towards the city, one of a long line of exhausted men and horses. A trail of corpses led from the moorings all the way to the battlefield; figures moved among the dead and dying, some looting, others looking to aid the wounded of our side or else searching for kin and friends. Enemy wounded we slew, thinking of the defiled dead of Fulford Gate close by: the onlookers from the city and nearby villages were no more merciful. I saw one Norseman, entrails spilling from an axe-wound, try to crawl away from a group of women who screamed abuse, then flung stones until he lay still and did not move again.

The luck that had brought me safe through the fighting in Flanders and Maine had not deserted me. I was unscathed and while Tiw limped from a sword-slash to his shoulder, the wound, though bloody, was not serious. In the haze of tiredness which follows the ecstasy of battle, I stumbled through the South Gate after the others. The stench of the city filled my nostrils as it had earlier that same day but it could not overcome the taste and smell of blood: that stayed with me for days after. My mail and clothes were splattered with mud and gore; my sword-arm was reddened to the elbow but none of the blood was mine.

I do not know how many hours passed between entering the city and the moment I found myself seated at a long table in a massive timbered hall, free at last of coif and helm, an ale-horn in one hand, a hunk of bread in the other. There was a great clamour all around as men talked off the lingering battle-frenzy, reliving the moments of individual triumph which go to make up a great victory. Memories of terror, a sword or spear-thrust that just misses, a breaking sword, a comrade hacked to pieces before one's eyes, they would come later, in nightmares. Now was the time for celebration and as ale and mead fired the boasting I wondered at my detachment, recalled Toli's assertion that war is for the young. I drained the ale-horn at a gulp, lurched to my feet and at that moment Martin entered the hall. He paused and gazed all about then, seeing me, looked relieved. I pushed my way through the throng and followed him outside.

'Thank God you're safe.' He looked searchingly at my stained mail, clothes, skin. 'I found Eadric but' - he grimaced and shook his head – 'I don't know how long he'll live. They took the wounded to the abbey until that was full: he must have been among the first brought in. He took a sword-thrust to the thigh: it went clean through his hauberk.'

We made our way through the narrow streets. They were crowded, god-fearing townsfolk scurrying from drunken fighters while the more enterprising (or less scrupulous), tried to sell us weapons and armour scavenged from the battlegrounds. Above the noise I thought to hear the cawing of carrion birds, and shuddered. Like most fighters, one of my worst fears was to find myself mortally wounded on such a field of death, with crows and ravens hopping in to peck at my eyes and flesh and being helpless to prevent it. But if that was the stuff of nightmares, the horror that met my eyes inside York abbey that day was like some vision of purgatory where men's soul's writhe in anticipation of Judgement, a foretaste of Hell.

So many had died or been maimed by my sword and spear, I believed myself inured to men's suffering. By the time I was twenty I had seen human bodies split like sheep's carcases; blood and brains burst from cloven skulls; the shock in a man's eyes when his guts slither from a belly wound. In Flanders, where I was a leader of men, I grew used to assessing how long the wounded might live: some I gave the mercy of the sword to save a slow and agonizing death. But that low-roofed building where men and boys lay on straw sodden with blood and excrement, so close they were almost atop one another, the animal whimpering and mewling, the pestilential stench, made my senses reel. I had to put one hand against the door-jamb to steady myself, swallow the vomit which rushed into my mouth. In the aftermath of battle, when you lean wearily upon your sword and look with a kind of wonder at the carnage, there may be some escape from the horrors: the vault of sky above, a breath of wind bearing the scent of trees or the sea. Here, in the stinking semi-darkness, there was none.

Martin, who had been there earlier, did not hesitate. Nodding to one of the priests who crouched like gore-crows beside the dying, he made his way to the back of the building. I followed, stepping over men some of whom lay mute and still as if already dead; others who cringed, maybe seeing the enemy that had struck them down in my mailed and belted figure. As I picked my way between them, I reflected that these were the strongest of the wounded: they had already lasted five days since Fulford Gate.

Without Martin, I doubt I would have recognized my foster-brother. His face, always lean, was skull-like, sunken, masked with blood. A dirty rag was knotted as a bandage around his head; his right thigh bound with what looked like strips torn from a cloak, caked with filth. His byrnie, ancient scale-armour which, I suspect, had belonged to Toli, still lay beside him. I picked it up, saw the rents in the long leg-flaps back and front, and knew the blade must have pierced his thigh right through.

'Eadric!' Martin's voice was low but urgent. Maybe I had seen too many die: hope failed me at the first sight of Eadric's face. But as Martin persisted, his eyes opened and fixed on me: he stared as if peering from a great depth then licked his lips. So intense was his gaze, so obvious his need to speak, I found myself leaning close. His breath was hot and foul against my face. He whispered, 'Take me home.'

Nine years I had lived an exile, fighting in foreign lands without a care as to where my body would lie should I be slain because the dead are dead and there was no-one to mourn my passing in my own land. I thought of Eadric's anger when he had considered the possibility of his death in battle, then imagined how it would be to being that news to Ymma and Toli, to admit I had abandoned him in a place as foreign to them as Byzantium was to me instead of bringing him home so that they could bid farewell. Eadric gasped and quivered, his eyes rolled up, the whites gleaming, then his eyelids fluttered and closed. Martin was watching him, transfixed. I said, 'Find his horse, then bring it along with ours. We ride south tonight.'

'He'll never make it.' He stared at me, appalled. 'What will you do: tie him across the saddle?'

'You think he'll live if he stays here?' My answer was brutal because I was unsure of myself, my mind dulled by the same weariness that made my limbs seem heavy as clay. 'Do as I say or find another master.'

He stared at me a moment longer then left without a word, picking his way carefully between the stricken. I took his place beside Eadric, watching the shuddering movement of his chest with a kind of dull fascination. My eyelids weighed like lead, the putrid air cloyed in my lungs, I tipped forward . . .

A hand shook me roughly awake: Martin's face was lurid in the flare from a tallow lamp. While it had been early evening when we had come here, it was now night. Eadric groaned and shifted restlessly, disturbed maybe by the light, but he did not waken.

'The horses are outside.' Martin's voice was low and harsh, his eyes unreadable. 'Tiw is lame; Eadric's died at Fulford. I managed to buy a pony but I paid more than twice its worth: sound horses are rare as hen's teeth in this city.'

'Then let us go.' I gave him Eadric's byrnie (his sword must have been lost in the marsh or stolen), and clambered to my feet, every muscle crying out in protest. Then I bent forward, took my foster-brother's arm across my shoulders, and hoisted him up. Although of slender build, he was taller than me: it took all my strength to raise him. I half-dragged, half-carried him to the door, shoving aside those lying in our path with my feet. Eadric gasped and moaned as his damaged leg was twisted and bumped along the ground but though Martin came to help when we reached the courtyard, there was nothing we could do to relieve his pain.

The pony was barely thirteen hands, a shaggy black beast which stood prudently beyond range of Swallow's teeth. One of the monks watched in silent disapproval as we slung Eadric over the palfrey's saddle like a sack of grain and wrapped a cloak around him. The horses snorted and shifted restlessly at the smell of fresh blood. As I mounted Swallow and Martin scrambled bareback on the pony, I had to grit my teeth to focus my mind on the journey. All my being screamed for rest, for somewhere dark and quiet where I could lie down and sleep. Yet the compulsion to go home was stronger.

The gate-guards looked upon us as if we were mad when we asked to be let out. It was a cloudy night without moon or stars and they must have wondered why two men should go to such trouble to take what appeared to be a corpse away when the slain were piled in great heaps on the other side of the city wall. But eventually they let us through and soon we were past the marshes and their dead, the reek of carrion, and were on the road south, the same road the Vikings had taken earlier in the day. The horses settled down and the pony ambled at a steady, even pace which belied its poor appearance though Martin's feet hung almost to the ground. From Eadric came not a sound but I refused to contemplate the possibility that he was already dead. Tiw, who had been limping heavily when we set out, moved more freely as the stiffness in his wounded shoulder wore off but from his drooping head I knew he needed rest as much as I after the journey north and the battle.

Afterwards I realized I must have slept in the saddle for as long as I was awake that night. Whenever some unevenness in Swallow's pace or an untoward sound jerked me awake I would look across to see Martin sway and put a hand out to steady him as he must have done for me. The horses plodded slowly, urged on, I suppose, by the automatic touch of our heels. No-one else was on the road: King's messengers bearing news of our victory would have left long ago. Occasionally dogs barked from roadside settlements but otherwise there was only the sound of hooves, the calls of hunting owls, squeak and scuffle of mice in the hedges.

When the sky lightened with a dawn grey as ash, we were still only just beyond Riccall. Looking to the north-west, the masts of Hardrada's ships were visible across the fields. Harold, ever prudent, had left men to guard the sorry remnants of the Norwegian force and a group of five hus-carls stopped us when we reached the river crossing at Selby. These came to meet us with lowered spears until they realized what we were, then let us pass, wishing us god-speed. Seeing Eadric slung across the saddle they stared incredulously: no doubt they also thought us mad. We were about to ride on when someone shouted my name.

So focused had I been on the fighting and my foster-brother's fate, I had not thought once of the men he had taken with him. Now, as the giant form of Acer the Hard ran from a small copse (where many men were camped), I was relieved that he at least, doughty Fen-wolf, had survived.

As he drew near, his pace slowed. His broad, usually cheerful face was grim, drawn with weariness, his clothes bloodstained save where his leather armour had covered them. He put a hand out for Swallow to sniff then, when the mare flattened her ears and bared her teeth in threat, pushed her head aside and came to stand at her shoulder, head bowed.

'There are only three of us left alive and two of them are wounded,' he said bluntly. 'We were trapped in the marsh: the only way out was through Viking swords and axes. Osgood drowned before my eyes – I couldn't reach him.' He hesitated and at last looked up to meet my gaze, his eyes red-rimmed and bloodshot. 'I saw Eadric fall: he must be dead. You know what it's like when a shieldwall fails, Hereward, there was nothing but slaughter. Some of us made it back to York then the bastards in charge of the city gave us over as hostages, stripped of weapons and armour.' He paused and gave a sudden, terrible grin. 'I got better yesterday though: a damascene-bladed sword and a mail hauberk you would envy.'

'Eadric is here,' I said and his expression switched to astonishment as he registered what lay across the chestnut's back. 'We are going home. Will you come with us?'

'Is he dead?' Acer went to the wounded man's head, bent to see into his face then straightened and looked at me accusingly. 'God's grace, Hereward, is this the best you could do? You must be losing your touch.'

Before I could respond, he was striding away towards a hovel I had barely noticed, huddled as it was behind a great stack of logs. There was a tumult of furious barking, sharply cut off, and men's voices raised in heated argument. After a while the noise abated and Acer appeared, dragging a small cart by the yoke-pole. It was such a vehicle as peddlers use, two-wheeled and flat.

'I told them to thank God we're not Vikings,' was all he said, then we woke Martin who was snoring quietly over the pony's neck and between us lifted Eadric down off the horse and onto the cart.

He was still alive: he whimpered as we laid him down and straightened his legs but his skin was burning hot and when Martin sniffed the bindings on his thigh, he grimaced and shook his head. I refused to think on what this signified but helped harness pony and palfrey to the yoke-pole, using a rope Acer had taken from the steading to make crude traces. We waited while he went to fetch his gear and bid his comrades farewell: he threw a cloak-wrapped bundle onto the cart and waved to the hus-carls who were watching with undisguised amusement. 'Let's go.'

After that, the journey became a little easier though slow, for we were held to walking pace. We took turns to go on foot and ride on the cart for Acer's horse, like Eadric's, had been lost at Fulford Gate. Swallow and Tiw plodded behind, half-asleep. Mired with mud and dried blood, we must have looked more like survivors of some dreadful catastrophe than triumphant victors. Folk stared and some fled but once they realized we were not Tostig's men, we received much kindness. Food and ale were brought out to us; crones clucked their tongues as Eadric moaned and tossed in the throes of a mounting fever and some gave us foul-smelling concoctions to smear on his wounds or pour down his throat. All these people were eager for news for we were passing through Morcar's lands and they had heard nothing since their menfolk had left for Fulford Gate.

Looking at their anxious faces, we tempered tidings of the slaughter in the marsh, concentrating rather on the victory at Stamford Bridge: they would find out soon enough whether those they loved would return. And we did not linger though our bodies cried out for the hospitality they offered: a place to sleep, fodder or grazing for the horses, hot food. The road stretched ahead, straight as a spear-shaft for the most part, and we plodded along mindlessly, as if caught in an unending dream. Occasionally horsemen galloped past, King's thegn's taking messages south but few others overtook us although we were travelling slowly. I guessed that most that had fought would be sleeping off their exhaustion and aching heads from the celebrations which must have drained every wine-skin and ale-cask in the city.

On the second morning we met Gamal and Siward with eight others riding north on an assortment of beasts ranging from Ulfkil's own bay palfrey to scrubby ponies. Their disappointment at having missed the fight was tempered by grief for friends and kin from Bourne who would not return: they looked upon Eadric with ill-concealed dismay. Half we sent to find and bring back Acer's wounded comrades at Selby, the rest turned round and journeyed with us for a while though they kept to themselves, as if ashamed. After a day, I sent them ahead with news of our return and they seemed glad to go. Only afterwards did I realize they were daunted by our appearance: to those that had never seen war, our drawn faces and blood-stained clothing were frightening in themselves

The journey we had achieved in two nights going north took more than twice as long at walking pace and as Eadric sank into a stupor, none of us believed he would reach Bourne alive. Indeed, having seen his leg- wound when a travelling healer tended it, the wonder was that he had lived so long. There was a hole through the muscle of his thigh I could have put three fingers in and splinters of bone emerged with the pus that squirted under the healer's hands. Yet as we crawled our way along the road, still he clung to life.

It was maybe four days from the Selby river-crossing that we reached Grantham and knew another day's journey would see us home. We rested that night, staying with a kinsman of Acer's. He and his wife looked at me curiously though we had never met before: tales of the Fen-wolves' exploits had been embellished to heroic proportions by Acer's boasting over the years. I cradled my bowl of ale and drank sparingly for Eadric had lain quiet all day, his breathing shallow, and I had resolved to keep vigil over him that night.

The others had settled down to sleep when I went outside and took my place beside Eadric (we dared not move him from the cart). I prayed awhile for his safe return, then talked softly of Bourne and his family, willing life into him with my words.

My voice had sunk to a murmur and, in truth, I was half-asleep, when a horse galloped by. The cottage was screened from the road by a thick hedge but though I saw nothing, there was something disturbing about the urgency of that gallop, a slight irregularity as if the animal were lame or near foundering yet being forced on to some desperate purpose. I listened until the hoofbeats faded into the night-time quiet yet my uneasiness lingered. When at last sleep overcame me, it was punctuated by the dreadful dreams that always follow fighting, where the horror and fear return and one wakes sweat-drenched and gasping, longing for dawn.

We set off soon after daybreak. It was a mist-hung autumn morning, the vegetation dew-netted, birdsong oddly muted. The horses were fractious (perhaps they also had been disturbed by the hoofbeats in the night), but no-one complained of broken sleep so I held my tongue. Eadric lay unmoving and silent but no stench of putrefaction came from the bindings on his thigh so it seemed the healer's salves had done some good. Acer shouted a cheerful farewell to his kin, then there was only the unreeling road, Tiw's squeal whenever Swallow nipped him for straying onto her territory, the creak of the cart and rumble of wheels, steady hoofbeats and a low drone as Martin hummed to himself as he walked.

The mist had cleared when a horseman appeared in the distance. Although only a speck at first, he was coming at full gallop: when he drew close we saw that his horse was sweat-lathered, its nostrils flaring crimson. We had no need to make way for Ermine Street was wide enough that twelve could ride abreast along most of its length and I think he would have ridden straight past save that his eyes registered the mail and weapons piled on the cart with the wounded man; the magnificence of the warhorse tethered behind. Then he brought his mount to a plunging halt and demanded our names and allegiance.

The peremptory nature of his questions breached all codes of courtesy but there was a kind of grim desperation in his manner which excused him. He was plainly clad, without mail to facilitate swift riding, yet his sword was no ordinary man's weapon. Thus instead of taking offence, I told him briefly who we were, that we were going home after the victory at York. He gave a wry smile and stood in his stirrups to ease his panting horse, then said, 'I think you will not bide long there, wherever you are headed. William the Bastard landed at Pevensey two days ago: his men are ravaging the country up to the London Road. Best raise what men you can and make ready to march south. I'm on my way to warn the King: he'll be here the day after tomorrow is my guess.'

'We've just fought two bloody battles: the levy from his manor' – Acer jerked his thumb at Eadric – 'was butchered. You think the rest will be willing? Look at the state of us!'

The man grimaced and gathered his reins. 'Make your complaints to William of Normandy, not me. Head for London is my advice: the fyrd from East Anglia and Wessex are mustering there. God keep you!'

'God speed you.' We watched in silence as he spurred his weary horse away then, as we turned again to the road, Acer gave a harsh laugh. 'So we were at the wrong fight after all. Still, once he hears of Tostig and Hardrada's fate, maybe this Norman bastard'll take fright and sail for home.'

'It would save us a journey if he did,' Martin replied. 'If the fyrd had been where they were all summer, I doubt he'd have landed. He must have heard of the attack in the north. What do you think, Hereward?'

I looked eastwards across the fields where cattle and sheep grazed on the stubble, at an eight-ox team ploughing in the distance with seagulls wheeling and crying in its wake.

'I think we've a hard fight ahead,' I said thoughtfully. 'I know Normans: they're better trained and equipped than Hardrada's men and they fight from horseback. But with Harold Godwineson leading us, we shall win.'

Acer nodded. 'No horse will charge into a set spear-hedge. And how many can they have brought on a sea-crossing?'

'How many ships have landed?' Martin slapped the hindquarters of the pony and it quickened its pace. 'Best not make judgements until we've some idea of the truth. We'll find out soon enough what kind of foe we face.'

We lapsed into reflective silence but kept to a brisk walk all morning, having left Ermine Street to take the tracks which lead to the old road soon after encountering the messenger. The horses sensed our urgency and Tiw's shoulder wound split open as he jogged and shied but it bled little and cleanly. Eadric seemed more stable that morning: his fever had abated and his expression was serene as he slept, undisturbed by the jolting of the cart. I had toyed with the idea of riding ahead but it seemed unfair on the others; only when the turn-off to Laughton came into view did I untie Swallow, clamber into the saddle and set her galloping towards the Hall. Now that what we had dreaded had happened, I grudged every moment spent needlessly away.

The sound of hooves brought Turfrida running, Aedgifu struggling in her arms. Recognizing me, she let the child go and waited, hands hanging at her sides, a look of utter relief on her face. Though Siward had arrived the day before, she dared not believe I was safe until she saw me. I slid to the ground and embraced her while Aedgifu pushed jealously between us to be hugged in turn. Aelgytha appeared from the stream a moment later, almost dropped her dripping pail in surprise, then, once Turfrida and I had broken apart, came to greet me.

Their joy turned to consternation when I told them of Eadric's wound and that of those who had gone with him, only three survived with Acer alone fit to return with us. Siward, fearing to say too much, had told them only that Eadric was hurt and Martin and I unscathed. I said nothing of the Norman invasion but there was no need: they had heard it from a staller who had ridden from Borough to raise the alarm.

'Toli and Cole One-Hand are at Bourne,' Turfrida said. 'They wanted to make sure the defences are finished before any answer the King's summons.'

The cart, drawn by its ill-matched pair, had just come into view when I remounted Swallow. The mare was fresh enough for the journey to Bourne and back: no horse could match her stamina.

'Make Eadric as comfortable as you can,' I said. 'I'll bring Ymma back with Toli.'

By the time we returned, Ymma riding pillion on Toli's broad-backed grey, Eadric had been settled on a pallet in the Hall, Aelgytha was boiling a chicken to make broth and Martin had seen to the horses, letting his chestnut and the black pony loose to graze whilst confining Tiw to the stable. Not wishing to witness Toli and Ymma's distress when they saw Eadric, I unharnessed the mare and led her to drink at the stream while they went inside. Once Swallow was grazing with the others, I wandered to the stable and there Turfrida found me washing blood from the stallion's shoulder.

She did not speak, just looked then put her arms around to hold me. Breathing in the warm scent of her, my senses surged with the desire that comes when one has been within an iron-ring's thickness of death, a need that is an affirmation of life itself. I lifted her and she locked her legs around me and the horse calmly champed his hay while we coupled frenziedly until at last I was lost and Turfrida cried out, making Tiw look round. We sank to the floor, spent, sated, panting.

When we had recovered our breath, she knelt and pulled her clothes into order, then regarded me with an odd, almost defiant expression. 'Hereward, must you go south?' she asked.

I had lain flat on my back in the straw, watching her. Now I levered myself into a sitting position and my anger flared because she knew I was bound to go: my fealty, like that of every free man in England lay first with my King.

'You know I must.' My voice was flat but Tiw sensed my fury and lifted his head, nostrils wide. 'The need is even greater with Eadric wounded. Someone must lead what remains of our levy. We leave in two days. Without the whole fyrd, we won't win.'

'I prayed your fighting days were over when we left Flanders,' she muttered.

'I know.' My anger melted into pity for she was struggling to hold back tears. 'But I am a man Normans find hard to kill. Have faith, love. If God so wills, I shall return, if not, well likely enough ill will befall me wherever I am, here or with the King's force. There is no escaping fate, Turfrida.'

She nodded and I took her in my arms and held her while she wept quietly. When she was calm, I bathed her face from the stallion's water-pail, then led her to the Hall. But though she seemed contained and self-assured as usual, I sensed that her fears had not been assuaged and did all I could to avoid being alone with her that evening.

That night I sank into slumber as black and bottomless as mire to be woken long after dawn by excited chatter in which I thought to catch Eadric's voice. Feeling almost as weary as when I had lain down, I rose and made my way into the main hall, fastening my belt as I went. Toli, Aelgytha, Turfrida and Ymma were gathered round Eadric's pallet. As I approached, they broke off their talk and moved aside. Eadric was sitting up. His face was like that of an animated corpse, chalk-white and drawn but his eyes, though sunken, were clear. Seeing me, he grinned weakly.

Aelgytha, naturally, attributed his seemingly miraculous recovery to the chicken broth she had forced down his throat during the night, against the wishes of Ymma and Toli who had protested that he should be allowed to live or die in peace, according to God's will. Whatever the cause, Aelgytha alone had believed Eadric would live and Ymma thanked her repeatedly whilst holding onto her husband's hand like someone drowning, their babe clutched to her breast. When Martin came in a little later, Aedgifu riding on his shoulders, the women were busy renewing the poultice on Eadric's leg while Toli and I talked in low voices of the muster.

Seeing Eadric awake, Aedgifu shrieked in delight and kicked her mount forward with such violence that Martin coughed and spluttered. The noise made Turfrida look up. She smiled at our daughter but then her glance sought mine, a strange, unreadable look that sent a chill through me. I called Martin and he put the child down and came outside. Beyond sight of the women, Toli's face was grim.

'Four kings I have outlived,' he said as we walked to the field to catch the horses. 'I pray I do not see the end of Harold Godwineson also. It would be an ill thing for this land if another foreigner took the throne.'

'That will not happen.' Swallow came to my hand and I rubbed the broad patch between her eyes, took hold her mane to lead her to the yard. 'Hardrada and Tostig could not withstand him: we'll send this Norman bastard back to France.'

'God grant it so,' he answered, fervently.

Martin and I rode many miles that day, covering all of Aveland Wapentake and most of Ness, visiting other thegns to plan the muster. Morcar's lands alone we passed by, whose men had already been lost or wounded at Fulford Gate. Of the rest, most were willing to march upon the morrow and many of the manors were already teeming with men and horses. There, the air was filled with the sounds of whetstone against blade, clang of hammer against anvil in the forges where horses were being shod and hasty repairs made to weapons and harness. The smell of baking wafted from every cottage for each man of the fyrd must travel with his own food.

I returned to Laughton by way of the marshes for the Fen-folk were as subject to the levy as the rest. They alone seemed reluctant to answer the King's summons. I heard it muttered that while an Atheling still lived, Harold Godwineson was no less a usurper than William of Normandy. When I asked after Rahere, none could, or would, tell me his whereabouts. After ordering their men to gather at Toli's Hall at first light, I rode away but Swallow was nervous, shying at every wind-stirred movement of leaf and stem and I also was uneasy, feeling unseen eyes watching from the shelter of the reed-beds.

Martin, who had gone to the villages around Lound, had done well: upwards of fifty men were gathered in the yard on my return. Some were grey-beards, others with hair barely pricking their chins but all were governed by the same excitement: they fingered the swords, knives or axes at their belts in eager anticipation. Someone had breached a cask of ale and the boasting and singing began soon after sunset. The night was fine so we lit a great fire in the middle of the yard and shouted our defiance to the stars while the picketed horses shifted uneasily and the women watched in apprehensive silence from the doorway of the Hall.

Only one man in Laughton did not get drunk that night and that was only because Aelgytha stood guard like a sow protective of its young while Ymma, exhausted, slept. Chicken broth and water was all Aelgytha allowed to pass Eadric's lips. Between relief at his son's recovery and fear of what might happen to the rest of us, Toli did not stint and had to be carried senseless to his pallet. Turfrida chided me for letting the old man get into such a state but I knew her sharpness stemmed from anxiety and silenced her with a clumsy kiss before reeling out again into the yard.

The blaze sent sparks shooting heavenwards and made men's eyes gleam red as they joined in heroic lays and sagas which made the blood rush like fire through our veins. Every one of us was invincible that night, our weapons forged from earth-iron and lightning, our thirst and strength unquenchable. If Grendel himself had stalked in from the fens, we would have sent him howling back. Our King had outwitted and outfought the dreaded warrior-king of Norway: we would follow him to the ends of the earth, aye and beyond (by now someone had discovered a skin of mead in one of the cottages); the usurpers would hear our war-shout and flee in terror and we would pursue them to the sea until the waves turned red with Norman blood.

As the mead took hold, the mood became more sombre: we swore fealty to one another so that any man who failed to help a comrade would be God-cursed; the tales became maudlin and, one by one, the men sank into a stupor. A sokeman whose grandmother had been a Wealhas slave began what he called 'The Lament for the Fallen' in the old British tongue: though no-one else understood the words, its slow, sonorous music, both sad and stirring, made the meaning plain enough. After that, a mournful, reflective quiet fell, the sound of snoring rose above the crackle of the fire and I staggered to my pallet where Turfrida lay waiting. I had just time to register her anger, pawed ineffectually in an effort to appease her, then sank into drink-sodden oblivion.

It seemed I had barely closed my eyes when a hand shook me awake. It was Turfrida: when I groaned and rolled over, away from the hearthlight and pale gleam of dawn, she pulled the bedding off me. My head was pounding, my stomach sour and when Aedgifu climbed atop and began to pummel me with her fists, laughing with glee, her clear young voice seemed to split my skull. I sat up with an effort, pushed the child gently aside and saw Turfrida standing by the bed, hands planted on hips, regarding me with weary forbearance.

'The men from the Fens have come,' she said. 'They're outside in the yard, doubtless wondering why they made the effort when the rest are still snoring in the dirt like pigs. Martin is trying to wake them. It was today you intended to leave?'

It was not the first time I had got drunk before leaving on campaign but this time I detected beneath her sarcasm a deeper hurt. My tongue was dry as parchment. I lurched to my feet and embraced her, mumbling incoherently 'I will return, I swear it'; tried to ignore the fact that she was like a wooden post in my arms and had turned her head to avoid the foulness of my breath. Aedgifu tugged at my tunic so I picked her up and hugged her, made her promise to look after her mother in my stead. Then, aware of Turfrida's gaze, hard and unreadable still, I put the child down and went outside to rouse the mighty warriors of the night, now reduced to an assortment of sorry wretches. Some, sprawled beside puddles of vomit, snored on despite the best efforts of the Fen-men, Martin and myself to wake them.

It must have been close upon midday when we left. Most of the horses around Bourne had been requisitioned when Eadric answered Morcar's summons and none had returned, but in any case, the fyrd went mainly on foot. The cart Turfrida and I had brought from Flanders was piled high with weapons, armour and provisions. Although riding, even I went without my hauberk that day: so ill did I feel, I could not countenance the extra weight though it might have helped sweat out the dregs of mead.

Eadric insisted on joining the leave-taking. He hopped from his pallet, supported by Aelgytha and Turfrida. Toli was still asleep despite the noise from the yard and the squalling of his grandson. I had not the heart to wake him and see his stricken face as we rode away, men he had known from boyhood who would not all return. It was a simple fact of war that even when fighting could be avoided, men still died through mischance or the sicknesses that come whenever large numbers are camped together.

As I led Tiw from the stable, Aedgifu's cries joined the screaming of the babe but when I went to bid farewell it was to discover that it was not my departure she mourned but the loss of her kitten, which had disappeared during the night. To quieten her, I promised another if the first could not be found. Then, as Martin came to tell me the men were as ready as they would ever be, I felt Turfrida's hand on my arm. The look upon her face acted as a balm to the fear which lurked behind my sore head and sour stomach: that if I returned, it would be to find her gone to Flanders, taking our child with her.

'I will wait,' she said. Her eyes were clear and calm, her expression serene and I could find no words to answer but laid my hand briefly against her face, then put my foot in the stirrup and swung into the saddle. From where she was tethered at the back of the cart, Swallow gave a jealous neigh, the driver clucked his tongue and slapped the reins against the mules' hindquarters and we were away, those on foot going in front because the rest were held to their pace.

I did not look back but when we reached the old road and turned south, Aedgifu's wail came clear across the fields and I knew that this time it had naught to do with a lost kitten.

4. London Waiting

Although we set off far later than planned, those we had arranged to meet waited: in a muster there are always delays. The men of Borough, led by Abbot Leofric, had left the previous day but townsfolk lined the narrow streets to wish us God-speed and Bishop Athelric blessed us from the abbey wall, surrounded by monks who called their own farewells. One stood a little apart, staring down in silence and my hand went to shield my face before I was aware of it. By the time I realized and lowered it from shame, he had disappeared though my flesh crawled, remembering eyes sunk in folds of fat and soft damp hands like something foul one finds under a stone. Martin, riding at my side, also saw him: as we passed through the burgh gates, he glanced across and began: 'Wasn't that – ' then fell abruptly silent. What he knew or guessed of my time as a novice I do not know but my expression must have warned him not to speak of Brand, my uncle, again. That fleeting glimpse was enough to unsettle my mood and sleep for the rest of the journey. Like a weeping sore, the memories festered.

Three days it took to reach London, a city Edward the Pious had made greater than Winchester. The road was chaotic with men marching south; choked with supply wagons drawn by oxen whose flanks streamed blood from the goad: the same urgency gripped us all. Yet we rested at night for this was no desperate race such as our ride to York had been but a full muster of the fyrd. As we gathered in makeshift camps by the road, I doubt there was one man who did not believe we were about to join the greatest force ever assembled in England, that we would sweep away the Normans as one swats a gadfly. Even I, who knew the enemy's might in arms, was certain our victory was assured simply by weight of numbers: a cornered wolf may be torn apart by a pack of curs. What none of us imagined was that the King would march without us.

Maybe the quiet of the Essex countryside, the silent, almost hostile stares of those who stood to watch us pass should have warned us. There were rumours of a great host leaving London, spears and helms glittering in the sunlight but we dismissed them as idle gossip. When we came within sight of the walls and huddled buildings, all dwarfed by the tower of Edward's Minster, there was no mass of men and horses encamped in the meads outside so we assumed they were gathered on the south side of the river. The gates opened and a single rider came out.

His dress and disdainful manner identified the man as one of the King's hus-carls but his face was disfigured by a sword-cut which crossed his nose and left cheek and was barely scabbed over. His speech was marred by the wound but though necessarily brief, the message was clear: Harold and his brothers had already marched for Pevensey where William the Bastard had set up a fort. The King had left orders that the main part of the fyrd was to stay in London. He was confident that his hus-carls and the levy from Godwineson lands would suffice to drive the Normans into the sea. There was no need for the rest to join him until they were called for.

A murmur of anger and disappointment arose as the news spread and I heard Acer the Hard, who had pushed to the front, say loudly: 'Well then, if the men of Mercia aren't good enough for Harold Godwineson, I say we turn round and go home. The Normans have landed on his shores, not ours: let him deal with them!'

This suggestion was met by a growl of assent and the messenger's eyes narrowed as others began to jostle and shout their support. His arrogance irked me: before the assembly turned to a mob, I raised myself in the saddle, turning to face them. Behind the more vociferous, weary men leaned on their spears or squatted on the ground but all were equally resentful at what they viewed as a dismissal.

'Without Harold Godwineson, you would be fighting Tostig and Hardrada's men in your own steadings!' I shouted. 'Hundreds of Mercians died at Fulford Gate and their deaths would have been in vain without the King's force. We all swore fealty when we came of age to bear arms: let those who are faithless go crawling home and when the rest of us return, glorying in renown, they will be objects of scorn. I am Hereward, Eorl Leofric's son, and I say there will be no enmity between men of different eorldoms. Harold Godwineson is no fool: Stamford Bridge proved that. He knows more of Norman numbers and position than us, therefore we shall obey his orders. That is the sworn duty of every free man, thegn or plough-boy, and if any here disputes it, let him stand forward!'

My eyes locked with Acer's and for a moment I thought he might rise to the challenge for his gaze was unflinching. But perhaps realizing that once he did so there was no going back, that he would have to fight me, a comrade of the Fen-wolves, and then, if I were slain, the other thegns who stood around me, he shrugged and grinned, saying lightly, 'Ach well, it was worth a try. Still, they say London is the greatest burgh in England. Let's see what it has to offer men of proper mettle.'

The King and his men may have left but the narrow alleyways of the city were crowded with their women, children and slaves, and those tradesmen that always follow armies, selling everything from swords to holy relics. I noticed much work of Norse origin amongst the weapons and jewellery, presumably looted from the battlefields around York. Our guide, whose manner had become more respectful since my speech, brought us to the old Roman fort on its mound beside the river. It guarded a wooden bridge, whose timbers were black with age. The river, wider than the Nene at Borough, was foul with rubbish and ordure from the houses and flowed sluggishly but from the weed which clung to the posts I guessed the tide was on the turn. A dead dog revolved slowly in an eddy between the piles; the air was full of the raucous screaming of gulls as they squabbled for possession.

It was here we were told that the city was full and we must camp outside the walls by Southwark with the rest of the fyrd who had arrived late. By now, with the weariness of the journey and the disappointment of being left behind, I was past caring overmuch, desiring only a horn of ale to quench my thirst followed by sleep: from their expressions, most of the men felt likewise. But when I asked by whose order this had been decreed and the hus-carl answered uncomfortably that Eorl Edwin of Mercia had charge of the burgh, it was as if I had been doused in icy water. I stared at the man in disbelief, heard Acer's harsh laugh as he realized the irony of his protest outside the walls. Sensing my anger, Tiw shook his head and struck the ground with his forefoot.

'Edwin?' The word came out as a strangled croak and in the corner of my eye I saw concern spread across Martin's face. He gave an almost imperceptible shake of the head, a signal that had long existed between us to warn when I was close to overstepping some mark of propriety. With an effort I mastered myself, gave orders that Martin and Acer should lead the others and make camp. Then, when the long file had begun to cross the bridge, I demanded Edwin's whereabouts of the hus-carl. He gave it reluctantly and I turned the war-horse and rode towards the mound where crude wood and thatch buildings had been added to the flint and brick of Roman stone-craft, making a sizeable fortress.

Edwin had had his own retinue of hus-carls but most must have fallen at Fulford Gate. To my embittered eye the gate-guards seemed hardly of an age to bear arms: some were beardless. When they sought to prevent me entering, I growled my name and lineage and they stood aside, clearly at a loss as to what to do. I rode though the short tunnel which penetrated the massive width of the outer wall. A cobbled yard lay beyond, overlooked by cramped stone houses, a massive timbered hall, stables and a makeshift forge where a smith was hammering a glowing sword-blade.

As I drew rein, a boy ran to take my horse and when I dismounted, offered to carry the coif and helm I had worn in anticipation of riding straight to meet the Normans. However slow-witted the gate-guards appeared, it seemed they had some way of sending messages swiftly inside for barely had I straightened and settled sword-belt and mail (after a long ride, the clothes underneath became twisted and stuck to my skin with sweat), when a man in full war-gear came to meet me. He was grim of face and limped heavily but his grey-eyed gaze was keen and appraising. Under his scrutiny, the force of my ire lessened: he was a man whose very appearance inspired trust.

'We would have given you and your men a better welcome had we known you were coming,' he said. 'Thorfin of Berwick is my name. I saw you after Stamford Bridge but I doubt you noticed me: I was bleeding like a stuck pig in the dark when you took your wounded kinsman away. Did he live?'

'Aye,' I replied. 'But he's not yet on his feet, nor sorry to be missing this fight, I think.'

His expression was suddenly guarded. 'You have been in Flanders and Maine, so I was told. What are the Normans like, as enemies?'

'*Formidable*,' I answered deliberately then, seeing he did not understand, added, 'They're a match for any of Harold Godwineson's hus-carls. They use horses to charge with and many have cross-bows whose bolts pierce any mail. But we are in our own land and have the advantage of numbers, or so I guess. Do you know how many ships came?'

'Upwards of two hundred I have heard,' he said grimly. 'There is rumour that more land every day. And it is not only Normans we face: the men of Brittany and Flanders have flocked to the promise of riches and renown, all in the name of God and Pope.'

As we talked, he led me into one of the stone buildings and along a dark corridor until we came to an iron-studded oaken door.

'Why couldn't the King wait?' I asked, for Thorfin did not move to open it at once. 'There must be thousands standing idle here: much of the Mercian levy has yet to arrive. Why such haste?'

He grimaced, the lines of his face stark as if cut by a knife. 'You saw Harold at Stamford Bridge,' he replied, his voice barely more than a whisper. 'There he was inspired to avenge the slaughter at Fulford Gate and the slight to himself from Tostig. Now he is like a man possessed. All his thought was to pin William's force south of the London Road, maybe fearing he could not be held once he broke beyond. Eorl Edwin tried to persuade him to wait but the King was deaf to all counsel, even that of his brother, Gyrd, who offered to lead the force. And news was coming in all the time: William sent his men all over Sussex to raid and plunder without hold or mercy. Maybe it was a deliberate ploy to goad Harold into moving before all the fyrd could assemble. Anyway, whatever the truth of it, the King is gone and his brothers with him. Who knows what was in his mind?'

I had barely time to assimilate this when he thrust open the door. The room beyond was small but although windowless, well-lit by beeswax candles set on a large table. Its surface was littered with documents; seated on the far side was my nephew, Edwin. A man dressed and tonsured as a cleric stood at his shoulder, scrutinising some kind of list.

Although I had not seen Edwin since he was a boy, it was the other who commanded my attention. He possessed a natural air of authority though he did not look up from reading as I walked to the table. By contrast, Edwin's eyes had not left my face since the door opened; he rose as courtesy demanded then bade me sit on a stool which stood to one side. I refused the invitation: like most warriors, I dislike sitting with my back to a door. He resumed his own seat with obvious unease.

'I am glad you returned after King Edward's death,' he said after a long silence. 'We have need of hard-handed fighters.'

'A pity then that Harold did not wait for us,' I replied sourly, irritated by the veiled reference to my exile. 'Where is Morcar: still resting after Fulford Gate?'

At this, the cleric raised his head. His face was such as Saint Peter is sometimes depicted: stern of aspect with deep-set, piercing eyes. Those eyes would, I guessed, turn to ice in anger but he was watching me with a kind of ironic amusement as Edwin cleared his throat then answered levelly: 'He was wounded but went to fetch the Atheling from the north: we expect them tomorrow.' He paused, considering his next words and, I realized later, gathering courage to speak what must have preyed long upon his mind. 'Let there be no bad blood between us, Hereward. We are kinsmen, after all. My father disposed of your lands when Morcar and I were barely old enough to bear arms. As to the eorldom: you know as well as I that succession passes from father to son, or else is decided by King's decree.'

He was only a few years younger than I but they yawned like a gulf between us. Despite his status, he seemed a youth beside all I had experienced. He flicked a fingernail nervously while his gaze traversed my mail, sword, hands, everything except rising to meet my eyes. His own face, pale in the candlelight, was still bruised around eye-sockets and mouth: I guessed he had received rough treatment as Hardrada and Tostig's hostage.

'What, then, would you have done in Aelfgar's stead?' I asked, not because I thought anything would change but that I needed to know before deciding how to deal with this young man and his brother. The simple fact of their birth was reason enough for me to hate them.

He hesitated. 'I cannot speak for my father,' he said at last, 'But your own deeds outlawed you. Maybe I would have done no differently at the time. Yet I think you have been harshly used. You had only to ask and I would have gifted an estate to you on your return.'

I stared and now his clear grey eyes met mine without flinching. The taste of bile rushed into my mouth and I swallowed loudly, fighting for control. While he had spoken honestly, he understood me well enough to know that I would have returned to exile before begging my nephews for land.

'Bourne, for instance?' The words seemed to choke in my throat. 'Is Morcar so kindly disposed towards me?'

'You will have to ask him yourself.' With every moment Edwin's assurance increased: I knew he thought he had the measure of me. But as I stood irresolute, torn between leaning over to shake him like an insolent child and laughing the whole matter off as a bitter jest, he rose to his feet and said passionately, 'Hereward, believe me: in all the years since I was made Eorl, I have dreaded this meeting. My father, your half-brother, feared you more than any man, thinking one day you would avenge your honour by slaying Morcar and I. Yet there was never enmity between us as boys. Let us be allies, if not friends.'

His heartfelt fervour made me realize at last that he was no more responsible for the legacy of his birth than I.

'Your father thought ill if he believed that of me,' I said after a moment's silence in which the cleric looked at each of us with a shrewd, appraising glance. 'I was a landless outlaw: I turned my back on home and kin as they had rejected me. Maybe I might have challenged Morcar for lordship of Bourne on my return but I will not now oust Eadric, Toli's son, from his place. You and your brother never wronged me: you have nothing to fear. I have settled at Laughton and am content.'

'Good.' Relief settled on his broad, pleasant features and he sat down, smiling. An awkward silence grew, neither of us sure what more to say after so long. The cleric, having dropped all pretence of reading, cleared his throat meaningfully.

'I shall introduce myself, since Edwin seems to have overlooked my presence,' he said. His voice was deep and resonant, compelling even though his words were light. 'I am Aldred, Bishop of York. Your renown precedes you, *miles* Hereward. I heard you were in Flanders, then rode to our aid at Stamford Bridge. The people of York, not least those held hostage, are in your debt.'

I had learned to disregard flattery from those who fawned in hope of gain but from this man, who had presided over Harold Godwineson's coronation and was one of the most powerful churchmen in the land, it was worth something. Yet there was an expectant, almost mocking light in his eyes as he watched me and it made me uncomfortable. Eventually, I inclined my head in acknowledgement, saying, 'Many died or were gravely wounded in the fight to keep the Viking force at bay: it is them you should thank.' And as his gaze did not waver, I added, 'By your leave, I must go and see to my men.'

Aldred nodded slightly in assent and again I thought to detect a hint of amusement in his gaze. But before I could be sure, he bent his head to peruse his parchment. Edwin got to his feet and came to bid farewell. He had to squeeze between wall and table to get round for he had matured into a sturdily built man, a head taller than me. I have heard it said that the two of us looked more akin than he and Morcar, who was slight and quick, brown-haired but with the same grey eyes as his brother. Edwin and I were both fair in colouring but he was clean-shaven save for his moustaches which hung below the level of his chin according to English fashion. His hair was trimmed shoulder-length while mine, to Turfrida's chagrin, hung half-way down my back. He took my right hand between his, gripping it firmly before releasing it and saying, 'I'll come to the camp tomorrow: Morcar and Edgar should see what force we have. I'll send a man with you now so we can find you. There were several thousand there this morning and more have been coming in.'

Thorfin was waiting outside and seemed glad to accompany me. We talked of the fighting at York and I learned he was a kinsman of the renowned Siward Beorn. Siward had, Thorfin told me, been instrumental in Tostig's first flight from the Humber, bribing his men to abandon him so that he was left with only three ships to sail to Scotland.

'I'm of Norwegian blood myself,' Thorfin said, 'but gold does not tempt my soul as it does the Vikings'. More pity that William of Normandy has forgotten his ancestry: his ambition would have been simply appeased could he have been bought so easily.'

'I think his price would have been too high even for the Church's coffers,' I replied, only half-jesting. 'And he has not forgotten all the customs of his forbears: the repaying of insults with blood for one.'

'Aye.' Thorfin ordered the gate-guards to let us out into the stink and bustle of the street. Fully armed as we were, folk parted swiftly to let us through yet it still took an inordinate length of time to reach and cross the narrow bridge. There was no wall on the other side though there was a cluster of mean-looking hovels: for London, the river itself was defence enough. Save at neap tides, it could not be forded within twenty miles up or downstream of the burgh and the bridge was the only foot-crossing in all that distance.

We found the men of Aveland, Barholm and Ness camped miserably on the edge of a marsh well south of the bridge. All the driest areas had long been claimed: men had camped in these fields for months and there was nothing left fit to eat or burn. In places the wet ground was churned into knee-deep mire by the passage of hooves and wheels and the whole area stank from the ordure of thousands of men and beasts combined with the ordinary refuse of living: bones and entrails of slaughtered animals, rotting kale-stalks and the like. The river flowed past it all and the camp added to the filth carried downstream from the town but women still washed clothes on the muddy banks and there was no other water to drink.

Made to sleep on bare mud with no fires and only the food they had brought with them to eat, men's discontent turned swiftly to rancour. Nearly all gathered there were from Mercia but this did not prevent fights breaking out over the smallest matter: claims over patches of trampled grass to feed horses; accusations of theft; disputes over bramble bushes (the only vegetation left standing), which were being uprooted and burned as men became desperate for warmth. There was no tree, fence or gate left standing for miles on this side of the Thames. Thorfin told me that a squabble over a branch lodged against the bridge led to the deaths of three men: one having drowned while trying to retrieve it, the others slain in the fight which ensued once the precious fuel had been dragged ashore. Such incidents, however, paled into insignificance compared with the bloody flux which had already laid hundreds low. 'If we don't march soon,' he confided in a low tone, 'more than half this force will be too sick to walk, let alone fight. You'll know how quickly such pestilence spreads when so many are camped together. Foul air rises from the river every morning.'

A cool wind was rising from the west even as he spoke: there was a damp edge to it which promised rain.

'Does Edwin know this?' I asked incredulously. 'We haven't come to starve or shit our lives away waiting for the King's call. My men only have enough food for two more days.'

'He must be blind if he can't see it for himself,' he replied. 'But he is young: he won't march until the command comes. The land hereabouts was stripped months ago when the fyrd was first mustered: even in the city food is scarce.' He paused and shook his head. 'It's October now: things won't be improved by us squatting in the mud like frogs. God grant the King sends soon.'

'Aye.' I saw Martin standing dejectedly where the horses were tethered in a fetlock-deep morass of mud and dung. Seeing me, he tried to look more cheerful but I guessed he had had a trying time keeping peace among our men. Thorfin nodded to him then took his leave, promising to return on the morrow, 'God grant with better tidings.'

With sunset came rain, a thin, cold drizzle which increased to a steady downpour. Martin and I fared better than most for we slept on the cart (mainly to ensure than no-one attempted to steal the food, weapons and armour stored there), but it was still a miserable night. Only eorls and the most powerful thegns had lodgings within the city; the rest of the fyrd huddled round pathetic fires of refuse while the luckiest sheltered inside benders inherited from those who had left with the King. Such constructions were few and, I heard, many had been destroyed by Edwin's hus-carls because of bitter fighting over their possession.

Morning brought little comfort to the thousands of hungry, weary men all now soaked to the skin. None had deserted in the night but I knew that if conditions did not improve, many would, having completed their forty days' service in the summer muster. From curiosity, I wandered the camp with Martin at my side, leaving Acer to guard the cart and horses. Most of my fighting previously had been as part of an organised army composed of men like the hus-carls whose profession was war. This host of thegns and freemen seemed almost a rabble by compare: some of the peasants were armed only with billhooks or cudgels and had no protection save what a leather jerkin could provide. I gnawed thoughtfully on a hunk of dry bread and watched a group of four bear a cloak-wrapped corpse to where the wattle and thatch of a tiny church stood isolated amid the squalor.

'That's the third today.' A young lad squatting on his heels to burnish a sword half as tall as he, caught my eye. 'If we're stuck here much longer, Duke William'll walk in over our corpses without having to strike a blow.'

He paused before adding wildly: 'They're saying this land is God-cursed, that the long-haired star was a sign and the King has been struck with madness. That's why he left without us.'

He was smiling as he spoke but something in his eyes chilled me.

'Who says?' Martin asked, grinning in return and I wondered he did not sense the boy's earnestness.

'Who doesn't?' The lad waved vaguely across the camp. 'My brother's a priest: he reckons this is Purgatory. Soon we'll be in Hell.'

He was an untried boy with a northern accent, likely enough the younger son or brother of a thegn killed at Fulford Gate, sent to make up the numbers. I never saw him again but wondered after if he had lived to recall those words, recognizing them for what they were. True prophecy ever comes unwittingly from the mouth that speaks it, so I was taught to believe.

Returning to our part of the camp, I had men dig shallow pits and line them with charcoal to collect drinking water (a trick of the Fen-folk I had learned from Rahere). This at least kept some occupied while the others Acer turned to weapons-training. The movement restored warmth to hands and feet numbed through cold and damp but they complained bitterly when we admonished slovenly sword and cudgel play, saying no man could fight on an empty stomach. All across the field groups were engaged in similar activity but large numbers were gathering at the bridge. Soon a clamour arose as Edwin crossed, surrounded by his men. The crowd fell quiet as he spoke: it was then I noticed Morcar standing hunched at his brother's shoulder, his left arm bound in a sling. I did not envy them, facing a hostile throng of frustrated, hungry and armed men but whatever news Edwin brought, his listeners did not dispute it and dispersed sullenly to their patches of mud.

True to his word, Edwin came across to me, guided by Thorfin. The tall northerner looked ill, his skin sallow and beaded with sweat but I did not get the chance to speak with him. Morcar, who accompanied them, was as eager to make peace with me as his brother had been the day before. Though ten years older than when I had last seen him, I detected the timid boy of the past in the nervousness of his manner: he met my eyes fleetingly and bit his nails as we talked. There was no sign of young Edgar, the Atheling, and when I asked after him, Morcar glanced round as if fearful of being overheard before disclosing he was safe in the fort. It was then that I wondered whether it was at the King's command they had brought him south or for another, darker purpose of their own.

The levy in the north having been decimated by the fighting against Tostig and Hardrada, Morcar had brought only a few hundred. He surveyed the mass gathered between the hovels of Southwark and the marsh with a weary, appraising eye and shook his head. 'I am minded to join the King tomorrow whether or not his call comes,' he said. 'What kind of ill-fortune is on us that the fyrd should stand guard nearly all summer to no avail, then we are attacked north and south within a fortnight? If Harold Godwineson has no need of us, then we should return home. No good is being served by sitting here.'

It was in my mind to point out that he, housed with his brother in the fort, would suffer no great discomfort from delay but his face also bore the marks of violence: his nose was flattened and twisted; the bruising extended to his eyesockets. Though they were not, according to Acer, wholly to blame for the disaster at Fulford Gate, the humiliation of that defeat must have been hard to bear yet, I reflected, he and Edwin had still answered the King's summons. Morcar appeared agitated; he must have been on the edge of utter exhaustion. In that moment I pitied him.

'I doubt there is one man here who would not willingly march today,' I told him. 'You can see for yourself how they've been living. Aye and dying too, from the flux and fights over food and fuel. If we don't move soon, they'll be set on the homeward trail anyway and no blame to them.'

The brothers looked at one another askance and Thorfin smiled: hitherto I doubt anyone had spoken so bluntly. Edwin, fingering the pommel of his sword, said uneasily, 'I am charged with holding this city: I cannot leave it undefended. No man under my command will leave until the King sends word.'

They stared at each other and the tension between them stretched like a drawn bowstring. Then Morcar said, with a breath of laughter, 'Do as you will with your levy and any others who will stay: the rest I lead south tomorrow.' He looked across the field to the dilapidated hovels, the bridge, the fort on its mound and the looming stone hulk of West Minster. 'But you are right brother: London must not be abandoned. Whoever holds this city controls the south of England, Wessex not least.'

A glance of understanding passed between the two and the tension dissipated. Edwin gave a grim smile, turned his gaze upon me. 'What of you, Hereward. Will you march or stay?'

'I did not bring my men to sit idle in the mud,' I replied. 'I am a fighter, no statesman or staller. We will go south.'

The prospect of action relieved the tedium. I gathered the thegns of Aveland, Barholm and Ness and gave them the choice of marching to join the King or staying to reinforce the guard on the city. None elected to stay thus the air was soon full of the sounds of whetstone against blade and the chatter of men roused from gloom to anticipation. The sun came out and most of us walked about half-naked, enjoying its warmth. Our mood was further lightened by the arrival of supplies, the ox-wagons we had passed on the way having been delayed by the rain. Only those sick with the flux or bound to stay behind were unaffected by the excitement: even Martin, who was often in dour mood before fighting, whistled as he burnished my hauberk and weapons, honed his axe-blade to hair-cutting sharpness. So involved were we in preparation, none of us stopped to wonder why no word had come from the King, who must have reached his destination the day before. The hours passed in more weapons practice for the fyrd, a final checking of harness and weapons and at nightfall, for the first time in days, men lay down to sleep with full bellies and a new sense of purpose.

Usually I have no difficulty in sleeping before a fight: it was, in any case, two days' hard march to the apple tree near Hastings where Harold had originally intended to muster. But that night I could not settle. Like a green lad preparing to face his first shieldwall I tossed and turned while thoughts of Turfrida achieved only a desperate yearning to be home. Remembering my warning to Eadric, I pushed such longings aside and eventually pulled my cloak close and wandered the camp in the bright moonlight. Under that eerie radiance, the muddy field looked disturbingly akin to the marshes around Fulford Gate save that here the figures stretched or huddled on the ground were asleep, not dead. I shivered and hurried back to the cart where Martin lay snoring; when I lay down this time I fell into an uneasy slumber.

It was still dark, with a pale glimmer in the east, when I was woken by men stirring all around. An indefinable sense of dread hung over the camp and I buckled on my swordbelt before joining the slow but inexorable movement towards the bridge, Martin at my shoulder. Torches appeared on the other side: as they were carried across, their flaring light revealed a great throng gathered around the bridge, townsfolk on the northern side, the fyrd on the south. All these people stood still and silent, waiting. Martin and I pushed our way through until we could clearly see those for whom the torchbearers had acted as escort. Edwin and Morcar were there but all eyes were on the tall figure that stood before them, the gaunt lines of his face stark in the torchlight. A cold hand seemed to grasp my heart when I recognized Aldred, Bishop of York: no ordinary occurrence could have caused him to address a gathering at such an hour. In the flickering light the river flowed blackly, like a torrent of blood.

Those in the north would not know it for a week or more but I doubt there is a single man, woman or child in England who cannot remember exactly where they were and what doing when they heard that news. Aldred was a plain speaker but had he not been, every word would have struck his listeners with no less force. Harold Godwineson and his brothers had been slain in a great battle near Hastings. The hus-carls had fought on but in the end the last of them despaired and fled, following what remained of the fyrd. It was a defeat more devastating than Fulford Gate and this time there was no King to rally a second force and turn disaster into triumph.

We listened in stunned silence as Aldred began to pray, his voice dry and harsh, that of a man focused on the necessity of the moment to the exclusion of all else. He blessed us all, commended the souls of the slain to the Almighty, then turned and made his way back over the bridge. Edwin did not speak: he and Morcar walked with the bishop and the torchbearers followed. There was, in any case, nothing to say.

The rest of that day passed in a kind of daze. Disbelief was followed swiftly by outrage which turned to resentful anger. There was not one man there who did not believe the outcome would have been different if Harold had waited for us.

As the hours passed, the true magnitude of the defeat dawned, fed by the accounts of those who began to trickle in from the south: women and children fleeing the ravaging of the Sussex countryside; wounded men on foundered horses who babbled incoherently of Norman feints and charges; of the King's fall, his eye pierced by an arrow; of routed men hacked to pieces in quiet lanes. There were tales of the red-haired Bastard riding his charger triumphantly over Harold Godwineson's mutilated corpse yet even as the extent of the slaughter became clear, still we did not comprehend what it meant for us. It was as if we were hearing a gleeman's tale, vivid and moving yet detached from reality. That day and the days which followed passed like a dream: we felt that at any moment we might awaken to find that the King had returned victorious, that we could go home, that nothing had changed. But there was no awakening

I think it was that evening but it might have been the next when Thorfin came to fetch me. By then a kind of sullen defiance had settled on the camp, melded from grief and anger. With the arrival of more refugees, the tale of the battle had reached epic proportions, concentrating all the fears which lurk in warriors' minds into a picture of desperate struggle and slaughter. No-one had yet deserted but there was a growing tension, that of embittered men forced to idleness. Aye, those first days there was no fear, only a growing lust for revenge.

Martin and I were discussing whether to send one of the youngsters from Laughton or Rippingale back with news, when I saw the tall northerner pick his way towards us. He was limping heavily and looked more haggard than ever: when he gripped my arm, it took all my willpower not to recoil at his reek of stale sweat and rotting flesh. Yet his voice was calm as he conveyed his lord Edwin's greeting and bade me come with him.

I went from curiosity as to my nephew's intentions but as Thorfin stumbled on the treacherous ground, did not question him. He was a man for whom I felt a natural empathy and I had seen enough die from wound-fever to know he would be lucky to see another dawn. Compared to what he faced, my concerns seemed petty.

Thorfin was eager to talk but his speech was all of home, the great river beside which the Thames seemed a muddy brook, the green rolling hills, his family, the beloved eldest son who had drowned in the carnage at Fulford Gate. He spoke without self-pity though he must have understood he would never see home or kin again. Only when we reached the door of the council chamber did his manner change. He turned suddenly, took my shoulders in a grip that even through my hauberk I felt hold fast as a falcon's talons, and leaned forward until his face was but a handsbreadth from mine. I almost gagged in his putrid breath as his sunken eyes, glittering with fever, locked with mine.

'Listen, Hereward.' His voice was a harsh whisper, fervent, compelling. 'It takes no great wit to guess what your nephews and the bishops are planning. They will proclaim the Atheling King and try to muster a force that will push the Normans back.' He paused and shook his head as if to dispel a blinding fog: his breath rasped in his throat. 'But Edgar is still a boy: he has already been passed over in favour of Harold Godwineson and men have not forgotten what happened at Fulford Gate under Edwin and Morcar's command. If they muster at York, over-winter there and strike ere spring brings more Norman ships, then there is a chance. But to stay here is madness: we are too few to repel William's force and there are none to aid us. All the Bastard has to do is surround the city and starve it into submission.'

His speech ended in a groan, his hands fell from my shoulders and he staggered. I steadied and eased him to the ground where he sat gasping for breath, head lolling. There was no-one about in the dim corridor. I crouched, wondering whether to call for help but with an effort Thorfin raised his head. His gaze wandered and I reached out to touch his shoulder.

'Listen.' He shut his eyes, all his will concentrated on forming words. 'For God's sake, take your men and go before it is too late. Mine are bound to Edwin but you are free. There must be some left to fight after London is taken.'

His breath hissed against clenched teeth, his eyes closed and he slumped forward. His limbs twitched as if attached to jerking strings.

'I will have him taken where he can be properly tended.' Edwin's voice startled me and I scrambled to my feet, wondering how long he had been there. He shouted for the guard and two mail-clad men came running. Their faces were hollow with weariness, their eyes red-rimmed and there was something in their manner, a kind of sullen diffidence, which disturbed me. They hoisted Thorfin between them and half-dragged, half-carried him away.

'The fool refused to rest,' Edwin said angrily. 'He took a spear-thrust in the groin at Fulford Gate: he was lucky not to die that day. I can't afford to lose men like him through wilful stubbornness.'

I said nothing but followed him into the dimly lit room where Morcar and Bishop Aldred were already sitting at the table. With them was a lad of about fourteen, tall and sturdy, dressed in a fine woollen tunic with richly coloured borders. A long dagger hung in a gold-embossed scabbard at his side. His was an open and pleasant face, framed by light brown hair which was neatly trimmed to his shoulders but he was very pale, the hollows of his eye-sockets purple with weariness though I guessed he would have shed few tears over the spilling of Godwineson blood. His clear grey eyes rested on me with a kind of detached interest, like one appraising a horse he knows he will not buy.

'Edgar Atheling.' I bent my knee as fitting before one of royal blood while Edwin told him my name and lineage. The lad's gaze sharpened but he did not speak, deferring to his elders without question. He knew well enough that he was but a gaming piece to these men who were all that remained of the Witan, the governing council of England.

'I have heard much of you.' I spun round, hand on swordhilt for I had not seen the fifth man in the room, standing beside the door like a shadow. Heavily cloaked, he possessed the deliberate self-effacement of an assassin though when he pushed back his hood I saw that he was older than Aldred. His visage was saintly, white of hair and beard (both were long and unkempt), lean to the point of emaciation. His deep-set eyes commanded attention: of greenish hue, they seemed lit from within by a kind of passion though what hunger drove him I could not tell.

'Stigand came from Canterbury this morning,' Morcar said and I knew then why the old man's gaze had sent a thrill of dread to my very core. It was like looking into the eyes of Fate. He it was who, while reviled and excommunicated by Rome, had yet clung to the Archbishopric of Canterbury and set a Godwineson on the throne of England.

Edwin passed a hand across his eyes. 'I take it you've heard the news, Hereward?'

I stared, unsure whether he was mocking me.

'Not of the battle.' He glanced towards his brother. 'Duke William has returned to Pevensey. He expects all that remains of the Witan to submit to him there and swear allegiance. He is waiting.'

My mouth was dry. 'And when they do not?'

He shrugged as if the question were irrelevant.

'William of Normandy is a usurping bastard with no legal claim on the kingship.' His gaze went briefly to the boy. Edgar stood with downcast eyes, his demeanour one of quiet resignation like a bull-calf penned for slaughter. When Edwin's eyes returned to mine they were unreadable: he waited as if expecting some comment. But I said nothing. Knowing their intent, somehow all seemed unreal as if the main protagonists were acting parts in a mummer's play. Detached from the main drama, I wondered why I had been summoned.

'Harold Godwineson and his brothers are dead: that is God's will and cannot be changed,' said Stigand. His voice, in contrast to Aldred's harshness, was soft and subtle, practised in whispering cunning counsel to the most powerful in the land. 'But we have a new King: the old blood has returned to claim its own. Against the Atheling, Duke William has no quarrel. The folk of London embrace him; Eorls Edwin and Morcar have sworn fealty: if the Normans will not leave of their own accord, we shall muster under Edgar's banner and drive them out.'

Stigand could have persuaded a river to run uphill, as the saying goes. So reasonable was his tone it seemed that the Normans were already defeated. But Aldred stirred impatiently.

'And where are the men that will flock to the Atheling's cause?' he asked. 'Three battles in as many weeks have not been without cost, though one so exalted may not have noticed. If we called on every bondsman and slave left in southern England, it would not be enough. The men who have waited here are sick with the flux and we have but little food. We must strike now, with what force we have, in the hope of taking the Usurper by surprise or we must go north and muster at York. There we can regain strength and acclaim Edgar King before marching back. That is the choice before us.'

Edwin and Morcar exchanged glances, then the elder said carefully, 'Hereward, of all of us you are most experienced in war. In our place, what would you do?'

There was a note almost of apology in his tone and I realized he was thinking that if circumstances had been different, I might indeed have been sitting in his place. And maybe it was that or else the culmination of many things: the miles I had covered in the past weeks, the battle, the strain of getting Eadric home alive, the effort to come south only to sit idle and frustrated in the mud while two days' march away the King who had led us to victory at Stamford Bridge was being butchered. Aye and Thorfin's talk of home and kin had also affected me for his face filled my mind's eye as cold, seething anger possessed me.

'In your place, nephew, I would be halfway to Pevensey by now,' I replied. 'We must hit hard, with whatever men we have, before ships bring reinforcements and William moves north. If he is truly expecting us to submit, that time is a gift, but he will not wait forever. We must strike before he loses patience. Otherwise, I am with Aldred. Our only hope is to retreat deep into Mercia, maybe to York, and recover strength, then attack in winter. But by then London will have been taken and it will be a bitter fight to get it back.'

Without realizing it, I had moved forward as if impelled by the force of my words: when I finished it was to find myself leaning over the table on clenched fists, eyes fixed on Edwin's. He returned my gaze for a moment then glanced towards the others, seeking guidance. An uncomfortable silence fell. Edgar half-opened his mouth, closed it again and stared intently at a knot in the oak table-top. Feeling suddenly self-conscious, I straightened and stepped backwards until I could see the churchmen's faces. Aldred, catching my eye, inclined his head slightly in silent acknowledgement but Stigand's gaunt features expressed a kind of pitying forbearance, as at the fulfilment of some long-held expectation.

'Such a strategy becomes one who is a warrior,' he said smoothly. 'But there is more to be considered than renown in battle. If we march now and lose, it may make a song worthy of heroes but there will be nothing to stop the Normans claiming the whole of England. To strike now is to stake all on one throw. London has walls that can be long defended while men rally to King Edgar's cause. We must wait until we have the numbers to assure victory.'

'Maybe you will wait long,' Aldred muttered sardonically. 'And what is to prevent William surrounding the city, cutting off supplies and starving us out?'

'There is the river,' Morcar pointed out. 'We will hold the bridge to the last man.'

'Aye, and when he falls?' I thought of the Vikings' desperate attempt to hold the bridge at Stamford, how we had heaved their corpses into the river to clear our way, and could curb my impatience no longer: each passing moment was time wasted. 'The sea did not stop the Bastard: you think he'll balk at the Thames, on which he could sail into the very heart of the city? We must strike now or retreat north. Let London be the bone one flings a vicious hound while the spear is sharpened that will silence it forever.'

Edwin frowned and rubbed his forefinger across his front teeth while Morcar shrugged: both seemed loth to speak. The boy, Edgar, looked up and from the stubborn set of his mouth and the directness of his gaze I guessed he had made some decision from which he would not be easily swayed.

'The people of this city have pledged to support me,' he said quietly. 'What sort of king will I prove myself if I abandon them now?'

I glanced helplessly at Aldred but his face was impassive. He knew the Atheling better than I: maybe he understood the futility of argument. Though young, Edgar possessed a natural air of authority which no doubt stemmed from his childhood at the courts of some of the most powerful in Europe and he was the future King: he would remember those that thwarted him. But a kind of recklessness overtook me. I could not stand by and let a green lad send us to ruin for no other cause than pride.

'If we move now, you will have no need to forsake them; if not, have them leave the city,' I said. 'If you refuse both, you will not be King.'

Stunned silence followed and a slow flush mantled the boy's face though he did not lower his gaze. His mouth tightened to a thin line but his eyes conveyed the belligerence of a defiant child rather than a man's anger. There came a low chuckle, dry and mirthless, from Stigand while Edwin and Morcar exchanged embarrassed glances. I was there, after all, at their invitation.

'That is wise counsel, if roughly spoken,' Aldred said calmly. 'You cannot ask a man his opinion then condemn him for giving it. If my word carries any weight here, I agree with Hereward. But if we strike now, we must be swift and resolute. We cannot afford to lose another day.'

'The fyrd were ready to go yesterday, along with your men.' I appealed to Morcar. 'If we leave at dawn, we can reach Pevensey before the Bastard crosses the London Road. It will take time to get his force in marching order: with luck we'll catch them unawares. Once cut off from the ships they are ours!'

It took only the space between one heartbeat and the next for me to realize no-one in that room, not even Aldred, shared my eagerness. Maybe they really believed they could hold London against the full might of William's force, an army which had wiped out the King's hus-carls and most of the thegns of southern England in one battle. And, also, the memory of Fulford Gate must have weighed heavily upon my nephews. Their confidence as war-leaders had been shattered by the magnitude of that defeat and in a warrior self-belief is everything, the difference between winning and losing, life and death. They shifted uneasily, avoiding my gaze, and I sensed then they would not march south. Yet I made one last effort for it seemed to me that this was our great chance for lasting victory, to rid ourselves of the Normans once and for all.

'The men are crying out for vengeance,' I said. 'They are ready to take lives for those slain at Hastings but give them a new king to follow as well as a dead king to avenge and they will fight to the last drop of their blood. We should use that eagerness for it will not last forever. If they are forced to sit idle in the mud while enemies ravage our lands, their anger will turn against you, their leaders. Many may prefer to die defending their own homes rather than a city they have not even been allowed to enter. Unwilling men do not make good fighters, however desperate the cause.'

Of the five, I think Edgar alone was persuaded by this argument but the Atheling was, as yet, powerless.

'You are but recently returned from exile, I believe,' Stigand said softly and his eyes were suddenly like polished stones. 'You are too quick to doubt the loyalty of the fyrd. It is simple enough to understand that if London is taken, England is lost.'

'Only the south,' Morcar muttered, casting a meaningful look at Aldred. But the bishop spread his hands in a gesture of resignation and bowed his head, obviously unwilling to challenge Stigand who was, after all, his superior.

Edwin, who had listened to the debate with grim concentration, pushed back his chair and regarded the two churchmen with a kind of weary forbearance.

'We shall wait,' he said at last, heavily. 'I will not send men blindly against so hard-handed a foe, marching our whole force on the off-chance of catching the Normans unawares. The risk is too great. We must send out scouts and wait for their report while we gather more men here. Then, if William comes, we shall be ready. Meantime, Edgar will be acclaimed King for, as has been said, against him there is no quarrel: his claim is just. Even the Pope cannot refute his right.'

'He has already endorsed William.' Through my anger I detected an edge of amusement to Aldred's tone. 'Even the Pope cannot uphold two claims to the same throne. Nor will he support any English claimant while my lord Stigand' – he inclined his head ironically – 'holds an archbishopric without licence from the Church of Rome.'

'There is nothing to be gained if we quarrel.' As the two churchmen glared at one another, Edwin rose and leant upon the table exactly as I had done earlier: I am sure at that moment he wished himself far away. 'I have stated our strategy: now we must act upon it. Spies will be sent out at once: no doubt news is coming in from the south all the time.' He glanced at his brother who, beneath his weariness, seemed apprehensive. 'Morcar, you are charged with defending this city. Have the walls patched up and the people armed. And the fyrd must be brought within.' He sighed and his bloodshot eyes met mine at last. 'Hereward, our thanks for your counsel. Time will prove the wisdom of this choice but we have the whole kingdom to consider.'

I stared bitterly and he could not withstand my gaze and looked away.

'May God guide you,' I said and the words choked in my throat. 'But if you will not let us march south now, I would have your leave to take my men home. For this also I would add: you will end up like ducks on an eel-pond, too fearful of the hawk's shadow to heed the pike circling beneath. When the Bastard moves north of the London Road, will you still wait? You asked my counsel: if you choose to ignore it, that is upon your heads. But I will not condemn my men to a fight they cannot win.'

They stared as if unable to believe what they heard but I was past caring. Then Stigand asked, with a kind of smug satisfaction, 'Is it your wish to be exiled again, son of Leofric? That is sedition.'

Edwin's gaze was fixed on mine and beneath the weariness stamped upon his features I read regret and a grudging respect. He shook his head almost imperceptibly, warning me to say no more but it was too late. There was that in the Archbishop's nature, a kind of lazy malice (like that of a cat which delights in tormenting its prey), which provoked me and I could no more ignore it than one can disdain the bite of a gadfly.

'The abbots of Borough and Croyland will not thank me if no man returns to tend their lands,' I answered. 'And,' I added meaningfully, borne by the force of my anger as a leaf is swept away on a flood tide, 'my fealty lies also with the King of England.'

At this, Edwin exhaled slowly, like the last breath of a dying man, while Morcar studied his knuckles. The Atheling, who had seemed lost in his own thoughts while we talked, leant forward and his gaze was suddenly keen and penetrating.

'I am rightful king,' he said, his voice so hard and clear that even Stigand seemed disconcerted. 'Are you disputing my claim?'

'No.' I inclined my head a little in acknowledgement of his status but our eyes remained locked. 'I meant no disrespect. But you have heard the arguments and, I think, do not lack courage. Will you therefore command me to stay against my own counsel?'

My mind had slipped into battle-focus: it was as if the others in the room were meaningless shadows. Yet for all the arrogance of his royal upbringing, Edgar was still a tyro. After what seemed an eternity but which must have lasted at most the space of five heartbeats, he glanced at Stigand and licked his lips before his gaze returned to me.

'No,' he said quietly. 'I want men who will follow me gladly. Yet when I am King, I shall expect such service from you as is due from all free men in England.'

'And you shall have it,' I replied simply. 'You, above all others, have rightful claim. But if you stay here and wait for the Bastard to move first, you may never come into your inheritance.'

'Enough!' Edwin's voice was stern but I guessed his impatience stemmed from worry rather than anger. 'We have decided our strategy. There is no more we need from you, Hereward. Go your way and if you can devise some means whereby you and your men leave without causing more desertions, you have my gratitude.'

To his credit, he did not accuse me of faint-heartedness: perhaps he did not dare. But it was there in the barely veiled contempt of Stigand's expression and the atheling's hard glance as I took my leave. Morcar said nothing, nor did he look up as I turned towards the door.

'I think I can help.' Aldred, calm and self-assured, followed me out and closed the door. The corridor was empty yet he took hold my arm and leant forward confidentially.

'I would have you know that I agree with you though I favour withdrawal to the north rather than outright attack,' he said. 'To my mind we lack the numbers for certain victory. Nonetheless, I shall stay here for good or ill: I do not think it Duke William's purpose to oust those endorsed by the Pope while he marches under the pontiff's banner.' He paused and sighed. 'Still, the Almighty works in ways beyond man's comprehension. Abbot Leofric of Borough is sick: he has conveyed a wish to go home that his abbey may be blessed by his death. As one of his men, it is your duty to escort him, with an armed band to ensure his safety. If you go today he may even reach Borough alive.'

'God grant it so,' I said, grateful for circumstances which allowed me and my men to leave without censure. Aldred gave a brief smile like a gleam of sunlight on a bleak winter's day then added gravely, 'If you had fought alongside Harold Godwineson you would likely be dead; as it is you have the chance to bring peace to one who has served our Lord and the people well for many years. Do not therefore think lightly of this task. There is no foreseeing God's grace or the fate of men: we must act each as we think best, according to conscience. No more can be asked of us than that.'

5. The Sack of Bourne

While we argued over whether to march south from London, William's force at Pevensey was disabled by the same deadly flux our men had suffered at Southwark. Had we attacked then, our victory would have been assured. But this we only learned when it was too late. Such was God's will.

The sickness had reduced Abbot Leofric to a skin-clothed skeleton. He babbled in a raging fever at the start of our journey then sank into a stupor. The stench from his soiled robes and bedding turned the stomachs of the hardiest: only the novice and priest who tended him could bear to be near for long. Before we were halfway home the former had joined his master on the cart, too weak to go to the verge to void his bowels.

As Aldred suggested, we left London the day of that fateful debate. I deemed it prudent to go before Edgar changed his mind and chose to outlaw me as one of his first acts as King. The true reason for our departure I told no-one, even Martin: the envy on the faces of those doomed to stay behind shamed me. No doubt many of my men wondered why a sick abbot (albeit one of the most revered in the land), should merit an escort of more than two hundred but they were too relieved at the prospect of going home to ask questions. The tales coming in from the south were enough to make the most steadfast quail and it seemed to me that many more days of enforced idleness would turn the frustration of the fyrd to rebellion. Edwin and Morcar had an impossible task keeping thousands of hungry, wretched men willing to fight whilst delaying that very moment by refusing to leave the supposed safety of the city.

That, though, was no longer my concern: my mission was to see that Leofric reached Borough alive. We moved at greater speed than on the southward journey, spurred by the hostility of many of the roadside vills whose men had marched with the Godwinesons and would not return. Only when we reached our own shire were we welcomed and then we began to lose men as they departed for their homes. Two days after leaving London we saw the smear of smoke over the potteries at Stamford, then the tower of Borough minster between the trees. Sensing our excitement, the mules quickened their pace (the abbot was past feeling the jolts as the wagon bounced along the ruts); workers in the fields paused a moment to stare then ran to ask whether news of a great battle and the King's death were true. We answered that Edgar Atheling was likely to be proclaimed soon and told them to pray for the soul of their abbot whom we were bearing home, gravely ill. Then the welfare of Leofric, who was deeply beloved for his fair dealings with folk of all kinds, overwhelmed the news of defeat and invasion which here seemed unreal, like tidings from some far-away land or of events long past, remote from daily life in this corner of the world.

The gates of the burgh were open and townsfolk flocked to meet us, the press becoming so thick that Acer and I had to ride ahead, swords drawn, to clear the way. Someone must have warned the abbey of our approach because the bishop and a retinue of monks awaited us in the yard. Leofric, who by now looked more corpse than living man, gave a groaning sigh as he was lifted from the cart onto a pallet: one novice turned away, retching at the stench. But the abbot was still alive. In that at least I had not failed.

Martin, I and the other men from Aveland Wapentake did not linger though the bishop invited us to take refreshment in the abbey. We were all eager to get home: as with any journey, the last few miles seemed the longest. And also I had seen who hung at Athelric's shoulder, looking upon the stricken abbot with a strange mixture of pity and anticipation. Before my uncle could acknowledge me, I mounted Tiw and we clattered out of the yard and down the long street to the North Gate under the gaze of bewildered townsfolk.

Once within Ness bounds Martin and I let the horses have their heads, the palfrey keeping up gamely with Tiw's long-striding gallop. We did not stop at Bourne, nor did I allow the stallion to slacken pace as the marshes spread to our right. By the time we reached the Laughton track Tiw's neck and shoulders were lathered and Martin's chestnut was dark with sweat but both horses sensed our urgency and charged towards the huddle of buildings as if at the end of a desperate race.

Alerted by the sound of hooves, Turfrida ran from the Hall as we clattered into the yard, Toli following closely with Aedgifu's hand gripped in his. There was alarm on their faces but I told them no emergency had brought us at such speed, only our longing for home. And then I slipped from the stallion's back into the embrace of my wife and child and we stood a moment in silent communion, taking comfort from one another, thankful for the fate which had spared me once again when so many had died.

It was maybe a week later that we heard of Abbot Leofric's passing. All Borough mourned (this loss struck more deeply here than the death of the King since burgh and shire had ever been distrustful of the Godwinesons), but the monk's choice of Brand as his successor was wholeheartedly endorsed. Only Martin could have guessed the true cause of my foul mood which began on hearing this and worsened as the days grew shorter and gales boomed in from the east.

Those closest to me bore the brunt of my ire which Turfrida at least attributed to the news carried up Ermine Street by dispossessed and starving folk moving desperately northwards. Duke William had waited while his men regained strength and the slain were replaced by more boatloads of mercenaries and horses (though it was now November, there was no shortage of those prepared to risk the perilous crossing for the promise of land and gold). Then, as no eorl or thegn came to submit at Pevensey, he unleashed his force to ravage all Sussex, Kent and Wessex, lands formerly held by the Godwinesons and now utterly defenceless, most of their menfolk having been lost at York or Hastings.

It is a measure of the strange unreality of that time, when all was still uncertain, that the people who supported Brand urged him to seek confirmation of his abbacy from the Atheling. It was my secret hope he would fall sick or be slain by Normans on the way but he reached London safely and Edgar welcomed him. By then Edwin and Morcar, perhaps realizing the futility of trying to hold the city, had returned to their estates in the north. Winchester, the ancient Saxon capital, and Canterbury had already submitted and William's force was sacking Oxfordshire, moving inexorably south-east: it could only be days before London itself was besieged. Whether the fyrd was still camped wretchedly in the mud outside the walls at that time I never heard but the situation inside was said to be dire for no new supplies had reached the city since our leaving it. Many must have died from lack of food and warmth before a Norman came within ten leagues of West Minster.

Driven by a restlessness I could not assuage, I took to riding abroad for tidings despite the short days and foul weather, calling in at Bourne whenever the temptation of a warm fire and a cup of mead on the way home overcame my bleak mood. Eadric welcomed me but I sensed a reticence in his manner, almost as if he were afraid. When Ymma was within hearing we talked of the estate and the season, a tree fallen across a track or a missing ewe, but whenever she went to tend their child (which was still small for its age), our discussion turned to the war. While William's force now ravaged the south at will, none of the Witan had submitted, nor had they proclaimed Edgar King.

'It's too late now,' Eadric remarked one day as he came out into the yard to bid farewell. He walked with a pronounced limp, leaning heavily on a crutch for his wound was still not fully healed. (Earlier that afternoon a long splinter of bone had emerged with the pus that leaked from the hole in his thigh). 'We're doomed to a foreign King, like it or not. But if he rules like Cnut it may not be too bad. If a Norman geld is imposed on the south it'll be recompense for the Danegeld they escaped last time.'

It was a grey, blustery day and geese flew overhead on the way to roosting grounds near the sea: the air was full of their haunting cries. A lad with a crooked nose brought Tiw. I took the reins but did not mount straightway, disturbed by Eadric's mien. He had lost weight since being wounded, his visage had grown haggard and his hair was streaked with grey but it was not these physical changes that alarmed me.

'I am no longer fit to fight, even to defend my own home,' he said suddenly. 'Will you bring Turfrida and Toli and settle here? We have at least built some defences: Laughton has none. Ymma agrees: it will be safer for us all to be together if the Normans come. We could build you your own house.'

I stared, astounded, and he lowered his gaze while a look almost of shame settled on his features. For a moment I pitied him: though not a proud man nor a warrior born, it must have cost much in self-esteem to plead thus. As I hesitated (in truth I did not know how to answer), he reached out and grasped my wrists.

'At least consider it,' he said fervently. 'What will you do if they ravage this land like the south? You cannot hold out at Laughton.'

'Nor here, if they come in force.' I pulled away and swung astride the stallion. 'But I will think on it, I promise.'

On the way home I decided that a move to Bourne would serve no purpose and said nothing of it to Turfrida.

By the time I saw Eadric again, events had eclipsed our own concerns. Despite their oaths to uphold the Atheling's claim, the Witan did not wait for William to besiege London but instead went to meet him at Berkhampstead. There they submitted and swore fealty, giving hostages as surety of good faith. Edwin and Morcar were still in the north but their oaths were given by proxy. Archbishops Stigand and Aldred knelt before the usurper as did the boy, Edgar, who was greeted as a kinsman and promised honour in the Bastard's court. The only sour note in the exchange of oaths and promises was that William knew of Brand's application to the Atheling for his abbacy, a fact which the Norman took as a grave insult. Only Aldred's intervention saved my uncle from imprisonment or exile, that and the payment of forty marks in gold, a huge sum though one that Gildenborough could well afford. In return, Brand gained not only confirmation of his abbacy but also that of the abbey's rights to lands it had held for generations. This last should have warned us of what was to come but so stunned were we by the rapid capitulation of our leaders, no-one wondered why the holding of land should be subject to question. For those of us who had not yet seen any Norman, it seemed unbelievable that we were living in an occupied country and the world as we knew it had changed forever. Even when we heard that the submissions had done nothing to stem the plundering of hall, cot and church by William's men, still it seemed that it was happening somewhere far away and to folk different from ourselves.

The Midwinter Solstice came and went, the wind swung to the east and it snowed. Only the children were delighted by this: for the rest of us it meant that precious stores of hay were used up and labour in the fields, clearing ditches, stone-picking, hedge-laying came to a standstill. The meres froze hard and only the main river channels remained free of ice. At Turfrida's insistence I sent Cole One-Hand to the reed-cutters with a bag of grain and a couple of sheepskins and they sent a stick of dried eels in return. Of Rahere no-one had heard.

At Christmas the weather eased and the tracks, though slushy, were passable. We all went to Croyland on Christmas Eve as was the custom in those parts and Ulfkil, after blessing us, told us that as the angels had promised peace and goodwill to all men at the Christ-child's birth, so our new King had pledged to all who offered him fealty. Remembering the abbot's warning when I had sought loanland, I wondered what had made him change his mind towards a man who was both usurper and bastard-born. But Ulfkil was foremost a pragmatist: he sought to protect his abbey's interests as Brand had done for Borough.

It was on Christmas Day that William was hallowed King in West Minster though we heard of it only after Brand's return to Borough in mid-January. Aldred presided at the coronation; all the surviving members of the Witan, including eorls Edwin, Morcar and Waltheof were present and this time William pledged to be as good and true a king as had ever ruled England, rewarding fealty and punishing sedition. The atheling, Edgar, was also there, watching those who had pledged to support him pay homage to the usurper for a second time yet he had lived most of his life in exile at one court or another; maybe he was simply glad to be alive and whole. At any rate, William appeared remarkably tolerant of those who had formerly opposed him and I suspect that the atheling made the same judgement as the rest, mistaking clemency for weakness.

Although some of the Witan maintained their positions that first winter, distrust not loyalty sprang from the seed of the Usurper's coronation. It began in London even as the King was being anointed. The Norman guard was nervous: mistaking the townsfolk's roar of acclamation for a riot, they set fire to the buildings between which the crowd was packed. All that part of the city save the Minster itself was made of wood: the fire spread quickly and most of those inside the abbey fled in panic. William, it was said, stood pale and trembling while the rites were scrambled around him but he soon regained his composure. No sooner were the fires out than the wooden fort by the bridge was pulled down and a stone keep erected in its place. This was the core of a grim and impregnable castle, a statement in stone of Norman ambition. As he moved to secure the lands he had overtaken, those misguided enough to have believed his promises discovered how they had been betrayed.

In most of the South it was easy. Almost a whole generation of thegns and ealdormen had died at Hastings and writs were issued ceding their lands to men of William's choosing. Only the abbeys kept their holdings: as yet he dare not challenge the Church. Those that had survived the fighting or, for some reason missed it, had to pay recompense to keep their lands and if they could not, it was forfeit to the King. And as a master-stroke, when complaints were made through the courts, it was decreed that since Harold Godwineson had unlawfully taken the throne to which the Norman was rightful heir, the date of William's succession should be that of Edward the Confessor's death. Any man who had answered Harold's call to arms was therefore a traitor and his property could be confiscated in the King's name.

This last I heard from Ulfkil, having ridden to Croyland on Toli's behalf. Since Eadric's wounding, the old man had become quiet and withdrawn until only Aedgifu seemed able to penetrate his melancholy. (No doubt my own ill-humour had not helped). Winter is never a good time for the aged and he had caught a chill after walking to Bourne in a rainstorm. After that he was left with a persistent cough and barely stirred, sitting hunched beside the hearth all day like a dotard. If he spoke to Turfrida or I it was to berate the fact he had lived long enough to see another king dead and all the might of England defeated, and he repeated Eadgytha's warning until our ears were weary.

With Bourne grievously short-handed since the slaughter at Fulford Gate, the church at Laughton had not progressed beyond foundations and this also preyed on Toli's mind until he accused us of deliberately staying the work in the hope that he would die ere we had to pay for it. Preoccupied with other matters, I did not take offence but Turfrida was deeply hurt and begged me to fetch the abbot who, she hoped, would assuage the old man's fears.

There was a gale blowing as Swallow picked her way through the mud; plovers dived and swooped all around, their strident calls sounding clear above the roar of the wind. The wild weather complemented my mood yet I looked forward to a warm hearth and cup of mulled wine with the abbot. Ulfkil greeted me courteously though he seemed surprised to see me. I tied Swallow in the yard and followed him inside. The long hall was filled with peat-smoke blown back through the vents and the blue-grey haze exacerbated the darkness for the fire was but a heap of smouldering embers.

'There are evil times ahead,' was the abbot's opening statement as he handed me a steaming bowl of wine. He told me the news from the south in a tone of grim resignation and listened with ill-disguised impatience as I related the tale of Toli's decline.

'Do not mistake me: the soul of one man is more precious in the eyes of God than all the wealth of Gildenborough,' he said when I had finished, and sighed. The wind howled in the rafters and Ulfkil drew his heavy robes about himself to keep out the draught. 'I will come to Laughton when I can - we are short of horses – though I do not know what I can do for the old man if he is so weary of life. Eadric's wound is healing is it not?'

'Aye, but the mending is slow: he cannot yet sit a horse.' I rose, for the afternoon was passing and nightfall would be swift. 'Come as soon as you may, for I doubt Toli will live to see his church finished.'

'I shall try.' Ulfkil's expression was thoughtful as he escorted me to the yard. 'It may be that we see the loss of much that is dear to us this spring, some things we do not even consider of consequence, yet we shall rue their passing. Still, God's will be done.'

The storm worsened: the gale flung stinging sleet into my face as the mare plodded homewards. Her thick coat was soaked into dark curls by the time we reached the Laughton turn and smelt hearth-smoke. Had I not been half-blinded by the sleet, I might have noticed fresh hoofmarks in the mud: as it was, when Swallow began to jog, I assumed that, like me, she was looking forward to shelter and food.

So loud was the roar of the wind in the trees and the rushing of the swollen stream, no-one heeded our arrival. I drew rein in the yard and swung down from the saddle, shivering at the touch of wet clothes against my skin. To my surprise, Toli's hounds were huddled miserably in the doorway of the Hall: usually they sprawled by the hearth like living rugs. They followed as I led Swallow to the stable, then the mare gave a strident, challenging neigh and I saw a white mule tethered in her stall.

No-one I knew between Folkingham and Bourne possessed such a beast yet even then I felt only a spurt of annoyance that my own horse should have been so casually ousted from her place. Tiw stood half-asleep in the adjacent pen. I tied Swallow firmly alongside and grasped the mule's bridle to lead it out. So engrossed was I (for the beast was unwilling), I did not notice Cole One-Hand enter the stable until the mare gave a warning snort.

'Hereward.' His voice was low. 'I'll deal with this. You'd better get inside: you have a visitor.'

Disturbed by his tone, I did not wait to ask who it was but hurried across the yard. The rooms at the back were deserted, the fire low. I flung my sodden cloak into a corner and put fresh wood on the fire then hesitated, hearing a voice from within. Smooth and unctuous, it made my skin crawl though I could not place it. I pushed open the door and the vague apprehension which had begun to form in my mind became a dreadful certainty. As I entered the room a fist seemed to press against my throat so that I could hardly breathe and icy sweat bathed my skin.

After Yule we had pulled a table and carven chair close to the fire for Toli who refused to leave the draughty hall for the comfort of our smaller rooms. Abbot Brand was ensconced there now, dandling Aedgifu on his knee while the old man and Turfrida sat side by side on the bench. The priest seemed to be telling a tale and so engrossed were the two, neither noticed my arrival. But Turfrida glanced round and a look of relief settled on her features though it turned swiftly to dismay as I strode across the hall, grasping my sword in both hands, ready to sweep it from the scabbard.

Something, maybe the sound of my footsteps or the woman's tension, broke the spell Brand's voice had laid upon the child. Both turned their heads and Aedgifu's chubby face froze in horror: never before had she seen me in my wrath. But she did not scramble from the abbot's lap to her mother's and I saw that he was holding her gently but firmly round the waist. Then the anger which had sprung like fire in my blood was effaced by fear. Toli looked up as I stood beside the table but his eyes were bleared and dull and it was as if he did not know me.

'Hereward.' Brand inclined his head in mocking acknowledgement. 'Had I known you were so fortunate in wife and child, I would have called sooner. As it is, the hour grows late. I must leave now else I will be journeying to Croyland in the dark. I am sorry to have missed you.'

Turfrida drew breath: before she offered him a bed I said forcefully, 'Then let me at least escort you to the stable. I am sure the Almighty will guide your mule's feet, however wild the night.'

Ignoring Turfrida's hard look and Aedgifu's obvious disappointment, I let go my sword and gestured to the main door. It took an inordinate amount of effort to do so for my fingers had locked as if reluctant to obey my will. My mind reeled between anger and unutterable relief that Aedgifu was safe.

Brand did not speak until we were outside. I shut the door, having let the dogs slink within: when I turned, the abbot blocked my way. Although he must have been close to sixty, fat had smoothed the effects of age so that he appeared much younger; his lips had lost none of their fleshiness and his eyes, bright with a kind of gleeful malice, peered from between corpulent lids so that to me there was something obscene in his every glance.

'I would hardly have recognized you,' he said softly, leaning close so that I could hear his words above the roar of the gale. 'Fell and stern you are become yet I deem the fallen angel that once looked from your eyes still dwells within.' He paused to lick his lips and despite the fact that I was no trammelled boy but a warrior in the fullness of his strength, I shuddered. 'A pity that you have no son. Many have passed through my hands in the last years but none so good as you. Maybe I should try a girl.'

Since returning from London I had taken to wearing a dagger all my waking hours. The blade was at his throat before he could draw breath. He stared at me undaunted.

'If you touch a hair of my daughter's head, you die.' Rage and fear choked me. I pressed a little harder and a few drops of blood sprang beneath the blade. He let out a clotted gasp and the pupils of his eyes widened.

'Dear me, nephew.' His voice shook as I lowered the weapon but not from fear: a waft of smell and heat arose from him that made my gorge rise. 'You must learn to curb your temper. When our Norman friends arrive, no doubt it will interest them to learn what a firebrand they have on their doorstep. A true touch of the Fen-wolf. Do not forget under what terms you hold loanland: Croyland also comes under Bishop Athelric's see.'

'Go!' I was breathing hard, fighting for control though even now he held a power over me I could not contest, as if by degrading and humiliating me as a boy he had somehow hamstrung a vital element of my will. Though with my whole being I longed to stab the life out of him, I could not do it and that he knew. 'I have kept my agreements. It may be that the Normans will not look kindly upon a corrupt abbot.'

'Corrupt?' He moved away a little and the wind whipped out the folds of his cloak like flapping wings. 'Oh come now, of what would you accuse me? I have heard their Church frowns upon marriage of the clergy, not their sins, for we are all sinners, Hereward. Would you rather they learned of you as 'Thegn of Laughton' or 'Abbot Brand's boy'? It might surprise your wife who knows so little of your past, aye, and little Aedgifu, who thinks her father such a hero.'

I do not know what would have happened had not Martin chosen that moment to lead Brand's mule into the yard. Afterwards I realized he must have listened to all that transpired between the abbot, Turfrida and Toli from our private rooms then, hearing my arrival, made himself scarce, not wanting to tell me who was there. Seeing him, I felt an immense relief, a release of tension like the snapping of a bowstring. I found myself smiling as I sheathed the dagger and pointed to the mule. 'Get on, Brand.'

He gathered his cloak close about himself and looked at me expectantly, waiting, I think for me to lay hands on him again. But I said firmly, 'Whatever happens with the loanland, Laughton is mine. Come here again and I'll cut you. Then we'll see which of us is the boy.'

He forced a smile at that but his eyes glared unutterable hatred. 'This land may be yours now,' he hissed, 'but there is a new king and it is widely known who led the men of this wapentake against him. Think well upon your position before threatening those to whom you owe fealty.'

With that, he turned on his heel, ordering Martin to lead the mule to the stone block where he heaved himself into the saddle. I watched unmoving as he rode away, the mule jibbing as sleet slashed into them: when I looked back into the yard, Martin was not there.

Knowing that Turfrida would demand an explanation for my discourtesy towards one who was not only a powerful churchman but also my liege-lord and kin, I went to the stable, needing time to think. Swallow was eating hay contentedly: her well-being made me aware that I was hungry and shivering, my wet clothes chilled from standing outside. Rather than face Turfrida before I had regained composure, I moved to the mare's shoulder and put my arms around her neck. Some days she would have swung her head to bite but as I pressed close to feel her warmth, she whickered softly and nuzzled my thigh as if to comfort a foal.

'Hereward.' I do not know how long I stood there, eyes closed, breathing in the scents of hay and horse-dung and the smell of the mare, letting the horses' champing and soft breathing soothe me, before Martin's voice jerked me from my reverie. 'You cannot stay here like this. Come inside. Turfrida will be worried.'

I was slow to meet his gaze, dreading to see pity there but he was watching me with a kind of loving forbearance, that of a brother rather than servant.

'Hereward!' By now it was almost fully dark and the sleet formed a pale blur as it swirled between the buildings. The stable shook as another gust slammed into it but the horses chewed on, unperturbed.

'Alright then.' He shrugged, shook his head in exasperation. 'Stay here and sulk like a child. But the longer you leave it, the more Turfrida will nag. Women are like that.'

'I'll come.' Until that moment I had succeeded in holding my mind still, avoiding thought of the implications of Brand's visit. The very sight and smell of him had made me want to vomit, as if my flesh recalled what he had forced upon me as a boy.

'Listen.' Martin took hold my arm as I stepped reluctantly from the mare. He leaned close and his voice was little more than a bare whisper. 'Brand cannot touch you now. Whatever hold he may once have had over you, all that is finished. It's a long time since I found you in the marshes.'

In all the years since I had run through the Bolhithe Gate and escaped by means of the river, I had never asked Martin what he thought had happened. Nor had he spoken of it save in vague terms though he must have guessed most of the truth from the marks upon my body. Though he was my father's man, he had abandoned that service to follow me into exile; since boyhood he had been my friend and protector though officially a servant. Sometimes I wondered whether he preferred men to women, for he had never married nor, as far as I knew, had any sexual relationship with a woman but as the same went for boys and men, I accepted him for what he was: he never wavered in loyalty. His eyes were dark and intent as he watched for my response, sensitive to my pain as if it were his own.

'Aye.' I had to force the words: my tongue seemed slow and heavy. 'But sometimes the past cannot easily be pushed aside.'

'It is over,' he said fervently. 'And I doubt Brand will hurry to return. You did well not to slit his throat. At least you don't have to explain that to Turfrida!'

It was a poor and bitter jest but there was truth in it and it did something to dispel the foreboding that weighed upon me. We stared at each other a moment longer, then he let go my arm. 'Come on: she'll have food ready by now.'

We entered the living room behind the hall to find Turfrida and the child preparing pease and bread. Toli sat on the bench and I wondered how they had persuaded him there until, drawing close, I saw that he probably had no idea where he was. Turfrida regarded me with studied patience but Aedgifu scowled and stirred the pot angrily as I stripped off my wet clothes and found a dry tunic.

'Why did you send my uncle away?' she demanded when I crouched beside the hearth. 'I liked him. He told me stories and made me laugh.'

I glanced at Turfrida but her face was unreadable.

'Brand is not your uncle,' I replied and a hand seemed to grasp my bowels as I recalled his threat. 'What kind of stories did he tell?'

She stopped stirring and her brow creased in a look of such concentration, it wrung my heart.

'There was one about a man called Samson who lived in a hot land a long time ago. God made him very strong because his hair was longer than anyone else's and he slew thousands of warriors when they tried to capture him. But his enemies sent a wicked woman to discover his secret and he opened his heart to her and she cut off his hair and made him weaker than a babe. So then he couldn't fight any more and they put out his eyes and chained him and made fun of him and he was very angry but he couldn't do anything because he was blind and his strength had left him.' She paused for breath and frowned, her eyes bright in the leaping firelight, then whispered confidentially, 'Then one day they took him to their temple and tied him between two pillars. And he called on God for help and pushed the pillars apart and the temple fell down, squashing all the evil men and women and Samson died too.' She resumed stirring hastily as Turfrida laid a finger on her head but her eyes went to the hair which hung in wet hanks about my shoulders, then to clean-shaven Martin who sat nearby. 'Is that why you're the best fighter? Would you be weak if I cut off all your hair?'

I did not answer straightway, wondering why Brand should have chosen this of all stories. Turfrida gave me a sharp glance then said lightly to the child: 'Ah, so that's it! Since I met your father I've tried to make him look more civilized, thinking if Martin could do it why not Hereward? Still, think on this, Aedgifu: I must be strongest of all because my hair is twice as long and soon yours will match your father's.'

'Then we shall rule this house and invite who we like!' Aedgifu abandoned the pot and skipped gleefully round the hearth to come at me. 'You won't be able to stop us!'

'Is that so?' I caught hold her waist and swung her, shrieking with delight, up over my head. 'And will you take my place when it comes to the running of the estates and marching to fight, little warrior?'

'If you let me ride the black pony I'll come!' she squeaked. I pulled her across my shoulder and down into my lap where she wriggled helplessly as I tickled her. 'William the Norman will run back across the sea when he sees us!'

'Ach well then, I'd better teach you to ride once the weather eases,' I replied gravely. 'The sooner we scare him away the better.'

'Yes!' The delight on the child's face was countered by Turfrida's tight lips but I ignored her for it was high time Aedgifu learned to handle a mount on her own. If the Normans raided here as they had in the south, I knew in my heart that there might be no option but to take to a fugitive life in wood or fen: our lives might depend on our horses. Even Bourne, semi-fortified as it was, could not be held long against concerted attack: it would become a trap rather than refuge.

'Eat.' While I mused, the child jogging on my knee, Turfrida had doled the thick pease porridge onto trenchers and torn a flat loaf into hunks. We ate in companionable silence (though Toli only picked and mumbled at his portion) while the wind moaned in the rafters. Drowsiness overtook me with the warmth of the room and the comfort of a full belly. I gathered the child into my arms and lay back contentedly and Brand's threats seemed no more substantial than the smoke eddying out through the roof vents.

Days passed and England lay under the pall of an uneasy peace while the few surviving eorls and thegns of the southern shires paid homage to the King and tried to redeem their lands with silver. As yet, no Norman force had moved north of Watling Street but we watched and waited with trepidation. After Brand's visit I stayed close to Laughton, rarely visiting the abbey's lands in Barholm Hundred but on the occasions I ventured there, I called on neighbouring thegns to discuss our response should the usurpers come so far. Uncertainty tainted every aspect of our lives yet ordinary folk went about their labour much as they had always done, assuming that a change of overlord would make little difference to the slow rhythm of their existence. Infields still had to be ploughed and sown; sheep were heavy with lamb and the geese which flew in from the marshes to graze grew restless as the days lengthened.

Much of the shire was under the eorldom of Morcar. We assumed he must have redeemed estates like Bourne when he swore allegiance to the King at Christmas. Only later did we discover that he had been permitted to keep only some of his poorest lands in the north. The rich tillage of Lincolnshire had been used to pay off those of William's supporters not already granted fiefdoms in the south and the only reason no Norman had been seen in our parts was that they had not yet sought to make their claim.

The year turned and Turfrida's belly swelled. Whenever I came home, weary from riding out for news or minding the spring sowing, the sight of her eased my anxiety. She radiated that contained well-being that resides in all healthy women when they are with child. Indeed, only Toli seemed ailing that spring: Eadric's wound had healed over at last and though left with a lasting lameness, he could at least ride a horse again. Ymma and the child were also well and sometimes the three of them came over to see the old man. Toli rarely spoke these days (save in complaint), yet he would hold the babe in his gnarled and palsied hands as though fearful it might break, peering into its eyes as if the answer to some profound question resided there. Ulfkil visited just before Ash Wednesday but the abbot could offer little comfort when Toli broke his silence to ask why, if God were merciful, a dotard such as he should be forced to live so far beyond his years that every moment was a burden. In an effort to appease the old man, we went on with the construction of Eadgytha's church. It seemed almost that by continuing those tasks begun before the defeat at Hastings, Norman encroachment could somehow be stayed.

By Easter the first courses of stonework were laid and we persuaded Toli outside to see. He blinked like a mole at the brightness of full daylight and pressed his finger into the rough lime mortar, ignoring the frowns of the two clinchmen. One of these was Thorald, youngest brother of Thorkil of the Fen-wolves and one of the more promising of those who had marched with the fyrd to London. He asked if we would be doing weapons practice again now that winter was over and I agreed to train those who were willing. It took no great wit to guess that such skills would be needed sooner rather than later: rumour was already rife of small-scale rebellions, the killing of Norman knights as they tried to take over the lands of those slain at Hastings or outlawed after. And yet, in our ignorance, hope lingered that we would be left to live as we were. The surviving members of the Witan were still at the new King's court: we waited to see what power would be granted them.

Doubts grew when we heard that William had taken them with him when he returned to Normandy soon after Easter. The boy Edgar, eorls Edwin, Morcar and Waltheof along with Archbishop Stigand were among those chosen as unwilling guests. Whether or not they believed the Bastard's promise of honourable treatment, his true intent was revealed at Rouen where these last representatives of English nobility were paraded like captives before baying crowds, stripped of their weapons and surrounded by guards. I have heard that all bore themselves proudly but the humiliation of being put on public display must have been hard to bear. Indeed, if William thought to cow his rivals by such an act, he gravely misjudged their nature: no hatred is so bitter as that rooted in shame. Where there had been distrust, resentment festered. The King's treatment of those who could have been his allies was further proof that his promises were empty and his pledge to reward fealty with honour a lie when applied to those of English blood.

With those he mistrusted taken from where they could do most harm, William left England in the hands of his half-brother, Bishop Odo of Bayeux, and William FitzOsbern, one-time Steward of Normandy, now Eorl of Hereford. Odo's rule was confined to those areas south of the Thames already subjugated by Norman ravaging prior to William's coronation but FitzOsbern's aegis included East Anglia and Mercia up to the Humber. When that news reached us, most folk buried their silver and few travelled far from home lest they return to find themselves dispossessed.

Bishop Odo I knew by reputation; of FitzOsbern I had heard enough in Flanders to understand that the appointment boded ill. Yet by the time lambing started no Normans had been seen in our part of the country save a few heavily armed bands riding north along Ermine Street, presumably to assess the richness of the usurper's realm. Maybe the two had their hands full enforcing the disposal of fiefdoms south of Watling Street, the line of the old Danelaw, for we heard rumours that Edwin had been given power over Morcar's lands and, along with Waltheof of Bernicia, would run the north of England as a separate province, paying geld to King William but operating under English law. Remembering Thorfin's warning, I treated such tales with the contempt they deserved for Edwin's standing in Northumbria had never recovered from the defeat at Fulford Gate. Later tidings that Copsige, Tostig Godwineson's deputy, had been appointed to collect taxes from York precluded any possibility of peace in the North: he was hated as much as any foreigner. Yet we still continued with the daily chores that attend the running of estates, the small joys and ills of the household, much as harvest mice build their nests and tend their young, hearing the approaching scythes and distant barking of dogs without comprehension until all is torn apart.

Under my guidance, Eadric improved the defences at Bourne. The gates were strengthened with wooden platforms from which men could shoot down on attackers from behind a stout palisade no spear or arrow could penetrate. Lack of labour meant that the ditch which should have surrounded the whole settlement only extended a little way to either side of the gates but to anyone approaching from the road it still presented a formidable barrier. I thought with envy of the stone-built castles of Flanders and Maine and toyed with the idea of sending Turfrida and Aedgifu back until it became clear what we could expect from Norman rule. But I knew she would refuse to go without me and I could not countenance abandoning my homeland so easily after years of exile: to do so would be to admit defeat. Thus I did not mention the matter and she, understanding my nature, never spoke of leaving.

The year dragged on through shearing and haymaking to midsummer. We heard that a castle was being built in Norwich and rumour came of rebellion in the west led by a dispossessed thegn called Eadric who, with Gruffydd of Wales, attacked the Norman stronghold at Hereford. There was insurrection on a smaller scale all over the south as those with nothing left to lose took revenge on Normans arrogant or foolish enough to travel alone. Retribution was swift: once a killer's identity was discovered, his vill was burnt to the ground, his neighbours and kin robbed and beaten. The dispossessed fled to Europe or Ireland if they had the means; trudged the long road to Scotland where King Malcolm had offered sanctuary, or else took to a fugitive life in the woods and hills. Some passed Laughton on their way north, shunning the routes favoured by the usurpers. These we gave food and shelter for a few nights, listening with a kind of pitying detachment as they spoke of widespread pillage, rape, burning. Many urged us to take all we could and flee while we had the chance but the more I heard, the firmer grew my resolve to stay.

It was soon after Midsummer that Cole One-Hand brought the news we had long dreaded. Upwards of four score Norman knights had ridden into Borough as escort to a number of King's officers. To these, every free man in the shire was to pledge allegiance and pay seisin. Anyone refusing to attend the Hundred Courts at which the oaths were to be taken and payment made would, by default, be outlawed, their land forfeit to the King. The cases of those who had marched against the Bastard would also be considered: against some of these writs had already been issued and their estates would be taken over forthwith.

'The Court for Aveland Wapentake is set for Lammas Day,' Cole said. 'At least by then we'll know what to expect: they're working through the shire hundred by hundred.'

'Like a creeping plague,' Turfrida remarked, glancing anxiously at me. 'Do we have enough silver to redeem Laughton? Toli has nothing: he used it to pay geld last year.'

'Maybe.' To my own amazement I felt no anger, only a kind of dull resentment that what we had tried to think away had come at last. The reeve's gaze was fixed upon me: the lives of more than my own family would be affected if we lost the estate. 'But it is a month yet to Lammas. Much may happen in that time.'

Turfrida caught my eye meaningfully as I turned to go (the start of hay harvest had been delayed again at Rippingale and I wanted to check it had all been cut). I paused to lay my hand against her cheek in a gesture of reassurance (it was about the end of July that our child was due), and murmured, 'Do not fret, love, all will yet be well' but riding away I was not sure which of us I had been trying hardest to convince.

It was on a day when the sky was blue as a thrush's egg and the marshes shimmered with heat-haze that we learned the true nature of the occupation. I had taken Aedgifu with me to the monk's demesne farm so that Turfrida could rest (in the last stage of her pregnancy she found the heat trying). The black pony, glossy with summer grazing, trotted valiantly alongside Tiw but its short stride was not the reason the journey took twice as long as usual. At every cot it seemed someone wanted to speak with the child, offering a cup of milk or a toy fashioned from reeds or withies that their own children had outgrown. Showered with gifts and good wishes, Aedgifu was in no mood to hurry home once my business was finished but as the shadows lengthened I was assailed by a vague unease, a prescience of something wrong. With every mile this anxiety deepened until in the end I set the child before me and urged Tiw to a canter, the pony galloping beside.

We entered the yard to find Turfrida pacing heavily back and forth in the shade cast by the Hall while Toli and Aelgytha sat side by side on the stone block. At first I thought Turfrida's labour had begun but as she came to meet us I saw that her face, while pale and strained, did not exhibit the intense inward focus of a woman in childbirth.

'What is it?' I laid a finger against Aedgifu's lips to stay her chatter then handed her down, Turfrida bending awkwardly to let the child slip to the ground. Tiw nuzzled my wife's tunic as I dismounted for she often kept a crust of bannock there for the horses. I pushed his head away lest he be too rough and caught the pony's bridle as it pushed jealously alongside.

'Cole One-Hand went to Lound to check on the wheat,' she said. 'On the way back he saw a band of Normans take the Bourne track.'

I glanced south for it had long been arranged between Eadric and I that we would light warning beacons if attacked. No smoke marred the cloudless sky, nor was there any untoward sound above the low hum of insects, the ripple of water, slow rustle of hooves on baked earth as beasts went to drink at the stream.

'Likely enough they've gone to assess the estate,' I replied. 'It will save Eadric negotiating at the Hundred Court. He would have signalled or sent a message if something were amiss.'

My dismissiveness was feigned: before Turfrida discerned my true discomfiture I turned to lead the horses to the stable. She laid a hand on my arm to stay me.

'They were fully armed,' she said. 'Why should that be if their intent was peaceful?'

'They are occupiers of a hostile land,' I answered. 'Many have been slain on visits to seemingly quiet manors. Have you forgotten how I went thus in Flanders for fear of an assassin's knife or arrow?'

She considered this. 'Then promise that you will go to Bourne at first light, to make sure all is well.'

'Aye, alright.' Shrugging off her hand I led the horses to the lean-to where I rubbed them down and turned them loose to graze. But I could not ignore my disquiet and against my usual custom caught Swallow and stabled her behind the Hall.

It was a still, cloudless evening yet the hounds would not settle as we sat around the hearth: afterwards I wondered what they had heard that we could not. And maybe it was the same instinct which compels birds and wild beasts to flock when danger threatens that made the folk of Laughton congregate in the Hall that night. All had heard the news and as speculation as to the Normans' purpose grew, so did our fears. When Martin came in after nightfall (from visiting the Fen-folk as had been his habit since boyhood - where he went and for what reason I never asked -), his face was grim.

'News travels fast across the water,' he said. 'The Normans reached Bourne mid-afternoon and they had not left by evening.' He took a bowl of ale gratefully from Turfrida, drained it then caught hold my arm and drew me aside. 'We should ride over without delay. Screams have been heard and the gates are shut.'

'When was this?' A fist seemed to close around my guts. 'Tell me you came straight here!'

'Of course.' His voice was low and urgent. 'It may have been no more than children playing. But we should go nonetheless.'

I glanced across the Hall. Groups of men and women discussed the Normans in low voices while children pelted between the benches in a wild game. Turfrida, leaning back a little against the weight of her swollen belly was talking earnestly with Aelgytha and Ade, the shepherd's wife, while Toli sat hunched in his chair, apparently oblivious to all. Yet when my gaze fell upon him he looked up. His eyes gleamed red in the firelight.

'Come,' I said to Martin. He followed me into the room where my arms were kept but no-one seemed to mark our leaving. I closed the door. 'The child is due soon: if ill befalls me, I would know that Turfrida is safe in your care.'

He argued as I pulled the hauberk over my ordinary clothes though his role had ever been thus, to give me peace of mind when I went to fight.

'Say nothing of where I am,' I warned. 'If she asks, I've gone to check on the cattle.'

'In war-gear?' he asked as I buckled on my swordbelt and settled the long knife that hung to my right, then as I strode towards the back door, added anxiously: 'What about your helm? It will hide your hair: in the darkness they may mistake you for one of theirs.'

This was good counsel. I donned coif and helm while Martin ran to harness the mare. With each moment my foreboding increased. It seemed an age before Swallow was ready and I swung into the saddle though it can only have been as long as it takes to down a horn of mead: I dreaded lest Turfrida come out and see me. But she did not and I thanked God that at least I did not have her anxiety upon my conscience, praying at the same time that I would return unscathed.

So clear was the night that the light of stars and quarter moon cast shadows on the track which ran like a pale ribbon beneath Swallow's hooves. In the stillness, the distant roar of the sea was a constant background to the sound of galloping: sensing my urgency, the mare went like the wind. Indeed, that ride seemed like something from a dream. As the empty landscape unreeled around us it was as if Swallow and I were the only living things in all the world.

I did not check her until we reached the track to Bourne. At the junction I pulled her to a standstill and our senses strained for the slightest sound or movement. Beyond the mare's breathing and my own, there was nothing untoward, only the night-time rustle of mice in the grass, croak of frogs from the eel-pond and ditches, the distant hoo-wic! of a hunting owl. I urged Swallow on and she walked warily up the track, head held high, ears pricked. When I laid a hand on her neck she shivered but did not falter.

I turned the mare onto the verge to deaden the sound of our approach; about three spearthrows from the gates I dismounted. The palisade formed a solid black wall against a lurid red glow but there was no smoke save that pouring from the roof-vents of the Hall, a dark hulk against the starlit sky.

Cautiously I led Swallow forward and a raucous burst of noise made her jib nervously: drunken shouts and laughter amidst which, sharply cut off, was a woman's cry.

We had cleared a killing ground within arrowshot of the defences and I hesitated at the edge, scanning the outer wall for a guard. Nothing moved but as more noise came from the Hall I noticed something stuck above the gates which made me leave Swallow and run forward. When I saw what it was, I stopped in my tracks and stared numbly, stricken, thinking: 'This cannot be.'

Eadric's head was rammed upon the spike like a felon's. Blood glistened like tar where it had run down the wooden pole. The greenish-white starlight illuminated the face in stark detail; his hair hung about it in dark hanks.

I have seen many men's faces set in death, including those slain by my own hand, but none so terrible. Eadric's visage was fixed in an expression of grief and outrage, of utter incomprehension. He had looked like that when in a fit of jealousy as a boy I burned a parchment he had been working on for weeks, decorating the borders of a psalm he had copied for his parents. It was the look of one whose trust has been betrayed beyond the limits of any imagined possibility and maybe it was the shame of that memory, hitherto forgotten, which lent me strength to climb the gate we had thought to have made unassailable by its very height, to haul myself over the pointed stakes onto the guard's platform and, once there, to ease the severed head from the pole. As I lifted it and kissed the cold brow, my hands shook with grief and rage. Blood clung stickily to my fingers. I took off my cloak, wrapped the head and laid it carefully in the darkest corner. Whether I wept I do not know but I promised to avenge him ere the night was over. From that moment to when I was with Turfrida again my mind was cold, detached, channelled into battle-focus so clear I felt invincible. As I turned and looked down into the yard, it was as if I viewed myself from the outside.

The source of the lurid light was the Hall itself. The doors stood wide open and half the winter wood store must have been piled on the hearth, maybe the faggots stacked as a warning beacon were there. The flames cast jagged shadows into the yard: the flaring light picked out Eadric's body at the end of a heavy blood trail. Beside the stables, the dark forms of horses shifted restlessly. I counted eight but that gave me only the least number of enemies for the horses lost at Fulford Gate had never been replaced and there was room for eight more inside. Beyond the stable and forge I could just make out the roofs of the labourer's cots but though smoke spiralled from some of them, there was no light or sound of activity. I guessed their inhabitants must be hiding or else were already inside the hall.

The sound of drunken singing swelled into the night and someone began to play a dance tune on a pipe. The playing faltered at first and mocking laughter accompanied it; fists thumped on tables to keep the rhythm. At intervals came the notes of a harp, heartbreakingly pure amid the cacophony.

I took a last look round, saw that Swallow was safe beneath the trees, her roan colour making her all but invisible in the dappled starlight. As I turned again to the yard I noticed other corpses: two dogs lay near the gates with cloven skulls and a sheep's innards were piled on its bloody skin a few paces from where Eadric sprawled, hands bound behimd his back. I climbed down the ladder and ran across the open space, keeping to shadow where I could. Close to the Hall, the air was thick with the stench of blood and the acrid reek of charred flesh.

As I peered carefully round the door, my mind remained clear and calm though the scene within revolted me to the depths of my soul. The fire had been built to a roaring pyre: had it been a windy night, the Hall would have been ablaze. Norman knights slumped or sat at the table in various stages of drunkenness, waited on by the women of Bourne while at the other end of the long hall, a thick-set man rutted on a naked girl roped to the box-bed. The door to the private rooms gaped blackly but there was no sign of Ymma or the babe. The player was the stable-boy with a crooked nose: as he fingered his pipe, his eyes were fixed agonisingly on the girl. No other men or boys from the estate were there (most had, of course, died outside York); of the Normans I counted fourteen. As I watched, one of those slumped at the table slid off the bench and settled on the floor in a mead-sodden heap. A heavily bearded, grim-faced man made some comment and shouted for more drink. It was brought by the crone who had acted as midwife at the birth of Eadric's son. Even she had not escaped the raiders' attention: her tunic was ripped open to expose her breasts, flaccid flaps of skin hanging almost to her waist.

All this I saw in an instant, being concerned only with how my enemies were armed and their drunkenness: the details I remembered after. In the heat of the room (which even where I stood was like the breath of a forge), most had stripped off their hauberks and some had laid their belts aside, no doubt to leave them unencumbered while they assaulted the women. Hunks of meat, spitted on swords, lay charring in the embers.

I entered the hall with my sword sheathed, needing to get close before they guessed my intent. My helm and hauberk were of foreign make; no doubt those who saw me assumed I was a Flemish comrade. The first three did not even know I was there: I struck them from behind, bringing Brain-biter's pommel down on their heads with all the force I could muster. Stupefied by mead (which to those unused to it acts like fermenting apples on swine), the others simply stared. I slew five before the remainder even thought of their own weapons: some died as they scrabbled for swords they had forgotten had been laid aside. The music stopped as a sixth man crashed to the floor and the pipe-player snatched a sword from the ground and ran towards the bed.

I keened aloud as I killed them, those things in the shapes of men who had slain my foster-brother and defiled my father's hall. Only the bearded man put up real resistance but there was fear in his eyes as he looked into my face: he saw his death there. He was still wearing his mail-coat but his head was unprotected. I struck him a shoulder-blow which brought him to his knees, then clove his skull. The harpist, a light-boned youth who seemed barely old enough to bear arms, knelt and begged for mercy but I slew him with no more compunction than the others and kicked his instrument into the fire. That left only the drunken sot sprawled beneath the table. My sword seemed suddenly leaden in my hands but I bent to drag him out and, in doing so, saw Martin framed in the doorway.

His face was pale and anguished but he did not move or speak as I slaughtered the drunkard even as the man began to protest my rough handling. Blood sprayed my face and I wiped it away with a gore-smeared hand, looking around to make sure no Norman remained alive. All were dead: the stable-boy had stabbed the one ravishing the girl then untied her. I leant panting on my sword and felt no joy or satisfaction, only an immeasurable weariness. The interior of the hall looked like some nightmarish charnel-house, a slaughter-pit where the victims were men instead of beasts. Everywhere I looked seemed red, from the glow of the fire and splattered blood, but my eyes were drawn to a dark patch on the earthen floor from which a heavy trail led outside, the spot where Eadric had been killed. I pulled off my helm and coif, let them drop to the ground.

'Hereward.' Many times Martin had tended me after fighting but now there was a note of pity in his tone I had never heard before. Unable to bear his gaze, I looked away and found Ymma and then the meld of anger and grief that had made me invincible turned to something darker. It lodged like a boulder at the very core of me.

She must have been there all along, hidden by the shadow of one of the doors, her back against the wall. Her legs were bent and splayed like those of a woman in childbirth; her tunic was ripped open from neck to hem. Her breasts, belly and thighs were dabbled with blood and nameless filth, her eyes stared sightlessly from a face devoid of expression, that of one who has lived through the unendurable.

'Hereward!' Martin's voice was insistent. He picked up a cloak and draped it round the shoulders of the girl the stable-boy had rescued and now helped towards the door. She clung to the lad, barely able to stand and he pulled the cloak close to hide her nakedness. Close to, they were clearly brother and sister.

'What are you doing here?' I was angry with Martin for disobeying orders. 'I told you to stay with Turfrida.'

'It was she sent me,' he replied defensively. 'She berated me for letting you go alone.' He looked round at the carnage, adding dryly: 'I was too late anyway.'

'Aye.' In the silence which followed, weariness overwhelmed me so that it became an effort even to breathe. Women began to move amongst the corpses like people trapped in some kind of dream, stupefied by shock, dazed. The stable-boy, his sister clutched against him, stared at the blood-stained sword in his right hand as if he did not know how it had got there. His face was white and strained like that of one who wants to vomit but cannot.

Martin was watching me expectantly. My throat was parched and I longed to go somewhere quiet to rest and think but there was something more to do before my promise to Eadric was fulfilled. 'See to Ymma,' I said.

He nodded and I think he guessed what was in my mind because his mouth tightened and he looked away as I knelt beside the dead drunkard and drew my knife. But before I started (the neckbone was already smashed so it was a cutting job), he asked suddenly, 'Where is their child?'

Since entering the Hall my mind had been focused on killing: the significance of Ymma's swollen breasts and the trails of milk down her belly had not registered. A woman's cry and men's laughter I had heard but no babe's squalling. I glanced at her but she still stared blankly into a void no-one could reach.

'Some-one must know.' I turned my eyes to the mess of flesh and bone beneath my hands and a wave of revulsion made me shudder. 'Look in their rooms: he may be there.'

'My lord.' The stable-boy stepped forward drawing the girl with him. Her face was turned into his shoulder as if to hide. 'They – the bairn is dead.'

He faltered and glanced at Ymma and it was as if the sight of her steadied his resolve for he swallowed hard and began to relate what had happened in a voice which grew more confident with every word.

My blood turned chill as I listened. I thought I had seen the limits of the evils men will inflict on others of their kind in the fighting through Scaldemariland and Maine: many of my comrades had delighted in torturing the flesh of those weaker than themselves, taking rape and pillage as a victor's dues. Yet as the boy revealed what the Normans had done the gorge rose in my throat, not from shock or horror but because I understood that kind of cruelty too well. When his tale was finished I asked whether he knew what had become of the child's body but he shrugged. I heard a kind of choking sob yet meeting my gaze Martin, whose face expressed the anguish I had not begun to feel, forced control on himself and crouched beside Ymma.

I turned back to the stable-boy. 'What is your name?'

He was watching me fearfully, making me wonder how I must appear.

'Wuleric, my lord.'

'Can you ride?'

'Yes.'

'Then go with all speed to Acer the Hard at Witham. Have him come back with you. Tell him there is Wolves' work here. Take two of the *destriers* but be careful: they are warhorses and may be dangerous to strangers.' I paused for a set, hard look had settled on his features and his hand tightened on the sword as the girl moaned and pressed harder against him. 'I will have the women care for your sister, do not fear. You have done well tonight, Wuleric.'

Since first given leadership of men in Flanders I have understood the value of praise. Here it was sincerely given and the lad's stubborn look faded. The crone came to take his sister and he released her gently into her care.

'Thank you, my lord.' He inclined his head, tried awkwardly to thrust the sword inside the rope that bound his tunic.

'Take a proper sword-belt and scabbard,' I said. 'This carrion no longer needs them.'

By now some of the women had recovered from shock to a kind of unreasoning anger. They bent to strip the dead while one, a middle-aged woman with greying hair and a face bloodied and bruised by the Normans' rough treatment, picked up a sword and stabbed it repeatedly into the groin of the man who, I assumed, had raped her. A deep grunt of satisfaction accompanied every thrust; the crone shook her head and guided Wuleric's sister outside. The lad himself, having chosen and buckled on a knight's belt with self-consciousness painful to behold, hurried out after. A few moments later came the soft whicker of horses followed by the clatter of hooves as he headed for Witham.

Whether he paused at the cottages or it was through that strange diffusion by which news travels through small settlements I know not but soon after Wuleric's departure, the men of Bourne hurried to the hall. They were few, maybe twelve in all, old men and young boys and all carried weapons of some kind: sickles, clubs, bows. They halted in the entrance, stared. The women stripping or mutilating the corpses stopped and met the appalled eyes of their husbands and sons with a kind of ashamed defiance; the one with the sword let it fall from her hand and began to sob and tremble.

I got to my feet, sensing chaos encroach: black raven's wings seemed to beat inside my skull. As if from a dream I heard my voice ordering some of the men to guard the gates, to let no stranger enter; others I set to help the women strip the slain and drag them into the yard. I stood and watched with a kind of terrible detachment until I was sure they obeyed and then I fetched Eadric's head from the guard-post. Maybe I was not in my right mind but it seemed fitting to untie his hands, to prop his body against the wall and arrange his head in his lap (it would not balance on the ragged stump of his neckbone), so that he could witness his avenging.

It was when all fourteen had been dragged out, naked and bloody, that I regretted not keeping at least one alive so that Eadric's face would be the last thing they saw before they died. When they lay in a row, I borrowed Martin's axe and hacked off their heads. These I gathered into a fallen cloak, slung the bundle on my shoulder and clambered back onto the platform. The peasant on guard cowered into the corner, his face rigid with terror but I heeded him no more than the eyes of those now gathered in the yard. They watched in silence as I rammed my trophies onto the spiked posts of the palisade, saving the highest, where Eadric's head had been impaled, for the bearded leader. His cloven skull had been bound neatly with a length of cloth to prevent it splitting apart but I do not recall doing it. Close to, the visage was familiar but I was in no mood to put names to faces as I climbed back into the yard.

The Bourne folk watched me with dread and did not speak: their craven fear irritated me and I told them roughly to go home. They scurried into the darkness like frightened sheep as I picked up the axe from where it was propped against a corpse and cleaned the blade on the cloak which still dragged from my hand. Eadric's eyes stared blankly from the rigor of his face: I could do no more for him. I knelt and laid the bloody cloak gently to cover him, was overwhelmed by a sense of futility like a black tide. If I slew every Norman in England it would not bring my foster-brother and his son back to life, nor undo the defilement of the women.

How long I stayed there I do not know. Martin roused and guided me into the hall. My mind was blank with exhaustion more profound than I had ever known, even on the way home after the fight at Stamford Bridge. He sat me down, put a cup of mead in my hand. 'Drink.'

The fire had burned to a heap of glowing embers. I scratched idly at a blood-splotch on the table, unsheathed Brain-biter and laid the sword before me, noting how the blade was notched and blunted.

'Hereward, listen.' Martin sat on the bench opposite. His face was stark in the ruddy light, drawn with grief and worry. 'Once word of this gets out, the Normans will not stop until you are dead and God knows how many others. We must fetch Turfrida and Aedgifu, go deep into the Fens or Brunneswald. We cannot stay here or at Laughton.'

The embers reflected in the sword-blade, made it seem that in places the metal was red-hot from the forge; where blood-smeared it appeared rust-eaten. My mind was slow: thoughts slid like eels from my grasp and yet my resolve was set, immutable as stone.

'No,' I said. 'We will make this a place of fear for anyone of Norman blood. This is not the south where they have usurped the lands of dead men. Here they will have to fight for every blade of grass they tread. I will not run away. Bourne is mine by right. I shall return and make it my home.'

He stared, aghast. 'Have you lost your wits? You've heard what happened at Hastings! Those you slew tonight were mostly drunk, weaponless. Do you think it'll be so easy a second time? There are maybe fifty men of the fyrd in the villages hereabouts though they owe you no fealty: you think they'll withstand a score of Norman knights or even answer your call, knowing what'll happen to their womenfolk when they're slain? This is madness: I want no part of it.'

'Go, then.' It was as if I had become a thing of wood: looking into his stricken face I felt nothing. 'I want no man of faint heart or doubting mind with me. The Fen-wolves will answer my call.'

'The Fen-wolves?' He shook his head incredulously. 'What of your agreements with the abbeys?'

'Those tenancies were void the moment I found Eadric's head stuck on the gates,' I replied. 'Abbot Brand will rejoice to hear this news, that I have fulfilled his expectations. If he licks the right Norman arses, they might even add Bourne to the abbey's lands. But they will have to take it first.'

Martin's gaze sharpened as if I had said something startling but further argument was precluded by a nervous sounding challenge from those on watch and the noise of horses entering the yard. A few moments later Acer strode into the hall, followed by the lad. Wuleric must have ridden at breakneck speed to reach Witham and return so quickly but if anything he seemed more self-possessed than when he had set out.

'Dear God, Hereward.' Acer could not conceal his shock as he surveyed the room though he must have heard the tale of the attack on the way. His gaze settled on me. 'Are you hurt? You look as if you've bathed in blood.'

'It's not mine,' I said. 'But there is still work to do. I want the Norman carrion taken deep into the Brunneswald. Open the carcasses for the wolves and wild pigs. Martin and I must tend Eadric and return to Laughton.'

'Wuleric said –' he began but the words stuck in his throat. He made a helpless gesture of resignation and disgust, blurted, 'I'll do it gladly. Come on lad, we'll need a cart and a strong beast to draw it.'

The two left hurriedly and I glanced at Martin. There was a curious tension in his face as if he were fighting to contain laughter or tears. Unable to withstand my gaze, he bent his head but as I lurched to my feet and slid my sword, fouled as it was, into its sheath, he stepped away and crouched by the dark patch where Eadric had been slain. He pressed his hand against the stained earth as if renewing or sealing a pledge, then followed me into the yard without a word.

We bore Eadric's body to the church and arranged it as best we could on the altar, wrapping the cloak around to make it appear whole. I washed most of the blood from his crushed nose and split lips but nothing could alter the terrible expression in which the features were set, nor would the eyelids close. In the end we took down one of the wall hangings and covered him with that but as I walked away I seemed to feel his gaze upon me, sad, reproachful. In his direst need, I had not been there.

By the time we returned to the hall, Acer and Wuleric were throwing the headless corpses onto a two-wheeled cart used to transport game from the forest. Two oxen stood placidly in the traces, seemingly unaffected by the stench which arose as the bodies were moved but the horses tethered near the stables whinnied and shifted nervously.

'I left my horse near Swallow,' Martin said as we crossed the threshold. 'Someone must ride to Laughton. Toli and Turfrida will be half-mad with worry by now.'

'Toli – ' Up till then I had not thought how I would break the news to him but knew it should come from my lips. 'Get the horses,' I said roughly. 'I'll fetch Ymma. I promised to look after her.'

The eastern sky was ashen with dawn. By that pale light I caught Martin's glance and read such tender and profound compassion there, it shook me to the core. Then he turned and hurried towards the gates.

The two women guarding Ymma were reluctant to let me near though she was still in a state of stupefaction. They had washed and dressed her in a clean shift but she had not spoken and lay curled on the bed like a frightened child. Ignoring the women's protests, I lifted and cradled her against my chest. She whimpered, trembling like a wounded deer as I carried her.

Ymma was lighter in bone and build than Turfrida yet in my weariness her weight made the length of the hall seem unending. When I reached the door I paused, the breath sobbing in my throat, and laid her down. Martin was waiting with Swallow and the palfrey while Acer and Wuleric threw bloodstained cloaks over the corpses on the cart. The giant Fen-wolf grinned when he saw me and opened his mouth to speak but I shook my head and then he noticed the woman propped against the wall.

'I'll make sure none of these bastards is ever found,' he said softly. 'Death was too good for them.'

I mounted Swallow and Acer lifted Ymma into my arms. I asked him quietly to search for the babe's body, hoping she could not hear. Then we left, the crowd at the gates staring awestruck at my bloodstained appearance.

We rode swiftly and in silence. In the growing light there was no need to hold the horses in, Swallow being in any case sure-footed as a pony. The woman weighed heavy in my arms, her head lolled against my shoulder. Only the movement of her ribs against my arm assured me that she was alive: she uttered not a sound. I longed for home, for Turfrida to comfort me, to smell hearth-smoke and the baking breakfast bannock instead of the cloying reek of blood.

The sound of hooves brought Cole One-Hand and Aelgytha running from their cottage, the reeve brandishing a cudgel, she wielding a long knife. At the sight of me they dropped the weapons. A moment later Toli came from the Hall followed by Turfrida, supporting her swollen belly with her hands. I brought Swallow to a standstill, let the reins drop. My eyes sought Turfrida's even as Aelgytha let out a sharp cry. A kind of hiccupping came from Toli's throat: he put out his hands as if struck blind and Aelgytha guided him to the mounting-block where he sat looking stunned. Turfrida walked heavily to Swallow's head, her gaze never leaving my face.

'What happened?'

'They slew Eadric, raped the women.' My voice was harsh, expressionless. 'His head was stuck on the gatepost. Fourteen of them: all dead now. I killed all but one and the stable-boy slew him.'

'Hereward,' Turfrida's voice was calm. 'Where is their child?'

I licked my lips, felt grief mounting like a dark wave to engulf me, fought to keep control. 'We couldn't find him. Wuleric said they killed him, then Eadric when he would not – I failed them, Turfrida.'

My voice caught in my throat: I could not bear her quiet self-possession.

'Shh, love.' She knew me too well to argue, motioned Cole to take Ymma. Her body slid from my arms into his and I heard Turfrida gasp at what had been concealed while I held her, the blood and filth which caked my hauberk and clothes. Afterwards I realized even my hair was matted with it.

Drumming hoofbeats sounded from the field: even with a double load Swallow had left Martin's palfrey far behind. Certain it was he, I did not bother to look round. Indeed, I remember little more of that morning save that when I had dismounted and Turfrida led me towards the Hall, I met Toli's gaze and his face was like a mask of death, stark and terrible, his expression one of mute accusation. I looked away quickly, stumbled in my weariness, glanced up to see Aedgifu framed in the doorway. She stood frozen, mouth an oblong gash, eyes fixed on me in terror. I called her name but she let out a shrill scream, turned on her heel and ran into the semi-darkness of the hall.

'You look like a ghost,' Turfrida explained tiredly. 'She'll be alright when you're clean and rested. Take off that hauberk and sleep.'

She led me to a pallet in the main hall (I was too stupefied to ask why), and helped me unbuckle my swordbelt. As she straightened, she gasped and put one hand to her belly but a black tide suffused my blood that I could not resist. I pulled off my mail-coat, lay down and my mind floated into merciful oblivion.

6. Dispossession

Our second daughter was born that same day and we decided to call her Godgifu. It seemed beyond all reason that so fragile and precious a life should come after a night of blood and death. And, too, she came like a gift from God to Ymma who, bereft of her own child, took some comfort from suckling ours. That idea had been Aelgytha's but while Turfrida embraced it willingly, I found it hard to accept there was no jealousy between the two women. In truth it was a boon for all of us, for they took turns to wait up with the child at night and with the extra milk the babe, who was small, having been born a week or two early, thrived.

The birth precluded our immediate removal to Bourne. In any case, Ymma was in no state to return to her home, defiled as it was. Uncertain what best to do, I spent much time riding between the two estates and escorted Toli, Aelgytha and Cole One-Hand to tend Eadric's body. Once there, the old man refused to leave, keeping vigil in the church day and night, refusing food and shrugging off the blanket the others draped around his shoulders. He moved only to go to the midden: when I saw his face, my heart was wrenched. Death was stamped there clearly as upon his son's.

News of the attack and my vengeance spread swiftly across the countryside and was soon wildly exaggerated. Had half the tales been true we should have had no fear of Norman reprisals but during those first days we kept horses harnessed in the pens and anxiety gnawed me each moment I was away from those I loved for fear of what might happen to them. Yet one day became three and the lads I sent to spy in Borough reported that a full score of knights had been called west where there was insurrection on a far larger scale. Abbot Brand appealed for calm and condemned the killings, warning that anyone tempted to similar action would face judgement in Heaven far worse than anything the King's men could mete out. Turfrida looked worried when she heard this - her faith was a simple and pure one - but I knew my uncle was pandering to his Norman allies. As for the rest, I had submitted to God's judgement long ago: the stain on my soul would hardly be deepened by the slaying of men who had themselves offended so gravely against His law.

Meantime, the King's sheriffs worked their way through Mercia as if nothing had happened and maybe this was why no Normans marched upon us: they were pledged to a greater purpose. Many of the dispossessed, both thegns and sokemen, made their way to Bourne which rumour had made into an impregnable stronghold offering sanctuary to anyone in need. Though we quickly disabused them of this (to anyone who had seen a Norman castle, Bourne was clearly no fortress), they were welcome: the estate was desperately short of labour after the slaughter at Fulford. But we made no promises of safety or even of fighting. Despite my rash words after the raid I knew that if the Normans were to be defeated, all who opposed them must be united in a single force. As yet, the Atheling and other members of the Witan were the Bastard's unwilling guests in Normandy.

The fourth day after the raid, we took Eadric for burial at Croyland. Martin and I made the mule-wagon as comfortable as we could for Turfrida, Ymma and the children. The delight of having a baby sister had, it seemed wiped all memory of my blood-drenched figure from Aedgifu's mind and she happily accepted Ymma as Godgifu's foster-mother. As the cart creaked along the old road, she took turns holding the reins with Aelgytha and chatted non-stop all the way to Bourne, oblivious to the grief that weighed so heavily on the rest of us.

I did not want Ymma and Turfrida to see the things stuck on the palisade that morning, nor enter the hall which, despite the efforts of Ade and the others, still bore marks of the attack. When we reached the turn to the manor, the women and children waited at the end of the track while Martin and I rode swiftly to meet the funeral procession.

From respect and love, we had decided to carry Eadric to his grave rather than have his body borne on a cart thus instead of being wrapped in a simple cloth as was the usual custom, Aldwin the carpenter had fashioned him a rough wooden coffin. The lid was left off so that Ymma could bid farewell though I hoped she would not for the rigor of his face was no less dreadful by daylight than when I had first seen it. Toli rose from his vigil and followed as Martin Lightfoot, Acer, Cole One-Hand and I lifted the coffin onto our shoulders and paced slowly across the yard and through the gates, passing under the crow-pecked heads of Eadric's killers.

Those who had recently joined us and had not known him, we left to guard Bourne but all the folk of the estate and neighbouring vills formed a great crowd. Eadric had been well-loved, the manner of his death an outrage. When we paused at the old road and laid the coffin down so that Ymma could look upon her beloved there was utter silence: even the children understood the solemnity of that moment. Toli watched stone-faced as his daughter-in-law bent over the corpse and ignored our whispered pleas for him to ride with the women. When we set off, he took his place behind the coffin as was his right, the cart and crowd of mourners following close on his heels. His mouth was set in an obstinate line and his eyes stared straight ahead, sightlessly.

Despite his frailty, the old man made it to Croyland on his own feet. It was through sheer will-power and because we stopped every-so-often to change pall-bearers. The marshes shimmered with heat-haze and the scent of hay hung over the fields where new-mown grass lay drying in the sun. From behind came the sounds of a baby crying and Aedgifu's clear laughter. It seemed wrong that the bright world should continue seemingly unchanged by the cruelty of men, that hay needed to be gathered and swallows darted overhead while Eadric, who had aspired only to live in peace, had died in torment, would never again walk the fields he had known since boyhood nor sit in quiet contentment in the home he had fashioned for his wife and child. Overwhelmed by grief, I looked round and met Turfrida's steady gaze: comforted a little I turned my eyes ahead and saw the abbey buildings amongst the trees.

Ulfkil and a group of monks stood waiting at the gates. They followed as the coffin was carried into the church. Toli staggered and almost fell at the threshold. Two monks hurried to steady and support him but once he had recovered his balance, he shoved them aside and knelt defiantly beside the bier. Ymma stood on the other side, composed and silent. Since seeing Eadric's face she had neither keened nor wept but her face was taut with grief, white as a stripped tendon. I took my place with Turfrida, behind Eadric's blood-kin.

The abbot glanced searchingly at me before beginning the service but it was not until my foster-brother's body had been consigned to the earth and most of the mourners had begun the long walk home that Ulfkil sought me out.

'That Eadric, of all men, should have died thus grieves me beyond telling.' The abbot stared at the shallow mound and sighed before looking up: the keenness of his gaze was discomfiting. 'But the manner of your revenge I cannot condone. Nor can I risk forfeiture of this abbey's lands by supporting a known rebel though my heart tells me you acted in good faith. Whether or not your loanland still belongs to St. Guthlac's after Lammas Day, the agreement between us is now void. And heed this also: it is only because you slew De Warenne, leaving half the knights at Borough leaderless while the rest marched west, that they have not yet tried to take you. Whichever meets first, shire or hundred court, you will be declared outlaw and then they will hunt you down.'

Though he had spoken only what I had already guessed, I stood silent while bitterness swelled within me like a rolling wave. And the name of De Warenne was like an echo from the past: I understood why the bearded man had seemed familiar. The Norman who ambushed me after I had bested him in single combat was of that kin, most likely a brother.

'Hereward, you cannot stay in England,' Ulfkil continued fervently. 'Go to your wife's land in Flanders and raise your children in peace. For it is in my mind that what happened at Bourne is only the beginning. I do not want to be burying you in a few weeks time.'

'I have lived long enough in exile,' I answered. 'And for me, Flanders is no refuge: I have enemies there also.'

He looked at me with a kind of sorrowful forbearance. 'Then you must understand this,' he said. 'This abbey will always welcome the weak and dispossessed who seek God's sanctuary in times of trouble. But outlaws and rebels we will not shelter, however dire their need.'

Recalling his words when I had come seeking loanland, I smiled grimly. 'That is clear enough. But Ulfkil, where does your allegiance lie? If the Witan calls us to unite in the Atheling's name, will you support him, though all his followers be outlaws by Norman decree?'

His gaze left mine and he turned to stare across the shimmering marshes towards the sea.

'If that happens, it is for each man to decide according to his conscience,' he replied gravely. 'I must answer to God, no earthly king. But do not forget: St. Guthlac's is part of Gildenborough. I am not free to do as my heart might bid.'

There was an odd hesitancy to these last words which caught my attention, alerted me to something on the edge of memory I could not quite recall. He swung round suddenly to face me and in his lean and tired features, his deep-set eyes, I read a strange mixture of compassion and anger, the look of one forced to act against their will.

'If you are resolved to stay, then so be it,' he said at last. 'You were ever headstrong. But heed this warning, though it has not come from my lips should anyone ask. I do not know what lies between you and Abbot Brand but you should be wary. He is greedy for land and power and he will betray his own kin to get them, have no doubt.'

'There is no love lost between us,' I replied. Yet despite my loathing of my uncle, my mind shied from the implication that he was behind the sack of Bourne.

Ulfkil regarded me steadily. 'I will pray for you and all your kin as well as Eadric's soul,' he said. 'Remember, in the end it is God's mercy that matters, not the deeds of men. Be at peace.'

Fearing what he might read from my face, I bent my head. To my relief Turfrida, who must have been watching, came over a moment later to say it was time to leave. Ulfkil greeted her kindly, blessed the babe and went to find Ymma.

'You could have done no other, love.' Turfrida put her free arm around me and I leant against her a little, feeling muscles stiffened by pall-bearing stretch painfully. 'Whatever happens, while I live I will be here to comfort you. You have not failed.'

I had no words to reply but bent my lips to her head, breathed in the smell of her hair mingled with the scents of earth, fen and hay, and silently blessed the fate that had brought us together.

Stricken, Toli refused to leave the graveside. Not even Aedgifu's tearful pleading could induce him to rise. As the shadows lengthened and a late afternoon breeze bent the reeds, he sat on the ground, silent and immovable as a boulder. Neither Ymma nor Turfrida could break his stubborn silence and when I knelt to speak with him, he stared at me with a kind of mute accusation I could not long withstand after the abbot's hints.

'Stay then!' I gave up in exasperation and clambered awkwardly to my feet. 'You will get small comfort from the dead. Does it mean nothing that Ymma and Aedgifu love and need you still; have you no gratitude towards Aelgytha and Cole One-Hand, who have cared for you all these years? Come home when it suits you: we must leave now. Will you not even honour your son and grandson at their death-feast?'

Anger penetrated where tenderness could not. He raised his head and his faded eyes met mine with a fierceness that shook me to the core. These past days he had seemed stunned by grief: we were accustomed to vacancy in that age-seamed face, not passion.

'My home is with Eadgytha and Eadric; I have no other,' he said. 'Did I not say to you upon your return that I had lived too long? I do not want to see you slain and my land taken by these Norman usurpers, nor will I become a fugitive in my own country, forced to the life of a beggar or outlaw.' He paused, reached out to grasp my hand. 'You pledged to honour me as a father, therefore grant me the respect due from a loving son and do not seek to cross my will. Then you will have my blessing.'

Such quiet dignity clothed him, I could not argue. Instead, I knelt to embrace him. At first he was inert as a wooden post but then released my hand and returned the gesture with astounding strength.

'God's grace upon you, Toli,' I murmured. 'Your will is your own and you have had my love since the day you and Eadgytha took me into your care. But there is still hope and the Normans may find me a hard man to kill.'

He let go and pulled away a little, his gaze on the raw patch of earth where Eadric lay. 'I am too old and weary for hope in this world,' he said. 'I shall wait here until God sees fit to take me. Then I shall be content.'

I had no words to answer but touched him briefly on the shoulder as I rose. As I walked to the cart where Martin and Cole One-Hand waited with the women and children, I felt the old man's gaze upon me but did not look back. When I reached the others, I shook my head and Ulfkil, who had been watching from a discreet distance, came to join us.

'I will make sure no harm befalls him,' he said quietly. 'And I will send to Laughton if there is any change. But in truth, do not look for his return. Half of that old man died with Eadgytha and though your arrival gave him a brief respite, Hereward, there comes a time when the most stoic of men says 'Enough'. The world is changing and Toli has ever been a man of peace. Eadric's death is too much. Pray that God's mercy releases him soon from grief and forgive his weakness. He is aged and weary: he cannot bear the burden of his life much longer.'

From where she sat on the cart between Turfrida and Aelgytha, Ymma stirred impatiently. Her face, tense and hollow-cheeked, was like a mask.

'I will pray for his soul, but I will not forgive him if he dies,' she said bitterly. 'He has only lost a son. Where was God's mercy five nights ago?

The greater burden is on those who must go on living.'

'The mercy of God is infinite,' Ulfkil replied. 'Yet his will is not for us to divine but rather to accept, however hard it seems. And take solace from this: the perpetrators of this evil will not escape his judgement.'

Ymma looked away and Turfrida, the babe asleep in the crook of one arm, reached out to embrace her with the other. Ulfkil made a strange gesture of resignation, turned to look across the graveyard to where Toli sat motionless, his shadow flung across the graves of his wife and son.

'May the mercy of God be upon us all,' the abbot murmured, then nodded slightly in farewell and made his way back to the church, head bent in an attitude of deep contemplation.

The sun had sunk behind the trees and the yard was dark with shadow when we rode through the gates of Bourne. Ymma looked expressionlessly at the row of severed heads but Turfrida could not conceal her revulsion. Her eyes sought mine as if she were unable to equate such a deed with the husband she knew and loved.

'It was necessary,' I told her quietly as we walked together towards the Hall. 'I am no butcher but I could do no other. They stuck Eadric's head there: it was fitting to do the same to them.'

The folk of Bourne had worked hard in Ymma's absence. In the Hall the furniture had been scrubbed; fresh reeds and herbs were strewn upon the floor; the bedding where Wuleric's sister was raped had been burned and replaced. Even the hearth had been scraped and cleaned and a new fire kindled as if to symbolise a fresh beginning. But some traces of that dreadful night still remained: dark stains in the yard marked where Eadric's body had lain and his killers been decapitated; fine destriers still occupied the stables; Norman mail and weapons were hidden in labourers' cots. And while those heads grinned down from their spikes, none would forget how they had got there.

The noise of merriment from within the Hall ceased abruptly when we entered. An awkward, embarrassed silence fell as if those there to celebrate Eadric's life were suddenly reminded of how he had died and were ashamed. But Ymma, her face still pale and drawn, stepped forward and said: 'You who knew him must understand how Eadric loved and honoured life. He was no war-monger to deprive mothers of their sons, wives of husbands, children of fathers. Norman brigands, King's men, slew him and our baby son but they could not touch what was between us, Eadric and I. They now feed the wolves and ravens but he is in God's keeping. They are less than the dirt beneath our feet but he will never be forgotten while those who loved him live on. Beloved husband, loyal son, faithful friend: remember him with thanks and joy and be not ashamed to drink and dance and sing tonight in his memory, nor dwell on the evil times that have come upon us but pledge rather to live each day as if it were your best and last.'

A low murmur of sympathy greeted this speech. Ymma stood straight and tall; her hair, wound about her head like a coronet, gleamed with the lustre of a freshly peeled willow wand yet her eyes glittered in the firelight: she was close to tears. An expectant silence fell. Turfrida nudged me in the ribs and hissed, 'In Toli's absence it is for you to speak, Hereward. You and Eadric were closer than most brothers.'

Deeds have ever served my purpose better than speech; humbled by Ymma's dignity and candour, I simply repeated Turfrida's words, adding that though I had avenged Eadric as best I could, his killers' blood would not restore him to us, nor undo what had been done to his son and the women of Bourne. And then, remembering the abbot's inference, my voice failed. I snatched a drinking horn and pledged the slain while guilt rose to choke me.

No doubt those watching assumed grief snared my tongue. I caught pitying glances as I gulped honey-beer like water. Ymma came to thank me but I made some excuse and blundered out, fearing what she might read from my eyes.

The gates were shut and barred but no-one stood on watch. The newcomers who had guarded the palisade by day probably thought they had done enough: after all, they bore no allegiance to Eadric, Morcar or myself. I crossed the yard and leaned aimlessly against the watch-tower as folk spilled outside to talk, escaping the noise within as ale flowed and grief was tempered by reminiscence and tales. Someone began 'The Battle of Maldon' and the slow, stirring music seemed a fitting elegy to my foster-brother though the protagonists of that epic were far from his quiet, peace-loving nature.

Turfrida had not followed me, doubtless she was busy with the children. When it became clear she would not come out, I climbed up to the guard-platform to be alone. At least no-one was likely to join me unasked: the stench from the spiked heads was enough to turn the stomachs of all save the battle-hardened or witless. I looked out along the pale line of the track to the marshes then, seeing nothing move, sat down, my back against the rough-hewn posts of the palisade.

The drink I had flung down my throat was not without effect. My thoughts ran in a seemingly endless spiral; the cacophony from the Hall irked me. And yet the focus of my mind was set towards a single goal, something that had nagged since the night of the raid but which, up till now, I had avoided because the question seemed unanswerable. Of all the estates in the shire, even the Wapentake, why had De Warenne and his men chosen to attack Bourne when it was neither the richest manor in the area, nor closest to Borough?

A burst of laughter broke my introspection and I cursed silently and bit my knuckles. I had only Wuleric's account of what had happened here that day and he had not seen all. Now, in the light of Ulfkil's warning, I needed the truth. Until I was sure of Brand's involvement, I could never be easy in my mind, suspecting that he might have revenged himself upon me by instigating a raid on my rightful home, knowing that Eadric and I were as kin. Like a child picking at a scab to find out what lies beneath, I thought the pain of discovery would be countered by the ending of uncertainty.

I do not know how long I sat there. The noise from the gathering subsided as a more reflective mood prevailed: someone began to play slow airs on a pipe and the pure, haunting notes seemed to pierce my heart. Drawn by the music and the warmth of the fire, the folk in the yard moved inside for the night air was growing chill as mist crept in from the marshes. I shivered and told myself I was doing no good by brooding alone, that by now my absence would have been noticed and Eadric deserved at least that I should join his wake.

It was as I got heavily to my feet that I heard a stealthy footstep on the ladder. I held my breath, hand on dagger-hilt (Brain-biter and my hauberk were hidden under the rugs piled on the wagon), then thought, 'What enemy could be here? Most likely it is some couple come to find a quiet place for their love-making, too drunk or besotted to heed the stench.' Not wishing to startle them, I cleared my throat and moved forward and the astonishment was mine. There was no mistaking the pale face that looked up, the crown of braided hair gleaming silver in the diffuse moonlight. She took my hand and climbed onto the platform, wrinkling her nose at the carrion-reek. Her gaze strayed briefly to the spiked heads then rested on my face.

'I expected to find you here,' she said.

'Did you?' The words hung in the air between us. Discomfited by her calmness, her very presence, I could think of nothing else to say, not knowing what she expected of me or why she should have sought me out.

'Oh yes.' Her eyes, glossed and unreadable in the pale light, held mine; there was tension beneath her apparent self-assurance, a kind of restless energy, barely contained. I wondered suddenly whether she had screamed when they raped her or endured it in silence then, ashamed of such a thought, lowered my gaze in confusion.

'I understand more than you know.' She had not moved yet I felt as if I stood naked before her, was daunted by her intensity. 'Eadric spoke of you often, even before your return. Before they slew him, he called God's curse upon them but he said also that you would avenge us.'

'Ymma.' Uncomfortable under that steady gaze, I moved back to the palisade, turned to look over. The track glimmered, the trees were black clawing shapes in the mist but it was not the chill air that made me shiver. 'What happened that day? How did they get in? I told Eadric to be careful. Why didn't he light the beacon? Had I come sooner, he might still be alive.'

'No, then you would be dead too.' She moved to stand beside me, her tread almost silent on the bare wood. 'They were cautious until they were sure of our numbers. We did not even suspect their intent until they slew the dogs and by then it was too late: they barred the gates and set a watch so that what should have been our sanctuary became instead a trap.' Her voice faltered and she edged closer and though we were not touching, the heat of her body smote my skin.

'The gates were closed when they arrived.' When she resumed her tale it was almost as if she were relating the experiences of someone else: her tone was emotionless, detached. 'Oda Crook-back was on watch and he was loth to let them in. But they shouted that they had come in the King's name to assess the land for geld and they waved a parchment hung with a red seal as proof. Oda called Eadric and he told him to open the gates. I think he was reluctant but you knew my husband, Hereward: law-abiding, given to trust rather than suspicion. Only when he looked closely at the writ did he begin to realize his mistake for though he could not read French, he could see nothing written there relating to Morcar or to Bourne. I had come out at the sound of hooves and was dismayed by the strangers' warlike manner and number. Eadric tried to reassure me that they were there on the King's business but I could tell he was uneasy because he bade me go to our rooms with the babe and keep the doors closed. And so I did but once Toli was settled, I returned to the Hall and watched from the doorway though none could see me from outside.

'They were courteous enough at first and made a great show of inspecting the buildings but I think it was possible resistance they were noting, not the value of the estate. When they realized how few able men we had, their mood changed. The dogs sensed it: they went up to the leader, a tall, bearded man who said his name was Frederick de Warenne, and growled as he demanded food and wine. When Eadric argued he need not provide anything, they pushed him roughly to the ground and as the dogs rushed to his defence, they slew two and the rest fled.

'I ran to our rooms but I was not quick enough. They saw me fumble with the doors as they dragged Eadric inside, and ordered me to serve them. There was not food enough in the Hall so I went to the cottages and, with the other women, brought back all we could find. We put the food on the table and bade the Normans eat.

'Eadric watched quietly as we went round with the ale but the Normans were not satisfied. As the drink took hold, they began to insult him and when he would not rise to their taunts they grabbed Ade, the beldame, and tore her clothes open, then made fun of her. When Eadric protested, they struck him down and tied his hands behind his back. One held him by the hair so that he was forced to watch what happened next.

'I did not flee. They were too many and I feared what they would do to Eadric if I ran. And Toli was asleep in the other room. They dragged me to the table and bent me over, then rutted upon me like animals, one by one. When they were done, they threw me to the floor and I crawled to the shelter of the wall, hardly knowing where I was. I could not bear to look at

Eadric, from shame and fear of what his face might tell.

'They settled down to drink for a while but their mood became crueller. Wuleric came in to ask whether their horses should be fed. A red-haired Norman with a twisted nose told him to fetch a sheep because they were hungry for fresh meat. It was butchered outside and some of them spitted bloody hunks on their swords and laid them in the fire but they soon forgot it. They called for music and when Wuleric took out his pipe, pulled Eadric to his feet and ordered him to demonstrate English dancing. When he refused, they took out their daggers and pricked him with the points but he would not move. Then Toli began to cry from the other room.'

Her voice failed and she put a hand to her mouth, fighting for control. In pity, I took her in my arms. So tense was she, her body shook to her heartbeat. Then, at last, she looked up and her eyes sought mine like those of someone drowning who sees help an arm's length away.

'De Warenne strode up the Hall and I watched him go,' she whispered. 'He drew his sword as he entered our room and Toli began to scream. Such screams you have never heard: they tore me apart. Then De Warenne came back. I could not see what he had done till he threw my babe in my lap, bloody and writhing, still screaming: the blade had pierced him through the stomach. They shouted at me to quieten him but after a few moments, De Warenne snatched him from my arms and took him outside and then the screaming stopped. When he returned, De Warenne's hands were bloodied to the wrist. He thrust them into Eadric's face and told him to lick them clean like the lame dog he was.'

She hesitated and licked her lips but her eyes were fixed on mine. I could no more have looked away than sprouted wings to fly.

'Eadric stared at De Warenne and cursed him in the name of God and all the saints and martyrs amongst whom, he said, our child should be numbered because he was free of any sin. And he told him also that the wrongs perpetrated upon us would be avenged by his foster-brother Hereward, son of Eorl Leofric, who lived nearby. But De Warenne laughed and poured scorn upon you. "Hereward," he sneered at last. "Is that the same man who stole the tribute of Scaldemariland from its rightful keeper, then fled to England like a cringing cur? I will show him how renegades and traitors are dealt with in this land." And he swung his sword and struck off Eadric's head with a single blow, then called Wuleric to drag the body out, still twitching in its blood.

'I remember little of what happened after that. They built the fire to a great blaze and for a while I willed it to spread and burn the Hall and all of us to ash. A girl was screaming somewhere but it was as if I had turned into something made of wood: I did not care any more. Even when you slew them it mattered little. I knew their deaths would not bring Eadric or Toli back, nor undo what they had done to me. They had destroyed and defiled our world and their seed was still inside me, filth lodged in my womb that I could not flush out.'

A clammy sweat bathed me: I too understood the ignominy of helplessness. Her tone, though low and measured, could not conceal her revulsion. Memories I had thought long buried came crowding in; pain griped my bowels. In an attempt to hide my distress I released her and stepped away but she moved between me and the ladder, fumbling at her clothes.

'Help me.' It was a kind of groaning whisper; she had undone her tunic to expose her breasts. The mist swirled and as she lifted her arms to take my face between her hands, the moonlight made her skin seem smooth and flawless as alabaster: my head swam at the scent rising from her body. Her gaze, clear even in that lambent radiance, seemed to swallow mine. 'I do not want to bear a Norman's babe. Make love to me now and I swear no-one will ever know. If a child comes of our union, I shall claim it is Eadric's.'

I stood as if pole-axed, appalled, spellbound: she lowered one hand and pressed it into the small of my back and at that touch my loins seemed to melt. I gasped, 'You want to share Turfrida's husband as well as her child – is that what Eadric would have wanted?' but in truth Turfrida was far from my mind as desire swept through me and my heart lurched.

'He would not want his killer's bastard nestling in my womb!' she spat and for an instant I glimpsed the madness that dwelt beneath her outward calm though it was swiftly masked and her tone grew low and sorrowful. 'Eadric changed after Fulford Gate. That he had led so many to slaughter weighed heavily upon him. He told me he did not wish to bring more children into a world where they would likely end in the maws of crows and ravens ere they had seen twenty years and so he hardly touched me. He was stubborn as his father. Yet I am sure he would rather I bore your child than any other's.'

I drew a shuddering breath but it was as if I were mazed: I could not summon strength to push her away.

'Choose someone else,' I said at last, with an effort. 'Why not Martin Lightfoot? He is a good and kind man and he has no wife.'

'Martin?' She made no attempt to conceal her scorn. 'He is a hound that follows one master, or had you not noticed? But no, Hereward,' her voice softened, seemed to caress my whole being, 'it is you I want. Will you not complete your vengeance by displacing the usurper's seed?'

'No.' A shiver ran though me as she drew her hand down my neck to rest upon my chest. 'I cannot.' And I tore my gaze from hers and looked to the ladder where lay my escape.

She clung to me then, grasping my clothes and pressing herself against me. The heat of her was like the breath from a potter's kiln and it was as if her madness seeped into me with that contact. It was summer: only a thin layer of woollen cloth separated us. With a tantalising, lingering deliberation, she moved her hand from my chest to draw up the hem of my tunic, keeping the other in the hollow of my back. I think I muttered 'No' but it sounded as an incoherent moan, a groan of longing as she slid her hand up my thigh and then I trembled, a molten heat sprang from my loins to suffuse my whole body, my head reeled. All else ceased to exist: there was only the woman, the need to possess and be possessed, all-consuming, overwhelming, unstoppable. Her mouth sought mine: darkness swirled: it seemed that I was drowning.

She cried out as my seed spurted into her but I was transported beyond coherent thought by the pulsing tide that coursed through us. And then, swiftly, came the ebb. Awareness of the world impinged: dank air chilled my skin; a burst of clapping sounded from the Hall. Ymma's face was upturned, mouth hanging open, a visage slack, sated, eyes glazed in the diffuse moonlight. Her breasts glistened with milk and saliva.

My body was weak and spent, her weight suddenly insupportable. I pushed her away and she fell sprawling on the platform. For a moment she was still, then felt between her legs and held up her hand. Her fingers were slick with our mingled juices. She licked them deliberately, eyes fixed on my face, gloating, triumphant.

'Since you first came to our Hall, it has been you I wanted,' she said.

I stared, stunned, and a keen wind seemed to sing through every fibre of my being, scouring away any lingering pleasure I had taken from our coupling. I realized then what I had done, betraying not only my wife but Eadric also, the sacred trust he had placed in me. Anguish must have been written clearly in my expression because she clutched at her gaping tunic to hide her swollen breasts but there was no shame or remorse in her action, only a dawning fear.

'At least Eadric died before he found out what you are!' I could barely force out the words: it was as if a noose had tightened about my neck. 'How many others have there been?'

She clambered to her feet but her eyes remained fixed on mine. Even in that wan light I saw the blood gather in her face.

'You men, you understand nothing!' she spat. 'I loved Eadric and if I yearned to join my flesh with yours, I did not do so, knowing how the mere thought would hurt him. If I now bear a child, there is a chance it is yours: had I believed a Norman bastard was spawning in my womb I would have tried to kill it and that is a worse sin than for a widow to lie with a man. No one will know the truth but us. I am no whore.'

'But what of Turfrida?' With each passing moment, my anguish increased. 'Were I a free man it would be different. But I have my own family and I have never thought of you save as Eadric's wife.'

'Your deeds belie your words.' There was a hardness to her tone that sent a chill through me. 'And I doubt this is the first secret you have kept from Turfrida. I am sure Martin could tell a tale if he were pressed: it is well known how you came to Toli's Hall as a boy. Or if not him, then maybe

Abbot Brand, your uncle.'

At this, the platform beneath my feet seemed to tilt and my blood turned to ice. 'What do you mean?'

'De Warenne called you other things besides thief and traitor.' She seemed to savour every word. '"Abbot's boy" he named you, said you belonged heart and soul to Gildenborough. I would have thought nothing of it had I not been watching Eadric's face. Up till then he had defied them: his anger and hatred were stronger than his fear. But when he heard that, his shock was that of one who realizes a truth which should have been plain before, that he has been betrayed by one he most trusts. For Abbot Brand came to Laughton a few weeks ago, did he not? No smoke without fire, Hereward.'

'He could not have thought that!' I could hardly speak: vomit rose scalding in my throat. 'I would have died rather than betray him!'

Stark in my mind was the image of Eadric's head stuck but a spearlength from where I stood; his expression of grief and baffled outrage. I remembered telling him briefly of my uncle's visit: that, combined with De Warenne's insinuations, might have been enough to sow doubt in his mind. I stood stricken, saw Ymma's expression change from triumph to pity and then anger came to my rescue, the blind, unreasoning rage sprung from grief and shame.

'If you breathe a word of this, even in confession, I'll kill you.' I lunged past her, grasped the ladder, began to climb down. She twisted round to watch me, called, 'Hereward, wait!' in a voice plaintive as a curlew's call then, when I did not pause, added harshly: 'You would be foresworn then: you promised to protect me and our child!'

'Then I will only cut out your tongue.' I reached the bottom of the ladder and hesitated. From the hall came the sound of singing but it was as if it belonged to another world. The mist made looming cliffs of the palisade and buildings; the wide emptiness of the yard seemed immeasurable. Only the knowledge that Ymma was watching gave me strength to cross that space. My anger had not abated but having no outlet it turned inwards, becoming that burning ember I knew of old, lodged at the very heart of me, feeding on guilt.

I could not face Martin, Acer, even Wuleric; what I would tell Turfrida I had not begun to contemplate. Turning towards the stables I realized that Ymma's sweat, her milk, the reek of sex clung to me and the gorge rose in my throat. I went to the water trough, washed as best I could without stripping: folk might enter the yard at any moment. With the dank chill from the mist, I began to shiver, staggered past the stables, found myself outside the church. At least there I would be in shelter and alone. I pulled open the heavy oak door.

It was relatively dark inside for the windows, expensively glazed, were small and set high. Having closed the door I stood with my back against the wall while my eyes adjusted. Images of the saints stared accusingly from their wall hangings; my skin prickled. I felt a presence there, something unseen yet sentient and waited, conscious of every breath, every heartbeat. Time seemed to slow.

Voices sounded in the yard as some of the Bourne folk left the Hall. Amongst them was Ymma's, bidding farewell, and then the dread that held me in thrall dissipated in a wave of grief I could not contain. Hardly knowing what I did, I stumbled forward.

The gilded crucifix gleamed coldly as I stood before the altar. I thought of Eadric's body lying there, his face set in that terrible expression which I now understood too well. I sank to my knees and all that I could not express in words burst from me in a groan and then at last I wept.

How long that spasm lasted I do not know but when it was over I felt exhausted, wrung to the depths of my soul. The stone floor was hard and cold, I was shaking as if with ague. There was no sound now from yard or Hall and the light was fainter than before: the mist must have thickened to fog. I clambered stiffly to my feet and made my way to one of the benches set against the wall. For all the outpouring of grief, my situation was unchanged: I had still to face my wife and children aye, and Ymma herself. Suddenly I thought of Toli, keeping his vigil beside Eadric's grave, how he had loved and blessed me, and then I ground my teeth and bowed my head to my knees, hands clenched before me, praying that he would never discover what had happened between Ymma and me, nor hear of De Warenne's slander. And I begged that God would grant him the swift and painless death he desired, because I knew that if Ymma was with child, I could not look that old man, my foster-father, in the eye and pretend Eadric was the sire.

As I sat there, I felt again that presence I had sensed on entering the church, thought to hear breathing other than my own. Beyond the nightmares which haunt the sleep of warriors, I had always scorned tales of ghosts wreaking vengeance on their killers or coming to warn their beloved of evils to come. Now, thinking of how I had wronged Eadric, a clammy sweat bathed me. At the faint sound of footsteps, my muscles seemed to turn to water: I could not move.

'Hereward.' I jerked upright at the sound of my name, stared wildly, back pressed against the wall. A tall figure loomed, dark and featureless against the light from the window high above the altar.

'It's me, Martin.' I let out a long sigh as he bent close and put a hand on my shoulder but though I was reassured by his touch, my mind darted like a rat in a trap, fearing he would smell Ymma on me.

'How long have you been here?' I shrugged away his hand, lurched to my feet. He withdrew a little but his eyes did not leave my face.

'Since before you came.' He hesitated and I sensed his discomfiture keenly as I felt my own shame. 'I would have spoken but I could not, nor leave without your knowing. Do not be ashamed or angry. By the depth of your grief is Eadric honoured.'

A breath of bitter laughter escaped me at this but I could find no words to reply. He tilted his head slightly, regarding me with a mixture of pity and bewilderment. 'Hereward, you're shaking. Come into the Hall. There's thick fog outside: can't you smell it? It'll be warm by the fire.'

'Why are you here?' I was shivering so violently, I could barely keep my voice steady. He guided me towards the door, hesitated with his hand on the latch.

'I needed to think.' For a moment it seemed he would elaborate but he thought better of it and pushed the door open. Thick tendrils of fog seeped past and I shuddered.

'Come on, let's get some ale into you.' He steered me outside, shut the door and guided me across the yard, his arm across my shoulders. 'If any's left by now!'

Of the crowd that had come to the wake, only a few remained in the Hall. Most of these were slumped at the tables or lay in drink-sodden slumber here and there on the floor. The fire had burned to a heap of glowing embers around which a group of men sat talking earnestly in hushed voices. There was no sign of the women but a babe's wailing betrayed their occupation of the private rooms.

'Where've you been?' Acer's speech was only slightly slurred. 'Ymma was looking for you. Turfrida took the children to bed hours ago – she said not to disturb them.'

'Since when have I been answerable to anyone here?' The words came out with more vehemence than I had intended and the big man shrugged, looking hurt. I crouched beside the hearth and poked the embers into life with a half-burned log adding quietly, 'I was on watch, up by the gates. But there's nothing to see now but fog.'

At this the lad, Wuleric, cast me a swift, questioning glance but he made no comment and I relaxed as warmth spread through my blood.

'Maybe someone should stand guard nonetheless.' Martin stretched and looked round hopefully but no-one volunteered.

'Ach, no: bide where you are.' Acer leant forward and spat into the fire. 'Those foreign bastards won't come tonight, they're too scared of blundering into the fen or Hereward here. They'll stay quiet until reinforcements arrive and that won't be until the trouble in the West's sorted, never if God wills.'

The talk turned inevitably to what we should do if and when the Normans returned in force, degenerating at length into the usual boasting of men contemptuous of an enemy they have not yet faced. I stared into the embers, only half listening until one of the newcomers, a dispossessed thegn from Oxfordshire, spoke of holding Bourne as a rallying point for all the folk of Mercia.

'Have you ever been in a siege?' I asked wearily. 'Bourne is indefensible save against a force of five score or less and even then we could not hold it long. It has no secure supply line and only one source of water. They would foul the stream with the carcases of our own beasts, throw fire in with their catapults, then sit and starve us into submission. We must find a stronger place, or wait. Anyway, unless all those prepared to fight are united in a single force, we will never rid our land of these usurpers. Otherwise, as rebels, we would be forced to live as fugitives. Maybe, for a while, we could hurt them, like wolves harrying a flock. But that is no life for any man, least of all for his family and in the end, though we might slay many of the enemy, the choice would come between submission and death. I would not force that on anyone. We must bide our time and pray that the Witan has not forgotten us. One day the call to arms will come and then we shall chase the Bastard and his cronies back to France.'

'That's easy to say,' Acer grumbled. 'But who is this great leader that will rally us? And more to the point, where is he? Harold Godwineson: there was a man we would have flocked to but Edgar Atheling is still an untried boy.'

'Edwin and Morcar might do it and Waltheof is still powerful,' said Siward. 'In the Atheling's name of course: he is rightful King after all.'

'Edwin and Morcar?' Acer almost choked with outrage. 'Ask the survivors of Fulford Gate what kind of war leaders they are. You won't find many in Northumbria no, nor Mercia, willing to follow them.'

The argument went back and forth but with the combined heat of the fire and the effects of strong ale, I could hardly keep my eyes open. The last thing I remember of that night is someone putting a cloak or blanket around my shoulders and then I sank into sleep that was like a black tide.

Next morning, Turfrida was deeply disappointed when Ymma refused to return to Laughton but I was hard-put to conceal my relief.

'If the Normans come again, what worse can they do?' she asked when Turfrida began to argue. 'And though I have suckled Godgifu like my own child, she is not and I must learn to live without my babe as without Eadric.' She paused and glanced sidelong at me. 'Though God grant his child stirs in my womb, that something more than memory remains of him.'

'I shall pray for you.' Turfrida stepped forward and the two embraced, squashing Godgifu in the process. She yelled in protest, thus what had begun in sorrow ended in laughter. Yet as I rode through the gates not long after, the heads seemed to leer down from their spikes, mocking me.

Threads of mist still hung about the marshes but above us the sky was clear and the steady beat of hooves on the track seemed almost an intrusion into the stillness. Even Aedgifu was quiet for a while, lying with her head in her mother's lap. Godgifu, a lambskin-wrapped bundle, was sound asleep on the seat beside them. Martin rode on the opposite side of the cart and every-so-often I caught him watching me thoughtfully. But he said nothing.

'Maybe one of you should go to Croyland,' Turfrida suggested at length. 'Perhaps Toli will have changed his mind. Folk do not often die of grief and it is a long way for an old man to walk alone.'

'He'll change his mind when the Nene runs uphill.' Aelgytha slapped the reins against the mules' hindquarters and they quickened their pace a little. 'He was weary enough of life before the raid on Bourne; Eadric's death he will never learn to bear. If he believes his time has come, who are we to gainsay him?'

'No-one should have to die without kin or friends to comfort them,' Turfrida replied shortly. 'Hereward, he thinks of you as his son. Let him know he is not alone.'

I stared across the empty marshes. Distant heat-haze made the reed-beds shimmer as the last of the fog dissipated.

'We made our farewell yesterday, by Eadric's grave,' I said at last, knowing that whatever happened, I did not want to look into that old man's face again lest he read the truth from mine. 'I do not think he wants to see anyone. Maybe I shall go tomorrow.'

'By then it will likely be too late.' Turfrida's face had tightened. She cast me a swift, angry glance then muttered, 'I did not think you could be so hard towards those that love you.'

'Maybe there are things between us you do not know.' I regretted these words as soon as they left my lips but they could not be unsaid. As I heeled Tiw forward to escape, a moorhen broke cover right under the stallion's nose and he shied violently, startling the mules and Martin's palfrey. The jolting of the cart made Aedgifu cry out in half-fearful delight and woke the babe so that by the time order was restored and Godgifu suckling contentedly, it seemed the argument was over. But as Martin and I jogged a little ahead, I seemed to feel Turfrida's gaze like two fingers boring into my back and knew she had neither forgotten nor forgiven my seeming lack of care.

As Lammas Day approached and the wheat and barley began to ripen, I had no choice but to push other concerns aside and think upon our future. Ulfkil's counsel and the drunken conversation at Eadric's wake pointed the way clearly enough: to seek shelter with Turfrida's father in Flanders. The Normans had not yet made full claim on the lands of the old Danegeld but I knew that as soon as more men were committed to Borough and the new castle at Lincoln, they would seek vengeance for De Warenne and his men. Bourne could not be held against them; Laughton was an open farmstead: if caught there, we would die swiftly. And yet I had already lived nine years in exile: to abandon folk like Wuleric and his sister, Aelgytha and Cole One-Hand, Acer and all my comrades of the Fen-wolves; to forsake the land of my birth for which I had yearned from the moment of leaving it, I could barely countenance. Reason dictated that we should go while we had the chance but my heart was set against it from the first. When I asked Turfrida, she looked at me with a kind of sorrowful forbearance and said quietly, 'I have told you already: my place is with you and our children. I will follow you to Flanders or into the Brunneswald. But if we cross the sea, there will be no returning: I do not want our daughters torn between two worlds.' In the end I delayed my decision and resolved to go secretly to the Wapentake on Lammas Day. There the fate of our lands would be decreed and circumstances likely force me to a choice.

Turfrida did not argue, knowing my mind was set but Martin tried to dissuade me with such passion that in the end I told him to hold his tongue or else leave my service. He desisted then but when Cole One-hand and I prepared to leave on the appointed day, he refused to join us, saying darkly that someone should remain to look after my family if I were taken.

Knowing what was at stake, nearly all the folk of Ness and Aveland gathered for that meeting though only those elected to the Wapentake were permitted to speak. I wore some old clothes of Toli's with a heavily patched cloak that belonged to Cole One-Hand and bore no sword though my dagger was strapped at my back. My disguise was aided by wet and blustery weather which meant my cloak and hood would go unmarked. Martin, resigned at last to my going, insisted that we take Swallow lest I need a swift escape. Mud-plastered and rain-soaked, the mare looked more broken-down than ever and Cole, who had felt her teeth more than once, agreed reluctantly to lead her.

The gathering was at the Hundred-Stone, a time-pocked boulder of hard grey limestone which stood at the boundary between Ness and Aveland. It was not far from Bourne yet though many were already waiting when we arrived, I did not see Ymma. Cole One-Hand, who was spokesman for Aveland Wapentake, handed Swallow's reins thankfully to Wuleric who fondled the mare's head while his eyes searched the crowd. They spoke quietly together then the lad led the horse away, giving no sign that he knew me. More folk were coming in all the time; I pulled my hood over to shadow my face and worked my way to the back where I could see and hear what was happening yet still be within reach of Swallow.

We waited while rain seeped through our clothes. The wind rose roaring in the trees and torn leaves stuck against wet skin and sodden cloaks. Folk began to grumble and shift restlessly, miserable children whined, the few horses swung their quarters into the driving rain and stood hunched, eyes half-closed. Some families, those who were bonded to a thegn and had come from curiosity, trudged away. These had no say and were tied to their land-lord: it made little difference who their master was, so long as he dealt fairly with them.

The muttering of the crowd grew louder and more agitated as annoyance turned to alarm. It was long past midday, the traditional time for the wapentake to begin. Someone shouted angrily that the meeting was a ploy and that while we stood like sheep in the rain, our homes were being plundered. Everyone knew of the raid on Bourne and its aftermath: a tall, dark-haired man I did not recognize yelled at Cole One-Hand that if the Normans were attacking manors in Ness and Aveland it was his master, Hereward's, fault, for they were simply avenging those he had slain. And when others shouted that Eadric had been killed first, he stared them down scornfully, saying, 'Then if Hereward was taking the blood-price for his foster-brother, where is he? If his cause were just, he should put it before the hundred-court!'

Frustration and fear were turning the mood ugly. Cole strove to keep the peace as the dark-haired man continued to argue and folk from Laughton and Bourne began to jostle his supporters whom they accused of being Norman cronies. I kept my head lowered, fighting for control because with all my being I longed to stride into the crowd, take my slanderer by the throat and challenge him to fight. But then a woman standing at the edge of the crowd on the track to Borough shouted, 'Quiet, fools, they're coming!' and then a dreadful hush fell as the muffled thudding of many hoofbeats sounded.

Even I, seasoned fighter as I was, felt a thrill of fear when the first knights rode into view. Without spear or mail I felt naked. Now I understood why the mere sight of armed horsemen makes the poor and disenfranchised flee: an appalling sense of vulnerability. As the Normans rode up to the very edge of the crowd it was not simply the overbearing power of their physical presence that cowed all there but the coldness with which their eyes scanned the assembly, as if assessing whether anyone was worthy of their attention.

Twenty had come but they were not all knights. The crowd gave way until the horsemen stood inside a wide semicircle and then others, hitherto unseen, urged their mounts to the fore. One was a tall man with a pock-marked face and the shaven chin and short hair favoured by the Normans, mounted on a grey palfrey. As a King's officer, a Sheriff, he wore no hauberk but the hang of his cloak betrayed a longsword at his side. The other was my uncle. Instead of a mule he rode a chestnut gelding broad-backed as Toli's grey. He pushed back his hood and surveyed the crowd with a kind of sanctimonious superiority.

I had despised him before but after the raid on Bourne, my hatred returned with a force I had not experienced since boyhood. I stood with eyes downcast, reliving the moment long ago when, after escaping him through the Bolhithe Gate, I had awoken on a Fenland mudbank. Then, my body racked by choking, slime squirting between my hands, I had tried vainly to put off the realization that having submitted myself to God's judgement in the Deeping Pool, I had been found guilty and condemned to life instead of drowning. I remembered being lifted, a voice whispering my name but all was vague compared to that which consumed me: a loathing of God, of Brand, my father, myself, that went to the very depths of my soul. Now it seemed to me that if his eyes met mine, he could not but recognize that force, would call the knights to ride me down. I kept my head bowed, watching from under my brows but the effort required to remain still and silent made me tremble.

Satisfied that no-one in the crowd posed a threat, the pock-marked sheriff unbuckled a leather wallet fastened to his mount's pectoral strap and, heedless of the rain, took out a parchment which he unrolled with a kind of exaggerated deliberation. A large red seal hung from it. I wondered if the writ was any more valid than that which had gained De Warenne entry to Bourne. The crowd watched his every movement with fearful expectancy but few dared look into his face, so terrified were they of attracting his attention.

He began to read in rapid French, making no attempt to raise his voice. In any case, those that understood anything he said could have been counted on the fingers of one hand. What I heard above the relentless dripping of rain, the soughing of the wind and the milling of bewildered people was clear enough, yet so strange was it to hear names I had known since boyhood embedded in a foreign tongue, I listened at first without fully comprehending.

The Norman finished speaking and let the parchment spring back on itself while his audience stared in silent confusion. A slight condescending smile twisted his lips then he handed the writ to Brand who unrolled it with a look of distaste. The ink had run in the rain and was staining his fingers.

'There are two matters to be brought before the Wapentake,' he said. 'The first is the disposal of lands. Those loyal to King William may keep their holdings by swearing fealty and by payment of silver equivalent to their land-geld, or whatever amount the King's men deem fit. All others, those who traitorously followed the renegade Harold Godwineson, are henceforth declared outlaw and, by ancient decree, their lands and possessions are forfeit to the King and will be given to worthy men.'

A low murmur met these words but as the knights' cold glance raked us over, none dared speak. Brand cleared his throat, then continued, 'Written here are the names of all those within Ness and Aveland known to have marched against the King. Know then that once your name is spoken, you are outside the law, having no right to land or property, no recourse to the courts. But as the King is mighty, so is he also magnanimous. Three days grace is granted you and if you are then found within the bounds of his kingdom, any man may slay you with impunity and you will find no sanctuary. Thegn or sokemen, all will be condemned in the eyes of man and God, for he does not love traitors.'

Again he paused but this time there was utter silence. Almost every able-bodied freeman there had flocked to Harold Godwineson's banner the year before, though few had seen actual fighting. But for most this was their first encounter with Normans and these looked not at Brand but at the waiting horsemen. The streaming rain seemed to meld the horses and riders into single beings, iron-clad, invincible. As they listened, the fear of the crowd became almost palpable.

'Before I read the list and take oaths and silver from those loyal to the true King, there is another matter.' For the first time, Brand seemed ill-at-ease. He glanced towards the sheriff as if seeking reassurance. The Norman stared back with undisguised contempt and Brand looked quickly away. (Any illusions he had harboured as to his standing amongst his new masters must have been dis-pelled in that moment: it was clear that he was despised rather than respected.)

'Of the events at Bourne, I need hardly speak.' The abbot's gaze passed searchingly over the assembly, no doubt sure I could not have stayed away. I hunched my head between my shoulders and half-turned and it was then I noticed familiar figures close by: the massive form of Acer the Hard; Siward the Red standing but a spearlength away, hood thrown back in defiance of the rain so that his bright hair was soaked and darkened; Gamal Longbow, a master of self-effacement, beside him, nondescript-looking as any bondsman. No order had I given to these, my old comrades, but they had moved surreptitiously to form a protective guard and my heart was gladdened by their stubborn loyalty.

'Eadric, son of Toli, defied officers on the King's business and paid for that folly with his life: had he not died then, he would now be outlawed.' Brand's tone was calm, reasonable. 'But the perpetrator of what followed, the slaughter in which one of the King's most renowned men was basely slain, will receive no mercy.'

A murmur arose all around, a sighing release of tension yet while most there had known Eadric and many had loved him, none spoke. Some, whose wives were close, reached out to them for comfort.

'You all know who this traitor is.' Despite Brand's bulk, his heavy jowls and thick eyelids, there was something predatory in the manner with which he surveyed the crowd. 'Hereward, son of Eorl Leofric, one-time Terror of the Fens, banished for crimes against church and king by his father's wish. From this day forward he is again made outlaw: he will be hunted down and slain. No sanctuary will he find in the churches of this land and any man or woman who shelters or otherwise aids him will be severely punished. No period of grace is granted him: his lands and property are forfeit. That is the law and the King's decree: those who dispute it do so at their own peril. Does any speak in defence of this wolf's-head?'

The silence which followed was like the silence of death, so profound that the sounds of wind and rain came loud. Then two of the knights exchanged some comment and began to laugh and the whole crowd seemed to shrink under their scorn; they hunched their heads into their shoulders even more, like crows caught in a rainstorm. None dared speak and I did not blame them: they were waiting to hear whether they also would be condemned. Brand, with a smile of smug satisfaction, started to unroll the parchment again when a woman's voice, shrill and strident, called: 'Eadric of Bourne was no traitor! He was killed for the sport of those who had already raped his wife and butchered his baby son. I was there: I saw it all. Aye and me also they shamed, a woman old enough to be your grand-dam! They were animals, not men. The deaths they got were too good for them!'

'Silence!' The sheriff signalled the nearest horsemen and they spurred their destriers forward. But the beldame, Ade, was so shrunken with age, cloaked and hooded in a throng of cloaked and hooded people, I do not think they could tell who had spoken. And so closely packed was the crowd that the horses, though trained for war, were clearly unsettled by the press of people that shoved against them.

'You don't frighten me!' Sensing her advantage, the crone began to taunt abbot and knights alike, calling Brand a Norman lap-dog in such choice language that the bravest in the crowd laughed and joined in. As the mood changed from despondency to a kind of reckless glee, some of the more vociferous pushed back their hoods, the better to deliver insults. But I watched with dread, knowing what would happen once the Normans were provoked into violence: simple slaughter, bloody and terrible.

'*À droit!*' The order cut through the rising clamour like an axe-blow. Utter silence fell and the ring of steel against leather and wood came clear as all the Normans drew their swords. It was done with an awful deliberation and their expressions left no doubt as to their intent. Horror now gripped the crowd as those closest to the horses tried to get away, pushing and shoving their neighbours in panic. I felt for my dagger as the Normans urged their mounts forward: a woman screamed as she was forced helplessly to the ground. Time seemed to slow as it always does in the moments between the unsheathing of weapons and onset.

'*Halt!*' Whatever else they might be, these Norman knights were disciplined. They pulled up their horses and some moved backwards to give the crowd space but there was no pity in their faces, only contempt. The sheriff spoke to them in such rapid French, interspersed with their own dialect, I was hard put to understand: the gist of it was that there was nothing to be gained by slaying those who would work their new estates. The word he used for the labourers was 'villan' and then I pitied these folk, freemen all, who listened in bewilderment as their future was decided. From now on they were bound to their new landlords, their status little better than slaves'. When the sheriff had finished, none of his men argued but some looked disappointed at losing a chance to slay more English and one swung his horse round, deliberately knocking over an old man, and then rode as if to trample him as he scrambled desperately away.

'*Continuez.*' An uneasy calm fell on the assembly as the dotard was helped to his feet. Brand perused his parchment and began to call out the names of those deemed traitors. His voice was clear, with an edge of triumph that made my skin prickle, and I would willingly have taken on all those knights in order to reach my uncle and strike him down. But at that moment a hand descended on my shoulder and a familiar voice hissed: 'Come away now, while you have the chance. There's nothing to be gained by staying.'

After all we had been through over the years I should have known that for all his protests, Martin would not be able to stay away. By now, those hoping to hold their lands by swearing fealty had come forward; a servant brought a mule laden with leather bags to take their silver. No-one protested at the injustice of having to buy land they had inherited from their forefathers: maybe they were simply glad to avoid the fate of the dispossessed. As the first thegn knelt in the mud to make his oath, Martin whispered in my ear but still I hesitated for there was something chilling about the method by which all our lives were being destroyed.

'Hereward!' Martin's rain-beaded face was pale and tense. That he had forgotten himself so far as to speak my name was enough to persuade me to follow. Wuleric, sensible as ever, had moved so that Swallow was screened from the Normans by the massive oak.

'What is it?' I glanced back to make sure our departure had gone unnoticed. Acer leant against the tree watching the proceedings with apparent disinterest but, I knew, with an ear for what was happening behind.

'Ulfkil sent to Bourne and Ymma had a lad ride over. Toli died last night. You'd better get back to Laughton and take all you can before these bastards' - he jerked his head towards the Normans – 'come to take possession.'

Martin had left his palfrey tied in a copse at the edge of Bourne lands. Swallow greeted it with a strident neigh and tried to lash out as he mounted and turned alongside. We rode slowly at first, not wishing to attract the attention of hostile eyes, and the horses jibbed at the wind-driven rain. The news of Toli's death weighed within me like a boulder but I did not yet feel grief, only a kind of dull resentment. Noting how the half-ripe wheat and barley was being battered by the gale almost I laughed aloud for it did not matter. I no longer possessed any land by birth or tenure, nor any rights, and this grain would go to stuff Norman bellies and pay Norman taxes while the folk who laboured to harvest, thresh and winnow it would be grateful for gleanings to see them through the winter.

The roofs of Laughton came into view at last, seeming to cower in their hollow under that hard grey light. Maybe it was the fact of Toli's death combined with my outlawing that lent the place a desolate look. Smoke spiralled from beneath the rain-blackened thatch and there was no-one to be seen as we rode into the puddled yard and drew rein. The low hills and marsh beyond were rain-veiled and bleak and rooks cawed from the elms as if mocking us.

The doors to the Hall were shut but Aedgifu must have been looking out for us through the chinks: barely had we dismounted when I heard her call an excited welcome. She struggled to open the door in the gusty wind. I gave Swallow's reins to Martin and went to help. Such trust and gladness was in her face as I picked her up and entered that my heart seemed to twist within my ribcage; the weight of the news I bore seemed suddenly insupportable. The main hall was smoky from green wood on the hearth but light shone from the rooms beyond. I stood hesitant in the doorway to our living chamber and Turfrida, who was suckling Godgifu, settled the babe in the crook of her arm and came to meet me, her expression one of grave expectancy.

'I have been outlawed and dispossessed,' I told her, and my voice seemed hardly my own, harsh, barely coherent. 'You would have done better to have stayed in Flanders, Turfrida. Henceforth I am a hunted man.'

She shook her head, felt my clothes, then reached up and touched my face with such tenderness, my loins seemed to melt.

'Get dry and warm, then we will think on the rest,' was all she said. 'None of this is unexpected, even Toli's death. Would you rather have stood by and let the sack of Bourne go unavenged?'

I had already dropped my cloak on the ground and was unbuckling my belt but at these words I froze. It was as if a great void opened suddenly inside me. I dropped to my knees beside the clothes-chest and a great howl rose from my very core as I thought of Brand's cunning and how I had betrayed those I loved best, the living and the dead. Only by clenching my teeth did I restrain that cry: Aedgifu watched with frightened eyes as I fought for control. Then Turfrida knelt before me. She put her arms around to hold me. I leant my head in the hollow between her neck and shoulder and the balm of her compassion seemed to flow into me with the warmth of her body, soothing the rawness of my grief and anger.

'Do not despair,' she murmured. 'For a season, even a year maybe, these Normans may think to rule here but their arrogance will be their downfall. Yours is a stubborn people, Hereward, and steadfast: the time will come when the usurpers are forced back to France. While such men as you live still, there is hope: only one battle has been lost, not the war. We shall take to the woods or fens for the winter then, come spring, the dispossessed will reclaim their own. Have faith, my love.'

Her strength against my uncertainty shamed me but I had lived in the forest during the days of the Fen-wolves (though our short sojourns in the Brunneswald were but play compared with the prospect of surviving the winter there with a wife and children to support), while she had spent her girlhood in a stone-built castle, secure, lacking neither food nor warmth.

'I should send you to your father,' I said. 'There you would be safe and the children too. From now I can be slain with impunity and if I die, you will become the sport of the first Norman that finds you. And whether we bide in forest or fenland, it will be a hard life. Go to Flanders and I will join you when I can.'

She leant back on her heels and her grey eyes regarded me steadily. 'I will not be parted from you,' she replied. 'And I have told you already: if we go to Flanders, there will be no returning, indeed there would be no need. But I shall willingly endure any hardship if you are resolved to stay. This is our home, and it is worth fighting for.'

I understood suddenly that it was not the ancient timber hall, the rolling acres of Laughton she meant but that deep sense of belonging only returned exiles come to recognize, the tie to the place of one's birth that goes deeper than tenure of land but is ingrained from the soil, the water, the very air one breathes. And yet she was far from her homeland. I searched for any trace of regret or yearning in her face and, seeing none, wondered if it might be different for women who may bind themselves so deeply to a man that love transcends all other loyalties.

'Then we will stay,' I said, 'unless a time comes when the choice is between exile and certain death. We have friends here and I doubt the Fen-wolves will remain idle long. But are you sure on this, Turfrida?'

'If we went to Flanders, you would be ever chafing to be here,' she replied simply. 'And you have enemies there also. Maybe it is not our fate to live in peace.'

I shivered at her tone, which was one of quiet resignation. 'I will do all I can to protect you and our daughters,' I said, and she smiled faintly, rose and delved in the clothes-chest.

'Put this on or you'll die from lung-fever before Norman swords get you.' She flung a thick woollen tunic at me, then went to our pallet where Godgifu had begun to grizzle softly. I stripped off my wet clothes and pulled on the dry, watching Turfrida suckle our child, her expression calm and serene as a painted Madonna's, and for a lingering moment it was possible to believe that the warmth and security of that room compassed our world.

An instant later, Martin entered and the illusion was shattered. His face was pale and strained, his hair rain-plastered to his face. 'Rahere has come,' he said.

I went out to see the tall Fen-man in the draughty space of the main hall, Martin at my shoulder. Rahere was crouched by the smouldering fire and his eyes gleamed red as he lifted his head. If possible, he seemed even leaner than before and there was a latent ferocity to his manner like that of a feral cat or half-tame wolf, dangerous even when quiet.

'So, will you take to the Wild, or have the comforts of hall and hearth softened you?' he asked sardonically. 'News of your outlawing has spread like wildfire. Or has your woman persuaded you to flee back across the sea?'

'If you have nothing but insults for me then leave ere I take offence,' I replied harshly. 'I have never fled from any foe: I will not start now. Why are you here?'

Rahere's teeth glinted in the firelight. 'I bear a message from Ulfkil of Croyland. He offers sanctuary to your wife and children and also to Ymma of Bourne, if the women pledge themselves to St. Guthlac's.' He hesitated, then added slyly, 'But I have another offer. There are many hiding places in the Fens and no Norman has yet ventured there. Your family could be safe while we make the marshes a place where no foreigner dares tread. Is that not better than skulking in the woods?'

Beside me I heard Martin shift slightly in disapproval but he said nothing. Rahere's eyes were fixed hungrily on mine and I wondered at his fervour, for he had ever shunned the company of others.

'I will think on it,' I said at last. 'But the Fens are no place for a babe in winter.'

'The woods are crawling with fugitives,' he replied. 'Their number increases every day: soon they will starve. But in the marshes there are always fish and birds to be caught and it is nigh on harvest: you could bring grain enough for a vill. Why let the Normans have it?'

It had turned into a damp summer and thinking I discerned the motive behind Rahere's plea, I laughed softly.

'So the Gyrwas fear rye-blight, do they?' My tone was ironic and Rahere drew himself up, eyes narrowed. But I had no wish to antagonize him and added more gently, 'You are right: why should the usurpers have everything? But those who raised the crops are also due a share. While it is in my power, I will make sure your people see though the winter, Rahere. And maybe soon the Fen-wolves' howl will sound again across this land.'

Rahere grinned and rose with the litheness of a youth though he was older by far than I.

'Aye.' He bent his head in half-mocking obeisance. 'I shall wait at Croyland after Toli's burial. Will Ymma come with you?'

'I do not know.' I escorted him to the door, ignoring the grey-muzzled hounds which had risen from their place by the hearth and followed, hackles bristling at the Fen-man's alien smell. Rahere nodded in farewell and walked across the yard. As he strode away it seemed that the streaming rain passed through him, as if his lean frame was without substance. I stared, then chided myself for a fool and went back inside, barring the door behind.

'Are you mad?' Martin, who had stayed by the hearth, had shed his sodden cloak and kicked the smouldering logs into flame. 'For God's sake, will you see sense? Go into exile while you can. If not Flanders, then to Scotland or Den-mark. King Swein would welcome you as Leofric's son and he may yet send a force against the Bastard: he has a claim to the kingship, after all. How long do you think you'll last as a hunted man with a wife and two small children in tow? At least give Turfrida the chance of safety. It's not fair to expect her to live as a fugitive.'

'Fair?' Borne by the force of an unreasoning anger, I strode across the hall and grasped his shoulders to stare into his face. 'What has fairness to do with any of this? Turfrida is my wife and she has chosen to stay, for good or ill. But you may leave now if you wish. I am an outlaw and cannot hold you to my service.'

His expression was anguished but his gaze was unflinching and he did not try to pull away though the bones of his shoulders were rigid beneath my grip.

'If you order me to go, I will,' he said. 'Yet I had hoped you thought of me as friend rather than servant. For it is as a friend that I tell you this: lands you have lost, aye, and foster-kin also to the Normans. But if you stay, you will lose everything, all that is dearest to your heart and likely enough your life also. In the end, this stubbornness will destroy you.'

He spoke with such passion it shook me to the core. I took my hands from his shoulders and turned away but he grasped my arm and wrenched me round so that, taken by surprise, I staggered.

'When I found you that day in the marsh, I vowed to aid and protect you.' His voice was low and fervent. 'I know what happened at Eadric's wake: I saw you and Ymma on the guard-platform. That I could forgive, for there was a kind of madness about Bourne that night. But this is pure folly. Is it your purpose to seek death, to see Turfrida defiled and your daughters slain?'

I stared at him aghast, recalled how he had waited in the church and, had there been a trace of pity or scorn in his expression, might have struck him down from anger and shame. But there was none, nor any fear, only a kind of sorrowful forbearance. When I could trust my voice, I demanded: 'Who gives you the right to question me?' but the words came forced, like a death-gasp. Between rage and guilt, my thoughts ran haphazard, harried by doubt and uncertainty. Only one thing was clear in my mind and I clung to it as a shipwrecked sailor a spar though the current may be sweeping him far from shore: 'I will not run away.'

Martin shook his head in disbelief. 'You are worse than Toli,' he muttered, 'yet I will not leave now when you have most need of friends. God grant this does not lead to all our deaths.'

'We shall all die one day,' I replied. 'But it is the manner of a man's death and how it is remembered that matters, not the mere fact of it. This is our land, and if it takes our deaths to rid it of the usurpers, that is a price I am willing to pay.'

Martin grimaced and glanced to where light spilled from the antechamber. Thence came the sound of a gentle lullaby which melded with the soft flare from the burning logs and the hiss of rain on the thatch.

'And them?'

'Do not seek to come between a man and his woman, Martin,' I warned. 'Turfrida is no fool and she has chosen to stay.'

'What did you expect?' he asked and his eyes were suddenly hard. 'She is your wife: you are the father of her children. If she ever forsakes you, it will be through your fault, not hers.' He hesitated then added quietly, 'You wrong her by your silence over Ymma. She loves you enough to forgive one indiscretion, especially if a child comes of it. Still, she will not learn of it from me.'

His gaze held mine with a fierce, almost possessive intensity. Remembering Ymma's description, I felt suddenly uncomfortable, as if I had glimpsed a part of his nature he had long sought to conceal.

'I must speak with her.' I turned abruptly and strode swiftly towards the sound of singing but I felt his attention the whole length of the Hall, like a hand pressed between my shoulder-blades.

Turfrida listened calmly when I told her of Rahere's offer, then set her clear, penetrating gaze upon me and asked quietly, 'And what were you and Martin arguing over so intently? Does he not wish to stay?'

'Ach, Martin!' I sat down on the pallet where Godgifu lay pummelling the air with tiny fists, absent-mindedly gave her my hand to grasp. 'He should have been born a woman. He thinks only of our safety, not what is happening in this land.'

'Then at least one of you has sense,' she said drily. 'Have you given thought to the morrow: that if the Normans have heard of Toli's death, they will likely try to trap you at Croyland? We cannot go to his funeral, Hereward, dear though he was to your heart.'

I heard these words with only half my mind, being astonished at the strength in the babe's fingers, the blind questing for life in that frail shell of flesh as she pulled my forefinger to her mouth and began to suck.

'We will find a way,' I said at last. 'If my enemies want me, they know where to come. Yet I do not hear them hammering at the door.'

Turfrida frowned, considering, then as Godgifu, realizing her efforts to suckle my hand were futile, began to cry, came and sat beside me, picking up the babe and freeing her breast in one easy movement. Aedgifu, who had been diligently stringing peas, laid awl and yarn aside and pushed jealously against her mother's knees. I bent, lifted her onto my lap and tried to ignore her eager questions as to where we would go and would we live in a stilt house like Edda's and was it true that if you ate enough eels, you would be able to breathe underwater like a fish, looked helplessly at Turfrida who said sternly that if she did not finish the peas, she would be left behind. The child slid off my knee with a swift, resentful glance and resumed her task in sullen silence.

'What of your promise to Eadric?' Turfrida asked when Godgifu was settled. 'Ymma cannot stay at Bourne alone.'

'That is for her to decide.' My guts churned and I looked away. 'She must have kin that would shelter her.'

Turfrida said nothing but there was disapproval in her stillness.

The tension between us was broken by the arrival of Cole One-Hand and Siward the Red. They had entered via the main hall: Martin stood a little behind them and his face was grave. The two crouched gratefully beside the fire for while it was not cold, they were drenched. Their clothes began to steam even as Cole raised his grizzled head.

'It was a good thing you left when you did,' he said, nodding thanks as Turfrida handed him a bowl of ale. 'Acer almost went berserk when they outlawed him: he was lucky they didn't kill him there and then.' He drank and shook his head. 'The Sheriff must have gone through old Court records, else it was the abbot revenging himself for the harrying he and his monks suffered in the past. Every one of the Fen-wolves has been outlawed and all their kin dispossessed. Bourne, Laughton, nearly all the estates around here have been ceded to a Breton named Ogier. These are evil times, Hereward. No thegn hereabouts has kept his land. Some swore fealty and still lost everything.'

I stared into the fire and it seemed to me suddenly that fighting the remorseless spread of these usurpers was like trying to stop the tide with one's hands.

'What will they do then, those turned from their homes?' Turfrida asked sharply. 'And what of you and Aelgytha and all the others who live here?'

Cole shrugged and his shrewd, kindly face looked old and weary. 'For us, at least we have a roof over our heads. But I do not think our new master will treat freemen differently from slaves. As for the others: who knows? Those with money or kin in foreign lands will flee. Most have no choice but the forest.' He paused and I felt his gaze keenly as if he had touched me. 'Those who were Fen-wolves and their kind will likely look to you for leadership.'

I saw Martin stiffen and bite his lip but he did not speak.

'This is not the time,' I said. 'Let us see the winter through first. We must gather strength, find out what the Normans intend. It is best to learn something of an enemy before striking.'

'Aye.' Cole smiled wanly. 'At any rate, we have a little time left. Brand let slip that Ogier the Breton is in Normandy. I do not think any claim will be made here until the King returns and the force in Borough is increased.'

'We shall know if there is need for fear by what they do tomorrow,' Martin said, grimly.

7. The Unquiet Winter

In the end, there was no sign of the Normans north of Borough the day of Toli's funeral. Turfrida, the children, Martin and I travelled to Croyland by hidden ways through the fens, leaving the horses with the reed-cutters and taking to the water. A taciturn boatman punted us through the winding channels in silence and we spoke little. It was one of those clear, rain-washed mornings when every reed is sharp-etched: buntings and warblers flitted in the striped shadows and once I saw a stork which stared imperiously before launching itself with a graceful leap. The beauty of its flight was lost on the boatman who remarked that they made good eating but were hard to catch and Martin and I exchanged glances. Before long, our own survival might depend on our hunting skills.

Not only the inhabitants of Laughton but folk from Bourne and neighbouring settlements as far afield as Folkingham and Witham had gathered in the church and graveyard. The mere fact of coming together for a purpose of their own was comforting to those who had but yesterday witnessed the shattering of the old order and now awaited the arrival of new masters or lives as outlaws with trepidation. As Ulfkil commended Toli's soul to the Almighty and Aelgytha and Ymma scattered earth into the grave, Acer caught my eye. When it was seemly to do so, I followed him to a clump of willows beside the river. Many of the Fen-wolves were already waiting there, along with young Wuleric and Thorkil's son, Thorald. Rahere stood a little apart, leaning on his great bow.

'Have you decided?' he asked. 'Is it to be forest or fens for you and your kin?'

'The Breton who has usurped my land is yet in Normandy,' I answered. 'We have still a little time. It is easy to declare a man outlaw but there are not enough Normans in the shire to hunt us all, nor do I think they will attempt it, not until their number is increased. If we can get the harvest in, we will not starve this winter but if we take to the wild now, there is no such surety.'

He looked at me curiously, gave a faint smile then nodded as if he had expected nothing else. Acer was not so circumspect.

'Is this how it is to be from now on?' he demanded. 'Are we going to stand by and let them take everything unchallenged? I thought you were a fighter, Hereward!'

'What purpose will it serve if every freeman left in England dies trying to protect his home?' I countered. 'Slaying a few of the bastards here and there will not drive them out. When the Atheling returns, we must unite under one banner. And,' I lowered my voice, 'there is much we can do in the meantime. Harvest everything you can, find places deep in the fens or the Brunneswald to store it. When the time is right, I will fire Toli's Hall as our signal. We will make this a place for our enemies to fear and when the Witan's call comes, we shall be ready.'

Acer and Martin looked at one another askance but the others grinned and some stroked the handles of their daggers in anticipation. The youngsters seemed abashed. Wuleric, who still wore the knight's belt he had taken after the slaughter at Bourne, asked hesitantly, 'Will you have us, Thorald and me? Can we join you?'

'You have already proved yourself,' I told him. 'You have but to name your sword. As for you, Thorald, you are welcome. You shall be the Life-reaver, like your father. But know this: the oath you must swear is binding and if you break our trust, the penalty is death. And understand that your fealty to us outweighs all others, to lord and kin aye, and to your rightful king, when he comes into his own again. Is that clear?'

They nodded, daunted by my sternness as I had intended, for oaths which bind a man for life should not be taken lightly. Then, under cover of the willows whose leaves tossed silver in a breath of wind from the west, they knelt and swore allegiance to the Fen-wolves, hands laid upon the blade of my dagger. When they arose and the others clapped them on the back in welcome, there was new hope in all their faces.

As before the fateful meeting of the Wapentake, our lives settled to an uneasy stasis. We lived much as we had the year before only now, instead of awaiting our King's summons to march against the invaders, we were on constant alert for bands of knights sent to claim usurped estates. Like me, most of the dispossessed stayed to gather the harvest and, once that was over, lingered. It is hard for any man, be he thegn or bondsman, to uproot from lands his family may have tended for generations on no more than an illegal writ and a threat, and in those golden days of late summer it sometimes seemed as if the events since Stamford Bridge were a bad dream from which we would soon awaken. But at Laughton, the foundations of Toli's church which would never now be completed, served as a constant reminder of all we had lost. And, like our neighbours, our household goods were stripped to the bare minimum, most of our clothes, food and bedding having being packed lest the alarm be given.

Stripped of my loanland, I no longer went regularly to Witham or Rippingale. But to Bourne I was bound to go, not only because of my promise to Eadric but because it still drew those fleeing north and I was eager for news. Turfrida often rode with me, Godgifu strapped at her breast in a sling she had fashioned for our flight while Aedgifu trotted the black pony alongside, sometimes veering off the track to jump the wayside ditches or chase sheep. She was fearless, sticking to the animal's back with the tenacity of a burr yet though I shared Turfrida's anxiety, nothing would have induced me to admit it. For while I knew how easily the strongest man may be maimed or killed by a misplaced hoof or a fall, pride I felt also and when Turfrida urged the child to be more careful, I praised her skill and the look in her eyes then was worth any amount of trepidation.

From folk from the south we learned of rebellion in Kent which, with continuing insurrection from Eadric the Wild in the west, was sufficient to divert Norman interest from our part of Mercia. Bishop Odo's hand had been harsh: refugees spoke of women and children burned alive in their houses, corpses hanging from trees like rotting fruit. Attacks like the one on Bourne, to us an outrage, were so common in the southern shires as to be unremarkable, only there the perpetrators went largely unpunished. The women in those lands, formerly under Godwineson rule, were mostly widows and thus helpless.

We worked even harder than usual to gather the harvest and distributed the grain to all that had helped bring it in. Even a contingent of Fen-folk came for much of the rye was blighted. Even this did not go to waste. While good wheat, barley and oats were stored in pits dug in secret places in the woods and fields, we heaped the spoiled grain in the granaries. This was the Norman's share and old talismans hung to protect the harvest were taken down and burned in the hope that the blight would poison them.

The bittersweet happiness of early autumn was even more poignant this year than last. There were the simple satisfactions of fruit-picking; seeing pigs grow fat on beech-mast and acorns; smoke hung in the air from where eels and fish were being cured. But this time, as we walked home with baskets of hazelnuts gathered from the woods or apples, dusky green and red in the soft autumn light, we knew in our hearts that we were clinging to a way of life which no longer existed, held by the deep-rooted fear that once we left our lands, we might never return. On some estates they even began the autumn ploughing as if nothing had changed. But at Laughton and Bourne sheep and cattle grazed the stubble and though crows stalked the shorn fields, no ox-teams plodded there.

By day we could almost forget but the nights were a different matter. Although to our knowledge the Normans had never begun any raid after dark, my senses pricked to every untoward sound and I kept Brain-biter within reach at all times. We stabled the horses close at hand and whenever the moon was bright, Martin and I took turns keeping watch. There was no real need for the Normans were being watched, yet somehow it made us feel better.

Though we had lived with uncertainty for more than a year, waiting gnaws a man's mind until at length he may act simply to make his path clear before him, for good or ill. As the days shortened and the first breath of winter blew with the easterly gales, I grew irritable and restless. Though the Normans had not come to make their claim, still there was no word from the surviving members of the Witan, nor the Atheling, upon whom our hopes rested.

Having no outlet in action, my frustration turned inward, spawning lurid nightmares such as I had last experienced in boyhood. The raid at Bourne I relived only this time the Normans forced Turfrida to watch as I was stripped, tied down and subjected to the same degradation I had suffered as an oblate (Ymma and Eadric laughed as Brand stepped forward for a turn, my foster-brother holding his lopped head by the hair while blood spouted from his neck). And of the Fairy Bear I dreamt. Its long teeth clashed in my jaws; my fingers were curved claws; I hurled myself at the bars of an iron cage as my enemies poked me with their spears, felt the points prick and howled in pain and futile rage.

From such dreams I would wake sweat-drenched, groping in the dark for something familiar. Sometimes my own cries woke me and then I would lie rigid, wondering what I might have spoken aloud, as Turfrida held and tried to comfort me. But it seemed that my ravings were not incriminating, for never did she make any accusation though she became exasperated then frustrated in her turn as broken night followed broken night and I refused to reveal either the content of the nightmares or their likely cause. With Godgifu's demands (unlike Aedgifu, who had been a contented and placid babe, she seldom settled easily and would sometimes scream for hours at a time), I wondered at Turfrida's strength for though her face was drawn and dark circles etched under her eyes, she remained calm and self-assured as ever. Indeed, looking back, it was her sagacity and unquestioning faith that saved me from despair in those days of lingering uncertainty. Only in sleep, I was beyond her aid.

Close on the anniversary of Harold Godwineson's death, Turfrida told me Ymma was with child. In truth, I had already guessed it. Whilst I avoided being alone with her, I could not go to Bourne and wholly ignore Ymma without raising Turfrida's suspicions and I had noticed she exhibited the focused vitality which makes pregnant women seem to glow with well-being, as if their very flesh is celebrating their fecundity.

'She is certain it is Eadric's,' Turfrida confided as we rode back. 'Maybe we will never know for sure: Ymma is of Danish descent and the Normans also are of Viking stock. But she believes it his and that is well. It will be raised as Eadric's son or daughter and the truth of its blood will make no difference.' She paused and glanced across the marshes to the distant tree clump which marked Croyland Abbey. 'If our children outlive us, maybe we do not wholly die. Not while they remember us.'

There was a wistful note to her tone I had rarely heard. Disconcerted, I said, 'For me, I wished my parents dead ere I was ten years old. I would rather earn fame by driving the invaders from our land.'

She nodded but her eyes remained inward-looking and remote. 'For men, who live for renown, it may be so,' she murmured. 'But for women?' She glanced at the bundle she held close as she rode. 'Life can be lost so easily, Hereward, like a flame pinched out between finger and thumb. Do you never wonder: what is it for? A summer fever, a spearthrust, and it is finished.'

I forced Swallow closer to the palfrey. Never before had Turfrida spoken like this and I realized she was afraid.

'If you wish, we can still go into exile,' I said. 'But storms will soon close the sea-road from the Humber and I cannot travel openly through southern England.'

She looked into my eyes with such tenderness, my heart was wrenched.

'We have made that choice,' she answered steadily. 'Do not heed my mood, love. I am tired, that is all and winter approaches.'

'As long as I have breath, I will look after you,' I promised. 'And one day Laughton will be ours again, I swear it. We shall yet be avenged upon those who have wronged us.'

She shifted the babe from one arm to the other and stared out across the reedbeds, sere under grey-scudding clouds. 'Then I pray our daughters are not left fatherless ere that comes to pass,' she murmured.

'We shall see them bear our grandchildren,' I said and she shook her head. For a moment my heart quailed, until I saw her lips were curved in a secret smile.

Days passed, leaves fell and young cattle were brought in from the marshes for slaughter. As the weather worsened, Turfrida urged me to move back to Bourne, arguing that if the need arose, we could escape to the fens or woods no less swiftly than from Toli's Hall and that there at least we had a chance to defend ourselves should the Normans came in force. But her real reason was concern for Ymma, who made no secret that she was with child and yet insisted on staying in her home as long as possible. As the heads stuck above the gates decayed to grinning skulls hung with rags of skin and tufts of bleached hair, this was her own gesture of defiance: to live on as if the cruelty of the raid could not touch her. But for me, every trip there was torment for though Ymma did not attempt to importune me, sometimes she caught my eye and smiled knowingly and then I would feel the blood rise to my face while my guts griped from shame and fear.

Turfrida, my helpmeet, who knew me better than any other, how could she have failed to notice the tension between Ymma and I? To me, whose guilt was clear as a brand, it seemed inconceivable that she should not suspect but her trust in me was complete: she did not contemplate the possibility that I could be unfaithful. When my self-loathing grew to the point that I could hardly bear her to touch me, it was not to her friend that she looked for the cause but the past which I had so long concealed. For my nightmares had not ceased and though for a while I spurned sleep in an effort to hold them off, weariness only exacerbated the horrors.

'It is time you told the truth,' she said at last one night after I had woken us all. 'What has your uncle done that haunts you so?'

'Brand?' My dissimulation sounded false even to my own ears. Turfrida propped herself on one elbow and her eyes gleamed in the dim glow of the hearth embers. I lay utterly still while fresh sweat broke out on my already wet skin.

'These past weeks I have listened while you cried out in your sleep and I have held my tongue, hoping that one day you would confide in me.' Her voice shook with barely contained fury. 'Do you know what that is like: to listen helplessly to the one you love best in torment night after night? Do not try to deny it: there must be some cause. And the abbot's name has spilled more than once from your lips.'

I lay silent, mind racing. From her tone I knew she would not lightly give up.

'Brand has ever hated me because I would not submit to my parent's wish and chose a knight's belt over a monk's habit,' I muttered at last. 'But it is how I failed Eadric that preys upon my mind.'

She snorted sceptically but my mouth was clamped shut and I determined to say no more. An oppressive silence fell, then she said quietly, 'I am not a fool. There should be no secrets between a man and his wife but since you do not trust me, I cannot force you to speak.' And she turned abruptly away while her words sank to the very core of me, like drops of molten lead fallen onto naked flesh.

In the end I yielded to Turfrida's desire to move. In my wretchedness, it seemed to make no difference where we were. Thus on a cold, windswept day towards the end of November we loaded the wagon and set off, leaving Cole One-Hand and Aelgytha in charge of Laughton. No condition of tenure was laid upon them save to keep firewood stacked against the walls of Toli's Hall. I had not forgotten my promise to the Fen-wolves.

'At least for a while I can pretend to be thegn,' Cole remarked, with an odd, half-regretful smile. But Aelgytha stood downcast and shook her head and there were tears in her eyes unrelated to the bitterness of the wind. She was a stoic and practical woman and I think she knew our departure marked a change that was both inevitable and irrevocable. When we reached the old road and turned south, I glanced back across the drab fields, the huddle of buildings under the gaunt elms, the half-built church, and was assailed by a sense of loss that pierced my heart. But Swallow was in irritable mood, snaking her head at the black pony which bore Aedgifu, and so I gathered up the reins and concentrated on the road and did not look back again.

The hall at Bourne was crowded with folk seeking refuge from the Norman threat. Most were from outlying vills but their numbers were swelled by refugees from the south who hoped for a muster ere the new lords came to take possession. Of the Fen-wolves, Acer the Hard and Siward the Red had brought their families from Witham while for Wuleric and his kin this was already home. As we approached the gates, the lad on guard shouted a welcome and many spilled from the Hall to greet us. Ymma, the swell of her pregnancy concealed beneath thick winter clothing, was grave and courteous, insisting that we share her private rooms, an invitation accepted gladly by Turfrida. As we crossed the hall, Aedgifu spotted a friend and darted to join a gang of children rushing in a wild game around the benches, cursed good-naturedly by folk who sat talking, tending weapons or, on the part of the women, spinning wool in the areas of floor they had taken as their own, piling scant possessions to mark their claims. Only two spaces in that great building were unoccupied: the area surrounding the hearth where a great log burned, and the stained patch where Eadric had died. All avoided treading there, as if his ill-fortune might somehow taint them. Even I, who believed in no such superstition, skirted that mark. More than once I caught Martin staring at it with a kind of dread.

A week after our arrival, Morcar came unlooked-for. Life at Bourne was strangely like being on campaign. There was that atmosphere of tense expectancy, the sounds of whetstone against blade as men sharpened weapons already honed and gleaming; the half-wistful, half-fearful expressions of women who understood the impermanence of such an existence yet waited stoically for their fates to unfold. Only the very young, blithe in ignorance, lived fully in those days, eating, sleeping, playing or listening enthralled as someone from the southern shires, remote to the children as Heorot or Byzantium, told a tale. For the rest of us, we spoke little of the future lest by voicing our fears we should somehow precipitate them. The Norman garrison at Borough remained weak and they did not venture north or east of Witham but I heard that William de Warenne was building a fortified steading at Acre in Norfolk and had sworn revenge on his brother's killer.

Morcar arrived on a clear, cold morning when every surface was furred with frost. I was with Wuleric and Martin, schooling some of the *destriers* that had belonged to the raiders, when Turfrida came to find me. She had never met my nephew before and at first I did not believe her, no news having reached us of the Witan's return. But even as I swung down from the saddle and handed the reins to Martin, I saw Morcar's tall, slight figure striding across the yard. When he was close, I noticed that his richly dyed cloak was much patched at the hem, his face pale and gaunt beneath an ill-kempt beard. His eyes glittered as if he were in the throes of fever as he reached out to grasp my hands but his touch was warm and sure.

'I am glad to find you here,' he said. 'News of your feat is widespread: mere mention of Bourne has the Normans frowning. Is it true they slew Eadric?'

'His head was stuck where theirs are now,' I replied. 'In truth, they were all drunk: the slaying of them was no deed worthy of renown. But Wuleric here killed one who raped his sister.'

'God damn them all,' Morcar said fervently. 'I have witnessed enough these past months that the sight of the bastards has me reaching for my dagger. But as yet not one has died by my hand and that is a shame worse than any humiliation they could inflict. As honoured guests we would be treated, that was their promise as we boarded the ships for Normandy. Then, when we reached Rouen, Bastard William's home town, they paraded us through the streets like captives, stripped of weapons and armour. We bore it as best we could. Pride at least remained to us, or so we told ourselves, but it was hard. Afterwards, we were prisoners in all but name, kept within castle walls ostensibly for our own safety. But at least one good thing came of it: those who had thought to trust our new overlords soon swore undying hatred beneath their oaths of fealty. All save my brother and the churchmen. Still, he is a strange man, the Usurper. He could have had us slain and thus rid himself of powerful enemies at one stroke but instead he let us go. And yet have you heard what he did to Harold Godwineson?'

'We heard he was mutilated and the pieces buried at Pevensey,' I replied. 'And that the Bastard feasted his war-leaders amongst our dead. But the last we discounted: even Harald Hardrada would have had more respect.'

'Aye, but William claimed Harold Godwineson was a renegade and usurper, an oathbreaker, nithing.' Morcar's tone was bitter; he glanced at me sidelong as we walked towards the Hall. 'They hacked off his limbs and balls while he was still alive, then the Bastard rode his horse over: only his byrnie held his torso together. They buried what was left on the shore, laying a great rock over to stop anyone moving him to consecrated ground. When his mother and Edith Swan-Neck came to beg for the corpse, William refused though they offered the keys of Winchester in exchange. He told them he would take the burghs of England with or without their leave, that a faithless dog deserved a cur's burial, and sent them away.' He hesitated and looked about as if fearful of being overheard before adding, 'Rumour says that the women went to the beach at night and removed the stone themselves, then took the King for secret burial. When William came to Winchester, they handed the keys over anyway, all the fighting men of Wessex being dead or scattered. As for the rest: what you heard is true. After the battle, they set up a table and benches looted from a nearby hall and celebrated their victory where the King and his hus-carls had fallen, with the wounded crying out and dying in the dark all around. A strange man indeed, this Duke. It is said that he worships the old gods, that deer are sacred to him though hunting is his greatest pleasure. His words mean nothing, his promises have proved empty and yet he spares those he knows most oppose him. Aye, a man who cannot be trusted yet who appears to trust his enemies. But cross him and he is utterly ruthless, without mercy. We must never forget what happened to our King.'

He had stopped and now reached out to grasp my shoulders, eyes blazing. I stared back, answered deliberately, 'I need no more reason to hate the Normans than what happened here. And that was no rare occurrence if half those who have sought shelter with us are to be believed. I will not rest until this land is free of them.'

He gave a half-rueful smile but there was no mockery in it.

'That is my feeling also,' he said, letting his hands fall. 'But we are weak, Hereward, and there are those that should have stood with us who cannot be trusted.' He hesitated and looked away, seeming suddenly very young beneath the rough hair and beard. 'My brother among them. He has kept his eorldom in return for fealty and William ceded him mine also, promising his sister in marriage if Edwin keeps Mercia and Northumbria quiet. Never did I think a kinsman of mine could be so easily bought. He has betrayed us.'

There was shame and disgust in his tone. He half-turned and spat as if to rid his mouth of a bad taste.

'If your redeing of the Bastard is right, Edwin may soon come to regret his choice,' I remarked. 'Anyway, it is not your doing, nor are we Godwinesons to fight brother against brother. But without a united Witan, we cannot win this war.'

'There is no Witan,' he replied bluntly. 'Not with any power. We need the Danes or Scots to back our cause if we are to have any chance. Norman numbers increase and we become fewer. Our only hope lies in the North.'

We had reached the church and stood to watch the activity in the yard. It was crowded with folk going about their daily business. Some tended beasts; a woman twirled a distaff as she chivvied a gaggle of children to the stream, Ulf the Simple panted at the bellows in the forge where the din of hammer against anvil told of a plough-share being fashioned or a blade straightened. Morcar watched in silence for a while then gestured towards the church door. 'Let's go somewhere quiet.'

It was cold and smelt of damp lime inside but the painted figures of the saints seemed to stand out from the walls in the clear light. Morcar crossed himself, then said quietly, 'I could not believe it when I heard how Eadric died. Of all men, he least deserved such an end. Once I offered him a place as a hus-carl but he refused, saying the stewardship of Bourne was all he wanted. I have never known a man so lacking in ambition nor so unwarlike. Yet he was esteemed by all the folk on the estate for his even-handedness and understanding. He was born for a more peaceful age. How did Toli take the news?'

'Toli died not long after Eadric,' I told him. 'The old man was never the same after Eadric returned wounded from Fulford Gate. To lose son and grandson at the hands of Norman raiders was too much. He wearied of life and God was merciful. They are buried at Croyland, all save the babe whose body we never found. I took such revenge as I could and for that I am outlawed and my land forfeited to a Breton named Ogier.'

My voice trailed into silence: until that moment I had forgotten that Morcar was rightful Lord of Bourne and had himself failed to keep it. But at mention of that name, a shadow seemed to cross his face and he clenched his right hand until the knuckles stood out white.

'I also am dispossessed,' he said. 'But I have not yet been declared outlaw. William would not dare until he has secured Mercia. He needs Edwin on his list of allies though he has stripped the best lands from his eorldoms, including Bourne, and given them to his most trusted followers. Once the Bastard thinks himself safe, Edwin also will lose everything and then he will face the same choice as the rest of us: to flee into hiding or exile. Indeed, I half-expected to find you returned to Flanders. There will soon be a price on your head if there is not already.'

I shrugged. 'I have friends and comrades here and there are those in Flanders who would gladly hand me in chains to William of Normandy. For good or ill, Turfrida and I will remain here unless a time comes when all hope of victory is lost.'

He glanced towards the altar where the carven figure of Christ hung twisted on his cross, mouth agape in hewn agony.

'Rebellion is planned in the north next year.' His voice sank to little more than a whisper. 'William's man in York, Copsige, has been replaced by his killer's cousin, Gospatrick, who is a close friend of the Atheling. They will arrive in the south with the Bastard's entourage at Christmas but they will not stay long at court. Messages have been sent to Sweyn of Denmark and Harold Godwineson's sons in Ireland, calling for aid. And Malcolm of Scotland fears the Normans have an eye on his kingdom.'

I was silent, considering, asked carefully, 'And all these will unite under the Atheling's banner?'

He nodded. 'He is older now: most consider him more man than boy. And though he was forced to swear fealty, he has not crawled to the Normans like some.' Seeing my incredulous look, he spread his hands out wide. 'You know as well as I that oaths made to the faithless are not binding.'

'I have not sworn fealty to any Norman,' I said. 'And those they outlaw are free of any such bond, being outside the King's protection. They will learn that men are dangerous who have nothing left to lose.'

A reflective silence fell between us. Morcar stood with his head bowed as if in prayer. Without mail, he was so slight of build that he looked almost a youth yet it seemed to me he had changed much since I saw him last. The humiliation of defeat, and Edwin's treachery, had left their mark. There was a new air of reserved caution in his manner.

'What, then, will you do?' I asked at last. 'For myself, I shall not yet dispute this Breton's claim. But I have comrades here I cannot forsake. Turfrida and I will take to the Wild for the winter, though to all appearances we will have gone to Flanders. When the call comes from the North, my men and I will be ready.'

'Good.' His clear grey eyes were narrowed and fierce. 'I am headed for

York to meet Gospatrick, and Marleswein of Lincoln. If the Bastard raises taxes again there'll be trouble. Aldred tried to keep the peace last time and Copsige's death was the result.' He paused, looked at me doubtfully. 'We must gather in the north and sweep south with a force greater than this land has ever seen to drive these Normans out. When we strike, it must be hard.'

'Aye.' I clapped him on the shoulder, conveying more confidence than I felt. 'Come on, you must be hungry and thirsty. For now we are well provisioned: it was a good harvest. And anything we eat, the Normans will not get.'

He grinned at that and followed me into the warm fug of the crowded hall.

Morcar stayed at Bourne for several days. He had only two men with him, one of whom was a cousin of Thorfin's. (As I guessed, that stalwart fighter had died of wound-fever the day I left London. I praised his memory as was his due but in my heart felt dismay for we could ill afford to lose such men.)

To seal my pledge, I gave them half the raiders' *destriers*. Horses were of limited use in the Fenland, hard to provide for in the forest and I was loth to slaughter them, the only other way to keep them from Norman hands. Morcar was well pleased with the gift and thanked me many times.

The three left at dawn as a gale blew in from the west. As I watched them ride away, the horses skittish, the men's cloaks billowing in the wind, I wondered what might befall ere I saw my nephew again. He had told me much I had not yet related to Turfrida or Martin, not least of which was the nature of Ogier the Breton. It was enough that we would soon be forced to the life of fugitives: I saw no reason to deepen their anxiety with hearsay.

News of the Bastard's return came a few days after Morcar's departure. We made preparations to leave Bourne, much to the disappointment of those who had sought refuge there. All save the Fen-wolves were told we would bide with Turfrida's kin in Flanders until spring and doubtless many believed they had seen the last of us. The skulls spiked above the gates were reason enough for us to stay away.

I left Turfrida to tell Ymma that we would go when Ogier reached Borough. The first bloom of Ymma's pregnancy had faded and she looked pale and tired. From where I knelt to roast chestnuts for Aedgifu I heard the women arguing but at first their words were inaudible above the flare of the fire and the noise from the inner hall.

'You have kin still in East Anglia,' Turfrida insisted at last. 'You will be safer there than with us. If you stay here, who knows what this Breton will do? At worst, you will be slain or used as a whore, at best he may force you to be his wife to strengthen his hold on the estate. Could you do that with Eadric's child growing in your womb?'

The pitch of her tone had increased and I glanced up to find Ymma staring defiantly at me.

'Is this how you honour your promises?' she asked scornfully. 'I thought you would keep a pledge to your foster-brother but all men are alike it seems: faithful only when it suits them. Do I have no choice in this?'

'My oath was to protect you,' I answered, uncomfortably aware of the hidden meaning in her words. 'What would you have me do: risk all our lives in defence of Bourne or lead you to an outlaw's existence in the wild? You are with child - do you want it born in a reed shelter or forest humpy?'

'I would slow you down should you need to flee, is that it?' Ymma made no attempt to conceal her bitterness and Aedgifu pressed against me like a frightened animal.

'Aye, maybe.' My anger flared, and Ymma's lips curved in a faint, insolent smile though her eyes remained cold. 'If we all die at Norman hands because of you, how then is my promise to Eadric fulfilled? I will escort you to safety if you wish but you cannot stay with us.'

'For that I should be grateful, I suppose?' Ymma's face was stark in the flaring firelight; her fair hair gleamed like bronze. Turfrida, puzzled by our intensity, glanced one to the other, seeking understanding. From where she lay amid a tangle of blankets and furs, Godgifu began to cry.

'I have been outlawed,' I replied, speaking slowly and clearly as if to a dull-ard. 'The man chosen by William the Bastard as new lord of these lands will soon come to claim them. By being with me, you would place yourself outside the law, be hunted like a beast. I will not bear that blame.'

We stared at each other like cats on the verge of fighting: the world contracted to the sharpness of battle-focus as if it were an enemy I faced.

'There is another choice.' Turfrida's clear eyes regarded us steadily as she settled babe at breast. 'Ulfkil has offered sanctuary at Croyland. There is no sin in bearing a child conceived in wedlock that is born fatherless. If you wish to remain here for Eadric's sake, what better place than where he lies?'

So obvious and reasonable was this solution, we stared at her like guilty children. Yet as Ymma hesitated, I thought of the insidious power of the Church, how a child born in an abbey would be bound to serve it, and the irony that a child of mine might suffer the same degradations was like a knife turning in my guts.

'Then I will seek Sanctuary,' Ymma said flatly. 'Though not from piety but so that my son might one day regain his birthright.' Her eyes rested unwaveringly upon mine and I felt blood gather to the nape of my neck as if a burning hand lay there. 'This charge I lay upon you, Hereward, in memory of Eadric and Toli, the elder and the young: to drive the usurpers out. And then I shall return to Bourne.'

There was a strange meld of sorrow and defiance in her tone but her gaze conveyed need, fierce as a white flame. Against my will, my loins tightened and I trembled. Aedgifu, who was still nestled close, withdrew a little, asked innocently, 'You're shivering – are you sick?'

'No, love.' I tore my gaze from Ymma's, noted her smug, secret smile and stroked the child as if she were a talisman to ward off evil. 'Perhaps someone walked over my grave.'

'Don't say that!' Aedgifu, distressed, turned under my hand and drove her head into my side as if to burrow through the ribs. I pulled her up and hugged her and lust dissolved under a surge of love for my daughter, pure and unconditional as my desire for Ymma was base.

'Nothing bad will happen while I have you with me,' I murmured to the child. 'I will keep us safe from harm, I promise.'

Turfrida, occupied with the babe, did not catch these words; Ymma looked on with a cool detachment verging on disdain but Martin muttered something under his breath, either watchword or prayer, and would not meet my eyes.

Long afterwards we realized Bastard William's return at Yule was due largely to distrust of Bishop Odo, his half-brother, and William FitzOsbeorn, whose abuses of power in the southern shires dismayed even their own knights. Having decided to assert his authority on his officers, he came in state, bringing the remnant of the old English order he had held hostage (how Morcar escaped early, I never heard). The Atheling went north to Scotland at the first opportunity but my nephew, Edwin, stayed at court while William took the main part of his force to Exeter where the townsfolk, incensed by the exorbitant geld exacted upon them, had barred the gates against their new overlords. The rebellion was led by Gytha, Harold Godwineson's dam.

News of this sedition (which ended when the prominent churchmen of the burgh sued for peace), reached us only after it was over and Gytha had fled towards Bristol. She was not pursued but a stone castle was begun straightway, built and paid for by the people. Other burghs capitulated swiftly after that but the imposition of heavy taxes continued and resentment festered beneath an uneasy peace. Once finished with Exeter, the Bastard's force turned back towards London, encountering little trouble on the way because most of those who might have resisted had fallen in the battles of the previous year. The Usurper and his court thus celebrated the birth of Christ in joyful mood while all across the country folk waited fearfully for what he might do next.

With rebellion quelled in the south and a truce declared with Eadric the Wild and his Welsh allies, it was inevitable that the Norman presence in Mercia would increase. William de Warenne had completed his *donjon*; now Ogier the Breton came to claim his fiefdom. Whether by chance or because he heard by whose hand Eadric of Bourne had been avenged, I do not know but an old enemy of mine, Ivo Taillebois, rode with him. When this news reached my ears, I knew it was time to go. As we had long planned, we loaded the cart and I bundled my weapons and tied them to Tiw's saddle. The remaining destriers I gave to those Fen-wolves who were accomplished enough horsemen to handle them for we could not take them with us. It would be hard enough to feed the animals we already owned.

While Turfrida, hindered rather than helped by Aedgifu, made ready to depart, Martin and I escorted Ymma to Croyland. She did not go willingly but could not argue against Turfrida's common sense. It was a raw January day and the marshes looked bleak and desolate. Even the thickness of a winter cloak over my hauberk, jerkin and shirt could not keep out the biting wind which, as we rode, backed from east to north. Ymma sat hunched over the pommel of her saddle, her face pinched with cold. The air bore the metallic tang which presages snow.

We spoke little on that journey. Martin's presence curbed Ymma's tongue and I had nothing to say to her. And yet I could not be wholly indifferent: after all, she might bear me a son. When we came through the gates at last and shivering novices ran to take the horses, it was but a matter of courtesy for me to help her dismount. She took my proffered hand and pressed it for a moment against her swollen belly with such subtlety, no-one saw. The intimacy of the gesture jarred like a sword-blow then, before I could recover, she stood up in the stirrups and swung down. For an instant, the space of a heartbeat, her face was close to mine. She whispered, 'It is your son's mother, not the bride of Christ I shall be'; next moment she was bending her knee before the abbot, who had come to greet her.

'You are welcome, Ymma of Bourne,' he said, raising her and looking searchingly into her face. She returned his gaze without flinching and I wondered at her boldness (though it was not she who had broken her marriage vows). Ulfkil blessed her and gestured to a nun who waited a little apart, face hardly visible beneath her cowl.

'Hereward.' As Ymma was led away (I could not help thinking of a prisoner under guard), Ulfkil turned to me. He seemed more careworn than before yet his expression was kindly. I inclined my head, more to hide my face than from respect: shame writhed like a worm beneath my ribs.

'Is it true you are returning to Flanders?' His directness disconcerted me and I hesitated, only for an instant but enough to arouse suspicion in one who knew me.

'For a while.' I glanced towards the iron-studded door which shut Ymma from the outside world. 'Make sure she is well cared for, and the child also.'

He nodded yet his gaze had sharpened and he half-opened his mouth to speak. But he was too wise to voice accusations based on speculation.

'You need not fear on that account,' he said at last. 'God keep you, Hereward, wherever you are. I will pray for the safety of you and yours.'

My thanks choked in my throat and his eyes rested thoughtfully on me as I took Swallow from Martin and swung into the saddle. Though I did not look back as we rode away, I seemed to feel the keenness of his gaze long after we must have been lost to view.

The journey to the reed-cutter's settlement was one of the hardest I have known. It began to snow as Martin and I clattered into Laughton and Turfrida's face was anxious when we set off. The children were bundled in layers of furs against the cold, the babe wrapped in Turfrida's mantle while Aedgifu rode before me, cradled in my arms. Her black pony, laden with bedding and fodder, plodded behind the mule-cart. By the time we reached the track through the marshes a fierce blizzard was blowing. So treacherous did the ground become that even Swallow began to peck and slide and at length we were forced to dismount. I carried Aedgifu while Turfrida struggled alongside, preferring to walk than ride in the cart.

In the end, it was the horses that saved us. All save Acer, who hauled and drove the mules along, we walked at their shoulders so that their bodies shielded us from the blast of the gale, urging them on whenever they slowed. Their instinct was to halt and wait the blizzard out but to stop would have been death to the children and maybe us also. Close to utter exhaustion, we walked through the settlement without knowing it. Tiw suddenly halted and refused to move: between gusts, the black swirl of the river appeared before us. A moment later, dogs began to bark and a narrow chink of light shone and widened as a door was opened. Two figures, made stout by layers of clothing, came down the ladder. One bore a flaming brand which flared and guttered in the wind.

'Get inside.' It was the crone, Edda, who bore the torch. 'Go! It's not too late for the bairns to die of cold. Get them inside.'

By God's grace, both children seemed none the worse for their experience. I helped Martin and Acer tend the animals then we sat thankfully by the fire, drinking hot furmenty laced with honey while the blizzard howled in the rafters and shook the whole building, drowning the sounds of river and roaring sea.

Next day the wind went round to the west and there was a swift thaw which made the tracks all but impassable. As we had planned, Acer took the mule-cart back to the old road and thence to his kinsfolk at Grantham, for he intended selling the beasts to refugees fleeing north to the Humber. Once rid of them, Acer had decided to take to the Brunneswald, there to await my signal with other Fen-wolves. As we watched him walk away, the mules jibbing and sliding in the slush, Turfrida, who stood beside me with the babe in the crook of her arm, smiled wistfully. I reached out, pulled her close, breathed in the tang of peat-smoke which clung to her hair and clothes, and promised that a time would come when we would live on our own lands again, free from fear.

If the summer had passed in a dream-like haze until the sack of Bourne, the time spent with the reed-cutters seemed even further removed from the realities of oppression and want which characterised that winter south of the Danelaw. We built defences as best we could, digging a ditch across the track and erecting screens of hurdles behind which an archer could hide and cover the hythe where boats landed. One day we sailed to the coast with fishermen who came to trade for eels and brought back baskets of rounded flints for slingstones. Those large enough to fit into the palm of a man's hand and with a hole worn through, we picked out to make hunter's bolases. Rahere had long since instructed the Fen-wolves in their use to hunt long-legged birds - storks, cranes, bitterns - in the marshes; with longer thongs and heavier stones, I thought they might be effective against horses, even men. The time was long past when honour precluded the use of such a weapon.

Weeks passed and we recovered from the coughs and colds which affected us all after our journey. There was no shortage of food and with the five of us huddled together with Edda, her daughter and four grandchildren, there was always a warm fug in the dwelling-hut though sometimes peat-smoke hung so thick in the air, our eyes streamed and we were forced outside to clear our aching heads.

Turfrida's initial wariness of the matriarch was assuaged by the old woman's kindness for once Edda realized my wife posed no challenge to her authority, she treated us like kin. When, during a period of heavy rain, Godgifu succumbed to a fever, it was the crone who insisted on sitting with her day and night as water flowed beneath the hut, forcing some foul-smelling brew down the infant's throat and comforting Turfrida who feared the child might die. After two days, the fever broke and Edda told us she was out of danger. We gave thanks to God for his grace in sparing her and Turfrida whispered that maybe the babe's recovery was a sign that all would yet be well.

Next day, news came that Ogier the Breton had visited Bourne.

These tidings were brought by a fisherman, a cousin to Gamal Longbow, who looked at me expectantly, as if I should don mail and helm and ride to meet the challenge straightway. But it transpired that though the Breton had ridden with an escort of a score of knights, amongst whom Ivo Taillebois was numbered, they had not stayed long, returning to Borough ere nightfall. Indeed, over the next weeks, our enemies made no further move to occupy either Bourne or Laughton (though they made their presence felt by the usual bullying of the poor and helpless), and as they bided their time, so also did I. There was little to be gained by attacking now, when they would be most on their guard. With so few men and limited arms, our only hope lay in the tactics of rebels such as Eadric the Wild: to attack, then disappear in the cover of wood and fen. This was a strategy the Fen-wolves had long perfected though none of us had expected to use it against so bitter a foe when, as youths, we harried my father's men or the monks of Borough. For now I was content to let the Normans grow comfortable and complacent, thinking the country subjugated and themselves secure. Like a bull that finds new pasture and settles down to graze heedless of the wolf-pack gathering at the forest's edge, they would be easy prey when we struck at last.

Though the Normans were relatively quiet in our part of the world, it was not so elsewhere. The oppression and castle-building continued relentlessly in the south while from the north came news that Gospatrick, unable to collect the heavy taxes imposed upon the people of York (their stubbornness was no doubt exacerbated by Aldred's pleading), had taken his men into Scotland to join Marleswein and the Atheling at King Malcolm's court. Remembering Morcar's words, even such scant news kindled hope of full-scale rebellion but having heard nothing of my nephew's whereabouts, I waited before rousing the Fen-wolves. I did not want to alert enemies to our presence until it was necessary.

It was now the hardest time of year, the grim end of winter when stores of grain and fodder begin to run out ere the new grass springs. The wild geese were restless and their mournful cries sounded through the twilight like the warhorns of long-dead warriors. Although we could survive by hunting and fishing, the horses suffered greatly, their hooves weakening on the soft ground, their ribs showing stark through coats grown long and thick as a bear's pelt. Swallow, foaled on a marshy island in Scaldemariland, was least affected, for she would browse on reeds and even seaweed but Tiw and the palfrey spurned such coarse fodder and began to starve. The black pony, Midnight, was tougher: it would chew any plant remotely edible but greed proved its undoing when it strayed into a fen and became stuck. Luckily Martin found it before Aedgifu and slew it with a single arrowshot before it drowned. By next dawn, the body had disappeared, sucked deep into the mire.

My daughter took the news of her beloved pony's death with a stoicism that amazed me. If she shed tears, it was not within my sight or hearing. To spare them a similar fate, we took to leading the horses along the treacherous marshland paths in search of better grazing and allowed Aedgifu to cling to the palfrey's back. So dulled was it by starvation, it did not react even when a snipe broke cover under its nose. Sometimes Turfrida joined us, the babe in its sling at her breast. It was to escape the confines of the settlement that she came, for there we were never alone, yet in truth I dreaded these occasions: it was then, before her artless trust and candour, I felt my guilt most keenly. And when one fine afternoon she drew me away from the others into a little clump of alders whose roots formed an islet upstanding from the marsh, hung the sling containing the sleeping babe on a branch and laid a hand against my face, murmuring 'Come, it has been long enough', I was overtaken not by desire but a rush of shame and self-hatred that made my senses reel. I pushed her away and leant against a tree, devoid of strength.

'What is it with you?' I raised my head to find her standing at arm's length, rigid, staring with eyes like flint. 'I am your wife, Hereward. Do I not at least deserve to know what is wrong? You were not so revolted by me after Aedgifu's birth. Or have you some other reason to spurn me?'

Seldom had I known her so angry. The tight control she kept of her voice was worse than any wild rant.

'A man's body does not always obey his will,' I muttered at last. 'You have done nothing wrong. It is not your fault.'

She folded her arms and regarded me steadily, head tilted slightly as if I were some curious and alien object.

'I am neither blind nor deaf,' she said quietly. 'Something preys upon your mind and it grieves me beyond telling that you will not share it. You know I would never betray you.'

Each word struck to the very core of me and I longed to confess the truth though by it I might lose her trust forever. But something constrained me. Having disappointed her as a man, I could not bring myself to admit that I had failed also as a husband. Pride or shame - I know not which (indeed, it seems at times that they are sides of the same coin) – fettered my tongue and I did not speak but forced myself to take her in my arms. She resisted at first then, perhaps realizing the futility of argument, laid her head against my shoulder and returned the embrace. But I sensed her unhappiness and then I cursed the fate which had brought us to this pass, my own weakness, though I knew with a deep and irreconcilable sorrow that what is done cannot be undone.

Turfrida treated me with firm, almost detached forbearance after that day and if nightmares woke me, she held and comforted me like a fractious child rather than lover and husband. In the end I took to sleeping during the day and prowling the countryside by night. Dark and bitter were my thoughts as I ranged field, wood and marsh, wandering as far as Folkingham and Bourne in an effort to wear off my frustration. Often I was tempted to fire Toli's Hall and raise the Fen-wolves simply to prove my manhood. But I told myself I had no right to sacrifice the lives of comrades for the sake of my pride and so let them be. Ogier and his men were still at Borough: we could not attack them there.

Martin, ever sensitive to my mood, guessed the cause straightway. He bore the brunt of my anger for I was careful not to upset Turfrida or the children, fearing she might change her mind and return to Flanders. At first he accompanied me on my night-time forays but when, irked by his unquestioning devotion, I shouted that if I had wanted a hound to dog my heels I would have taken one from Bourne (I yelled the insult without thought of Ymma's words), he turned back, affronted, and thereafter avoided me as best he could.

Thus we continued as dank winter turned to spring, existing in a kind of half-life, secretly resenting our dependence on our hosts, irritated by each other as any confined animal, forced to recognize the immutability of its imprisonment, turns upon its companions in mindless fury. Yet Turfrida and Martin did not forsake me nor speak of leaving. In our hearts we were sustained by the belief that our situation was temporary, that come autumn the Normans would have gone and we could return to our homes, free to resume our lives as before.

The geese winged northwards with the last of the winter gales; the days lengthened and new reeds sprang green through the rotting husks of the old. My mood improved (it was impossible to remain morose with Aedgifu and the other children running mad as hares, intoxicated by the sun), and Turfrida it seemed had forgiven me: she became warm and loving as ever. Mind focused on the coming fight, I gave up my nocturnal wanderings and the nightmares, though no less potent, diminished in frequency. Ymma and Croyland seemed a world away. I had not ventured within sight of the abbey since leaving her there.

Ogier the Breton moved into Bourne with a retinue of knights on Ash Wednesday, to the consternation of all who had begun to believe he would never come. Rumour had it that as he rode through the gates, the skull of De Warenne fell from its spike and shattered at his horse's feet, startling the beast so that he was almost thrown. Whether there was any truth to the tale I do not know; maybe some enterprising soul loosened the rotting rag that held the skull together or else risked their life by hiding on the guard-platform and throwing it down, escaping in the confusion which followed. Either way, news of the omen spread like wildfire amidst a populace beginning to understand the difference between life as free labourers and serfdom. The Normans reacted by taking down the remaining skulls and ordering the destruction of the church built by Aelfgar, as if their God were somehow different to ours. A week later, having established their hold on Bourne by forcing every man, woman and child to swear fealty to their new overlord, they moved on to Laughton. There they scattered the half-built walls of Toli's church in contempt and ousted Cole and Aelgytha from the Hall though once this was done and our rooms at the back smashed to pieces, they returned to Bourne. Turfrida remarked that maybe they had seen my name inscribed in the daub by our doorway. No detail was too small to escape their notice if it hinted at insurrection.

Though I had promised to rouse the Fen-wolves as soon as the enemy made their move, still I delayed though I knew the patience of those that had over-wintered in the depths of the Brunneswald must have worn thin. The responsibility of leadership weighed on me as never before. While hundreds had been under my command in Flanders and Maine, they had been part of a greater force and I had obeyed the orders of my patron, no matter what the objectives. Without knowing when the full might of the atheling's force would be unleashed, I was loth to risk the lives of my men in mere skirmishes. It was clear that nothing less than outright war would oust the Normans now.

Relief came at last in the form of a message in the name of Edgar Atheling. It was timed to reach every thegn left in England by Easter and was, ostensibly, no more than an exhortation to celebrate Christ's resurrection: 'Rejoice, for the true King is come again. Death has no hold on him and the meek and oppressed he shall exalt over the usurpers. Arise as Christ is arisen!' A heavy and secret oath was added, designed to make sure of the fealty of all that took it: no man was contemptuous enough of God to swear his soul away lightly. Nothing was written lest it fall into enemy hands but a token validated the message, a broken arrow-shaft representing the fatal flight that had robbed us of Harold Godwineson, a reminder that his death and the desecration of his body had still to be avenged. Message and token passed man to man, vill to vill so that no unusual number of travellers would be evident and the most eager recipients (myself included), sent out not one but several messengers to spread the word more swiftly. Within a few days of its instigation, the message had reached every corner of England and further, wherever the dispossessed had spread. And though some of its carriers were doubtless caught with the token in their hands, I never heard that any man betrayed the kin or friend from whom he had received it, nor the true nature of the message he bore.

Only those who have suffered the ignominy of utter helplessness will understand the hope engendered by those simple words, an oath, a broken arrow. To those who had felt forsaken, leaderless and lost, it gave a new sense of resolve. Bound by solemn words, the humblest ploughboy, little more than a slave in the eyes of his new masters, felt empowered. Rusty weapons were taken from hiding places in the thatch of labourer's cots while in the glades of the Brunneswald men like Acer the Hard taught lads the rudiments of fighting though their only weapon might be a stout stave. I watched and waited im-patiently for tidings from the north, a message from Morcar warning me to be ready but days passed into weeks and still no news came save that Edwin had left the Bastard's court and gone into Mercia. Whether he had fled, rueing his treachery as I had predicted, or was on some errand of the King's, was a matter of much conjecture until, as April turned to May and the air again clamoured with the bleating of sheep and lambs, William brought his wife, Mathilde, to England to be made Queen.

The pomp of this event ranked with the Bastard's coronation and whether a deliberate ploy or no, it served to demonstrate how completely the south had been subjugated. By now, few remaining members of the old Witan retained any position of power: the ceremony was conducted by Norman churchmen and with Norman witnesses. My nephew, Edwin, was conspicuous by his absence and to those who knew him this was proof that he had at last realized the error of his ways. His spurning of so momentous a court occasion was, in itself, an act of sedition.

In the fastness of the Fens we continued from day to day as before. Sporadic rebellion broke out all around the country but still no call to arms came from the north. Then, maybe a fortnight after Mathilde's accession, we heard that the Bastard was on the road again with the core of his force, his purpose to secure Mercia. Sure that this would prompt Edwin and Morcar to instigate the rising, I bade Gamal Longbow (who had brought the tidings), to warn the Fen-wolves and others in the Hundred who had taken the Easter Oath to make ready. But days passed and we heard nothing more until news came that my nephews had met William at Warwick and there knelt in submission to repledge their oaths of allegiance. Maybe by doing so they hoped to stay the Normans' inexorable progress, the relentless castle-building, but if so, they were to be quickly disappointed. The Bastard accepted their homage, ordered a new motte and bailey begun and Edwin and Morcar fled to the Welsh borderland. From that moment it was clear that there would be no deciding fight that year. With their capitulation, our hopes failed.

Close on this news, which came like a punch in the belly, Acer told me it was being whispered amongst some in the Brunneswald that the Fen-wolves had not been raised because I had made a secret agreement with the abbey for protection in return for peace. My face must have betrayed my feelings because when he had finished (no other would have dared tell me), Acer took a step backwards and kept his eyes downcast. He had found me fletching arrows. I grasped the one I was working on between my hands and bent it with such force that the slender shaft snapped. I threw the pieces in the river, lunged to my feet.

'Who says this?' My voice was a low hiss. 'Let them speak it to my face: we will see then who is afraid!'

'Ach, I should have kept my mouth shut.' Acer exchanged a meaningful glance with Martin, who stood nearby. 'Let it go, Hereward. They're tired of scraping a living in the forest, watching their bairns go hungry while the Normans do as they wish. We were all waiting for the fight to begin in earnest: now your nephews have given in without a blow being struck. Small wonder they're losing faith in those that should have led them. If you submit as well, there is no hope. The Normans will simply have walked in and taken over with no-one having the guts to stand against them.'

I was silent while my initial flare of rage was overtaken by a strange calmness. Often I have found that as hope fails, resolve may harden and I felt it now as a kind of ecstasy, a certainty that the time had come to act. It was akin to the moment when shieldwalls meet and one's being is given wholly to battle-joy, that clear unquestioning faith in the strength of one's sword-arm, trust in those who stand beside you, the belief that fate has decreed your death for another day.

'Aye, we have waited long enough and for what?' I half-turned to look towards Toli's Hall. 'Acer – you're like a bear: a shadow in the woods but a giant in the open – stay here and if ill befalls me, the leadership of the Wolves is yours. Martin – bring me a firepot and Brain-biter - and not a word to Turfrida of what's happening. Go!'

Acer smiled grimly and Martin cast me a swift, despairing glance then obeyed without speaking. I went to the pen where the horses were kept. With the spring grazing, they had recovered from the privations of the winter. The mare nickered at the sight of me and I slipped a rope halter on her and led her out. For what I intended, speed was of the essence; I would go lightly armed and if I needed to escape on foot across the marshes, Swallow would find her own way home.

There was a little-known path running parallel to the line of the old road. When Martin returned and I had buckled on my swordbelt, mounted the mare bareback and taken the fire-pot in my hand, I looked for the gap between reed-beds which marked the way. My servant's face was anguished and he opened his mouth as if to speak, hesitated, then blurted: 'Turfrida will not forgive us if this madness leads to your death.'

'She will understand,' I answered, heeling Swallow forward, and a fey mood took me so that almost I laughed aloud. 'This day no harm can befall me!'

During that ride it did indeed seem that the mare and I were shielded by some spell. Her hoofbeats were muffled by the dry, peaty soil and the marshland and pasture beyond were still, shimmering with heat-haze beneath the blue vault of sky. When a curlew flew up from a spearlength's distance, we saw it in the same instant and the same surprise jolted us both, then she shook her head as if chiding herself for startling. And as if also bewitched, the bird made no cry as it took to the air. It was as if all Creation, earth, air and water, held its breath.

A horse is hard to hide in open fields thus I had thought to leave Swallow tethered in the marshes near the road and go to Laughton on foot. But my recklessness brooked no such caution. The fire-pot hanging in its thongs from my left hand, I loosened Brain-biter in its sheath and urged the mare on. She cleared the ditches on either side of the old road and stretched out into her raking, tireless gallop across the pasture. The huddled roofs of Laughton and a wreath of hearth-smoke were just visible beyond the trees that grew beside the stream.

Using the trees as a screen, I did not slow the mare until we were within shouting distance of the Hall and then at a word she slackened pace. I slid from her back and crept to the stream, moving until the rear of the Hall, the lean-to and pen we had made for the horses were visible. Even at a distance, I saw that the walls and door of our private room had been smashed in, the roof torn down. Where the half-built church had stood was a pile of rubble: it had been utterly destroyed. All seemed deserted.

The despoilation of our home I noted with an odd detachment, having expected nothing less. I stood in the shadow of the trees while the water ran at my feet and flies danced in the air before me. One thing at least had not changed. Wood was stacked against the walls of the main Hall.

The heat from the firepot reddened my fingers yet I waited, hearing footsteps. A moment later Aelgytha came round the corner, a pail dangling from each hand. She made her way to the watering place where the bank of the stream was trampled flat, set down the pails and stretched. When I hissed her name, she froze and looked around warily before hurrying towards me. I leapt the stream and pulled her into the shadow of a hawthorn.

'What are you doing here?' Her face, once hale, was drawn; her hair hung in a loose tangle down her back. 'Go, quickly: Ogier and his men will come today to check on the sheep.'

'How are you Aelgytha?' I drew my forefinger down the line of the scar on her cheek. 'And Cole: is he well?'

She grimaced and looked down in an effort to hide her distress. 'He tries, Hereward. He has always been a hard worker, wanting to do the best by those in his care. But the Normans treat us like slaves and half the time we don't understand what they want because they speak only in their own accursed tongue and will not deign to use ours. They' - she swallowed to restrain a sob – 'when we could not gather all the grain they wanted, they blamed Cole though it was the end of winter and we had nothing. They stripped him, tied him to a post and whipped him with an ox-goad until his ribs were laid bare. All the folk of Laughton were forced to watch and they would not let us tend him until a whole night had passed. Since then he has been abed: only these past days has he stirred abroad and he is too weak to do more than cross the yard. We thought he would die of despair like Toli. Only the children and the thought that you would avenge such injustice kept him with us. But it has been a long time waiting.'

'For God's sake, Aelgytha!' With my free hand I grasped her shoulder. 'Why did you not send word? Rumour reached us of beatings and the like but not that it was you.'

'He would not let me,' she replied defensively. 'He made all the witnesses swear silence. Knowing your temper he feared to be the cause of your capture or death. Ogier goes nowhere without at least twenty belted knights: he is always on the watch.'

'He will need to be,' I said grimly. 'No peace will he find here, I swear it. But Aelgytha, I am here to fire the Hall and raise the Fen-wolves. If Cole is blamed, the Normans will likely slay him. Come with me now to the marshes. The bastards have not yet ventured there.'

She smiled wanly. 'He will not leave,' she said. 'Do you think I haven't tried to persuade him, for the children's sake if not ours? Get on and do what you will and we shall weather what comes as we must. Cole will not abandon those he has overseen from plough-boys to sokemen, especially now. Folk think him humble but he is proud underneath, Hereward. And my place is at his side, come what may.'

I did not argue (no man defensive of his own pride should presume to question another's). Instead, I leant forward and kissed her on the forehead, respecting her stoicism and courage. She reached up and laid her hand against my face.

'Be swift,' she said, 'and know that you are in our thoughts. And remember us to Turfrida: maybe soon we shall meet again.'

'Come with me,' I insisted. 'These Normans are without mercy. You would be welcome, all of you.'

There were tears in her eyes as she shook her head and bent to pick up the pails. 'Do not linger.' Her voice shook. 'And understand this: not only the Fen-wolves will rejoice that the waiting is over.'

I watched as she filled the pails and walked slowly back to the hovels which had replaced the cots destroyed by Ogier and his men. She was stooped like an old woman but it was care and hunger that had worn her, not age. When she was out of sight, I ran to the wood-stack, cradling the fire-pot between my hands. After the winter there was less than a third of our original store left yet Cole and the others must have worked hard to save that much.

Since boyhood, fire has been my friend, one that has never betrayed me. The wind blowing from the marshes strengthened as I worked my way along the side of the Hall, setting small blazes wherever there was a gap in the daub. Flames leapt eagerly up the dry wattle inside and I knew that once the timbers were ablaze, no earthly power could save the building. Even when I set the ruins of our private rooms alight I felt no regret. That life was lost to us until we cleansed our lands of the invaders.

From the lean-to a horse snorted nervously and I hurried over and opened the gate. Toli's old grey was stabled there. I led it out and slapped it on the rump to send it away. Smoke streamed from the side of the hall and the crackle of flame grew to a steady roar. The horse hesitated, swinging this way, then that until as I moved to hit it again, it whinnied and dashed into the yard. Aelgytha must have raised the alarm because I heard voices, though no-one shouted or screamed. Even the dullest amongst them would have understood the significance of the blaze.

Once the flames had gained a hold, licking high around the eaves until the thatch began to burn, the wind died. Smoke towered into the sky, silver-white against the blue. Curtains of flame leapt twice as high as the building was tall. The heat of it smote my face and I moved back across the stream where the trees swayed in the wind of the burning. The roar of fire assailed my ears like the battering of surf against shingle, the boom of a mighty gale; it ran through my blood like fever, like battle-frenzy, until my scalp prickled with the power of it, this elemental force unleashed by my will. As I watched the flames run over the exposed roof-ridge, ancient carved timbers hewn by Toli's father, I was exalted. This marked the start of revenge: against those who had usurped my lands; the killers responsible for Eadric and Toli's deaths; the oppressors of free folk who wished to only to live in peace; against Brand and his kind, collaborators and betrayers.

How long I might have stood there had I not heard Swallow's neigh, strident even above the roar of the fire, I do not know. That sound brought me back to myself. Remembering Aelgytha's warning I scrambled up the bank, cast a last look back at the hall. A huge section of roof collapsed, sending sparks and pieces of burning thatch spiralling into the billowing smoke-cloud. So high was that plume, it must have been easily visible from Borough and Folkingham, even from glades deep in the Brunneswald.

Swallow was where I had left her but she was treading frantically from side to side, head craned high, white-rimmed eyes fixed on the fire. Seeing me, she whinnied again and stood still but when I reached her side she was trembling and her coat was dark with fear-sweat. Understanding her terror, I soothed her with hands and voice, then grasped her mane and pulled myself astride.

If she had gone swiftly before, now she ran like the wind and her long mane whipped my wrists. She cleared the ditch and crossed the old road and there, at the edge of the marsh, I checked her. She stood quietly, blowing hard not from exertion but the cessation of fear, and I stroked her neck automatically whilst watching the smoke roil upwards. There came a muffled roar as the remainder of the roof collapsed and the base of the smoke-pillar turned red, then, gradually, the smoke began to thin as a high wind smeared it across the sky. I could do no more. I turned the mare and we wended our way home while behind us the last wisps rose from the Hall and were lost.

Later that day, when the shadows were lengthening, Martin pointed out new streams of smoke coming from the direction of Laughton. The wind had picked up again, veering to the south, so we thought nothing of it, assuming the breeze had re-kindled smouldering timbers. Then, at twilight, a keening cry arose that was no utterance of bird or beast. Often I had heard such from women searching battlefields or the ruins of their homes. Martin and I exchanged glances and hurried towards the sound, picking up weapons on the way. Turfrida and Edda watched us go without speaking. Remembering the sack of Bourne the same dread gripped us all.

We found Aelgytha and her children thwarted by the ditch we had made across the track. She had sunk to the ground from exhaustion or despair but the eldest boy, a lad of maybe twelve years, whipped a knife from his belt and stood protectively before her as we waded across. He was easily disarmed and followed sullenly as Martin and I helped the woman to her feet, picked up the younger children and led the way to the settlement. We did not ask what had happened for they were barely capable of speech but Cole's absence told its own story.

Ogier and his knights had arrived soon after the collapse of the burning Hall, Aelgytha told us later. They must have ridden fast because their horses were panting and lathered. The Normans had the village men tend the beasts and while they were occupied, Cole was dragged from his cottage. He had been waiting for them but said nothing when they pointed at the smouldering ruin and demanded who was responsible. Even when, French gaining no answer, they interrogated him in broken English, still he kept up a stubborn silence though Aelgytha begged him to speak. Then Ogier ordered the remaining buildings fired, down to the meanest hovel.

By then, all the folk of Laughton had gathered, drawn by the noise and smoke. They watched helplessly as the questioning continued. Ogier was a man of little patience and when Cole had been kicked and beaten half-senseless and still nothing came from him but groans and curses, they dragged him to one of the elm trees. One found a rope, slung it over a branch, made a noose. This they put round Cole's neck and hoisted him, kicking and jerking, into the air.

Three times they did this, raising then lowering him just before he lost consciousness and each time he reached the ground, they loosened the noose and demanded again who had burned the Hall and to what purpose. The third time, his bowels broke. 'My arse has spoken for me,' he gasped when they brought him down and though his voice was cracked and discordant, the words came clear for all to hear. Ogier, his face dark with anger as was Cole's from strangulation, waved his hand and again Cole was hoisted high only this time they did not lower him but tied the rope's end fast, promising the same fate to anyone who cut the body down. Then they got on their horses, watched until Cole's feet stopped twitching and, laughing, rode away.

We went back that night, Martin and I, lightly armed with bow, axe and sword, carrying a pair of the iron-shod spades the Fen-folk use to cut peat. Aelgytha's children had succumbed to shock and exhaustion and were asleep but she insisted on joining us. The breeze from the south made the hanging corpse sway for no-one had dared touch it. We cut the rope and lowered Cole with reverence, then at Aelgytha's bidding, stripped away the soiled clothes. The air reeked of smoke and shit and Martin and I were glad to leave the tending of the body to the women and begin the grave for the sight of that corpse was enough to turn the stomach of the most battle-hardened, the face distorted and blackened with torn, protruding tongue and bloody eye-sockets where crows had pecked.

We buried him deep, within the enclosure of Toli's ruined church, and the folk of Laughton, ashamed of their fear, vied with each other to help. I spoke a brief eulogy, praising Cole's faithful service, his steadfastness and strength in refusing to submit or betray his friends. Then Aelgytha, calm and composed, strewed a handful of earth over him and stood a moment in silent prayer before the rest of us did likewise. When all were done, we filled the grave and cast ash and pieces of stone upon it so that only those who looked close might see how the ground had been disturbed. I did not put it past the Normans to dig him up and hang his corpse again once they discovered the grave.

As I had intended, the burning of Toli's Hall was marked as far north as Grantham and south to Borough and so many had now sought refuge in the Brunneswald, I think all the Fen-wolves heard the news ere the smoke dissipated. But by that strange chance which often brings life from death, hope from despair, the first of the gang to meet me after was Rahere and the tidings he brought were of birth, not killing. A son had been born to Ymma a day after we buried Cole. When Turfrida asked tentatively whether the child took after Eadric, the tall Fen-man grinned and said he had not seen but the serving woman he had spoken with insisted that the babe was fair as most born in these parts and sturdy. Ymma had been all night in labour.

'Thank God!' Turfrida exclaimed fervently then glanced towards Aelgytha who sat nearby, perhaps afraid of intruding on her grief. But Cole's widow did not react, she was helping Edda sort herbs and seemed oblivious to all else. As for me, my first thought was that if Ymma had died in childbed, our secret would have been safe forever. For so base a wish, I was swiftly punished.

'We must go and see them,' were Turfrida's next words. 'And it would be fitting to ask Abbot Ulfkil to intercede on Cole's behalf: after all, he lies in unhallowed ground. If we go by boat it will be safe enough'

'That is more than I dared hope.' Aelgytha looked up from her work and her eyes were bright with unshed tears. 'I would not ask anyone to risk their life for us but it would ease my heart to know his soul is safe.'

'Then it is settled.' Turfrida looked to me for confirmation. Caught between my promise to Eadric and respect for Cole One-Hand, I nodded. 'We shall leave at high tide tomorrow.'

The journey to Croyland was uneventful though for me every stroke of the paddle seemed significant, driving me ever closer to an encounter I dreaded. However my anxiety was needless. Weak still from the birth, Ymma was confined within the abbey walls and only Turfrida admitted, Godgifu grizzling in her arms (we had left Aedgifu behind because she seemed slightly feverish). Soon Ulfkil came out to talk to Aelgytha. At length she went into the church while the abbot joined me beside Eadric's grave.

'It was ill done to return so soon,' he said. 'Not least for your wife and children and maybe many others, of whom Cole One-Hand is but the first. These Normans do not forgive easily, nor do they forget. Go back while you may: you can do no good here. Our only hope is in peace.'

'You did not speak thus ere the usurpers came,' I retorted, perplexed until I realized he thought I had over-wintered in Flanders. 'And I have never been far away though rumour said otherwise. Would you have us lose everything without fighting for it? I did not think you would submit so easily.'

'The King's claim was endorsed by the Pope,' he answered wearily. 'I must do as my bishop and Abbot Brand tell me. Your presence here endangers all of us. The Normans will soon discover who fired Toli's Hall and then they will scour wood and fen until you are dead. Is that your purpose: to leave your children fatherless?'

'It is they that will find this land dangerous,' I replied angrily. 'And I will not be their quarry but their hunter. This abbey I will spare for Ymma's sake, but those who side with the Normans are my enemies.'

'More killing will not restore our land to us,' he said, with tired resignation. 'It is finished, Hereward. We have lost and must make the best of it we can.'

'I and my comrades will not submit while an atheling lives,' I said. 'We have a true King and he is no nurseling child. When his call comes, whose side will the Church take?'

'His call?' He shook his head. 'What came of the Easter Oath and the broken arrow?' He glanced away towards the distant sea. 'I pray that God will send us a sign but some say the Normans are a punishment for our past impieties. If that is so, fighting or submission will make no difference in the end.'

'That I will never believe.' The words came out more forcefully than I had intended and he looked up to meet my gaze with a kind of pitying forbearance. 'We will rid ourselves of the bastards as one culls a vicious cur, whether by paying geld to the Danes or allying with the North. It is not over.'

He shrugged. 'Then as I cannot persuade you to reason, I shall pray for you instead,' he said heavily. 'But this I must tell you and you may heed it as you will: you are set on a course that will be the death of many more who are your friends. And think well before you loose the Fen-wolves upon this country for it may be that the ordinary folk, bound to their new overlords, will pay the price of your vengeance.'

'We are at war, Ulfkil,' I pointed out with all the patience I could muster. 'Much must be risked on the chance of victory. Ask the people whether they would rather be free men under a Saxon thegn or Norman villans with no more rights than slaves, then tell me that my purpose is awry.'

Our eyes locked for a moment and he sighed. 'Maybe Toli was right: those of us who remember Cnut's rule have lived too long.' He seemed suddenly diminished, an old, weary man who had ruled his abbey with vigour and prudence for many years and now had no redress against Norman intervention. 'May God guard and guide you. But I can offer no other help than prayer.'

'Keep Ymma safe and that is more then enough,' I replied, pitying him. 'For I promised Eadric to protect her and would not be proved faithless.'

'While I am abbot, she will always have a place here,' he said. 'And the birth of her child has gladdened the hearts of many, that life should spring thus from grief. Do not fear on their account.'

Aelgytha seemed much comforted by our visit to the abbey but Turfrida was unusually withdrawn and hardly spoke as Martin and I paddled and poled the boat home. Fearing what Ymma might have revealed, I became awkward and clumsy in my handling of the craft and the silence between us grew ever more discomfiting as the reedbeds slipped to either side. Lost in her own thoughts, Aelgytha trailed one hand in the water while Martin corrected my wayward steering without reproof.

Later that evening, Turfrida confronted me. I was alone by the river, brooding on Ulfkil's words and the bitterness of fate which should have granted me a son I could not acknowledge to a woman I had taken in a moment of madness. So deep was my introspection, I did not hear her approach and yet she did not startle me. She came to where I was sitting on a heap of cockle shells left by generations of Fen-folk, but did not speak. The awkwardness between us was almost palpable and the lap and ripple of water against mud; wheeping of oystercatchers out on the sandbanks and distant call of a curlew seemed loud and intrusive. A babe's wail sounded from the settlement.

'I left Godgifu with Aelgytha,' Turfrida said. She sat down but made no attempt to touch me and stared into the water as if to read some profound meaning from the swirling current. Fear gripped me then for her very quietness betrayed the depth of her hurt.

'Turfrida –' I longed to take her in my arms, to lead her to the alder patch and join with her there, sharing the unquestioning loving-kindness that had been between us of old. But it was as if an unbreachable barrier had sprung between us through which we could see one another but not make contact, as if the weakness that constrained me when I encountered Brand again curbed my will. What I most desired I could not do and when Turfrida raised her head and I saw her pain, a strangling hand seemed to tighten round my throat.

'She says she will name the child Hereward,' she said at last and while her voice was steady, I knew it was only by great effort that she kept it so. 'Because you are their avenger. Save that it is a boy, it looks much as Aedgifu did as a suckling. I would have thought it more fitting she name it after its father. Then at least he would live on in memory.'

'While I live, Eadric will not be forgotten,' I replied, trying to keep my tone light as cold sweat bathed me. 'And all babes look much alike at that age, do they not? If she wishes to call the child after me she does me too much honour, but it is her choice, not ours.'

'Is that all?' Her eyes were cold, her voice hard. 'Even now, one of its eyes is darker than the other. Have you nothing else to say?'

'What should I say?' From fear and guilt I spoke more angrily than I had intended. 'Are you accusing me of lying with my foster-brother's wife when his body was scarcely cold? If so, out with it and have done!'

Often I have found when fighting with the odds against me that outright attack disconcerts the enemy and thus weakens them: so it was now. Instead of asking the question which would have undone all I had striven to preserve, Turfrida looked away ashamed, saying, 'Forgive me, my tongue outstripped my mind. You know how I have yearned to give you a son. When I saw the babe, I was jealous. But God has blessed us with two healthy daughters and boys often die young. I should be thankful, not fret over what cannot be changed. Compared with most, we are fortunate.'

'Aye, that is true.' I took her in my arms, pulling her close so that she could not see my face. 'And God knows, if we are forced to the woods it will be hard enough with two bairns in tow. There will be time enough to make sons when the Normans have been driven out. Trust me.'

Twilight was stealing across the marshes. She leant her head into the hollow of my shoulder and I held her quietly, with a tenderness that was like an open wound.

8. The Brunneswald

One should be careful what one speaks in the name of God. Aedgifu's fever rose and fell but it did not leave and as days passed we realized it must be ague, the dreaded marsh-fever. Edda told me grimly the illness had killed over half the reed-cutter's children one year, nor did it spare the strong and hale who sometimes succumbed as swiftly as the very old and young. And often it subsided so that the sufferer thought themselves cured until, when they were weak, it returned with greater ferocity than before.

Such was the nature of Aedgifu's sickness. We took turns to sit with her and sometimes she woke bright and hungry, asking why we looked so worried. But most nights her body grew so hot we thought it must scorch the linen she lay upon and she shook uncontrollably as I have seen wounded men do, just before they die. With each day, she grew weaker and her flesh seemed to melt away until the child that had been so sturdy was reduced to a skin-clothed skeleton, her eyes huge in a face become all bone.

Turfrida and I watched helplessly, racked by guilt. It seemed to me that if our daughter died, the blame would be all mine. And worse was the look on Turfrida's face for I read there the same anguish, only in her case it was wholly unjustified. To escape, to occupy mind and body so that for a while I could forget my wife's haunted eyes and our child's stick-like limbs and febrile gaze, I called upon the Fen-wolves. As in the past I had tried to wipe out boyhood shame in bloodshed, so now I took refuge from guilt by slaying Normans. It was almost as if nothing had changed since the days when, unable to strike directly at those that hurt me, I sought to prove myself against anyone within my reach. And now, as then, it was only a kind of unreasoning stubbornness which kept me from despair, a refusal to submit, like that of a wilful colt which fights the halter until its heart bursts.

Martin, I think, guessed much of what was on my mind. He loved Aedgifu as if she were his own but fearing maybe what I would do if she died, he seldom left my side. We rode deep into the Brunneswald to where Acer and his family, along with many others, had taken refuge in a glade of ancient oaks. Many of these, from the thickness of their boles, must have been saplings when the Iceni and Romans fought over this very land. Some, age-hollowed into branched husks, made good homes for the dispossessed; other less substantial shelters, humpies of skins stretched over wattle hoops, were scattered between the trees. A few seemed no more than chance accumulations of branch and fern save for the smouldering hearths in front.

When we entered the glade Swallow became nervous, sensing hidden watchers. Acer gave a piercing whistle as he strode to meet us and Gamal, along with several lads I recognized from Bourne, climbed or dropped from the branches where they had hidden to keep watch. All were armed with bow and knife and they grinned self-consciously when I complimented their wood-craft.

'No Norman bastard has yet ventured this far into the woods,' Gamal said. 'But when they do, we'll be ready.'

'They won't.' As I looked round the glade and took in the squalor beneath the leaf-filtered sunlight, the stench of ordure and refuse, anger formed a hard knot in my stomach. The children seemed healthy enough as they played together but the women's faces were hollow and weary. They glanced at Martin and I with the dull indifference of those who live with no thought of the future but scratch an existence from day to day because there is no choice. Once they realized we posed no threat, they turned back to their tasks, moving as if half-bemused. Old men stared sightlessly from tree-roots, dwelling in the past.

'We shall make the Brunneswald a place where no Norman dares tread,' I said fiercely. 'They'll find no peace hereabouts. We'll be the wolf-pack that harries them, appearing and disappearing like forest shadows. And at harvest time their share will be ours. They have gone too long unchallenged.'

Those first days of our campaign passed in a kind of dream. In their arrogance our enemies rode through the countryside without keeping proper look-out, thinking the population utterly subjugated. Armed only with bows, swords, long knives and balters, we moved swiftly through woods and along hedges grown wild from two years' neglect. Our first encounter, with three riders travelling the old road towards Bourne, passed in less time than it takes to sink a horn of ale: two died pierced by arrows before realizing they were under attack. The third, thrown when his horse stumbled and fell with its legs entangled in the thongs of a bolas, shouted a protest ere his head was hacked from his body. We stripped them of weapons and mail and left the bodies where they lay while the stricken horse we slew and butchered for meat. The others we hamstrung, *destriers* being weapons of war no less than swords and lances. Next day we ambushed a party of seven knights riding south along Ermine Street.

Acer and I alone wore mail in those first skirmishes. Our tactics relied upon speed and stealth and we were on foot: the weight of a mailcoat could mean the difference between life and death to those unused to it. If a mounted knight caught up with any of us, we were doomed with or without armour unless comrades were on hand: each of our lives depended on the skill and integrity of the others. When Thorald was struck down in that second encounter, there was a scramble out from the hedge whence we had sprung our attack and the Norman hesitated in the act of wheeling his mount to trample the lad then, seeing himself outnumbered, spurred his horse away.

The rest had been felled with javelins and arrows or else lay trapped beneath their struggling horses. I left them to the others while I knelt beside Thorald. He seemed stunned but as I pulled him into a sitting position, he gasped and clutched at his shoulder. He was lucky: it had been a clumsy blow and the gash in his upper arm was bloody but not serious. Once reassured he was not maimed for life, he grinned and apologised for his clumsiness.

Thorald was our second balter-man, responsible for bringing down any horses whose riders had escaped the missiles, and his throw had been poor, striking the animal's chest. Like a sling, the bolas required space for a proper cast thus the balter-men were usually the first of us to be exposed to danger. Had Norman horsemen used bows or javelins we would have been forced to a different strategy but they carried lances rather than throwing-spears and considered the bow a foot-soldier's weapon. Thus we persevered, for the bolas was easy to make, light to carry and, when used properly, could bring down a galloping horse in a single stride. The impact killed most riders at once or else injured them so badly it was simple knife-work to finish them.

We were merciless, remembering how Eadric and Cole had died, how we had been humiliated and dispossessed, our people reduced to serfdom. What we could not carry or had no use for once the corpses were stripped, we utterly destroyed, hacking harness and gear to pieces to prevent it being re-used. Yet the killing appeased neither our anger nor our lust for vengeance. Looking upon the carnage, breathing in the stench of blood and entrails, we felt satisfaction in a job well done but it was short-lived. In our hearts we knew these fights were but mere skirmishes and with every month that passed, the usurper's grip tightened. Already the year was turning towards another harvest-time.

Those first days I was able to keep my mind occupied with the day's work, the tally of dead, the value of the booty until the marshland came into view. A piercing anxiety would grip me then until we reached the settlement, fearing to hear sounds of mourning or worse, utter silence, Turfrida running towards me, face disordered by grief. But each day the scene was much the same, men and boys mending nets and traps or tending boats, women cleaning fish or weaving the reed baskets they took to sell in Borough at the spring and autumn fairs. Aedgifu clung to life, though by now she could barely lift her head to drink Edda's potions and the gruel that sustained her. I would tend my weapons and eat, then prepare for a night watching over the child to give Turfrida, become thin from worry and Godgifu's demands, a chance to rest.

A week after our first attack, I returned to find my wife talking earnestly with Rahere. He alone of the gang had not answered my signal but he had ever been his own man and I knew he would not break faith. They sat together on a great slab of driftwood with the babe sprawled on an old sheepskin at their feet and while they looked up at my approach, they did not rise. My initial dismay was stayed by the sight of Turfrida's face. She was smiling and seemed less anxious than when I had left at dawn.

'Aedgifu is sleeping,' she told me as I crouched by the river to wash the bloodstains from my hands and arms. 'A proper sleep, Hereward: the fever has left. Rahere saved her. We must reward him richly.'

'I have no use for gold or silver, lady.' The Fen-man's tone was dry and measured. 'And the sickness may yet return. For now, the child is safe but by next moon, who knows? The marsh-fever cannot be cured so easily.'

'Nonetheless, we are in your debt, Rahere.' I rose and stood staring down, one of the few occasions I had had the advantage of him. 'Yet it is ten days since Toli's Hall burned and the Fen-wolves have missed you. I thought you were eager for this fight.'

'Aye.' He leaned back a little and grinned. 'When you've finished playing hide and seek in the woods and draw the bastards into the Fens, then I'll join you. It seems you've had it easy up to now: soon it'll become interesting.'

Turfrida frowned. Though she knew well enough what I was doing, I had not told her details of the killings.

'We could do with your hand and eye,' I said, for Rahere's accuracy with bow and bolas was unsurpassed. 'We almost lost Thorald the other day – he cast the balter and missed.'

'Ach, let the youngsters get their hand in ere the Normans learn the game.' Rahere's drawl was laconic and a grim smile lingered about his lips. 'Have your fun while you can. I'm minded the bastards won't give up so easily. They have yet to punish those who buried Cole One-Hand, for instance.'

'They'll have to find them first.' I stared across the marshes to the rounded hills, the woods dark blue against the westering sun. 'And the manner of Cole's death has still to be avenged.'

'What will your woodsies do, then?' Rahere made no attempt to conceal his amusement. 'String Normans from every tree in Brunneswald? I tell you this, Hereward, and it is no jest: those that stay in the forest will submit before long. The place is hunted bare and someday a little bird will whisper in the Bastard's ear that woods can be set alight after a dry summer.'

He spoke with the contempt many of the Gyrwas bore the woodlanders and cottars who were their neighbours, a feeling that was returned wholeheartedly. It was widespread belief among ordinary folk that the Fen-dwellers had webbed feet and could breathe underwater as well as any fish.

'Reeds burn also.' The babe had begun to cry and Turfrida bent to pick her up, fumbling with her tunic to bare her breast. A strange, almost pained expression passed across Rahere's gaunt features; he licked his lips as if suddenly uncertain of himself and glanced to where Martin was sharpening his axe. In the same instant my servant raised his head and a look passed between them that I could not mistake, a kind of burning ardour.

Next moment, Martin attended once more to his weapons and Rahere rose to his feet with the barely contained ferocity so characteristic of him, yet I was shaken. Such a glance I had last met when Brand trembled beneath my dagger.

'So?' Rahere's voice broke my reverie. He was watching me with a kind of sardonic expectancy. 'When the woods fail, will you bring the fight to the fens?'

'Most of England is wood and field, nor marsh,' I pointed out. 'The day we rely on the fens to save us is the day we admit defeat. You have sworn fealty to me and my comrades Rahere, and we need you now. Would you be proved faithless after so long?'

His eyes grew wary. 'I have saved your child, Hereward: there is no need to insult me. When the true fight begins, I'll be there.'

'No insult was intended.' Martin had crossed to the horse-pen and I was uncomfortably aware that the Fen-man's gaze followed mine.

'It is a long time since he found you in the marshes but he has never forgotten,' Rahere murmured, his voice oddly strained then, as I glanced at him askance, he shook his head and strode swiftly to where his punt was moored. Within moments he had disappeared between the reed-beds.

'Hereward?' Turfrida's voice was sharp with anxiety. Fearing what she might read from my face, I took her in my arms, my eyes still on the rippling wake of Rahere's craft. 'What's wrong?'

'Nothing.' I fought down the foreboding that had risen like a dark wave, all my past gathering to overwhelm me. 'Let me see Aedgifu.'

The misgivings aroused by that encounter were effaced at the sight of our daughter, limbs spread in the abandon of an untroubled slumber, though her thinness wrung my heart. Yet when Martin came in at twilight, he flushed under my glance and avoided my gaze thereafter like one ashamed.

(As a hound with one master Ymma had described him. Now, for the first time, I wondered where his heart truly lay. Often we had each stepped between the other and death: I trusted him not only with my life but all those closest to me. Indeed, knowing much of my past and the truth of my relationship with Ymma, he understood me better then Turfrida in some ways. And yet a man's desires and sins must be accounted for between his own conscience and God, they are not for others to bear. That lesson I had learned in the waters of the Deeping Pool long ago.)

By next morning, refreshed by a night of unbroken sleep, it was as if that echo of the past had never been. Aedgifu woke long after the rest of us were up and about and though weak, she instantly took advantage of our relief at her recovery, demanding a new kitten and pony before she possessed the strength to sit unaided. But when she saw me don hauberk and swordbelt her mood changed. She stared, distraught, and begged me not to fight.

'Where is the young warrior who promised to ride at my side and chase our enemies away?' I asked, stroking her face with my forefinger. 'Get well, then we'll find you another pony. But only the brave heart gains reward.'

She pulled the covers over her head and giggled when I tickled her gently through them but Turfrida gave me a hard look. When I bade farewell, she nodded but did not reply. She knew that one day a fighting man's store of luck runs out and for her there was no choice but to endure the hours in the hope I would return unscathed. The lot of women I have never envied.

The weeks passed, the year turned once more through harvest. The Normans had grown wary for it was not only in our part of the country that they were attacked. Yet the Bastard's progress north was inexorable. Every strong fort or hall he came to he destroyed, then replaced with castles. Through the forced labour of those who had formerly been free was this achieved and where no natural defence of strategic sites existed, great mounds of earth and stone were raised while in the fields the ripe grain turned from golden to bleached white or mildewed grey then fell to the ground for lack of people to harvest it.

By now it was clear that the Normans had no intention of ruling as English kings, with the customs and laws evolved through years of governance by an elected witan. Their desire was simple: to force their law, their religion, their feudal system upon us, to destroy us so completely that no memory would remain of what had been before. Those not already slain, dispossessed or outlawed they wanted as their serfs, labourers bereft of land and rights, slaves in all but name. Now, as he returned south from York (from whence the Atheling, Gospatrick and Marleswein had fled at rumour of his approach and a new castle had been built), the Bastard heard what had been happening in the rest of the country, the ambushing and killing of his officers, many entrusted with the collection of geld. To counter this insurgency, he devised the murdrum fine.

In our parts ordinary folk clung to the belief that the Normans were but a passing thing, like blight or murrain, and many still looked to their rightful thegn for justice. Thus when the Fen-wolves were quiet, I often went to the Brunneswald or secret moots to hear and decide grievances. Turfrida begged me not to go for with Martin as my only companion I was in more danger then than when we went to fight: it would take only one person's treachery for me to be caught or slain. I reminded her how the secret of our very presence had been kept and told her that the day one of my own people betrayed me would be the day I wearied of life. But when I heard of the new law, I was dismayed for it epitomized the cunning and ruthlessness of Norman strategy. They understood how the lives of rebels and outlaws relied on the faith and support of ordinary folk, therefore it was this trust the murdrum fine was designed to break.

Under our laws, every man, woman and child, whether free or bonded, had their price, wergild set at a fixed fee according to their status. Thus if a king's thegn were slain his kin could demand wergild of £4 from his killer and if payment was refused, the slayer might be enslaved or outlawed according to hundred or shire court judgement. The Normans corrupted this tried and tested system by decreeing that the hundred in which a Norman was slain would be held responsible for his death and must pay recompense in full or else deliver the killer to the King's justice. The levels of the fines were so high that most hundreds could only dream of raising them, thus unless the murderer were found and handed over, payment was due in kind.

Wuleric brought this news. He watched my face with the trustful expectancy of a puppy and for a moment I resented the faith he and the others had in me as war-leader and thegn. And yet these were responsibilities I had brought upon myself: honour dictated that I should not forsake them. My face had set in a grimace. I forced a wry smile.

'We must be more careful henceforth, then,' I told him. 'Who is to judge whether a stripped and headless corpse is English or Norman? And if men simply disappear, no single hundred can be blamed.'

He went off to spread the tidings to others of the gang, his motley clothing of threadbare woollens and animal skins melding swiftly into the colours of the background vegetation. I watched him go with a mixture of pride and sorrow for it seemed to me that with laws like the murdrum fine, the days of the Fen-wolves were numbered. Whilst I doubted any local would deliberately betray us, no man knows until it happens how he will bear himself under torture or if his wife and children are threatened.

Though no castles had been imposed closer than Lincoln and Norwich, the harvest was late throughout the shire because Normans granted fiefdoms were demolishing the old halls and having fortified steadings built in their place, massive stone and timber constructions, often within defensive walls. Most of the labourer's cots were also destroyed and they were permitted to re-build only at a distance from their overlord's dwelling. Formerly, every man who was not a slave held land (for which he paid geld to his thegn), thus his home, cot or hovel, was sited in its own plot, riotous with herbs and vegetables. Now the ordinary folk had nothing save the paltry strips allotted by their new masters. Often it was common pasture that was ploughed to feed the villans, thus those who possessed animals had nowhere to graze them. The beasts were then slaughtered or incorporated into the landlord's herd: the man was fortunate who received payment for them. And those who had taken refuge in the forest were worse off. Deprived of the beans, peas and other staples they would normally have grown for themselves, they were hungry in what was usually the most bountiful season and, with every week, game became scarcer. Yet as before the invasion, few voiced their fears, as if by ignoring the threat they could nullify it, and now, as then, such belief was delusion.

Martin and I were away at moot deep in the Brunneswald when the Normans came to the reed-cutter's settlement. The place was no secret to those using the river. Boats stopped often to trade for eels and salt; many fisherfolk who were Edda's kin beached to pass the hours whilst waiting for the tide; others brought rafts to load with reeds for thatch. And maybe it was some zealous clerk, tallying rents in Borough, who discovered or remembered that there were many folk living in the far reaches of the Fens who had not yet paid tax to their new overlords. At any rate, geld was the excuse for their visit, as it had been for the sack of Bourne.

Perhaps, having lived there so long undisturbed, we had grown complacent. At any rate, Turfrida told me after, when a longship appeared from the direction of Borough, no-one paid much attention, expecting it to sail past. But a lad sitting on the bank to mend eel-traps watched it because such ships were rarely seen and when it turned straight for the hard where the reed-cutter's craft were drawn up, he shouted an alarm and ran to hide, having seen Norman knights on board.

It was harvest time: the settlement was deserted save for that boy, Edda, and Turfrida with our children. All the rest were busy in the little plots of rye and oats the Fen-folk grew wherever the ground was high enough and untainted by salt water. Weak still from her sickness, Aedgifu was sitting in the sun, sorting withies for the two women who wove baskets with the babe asleep on a rug beside them. Alerted by the boy's shout and the barking of the settlement dogs (an ill-bred assortment of curs which, owing to a diet of fish-scraps, were unusually fat and glossy), the women scrambled to their feet, the babe yowling in protest as Turfrida snatched her up. By then the ship had grounded.

Turfrida thrust the babe into Edda's arms and put her arms protectively around Aedgifu who had struggled to her feet and stood trembling as the Normans marched down a plank onto land. All wore mail and helms, the nose-pieces obscuring most of their faces so that they seemed barely human. Realizing the futility of running, Turfrida tried to comfort the terrified girl as best she could, and waited.

It was late afternoon when Martin and I returned. We had ridden far and fast that day and were weary. News of the murdrum fine had made the Fen-wolves uneasy. The arguments went back and forth: while no-one wanted to give up the fight, those with kin living as vassals worried what punishment might be inflicted upon them if slain Normans were found in their hundred. And something else which rankled with a few (of whom Acer was the most vociferous), was that so far we had not killed any of the hated landlords but only their knights and officers. In part, this was due to circumstance, many of these men being with the King, but after the first ambushes they travelled with so large a retinue of knights as to be untouchable. And I had seen what the Normans called punitive work on the borders of their own country: the massacre of every man, woman and child in a vill; the slaughter of livestock; the destruction of buildings and crops so that what had been prosperous farmland became waste. Such retribution had already been meted in the south upon those that resisted. I did not want it wreaked upon my people, my lands, in return for the slaying of men whom the Bastard would only replace with worse. Thus I argued that we should continue as we had begun, picking off sheriffs, tax-collectors and their escorts but sparing their lords until the full rebellion was in progress.

I was their leader: though they did not like it even Acer had to agree that our main purpose must be to keep the Normans out of the Brunneswald and Fens while we gathered our force. That we had already waited months for an empty summons and my nephews had forsaken our cause, none dared voice. There was no chance of a deciding fight until spring and the harvest looked to be a bad one: for now we must concentrate on gathering stores against the coming winter. To speak aloud our doubts seemed a betrayal of those who had already died at Norman hands.

With such matters my mind was occupied as we led the horses along a narrow path which wound between meres and alder clumps, a secret way through the marshes. We were within half a mile of the settlement when Swallow lifted her head and began to jog nervously. Martin said, 'There is smoke ahead.'

Even then we were slow to recognize danger. The smoke rose in a billowing white cloud yet we heard no shouts or screams and assumed the Fen-folk were burning off a patch of stubble as was their custom. We quietened the horses as best we could (the palfrey was quick to catch Swallow's fear), and went on. In places the ground rippled where we trod, a layer of matted vegetation concealing unfathomable mire. A curlew's call sounded from far away then, as if in answer, a child's shrill scream. And I ran, loosening Brain-biter in its sheath, my mind empty but for one thought: to reach the settlement. The voice was Aedgifu's.

The rising smoke had been seen by other eyes: the reed-cutters entered the open ground between huts and stacks at the same time as Martin and I. But while they paused to stare, I sprinted forward, letting go Swallow's reins and unsheathing my sword while a wordless howl of rage burst from my mouth.

It was too late. The ship was already beyond spear-range, being rowed swiftly upstream on the flood tide, not by Normans but fishermen and serfs from Borough pressed into service. Seeing me, the knights on board crowded to the stern and side of the vessel, causing it to heel dangerously; they waved their swords in mockery and yelled abuse. One, who from the glittering splendour of his arms and aloofness from the clamour, I took to be their leader, was attempting to fix a kind of dark ribbon to his lance. As I stood thigh-deep in the swirling water, panting with frustration, he straightened and turned, holding it aloft. It me took a moment to recognize Turfrida's hair: lest there should be any doubt, he shouted his men to silence then called: 'She will be mine when your head is stuck on a spike, outlaw!' His next words were lost in a burst of jeering laughter as the ship rounded the bend. It was my old foe, Ivo Taillebois. I called him to come back and fight me but they were gone.

I stood stunned by my impotence then the battle-focus, which had taken me blindly through the settlement, faded. I heard the ripple of the ship's wake, a child's sobbing, crackle of fire and the shouts of men; smelt smoke and a battle-ground stench. Cold fear clawed my belly. I turned, staggered out of the river, saw what they had done.

One of the reed-stacks was ablaze. A glance told me there was little chance of the fire spreading for those who had run from the fields were pulling the pile apart with pitchforks while others ran with pails of water to quench the flames. But as my eyes sought Turfrida and the children, they fixed upon what I had passed in my frenzy and vomit rose to scald my throat. Like some obscene standard or scorn-pole, the head of my war-horse, Tiw, was stuck on a staff which leaned drunkenly in the soft earth. His eye-sockets were bloody holes, his genitals had been stuffed into his gaping mouth, his entrails were heaped beneath. Flies buzzed and crawled over the glistening pile. A gore-trail led to the mutilated carcass in front of Edda's cot.

Swallow and the palfrey, terrified by the smoke, half-maddened by the stench of blood, were struggling to get away from Martin who was watching me with grave concern. In a voice that did not seem mine, I told him to take them away upwind. Afterwards I realized he would have done so before save that he wanted to be certain I would do nothing rash.

Turfrida and the crone were huddled together with the children between them and weakness flooded through me, seeing that all were alive. Then my wife raised her head and my heart lurched for her face was stark white and striped with blood from where they had hacked off her hair, cutting deep so that her scalp was cross-hatched with wounds.

Meeting my gaze, she let out a wordless cry and struggled to rise. The sword dropped from my grasp and I ran to hold her while Aedgifu clung to us.

Strange indeed is the way of Fate, the will of God. The rift that had grown between Turfrida and I since the night of Eadric's wake we had not the power to heal ourselves but through the cruelty of Ivo Taillebois it was breached at last. That night, as Martin and some of the reed-cutters cleared away Tiw's corpse (I tried not to heed the thud of axes into flesh, the splintering of bone), I took her in my arms and begged forgiveness for having been away when she most needed me.

'There is nothing to forgive,' she murmured, and her calmness was like a balm. 'They were too many. Had you been here, you would be dead. By God's grace what they planned for you they did to Tiw instead.' She paused and shuddered. 'I do not know if they expected to find us but they appeared so quickly – there was no time to run and hide. They caught me and tore away the children and they would have raped me then and maybe Aedgifu also, had Ivo Taillebois not seen and called a stop to it. But in return for our lives and to save the settlement being burned, he made me promise to be his wife after they kill you.' Her voice sank to a whisper and she pressed her forehead into the hollow of my shoulder. 'I should have defied them but Aedgifu was being held by one and they had laid Godgifu on the mud and the tide was rising: I wanted only that they should be spared. Aye, I would have lain willingly with any or all those bastards to save our daughters' lives.' She tried to pull away, face twisted in anguish but I held her firmly. 'What kind of wife is bought so easily? If they had raped me, my shame could be no less.'

'Hush, love.' I soothed her with voice and hands as I would have comforted Aedgifu after a nightmare and when she was quiet, led her to our pallet. We lay together, finding simple solace in our closeness and if ever there was a time I should have admitted the truth of my relationship with Ymma, it was then. But I was too afraid of shattering our new-found trust and thus kept my silence though I was to rue it bitterly.

We left the settlement at dawn next morning. Martin had seen that nothing remained of the stallion's carcass though the tight bellies of the dogs and cats testified to the fate of some of it. He confided long after that when he had come to return Brain-biter, he had found Turfrida and I asleep, limbs entwined and, not wishing to disturb us, kept watch alone.

With the discovery of the settlement, we knew the Normans would impose a heavy fine on the inhabitants, not least because they had harboured a proscribed outlaw. Our store of coin brought from Flanders had been increased by captured Norman geld and we paid our hosts richly, in part to compensate for the burnt reed-stack. At first Edda, the matriarch and their leader, refused to accept anything but when Turfrida pointed out patiently that the whole place and likely enough the marshland itself would be fired if the Normans were not paid, prudence triumphed over the old woman's pride. And there was a certain satisfaction to be gained from the knowledge that they were being given their own gold back again.

The loss of Tiw meant we had no choice but to travel on foot, loading all we could onto the backs of Swallow and the palfrey for the Fen-folk had no beasts of burden to lend, the river being their road. The safest course was to take Rahere's advice and go deeper into the fens but to live like a hunted otter, creeping from holt to holt whenever the hounds found my trail, was not in my nature. Instead, I resolved to join others of the gang in the Brunneswald.

Strangely, Turfrida seemed almost light-hearted that morning, as if the assault had cleared her mind of doubt or uncertainty. She talked long and earnestly with Edda and Aelgytha, who had decided to stay behind. Her strength and good sense had already made her a valued member of the reed-cutter's community and also, I think, she realized that a woman with three bairns in tow would only be a burden to us though she was wise enough not to say so. The sun's disc had just risen clear of the horizon when we turned our backs on river, stilted huts and reed-stacks, and took the winding path towards the old road and Laughton.

We gave the vill a wide berth and entered the forest close to the deserted saw-pit. Remembering the summer's day we had come here to collect wattle for our house, I felt a pang of nostalgia for it seemed to have happened in another, blessed, life. Turfrida, who had been walking a little behind with Godgifu cradled in her arms, moved forward and I saw that she was smiling wistfully beneath the cloth tied to cover her ravaged scalp. But ere I could speak, she shook her head as if to chide herself and walked on, eyes bent to the path.

When we reached Ermine Street, which slashes like a wound through the eastern margin of the Brunneswald, we paused. Martin was leading the palfrey with Aedgifu, still subdued by shock, clinging to the load. He handed the reins to Turfrida and clambered over the broken branches and other debris which now filled the ditch to see if the road was clear. Nothing stirred as far as the eye could see and we crossed hastily and followed a winding deer trail into the dense heart of the forest. As a precaution, Martin erased our tracks with a switch of broom for the ground was dry and dusty, then hurried after.

Acer was at the clearing's edge to meet us; unseen watchers must have reported our approach. His welcoming grin faded abruptly when I told him what had happened and he realized the significance of the horses' loads, Turfrida's bloody head-cloth, Aedgifu's unusual silence.

'God's curse upon them all,' he growled, lifting the child from the palfrey's back. 'The list of those who owe redress is getting long. Hereward: you can't let this pass.'

His voice was low but determined yet as he spoke he hugged Aedgifu who snuggled against him: despite his size and apparent fierceness, he was one of her favourites. At length she wriggled and he set her down and tousled her hair. Seeing some children from Bourne with whom she used to play, the child ran to join them.

'The Normans understand blood-feud,' I replied grimly. 'Ivo Taillebois will pay for this evil with his life. He knows me well enough to accept the challenge: there are old scores to settle between us.'

Acer grinned but Turfrida looked at me intently and I read a kind of pitying forbearance in her expression.

'Ivo Taillebois and his kind will not meet you on equal terms,' she said. 'You are an outlaw. They will hunt you like a beast and, should they catch you, they will hang you from a tree as a felon. If you challenge them, they will refuse.'

'What would you have me do then?' I asked. 'If this shame is not avenged it will be thought I am afraid.'

'Remove one Norman baron and another will take his place,' Turfrida insisted. 'You are leader of the Fen-wolves: you must use a wolf's cunning. Capture enough grain to see us and our friends through the winter and it will be a festering hurt to Norman pride that despite all the humiliations they have heaped upon us, we will not go away. And then, next year, we shall throw off their yoke forever.'

Acer and I stared at her in astonishment for it was as if she were privy to all that we had debated and argued over for weeks. Seeing our expressions, she gave a wry smile. 'Do not underestimate me because I am a woman,' she said. 'My hatred of them and what they are doing is no less than yours and may be all the more bitter because I cannot take up arms and must have the one I love best avenge me and risk death in the doing of it. But know this: if the day comes when Ivo Taillebois claims me as his wife, I shall seek sanctuary at Croyland or else take my own life before he has me to bed.'

She spoke with such fervour, my throat constricted from pride and love and I could not answer. Acer muttered, 'They will have to slay me and every other Fen-wolf first,' then looked across the clearing where the children were rounding up piglets for no other reason than sheer bedevilment. Squeals and shouts echoed between the trees as the frightened beasts darted here and there, chased remorselessly by the pack of children among which was Aedgifu, noisy and excited as the rest. Swallow and the palfrey shifted nervously as the tumult came closer. Though they were used to children and beasts I think the absence of the stallion unsettled them. As I calmed them, Acer cleared his throat. 'Seeing as you've joined us, we'd better find you somewhere fit to live.'

We built a humpy away from the others in a little hollow. It was surrounded by green-stained outcroppings of flinty chalk and a small spring-fed pool lay in the centre, from which water flowed to supply the whole camp. Hollies grew there and we sited our shelter in the cover of the tallest, whose branches hung to the ground. Beyond the hollow stood great beech trees and the ground there was thick with mast though around the spring thin grass grew.

When it was finished, the humpy had room for the four of us to lie down in comfort though it was not high enough for a man to stand upright. We made our hearth just in front of the opening so that some warmth would reach inside. Martin, who insisted on staying near, built a hide-covered lean-to such as hunters use under another holly. At a quick glance neither shelter was visible from outside the hollow.

In a way it was a blessing that we had only two horses to provide for. Feed in the forest was scarce and we could not turn them loose. Swallow, I knew, would find her way back to the rich pasture at Laughton. The animals owned by other fugitives (amongst them the *destriers* I had given to the Fen-wolves), were penned together in an adjacent clearing but we built another because the mare would not tolerate close confinement with strange horses. Wuleric promised to help look after them. Apart from Martin and me, he was the only man Swallow would allow to handle her.

By now, the core of the gang was living in the forest and many were eager to join us, lusting for vengeance against those who had dispossessed them and wanting to share our luck, for it was widely known that so far not one of us had been slain. To become Fen-wolves, such men had to prove themselves and as I did not know them, I formed them into separate bands, led by an established member of the gang and answerable to me. Any man who complained he did not need nurse-maiding or took umbrage at being treated the same as those he took to be inferior in wealth or status learned quickly that here there was no difference between former thegns and ploughboys. We had captured mail and arms to go round twice over and Acer and I made sure that any man or boy fit to bear a weapon was taught to use it well, whatever his history. At times the woodland rang so loud with the clang of blade against blade, the dull thud of javelin into target, I thought some enemy passing along Ermine Street must hear and we would be discovered. But weeks passed and, if anything, there seemed fewer Normans on the road than before. Their huntsmen we did not fear for they soon learned that if they ventured into the Brunneswald they would become the quarry of hunters fiercer and more skilled in woodcraft. In any case, after two years of feeding a growing horde of refugees, the forest was scarce in game of any kind.

Until our arrival, the fugitives had been living from day to day, the women occupied with feeding and caring for their families while the men dreamt of slaying Normans as they felled trees for fuel. Yet so often since the defeat at Hastings had hope been extinguished when erstwhile leaders capitulated, sullen resentment had replaced enthusiasm. When I spoke of a planned rising in the north I do not think many believed the next so-called rebellion would be any more successful than the last. They did not look so far ahead - as Turfrida was fond of pointing out, there was the winter to get through first - but that thought kept me from despair. Aye, that and an undying hatred which went far deeper. I had not forgotten Brand's role in the sack of Bourne nor how swiftly he had collaborated with the enemy. It was no coincidence that many of the tithe-wagons we ambushed from estates as far apart as Woolsthorpe and Thurlsby were bound for Borough Abbey.

Tithes were due all on one day and because the harvest was so late, most of the wagons were unguarded. Those driving the carts were our own people. Some, to whom fear had become a habit, grovelled shamelessly as we robbed them and from disgust and pity we let them go, bidding them tell their masters that the rightful owners had taken their due. Others handed the grain over almost with relief. Whilst they dared not openly defy their overlords, to have any portion of the harvest kept from Norman mouths and the church (which was much despised for its weakness), seemed almost an act of rebellion in itself. To save them being accused and punished, Martin gave receipts for what we had taken, written in English and signed in King Edgar's name.

This seemed a good idea until Ogier the Breton returned from campaigning with the Bastard and decreed that anyone found in possession of such a slip would be charged with sedition. Having no wish to increase the tally of innocent dead, we desisted and Ogier demanded a second tithe from the gleanings which were all the villans had to keep them through the winter. Even if the serfs had not already hidden their portion, the demand could not have been met but it gave the Normans another excuse to dole out beatings, rapes and burnings as the mood took them. Some of their victims sought sanctuary with us but most simply rebuilt their hovels and stayed on, knowing no other life than to work the land. Like a cur which fawns upon the hand that beats it they had adopted a kind of cringing servility as their strategy for survival. Turfrida urged me to pity them, saying that the weak could do no more than bear what was beyond their power to change but I told her roughly that if she believed that, we were already defeated. At any rate, we had taken enough grain to see us through the winter, though the number in camp had swelled to more than two hundred. Now all we could do was pray for a mild season without pestilence and that the Normans would not discover us.

The ambushes by which we gained the tithes were not without cost. None of the Fen-wolves was slain but one of the twins, Outi, lost a hand and was lucky to keep his life when the band he was with, returning along an open lane laden with bags of grain, met a group of ten knights including Frederick de Warenne. Torn between abandoning their plunder and fighting, the outlaws hesitated and that was their undoing. Two only escaped, Outi helping a young lad scramble away in the confusion of trampling hooves, hacking swords, the noise and chaos of slaughter. All the others were killed, news I heard with some relief, none having been taken alive to betray us. Outi was pursued by a single horseman who struck as he climbed out of the roadside ditch then, as he stared at the spouting stump where his hand had been, laughed and turned his horse to join the massacre. If the lad, Hakon, had not returned to bind the wound, Outi would likely have bled to death: they staggered into camp as we were about to send out searchers.

The annihilation of almost a whole band shocked us. Next morning I had all the fighters gather and made Outi, weak still from loss of blood, relate his tale. When he had finished, I told them sternly that gold and grain could be got elsewhere but lives were not so easily replaced.

'This is our land,' I concluded. 'It bred us: it is in our bones and our blood. Use it wisely and it will shelter and protect us for we cannot win this fight by force alone. Be wary, never cease watching for the enemy, keep to the woods and fens for there they cannot use their numbers or their horses to full effect. And henceforth any man caught in the open is undeserving of vengeance for to die thus is a mark of folly, not valour. Mourn the fallen but do not follow them. We have greater work ahead.'

They stared as a drowning man might look at a spar floating just within his grasp and many thanked me as I walked back to Turfrida and the children though I had spoken only what needed to be said. Yet in truth I was gnawed by anxiety, fearing that all our efforts were of no more significance than the sting of a gadfly to a bull. So far we had survived because no great force had been sent against us but the time comes when an irritated beast goes to the scratching post. Yet to admit such thoughts, even to Turfrida or Martin, would have achieved nothing; to own to doubt affronted to my pride. Nor was it in me to send others into danger without sharing it myself. Fighting I was born to and though I knew that one day I might be slain, I believed also that the day of my death was fated and was therefore unafraid.

Turfrida, wise to my moods, maybe understood more than she said for as her scalp mended, she became once more the calm and loving presence that had steadied me in the past. She did not speak again of Ymma and the babe nor of the attack that had driven us to this life in the Brunneswald but instead made of the humpy a home I was glad to return to at day's end. And such was her natural assurance, it was not long before she was called on to mediate in the petty quarrels that erupted from time to time between the camp women, becoming in her turn a kind of leader, much esteemed for her even-handedness and sagacity.

The leaves turned and the days began to shorten. For a while we suspended our attacks, letting the Normans think us dismayed by the slaughter of Outi's band but we were not idle for it was time to gather the harvest of the woods. Before, such work had been left to the women and children but it was not deemed safe to let them wander without armed escort. Desperate men of all kinds had been forced into the forest and the brigands that had always lurked there had not been ousted by Norman rule. These were such as knew no loyalty other than to their own rapacious natures and though at first a few tried to join us, by their deeds they were soon known and swiftly dealt with. For rape they were castrated and dragged deep into the forest to bleed their lives away; for theft they lost their hands and were driven out; for slaying, unless blood-feud could be proven, they were hanged. Once word spread that the Fen-wolves meted their own justice, such men avoided us but they skulked still within the forest bounds, having nowhere else to go. A woman alone was easy prey and though she might possess nothing more than the clothes she stood up in and a leather or wicker basket, that would not save her. Men reduced to wearing animal skins and rags would kill for a threadbare cloak and think nothing of it.

Those autumn days when Martin and I went with Turfrida and the children to forage for nuts, berries and fungi seemed after like a dream of happiness. The quiet of the deep woods wrapped us round and Aedgifu's clear laughter rang out like the call of a wild bird. It was as if we had returned to a world without the Normans. I lay upon my back, staring at the sky through interlaced branches, listening to the drone of insects and the chatter of the women and children as they worked, or else vied with Martin to climb high into the beech trees and shake down mast on which the pigs feasted. (That year we were not so desperate as to collect it for ourselves). Returning to our home amongst the hollies with Aedgifu sitting on my shoulders, for a while I could forget my cares. But some days we came across stark evidence of the truth: woodcutter's huts overtaken by bramble and bracken because they had all died at Fulford Gate; once the half-decayed corpse of a young woman, her slit throat gaping like a maw, and though we hurried past such reminders, we could not ignore them.

In the months since their capitulation at Warwick, we had heard nothing of my nephews save that their men were occupied in attacking Normans throughout north and west Mercia as we were doing in the east. A distant kinsman of Acer's from north of Grantham brought news that Edwin and Morcar intended to overwinter in Scotland at King Malcolm's court along with the atheling, Earl Waltheof, Gospatrick and Marleswein. Hearing this, I was tempted to join them, for they would plan the rising. But I could not ask Turfrida to travel so far through occupied land in winter, nor leave her alone so soon after Aedgifu's illness and Ivo Taillebois' attack. Nor was I prepared to abandon my comrades. Thus I returned a message stating that I and my men would be ready to fight when the time came and said nothing of it to Turfrida and the others. All over England the dispossessed did the same, then settled down in hide shelters or booths made of stones and cloth to wait out the winter while in the burghs, the castle-building continued relentlessly.

Geese winged their way from the north, filling the air with their haunting cries and we looked up through bare branches to see them wheel overhead, heading for the safety of the marshes. The sight and sound of them rekindled my restlessness: wild wanderers of land and ocean, they symbolised a kind of freedom I could not attain. Even news that Ogier the Breton and Ivo Taillebois had returned to Normandy, supposedly for fear of me, did not ease my frustration. Indeed the tales that had begun to circulate concerning the exploits of the Fen-wolves (exaggerated beyond belief by despairing folk eager for heroes in whom to put their faith), only increased my bitterness. The insult to me and those of my blood by the slaying of my war-horse and the despoilation of my wife had yet to be avenged and the hanging of Cole One-Hand also weighed heavily upon me, the perpetrators of these deeds being beyond my reach. Since the rousing of the Fen-wolves I had lost count of the Normans we had killed and maimed yet they had been swiftly replaced, often by men more brutal and uncompromising than the first. And being unwilling to venture into the fastness of the Brunneswald to confront us, the Normans punished the ordinary folk, demanding redress whether or not murdrum could be proved, and this also disturbed me for a man whose family is starving may be easily bought.

Mindful of how my dark mood had nearly estranged us in the past, this time I sought to assuage it by hunting, taking only a bow and dagger with a couple of deerhounds as my companions. The dogs had attached themselves to us from the motley pack which roamed the camp because Aedgifu fed them precious scraps from her trencher. Turfrida and I indulged her in this for she still suffered occasional nightmares about the killing of Tiw and it was good to have the hounds there as watchdogs. Lean and shaggy, they shadowed me as soon as they saw me prepare to set out alone, knowing there was the chance of fresh meat ahead. Yet I was more than likely to return empty-handed, deer having become scarce and warier than usual. As winter deepened, it was the sheep and cattle of estates bordering the forest which became my targets though I was careful to leave the bloody hides behind so that wolves, not serfs, might be blamed. But though my return after a successful hunt was greeted with relief, often as I knelt to butcher my kill I felt a kind of dull resentment rather than satisfaction, wishing that my enemies lay thus beneath my dagger instead of a young doe or heifer that should have been left to bear her young. And sometimes, when I handed the stained bag of meat and bones to Turfrida, I had to grit my teeth and turn away, unable to bear her gratitude when it was I that had forced her to a fugitive's life.

Thus the days passed and an uneasy quiet lay over the countryside as cold, damp and hunger became more immediate foes than the Normans. Common maladies turned deadly in folk weakened by lack of food and many were the deaths from lung-fever though by compare with others I remembered, that winter was not especially severe. Huddled with Turfrida and the children in our shelter, eyes stinging from the smoke, I thought regretfully of Toli's Hall burning as sleet drummed upon the skins that made our roof, and told myself we were fortunate compared with most. But the truth was we had no choice but to endure and in this we were no different to the poorest serf save that we were not forced to work when the ground was frozen hard as iron and the east wind chilled to the bone, but could take our ease by the fire.

We feasted when Outi, who since the loss of his hand seemed possessed by a kind of fey recklessness, organised a band of like-minded lads to raid the store at Bourne after the camp's supply of ale ran out. By luck they met no opposition, for most of his knights had gone with Ogier to Normandy yet as we celebrated their success, it made me feel old that I had not gone myself.

'Don't take it so hard,' Martin told me as I sat brooding by the great blaze in the centre of the clearing, round which an assortment of children danced to the beat of an improvised drum. 'We can't afford to risk good men on wild ventures. Let the youngsters have their fun. If they don't, there'll be trouble in camp: they can't sit idle.'

'Ach, maybe.' In my heart, I knew he was right. My own restlessness was proof enough and Martin himself had been on several of his mysterious expeditions into the Fenland since we had taken to the woods. And so I did not criticise but kept silence and perhaps that was enough. The talk that night was all of the fighting which lay ahead and the cruel, uncompromising nature of our enemies and that brought home the reality of our situation. Before setting out thereafter, Outi and the others told Acer or I what they planned.

It snowed heavily around Yule and even the children soon tired of the novelty as the ground turned to a muddy slush and everything became sodden. The horses, which up till now had withstood the privation and cold well, began to suffer. Swallow again proved hardiest but two of the destriers we slaughtered ere they sickened and fresh horsemeat made a welcome addition to our diet. The hides we gave to some newcomers from the north who possessed nothing more than the clothes they wore and a rusty sword.

These, a gaunt woman whose staring eyes made me wonder what horrors she had endured, with a lad of barely thirteen summers and a little girl of Aedgifu's age, arrived during a blizzard, having fled into the forest from a band of Normans travelling along Ermine Street. They had been advised to seek sanctuary at Borough by Athelwine, Bishop of Durham, who was brother to our own Bishop Athelric. I wondered why they had not gone further north since it was Norman rule they wished to escape but the boy told me blood-feud had closed Bernicia to them. Starving and half-frozen, Turfrida took them into her care and we made them welcome, for having discovered our refuge they could not be allowed to leave lest they betray us. They were, anyway, in no fit state to travel on.

The woman, whose name was Gerd, told us that the King's replacement for Gospatrick, Robert de Commines, was hated even more than Tostig God-wineson had been. Having harried the folk of York for every piece of gold and silver they possessed (and, the lad, Erik, added, anything else of value), De Commines had gone to Durham with five hundred knights, for that burgh had refused to pay the exorbitant geld levied upon it. There was nothing new in the tale of brutal pillage, dispossession and burning which followed save that this had happened not in the already subjugated south but well north of the old Danegeld. The northern eorldoms had long acted almost as vassal kingdoms with respect to whoever ruled in Winchester or London and while Yorkshire had lost thousands against Hardrada and Tostig, Bernicia could still muster a substantial force, all fiercely protective of their independence. Blood-feud and ancient rivalries had long prevented an alliance (Morcar had been chosen as Tostig's replacement in Northumbria simply because he was of a powerful kin remote from the tangled politics of the north), but now, Gerd said, men who would formerly have died rather than be seen in each other's company were plotting together, having realized that to stand alone against the Normans was to invite defeat. Bishop Athelwine, it was said, warned De Commines that his cruelty would have dire consequences but his words went unheeded.

At first I wondered that she should be so well informed but when, in the warmth of our humpy, she shed the layers of ragged cloth wrapped about her head and hands, it was clear she was of highborn blood for her skin was pale and smooth, her speech that of an educated woman. Although wary at first, when they saw the shelter that had been made for them and realized they had not fallen among brigands who would rob, then sell them as slaves into Scotland or Ireland, they relaxed their guard. Their lands in Northumbria had been seized by a neighbour following her husband's death at Fulford Gate and they had been sheltered by kin in York until these were dispossessed by the Normans. Although they would not disclose their lineage for fear of enemies, the boy let slip they were of Siward Beorn's kin. They thought Siward had gone to Scotland to join the atheling at King Malcolm's court.

Hearing this, I regretted not going north at the start of winter, for it seemed certain that the centre of the rising would be at York. My eagerness for news sent me out alone, ostensibly to bring back meat though my true intent was to intercept folk going south along Ermine Street who would exchange tidings for a piece of bannock and a draught of ale. Thus from such diverse sources as monks travelling from York to Borough or Ely; peddlers on their way to buy pots from Stamford; Norman messengers to whom I called in their own language, purporting to be a Flemish comrade, I learned that in the north events were moving swiftly from local insurrection to wider revolt. Early in the New Year the people of Durham, sick of the cruelties imposed upon them, besieged the bishop's house where Robert de Commines and his cronies were carousing, fired it and burned them all to death. Bishop Athelwine himself was not inside: it was rumoured he had told the rebel leaders when to strike. Whatever his personal involvement, that fire acted as the signal for outright rebellion not only in Northumbria but all England north of Watling Street. The next news was that Edgar Atheling along with Gospatrick, Marleswein and a force of thousands, was marching south to York.

This was the news we had anticipated and a ripple of excitement ran through the men in camp while the women's faces took on a guarded, closed look. The long months of waiting seemed suddenly condensed: it might have been two weeks since the defeat at Hastings instead of more than two years. Snow was still thick on the ground but though we knew the journey north would be slow, none of us cared. Any hardship we faced on the road was nothing compared with the frustration and tedium we had already endured. Had it been spring or summer, I would have gone by sea but at this time of year the risk of shipwreck was too great.

Turfrida knew better than to beg me not to go but her displeasure was clear from her quietness and increasing coolness towards Gerd and Erik (now nick-named Winter). Wide-eyed with a kind of half-fearful adulation, the lad hung around Acer and I, his sword strapped across his back.

'Better watch him or he'll be halfway to York before you blink,' Martin remarked one day when Erik had shadowed us to a moot of the Fen-wolves, hiding unnoticed behind a tree until Siward the Red went there to piss. The boy was trembling with fear when he was brought before me but once left alone, stood straight and looked me in the eye with a kind of reckless defiance. Acer, laughing, said he should be tried as a spy but when I asked why he had followed us, the lad answered that he was bound to avenge his mother's honour and regain the estates lost after his father's death. Recognizing something of my boyhood self in his pain and stubbornness, I made him my armour-bearer rather than send him back to camp. I had long decided that if I had to go north I would leave Turfrida and the children in Martin's care.

Our weapons and gear were ready; the women baked the hard bread that was the staple of the fyrd while we collected all the smoked and dried meat we could find. Then, the day before we were due to set off, Rahere arrived, laden with sticks of eels, his bow and light javelins slung across his back.

'News travels fast across the water,' he told me. 'The rebel force has reached York; their ships guard the Humber from the Mouth to the city. The Bastard won't stand by for long. Durham has already acclaimed Edgar Atheling as king.'

Looking into the Fen-man's face, the mocking challenge of his gaze, I felt suddenly that clarity which comes when fate takes hold and one must go with it or lose one's path. As if a voice had spoken it aloud, I knew we must delay no longer. I glanced past Rahere to where the Fen-wolves stood all around though I had not summoned them. They were watching me expectantly, save Martin who looked pointedly away.

'Then we shall leave now,' I said and a murmur arose, a breath of excited anticipation. 'But you, Rahere, I would have stay. If there is trouble, the women and children must be led to safety in the Fens.'

In the corner of my eye I saw Martin bow his head while the others ran to gather their gear and make their farewells. Rahere crouched to uncut the eels. I clapped my friend and servant on the back in an effort to cheer him up (I knew he was angry with me for leaving him behind), then went to find Turfrida.

'I'll be back before Easter,' I promised her. 'By then we'll have driven the Bastard south of Watling Street: this will be a free land again. And you will be safe here. Not all the Fen-wolves are coming north and Martin will look after you.'

It was a cool, grey day; fine drizzle made the trees drip and smoke from the cooking fires hung thick in the air. By that dismal light my wife looked care-worn and weary, hollow-cheeked with red-rimmed eyes. Godgifu began to cry from the hammock where she lay bundled in furs but Turfrida merely cast her an exasperated glance then followed as I slung the bundles containing my weapons and food on my shoulder and walked towards the horse-pen.

Wuleric was waiting there with Swallow and the bay destrier I now rode in place of Tiw already harnessed but seeing Turfrida's taut features, he made some excuse and left.

'There is no need for you to go,' Turfrida said in a low, strained voice as I tied the javelins to the war-horse's saddle. 'If you are right, the fight will come here soon enough. Why can't Acer lead the men north? It was not for this that I stayed with you.'

Focused on the task ahead, I did not heed the warning implicit in these words.

'I have waited long enough,' I replied. 'Would you have it said that Here-ward ignored the atheling's call and skulked in the woods instead of fighting? This is the beginning of the war that will rid us of the Normans once and for all: every fighter of renown is needed at York. I must go.'

Bitter reproach was in her glance yet she did not plead or berate me, simply bent her head. The hood of her cloak slipped back to reveal the scars cross-hatching her scalp beneath the growing hair and love and pity wrenched my heart. I reached out to touch her face but she tilted her head so that my hand fell away.

'You and the children will be safe here,' I insisted softly. 'Have faith, love.'

'And who will care for you or bring tidings of your death?' she asked and her eyes were hard yet bright with unshed tears. 'That boy?' She pointed scornfully at Erik who stood uncertainly beneath the dripping hollies. 'And I have heard no summons bidding you go. You are leaving because you are tired of all this' – she swept her arm to indicate the squalid camp – 'because in your heart you know you cannot beat the likes of De Warenne and Taillebois with a few ragged brigands!'

I stared and something seemed to jar deep within so that I could have tipped my head back and howled in grief I did not then understand. But only for the space of a single heartbeat did that feeling last before anger took me, a red molten surge that swept away thought and reason.

'Your tongue outstrips your mind, woman!' I raised my arm and struck her. The sound of the blow sounded clear across the camp. Turfrida's head snapped round with the force of it, her body span and she fell to her hands and knees just as Aedgifu ran up the slope. She stopped in her tracks as Turfrida spat out a broken tooth and slowly raised her head. Blood drooled from her mouth and split lip, a red welt had already sprung across her cheek. Her eyes were dark, the pupils wide with shock but gradually the grey returned. Aedgifu let out a shrill scream and flung herself at her mother, clinging as if the world was about to end. Cold to the very core, I watched as my wife wiped her bleeding mouth with her sleeve and sat back on her heels, gathering the sobbing child into her arms. Two pairs of eyes stared at me, one wide with fearful bewilderment, the other stone-like, unreadable.

'Turfrida – .' The name died on my lips. I stood torn between the desire to kneel and take them in my arms, begging forgiveness, and the lingering remnant of my anger. And then, knowing how she would rue her bitterness should I be wounded or slain, I turned and walked away. Turfrida made no sound but Aedgifu's muffled sobs and Godgifu's cries, which had risen to heart-rending shrieks, rang in my ears. When I reached the horses, the babe fell abruptly silent.

Young Erik averted his gaze as I led Swallow and the *destrier* out of the pen. I ignored him but Martin stood a little way down the slope, the tall figure of Rahere at his shoulder. A faintly sardonic smile twisted the Fen-man's lips but my servant's face was stricken. He looked past me to where Turfrida was tending the children.

'For God's sake, Hereward.' Martin stepped forward to block me. 'If you leave like this and ill befalls them, you'll never forgive yourself. Go to her now, before it's too late.'

'I warned you not to meddle between us.' I pushed past, the horses jibbing as they sensed my mood and when Martin caught hold my shoulder to stay me, dropped the reins and spun to face him, drawing my dagger in the same movement.

'Wait!' With a movement sudden and precise as a heron's the Fen-man caught the wrist of my dagger hand, his grip hard and immovable as iron. For an instant I strained against him, then Martin said urgently, 'Hereward, I will not fight you!' and something in his tone, which was both uncompromising and passionate, brought me back to myself.

It was like awakening from a fever-dream. The wood and leather of the dagger-hilt felt unreal to my hand. I sheathed it as Rahere let go and stepped away but Martin did not move. He jerked his head towards the hollow, saying quietly 'Go to them. I'll see to the rest.'

Turning, I saw my wife standing before the dark, dripping hollies. Smoke from our hearth-fire hung in the air around her. Godgifu was cradled in her arms, Aedgifu clung to her tunic: they stared back unblinkingly. Turfrida's face, swollen and bloody, betrayed nothing of her feelings. She was waiting to see what I would do but the child's visage was white and rigid with hate. Her gaze struck like a spearthrust. There was a challenge there I could not meet.

I stared back, then turned on my heel and walked to where Wuleric stood with the horses. In silence he handed me Swallow's reins and I swung into the saddle and rode away between the trees without a backward glance. Turfrida had insulted my honour: she understood my nature well enough to forgive a single blow struck in a moment of blind anger, such was my belief as I halted the mare where the Fen-wolves had gathered, shields, weapons and bags of food slung across their backs. The women stood to watch our departure with sullen resignation, children pressed close, but Turfrida was not there. All will be well, I told myself. On my return this will be forgotten in the joy of victory, that we have come into our own again. But what is done cannot be undone.

Part 2: The Last Stronghold

1. The Fight for York

It took more than a fortnight to reach York, forced as we were to use little-known tracks, keeping to the woods where we could, hurrying as much as the short days, sodden ground and our weariness allowed. We had only five horses of which two were loaded with as much gear and supplies as they could bear without breaking down; the others were used to scout ahead. Since Swallow would allow only me on her back, I rode guard on our line, eighty men in all, doughtiest fighters from the camp including the core of the Fen-wolves.

The countryside seemed ominously quiet although this may have been due to the foul weather. Of Normans we saw few and they did not see us as they rode by on well-fed *destriers* in groups of five or more. We resisted the temptation to attack for this was unfamiliar country and it was not our intention to alert our enemies to the force gathering in the north. Yet our anger and hatred smouldered for signs of the occupation were everywhere: decayed corpses hanging from trees; clusters of stick and mud hovels (which were all the villans were allowed), beside the burned ruins of what had been prosperous settlements while half a mile distant a Norman *donjon* would be stuck like a carbuncle upon once green land. We avoided such places when we could but sometimes serfs toiling in the wet fields would pause and stare towards us with a kind of unthinking curiosity, as if even the ability to fear had been bludgeoned from them. Often so plastered with mud was their skin, hair and clothing, they seemed hardly human but rather creatures fashioned from clay, dumb, unreasoning, knowing only servitude.

We approached York by the same road Martin and I had travelled with the wounded Eadric. At the Selby river crossing Swallow grew nervous and I warned the men to be on their guard, fearing an ambush. There was indeed an armed band lurking in the trees but they were Marleswein's men from north Lincolnshire. When I told them who we were, they bade us hurry on to York. From them we heard that the city had pledged allegiance to the Atheling and proclaimed him King despite the protestations of Archbishop Aldred but the castle itself was still in Norman hands. All Northumbria was in revolt but the leaders of the rebellion were waiting for Sweyn's ship-force from Denmark before moving south. After months of negotiation, the Danish King had finally pledged his support in return for gold.

(Hearing this, I felt the stirring of a doubt that was to deepen as the days passed. A man who sells himself to one side in war may be bought as easily by the other: I had not forgotten Thorfin's cynicism. But I told myself that if the whole of England rose at once, we could defeat the usurpers without help and forced my misgivings aside.)

After this news, even the bitter wind blowing across the low hills and boggy floodplains could not quell the mens' excitement. Their boasting and laughter rose above the rush of the gale through dead grass and sedge, its moan through clumps of trees whose bare branches tossed against an iron-grey sky. The shipwrights of Scotland and Northumbria had not been idle this past year. When we passed Riccall, the masts of at least forty warships were visible and Acer remarked that they would do to carry the defeated Normans back home. But when we came to where the road rises above the flat marsh and dyke, the bend in the river at Fulford Gate, a more sombre mood fell. All the Fen-wolves and most of the others had kin or friends who had died there. Only a few, like Acer, had survived the carnage.

Whether from lack of labour or poor leadership following Harold Godwineson's death I know not but the corpses heaped upon the battlefield had never been buried or burned but simply left to rot. After two and a half years, most were reduced to skeletons on which the skin seemed to have melted into shrunken rags; tufts of hair flapped in the wind from grinning and cloven skulls. Some of the piles were higher than I am tall though scavengers had been hard at work. Scattered bones littered the fields and marsh and even along the road white fragments stuck out from grass clumps. The skull of a horse stared emptily from where it had been flung into a hedge.

Erik and Wuleric, neither of whom had experienced war, stared at the heaps in horror: the magnitude of the slaughter was evident from the sheer mass of bones. Gamal Longbow, who had lost two brothers with Eadric's levy, made his way to where Acer and I rode at the head of the column.

'Did no-one tend them?' he asked incredulously. 'Is everyone here?'

'Ulfkil of Croyland told me once that any ground is sacred where folk have wept and called for God's help,' I said. 'And believe me, enough blood and tears have sunk into these fields to consecrate them for a thousand years. The dead are dead, Gamal.'

He shook his head disbelievingly and looked again across the marsh, half-flooded by winter rains. 'So many,' he muttered then bit his lip and walked on in silence, head bowed. I thought of those fields as I had first seen them, the stench and glutted packs of crows, and was sickened by the waste of it, all those thousands who had died for nothing because, in the end, theirs had not been the fight that mattered.

'Don't worry about them, lad.' Acer reached down from the height of his *destrier* to squeeze the young man's shoulder. 'They're past caring what happens. It's the living need our help.'

Veiled by driving rain, the walled city looked drear and forbidding and the gates were shut. The guards watched suspiciously as we approached for we all wore mail and helms of Norman make but when it became clear who we were, they welcomed us. From them we learned that Richard FitzRichard, castellan of York, and the Sheriff, William Malet (a name I recalled from Flanders), were trapped in the castle along with all the Normans that had escaped the rebels sweeping south from Durham. Edgar atheling was in the city, awaiting Bishop Aldred's approval to make him King. When I asked after my nephews, the guard knew nothing of them.

Those first days in York a kind of intoxicating anticipation affected us all, fighters and townsfolk alike. Though Aldred stubbornly refused to acclaim Edgar, it was the Witan that chose and made kings: when Edwin and Morcar arrived, the Archbishop would be over-ruled. In our minds we had a true King again; the tenuous Norman foothold in Northumbria had been removed; York, capital of the North, was in our hands, and it was inevitable that hunger would end the siege. Then we would stick the heads of FitzRichard and Malet over the city gate and raze the hated castle, symbol of oppression, to the ground.

Meantime, we trained our men in the flat pastures outside the east gate, kept guard on castle and city or went out to scour the countryside for food. With thousands already gathered and more arriving every day, supplies in the city were growing scarce. For amusement we taunted the besieged, yelling abuse and flinging refuse and ordure over the castle gate though to do so was not without risk: crossbowmen were stationed there. The Normans stared down in contemptuous silence for the most part: guessing they did not understand our speech, I taught my men (and they swiftly passed on to others), the insults in our enemies' accursed tongue I thought would strike deepest. After that the Normans became angrier and some shouted back, boasting that they had food enough to last a year while for water, God would provide all that was required.

This much was true: in the first weeks we were there, it rained almost every day. The Ouse burst its banks and the hovels closest to the river were washed away but no-one drowned. This was where the poorest inhabitants of the city lived and it seemed that the destruction of their homes by flooding was almost an annual event, for they simply took their sodden possessions to higher ground and waited for the waters to drop.

My comrades and I were fortunate in having arrived early enough to be accommodated within the city walls. As more arrived, some singly, others in bands of ten or more led by a thegn, occasionally a lesser eorl or dispossessed ealdorman with upwards of fifty, they were forced to camp outside. All avoided the southern side, fearful of the unhallowed dead, but the land before the other gates was soon crowded with makeshift shelters. Horses and pack-beasts grazed the surrounding pastures but though numbering hundreds, these gave little clue as to the size of the fighting force mustered, most such animals having been forfeited to the Normans.

Mindful of the counsel I had given in London, I was wary of the Atheling while Aldred, I suspect, deliberately avoided me. He now preached moderation and peace as if the Normans had already conquered the whole of England, making resistance futile. Acer and I, with Erik as our servant, were quartered in a house close to the abbey, thus I saw the Archbishop often as he made his way from his devotions at the Minster to the great Hall where Edgar held court. Most of the townsfolk, including our hosts, a bustling widow with six children and her ancient father, spoke of the Church with contempt almost as bitter as their hatred of the Normans, perceiving its refusal to acclaim the Atheling as weakness.

So diminished did Aldred appear, shuffling through the crowded street with one hand on a novice's shoulder for support, I felt a kind of grudging pity for I think conflicting loyalties to God, pope and king weighed heavily upon him. And yet despite the pressures which must have been exerted by Marleswein and Waltheof, to say nothing of Edgar himself, the old man steadfastly refused to change his mind. Perhaps he thought that if his obstinacy cost him his life, at least martyrdom would bring him peace.

The atmosphere of excitement was heightened when the castellan attempted to escape. A hail of arrows and cross-bow bolts from within the castle warned that something was nigh, that and the sound of trampling hoofbeats. Even as the watchers shouted an alarm, the gates swung open and a force of maybe fifty mounted knights charged out onto the bridge, the gates clanging shut as soon as the last *destrier's* tail was clear. But though the guard on the bridge was swiftly overwhelmed, being lightly armed and on foot, the press of folk at the other end was so thick that the horses were brought quickly to a standstill.

I was on the city wall talking with one of Waltheof's men, a thegn of some renown called Arnkell, when the sounds of fighting reached us: desperate shouting, clash of iron against iron, a horse's squeal. We glanced at one another then Arnkell said briefly, 'The castle' and we ran, unsheathing our swords as we went. I let him lead for he knew the city better than I; young Erik, who shadowed me wherever I went, was close on our heels. The noise increased as we drew closer, men's screams mixed with horses', and the dull thud of metal hacking into flesh.

So many folk were jostling to join in, the fight was almost over by the time we reached the bridge. The air reeked of blood and burst entrails; the mud underfoot squelched with gore. One Norman was still mounted: he kept his horse trampling in a tight circle and swung his sword to clear its path but the animal became half-mad with terror as the clamour of the crowd rose to a baying frenzy. Erik was carrying a spear, symbol of his status as my armour-bearer (or so he believed): I snatched and flung it as a gap opened. The beast crashed to the ground with a squeal of pain and fear and the mass of people closed over horse and rider like a wave. They jerked and shrieked as assorted weapons slashed and stabbed into them.

A strange silence fell when they were dead, then one or two of the townsfolk began to laugh and talk hysterically, as if they could not believe what they had done. As the crowd dispersed, many of them bloodied to knees and elbows, we saw the full extent of the massacre: slaughtered men and horses lay tangled together and amongst them lay the bodies of many women and children. From their cloven skulls and shoulders, I guessed these had been cut down as the knights tried to force their way through. Many of the Normans had been hacked to pieces save for their torsos which were protected by their hauberks. I thought of the desecration of Harold Godwineson's body and felt no pity as I pulled my spear from the *destrier's* chest and handed it back to Erik. The lad's face betrayed no emotion, as if such sights were commonplace and again I wondered what he had witnessed in the past.

We were picking our way between the corpses, curious as to the purpose of the sally, when Arnkell stopped abruptly and hissed softly between his teeth.

'This is a prize indeed!' he exclaimed as Erik and I helped dragged the body of a middle-aged, thickly-built man from beneath the carcass of his horse, a bay which must have been almost as magnificent as Tiw before being butchered by the mob. The rider's gear matched the splendour of his mount: his hauberk of fine ring-mail and helm were of Flemish make, the latter finely decorated with gold inlay. He had been speared through the mouth but there was no other mark on him. Arnkell unstrapped the helm with trembling fingers to expose a brutal, broken-nosed face that yet seemed somehow pathetic, the eyes bulging sightlessly, the mouth a gaping blood-filled maw.

'Richard FitzRichard, castellan of York,' Arnkell announced ironically, then straightened and surveyed the onlookers. 'Who slew this man or saw it done?'

A clamour arose as fighters and townsfolk (some of them women), vied to claim the kill. Realizing he would get no sense from them, Arnkell shrugged. 'Then let whoever has the sharpest axe cut off the head of this carrion and stick it on a pole before the castle gates. That'll tell the bastards what happens if they dare come out!'

A loud cheer greeted this speech. Someone shouted, 'Why not the others?'

The tall Northerner grinned. 'Aye, why not? But make sure this man's head is stuck highest so they know who he is.'

We left them to their butcher's work (Acer the Hard appeared at that moment, armed with a massive Viking axe which in his hands could cleave a man's body in twain with a single blow), and made our way to the main hall. News of the slaughter had preceded us and the Atheling, Waltheof and

Marleswein passed by as they went to view the carnage. In the years since I had last seen him, Edgar had matured into a young man of proud bearing but he avoided my gaze. Perhaps he remembered me from the council in London, the advice which might have seen the Normans routed and made him King had any possessed courage to take it. At Arnkell's triumphant news, Waltheof smiled grimly and exchanged glances with Marleswein. 'It's a start,' he muttered.

After that, life in the city settled to an uneasy calm. By now thousands were mustered but impatience grew as days passed and nothing happened. I was not privy to the counsels of the Atheling and his officers but rumour was rife that we would march south at Easter, joining up with Sweyn of Denmark's ship-force on the Humber. Yet we could not move until the castle at York was ours, in part because to leave a Norman stronghold at our backs was sheer folly but mainly because it was there that the gold which would buy Danish support was stored. There was much jesting over the irony that the force which would finally defeat the usurpers should be paid with Norman taxes but the laughter was bitter: no-one who lived north of Watling Street had forgotten the hardships imposed by the Danegeld.

Those of us who had waited in London those fateful days after the defeat at Hastings were assailed by foreboding as our leaders procrastinated. No assault was launched on the castle though in truth even I, who had been present at many sieges, had no idea how to begin this one. Built on a steep mound and surrounded by a ditch both deep and wide, the main fort could be reached only by a draw-bridge from the bailey. The latter was sited on the end of a narrow promontory formed by the confluence of the rivers Ouse and Foss and winter flooding had made it into an island. A bridge across the Foss connected it with the city. Both motte and bailey were ringed by high timber palisades and the bridges guarded by watchtowers. Attackers could therefore only approach from one direction and the Foss bridge was only wide enough for three horses to pass abreast. To a force lacking the most basic siege engines the place was im-pregnable.

A week after the killing of FitzRichard, a band of Waltheof's men, frustrated by inactivity, perhaps hoping to gain renown, attempted to break down the gate with a crude ram. The jeering defenders sent down a hail of arrows followed by pail-loads of red-hot sand. Some of the attackers with presence of mind to jump in the river lived, though they were horribly scarred, but most died in agony a few days later, flayed by the scalding grains trapped beneath their mail. Gamal, who helped carry some of the victims to the abbey, told me that when the monks tried to strip them of their clothes, their skins peeled away with the cloth, exposing the raw flesh beneath. Their screams could be heard right across the city.

After that, few dared venture onto the bridge and Norman scorn took on a new spite while the heads of the castellan and his men rotted on their stakes. William Malet again boasted that we would starve ere they felt a pang of hunger. Knowing I understood his language, he singled me out by name whenever he saw me, trying to lure me into bowshot by insulting my kin and honour. I disdained to acknowledge his taunts and it may be that my silence provoked him to indiscretion because it was to me he revealed that the Bastard was already on the road north, in response to their request for aid.

Maybe the purpose of FitzRichard's ill-fated sally had been to divert attention while a messenger slipped past the chaos and away. But it was three weeks after the massacre that William Malet first spoke of it and how he had received a reply was the greater mystery for no-one could enter or leave the castle without knowledge of our guards. Then, one day, Siward the Red sought me out. His lean and freckled face was troubled as he asked, 'Did you know a priest is visiting the Normans every day?'

The locals who made up the main guard on the bridge had, it seemed, been allowing a monk through without question. I was so angry at this lapse I could barely speak. I growled, 'Go to the bridge and I'll send another of the Fen-wolves to join you: at least I can trust my own men. When we've caught the traitor, we'll go to the King. Tell anyone who tries to stop you that they must answer to me.'

Twilight comes early in the north, even towards the end of winter. It was near pitch dark yet men had not gathered for the evening meal when Siward and young Hakon dragged their prey to the main Hall. He was a novice, a boy of maybe fourteen years whose eyes started wildly from his thin face. Acer and I were warming ourselves by the great fire in the centre of the hall when they flung the lad at our feet. He grovelled shamelessly, begging for mercy though he had not been ill-treated, merely roughly handled: a slave-woman would have had more pride. We watched with contempt until at last he fell silent, hunched on the floor like a beaten dog, unable to control his trembling. His white, soft hands fluttered on the flagstones; he stank of fear-sweat and urine.

At a nod from me, Acer grasped the lad's shoulders and hauled him to his knees, pinioning him so that he could barely move. He hung his head but Acer dragged it back by the hair so he had no choice but to look into my face as I demanded what he had been doing at the castle and who had sent him. There was no need to ask whence he came: there was only one abbey in York.

He stammered incoherently at first, saying he meant no harm: he was doing God's work as he had been instructed. But I was in no mood for a lengthy interrogation. I drew my sword and the blade reflected the firelight as if forged from flame.

'Don't kill me!' Panicking, the boy tried to throw himself sideways but Acer's grip was immoveable. 'Please! I was only doing my Lord Aldred's bidding! Even the Normans may receive God's grace. I've done no wrong!'

Hearing this, a cold, sick feeling lodged in my belly. Aldred still argued for moderation, not understanding the extent to which the Normans desired to destroy us. And his faith, like that of Ulfkil of Croyland, was fervent and simple. Whilst I doubted he would have agreed to open treachery, he might have been persuaded that by offering consecrated bread and wine, maybe even holy texts, to the besieged, he was obeying Christ's doctrine to love one's enemies. Once a precedent was set, it would have been easy for a Norman agent to insinuate himself into the Archbishop's trust. Messages might have been passing under our noses for weeks.

'Strip and search him well.' I slammed my sword back into its scabbard. 'The Bastard could be here within days. Where is Waltheof?'

As I strode from the hall, the boy squealed but I did not look round. It was raining again: splashing through the narrow streets which were wreathed with hearth-smoke, foul with stench of too many folk crowded together, I wondered what folly had brought me there when I could have been with Turfrida and our daughters, safe in the depths of the Brunneswald. Our little humpy amongst the hollies seemed suddenly a place of comfort and security. Climbing onto the city wall, I stared into the darkness and driving rain, looking south for the flaring torches of the enemy but there was only the splash of water against stone, the moan of the wind, and blackness, as if we had entered a night without end.

That evening a kind of madness affected us all, the fey recklessness which overtakes men who sense their doom closing upon them. News of the betrayal had spread swiftly to every corner of the city and the feasting hall was packed. The hapless novice had been incarcerated in a secret place for his own safety while the Atheling, Waltheof, Marleswein and Gospatrick held a war council. Archbishop Aldred had been questioned and protested his innocence, saying he had acted according to his conscience to bring God's grace to the enemy even as Christ had proscribed. Rather than have him hanged, Edgar merely confined him to the abbey under guard. But all this was, we knew, no more than shutting the stable door after the horse has bolted and slowly, like a creeping fog, fear spread across the city. Up till then the rebellion had met no real resistance in the north and to many it must have seemed almost a game, despite the failure to capture and hold any castle. Now, a reckoning was due. Listening to the boasting, seeing the eagerness with which men gulped their horns of ale or wine, I wondered suddenly what it had been like here the night before Edwin and Morcar's men went out to meet the Vikings at Fulford Gate.

It was that thought inspired me to gather the Fen-wolves ere the drinking began in earnest. They looked at me expectantly as I reminded them of their oaths. 'If the Bastard comes, he'll likely burn the ships at Riccall and Humber Mouth,' I told them. 'Therefore, if we lose this city we must go north into Bernicia. Fight hard but do not throw your lives away: there will be more fighting to come. And this I promise you: the day the Normans are defeated will dawn ere this year ends. If not, I'll take a woman's guise and have Turfrida teach me to weave for I shall deserve no better. And Acer here will spin the yarn for me. So fight well!'

They cheered at that and Siward the Red tipped back his head and gave the wolf's howl which had long heralded our attacks. The sound echoed through the hall and many looked round, puzzled, while some joined in, ignorant of its significance. Acer stepped forward, declaring fiercely: 'Skull-smiter!' and thus we chanted our sword-ode and grinned at each other as the joy known only to those bonded in danger surged through us, the kinship deeper than blood which can be ended only by death. We were the Fen-wolves, whose name struck fear into the usurpers' hearts, none of us had yet been slain by Norman hands and our loyalty to each other outweighed any other fealties. Whatever the next day brought, we knew the trust between us would not be broken.

For all that, there was a kind of desperation to our revelry that night. Some simply drank themselves senseless while others went out to find women. Those they brought back were mainly whores (for such come to ply their trade wherever fighting men gather), and these, tunics gaping to reveal their breasts, moved from man to man, flattering and enticing with their voices while their fingers felt for a money-pouch or carelessly fastened cloak pin to supplement their earnings. The lad, Erik, stared in open-mouthed amazement and Acer led him off for instruction, remarking it would be a sore waste for one of such mettle to die a virgin. When a fair-haired, clear-eyed girl entwined herself around me as I sat moodily at the mead-bench, I pushed her roughly away then, when she persisted, took her with no more thought than it takes to down a horn of ale. The brief oblivion I achieved gave me no pleasure, only a disgust which lingered like a bad taste in the mouth: her squirming and sly, sensual smile reminded me of Ymma. Seeing the girl depart to find more gratifying company, Acer winked knowingly but made no comment. I glared at him and soon left the noisy chaos of the hall for the crowded squalor of our lodgings but sleep long evaded me, so fierce was my longing for home and Turfrida.

I woke from a series of lurid and bloody dreams to a tumult of shouts, screams, the clash of weapons, and leapt from my pallet, fumbling for hauberk and swordbelt. Despite the noise, Acer lay snoring and Erik was curled on the floor, a beatific smile on his face. While the woman of the house tried frantically to gather her most treasured possessions into a cloak and her children wailed, I kicked my comrades awake. Hearing the sounds of conflict intensifying and growing louder with each passing moment, Acer sprang to his feet and struggled into his mailcoat, saying grimly, 'They've come, then.'

The journey the Bastard's force had achieved was no less a feat than our march to York under Harold Godwineson: while it had taken a little longer, it was done in the worst of the winter. Unable to cross the swollen Ouse, they had been forced west and approached the city from that direction, arriving sometime in the night. Where the previous evening there had been only empty, half-flooded fields, dawn revealed a host to those looking from the city walls.

How the Normans gained entry I never discovered. The swiftness of their march precluded the transport of siege engines: perhaps they had improvised a ram. Be that as it may, by the time Acer, Erik and I were armed, the streets were swarming with them.

Our hostess began to keen as we made ready to leave. I told her roughly to be silent and to bar the door against all comers until everything was quiet. She shut her mouth but her wild, staring eyes and look of terror, like that of a trapped animal, haunted me long after though I never knew her fate. By contrast, Erik's face was pale but determined; Acer's wore an expression of grim anticipation. We drew our swords, I exhorted the lad to stay close, then we opened the door.

I have been in some hard fights but none so desperate as that one in the narrow streets and muddy yards of York. The massacre of FitzRichard and his men was here reversed for the townsfolk had shut themselves in their houses or fled to the sanctuary of the Minster, thus the mounted knights had room to charge, wheel, slash at will. So sudden and unexpected was their incursion (and many of our men were befuddled by drink from the night before), there was no chance to rally resistance in any section of the city. All was chaos and noise, the yells of men and screaming of horses; the din of hooves, the clash and thud of weapons. Whenever we brought one knight down it seemed two more sprang to take his place. We fought with no coherent plan, simply to stay alive.

By chance, the three of us had made our way close to the abbey and were taking some respite behind a storehouse, the Normans having drawn off, when a deep horn call sounded from the direction of the castle. It was followed closely by a wolf's howl.

'Bastards are coming out,' Acer grumbled, meaning William Malet and his men. 'Now we'll have some fun. Come on!'

The battle-joy which comes when one embraces one's fate without fear swept over me then and an answering howl burst from my lips as I ran forward. Some of the streets were connected by winding alleys too narrow for an armed horseman to get through and these proved our salvation. Coming upon a band of knights who had surrounded maybe twenty rebels in a courtyard, we attacked from the side with such force that the Normans were disconcerted and wheeled away. Gamal, Siward the Red and several other comrades were there. Siward, who had seen the enemy from the city walls, shook his head ruefully. 'We're outnumbered two to one and that's without anyone from the castle. If we stay here, we'll die.'

'What kind of talk is that?' Acer spat disgustedly. 'What's happened to the Atheling and Waltheof? We're part of their force now: we leave when they do.'

There was no more time for talk. A group of fighters, who from their gear looked to be northerners, came flying round the corner, pursued by the Normans that had just left us. Arnkell was among the first: seeing me, he shouted at his men to stop. They had already stumbled to a confused standstill for at first sight the yard seemed closed. Finding themselves outnumbered, the horsemen pulled their mounts to a rearing halt. I snatched my spear from Erik, glanced sidelong at Acer who nodded in agreement. We had fought together long enough to know one another's minds without the need of speech.

No horse will charge headlong into a set spear-hedge but in the scramble for weapons and mail, most of the defenders had left their spears behind. We formed a line as best we could, swords making up the gaps, and edged backwards to gain protection from the buildings while the knights advanced. Arnkell, blood streaming from his left arm, moved through his men until he reached my shoulder.

'We must get out of the city!' he said hoarsely. 'Make for the south gate: it's our only chance! Word is, Edgar and Waltheof have already left.'

'So much for royal blood,' I muttered, while to my right Acer let out a string of curses. 'Very well, Arnkell, there's a way out behind us. Have your men pass through and pray there are no Normans waiting on the other side.'

Had William the Bastard known the city better, he could have stamped out all the leaders of the rebellion that day, save only my nephews who were ensconced deep in West Mercia. Having entered from the west he must have thought to trap most of us between William Malet's force, which sallied triumphantly from the castle, and his own knights. But the east and south gates were held by men from Lincolnshire and Yorkshire who had already felt the iron grip of Norman rule and they fought stubbornly to allow their comrades to escape into the flooded marshes around Fulford or towards Stamford. And the river also provided a way out though a perilous one, the Ouse being in spate.

We shouted and howled our war cries as the knights charged again but each time their horses swerved aside at the last moment and two fell as their hooves slid in the churned mud, much of which was already puddled with blood. The riders we slew while their horses struggled frantically to their feet, confusing the others. After what seemed like an age but can only have been as long as it takes to don a hauberk, Acer and I gained the relative safety of the alleyway. Most of the others had already left but the Fen-wolves were waiting, along with Arnkell and five of his men. He had taken advantage of the brief respite to bind his arm and seeing me glance at the blood-sodden rag, gave a sudden grin. 'Just a flesh-wound: one of your fighters stabbed the bastard as he was aiming the death-blow.'

I nodded then froze for above the screaming and shouting came the ordered clatter of many hooves. A paved road ran from the Foss Bridge to the south gate: I guessed a considerable force had been sent from the castle to capture it. A moment later a detachment of more than forty knights trotted past the alley entrance. Not one glanced towards us, their eyes were fixed on the road ahead. With their well-fed, glossy mounts, unstained cloaks, mail and weapons, they looked invincible. The metal of their helms gleamed in the grey light; some had pennons attached to their lances. I thought of Turfrida's hair stuck on Ivo Taillebois' spear and such hatred gripped me I trembled with the force of it.

'If we get through, what then?' Gamal asked suddenly. 'They'll cut us down like beanstalks once we're in the open.'

His question was directed at Acer, not me. Siward told me after that in those moments I seemed possessed by the madness of a berserker and none dared speak to me lest it be turned on them.

'When we get through we'll think about that,' Acer replied, not unkindly. 'Keep together and don't stop until we reach the gate. And remember: these Normans look as if they were born with iron skins and four legs but they bleed and die like any men once you get them on the ground. It's when their horses wear mail-coats we have to worry!'

A burst of reckless laughter greeted these words and again the battle-joy welled up in us, making us as one. Buoyed by it, borne on its surge, we howled like wolves and ran out of the alley.

Intense fighting happens as if in a dream, seeming to occupy a space outside time where the dealing of a single blow takes half a lifetime and the counter-stroke is over in an eyeblink. The road we ran down was already slippery with blood and gore: a heaving mass of mounted knights and men on foot was locked in combat before the gates. The opening was still wide enough for a wain to pass because bodies, dead and dying, blocked the heavy gates themselves but the Normans could neither surround nor charge there while the defence was so fierce. The whole group of knights we had seen ride past now stood between us and our comrades but to hesitate or turn back was to admit defeat. By now we were beyond fearing death.

In truth we were already weary, blood-splattered from our own wounds as well as our enemies'. Yet as we yelled again we felt neither tiredness nor pain and our exhilaration was heightened by the look of horror which fleeted across the faces of the Normans as we met them, inspired beyond our strength to hack and slay until the coming of darkness. Like ravening wolves, driven beyond reason by hate, we hurled ourselves at men and horses, Acer wielding his axe like a Norse god in his fury, young Erik keening his own war-song at my side. Blood sprayed; screams rent the air; a red haze and rasping thirst is all I remember of that fight, aye, and as it continued, a desperate longing for it to end ere my sword-arm failed.

Afterwards, much of it returned in dreams, jagged images of my sword slashing indiscriminately into the meat of men and horses; of a Norman looking wide-eyed into my face, maybe seeking mercy, half his jaw missing; of Douti struggling on the stones, his back broken after being ridden over;

of Hakon leaning against the twisted gates, hands clutching the broken lance stuck in his belly. But none of these things come willingly to my mind even now. I recall the quiet of aftermath, waking to myself in a crowded room which was, in fact, a byre; the feeling of astonishment at being alive and unscathed save for the odd gash which now stung beyond all reason; the dread of looking round to see who had lived and who was lost. Yet I do not remember how I got there.

'Most of us made it,' Acer said, for my question must have been clear upon my face. 'Douti is dead and Hakon missing. And Gamal here is lucky to have kept his head: young Erik was keeping a sharp eye out. We should make him the twin's replacement. He's quick with that old sword.'

The exhausted, pinched look on the lad's face vanished with the praise: Acer was not named 'the Hard' for nothing. And seeing the effect of his words and mindful of his reputation, the elder grimaced and added, 'Don't let it go to your head, lad, lest you lose it next time. I said you were quick, not skilful.'

'Ach, give the boy his due.' I yawned and stretched, stiffened muscles creaking in protest. 'Anyone who escaped the city is worthy of renown. There must be hundreds who died before they got near the gates. One thing's for certain though: next time the usurpers hear a wolf's howl, they'll think twice before clashing swords with us.'

They were too weary to cheer but nodded or grunted in agreement. Quiet descended on the byre, broken only by the steady stroke of blade against whetstone as men sharpened weapons notched and blunted by use, low talk as the fight was relived and compared with others, the moans of a wounded comrade bedded down in the straw. Arnkell, who sat with nodding head and bowed shoulders beside a small fire which seemed to produce more smoke than flame, suddenly stirred and looked round as if unsure where he was or how he had got there. When he saw me, he rose awkwardly, wincing as his wounded arm moved, and made his way outside.

I followed, for there was that in his face which needed no words to express. The men could take their ease, bind their wounds, tend weapons and gear, but they looked to us to lead them, to find shelter and food or, if that were impossible, to share their hardship. That responsibility I had taken freely and it had begun to tell after the slaughter of Outi's band but only now did I feel the full weight of it. With no clear idea of our position in relation to the rest of the rebel force (or, for that matter, the city), I did not even know which way safety lay.

It was dark with a thin rain blowing in from what I assumed to be the west: the air lacked that bitter edge which comes from the north and east. There was a dank, rooty smell of marsh and the rustle of reed-stems but no sound of lapping water so I guessed we were somewhere east of the flooded meads around Fulford. Hearth smoke was borne on the wind but there was no way of telling whence it came. It may have been from our own fire. No ruddy gleam betrayed the whereabouts of other fugitives or even York itself.

'They fought well, your men.' Arnkell drew me into the lee of the building where, from the stench, cow dung and rotting straw had been heaped for generations. 'But we'd all have been finished if they'd followed us beyond the gates.'

'They had enough to occupy them inside,' I replied grimly, recalling the shrill screams of women in the background as we retreated. 'It seems they had their orders and obeyed. Best not to dwell on what might have happened. We have to decide what to do now.'

'Aye.' I could see no more of his face than a faint blur but sensed his intent look and knew when he turned to stare into the blank darkness. 'This cannot be all. We must gather and attack the city before more Normans come from the south. If we give up now, the men will lose heart: it will be over.'

In the silence following this bald statement I heard raised voices from within, one of my men arguing with one of Arkell's, then a burst of laughter as the dispute was resolved by some growled comment from Acer.

'We'll not give up, not until the last of us is slain,' I said fiercely. 'In any case, what do we have to lose? Our families are living like animals in the forest; we survive by taking what we need and it is those who were our neighbours and friends who suffer for it. Many have already died for lack of food and shelter and it can only get worse unless the Normans are ousted. No, I will not submit, not while there is breath in me. I cannot.'

He said nothing for a while, daunted maybe by my fervour. Then he replied thoughtfully, 'It is not so in Bernicia, at least, not yet. But what has happened here and in Durham is warning enough of what we should expect.' He paused and sighed heavily. 'If we cannot retake York and do it properly this time, the rising will be all but over. For a lasting victory that will give us the whole of England, we need the Danes and the gold to buy them is stored in the castle. It is an evil chance that has lost us this city, Hereward.'

'At first light we must find the others who escaped,' I said, trying to ignore his despondency. 'And when we attack, it must be a concerted effort. We have men enough if the Atheling and Waltheof are still hereabouts. Bastard William fears what might happen in the north but he believes the south to be secure. That may give us our great chance. Edgar has a sizeable ship-force: we could lure the Normans here while he struck at London.'

'With whom?' His tone was one of utter weariness. 'Until we have the means to take their accursed castles, the south is lost. Look at what happened to your nephews last year. No, my friend, we must be patient a little longer and wait for Sweyn's ships.'

'My patience ran out when our refuge was despoiled, my wife humiliated, my war-horse butchered,' I said through gritted teeth. 'If the Atheling has no stomach for this fight, we'll shame him into action. If it's true he's gone north again, I'll wager Archbishop Aldred had a hand in it. But I cannot believe the others will have given up so easily.'

'Perhaps,' he replied doubtfully. 'If they're still alive.'

Dawn revealed a bleak landscape of rain-sodden pasture, criss-crossed by ditches which were full almost to bursting. We were on the floodplain of the Derwent, beyond the battleground of Fulford Gate and I guessed that Riccall, where the Atheling's ships had been moored, was less than an hour's walk away. Sheets of rain blotted out the horizon but the city was just visible in the murk. Great plumes of smoke rose from somewhere near the walls but we could not make out what was happening. Erik was first to offer to find out. With his northern accent, stripped of mailcoat and sword, he needed no artifice to pass as a local serf. He slipped a long hunting knife inside his tunic and covered his head and shoulders with a filthy piece of sacking we found in the byre. Then he slipped away towards the city while one of the few unscathed of Arnkell's men left for Riccall to discover the truth of Edgar's whereabouts.

Few times in my life have I known such anxiety as then, waiting for the spies to return. Others went out to forage (most of us had not eaten for a day), while the rest of us tended our wounds, made those who were seriously hurt as comfortable as possible, and kept look-out. If the Normans were hunting fugitives it was inevitable they would discover us, so obvious a refuge did this lonely byre provide. But time dragged past, the rain settled to a steady downpour and there was no sight or sound of enemy horsemen.

The scout who had gone to Riccall was first back. He was a gaunt, dour-looking man and shook his head grimly as he strode towards us, mired up to his knees.

'Edgar's gone, along with Gospatrick,' he reported. 'The ships that are left are making ready to sail, for fear the Normans will burn them. They're supposed to be mustering down the Humber, to join up with the Danes, but rumour says the atheling's gone straight to Scotland, to hide behind King Malcolm's throne. They've abandoned us, Arnkell.'

A gust of wind blew a stream of droplets from the rotting thatch on top of us (we were crouched outside to keep watch), and Arnkell swore and moved back into the gaping doorway. 'Have you heard anything of the others? Marleswein and Waltheof, the Bernicians?'

'No news of them had reached the ships.' The man stared south into the sheeting rain and spat as if to rid himself of a bad taste. 'They may be dead or perhaps they've sworn allegiance to save their skins.' He hesitated, then added quietly, 'Arnkell, we must get away while we can. Without Edgar and Gospatrick's men we'll be outnumbered once the Normans leave the city.'

It was fortunate that some of the foragers returned at that moment. Thorald and one of Arnkell's men each carried a slaughtered sheep across his shoulders; another bore a cloak-wrapped bundle of stolen victuals: stale bread, half a round cheese and a crock of honey. To exhausted and hungry men, the mere sight of food was enough to cause trouble: the initial murmur of relief soon turned to bickering over how it should be split. Arnkell and I exchanged weary glances and went to restore order though in truth only pride kept me from snatching and tearing at the food like a starving cur.

All was quiet and the smell of roasting meat rose tantalisingly into the air when the measured splosh of hooves sounded from close by. Cursing whoever stood on guard and had failed to raise the alarm, Arkell, Acer and I drew swords and moved cautiously into the doorway, expecting to see Norman horsemen approaching. It crossed my mind that it would be a poor thing to die in defence of a dilapidated cowshed then, instead of a warcry, laughter burst from my lips. Plodding across the wet field came Erik leading two *destriers*, my bay and Acer's chestnut. Swallow ambled behind, head hanging low, her rain-soaked coat sleeked to her ribs, making her appear little more than a walking skeleton. Since the start of the fighting, I had had no time to think of the horses other than to assume them taken but seeing the mare with whom I had shared so much, I realized suddenly how I would mourn her loss. I whistled and she flung up her rough-hewn, bony head, whickered and trotted around the others to meet me, snapping ill-naturedly as she passed them.

I stroked her neck and scratched her withers and she blew softly and nuzzled my face as if to welcome one of her own kind. Arnkell was having difficulty concealing his amusement at the obvious affection I bore a nag when the two stallions, though no match for Tiw, were at least of reasonable confirmation.

'Say a word against that bag of bones and Hereward'll have your head,' Acer said, half in earnest. 'And she'll likely defend him likewise. Don't let anyone fool you against betting against her in a race, either.'

Arnkell shook his head disbelievingly but was too wise to comment. Erik reached us; I pushed the mare away and she went to stand in the lee of the building.

'I thought the horses might be useful.' The lad's tone was level but there was a note of triumph in it. 'And they gave me an excuse if I was spotted on the road. But the harness I could not get.'

His eager, rain-beaded face grew serious as he remembered the real object of his foray. 'I went to the South Gate,' he said. 'It was shut: they've closed the city to all save those bearing the Bastard's seal. The gate-wards asked who I was and what I was doing there so I spun some yarn about my lord's wife sending me to look for a missing serf and some horses he had stolen. They asked who was my King and I told them I am a faithful servant of William of Normandy but we thought the missing man might have joined the rebels. Then they laughed and said we should look to the city walls because that was where the traitors' corpses would be hung or thrown after the leaders' heads had been stuck on spikes above the gates. His English was not good and I speak none of their accursed tongue but I think they are burning their dead and then they plan to build a second castle, to guard the west bank of the Ouse. I left ere they grew suspicious and walked east, knowing they'd be watching. Then I saw the horses grazing in a field. I caught the others easily enough but Swallow wouldn't let me near.' He paused and glanced at me with an odd mixture of wry amusement and awe. 'I don't know why she followed.'

Acer grunted. 'That horse is like Martin and Turfrida: it knows its master's will and answers to no other. You did well, lad. Are you sure you weren't followed?'

'As sure as anyone could be.' Erik frowned. 'I waited in the rain for what seemed half the day, then came back across the fields. All the Normans are still inside the city.' He glanced at Arnkell with a sudden grin that made him seemed boyish then sniffed the air hungrily. 'Maybe they don't like our weather. Is there anything to eat? My belly's cleaving to my backbone.'

'Aye.' The tall Northerner sheathed his sword deliberately. 'Get inside with you. And once you're fed and warm, get some mail on. There's more fighting ahead or I'm a Frank.'

The lad touched hand to brow in mocking obeisance, handed the halter ropes to Acer and went into the smoky fug of the byre. Acer rubbed his *destrier's* forehead, his expression unusually thoughtful. 'A second castle,' he muttered. 'What do we do now?'

As darkness gathered we moved to Stamford Bridge where the lie of the land offered a better defensive position than where we were though I sensed some of the Fen-wolves were uneasy at putting another river between ourselves and home. We crossed the bridge cautiously, smelling smoke on the wind and the horses snorted and jibbed as the slippery planks creaked and sagged under them. The roar of the river, swollen to a torrent, drowned all other sounds.

Our wariness was well-founded. As the last of us stepped down into the wet pasture, an ear-splitting whistle sounded from somewhere within a clump of hawthorn bushes but a spearthrow away. Of one mind, Acer and I ran forward to give the others space, unsheathing our weapons as we went then, as our comrades fanned out to form a shieldwall, figures appeared in the gloom, almost as if they had sprung from the earth itself. Some bore spears and others had arrows nocked to bows but as they drew closer and the foremost of them raised his right hand to halt the others, it was clear he was no Norman. Even in the semi-darkness, he loomed like a giant for he must have been close on seven feet tall; his long rain-draggled hair hung pale against the stuff of his cloak, his helm and sword-hilt gleamed with gold. From behind me, Erik gave a half-stifled cry of recognition and Arnkell strode forward, sheathing his sword.

The two embraced like brothers, then came to join us. The stranger was the renowned Siward Beorn, he who had thwarted Tostig Godwineson's first foray up the Humber.

'Hereward.' He surveyed my face with a keen, appraising glance as Arnkell introduced us. 'I have heard much of you and your men. All hard-handed fighters are welcome here. Waltheof wants us to attack the city the day after tomorrow, as soon as all the stragglers are in.'

'Attack?' Acer made no attempt to conceal his scorn and I saw Siward and Arnkell stiffen, put a warning hand on my old comrade's shoulder. With an effort, Acer bit back his next words and contented himself with hawking loudly and spitting to the side.

'Take us to your camp, then we can talk.' I was sharply aware of alarm growing behind me as Siward's words were repeated. 'Have you anything to drink – other than water, that is?'

The big man gave a shrewd grin, revealing a line of broken teeth. 'Aye, let there be no quarrels between us. Any enemy of the Norman bastards I count as friend.'

'If we cannot agree amongst ourselves, we are lost,' said Arnkell.

Waltheof and many of his men had gone to muster support from estates towards Humber Mouth but there was still a force of more than two thousand gathered on a low, wooded hill maybe two miles east of Stamford Bridge. From a distance their camp fires were visible only as faint, ruddy patches amongst the trees for they had been made in shallow pits, both to protect against the weather and for concealment. The effect was eerie, akin to the ghost-lights which flicker in the Fens, exacerbating the shadows. As we drew closer we could just make out figures huddled around the fires or standing guard amid the trees. The occasional glint of flame against polished metal marked where men moved or weapons were being tended but there was little sound other than the moan of the wind in the trees and the incessant drip of water. The roar of the river, diminished by distance, was no more than a faint murmur.

Siward led us to a hollow near the top of the hill where a large tent had been fashioned from hides and poles. Inside, the fire had burned down to a bed of glowing embers which Siward stirred to life and replenished from a stack of broken wood to the side. The flames revealed little else within: skins and rugs were piled in one corner and that was all.

'Edgar stayed here,' he said by way of explanation. 'He's sent Marleswein to rouse the Danes but when they'll answer our call, who knows?' He grimaced and in the flaring light an old scar which ran from the corner of his left eye to his mouth creased into a stark line. 'The atheling's returned to Scotland, in case you're wondering. He went unwillingly but we thought it best. William promised him an honourable place at court in return for his allegiance but so far the Bastard's pledges have proved somewhat empty.' He hesitated and banged the side of the tent with his fist, calling for someone to bring drink; when he turned to face us again, his expression was one of grim resignation. 'We're to pin the Normans here until Sweyn's ships enter the Humber.'

The breath hissed between my teeth and I exchanged incredulous glances with Acer while Arnkell squatted beside the fire and began to jab at the heart of it with a piece of stick. 'What surety do we have that the Danes will come?' he asked.

'None.' At that moment a heavily cloaked woman entered the tent. Her pock-marked face was thrown into cruel relief by the firelight as she bent to set out some horn cups which she filled with a dark syrupy metheglin whose tang came clear above the smells of wood-smoke and stale sweat. Siward almost snatched the cup she offered him but waited until we had all been served before growling, 'There's gold plundered from all the north stored in York: that will be lure enough. And there is always promise of more. The atheling is ready to agree another Danegeld if they help rid this land of the Normans. Whether he'd really do it is another matter.'

His eyes reflected the flames as he stared at us, maybe seeking to judge our resolve from our reaction, then grinned. 'Either way, we've got the Bastard trapped. Cut off its head and the snake dies. He'll not escape York alive.'

'Aye.' We raised our cups as if to seal a pledge and, following Siward's example, drained them at one draught though the stuff burned the gullet like fire, then spread a tingling warmth through stomach and lungs. Siward watched with a kind of sardonic amusement as Acer coughed and spluttered, then motioned the woman to re-fill our cups. Erik, standing by the tent door with my spear, looked on forbearingly as our talk turned from sober discussion to drunken boasting but where Martin's presence might have constrained me, the boy's provoked me to greater bragging. I remember stripping to the waist and wrestling with Siward, reeling to and fro around the blazing fire, then flames, looming faces, the taste and smell of the mead whirled into a nightmare vortex, a heaving through my blood, and darkness.

I woke long after dawn to find Acer snoring next to me in a puddle of vomit. Rain beat loud on the sagging skins of the tent and water dripped onto my shoulder: it was this had roused me. My head felt as if it would split at the slightest movement, my tongue was like cracked leather, the rest of me ached as if I had been beaten. With an effort I sat up, rubbed my eyes, groaned to make sure I was still in control of my voice, looked round blearily. There was no sign of Siward Beorn or Arnkell but Erik still stood on guard. His head drooped and he was leaning on my spear for support but though drowsing he was not asleep for he opened his eyes then stood abruptly straight, seeing me awake.

'Have you been there all night?' I drew my knees to my chest and laid my head upon them to hide my eyes from daylight as the boy dragged the tent-flaps open. It seemed to take all my will to form coherent speech.

'There was no need: here we are among friends.'

'They might have stabbed you in your sleep,' he said defensively. 'I am from Bernicia, my lord: maybe I know more of them than you.'

Even through the fuddleness from the mead the warning implicit in these words was clear. I scrambled clumsily to my feet, shedding the cloak that had been laid over as a blanket, retrieved my shirt and jerkin and pulled them on, shivering from the draught.

'Here, help me with that.' I waved towards my hauberk which lay near the depleted wood-pile and when the lad brought it to me, grasped his shoulders. He held himself still and did not recoil from the foulness of my breath nor my fierceness as I thrust my face almost into his.

'This is war, Erik,' I hissed. 'All other quarrels must be laid aside, even blood-feud. If the least of us fights among ourselves we have no force worth speaking of. Do you understand? We have but one purpose: to rid our land of the usurpers. If you will not accept that, I release you from my service.'

He stared but did not move as I took my hands away and something in his eyes, a mixture of hurt, disappointment and anger tightly controlled, struck like a spearthrust to the very heart of me. Such a look I had last seen on Turfrida's face as she watched me leave, a kind of mute accusation, and I turned abruptly and struggled into my mail-coat ere the lad noticed my discomfiture.

'Make me a Fen-wolf and I will renounce my feud,' he said quietly, handing over my sword-belt. 'Archbishop Aldred will mediate between me and my enemies. I think my father's spirit would be content with that.'

I stood with heaving stomach and reeling head, wondering at the boy's simple certainty and could have howled aloud or wept from grief I did not then understand. Instead I kicked Acer none too gently in the small of the back to rouse him. 'Very well. Name your sword and we'll meet at nightfall to take your oath.'

His eyes narrowed for a moment, then he bent his head. When he looked up again I could hardly bear the mixture of hope and adulation lightening his features.

'My sword already has a name,' he said.

By mid-afternoon I reckon a thousand more men had come to the hill, last of which were Waltheof's remaining hus-carls and the eorl himself. The rain had stopped but the air was heavy with moisture and the wind had veered inexorably to the east. It seemed to cut even through my mail, chilling my damp clothes as, with gathering darkness, I made my way to the clearing where I had told the Fen-wolves to meet. The place stank, for the whole area of woodland had been used as a latrine for days but at least it was deserted. As with all bands of men oath-bound in fealty, the secret of our ritual was jealously guarded for therein lay its potency.

Erik was liked and respected, therefore welcomed. When he had sworn allegiance, we chanted our sword-ode, adding 'Blood-Venger' to the end and then our wolf's paean rose between the dripping trees, echoing eerily in the hills. We listened as the howl faded into the moan of the wind and a more sombre mood fell as we honoured the dead (two more had succumbed to their wounds after being moved from the byre), and swore a swift and bitter revenge. Yet there was a kind of reticence beneath the praise-giving and when Gamal began the 'Battle of Maldon', dead silence fell. In the light of what we had witnessed and endured over the past days aye, and years, the heroism of the doomed King and his followers seemed futile, their valour empty. We realized suddenly that renown exists only while there are some left to sing of it.

'They're getting tired,' Acer remarked as we followed the gang back into camp. 'Not in body, at least no more than you and I, but in here.' He tapped his forehead meaningfully. 'Three years we'll have been hammering away at the Normans and it has made no difference save that during that time we've gone from being free men with homes and land to ragged outlaws, our wives and children left to scratch a living from the woods while we throw ourselves at the bastards like mad dogs. I tell you, Hereward, if we don't start winning soon, they'll despair and go home. Aye, and no blame to them.'

I listened in silence and a cold hand seemed to clutch my guts because I knew he was right and it was clear also that without the Danes, the best we could do was hold the Normans where they were. Yet even as this thought crossed my mind, I felt my resolve harden. To consider failure was a betrayal of my honour, my kin, all those unjustly killed at Norman hands.

'Not while I lead them,' I muttered.

The Council was held in the tent we had occupied the night before. Waltheof led the debate which swiftly degenerated into wrangling over strategy, some wanting to hide in the hills and wait until Sweyn's ship-force arrived while the rest of us, having the Bastard at last within our reach, argued for an attack on the city, our purpose to besiege and take the castle before another could be constructed.

Waltheof, tall, dark-haired and grim, eventually called for silence. 'Let those without the stomach for this fight leave now,' he declared. 'The Atheling is gathering a ship-force in Scotland; join him and wait until Sweyn of Denmark arrives. Then we shall scour this land clean of every trace of Norman blood. No-one who thus keeps faith with our true King may be called coward: there will be renown enough earned ere this year ends to keep the gleemen busy for a hundred years. Over those who choose to stay I claim no lordship but my men will attack the south gate at dawn. The Bastard is within our grasp. Let's not squander this chance.'

Most of those at that council owed the Eorl of Bernicia no allegiance and many had been shocked by the sheer brutal efficiency of the enemy, the ease with which they had won back the city. It was obvious at once who intended fleeing to Scotland because they looked at one another askance and avoided the eyes of the rest of us. Maybe, if Waltheof had reiterated the importance of re-taking the city; that whoever held York controlled the whole of northern England; that without the gold hoarded in the castle keep we had no surety of Danish support, more would have stayed. But by admitting these truths he would have betrayed our weakness, his own demise from one of the most powerful in the Witan to a landless fugitive, and he was a proud man. Ere daybreak more than half the men camped on the hill had slipped away, some to join the atheling but more, I suspect, to whatever homes and kin remained to them. When we mustered at Stamford bridge in the pre-dawn twilight I doubt there was more than a thousand of us left.

Those weeks of desperate fighting became like a nightmare from which one struggles to awaken and cannot. That first dawn attack took the usurpers by surprise: we stormed the gates and swept in recklessly ere they were aware of what was happening. But our joy at entering the city was short-lived. At full light hundreds of mounted knights sallied from the castle and this time, when we were at last routed, they pursued us, cutting down those who broke and tried to run away easily as a child switches nettles. A third of our force was slain or captured that first day and next morning the corpses were flung over or hung from the city walls, naked and bloody. Some of the captives were spared. Instead of being killed, they were set free, blinded or with both hands severed and the stumps seared, so that we would know what kind of mercy to expect.

To some, this further demonstration of Norman cruelty was enough incentive to fight on. There was, in any case, too much at stake simply to abandon the city although it was plain we could not take and hold it without reinforcements. We watched helplessly as a great swathe of wooden buildings was demolished and cleared and construction of a new castle mound began. While we harried every band of Normans entering or leaving through the north, south and east gates, the western side we could not attack so easily for the gate was well-manned and the road guarded. And at every skirmish we lost a few more men who were not replaced.

'We can't go on like this,' Acer said quietly as he helped me off with my hauberk, ten days before Easter. Erik was resting after dislocating his shoulder in an effort to fell a *destrier* single-handed. Most of us had been wounded by now though the core of the Fen-wolves remained able to fight. That very morning I had escaped death only through the stoutness of my mailcoat which turned aside my god-father, Gilbert de Ghent's, lance. He had not forgotten my defiance of him in Flanders: he mocked me as I struggled to my feet, saying he would return for my head when he'd worn out his current Saxon whore. He and Ivo Taillebois were old comrades and no doubt the latter had boasted of his raid on our refuge, his promise to Turfrida, her humiliation. The bitterness of the encounter was slow to leave and I stared at Acer blankly then sat on a half-rotted log and bent over, resting my head in my hands, letting exhaustion wash over me like a black tide. I was tired as were we all, hungry most of the time, resentful of those that had escaped to the safety of Scotland. Yet as Acer sat beside me and began to hone his sword, I remembered how Turfrida and I had parted, my promise to return as part of a liberating force. To go back defeated, having achieved nothing, would be an affront to my pride no subsequent victory could wholly mend.

'If we cannot take the city, we will go north to join the Atheling,' I said.

By the forced labour of more prisoners and the people of York, the new motte with its outer palisade of stout timbers, its keep and watch-platforms, was completed ere Easter, despite our efforts to prevent it. As soon as it was finished, the Bastard and most of his force returned south, leaving Gilbert de Ghent as castellan. From the cover of the marshes we watched them go, William mounted on a fine bay stallion, so sure of himself that he had left off his helm for it was a bright day and the spring sunshine warm. Surrounded by his knights he was untouchable and he looked about with the arrogance of one certain of his invincibility though his red hair made him an easy target amid the mail and dark surcoats of those around him. Crouched beside me in ground that oozed stinking black slime whenever our weight shifted, Gamal hissed between his teeth and stroked the curve of his bow longingly. But the Usurper was well beyond arrowshot and would remain so, thanks to the labour of thousands who had cleared the verges for almost the whole length of the Great North Road to make ambush all but impossible.

'Don't waste an arrow: the Bastard's unkillable,' Erik muttered, expressing a sentiment that had been rife since Hastings. 'He made a pact with the Devil ere he stepped on these shores. Why else d'you think the luck's run with him and so far against us? I was talking with one of Waltheof's men who was at Berkhampstead when the Witan swore allegiance. He said William's not like any other man. He doesn't drink or boast and when he stares at you, you freeze like a hare when the fox is close. His eyes are like stones: no one can tell what he's thinking. And he never laughs. Maybe he's not made of flesh and blood at all.'

The long line of men and horses had almost disappeared from view though the flash and glitter of their harness and weapons came clear across the distance.

'He's the bastard son of a serving wench,' I said dismissively, disturbed by the lad's awe. 'Any man born of woman can be slain. Don't believe everything you hear: wild tales swarm like flies around a turd when ignorant folk talk of what is beyond their understanding.'

'Aye, look at us,' said Gamal, grinning. 'We're Fen-wolves: like the berserkers of old we take the shape of beasts at will – that's why none of us has ever been caught.' He lowered his voice to a dramatic whisper. 'But to join us you must undergo a deadly trial and . . . '

'Enough!' Knowing how swiftly such nonsense spoken in jest could become entrenched lore through idle chatter, I decided to put a stop to it. 'The Bastard may be beyond our reach but we still have two castles to take. Back to camp.'

That night, Waltheof called me to his tent. Arnkell was also there but many others who had attended our first war council and stayed, had died since or, being badly wounded, had been carried home to live or die by God's will. We sat around the hearth on filthy sheepskins, staring into the red glow until our eyes smarted, each knowing what had to be said, none wanting to say it. In the haggard faces I saw reflected my own weariness.

'News has come from the north,' Waltheof began at last. 'Sweyn of Denmark has set a price for his ship-force. Three hundred he is prepared to send, under command of his sons, if we promise to meet his demands and hand over half any plunder gained during the fighting.' He hesitated, went on sardonically, 'But they will not be available – so the message says – until they have fulfilled other commitments. If they come, it will not be before summer's end.'

Disappointment, frustration, anger, all these flared within me for a moment then as suddenly disappeared as I forced calm on myself. 'What was the price?'

He named a sum which made us gasp, smiled grimly. 'More than twice that amount is stored here in York: Sweyn knows this. The atheling has a ship-force still and is adding to it all the time. The plan is to attack together from the Humber, take the city then sweep south. If necessary, the Danes will stay all winter and leave in spring when the Normans are finished.'

'So we've been wasting our time here, aye, and the lives of our men?' Arnkell made no attempt to hide his bitterness. 'We run away again while the likes of William Malet ravage our lands? Is that it?'

'I do not presume to command any of you,' Waltheof replied wearily. 'But we cannot take these castles alone. Nor are we fleeing in fear. Say rather that this is part of a greater strategy: a retreat to gather strength for the final fight. What better plan would you suggest?'

'As strategies go, it's better than nothing, if only to save our pride.' Siward Beorn stood with folded arms before the closed tent flaps; his shadow loomed behind him. 'But I know these Vikings: they cannot be trusted. What if the Bastard offers them a better price to stay away?'

A pained expression crossed Waltheof's face; he glanced at each of us in turn as if gauging our worth, then said quietly, 'Do not forget: Sweyn is of Cnut's blood. If needful, the Witan will uphold his claim over Edgar's.'

There was a faint smile on Arnkell's lips but the rest of us stared, astounded at such baldly stated treachery. Siward Beorn fingered his beard thoughtfully, his clear eyes suddenly hooded like a falcon's to hide his thoughts. 'It seems it is not only the Vikings who cannot be trusted,' he muttered but if Waltheof heard, he gave no sign. Silence fell as each of us considered the implications. I thought of the young atheling and wondered if he had guessed the frailty of the thread by which his life hung. Waltheof's speech made it clear that Marleswein, who had been sent as envoy to the Danish Court, must have been primed to offer the kingship should the promise of gold fail.

'Why should Sweyn believe those prepared to betray their own?' I asked at last, heavily. 'And do not forget how this land suffered under Cnut's sons. We might be ridding ourselves of the fox by letting in the wolf.'

Siward Beorn grunted in agreement while Waltheof nodded then spread out his hands as if to express a kind of helplessness, that of a man trapped by circumstance.

'Of course, it may be that the Witan would not follow my lead,' he said blandly. 'There are few of the old council left: we would have to elect a new one ere a king could be chosen. As Eorl Leofric's son and a man of rare renown, no doubt a place would be there for you, Hereward, and others of like mind.'

I bent my head, more to prevent him seeing my face than in acknowledgement. Siward Beorn let out a long breath of admiration.

'So let me get this right,' he said. 'We go north to join the Atheling in Scotland, return by the Humber when the Danes come, attack York, take its gold to pay off Sweyn's force, then move south, pushing the Normans back until we reach the sea. What of the Bastard's ships? And what's to stop the Vikings snatching the gold once York is taken, and leaving straightway?'

'The Danes will attack first along the south and east coasts: they have business in Ireland,' Waltheof replied with exaggerated patience. 'Every Norman ship they find will be destroyed. As to the gold: that's a risk we shall have to take. Even if Sweyn is suspicious of our offer of the kingship, still it will tempt him. And there is plunder to be gained in the south also.'

'Gildenborough was not so-called for nothing,' I added grimly. 'There are riches hoarded there that must rival the store of gold in York, enough to buy the Vikings for a year. Let them know that and they will come at least as far as Watling Street.'

Waltheof stared hard at me. 'Then I would have you and your men go south to make sure it stays in Borough until we need it. It is in the abbey's keeping?'

'Aye.' I could not wholly conceal my bitterness. 'I held land of them: I've seen some of the treasure with my own eyes. There are gold reliquaries, chalices, books studded with precious stones and I have heard of a gilded table and a gold crucifix it takes three men to lift. No abbey in the land is richer.'

'Good.' Waltheof sighed and scratched his head: the lice with which we were all infested had begun to stir in the warm fug of the tent. 'So far the Bastard has left the Church to itself for the most part: let us pray he does so for a little longer. But it may be as well to find a place where the gold can be defended, should it be needful to take it under your protection, Hereward.'

'I almost wish I could come with you,' Siward Beorn's eyes gleamed in the firelight. 'But it may be that the monks will give their gold willingly to our cause or am I mistaken in thinking the bishop is brother to Athelwine of Durham?'

'That may be but so far those of Borough have licked Norman hands like cringing curs,' I told him. 'In truth, I do not believe they'd give their wealth willingly to any man, be he Norman, Saxon or Viking. When the time comes, I'll know where to find it.'

'Have no doubt your loyalty will be rewarded.' Waltheof stretched and rose awkwardly to his feet. 'This Council is ended. I shall see you again, Hereward, when our force reaches Borough.'

'We'll be ready.' I inclined my head in acknowledgement and to my surprise he returned the gesture before striding out into the darkness. The giant, Siward, clapped me on the shoulder and I almost staggered under the unconscious weight of the blow.

'I look forward to fighting alongside you again,' he said. 'Wait for me before you go to fetch this gold.'

'That will depend on the Normans,' I answered. His clear eyes narrowed for a moment, then he gave a great guffaw and swept his hand from left to right.

'We'll drive them before us like sheep,' he said. 'Once they're out of their cursed castles, we have the measure of them now. When you hear our ships have entered the Humber, make ready. This time we'll have the bastards running for home!'

Acer and the others made no secret of their relief that we would be going home instead of to Scotland though they were less pleased when I told them we would not set out until after Easter, to cover the departure of Waltheof and his men. Arnkell also stayed for he had a fastness in the wild hills west of the city which he planned to strengthen and use as a rallying point for other disaffected folk of the region in preparation for the fight to come. Together we laid ambushes and even stormed the city wall to attack the new bailey one moonless night but the steep slopes and clinging mud slowed us and we were forced to retreat when barking dogs betrayed our presence and bowmen began shooting down. Though they loosed blindly in the darkness, so fierce was their response the arrows fell thick as hail and many found a mark.

It must have been obvious to our enemies that our numbers were much depleted because a few days after Waltheof's force had slipped away, William Malet and Gilbert de Ghent, who up till then had remained in the safety of their respective towers, emerged to harry the folk of York and the surrounding vills, those who had laboured to build the very castles from which they were now oppressed. Every day bands of mounted knights rode out, never numbering less then fifty, and while they may have suspected where we were, they did not risk an encounter with real fighters but instead wreaked vengeance on the poor and helpless. Sometimes when we entered a settlement to find food, we discovered only smoking ruins and the carcases of butchered livestock mingled with the sprawled bodies of women and children; the men would be hanging naked and mutilated from nearby trees. Where time allowed, we burned or buried the dead as best we could but more often than not we were forced to leave them as they were. Such wanton slaughter sickened us to the heart but it served to harden our resolve: we swore that whatever we found on our return home, we would not forget or forgive the cruelties inflicted here. Yet all this was but a foretaste of what was to come in the unhappy north.

2. Return to Bourne

No more Fen-wolves had died and I was still unscathed when, a few days after Easter, we at last turned our backs on York and set our faces for home. Arnkell embraced me as we made our farewells and we swore fealty to one another in the manner of blood brothers, Acer and a grim Northumbrian acting as witnesses. Then we parted, he leading his men west as we slipped south.

Avoiding settlements of any size, we passed unchallenged through the country. Labourers in the fields fled at the sound of hooves and trampling feet, the creak and jangle of mail and harness, or else stood watching in frightened huddles. Only rarely did any dare ask who we were and whether we formed the vanguard of a greater force come to rid them of their oppressors. We reassured these as best we could and hurried on. Their faces were full of desperate hope but we left them to their fate.

When we reached Lincolnshire the orchards were heavy with blossom, the air filled with the calling of young lambs, the rolling hills green with new grass. Many of the new overlords had gone to celebrate Easter in Winchester where the Bastard was holding court. Their estates we ravaged; any Normans we found, we harried and slew. While some reached the safety of the fortified steadings, they did not escape for the stone buildings were roofed with thatch or shingles and burned easily. We barred the doors and fired the eaves and though the screams of those trapped inside seemed to rend the air apart, shattering the springtime quiet of birdsong and insect hum, we felt no pity. Sometimes the serfs, fearing reprisals, begged us to leave without causing trouble but we paid them no more attention than one heeds the bawling of a cow as her bull-calf is led away to slaughter. Any Norman killed now was one less to fight in future.

It was maybe two weeks after setting out that we reached the northern margin of the Brunneswald. Passing beneath the twisted branches of its ancient oaks was like coming home. My senses quickened to the scents of leaf-mould and green leaves, a woodpecker's yammer; shafts of sunlight dappled the forest floor with light and shade. Sensitive as ever to my mood, Swallow lifted her head and picked up her feet. For the first time since leaving I was able to think of Turfrida and the children with joyful anticipation instead of longing.

Wuleric was guarding the way into camp, stretched like a cat along a great bough. He gave a piercing whistle to alert others to our arrival then dropped to the ground, bow in hand. His eyes surveyed us anxiously and I guessed he was trying to see who was missing. Though he was grinning with a kind of boyish relief at our return, he avoided my gaze.

'Of the Fen-wolves, only Douti was lost,' I told him. 'But many others fell. Is all well?'

He nodded, turned on his heel and began to walk swiftly along the narrow, twisting path. Alarmed by his apparent diffidence, I urged Swallow to lengthen her stride until the lad must have felt her breath on his neck. 'Wuleric – what's happened?' A cold hand seemed to tighten on my guts. 'Is Turfrida safe?'

He nodded again but did not speak. I leaned from the saddle, grasped his shoulder to wrench him round, saw he was afraid. Then, rather than bandy words, I pushed the mare to a trot, the fastest pace the nature of the path allowed. Erik, for once, did not shadow me. Maybe Wuleric prevented him or else he sensed this was not a time I needed my armour-bearer.

The stench of the middens scattered around its perimeter betrayed the presence of the camp before it came into view. By now, weathering and the accumulation of mould and leaves on their roofs made most of the shelters in the clearing indistinguishable from the background vegetation. Hearing hooves, women peered out of their doorways or rose to see what was happening. All were thin and dirty, their rags worn to the colour of earth: some looked more like fey creatures magicked from a handful of leaf-mould and twigs than human beings. They stared as if bemused as I rode past, their children standing mute beside them. None called a greeting or asked for news; they watched as if the figure of a horseman were something beyond their comprehension.

Dread gripped me. In the still air, smoke from the many hearths formed a pall which reached halfway up the trees, filtering the sunlight as if a malign spell lay upon the camp. Swallow snorted and shivered and I heeled her to a canter at the base of the slope, raced the last few strides to the holly-crowded hollow we had made our home.

Martin was sitting beside the stone-rimmed fireplace, trying to coax a blaze from a few sullen embers. He rose and came to take the mare without meeting my eyes. I sprang from the saddle, caught hold his shoulders, thrust my face almost into his. 'For God's sake, Martin, what has happened here? Where is Turfrida?'

Early spring is when the threat of starvation looms greatest yet it seemed to me his features were worn by grief rather than hunger. His eyes, sunken in bruised-looking sockets, held mine with the same meld of pity and fear I had seen in Wuleric's, only more intense. He jerked his head towards the shelter. 'She's inside. Go to her.'

There was no need. Hearing my voice, she came out, shuffling like an old woman, blinking in the bright daylight. I stared, stunned. In a few weeks, she seemed to have aged years. Godgifu, cradled in her arms, began to cry and she bent her head, murmuring to comfort the infant. I stared uncomprehendingly, waiting for Aedgifu to run out and greet me while a chill seemed to rise from the ground to freeze my blood. Then Turfrida looked up. Her grey eyes sought mine like those of someone drowning who sees help an arm's length away. She staggered and I went to her, enfolded her in my arms, felt her cling on as if she would never let go, her head pressed into the hollow of my shoulder while the babe squirmed between us. And I wanted to tip back my head and howl my loss to the sky so that all the world should hear and share in it but my men were gathered below, looking on in silence, and pride prevented my being so unmanned before them.

It was sickness that had taken her, Aedgifu my beloved, whose bright nature had lightened our lives, joy-bringer whose hair shone like oat-straw in the sun, now mouldering in a glade deep in the Brunneswald, her limbs stilled forever, her laughter silenced, mouth and eyes earth-stopped. Even as we hewed our way out through York's South Gate, she had lain delirious, shaking with ague as an aspen-leaf trembles in the breeze before being torn away. Many had been stricken with a cough at that time but with Aedgifu it had led to another bout of the marsh-sickness. This time the fever intensified despite all Rahere's efforts until, Turfrida told me, it wrenched the heart to see her bone-thin limbs jerk and shake with such force it seemed they must shatter. When death released her, they thanked God that she could rest in peace.

Those that had been there maybe took solace from such sentiments: for me there was no comfort. My grief was like a wave of the sea, a giant roller that picks up a hapless swimmer and bears him inexorably landwards until at last it slams him against the shore. I did not rest, I did not wait but held my wife until that first uncomprehending disbelief was replaced by a white rage. My mind was clear and cold yet fey. I kissed Turfrida, handed her to Aelgytha without wondering what she was doing there, mounted Swallow, called my men to follow. We were barely beyond sight of the camp, heading towards Bourne, when Martin forced his palfrey alongside.

'What are you doing?' His face and voice were anguished. I noticed that whilst girt with a sword he was without mail; his horse, grabbed from the pen, had neither saddle nor bridle, only a rope halter. This angered me and I did not answer. 'Where are we going?'

In the stillness of the afternoon the great trees stood like silent sentinels; clouds of insects danced in leaf-filtered shafts of sunlight; a wren's song, clear and poignant, sounded from close by: all these I noted but they were no longer part of my world. Like the Fairy Bear hurling itself against the bars of its cage I had only one thought, one purpose. The Normans had caused Aedgifu's death surely as if they had impaled her on a lance: had I not been dispossessed and outlawed she would not have caught the marsh-sickness; without them, we would still be living happily at Laughton: such was my reasoning. Toli's Hall, our home, was gone but Bourne, my patrimony, remained. We reached the edge of the wood and there I drew rein. Lambs gambolled in the rolling pastures; women toiled at planting and weeding the in-field; a horse whinnied from the yard. There was no sign of a single Norman: almost it seemed that nothing had changed since the day I returned from exile save for the wooden palisade built by Eadric and I. I smiled at the irony it might be used against me but knew it could not be held without a substantial force.

The Fen-wolves (no others had dared follow), gathered round in silence. They stared at the peaceful scene before them and some licked their lips or fingered their sword-hilts apprehensively, but none asked my intent. Even Acer, who rode at my right as usual, avoided my gaze. Martin alone had courage to question me. He leaned from my left (his palfrey shifting nervously as Swallow flattened her ears in threat), hissed urgently, 'Hereward, come away. This is madness!'

He was right but it was as if some external power had hold on me, rendering me invincible as when I had avenged Eadric. No weapon made by man could touch me. I stood up in the stirrups, drew the gleaming length of Brain-biter, tipped my face to the sky and let out the wolf's howl that had struck terror into the hearts of my enemies since I was a boy, only this time the cry seemed to rend my throat. I howled until I had no more breath while the others gave voice all around me, then launched Swallow down the slope.

Ugly and lean though she was, no horse could match my mare for speed and most of my men were on foot: soon they were left far behind. I heard Acer and Martin shout after me but heeded them no more than the crows which flapped up from a lamb's carcass at the thunder of hooves. The folk working in the fields had run for the settlement at the first wolf's howl; a shepherd stood and watched blank-faced with amazement while his dogs cowered in the grass at his feet. Ahead was the palisade, a solid fence of six-foot high pointed stakes. There was no guard platform on this western side but there was a gate, no different in outward appearance to any other section. In their terror or perhaps to aid us (for they can have been in no doubt who we were), the labourers had left it open.

Had I been in my right mind, I would have waited for the others although success in attack is all about impetus. Instead, I urged Swallow on. She charged through the gate and across the small inner paddock, piglets and chickens scattering in alarm while geese flapped and screeched, and on into the yard. There was no-one about but as I trotted the mare in a wide circle, brandishing my sword and shouting for the Normans to show themselves, I sensed eyes watching from the safety of the buildings. A horse whinnied from the stables, sparrows chattered in the eaves, then came rumbling hoofbeats and the yells of men as the Fen-wolves joined me.

The door of the Hall was closed. Acer dismounted and hammered upon the thick oak with the haft of his great axe, shouting to be let in else he would break down the door. Wuleric, sword in hand, went cautiously into the stables, Gamal at his shoulder. There was a startled cry: they returned dragging a boy of maybe ten years between them. I recognized him as the blacksmith's son.

'He says the Norman lord is gone,' Wuleric let the lad fall and he sat snivelling but did not try to run away. 'There's none here but a few servants.'

The truth of this was proven moments later when the great doors opened a chink. Acer thrust his axe into the gap and wrenched them apart. Eyes stared from the darkness on the other side: those who had fled the fields were huddled there. Most I knew from when we had lived at Bourne. Ade, the crone who had brought young Toli into the world and comforted Ymma after the raid, peered at me with her head tilted like a bird's, then hobbled out into the yard, calling the others to follow: 'All's well: it's young Hereward and his gang. They'll not harm us.'

They spilled silently into the yard, women and old men, hollow-cheeked, wary, distrustful. Then Wuleric strode forward to embrace the old woman and it was as if that act of affection opened a flood-gate. Suddenly they began to talk excitedly; they clustered round Acer asking whether it was over and the Normans had been defeated. Bile rushed into my mouth: I wheeled Swallow without any clear intent. A scream sounded from behind the Hall amid a flurry of noise akin to when the hounds close over a kill.

Some of my comrades followed as I cantered the mare through the narrow gap between church and wall to the rooms behind the main Hall. Siward the Red and Thorald had gone to watch this back door and shrewdly, rather than trying to force their way in, simply waited outside. Their patience had been well rewarded. Hearing the noise from the yard, three Normans had taken their chance to slip away unnoticed and walked straight into the trap.

One, who from the richness of his clothes I guessed to be a steward of some kind, lay moaning on the ground, hands pressed to his belly while a red stain spread beneath his fingers. A woman, young, dark-haired, knelt beside him while another man, barely more than a youth, stood defensively before them, dagger drawn. He was clean-shaven, dressed in a fine tunic of French cut and he met my gaze with the cold arrogance of his kind then spat defiantly on the ground.

He was brave or maybe the recklessness of despair inspired him but a green lad on foot has no chance against a seasoned fighter on horseback. I urged Swallow forward and, as he lunged, chopped off his dagger-hand. He stared disbelievingly at the stump and I swung the mare round and hacked down. The woman screamed like a trapped hare as the youth fell on top of her, his skull cloven. As she scrambled for the dagger, Siward dealt her a blow that sent her crashing down. Through the open door I thought I saw movement: more were inside. I sent Siward and some of the others round to flush them out, dismounted, handed Swallow's reins to Wuleric.

The woman moaned and began to crawl brokenly to where the man with the belly wound gasped and shuddered. Blood and saliva drooled from her mouth. The strength of her resolve horrified me: I knew that only death would stop her. I seemed to see myself from the outside as I stepped behind, grasped her hair and cut her throat. Blood spurted and gurgled, she sagged and I pushed her over with my foot, aware that my comrades were watching in appalled silence (it was an unspoken rule of ours that women and children should be spared unless they were known traitors). Only long after did I realize that she had reminded me of Turfrida as I had seen her before leaving for York.

Turning to the wounded man, I heard the clash of weapons from inside the Hall, followed by a man's death-grunt, sent the rest of my comrades to join the fight.

The steward's eyes were clouded with pain but he did not protest when I pulled his hands away to expose his wound. Maybe he thought I wanted to help him. Beneath his slashed tunic was a gaping slit. I saw the smooth darkness of liver, glistening coils of intestine, knew he might take days to die. I gripped his shoulders and pulled him into a sitting position. He cried aloud as his organs pushed against the wound, clapped his hands to the place to keep them in.

'Tell me where your master is and I will slay you quickly,' I told him. 'Else I will bind your hands and feet and let the pigs and dogs have you.'

Not understanding, he only moaned until I repeated my demand in his own tongue. Then he writhed beneath my hands and started to gabble, as if talking would somehow alter his situation.

From him I learned that Ogier the Breton had gone to join the Bastard at Winchester and was thence sailing home to see his wife and bring her back. He had taken all his men-at-arms and most of his servants, leaving no more than ten behind to run the estate. They had expected no trouble because all had been quiet: the outlaws in the Brunneswald were assumed to be dead or defeated. He spoke in gasps, eyes fixed on the dead woman.

I heard him out, then stooped to slash his throat. He died without struggling; next moment Siward and Acer came out of the Hall, followed by the others dragging Norman prisoners. Among them were two children, a boy and a girl. The boy, maybe four years old, kicked and tried to bite like a wildcat until Gamal struck him on the head and thrust him to the ground, half-stunned. The girl, who was perhaps Aedgifu's age, thin-faced and dark-haired, stared wide-eyed at the dead but made no sound. With them were three more men and two women. One of the men, bleeding heavily from a head wound, muttered what seemed an unending stream of obscenities as he was forced to kneel; the women, their faces mask-like with terror, clutched at one another, no doubt expecting to be raped. The other men, both young, looked upon us with contempt though from their dress they were only servants of some kind. They also were forced to their knees. I stepped forward, raised my reeking sword, felt the eyes of the Fen-wolves upon me as they waited to see what I would do. Then the man with the scalp-wound looked up and said in careful, heavily accented English: 'You are not men, you English, but animals and you will die like wolves in a trap.'

'Not today,' I replied and beheaded him with a single blow. Blood sprayed: the taste and stench of it cloyed in my mouth and nostrils. I thought of Eadric's head stuck on the gatepost; of Cole One-Hand's distorted, blood-blackened face; of Tiw, my war-horse, butchered, and little Aedgifu lying deep in woodland earth and a pain worse than any imagined death filled me. I think I cried aloud as I slew them, those kneeling men and women, hacking down to come at the darkness which had lodged deep inside me, a feeling of grief and futility immutable as stone. I heard screaming, thin and shrill as that of a hare caught by a weasel then hands gripped my shoulders and a voice said firmly in my ear, 'Hereward, no.'

My comrades stood in a silent ring and in that circle lay the seven dead, men and women tumbled on the ground as if a giant hand had picked them up and flung them down from a great height. Before me stood the two children, clinging to one another, the boy's face pressed into the hollow of the girl's shoulder. She stared at me defiantly though she was trembling. Her black gaze seemed to swallow mine and I looked away.

'Get them out of here.' My voice did not seem my own: harsh, expressionless. I looked at the bodies with a kind of dull resentment. 'Strip this carrion and dump it in the fen. No Norman will lie in Bourne earth.'

Usually they would have cheered but instead a low murmur of approval arose from the Fen-wolves, so wary were they of my mood. Someone, I think it was Gamal, led the children away. I never saw them again.

'Come.' Martin spoke as if to gentle a frightened or angry horse and I obeyed because nothing seemed to matter. An unutterable weariness had descended on me. I wanted only the black annihilation of sleep, to escape realization, to forget. Behind me came shouts and laughter as my comrades began to celebrate our return to Bourne but I stumbled as I walked, ignored their calls to join them, submitted to Martin's guiding hand like one bereft of will.

It was cool and dark and there was the sepulchral smell of damp stone and incense yet it took me some time to realize we were in the church. Almost I laughed, remembering how I had sought sanctuary there the night of Eadric's wake; Ymma's breasts in the moonlight, how her smell had clung to me even as I knelt before the altar. With an effort, I pushed memory aside and looked around though what I sought was no longer to be found in this world. The saints stared down from the walls as they had always done but the plain table was now adorned with a richly embroidered cloth and the bright enamel and gold idols of the Normans' faith. At the centre stood a painted wooden image of the Virgin and Child, the mother's head bent over the babe, her eyes grey, her hair beneath its cover dark like Turfrida's. The child's gilded hair shone in a shaft of sunlight falling through one of the high windows.

'You cannot bring her back,' Martin said softly. 'Let her go.'

I stared at my bloodstained hands. A black wave engulfed me, memory and grief unassuaged by the killing, and I would have cried aloud save that the breath choked in my throat. Then Martin put a hand on my shoulder and it was as if that contact breached a dam. My sobs seemed to wrench me apart until at last I was utterly spent. Then, after a while, I thanked him, rose and went outside.

Soon the bodies had been carted away and Norman heads again stared sightlessly from the spikes previously occupied by De Warenne and his brigands. I thought hard before displaying them thus but our occupation of Bourne was in itself an act of rebellion and it was my belief that the news would spread fear among the usurpers and hope to the oppressed. With the Fen-wolves and men from the Brunneswald I had a fighting force of sixty, not counting old men and boys who at need could wield a cudgel or axe, and of weapons there was no shortage because we found a great store in the outbuildings, enough for a small army. Some of these were finely balanced, well-wrought swords and lances from Normandy but others were rusty and of ancient pattern, spears and daggers looted from tenants.

When I asked the manor folk how they had fared under the Breton's lordship, they told me they had been robbed of anything of the slightest value, even to their iron cook-pots. Though given first choice of the hoard, most took back their old possessions despite their inferior quality, many of these having been passed down the generations. Their humble loyalty to the past was my men's gain for the Fen-wolves took the pick. What remained would be used to strengthen the defences, for it was my intention to lengthen and widen the ditch and set spears within so that no horse could cross without being impaled.

My mind was clear and cold as I directed my men and reassured the cottars that we meant them no harm but the knot of grief at the very core of me remained. Indeed, to all outward seeming I was the same man as before but part of me died that day along with those men and women, innocent perhaps as Aedgifu save that fate had made them Normans. Any vestige of mercy towards their kind had been scoured from my soul.

I sent Acer and some of the others to fetch all the folk from the woodland camp but Martin stayed behind.

'No Norman shall have Bourne while I live,' I told him as the procession of dispossessed emerged from the edge of the wood and began to cross the pasture. It was late afternoon. Horses dozed in the paddock, switching flies; the air was sweet with early hawthorn flowers. 'We should have stayed, not fled like frightened sheep when the Normans made their claim. Then Aedgifu would still be alive.'

He glanced at me and a look of pain fleeted across his features. 'Do not say that to Turfrida,' he warned. 'It was the marsh-fever that took Aedgifu: sometimes children die, you know that. And if we'd stayed, who knows what the Normans would have done? You cannot change the past, Hereward.'

I stared across the fields, seeking Turfrida amid the crowd, teeth clenched so tightly my jaw ached. So focused was I on controlling my anger, I did not hear Martin leave. When I looked round again it was to find myself alone.

While they had never been far apart, the reunion of those that had taken to the Brunneswald with their kin and friends who had stayed behind was joyful if only because the former now had a solid roof to look forward to and the others help in the fields and a life free of Normans. Many paused to thank me though some averted their eyes as if afraid. One face only I sought and as the line passed and still she did not appear fear gripped me that she was not there, that grief and resentment had turned her against me. I saw again her swollen, bloodied visage staring at me from the forest floor, the look of hate that had struck like a spear-thrust ere I left for York and coldness crept through my bowels.

Last of all she came, walking proud and erect, the babe in her arms, Aelgytha and, to my surprise, Rahere to either side. The tall Fen-man nodded gravely when we met and there was no trace of his usual sardonic wit in his eyes. He put a hand on Aelgytha's shoulder and steered her away to leave Turfrida and I alone.

She stood at arm's length, looked me over, taking in the blood which had dried to a rusty film on my skin and mail, the exhaustion that by now must have been clear for all to see, maybe the traces of my tears.

'How many?'

Her grey eyes were unreadable; her face blurred as I swayed in weariness. Remembering only kneeling figures, the thud of my blade into flesh and bone, the spray of blood, I shook my head.

'The women and children too?' Her voice was hard, insistent, cutting though the haze of tiredness and grief like a knife.

'Not the bairns.' My tongue was like a hunk of dried leather in my mouth. 'Turfrida?'

Godgifu let out a sudden cry, like that of a startled seabird, and began to wriggle. Turfrida lifted the child to her face, kissed her, then, with a strange expression that mingled love, exasperation and despair, thrust the babe into my arms.

'This is where comfort is to be found,' she said fiercely. 'In life, not death. When will you learn that grief cannot be washed away in blood? Do you think Aedgifu's soul will be gladdened by the slaying of innocent men, women and children?'

The babe squirmed in my arms and began to wail, disturbed no doubt by the hardness of my mailcoat, the stench of blood and sweat that clung to me. Turfrida's steady gaze held mine. There had been a note of defiance in her tone I did not understand and a hurt, baffled anger gathered deep within me.

'They were not innocent, they were Norman usurpers,' I growled, thrusting the child back at her. 'And I told you: the brats were spared.'

Godgifu began to yell and the din battered my ears: I could not think properly. Deftly, Turfrida opened her tunic and put the child to her breast but her eyes did not leave mine and in the forbearance of her gaze I realized suddenly the true nature of my rage. Guilt seemed to press upon me like a heavy and remorseless hand, stemming back to the day I had struck her for the wound to my pride and ridden away without a word of farewell.

'Turfrida.' The name came like a death-gasp. She shook her head slightly and stepped forward, putting her free arm around to hold me. I bent my head against hers, felt the softness of her hair against my face. Her steadfastness and the warmth of her compassion were like a balm; she murmured my name and I knew that beyond all reason I was forgiven.

Over the next few days we cleared every trace of Norman occupation from Bourne and built new homes for those who had had no proper roof since being dispossessed. No neighbouring estates now operated under Saxon thegns: those still living on the land of their forbears were, at best, in the position of stewards under Norman lords. Gilbert de Ghent, who held vast fiefdoms including manors at Folkingham and Witham was, of course, occupied at York; Ivo Taillebois and De Warenne were at Winchester where, we heard, my nephews had returned to court, perhaps realizing that cringing abasement was more likely to gain them their rights than rebellion. The Bastard, it seemed, forgave their inconstancy and Edwin stayed in the south but Morcar was more circumspect and returned to Mercia though he did not come to Bourne. Perhaps he assumed it was still in Norman hands or else when he heard the news (which spread like wildfire among the disaffected), was ashamed. Either way, we heard no more of them for some time though folk flocked from miles around to join us.

I knew in my heart that if a large force was sent against us, Bourne could not be held but my hope was that the Danes would reach the Humber and the Atheling's force sweep south ere that happened. At need we could return to the Brunneswald or the Fens and to that end I asked Rahere to find us a refuge in the marshes. With those from the camp and Bourne together with fugitives and rebels who joined us every day, we numbered more than two hundred.

'No need to look,' he told me with his wolf's grin. 'Ely is the place, if you can stomach the company of monks. Two thousand of us could live there with no-one the wiser, if the holy men kept their mouths shut. It's an island for more than half the year and only two roads in, one of which is impassable at high tide, the other with a ferry-ride at the end of a long causeway. Ay, it's a place rich in gold and tilth, best eels in all the Fens and I should know: I've been raiding the abbey's traps since I was tall enough to pole a boat.'

'I remember.' It was with my father that I had gone there as a child. Whilst I could not remember the reason for our visit, I recalled how I had been awestruck by the great stone-built abbey standing high above the surrounding fens as if set to guard against heathen raiders from the sea. A courtyard there was with arches that seemed to spring from the ground, stone carved by the will of skilled men to the greater glory of God; a hall hung with embroideries, tables set with golden cups and platters which gleamed in the firelight; a tall monk who stooped to bless me, his fingers like dry sticks in my hair, my father's reprimand when I flinched from that unwanted touch.

'The abbot, Thurstan, is no great admirer of your uncle,' Rahere said softly, his words coinciding so exactly with the run of my thoughts that I stared at him in astonishment. 'Long have their abbeys vied for gold, land and royal favour. And the folk of that country have ever wanted a true King, neither Godwineson nor foreigner. You would be hard put to find a better refuge.'

I thanked him and asked that he show Acer, Siward the Red and Wuleric the way to the Isle though the marshes so that someone could lead the others there if ill befell me. Martin, overhearing, looked at me askance, thinking such caution ill-omened but mindful of the task entrusted to me by Waltheof, I was more circumspect than before. And also, Aedgifu's death had affected me more than I dared admit even to myself. It had reiterated how precious was each moment spent with those I loved, how fragile the web of chance that kept them from harm. For myself, I feared death no more than before but I worried what would become of Turfrida and Godgifu if I were slain or captured and so planned our next attacks in such detail that old hands like Acer and Gamal complained there was no renown to be gained where success was assured.

While the Fen-wolves grumbled that the edge of danger was gone from our lives, more of the disaffected joined us. Of these I was wary and, ever mindful of the chance of treachery, laid upon them a heavy oath of fealty. None of the newcomers was privy to our plans until they had earned my trust, nor did we relax the rules which bound the Fen-wolves. Thus the core of my force remained unchanged, an elite to which the others aspired but few achieved.

The Norman occupation had done nothing to ease the hardships of the cottars of Bourne, short-handed since the carnage at Fulford Gate, therefore when we were not out raiding we laboured in the fields or ventured into the fens after fish and birds. There was a hidden purpose to the latter work. Mindful that one day we might be forced to a fugitive life, I wanted all who joined us to become as skilled in fen-craft as my comrades of the Wolves though to some from the south or west, the wild expanse of mere and marsh was an alien and dreadful place. Many had never set foot in a boat of any kind and regarded the slim reed punts of the Gyrwas as one unused to horses might look upon a powerful *destrier*. But pride and the knowledge that one day their lives might depend on such skills overcame their reluctance, spurred, no doubt by fear of drowning. The number able to swim I could count on the fingers of one hand.

In this manner, attacking Norman estates one day, sheep-shearing or hay-cutting the next, weeks passed. There was no word of Ogier the Breton, erstwhile Lord of Bourne, and lesser Normans who had been granted land in the area began to move to safer fiefdoms or back to Normandy, ostensibly to visit their wives. Indeed, so uncertain was the Bastard of his hold on the country, he sent Mathilde to the safety of Rouen. He was no fool: he knew our abandonment of York had not been a defeat but strategic withdrawal, must have guessed that a great force was massing against him somewhere beyond his reach.

Harold Godwineson's sons came from Ireland to raid along the south-west coast, perhaps hoping for support from those who had aided their mother's escape after the Exeter revolt but they were quickly repelled, not by Normans but locals who, like the Fen-folk, bore their kin no good-will. There were other small instances of insurgency, regions like ours where no Norman dared venture without an escort of two score knights, yet no concerted action was launched to quell it. From this I deemed that the Bastard, like us, was waiting.

Two years to the day after Eadric's death, Turfrida, Martin and I visited Croyland. Aelgytha came also though her thoughts seemed less with the dead than the man who strode protectively at her side, a seasoned fighter called Harald who had been with Eadric the Wild on the Welsh borders for a while. He must have seen upwards of forty years and from his dark hair and short, wiry stature had Welsh blood but he made Aelgytha laugh and I was happy for her, knowing how she had mourned Cole One-Hand.

It was a blustery day, the reed-stems clashing in the wind and seagulls crying overhead. Godgifu, who was sitting on my shoulders as we walked, let go my hair and lifted her hands as if to touch the wheeling birds. She had grown into a sturdy child, darker than Aedgifu and with her mother's grey eyes but while I loved her dearly, it was not with the passion I had felt for our firstborn. Of Ymma and our son I tried not to think, avoiding that pain as a horse shies from fire. Even when the buildings of the abbey appeared, squat and solid amid the rippling reeds and water, I pushed them from my mind though I could not wholly deny the dread and guilt which gathered as we crossed the wooden bridge and approached the gates.

Ulfkil welcomed us warily, unable in conscience to refuse us entry when we were come to pay our respects to the dead, uncertain how news of our visit might be received by the Normans. He looked careworn and tired and when we told him of Aedgifu's death, muttered something under his breath that sounded more like bitter curse than prayer. Pitying him, Turfrida laid her hand on his arm and the old churchman seemed to take more comfort from her than she from him.

A large number of the dispossessed from North Norfolk as well as Lincolnshire had taken refuge in the abbey. They stared uneasily at our weapons and mail as we made our way to the church and thence to the graveyard. The mounds under which Toli and Eadric lay had sunk a little and greened over, were studded with kingcups. The others knelt piously in the long grass and Godgifu crawled in pursuit of an azure dragonfly while I stared across the marshes, assailed by sudden despair. But I knew that to rail against fate is futile: it ill becomes a man to berate God like a woman scolding the flames that have scorched her baking bannock. I clenched my hands and turned again to the graves, became aware that the abbot was watching me intently.

We walked a few paces away and I saw that while the rest were absorbed in prayer, Martin's gaze followed me. When he was confident we could not be overheard, Ulfkil leant close.

'Ymma is gone,' he said quietly. 'With a young boy, she could not devote her life to Christ. She sent word to her kin in East Anglia and they came to fetch her a few days ago.' He paused, his face troubled. 'She asked me to tell you she will not let the child forget whence he came, that when he is old enough she will send him to you to learn the skills Eadric wanted to teach his son. And she said also that she would pray for you.'

I bowed my head, afraid of what my face might betray. The abbot's deep-set, piercing eyes regarded me steadily, without accusation, more a kind of pitying forbearance. I realized then that he knew or had guessed the truth, though if given in confession he would never divulge it.

'Then if you have cause to meet her again, thank her for her thoughts,' I said deliberately. 'And her son will always have a place with me, if I live so long.'

He gave a strange smile, as if he had expected no other reply, then nodded. 'I will make sure that the message reaches her.' He hesitated, added wistfully, 'He is a fine, strong boy, young Hereward. God keep the both of them.'

'Aye.' I inclined my head briefly in gratitude and acknowledgement. Ulfkil went to the graveside and began to intone a blessing but I looked eastward and prayed that one day I would see my son return to Bourne.

Had Aedgifu been alive, I think Turfrida would have been upset by Ymma's departure; as it was she took the news with a kind of bland acceptance that verged on indifference. She longed to give me a son: that Ymma should have borne two boys irked her though such is often the way of it. To see young Hereward so soon after losing our beloved daughter would have hurt her deeply; had she guessed the truth, she might have deserted me and taken Godgifu to Flanders. But as long as Ymma stayed away, my secret was safe and that knowledge was like the lifting of a great weight. Though I had not been conscious of it, that guilt, the fear of discovery, had haunted me since the day of the child's birth.

By the time hay harvest was over we had still heard nothing from the north. The uneasy peace continued and from Folkingham to Witham no Norman had been seen for weeks, so strongly did terror of the Fen-wolves lie there. My network of spies now covered all the Fenland and as far west as Northampton and a system of beacons was set up to warn of approaching enemies. But the days passed and no smoke rose to call us to arms. I began to wonder if, yet again, the seeds of rebellion had failed or the Danes betrayed us despite the promises of Waltheof and Marleswein.

Whenever I grew restless, Turfrida bade me look at the folk going about their work on the estate much as they had always done, the captured *destriers* grazing the paddocks, the ripening crops and fattening beasts, and be glad, for by my will and the swords of my men had this haven been secured. Yet though this was true, in my heart I knew that we had met no serious opposition in re-taking Bourne and to hold it might be a different matter.

I tried to be patient but the first hint that the tide was turning against my enemies came from Borough where Brand had been taken ill. Thorald, who was one of my best spies, brought news that Bishop Athelric had asked all the inhabitants of the burgh to pray for the abbot's speedy recovery. I spat into the fire then, aware of Martin's warning glance, asked what pestilence had struck my uncle down. The young man looked uncomfortable and replied that there had been no official disclosure but rumour was rife it was the King's Sickness. This was the malady which had brought the Confessor to his death-bed, the rottenness that turns a man's breath to honey and his extremities to a putrescent foulness. Imagining Brand's soft, grasping fingers turning black and sloughing off to useless stumps, his gross pudenda swelling like turgid wineskins until he screamed in helpless agony, I could not restrain a smile and had to turn away ere Turfrida saw. For days afterwards I was in gleeful mood though if anyone asked the cause I told them I was sure that the combined rebel and Danish forces would soon sweep down from the north.

When we did hear at last of the Danes, tidings came rather from the south. It was just before Lammas Day and I was assessing the barley, savouring the sweet, milky taste of the ripening kernels when I saw a rider approach. Outi One-Hand was with me. He whistled softly between his teeth and loosened his dagger in its sheath but I had already recognized horse and rider as Wuleric on the liveliest of the captured warhorses. He waved wildly and charged straight though the standing grain, brought the stallion to a rearing halt almost on top of us.

'The Vikings have attacked!' His face was alight with excitement; the horse snorted and tossed its head. I laid a hand on its neck to steady it, noting the muscles hard as iron, the hot, wet skin, while my mind raced.

'Where? How many?'

'All along the south coast: they came from Ireland. They're working their way round Kent.' The *destrier* sidestepped, away from my hand and I frowned: a warhorse should move only at its master's command. 'They say there are twelve score ships.' Aware of my displeasure through his enthusiasm, Wuleric sat straighter in the saddle and shortened rein, bringing the animal under control. 'Sweyn's brother, Osbjorn, and two of his sons are leading the ship-force. They're burning every Norman boat they find. The Bastard was in Winchester – there was nothing he could do!'

I was silent, letting the significance of the news sink in. The two watched me expectantly.

'Vikings are fickle allies,' I said at last, then seeing their faces falter, added quickly, 'but there is gold enough in this land to buy each of them thrice over. Once they enter the Humber we can be sure of them. This is the start of it lads, the fight that will rid us of the Normans once for all! Wuleric, spread the news as far as you can and tell the Fen-wolves to meet by Thor's Tree at sunset. The Fen-wolves only, mind, none of the others. Do you understand? And make sure Rahere comes.'

He grinned and nodded, then sent the horse from standstill to full gallop, heading for the hall. His excitement was infectious. Outi and I looked at one another, then at the trampled swathe through the barley and laughed from a mixture of joyous relief and apprehension.

'God knows, we've waited long enough,' Outi surveyed the stump of his right wrist regretfully. 'Will you take me with you when you go? I can fight as well as ever now and I've Douti's blood-price to take as well as this loss to avenge.'

There was desperation behind his earnestness. Since his twin brother's death he had rarely strung so many words together and I had no right to deny him vengeance.

'You will be there,' I promised.

Thor's Tree was an ancient lighting-blasted oak which stood alone in a sheep pasture just beyond sight of Bourne. Whether it had been named after the Thunderer who struck it or someone given the god's name, no-one knew but it was an old trysting place for lovers and those who wanted their affairs kept secret. Ever since I could remember, it came late to leaf so that we thought it had died at last; each spring, when the hawthorn flowers were fading, the first green buds would unfurl on the gnarled and twisted branches save those seared by the thunderbolt. Some of the ancients in the local vills, clinging to remnants of pagan custom, venerated the tree and occasionally votive rags or little carved figures could be found jammed into fissures in the bark. To the Fen-wolves it was simply a good place to meet, especially as all the gang now lived at Bourne, save Rahere who scorned all burgh-dwellers.

Wuleric's news had fired my comrades into reckless mood; some were already half-drunk when they reached the tree. I stood on a knotted root, my back against the rough trunk and some shouted my name while others howled our war-cry. Apart from myself and Turfrida, only Martin and those who had been in York understood the full significance of the tidings but the size of the ship-force alone suggested that the attacks were no mere raids for plunder. Two hundred and forty was the number Harald Hardrada had thought sufficient for an invasion.

Pushing aside thoughts of the warrior-king's failure, the fact that he also had begun at York intending to join a larger force even as Sweyn's sons were due to meet Edgar's, I raised my hand for silence. Their faces alive with hope, my comrades waited until someone, unable to bear the tension, yelled, 'Come on Hereward! When do we march?'

Laughter arose at his eagerness but it stopped abruptly when I said, 'This time, we do not.' They listened in bewildered silence as I told them we had been entrusted with a secret mission, that to accomplish it we must wait for the fight to come to us when the combined English and Danish force moved south.

They were my comrades, many of whom I had known since childhood, others whom I loved as brothers, but I was leader. They looked askance at one another as my words sank in and some muttered discontentedly but none dared voice open dissent. Then Acer, who stood at my right, chuckled grimly. 'At least we won't wear out our boots going north again,' he said. 'Anyway, I've had a bellyful of York though it'd have been good to see those cursed castles fall at last.'

'You'll see plenty of castles fall, aye and burn to the ground, ere this is over,' I promised. 'This time we have the measure of the bastards: with the Danes we'll outnumber them. This time we'll drive them back to the sea and with their ships destroyed they can swim for home!'

As they shouted their enthusiasm, I signalled Rahere who stood grim and taciturn amid the tumult.

'The Danes should be past Dover by now, working their way north,' I said quietly. 'If they come into the Wide Sea, let me know. I would meet these sons of Sweyn ere the real fighting starts. Men who can be bought once are always open to a higher bidder.'

His keen eyes narrowed but he did not speak, simply nodded in acknowledgement and strode away. I watched until he was lost to view then turned to Acer. 'Come on, let's celebrate the beginning of the end!'

Between disappointment at not marching straightway and anticipation of fierce fighting in the near future, the men went a little wild that night and most of the cottars hid behind barred doors for fear of being made sport of. I joined in the drinking for a while then, as the mead took hold and feat-challenging began, went to find Turfrida. She was in the back room with Aelgytha. I barred the door to keep out drunken intruders, unbuckled my swordbelt and laid the weapon aside. The women watched circumspectly as

I sat on the bed that had been Eadric and Ymma's. Godgifu crawled across the floor to my feet and grasped the hem of my tunic in an effort to stand.

'Were they angry?' Turfrida gestured towards the door behind which a raucous burst of noise told of someone's failure to reach the mead-bench.

'Surprised, maybe.' I shrugged, lifted the child onto my lap. 'We seem to have spent half a lifetime waiting for this fight to start in earnest. God grant we succeed this time, else we may as well give up. At least no-one's called me coward for not going north at once.'

Godgifu, seeking attention, reached out and pulled herself to her feet by hauling on my hair. I yelped and the women exchanged amused glances ere Turfrida came to rescue me. Behind her smile, her eyes were grave and as she lifted the child away, Aelgytha rose and left discretely through the back door. More shouting came from the hall, then a drinking song began.

'They must see there is nothing to be gained by marching to seek out war when it will come here anyway,' Turfrida said, setting Godgifu down to play with the wooden animals that had been her sister's. Her eyes were on the child yet her tone was apprehensive. 'The Normans will destroy everything in their path if they are forced to retreat. Do not leave us defenceless, love.'

She turned to meet my gaze and for the first time I saw fear lurking in her eyes. Her face was pale and worn by grief and anxiety; remembering how I had left her before, my heart was wrung. I rose and gathered her into my arms and we held one another while the child played, absorbed in her own world.

'I will make sure you are safe,' I promised, though even as I spoke a picture of my warhorse's head stuck on a spear, the sound of flies buzzing over his entrails, Ivo Taillebois' mocking laughter, filled my mind. And it seemed that Turfrida was thinking the same for she shuddered and pressed her head into the hollow of my shoulder. But a moment later she pulled away to look into my face and her eyes were hard.

'And how will you do that?' she asked bitterly. 'You have said often enough that Bourne cannot be held against serious attack. Will you hide me away like Ymma or have me skulk in the fens or woods until we lose our other child?'

Disconcerted by her reference to Ymma and her vehemence, I stared, wondering if her abrupt change in mood were due to her moon-time. But when I asked, she gave a derisive snort and said disgustedly, 'Ach, I should have expected no more from a man. I am not a brood-mare to be used, then moved from stable to pasture as the whim takes you.'

'I have never thought of you as such.' I watched, shaken, as she went to stand with her back against the door. The child played on, oblivious to all save her game; from inside the hall a shout marked the end of one song and the beginning of another; fists thumped tables to keep the beat. 'What, then, would you have me do?'

Her eyes held mine unwavering; the muscles of her face were taut. Silence stretched between us. When she spoke at last, the words came clearly spaced as drops of blood falling from a wound.

'If this rising fails like all the others, I would have you turn from the fight,' she said. 'Make peace with the King or if your pride prevents that, take me with you to Denmark or Flanders. Cnut was a wise man: he understood the futility of trying to stay the tide. Will you not heed his example?'

As when she had insulted the Fen-wolves ere I left for York, her lack of faith astounded me. And, as then, my anger flared but remembering what had happened last time, I contained it though the effort to do so took all my will.

'We are fighting Normans, not the sea,' I retorted. 'And this time we shall win. What has happened, Turfrida? You know I would cut off my sword-hand rather than submit to William, bastard ruler of a usurped land. Once, you had faith in me.'

A burst of cheering sounded from the hall but it seemed to come from another world. Sensing the tension between us, Godgifu left the toys and crawled towards Turfrida who bent to pick her up then cradled her, opening her tunic automatically. The sight of her breast, white and smooth against the rough cloth, evoked a rush of tenderness through me that had nothing to do with sex. I longed to take her in my arms, to shield her and our child from all that threatened us. But there was no compassion in Turfrida's eyes as she returned my gaze, only a kind of detached appraisal, as if I were a stranger.

'Since then I have lost my home and a child, to say nothing of my own honour,' she replied. 'You promised to return ere Easter. Weeks I waited while our daughter sank towards death in a shelter made of sticks and hides and no news came save that William had retaken York and hung the rebel dead from the city walls. I will not do that again, Hereward, living between despair and grief from day to day, not knowing if you are still alive. No, I would rather take a nun's veil. At least then I would not have to fear the likes of Ivo Taillebois, half-expecting him to ride into camp with all his men and your head hanging from his saddle!'

'That will not happen!' My voice had risen; with an effort I controlled it. 'Turfrida – I swear I will never desert you. Believe me!'

She smiled. 'Go to your men,' she said and it was only long after, when I had cause to recall this scene, that I recognized the wistfulness of her tone. 'They will be missing their leader.'

With that she turned to open the door and went outside after Aelgytha, the child still at her breast. Thinking we understood one another, I grabbed a piece of bannock and ate it hastily before returning to the hall where my comrades welcomed me as if I had been long away.

3. The Camp of Refuge

In late August the Danes entered the Humber where they were met by the Atheling's force of eight-score warships. These carried the core of the rebel army led by Edgar, Waltheof, Gospatrick and Marleswein. The rest marched from the north, joined all along the way by folk sick of want and oppression. York was their intended target and those who had been there earlier in the year must have felt some trepidation, knowing how well it was defended. But when they came within sight of the city, they found it already destroyed.

The smoke in the sky must have warned them but to find the place they had thought to liberate turned to a blackened ruin dismayed all save the Danes to whom a lump of molten metal was of as much worth as the most finely wrought reliquary, so long as it was gold. We heard that the castellans, Gilbert de Ghent and William Malet were responsible. Hearing of the approaching rebel force, they had fired the houses surrounding the castle lest their timbers be used to infill the defensive ditches. A strong wind had sprung from the south and the fire spread swiftly. Some said it was as if the wrath of God had passed over the city, great vortices of flame spiralling high above the buildings, destroying all in their path. The whole city was gutted save the ancient Roman walls and the castle towers on their mounds: abbey and minster were lost. That the usurpers had been spared while the bodies of hundreds of ordinary folk lay charred and twisted in the ashes of their homes was an added bitterness to the survivors who had lost the little that remained to them after years of oppression.

Archbishop Aldred died but a few days before the rebels' return to York. Torn between conflicting loyalties to his Church; the atheling whom he had upheld ere Hastings, then repeatedly denied; the Norman usurper he had anointed King, and the Pope, that distant power whose grasping desire had legitimised the Bastard's claim, he died weary and broken. Perhaps, hearing of the Danes' progress north, even he had realized that outright war was inevitable, that he was powerless to prevent it and God, in his mercy, saved him witnessing what was to follow in the land he had struggled to save. The Atheling must have hoped that this time the Archbishop would relent and acclaim him, thus strengthening his right to the throne: now this could never happen.

The arrival of the rebel force, which with the Danes numbered thousands, at least gave the people of York something to celebrate and they were welcomed with much rejoicing. Although the wooden towers on top of the mottes had survived the fire, huge gaps had been made in the palisades and the Normans could only watch and wait as the force approached, a tide of men swelled by enraged townsfolk who grabbed anything that could be used as a weapon as they swept through the rubble-strewn streets. They stormed both castles, overwhelming the garrisons by sheer weight of numbers, and massacred all they could find. Waltheof, it was said, felled more than twenty Normans single-handed as they attempted to flee though a postern gate.

Two men only survived the slaughter. Both castellans were captured with their wives and children. Even in defeat they acted with the cool arrogance of their kind, the men promising swift retribution, the women swearing by the Blessed Virgin that if raped, they would stay from their husbands for a year and strangle any babe they bore that might be of Saxon blood. They had, so far as I know, no cause to do so. Waltheof, who had them in his keeping, knew that while the ransom value of William Malet and Gilbert de Ghent was enough to safeguard his own head, abuse of the prisoners would be punished, should the rebellion fail. Thus they were closely guarded and Sweyn's sons, Cnut and Harald, kept away. There were widows enough in York and its environs to satisfy even a Viking horde, though doubtless many submitted unwillingly to their ravishing.

Elated by the ease of victory, there was much rejoicing amongst the liber-ating forces and messages were sent to every corner of England, calling on all able men to join the fight. It was towards the end of September that we heard the news and it made us all restless though we were bound to stay and safeguard Borough's treasure. To appease the disquiet that seethed beneath the surface, I sent Erik and Outi with a return message to Waltheof and the other leaders, confirming my purpose. So long was it since I had had parchment and quill to hand, the letters came blotted and awkward and I had Martin transcribe for me, ashamed as I was of my lack of skill.

'Maybe as a boy you should have paid more attention to lessons and less to beating up your fellows,' remarked Turfrida, who was watching with a sardonic eye while Godgifu played with a discarded quill. Martin, his head bent over his work, chuckled, then leaned back and handed over the pen for me to sign my name. With Erik going north, he was in good humour: a seemingly friendly but in truth bitter rivalry had sprung between them that I wanted to stamp out ere it turned to bloodshed.

'Aye, and would you have married me if I had been a soft-handed scribe?' I asked, and left before she could answer.

A day after the pair had ridden north on two of the *destriers*, ominous news came from the west. It seemed that the Bastard had been hunting in the Forest of Dean when he heard of the burning and capture of York. He was usually a man of icy self-possession but at these tidings, he was wroth. Within days his whole force had mustered and begun the journey north, wreaking destruction on every vill they passed.

As soon as we heard this, our excitement began to wane and hope was overtaken by dread. Once more we waited and though everyone on the estate was busy with preparations for winter, there was not one man, woman or child who, hearing hooves on the track, did not rush into the yard in expectation of news.

My enemies, Ivo Taillebois and William de Warenne, were with the Bastard, thus more to relieve our pent-up frustration than because we needed the supplies, we raided their estates yet again, slaying any Normans foolish enough to remain. Fine cloth, weapons, gold and silver we took but the freshly harvested grain we distributed to the poor. All the recipients blessed and thanked us then hid the stores where the Normans, if they returned, would not find it. Much of the harvest had been spoilt by rain that year: at least now the cottars would not starve.

As at other times when our futures hung on events beyond my control, an ungovernable restlessness gnawed me. With the Normans away, I rode openly about the country and every day our numbers at Bourne increased as those minded to fight joined us. But as news trickled from the north, we began to realize that there would be no glorious sweeping of the invaders from our land ere Christmas. Winter and the Bastard's swift response had thwarted our purpose yet again.

Soon after the third anniversary of our defeat at Hastings, Rahere sought me out, his gaunt face even grimmer than usual. News travels swiftly over water he was fond of saying and the season had not quite closed the sea-road. He had heard from a fisherman, who had been told by a merchant, that York had been abandoned by the rebels. The Danes had taken to their ships while the rest simply dispersed as soon as rumour of the Bastard's approach reached them.

Reason dictated that the burnt ruins of the city provided no stronghold yet I was not alone in bitterness at these tidings. Indeed it was then, three full years since the usurpers set foot on English soil, that the task we had taken upon ourselves weighed most heavily. We heard of sporadic fighting in west Mercia which drew the Bastard away from the environs of York but he left two of his most formidable commanders behind with orders to hold the city and keep the Danes penned north of the Humber. Prevented from sailing home by storms and knowing themselves safe from sea-borne attack, having destroyed the Normans' ships, the Vikings set up camp on the Isle of Axeholme and played a cat and mouse game, dodging back and forth across the Humber, refusing to engage in open fight. The Atheling, with Gospatrick, Marleswein, Waltheof and Siward Beorn had retreated to the wilds of Northumbria where Arnkell had established a refuge but the hostage castellans (along with much of York's store of gold), were handed into custody of Osbjorn, King Sweyn's brother, thus giving the Danes surety that the Bastard would negotiate if things went ill.

The rebellion in Mercia faded into a series of bloody skirmishes, the rebels taking to the woods as soon as the Normans were engaged so that they could not use their horses to full effect. It was rumoured that Morcar was involved. Edwin, who had stayed at court (presumably to protect his eorldom), but refused (or was not trusted), to march with the Bastard, now fled north, no doubt fearing he would be implicated by his brother's insurrection. I sent Thorald to find them for it seemed to me that if we joined forces, we could trap the main body of the Norman army along the borders of Mercia and Northumbria, calling for the Danes to close in from the east while the Atheling's men moved from the north. But by the time he reached Stafford, delayed by flooding, the chance was already lost. The news he brought on his return was that having quelled the uprising in Mercia, the Usurper, instead of heading south to London or Winchester as reason dictated, had stayed to oversee the building of a new castle at Nottingham, then marched his men north again.

That winter was one of the harshest in living memory. Heavy rain through October and into November turned every road to a morass and rivers burst their banks while the beech mast and acorns on which the pigs usually foraged rotted on the ground. At slaughter-time, all the beasts were thinner than usual and folk still camped in the Brunneswald, too afraid to seek refuge at Bourne or Croyland, crept out to beg for scraps at the gates though we had little to spare.

Outi and Erik, whom we had given up hope of seeing ere spring, assuming they had stayed with Waltheof, returned on a December day when a bitter east wind brought snow swirling in across the marshes and froze the churned mud of the yard into iron-hard pocks and ruts. So swathed in rags of cloth and animal skin were they that the guards took them for beggars. Only when Erik shouted that he was a Fen-wolf and named his sword were they allowed in: ever mindful of betrayal we were wary of all travellers. Once inside the hall, the pair huddled so close to the fire that their clothes steamed and all stared in horror when they pushed back the cloths wrapped round their faces, so startling was the change in them. The lad, Erik, always thin, looked as if his skin would barely stretch to cover his bones; Outi, who seemed stunned, was equally emaciated, his skin blotched with weeping sores. Their lips were cracked and bleeding: neither spoke.

Erik's mother, Gerd, and Ade the crone rushed to bring them warmed mead and the porridge of pease and barley which had become our staple while a crowd gathered as news spread of their return. I was out with Martin, checking on the cattle which we had driven from open pasture into the shelter of the woods, when a stable-lad came to fetch us. We hurried back as soon as we could but need not have worried about missing their tale. Erik was busy wolfing down food while Outi, who was so weak he had to be spoon-fed like a child, had not yet uttered a sound.

The crowd parted to let us through and Turfrida came to stand anxiously at my side for there was an air of desperation about the two that dismayed us all. At last Erik finished eating, laid his spoon down and took a long draught of mead. Until then he had avoided meeting anyone's gaze, even his mother's, but now he raised his head and his eyes, dark and huge in their sunken sockets, sought mine.

'The bastards,' he said, then shook his head as if to dislodge some dreadful memory. 'I thought I'd seen the worst of men when our home was destroyed but these Normans . . .' His voice trailed into silence but his gaze remained fixed on my face, as if to draw strength from my presence. 'I – we . . . ah God, how can I describe it?' He took a deep, shuddering breath, then as I told him to start at the beginning, smiled weakly and drank again. Whether it was the effect of the mead or the silent expectation of his audience I know not but when he spoke again his voice was calmer and, as his tale continued, it grew in strength as if the telling in some way dispelled the horror.

'The Normans got to York before us: my horse went lame and there was flooding everywhere,' he said. 'There was nothing left of the city, just broken walls and the mottes, everything else was charred ruin. It was chaos, folk trying to make a living from whatever they could find while the Normans forced them to rebuild the castles. Anyone who refused, however sick or weak, was beaten until they obeyed or died. Even Outi and I helped. By that time, bands of knights were scouring the countryside for rebels, pillaging and destroying as they went. When the Bastard went to quell the rising in Mercia, everyone thought that was the last they'd see of him, but he came back. What had happened up till then was only the start.

'The Vikings still held Gilbert de Ghent and William Malet, so William negotiated with them. He would let them overwinter on the Humber with foraging rights from the Trent to the Ouse if they promised peace and to return to Denmark in the spring. To back his word, he gave them gold and some supplies and they kept the hostages. The Danes got the worst of the bargain because once he was sure of them, the Bastard set his men to destroy everything in the shire, hall, cot, burgh, and all its people.'

There was a thump as Outi's head struck the table. He had passed out from exhaustion, the sudden change from cold to warmth. Erik watched dully as he was lifted from the bench and laid on a bearskin dragged a little way from the hearth for him. The lad's hand gripped his horn mead-cup as if it were a talisman to hold him in the living world.

'Go on.' I pulled Turfrida close for his words had struck a chill into all our hearts: what had happened elsewhere could be done here. Even the children listened in silence, spellbound by the mixture of bitterness, resentment and wonder in his tone as he resumed his tale.

That the two had escaped the slaughter was due in part to their skills in fieldcraft, more to luck and the fact that they were travelling south instead of attempting to escape north into Bernicia or Scotland like hundreds of the local populace. Of whole burghs razed to the ground he spoke, of farmsteads raided, the menfolk tortured and killed, the women beaten and raped before being impaled next to their children. The dead were left unburied, the maimed abandoned to die of their wounds and exposure, while those that survived the ravaging starved, all their stores of grain having been stolen, burned or spoiled, their livestock butchered and the carcases left to rot. The whole land was being laid to waste, Erik said, in a swathe of systematic slaying and destruction across all Yorkshire from the Humber to Durham, from the east coast to the west, deep into Cheshire, and then he shook his head and laid his hands, chapped and swollen with chilblains, palm upward on the table in a gesture of helpless resignation.

'They won't find it so easy if they try it here,' I said, for a murmur had arisen as soon as his tale was done, a whispering laden with fear and trepidation. 'Did you find Waltheof?'

'He had long left York by the time we got there,' Erik replied. 'We heard he was in the hills to the west but by then the Normans were holding and questioning all the travellers they could find. The trees beside the main roads are thick with the bodies of those who answered wrongly, who were suspected of being rebels. When at last we found the Northumbrians' camp, they had moved on and we were close to starving. Only the kites and crows are glutted in that land. We thought it best to return while we could, rather than risk dying of cold and hunger. And the Normans were hunting us.' He grimaced and licked his lips. 'Have you ever been hunted, Hereward? They were like hounds upon a wolf-trail: we thought they would never give up. But once we were well south of the Humber, suddenly they turned back. By then we were almost finished. If we hadn't found the carcass of a deer, still warm, we wouldn't have made it.'

'I'm glad to see you safe.' Ignoring the look of displeasure that fleeted across Martin's features, I poured the lad more mead. 'Long may the Wolves elude the Bastard's hounds. But surely he'll not lay waste the whole of England?'

'Na!' Acer screwed up his face and spat vociferously into the fire. 'He's clearing a killing ground to protect his gains from the Scots and Danes, aye and taking the chance to terrorise the rest of the country into submission. If Osbjorn keeps the agreement, it's over. Our fight is lost without his men.'

'Since when has a Viking ever kept his word?' Sensing their growing dismay, I looked fiercely from man to man, daring them to argue. None did, but not all withstood my gaze. Raiding and pillaging by gangs of outlaws or warbands was nothing new yet there was something deeply disturbing in this harrying of the north by the King's force, the annihilation of whole settlements not for plunder or even to gain land but as an end in itself. Seeing the tense, questioning faces all around, I felt the same dread but refused to acknowledge it. They were mine, the Fen-wolves, looking to me for leadership and hope and I vowed to myself that I would not let them despair.

'Osbjorn will not betray our cause,' I said firmly. 'He has kinsmen in Northumbria he would not wish to see dishonoured and there is still the gold of Borough to collect. Aye, and the castellans of York are in his care. Long may they remain so, for while they do, the Bastard will not attack the Danish ships. The fight is not over!'

A growling murmur of assent rose to a shout of defiance, momentarily drowning the moan of the wind in the thatch, the flare and crackle of the fire. But while the men soon forgot their anxiety in the flow of mead and ale, singing and feats, I could not ignore the feeling of apprehension that had lodged deep within nor the hardness of Turfrida's glance as she retired to our private rooms.

Thus we lived through the dark days of winter, going about with hands and feet wrapped in rags against the cold, eking out our supplies as desperate folk dragged themselves through the snow to beg at the gates. In the past such supplicants would have bound themselves in vassalage to the thegn of Bourne but as an outlaw I asked nothing of them but loyalty and to my knowledge, none ever betrayed me.

Few good tidings reached us in that time but in early December we heard that Abbot Brand had died, blind and mad, his body swollen and putrescent. So long had I prayed that my tormentor might meet such an end I felt little satisfaction at his demise. Indeed, having had no part in it, I was angry rather at my failure. Martin was careful not to mention his name in my hearing; Rahere, whom I suspected of knowing more of my past than I liked, eyed me strangely after hearing the news, nodded and went swiftly out. But Brand, as a collaborator, was not mourned by the folk of Bourne as his predecessor, Leofric, had been and events swiftly precluded the choosing of his successor.

The Bastard came south just before Christmas. First he outlawed Bishop Athelwine of Durham (whose involvement in the burning of Robert de Commines, the event that had led to the rebellion in York, could not be denied), then as he passed Northampton, he sent men to arrest Athelwine's brother, our own Bishop Athelric, for sedition. The arrival of eight score knights sent Borough into panic but none dared protest as the Bishop was led away in chains. I doubt whether Athelric had any involvement in his brother's schemes but he made a convenient scapegoat. At Bourne, we kept unceasing guard and look-out on all the roads within five miles of the hall but with their purpose achieved, the Normans rode away and an uneasy peace resumed.

With so many crowded into Hall, cots, even stables, it was inevitable that sickness would follow. Many old folk and children succumbed to the lung-fever and there were few who escaped coughs and colds which increased the misery of unremitting bad weather. Howling gales and snow made the simplest task difficult; weapons practice and guard duty became a kind of torture. Some grumbled that even the Normans would not attack in such weather but having heard how the Bastard had forced his men across the hills and lakeland of the north in similar conditions during his search for

Waltheof, I refused to relax my guard. I had learned through bitter experience how swiftly complacency can lead to disaster.

At last the days began to lengthen though snow lay long on the ground. As soon as the roads were passable, I sent Wuleric and Rahere to Borough with gifts of deer-skins and smoked eels for the monks. Bereft of bishop and abbot, it seemed to me that the abbey was vulnerable to the ambitions of rival churchmen who might seize its treasure, ostensibly for safe-keeping. Thus I bade my messengers bide in the town and keep watch for anything suspicious. With York lost, the gold of Borough was now the most potent means to keep the Danes loyal to our cause and I was determined not to lose it.

The season turned towards spring, thaw brought flooding and many of the sheep which had survived the bitter cold were swept away and drowned. So wet and heavy was the ground, even an eight-ox team could not pull a plough through it. One team, bogged down, panicked and two of the beasts escaped and ran amok. They were brought to a standstill with spears and arrows, Acer's deft axe-work felling them in the end but it was dangerous and bloody work and a sad waste of good draught-animals. After that, I called a halt to ploughing until the land had had a chance to dry, thus spring sowing was delayed.

Once the floods had subsided, tidings began to trickle in again. The Danish fleet remained in the Humber though the sea-road east was now open; the Atheling was in Scotland. Of Waltheof no news came until after Easter and then I could not believe it. Having evaded the Bastard's force in some of the roughest country and worst weather England could provide, he had gone as a supplicant to the Easter court at Westminster and formally submitted. In his turn, Gospatrick had begged mercy in return for fealty but rather than make the long journey from Scotland, he had done so by letter, perhaps fearing refusal. My nephews, ever indecisive, were again at court, presumably hoping that their detachment from the rebellion at York would earn them favour but they must have thought the Bastard blind and feeble-witted not to suspect their involvement in the Mercian uprising. For now, it seemed, they were tolerated, but when the court moved to Winchester to convene a Great Council, they must have felt distinctly uneasy: no other members of the old Witan were there. Encouraged by the Bastard's mood of clemency, Eadric the Wild also submitted. He was pardoned in return for fealty and promised a fiefdom, should he prove true.

It was as the council was in session that Sweyn of Denmark made his move, sailing to join his kinsmen moored in the Humber. The bitter winter had given way to a mild spring and with no Norman ships to harry them and the gale season over, the Danes were free to move as they willed. Yorkshire was a ravaged wasteland (many of Osbjorn's men had perished of hunger during the winter, William having reneged on his promise to send supplies), and there was nothing to be gained by sailing to Scotland. They waited for a favourable wind, then sailed out of the Humber and turned south.

Perhaps it was in part the need of gold to negate the Viking threat that the Bastard now attacked the Church. Those English bishops and abbots who had voiced dissent or scorned the Popery of the prelates imposed upon them were divested of office and imprisoned or outlawed. Some, like Athelwine of Borough, had already been caught and flung into the stinking prison-houses attached to nearly every castle; others were taken at the Council to which they had gone with the unthinking trust of lambs to the slaughter-pen. With those churchmen he distrusted dealt with, the Usurper demanded recompense from the abbeys in the form of property and gold. Ancient charters by which land had been claimed and held by the Church were destroyed and new ones imposed, granting estates which had been demesne land for monks as fiefdoms. All over the country, treasures, holy relics and thegn's gold held at the abbeys for safe-keeping were hidden in anticipation of those sent to take by force what was not submitted willingly.

It was at this same Great Council that a new abbot was appointed for Borough. Turold, formerly a monk of Fécamp, was a man of fearsome reputation. Rumour had it that as he accepted the appointment, he was told that since he behaved as a man of war rather than a monk, he was being sent where he could best use his skills. It seemed that my vengeance on the raiders of Bourne and subsequent activities had not gone unnoticed.

I pondered the significance of this choice long and deeply, knowing how easily Bourne could become trap rather than refuge, haunted by the fate of Borough's treasure. If the new abbot brought his retinue of knights (he was said to have two hundred in his service), it could only be a matter of time before he launched an attack on us while Borough would be all but unassailable, the gold beyond our reach. Acer and Martin looked startled when I told them we should make our move ere Turold arrived, then said they would follow wherever I led though God's curse fall upon them for desecrating the abbey. I said roughly that if God's curse had any potency in this life, our enemies would already be crawling on their bellies in the dust, then went to find Turfrida.

She eyed me circumspectly as I entered our chamber. She was busy setting up Ymma's loom while Godgifu played with a tangle of woollen yarn at her feet. The door was propped open to let in the sun. I paused to watch the deft, graceful movements of my wife's fingers as they threaded the weft and my shadow stretched towards her. She listened in silence to my plan and though her face remained still, a furrow appeared across her brow and her grey eyes hardened while her hands moved upon the loom, needing no thought to guide them.

'You cannot do this,' she said gravely when I had finished. 'If you succeed, they will hunt you down until you and all your men are dead or captured. And you have sworn fealty to the abbot of Borough, an oath made on holy ground before God. Hereward, you must not!'

'Since then I have been outlawed, and Leofric of Borough is long dead,' I replied. 'Would you have all the treasure of Gildenborough fall into Norman hands? That gold may be the price of ridding ourselves of them forever.'

'Ah, love.' She folded her arms and looked steadily at me. 'And where will you hide this priceless hoard? Here? I do not wish what befell Eadric and Ymma to happen to us. Nor will I stand by to see you slain.'

'Ely will be our refuge and our stronghold,' I replied. 'There we shall be safe and the Isle will provide all we need. We can return to Bourne when the Normans are gone.'

She stared, then bowed her head as if overcome by some sudden emotion though whether grief, anger or exasperation I could not tell. I longed to go to her, to take her in my arms and comfort her but something, a kind of awkwardness, constrained me. Godgifu stopped playing and began to cry. Turfrida bent automatically to pick her up and when she straightened and looked at me I saw that her eyes also were bright with tears.

'I will not go,' she said. 'You cannot win this fight, Hereward: it is too late. This will end in your death, if not the deaths of us all, and nothing will be gained by it. There is no dishonour in submitting: has not Waltheof just done so, to say nothing of your nephews? There is a place for us in Flanders with my father or else we could go to Scotland. Surely we would be welcome there?'

Such entreaty was in her voice it wrung my heart but my resolve remained unshaken.

'My purpose lies here,' I told her firmly. 'A task was entrusted to me and I am oath-bound to it though I die in the attempt. I am a fighter, Turfrida: would you have me cast aside sword and hauberk, bend my neck to the Norman yoke, from fear of death? I have misjudged you then: you know little of me if that is so.'

Godgifu began to struggle and Turfrida murmured in an effort to calm her then, this failing, set her down and gave a skein of wool to play with. Reassured, the child crawled to where her wooden animals were strewn on the floor, jabbering to herself in her own speech. We watched in silence for a while and the sunlight falling through the open door made a golden halo of her hair so that for an instant it seemed that it was Aedgifu who played there and we were back in Laughton, secure and content in a world free of Norman invaders.

Turfrida sighed heavily and the spell was broken.

'Do as you will then,' she said, 'but do not expect me to condone it or follow you blindly into a trap. For that is what the Isle will become if the Normans attack in force and you will die like a wolf in its lair, alone and raging against the fate which has brought it there. Enough grief I have endured these past years without that. Do my love and the life of our child mean so little to you?'

At these words, the thought of Ymma and my other child, the son I had never seen, sprang unbidden to my mind. With an effort I dismissed them but my discomfiture must have been evident from my expression because a look of puzzlement settled on Turfrida's face and she frowned.

'I learned young the futility of railing against fate,' I told her grimly. 'And I have never loved any woman as I love you. But this time we will win: even now the Danes are sailing south. And it would take all the Bastard's men to besiege the Isle. Believe me, we shall be safer there than anywhere else in England.'

She took a step forward and for a moment I thought she had relented and meant to embrace me. But then she stopped and stood rigid, hands clenched at her sides. Her eyes held mine so that I could not look away. 'Then you will not turn from this path? You will steal the treasure of Gildenborough and hide in the marshes like a common brigand? What happens when the Danes take the gold and sail away? That is all they have come for.'

'Better it fall into their hands than the Normans',' I retorted. 'Have you so little faith, Turfrida? Sweyn and Osbjorn are allies, not enemies and they love the Bastard no more than we.'

She looked at me with a kind of pitying forbearance that at once angered and dismayed me.

'I will not argue this,' she said at last, quietly. 'But you are a fool if you cannot see that these Vikings have no more honour than the raven they revere. They will tear the rebellion apart for the gold accrued to buy their fealty and then they will sail where the Normans cannot reach them.'

'You speak of what you do not understand,' I muttered, though she had but voiced my own doubts. 'The Danes will keep faith with or without the treasure. Has not the Bastard already tried to buy them off? And at need we have more to offer then gold.'

From the yard a horse whinnied and was answered by Swallow's strident neigh. Turfrida smiled wanly. 'Then I will speak no more of it,' she replied. 'Yet mark this, Hereward. If you are set on this course, I cannot stay you but I will not follow to see you slain or taken. Do you understand?'

There was a note of calm finality in her voice yet after so long, after all she had endured in the Fenland and Brunneswald, I could not believe she would forsake me.

'We will build a place of our own on the Isle,' I told her, 'somewhere no Norman or Viking can touch us. Do not be afraid.'

She shook her head like a child being told there are no ghosts lurking in the dark and I moved to take her in my arms, breathed in the warm smell of her: desire surged through my blood. Her expression was one of unutterable yearning as she lifted her face towards mine and her lips parted slightly; a faint moan escaped them. Then someone shouted my name and the moment was lost. Turfrida bent her head and I stepped away, hurried out to see what was happening.

A crowd had gathered in the yard. Seeing me, the Fen-wolves pushed to the front, grinning and jostling one another. Danish ships had been sighted off Humber. According to Rahere they would likely enter the Wide Sea within a week. The excitement was almost palpable. Fighters and cottars alike looked at me expectantly, knowing this was the news that marked the start of the full rebellion and, God willing, the end of the Norman occupation.

'Then make ready to leave,' I said. 'We muster on the Isle.'

In truth I knew it would be weeks ere all the rebel force could gather but I understood also how swiftly a fighting man's enthusiasm may turn to frustration if action is delayed. I sent Thorald with a message for King Sweyn, that we would await him on the Isle and that the gold of Borough was ready for the taking, lest he think to sail elsewhere. Then, with half my men and cottars skilled in building, I set off for Ely, my intention to set up a base, leaving the defence of Bourne and care of my wife and child to Martin Lightfoot and Acer. With Ogier the Breton in Normandy; Ivo Taillebois and De Warenne still at court; Gilbert de Ghent a hostage on a Danish warship, I was confident there would be no enemy attack in my absence.

We marched openly upon the road that day and our weapons and mail glittered in the sunlight. By luck it was a week of neap tides thus Rahere was able to guide us along the ancient northern way to the Isle. This road was, he warned, underwater most of the year as the banks which supported it over the most treacherous fens had long since fallen into disrepair. We reached the Isle with nothing worse than wet feet and this seemed a sign that fortune was turning in our favour. Indeed, it was as if we had reached a blessed land, a place untainted by Normans: a shepherd lad watched his newly-shorn sheep without fear; the spring barley and wheat already stood knee-high, nurtured by the rich tilth and mild clime; larksong echoed the shimmering of the spring air which made all the buildings of the abbey, the great stone tower of the Minster, waver like a mirage.

Though we passed it, we did not enter the abbey that day. I wanted first to speak with the Danes, to make sure of our common purpose. But I sent Outi and Wuleric to reassure Thurstan, the abbot, that we meant him and his monks no harm and the message they brought back was one of welcome (though faced with a hundred armed men soon to be swelled by a ship-force of thousands, the abbot had little choice but to be accommodating).

Rahere, who knew Ely and the marshes and channels surrounding it as well as any creature of the fens, had already suggested a site for our main camp, the place that would become home, weapons-hoard and granary in one, a land-base for the whole uprising. It was not my plan to build a fortress since the Isle itself would be our stronghold, thus a simple palisade would surround what was to become the 'Camp of Refuge', though in those first days, before other leaders joined us, it was known simply as 'Hereward's Camp'. Humps in the ground marked where there had once been a substantial settlement (indeed Rahere told me the place, Cratendune, had been the site of the first abbey on the Isle, destroyed by Vikings two hundred years before), but now there was only a barn in the midst of the pasture and a handful of fishermen's cots near the water's edge where the land curved round to form a natural harbour. Just over a mile south of the present abbey, the place guarded the main ways into the heart of the Isle from south, east and west, the most important of which was the river itself, and there was room enough on its gentle slopes for a force of several thousand to camp in relative comfort.

The folk living there were at first alarmed, thinking us Normans from our weapons and gear but as soon as they realized who we were, their fear turned to excitement and they offered themselves and their boats to our cause. I sent them to collect timber wherever they could find it while the rest of us marked out the camp according to what I remembered from my campaigning in Flanders. This done, Siward the Red, Wuleric and I (with Erik tagging along as usual), rode around the Isle to familiarise ourselves with every cot and patch of woodland, the vineyards and crops, where horses could be stabled and pastured, looking for weaknesses in the lie of the land which could be exploited by our enemies.

Most pilgrims coming to the shrine of Ely's saint, Etheldreda, travelled by the southern way using an ancient causeway and crossing the West River at a place called Aldreth. Looking down upon the raised track on the other side of the river, the ferry moored on a muddy bank, the line of poles which marked a route across the meres to the Isle, I sensed that this was the most vulnerable point on the Isle though it was a place where we could easily build defences. The land rose steeply from the meres to a high ridge, a gift to archers shooting down, and the causeway itself was narrow and looked to be in poor repair.

'We'll keep guard here,' I told my companions. 'That way we can keep an eye on whoever comes to the Isle. And from here our enemies will be visible a day's ride away. The Bastard can throw whatever force he likes at us but they won't take Ely while we live to defend it!'

Buildings of wood, thatch and hides are easily constructed and by the time the first Danish ships arrived we had the frames of the main storehouses and living huts complete, all within a wide ring of pointed stakes. The ancient barn became our mead-hall. Many of the Isle folk had come freely to join the labour, including some of the monks, although we were wary of the latter's motives, unsure how much of their support for the rebellion was based on contingency. We cleared a wide mooring area for ships so we were ready when, a few days later, Sweyn finally sailed up the Ouse escorted by a flotilla of fishing boats, punts, even rafts. The coming of the King of Denmark was a momentous occasion in the Fenland: all knew what it might signify and wanted to be a part of it.

An atmosphere of holiday prevailed those first days. Abbot Thurstan had pledged his support for the rebellion and sent a wagon-load of wine and mead as a token of goodwill so fighters, monks, Vikings and locals drank and feasted together. The Danish force numbered nearly two thousand. While the men made more shelters and indulged in games and feats, I joined their leaders to discuss strategy.

Waltheof had, as I suspected, made mention of Borough's treasure to tempt Sweyn south. It was not long before the Danish King asked me if rumours of a golden cross taller than a man and a table sheathed in gold were true. He was a man in the mould of Harald Hardrada, a grizzled giant with keen grey eyes, hands scar-seamed and calloused from a life-time's sea-faring and fighting. The two sons he had brought were markedly different in manner. Harald was a lighter-boned version of the King, stern of feature and steady in demeanour while the younger, Cnut, was restless and, from the scars which marred his face and arms, a reckless fighter. He regarded me with a kind of wary diffidence but I sensed challenge in his stance and resolved to treat him with caution: I wanted no trouble between my men and the Danes. Osbjorn, Sweyn's brother, was a quiet man, broad of shoulder and, I guessed, unassuming. While the others wore torques and arm-rings and their sword-belts, scabbards and cloak pins were encrusted with the intricate inlaid gold-work beloved by all Vikings, his dress was plainer though he wore a heavy gold ring on his right hand, symbol, I assumed, of his status.

Siward Beorn (who had joined the Danes soon after their arrival in the Humber, more I think as Waltheof's spy than from bonds of kinship), met me with joy and relief while Erik looked on with studied indifference. When the greetings were over, Siward took me to see the hostages, incarcerated in the hold of Osbjorn's ship. They were chained in a dark space barely large enough for them to lie flat but they seemed well fed though the stench in that confined space was enough to turn the stomach. Unkempt and filthy, they glared at us like caged animals. My one-time godfather, Gilbert de Ghent, grimaced and spat when I told him he should have stayed in Northumbria with his tame beasts rather than become the dog of a Norman bastard.

By the beginning of the last week in May the camp was well established. Remembering the squalor at Southwark, I made sure proper middens were dug well outside the palisade. At least here there was no question of drinking water being fouled because few in the Fenland drank anything but beer, mead and rainwater, most of the waterways being tidal and tainted with salt. Thus, despite the number of ships jostling in the harbour and surrounding channels, the crowding in the camp which became ever more marked as folk flocked to join us, we remained mercifully free of sickness. The Danes, despite their fearsome reputation, turned out to be a well-disciplined force, no wilder in drink than my own men though the local cottars kept their womenfolk close. Many were, in any case, close kin, the Fens being part of the old Danelaw.

The very form and situation of the Isle (which in truth was a series of islets of various sizes connected by fords or causeways), was our best defence but we augmented the natural features by building turf ramparts at the edge of the marsh at Aldreth and on top of the hill behind, from which the causeway and a broad expanse of the southern fens was visible all the way to the ridge where the Cambridge road ran. Halfway along the causeway was an ancient earthwork called Belsar's Hill and here we built a palisade on top of the ring-bank to serve as a check on all traffic to the Isle from the south. The narrowness of the causeway precluded it as a serious fortification but it would slow an invading force if manned by determined defenders. Watchtowers and beacons were sited at other high points of the Isle, to warn those in camp of enemies approaching by land or water. Then, preparations complete, we settled down to wait for the Atheling's ships.

Both Thorfin and Siward Beorn had warned of the Vikings' love of gold, fierce as the lust most men feel for a young and beautiful woman. It was not long ere Cnut Sweynson pestered me to launch our raid on Gildenborough. Mindful that once the treasure was on the Isle it might cause dissent, I was cautious for I had wanted to discuss a war-plan with the leaders of the rebellion, Edgar, Marleswein and Waltheof (the sincerity of whose submission I believed in no more than that of my nephews). But circumstances often overtake intention. In the last days of May, news came that the Great Council had been concluded and Turold, with a force of eight score knights, was on his way to take up his new appointment. He was expected to reach Borough in the first week of June.

Knowing Turold's reputation, I sent Erik to warn Martin and Acer and have them bring Turfrida to the safety of the Isle, along with the rest of the Fen-wolves and any of the Bourne folk who wanted to come. Bourne could not be defended against so large an enemy force: it was better abandoned. The spiked heads of Ogier's servants would greet the Normans and they would find nothing worth the taking within. I hoped they would be dismayed that I had eluded them and was still at large.

I was at the abbey the following day, negotiating for supplies (while Borough was richer in treasure, Ely was famous for wine, fruit and fish), when Erik sought me out, having returned alone. It was a still summer morning, swallows flying low over the water, the marshes shimmering with heat-haze but any joy in the day was swiftly dispelled by the lad's arrival. We had a system of boats and horses set up for swift travel across the fenland and he had clearly come at full speed: the *destrier* he rode into the yard where I was inspecting grain with the abbot was lathered and panting. Alarmed by his worried expression and the state of his mount, I glanced north-westwards but no smoke rose from the warning beacons at Bourne and

Witham.

'Martin bids you go at once to Bourne.' He sprang from the saddle while the horse stretched its neck to breathe, nostrils flaring red.

Aware that Thurstan was watching us with interest, I put a hand on Erik's shoulder and drew him into a doorway where we could speak privately. 'Why? What's happened?'

He flushed and would not meet my eyes. 'That was the message. He said only to make sure you went swiftly.'

Fear for Turfrida and Godgifu leapt to my throat and with it anger at the boy's reticence. I grasped his shoulders and thrust him against the wall, leaning forward until my face was but a handsbreadth from his. 'Tell me what's wrong!'

He had submitted meekly beneath my hands but from the stubborn set of his mouth I knew I would get no more from him. Glancing at the river, I saw that the tide was against me. To reach Bourne before nightfall I would have to ride the long way round, along the causeway from Aldreth.

The *destrier* stood exhausted, head hanging but it would have to do: we had requisitioned the abbey's few horses and they were pastured with the rest near Cratendune. I mounted and jerked hard on the reins to turn the animal. The monks stood and stared as I urged the horse to a halting gallop. Its breath was harsh and quick. I prayed it would not founder before I reached camp.

Those on guard gave the alarm as I forced the stallion down the slope and through the gates, no doubt they thought I brought momentous news. The horse staggered to a halt and stood trembling, blood-flecked foam dropping from its mouth. Men crowded round. I shouted for Wuleric to bring Swallow and reassured Thorald and Siward Beorn, who had come running, that I was on my way to Bourne but it was a private matter, such was my redeing of Martin's message.

It was only when we were off the Isle, galloping along the causeway past the half-built palisade at Belsar's Hill, that I recalled the unnatural quietness of my comrades as they watched me leave, a dreadful, suppressed expectancy like that of those who see a distant figure walking towards a patch of quicksand but are helpless to intervene. That others knew or guessed what had happened to those I loved but were afraid to tell me tainted my fear with resentment. I lashed Swallow's shoulders with the ends of the reins and she shook her head, laid back her ears and sprang forward as if a demon possessed her.

Sudden sickness, a raid by Normans or outlaws from the Brunneswald, an accident such as may befall any household: fire, a falling branch, a horse's kick, a dog's madness; all these possibilities thronged my mind as the mare ran on. The rhythm of her gallop became the pounding of blood in my head and when I turned her onto the winding track through the marshes to the Old Road, and saw the roofs of Bourne in the distance, Croyland Abbey to my right, my dread only increased for all seemed peaceful. A man cutting reeds with his children shouted and waved cheerfully; plovers wheeled and cried overhead, wings flashing in the sunshine. It seemed that in all the world I alone was afflicted by anxiety, aye and the mare also, whose coat was now black with sweat, eyes wild and white-rimmed as she galloped, sensing my urgency.

We turned at last onto the Bourne track and I straightened in the saddle and slackened rein, allowing Swallow to ease to a canter, then as the gates loomed before us, to a trot. The gates swung open, the yard was busy with people preparing to leave, bundles of possessions, half-loaded carts. I rode in and all stopped whatever they were doing to stare. Scanning the faces, those of friends and comrades, the cottars who had seemed as much a part of Bourne as the trees and buildings, I could not find those I sought. There was an odd, uneasy silence; people watched but avoided my gaze as I swung down from the saddle. I left Swallow standing where she was and strode towards the Hall and the crowd parted as if afraid though there was nothing save their own discomfiture to indicate anything amiss.

The doors of the hall were shut, unusual on a warm summer's day, and the fear that had subsided to a dull ache in my belly leapt again to my throat, made my palms prickle with sweat. My left hand went to the hilt of my sword and the familiar touch of oiled wood and leather comforted and steadied me.

I was but a few paces from them when the doors opened. Martin stood inside, his face pale and haggard. I strode past him and, to my astonishment, he closed the doors behind.

It was dark and cool inside. The fire had burned to a heap of glowing coals and though the door to our rooms stood wide, no light came from there. Martin walked to the hearth, for no reason than that it was a kind of focal point in the echoing emptiness of the hall. Sensing we were alone, I hurried after.

'She has gone.' My lifelong companion and servant stood hunched as if expecting me to strike him and did not look up but kept his eyes fixed on the embers.

'Gone?' I stared at him blankly. 'When? Why?'

From outside came the measured clop of hooves, the rising murmur of voices. I groped for the corner of a nearby mead-bench and sat down while anxiety turned to a deeper pain. Of all the contingencies I had worried over, that Turfrida might leave of her own volition had never occurred to me.

'Ah God, Hereward.' At last Martin raised his head and in the faint light from the louvres high under the eaves I read both exasperation and compassion in his face. 'Did she not give warning enough? She is a high-born woman with her own mind, not some cottar's chattel. It is not her wish to see you slain or broken by defeat.'

'She is my wife!' The anger born of humiliation effaced the emptiness I had barely begun to acknowledge. 'Where is she? She will join me at Ely whether she wills or not!'

Martin was watching me with a kind of wary forbearance. I noticed he bore no weapon, not even a dagger and, briefly, wondered why. When next he spoke, I knew.

'She has renounced you,' he said, speaking slowly and clearly as if to a recalcitrant child. 'She loves you still but too long have you gone your own way, heedless of her words and wishes. This fight against the Normans cannot last, nor can we win: you know that in your heart. Submit to the King and she will return to you: that was her message. And she bade me give you this.'

It was a curl of Aedgifu's hair, still bright with the sheen of oat-straw as it lay in my palm. Guilt swelled in my throat to choke me. I closed my hand upon the lock, feeling its softness, then flung it on the fire where it shrivelled and blackened, giving off a foul stench.

'She must think me woman-hearted as well as coward,' I muttered, then, at the look on Martin's face, added disgustedly, 'Is that what you think also, Lightfoot: that we are already defeated? If so, then you had better flee with Turfrida than stay where I can reach you. I want no doubters in my band.'

'I am your man until death,' he replied simply. 'But she did not doubt you, only the wisdom of the course you have set yourself. Nor has she gone far, hoping you would relent.'

'She is more of a fool than I thought then.' I rose to my feet and began to pace the length of the bench, disturbing the dogs sprawled beside the fire. 'We will fetch her back and when the Normans are driven from this land she will feel her shame. Where is she? Come on, Martin, I left her in your care. You did not let her go alone?'

'Acer escorted her.'

Martin's discomfiture was now so marked he did not need to say more and a bitter laugh escaped me. He stared, astonished, and I clapped a hand to his shoulder, pushed him towards the door. 'Get a horse: we must find her before she discovers the truth about Ymma's babe.'

No-one had dared tend Swallow, knowing her reputation, but she had made her own way to the water-trough. She turned her head and whickered softly as Martin and I entered the sunlit yard. Many folk were still gathered around the carts; I caught their sidelong glances and knew they must have been laughing at me, their renowned leader, forced to chase after his deserting wife like a cuckold. I caught Swallow and glared at the onlookers who fell silent from fear of my anger though I knew there would be one subject of conversation in Bourne that night. At least the gate-guards kept their eyes looking outward (though no doubt their ears pricked to every sound); they had been well instructed or else were afraid of attracting my displeasure. Of Acer there was no sign. Maybe he was embarrassed or afraid to meet me in such circumstances.

At last Martin clattered up on his chestnut and the gates swung open. I gave orders that all who wanted to leave for Ely should delay no longer, then we set off at an easy canter. The mare, matchless in stamina, seemed fresh almost as when we had left the Isle but the same could not be said of me. Every-so-often I stood in the stirrups, supposedly to survey the marshes and fields for enemies but in reality to stretch my aching muscles: it was long since I had ridden so far at speed. But in truth the weariness assailing me was less a physical ill than a kind of heart-sickness, a dull pain that intensified with each passing moment.

When we reached Croyland abbey, the gates were closed. Though no watchers were visible on the walls, my skin prickled when we drew rein; pride prevented me looking about. Martin rode forward and banged his fist on the iron-studded wood. Nothing happened. We waited and it seemed to me that I heard whispering but it may have been only the wind in the reeds and willows.

At last I could bear it no longer. I wheeled the mare round and looked up to the guard-posts, shouting for the abbot. There was a flurry of movement and a pigeon flapped heavily from a gap in the stonework: when next I looked up, Ulfkil stood there, arms folded, face stern, imperturbable. Under the steadfastness of that gaze my impatience seemed petty, that of an ill-disciplined child. I reined the mare in and inclined my head in brief acknowledgement.

'Has Ely so swiftly disappointed your needs that you must come to my door?' The abbot's tone was laconic but I sensed hidden meaning in these words. 'Go away, Hereward. There is nothing for you here.'

Fear leapt to my throat that Turfrida was no longer there, that she might already have set sail for Flanders, taking our child. I suppressed it with an effort.

'I have come for my wife,' I replied, with as much dignity as I could muster. 'Let her come out, then we shall leave in peace.'

Ulfkil's expression did not alter. 'That is for her to decide,' he said. 'She came seeking sanctuary and I have granted it according to my duty. Would you risk God's curse, eternal damnation, by violating the sanctity of this abbey by force?'

'She is my wife!' Someone sniggered from behind the shelter of the wall and a sense of helplessness overwhelmed me, of ignominy I had not felt since the day I escaped Brand through the Bolhithe Gate. An icy sweat sheathed my skin as I stared up at the abbot. Swallow tossed her head and snorted nervously.

'Aye.' Ulfkil frowned. 'And as such, is she not worthy of consideration? Think upon that, Hereward, ere you come demanding at my gates again. If you want her back, you know what you must do.'

The wild rage born of frustration boiled within me. I ground my teeth while my eyes scanned the walls though whether I sought a glimpse of my beloved or was looking for a weakness in the masonry, some line I could scale, I could not tell.

'She knows me better,' I growled at last. 'If she knew I was here, she would at least speak with me. You do ill to come between a man and his wife, Ulfkil.'

A faint smile curved his lips and he shook his head.

'That is not so,' he replied, 'and I deem she understands you better than you know. Make peace with the King and she will be yours again, that was the message she bade me give you. She loves you too well to stand by and see you defeated.'

A sound escaped me then, a kind of wordless groan. I lifted my clenched fist to my mouth and bit my knuckles as if pain could bring resolution.

'Hereward.' The abbot's voice was stern. 'Think upon what you are doing, what it will mean for the people of these Hundreds if the Normans take revenge by ravaging this land as they have the North. That will be upon your head if you continue your war-mongering.'

'This time we will win!' There was an unintended note of desperation in these words and it exacerbated my sense of helplessness. 'Would you have us lose everything without a fight? Do not assume these walls will protect you from the usurpers' greed.'

His eyes narrowed. He lifted one hand as if to bestow a benediction, then lowered it again.

'God is all the defence we need,' he said at last, simply. 'It is by His will that the Normans have come, perhaps to punish us for past impieties. You have much still to lose, Hereward, and if it is lost it will be through your fault, not theirs.'

'Pray, then, when Turold and his knights stand here instead of me,' I told him roughly. 'And bid Turfrida remember Eadric and Cole One-Hand ere she demands that I crawl on my belly before the Bastard. Aye, and ask if she has forgotten Aedgifu, our firstborn. I will not rest until every drop of Norman blood is scoured from this land.'

'I will pray for you,' he said meaningfully, and with that he turned and left.

Robbed of the chance to retaliate, I stared at the space where he had stood while the blood sang in my ears. Swallow snorted then snapped at the palfrey which Martin had forced alongside. No doubt his purpose was to console me but the shame of having my weakness laid bare not only before him, who knew me better than any save Turfrida, but the monks of Croyland who were, I was sure, crowded on the other side of the gates to listen, was too much. I had ridden far and fast that day and knew Swallow must be tired but I did not care. I wrenched her round and urged her on and she sprang into her raking gallop as if at the start of a race.

We reached the Isle at dusk for the tide had turned and we were able to use the ancient Roman causeway though in places the horses were forced to breast through. In my weariness I avoided thought of past or future, was conscious only of the chill air rising from the fens, the lap of water all around, the movement of the mare beneath me, still smooth and seemingly tireless despite the miles she had travelled. Martin, wisely, kept silence until we reached camp.

Our comrades greeted us eagerly, asking after kin and friends still at Bourne. When inquiries were made after Turfrida, who was much esteemed for her sagacity and kindness, I said only that she was at Croyland to pray for our success. While some cheered this news, Rahere avoided my gaze and Erik stared accusingly but if they knew or had guessed what had happened, I trusted their discretion.

I was lying alone in my hut, brooding bitterly upon Ulfkil's parting words when an argument began nearby. The voices were low and fierce. One was Martin's (he was outside, burnishing my sword), the other, with a Danish accent, was quick and fervent. Before their dispute could spark trouble I rose, hand on dagger hilt. Next moment the weighted hide curtain was thrust aside and Sweyn's son, Cnut, strode in, an apologetic Martin at his shoulder.

The young Dane was restive and passionate; recognizing something of myself in my wilder days in him, I resolved to be patient as he began a tirade accusing me of cowardice, of skulking behind the abbey's power like a child hiding in its mother's skirts while there were great deeds to do and lasting renown to be won.

'No man has ever called me coward to my face and lived,' I told him grimly when he paused to draw breath. 'But youth and ignorance excuse you this once, though I am told your father has many sons. Pick forty men skilled in arms and worthy of trust and have them ready tomorrow night. We strike Borough the following dawn. And next time you slander me, you die. Is that understood?'

He nodded, seeming at once daunted and excited, bent his head in acknowledgement and left. Martin watched thoughtfully, then gave Brain-biter into my hands. The long blade gleamed red in the firelight. I ran my palm along it, feeling the smooth blood-groove which ran half its length.

'You would slay the monks?' Martin asked at last, incredulously. 'For gold?'

'For that gold I will cut down any who stands in my path,' I replied. 'And you of all men should know I bear the monks of Borough no love.'

He looked at me with a mixture of pity and sorrow. 'Then by your leave, I will stay behind.'

'As you wish.' Something in his gaze reminded me of Turfrida's quiet defiance and I longed for him to go. 'I want no faint-hearts on this errand.'

He did not reply but his dark, lingering glance drove me to the mead-hall that night, to drink and forget amid the noise.

4. The Gold of Borough

Next morning numbers in camp were swelled by the arrival of the rest of the Fen-wolves and their kin from Bourne. They had brought as much food as their carts and draught-beasts could bear along with most of the estate's livestock, and looked at the lush pastures and burgeoning crops of the Isle with wonder. Only a few cottars remained behind. They were such as care little what master they serve so long as they have the same roof over their heads and these we did not miss, thinking them too afraid of reprisals to betray us. There was no room for the rest inside the palisade so they built their shelters in the fields beyond, secure in the knowledge that safety was not far to find should danger threaten. Their dogs bickered with those that regarded the camp as their own territory and whenever a serious fight occurred, a crowd gathered to watch and bet on the outcome.

I had Martin bring Acer to my hut straightway. The big man was awkward in my presence; he would not meet my eyes and shifted uneasily from foot to foot like a child being brought to account for stealing apples. I thanked him for the safe conduct of my wife and child to Croyland then gave him the same tale as the rest: that Turfrida had gone there to pray for our victory. He looked askance but then shrugged and nodded, obviously relieved that I bore him no blame. In any case, he knew as well as I that there was no room for disagreement between us. I had seen in Flanders how swiftly the slightest mis-understanding between leaders can lead to distrust and the formation of factions among the men. If that happened here, our cause was lost.

I was by the ships that evening, talking with Siward Beorn, when Outi brought news that eight-score Normans had ridden into Stamford a few hours before. A man dressed as a knight but tonsured as a monk was their leader; he bore a huge mace and had the Cross of Christ blazoned on his shield. Being travel-weary, they had decided to lodge there for the night. They would be in Borough by midday.

That we would be snatching the treasure from under Turold's very nose heightened the eagerness of those chosen for the raid: Cnut's forty along with a picked handful of Fen-wolves, and Siward Beorn. No-one slept that night. Our comrades crowded round as we checked our gear and weapons, offering advice no-one heeded and laying wagers on how much of the fabled gold we would bring back and which of us, Vikings or Fen-wolves, would steal most. It was good-natured banter for the most part but I noted the main protagonists for it had always been my fear that the treasure would cause trouble between the two forces. Martin stood a little apart making no effort to conceal his disapproval; our eyes met and I looked away, refusing to acknowledge him.

Dawn broke, a pale bar lightening the eastern sky, and we boarded the two warships that would bear us first down the Ouse and then upstream along the Nene to the Bolhithe Gate. There was little wind and few folk about so early yet the sails were unfurled to display the devices designed strike terror into the hearts of their victims: Land-Waster and All-Seeing Eye. The tide bore us swiftly and in the knowledge we would soon be rowing against it, we sat back and took our ease. Fishermen out to check their traps shouted and waved as we passed; the marshland stretched flat and still to either side and, high above, a few wisps of cloud shone red and gold. A harrier wheeled there, no more than a black speck, but its cry came clear even above the rush of water and thrum of the rigging and Acer and I exchanged glances and grinned, thinking it a good omen.

Proud of their skills in seamanship, the Danes seldom allowed others to man their ships but at the confluence of the rivers, we all bent to the oars and the craft, being low in draught, skimmed swiftly across the water although the flow was now against us. Even so, it was full daylight when we reached the bend in the river and saw St. Peter's tower rising against the sky. We paused in our rowing to stare a moment, the Danes no doubt lusting after the bright gold that lay within those walls, while we who owed fealty to the abbey were apprehensive. Then I thought of Brand and how I had been denied vengeance for the humiliations he and his cronies had inflicted upon me as a child and I tipped my head back and howled my warcry so that none should doubt who was attacking the abbey. Cnut, in whose ship I rode, looked startled as my comrades joined in, then he and his men added their voices so that the sound echoed in the stillness. As the ships swept under the looming rampart of the abbey wall and approached the jetties for which the Bolhithe Gate is named, figures scrambled frantically among the boats and scuttled for the safety of the burgh.

That there was no Norman garrison was evident from the lack of any kind of defensive action. Not a single arrow met us as our ships nosed in between the fishing and trading boats and we leapt ashore. But the momentum of the attack was checked when we reached the gate for it was shut and stoutly barred and though Acer and Cnut hewed it with their axes, the seasoned oak only flaked a little at each blow and the faces of the two soon ran with sweat.

The idea of being so easily thwarted irked me unbearably. We could, of course, simply have sailed round to the West Gate which I knew to be newer and of cruder craftsmanship, but it was here I had sworn revenge long ago and to enter the burgh another way would mean fighting through the narrow streets only to find ourselves on the wrong side of the main abbey gates. The Danes were busy destroying all the boats within reach, ostensibly to prevent their use in pursuit (though none were warships), and the din maddened me. I yelled for silence and Cnut grinned wildly and shouted at his men in their own tongue. They quietened a little, looked at me expectantly. From the other side of the gates came the sounds of urgent speech and running footsteps. Acer wiped his brow with the back of his hand and leant on his axe to recover his breath. 'What now?'

'Wait,' I told him though I had no idea what best to do. Then Cnut shouted in warning: one of the wrecked boats was on fire. The owner of the craft must have been about to cook his morning meal, for a small brazier set in the prow had overturned. Cnut's men were cursing and using oars and spears to fend the blazing planks from their ships. Like all seafarers, they feared fire as much as the fiercest storm.

Grinning, I called the Fen-wolves and had them gather all the timber they could find. We piled it against the gates, then set it alight. Once the danger to their ships was past, the Danes joined in, breaking up the jetties once all the wreckage was burned. We cheered as the flames licked up the gateposts and turned the iron bolts to a glowing red but none there understood how I longed to raze not only the gates but all the abbey to the ground so that no stone or timber remained to bear witness to my past.

Siward the Red and Gamal Longbow were posted at the water's edge to watch the wall from which a single archer could have caused swift carnage among us. They stiffened suddenly and following their gaze, I saw a monk standing there alone. He looked down in silence and some of the Danes jeered but the Fen-wolves remained quiet. Many had known him since he first came to the abbey as Abbot Leofric's scribe: Athelwold was his name. Though he had never caused me harm, I bore him no great good-will. He had been a faithful servant to my uncle, who had rewarded his service by making him Prior.

'What do you want?' he called, when all had paused to stare. 'This is holy ground and any man who desecrates it risks excommunication in this world and damnation in the next. Leave now ere it is too late!'

His eyes had passed over us each in turn and come to rest on Cnut who, scar-faced, bare-headed and grinning, his gold-twined mail glinting in the sun-light, looked more like some nightmarish figure from legend than living man.

'We've come to take your gold into safe-keeping, old man!' His men shouted their approval and brandished their weapons as Cnut strode forward. Athelwold returned the threat with disdainful silence.

'Let us in and we will spare you and your monks.' I pulled off my helm so that he would know me. 'Else we will burn the abbey to the ground and all those inside. It is no matter to us if the gold comes out molten: we'll have it either way.'

'It was an ill fate that turned you from oblate to outlaw,' he replied calmly. 'Oathbreaker and traitor I name you, for you are a sworn man of this abbey. Think well upon what you are doing.'

'The time for words is over,' I said. 'Turold is coming and he is no peaceful servant of God. Let us in or the ruin of the abbey will be upon your head. We come to save the treasures of Gildenborough from Norman greed.'

He hesitated and his brow furrowed as he stared at me, his gaze keen and penetrating. Then he shook his head as if to dispel some lingering doubt.

'I will not betray the treasure held here in trust to any man, least of all one outside the law and reviled by the King,' he said. 'If you want it, you will have to take it by force and every drop of blood spilt within these walls will weigh against you on Judgement Day. Therefore beware ere you bring fire and sword within these walls!'

With that he turned and left and his words seemed to have daunted even the Danes. Though their taunts followed him, they hung back from the gates while the Fen-wolves looked doubtfully at one another. But clearly as if my own voice spoke from the past I remembered my promise: 'One day I shall return and burn this place to the ground' and I snatched the axe from Acer's hand and smote the gates, heedless of the flames licking all around me, crying aloud my anger and exultation as I felt the burning wood give way. Showers of sparks spiralled high into the air as my comrades joined in and from the other side came screams and frantic calls for water though from the abbey there was no access to the river but the Bolhithe Gate. As the whinnying of terrified horses joined the tumult, we realized the fire must be spreading inside.

The gates crashed down at last and we ran through, those on the other side fleeing before us. I had snatched a flaming brand and others followed my example although the thatch of nearby buildings was already burning. Intoxicated by the promise of plunder and the terror of all that saw us, we set light to anything that would burn as we wended our way between the squalid hovels huddled between wall and abbey, thus our progress was marked by leaping flame. The minster tower reared ominously as we entered the cloisters and narrow corridors of the abbey; our warcries mingled with screams and the crackling of burning wood; our swords gleamed: none withstood us.

The monks scurried ahead like frightened sheep until we overtook and made them choose between joining us and death. None chose the latter, thus I had the steadiest of my comrades escort them back to the ships while the rest of us entered the minster itself, where the most precious of Borough's treasures were kept.

Reliquaries, jewel-encrusted books and vestments, statues of the saints we took: the great gold-sheathed table was hacked to pieces. The massive cross was too heavy even for Siward Beorn to lift so the Danes cut away the gold crown and bejewelled footrest and left the figure of Christ face down on the altar. There was too much to carry so we snatched wall-hangings and alter-cloths, heaped the treasure onto these and dragged them along the ground. Pieces of burning wood and thatch rained upon us as we made our way back to the hithe. Even the signal to return to the ships, a braying warhorn, was barely audible above the roar of flames.

One of the Danes was caught beneath a falling beam and died screaming but otherwise all Cnut's men and mine returned unscathed. Fifteen monks, including Athelwold and a deacon called Leofric, were waiting there under Acer's watchful eye. They boarded the ships reluctantly but I noticed that while the rest watched the inferno that engulfed all the abbey save the minster, along with much of the town, the Prior's attention was on the treasure piled at the mastheads of both ships.

The tide now bore us swiftly away while great plumes of smoke rose behind to sully the sky. Cnut, a number of gold crucifixes hung round his neck, laughed and sang, drunken as if from mead by our success but though relieved that the treasure was beyond Norman reach, I was more circumspect. I knew that Turold, who might arrive at any moment, would not lightly forgive the despoilation of his abbey nor the taking of the treasure, and that punitive action against the townsfolk might change the loyalty of those who had hitherto supported us. More pressingly, I worried that the gold would cause trouble with the Danes. Once it was in their possession, we would have no hold upon their fealty.

It was past midday when we reached Cratendune and everyone in camp flocked to meet us and hear our tale, the outcome of which was clear from the smear of smoke over Borough. They stared in amazement as we piled the treasure on the grass, gold gleaming and jewels glittering in the bright sunlight. Most of the captured monks wandered about in a state of bewilderment or knelt in prayer but Athelwold stood aloof and regarded the antics of the Danes and Fen-wolves as they began to celebrate, with disdain.

Once the ships were securely moored, we loaded treasure and captives onto carts and took them to the abbey. Thurstan received his unwilling guests with wary courtesy. There was little love lost between the churchmen, mainly because of fierce competition for holy relics and the pilgrims' gold they brought.

We feasted long and hard that night in the Great Hall of the abbey, the monks of Ely being keen to prove their table superior to that of Borough. Most of the gold was heaped on the dais at one end of the Hall but the most sacred relics had been taken to the church under the watchful eye of Athelwold. Sweyn and his sons drank and joined in the feat-challenging and wrestling with enthusiasm (so also, I noted with some amusement, did the monks of Ely), but as the night grew old I saw that the treasure was surrounded by Danes and some instinct warned me to be on my guard and drink no more. There was no trouble and by dawn we were all asleep but from then on, no English hand touched that hoard. By default rather than any conscious decision on my part it came under their guardianship and since that was, in the end, the purpose of taking it, I tried not to concern myself overmuch at how easily they had gained possession.

Had I known that messages were already passing between Sweyn the Cunning and William the Bastard, I would have acted differently. As it was, when Danish King asked permission to take a third of the gold onto his ships as surety of our good faith, I agreed, trusting the loyalty of the monks less than his.

The days following the raid were nervous ones for us. Having set off soon after dawn, Turold and his knights had arrived in Borough soon after we sailed away. He found the abbey a smouldering ruin save for the stone Minster which, by God's grace, was unscathed. All the monks were gone, fled or captured, save one who had been abandoned in the infirmary.

The town was grievously affected by the fire but that did not prevent the new abbot interrogating suspected rebels. Some of those caught and beaten by his men came eventually to the Isle, preferring to keep their pride and become outlaws rather than submit to the rule of one who considered that all Saxons should be slaves.

Where there is no line of retreat, attack is the best form of defence and Sweyn's sons, Siward Beorn, Acer and I led raids into the lands of William Malet and Gilbert de Ghent, penetrating deep into Norfolk and towards Cambridge as well their fiefdoms to the west. It was my purpose to unsettle the enemy while we augmented our supplies and strengthened the defences of the Isle, building walls of turf in the marshes at Aldreth behind which archers and spearmen could take cover, weakening the tide-damaged embankments of the old Roman road to the east until it was effectively unusable. And all the time we watched for ships from the north and asked fisherfolk and merchants for news, for it was still our belief that the Atheling's force would sail to join us.

Midsummer passed and our uneasiness grew. No news came from the north save that of famine and ruin. The harrying had not ceased and some believed it would not until every native-born man, woman and child was dead. Yet each week more fighters came to the Isle, many of high renown, who saw in the raid on Borough and the presence of the Danish force hope of the organised rebellion that had so far failed to materialize in nearly four years of occupation and oppression. To keep all these busy (for idleness swiftly breeds discontent and rancour amongst fighting men), I set them to work in the fields when they were not out raiding, hunting or fishing, and those who complained soon learned that on the Isle there was no distinction between former thegn and cottar when it came to tilling the land or fighting.

Our contribution was welcomed by the abbot for with so many mouths to feed the resources of the abbey were sorely stretched in terms of labour. It was a wet, cold summer but as Lammas Day came and went, the discomforts of the season were but a minor inconvenience compared with the fear that gnawed at the resolve even of the most steadfast. Harvest was approaching and still we had heard nothing from the Atheling or any other leaders of the rebellion. Even my nephews were ominously silent although I could not believe that their latest submissions to the Bastard were any more sincere than the first.

The only respite during that time of pelting rain and gales which flattened the wheat and barley in the fields and rotted the hay was the apparent quietness of our enemies. I put this down to the fact that we still held the hostages from York, to say nothing of the churchmen from Borough. Part of the Bastard's force was still engaged in the north, the rest were busy collecting tribute from the abbeys and overseeing the building of more castles. Every fiefdom of significant size now had its own motte and bailey, constructed by the forced labour of those who should have been tending the crops and livestock.

On the Isle we felt secure but increasingly isolated. When news came that Bishop Athelric, speaking from his prison cell, had excommunicated the desecrators of his abbey, Prior Athelwold, who preached interminably whenever we gathered in the Great Hall, promised forgiveness if we gave back the treasure. Sweyn told him, with a sardonic glance at me, that he was welcome to guard the gold himself if he was concerned for its safety and the prior thanked him gravely. After that, Athelwold and his closest companions were often found in the company of the Danes and I thought it a useful alliance for even Cnut made a show of piety when the prior was within hearing.

Worried that if the atheling did not make his move soon, Sweyn would decide to return home ere storms closed the sea-road for another winter, I sent messages north by sea and land, urging our leaders to remember Waltheof's promise. But the foul weather worsened and the messengers were delayed. One at least drowned in a storm which claimed many boats. The only news from the north came via ragged fugitives, driven into the Fens by need. Starvation was rife beyond the Humber, they said, and there were widespread rumours of children being butchered and eaten so desperate were the folk of that ravaged land. And they spoke bitterly of their oppressors who offered neither help nor pity but instead rode about the country to collect taxes. Any man who had somehow managed to cling to his own land, now found himself dispossessed and if he could not pay his tithes, he was hanged. There was no justice, no mercy, and without folk to tend it, the land itself was turning to waste, becoming a place of misery and death to all save Normans and the carrion-eaters, including feral dogs and pigs, that gorged on the swollen corpses that lay untended in vill and field.

Such tales we had heard before yet on the Isle it sometimes seemed hard to believe that so much wretchedness could exist within two days' ride. Whenever the fugitives arrived, they were treated kindly and their stories circulated around the camp so that no man forgot what kind of enemy we faced, what we were fighting for. But as the days passed and still no messages came, tensions grew and the slightest disagreement between my men and Sweyn's was likely to provoke a fight. Mercifully, no-one was killed, (due largely to the efforts of Acer and Osbjorn, who punished both sides with equal vigour), but I knew that without action soon, there would be serious trouble. Fighters who live for the renown earned by their swords do not take easily to enforced idleness. I felt the same restlessness, the same frustration at our so-called leaders' hesitation. They knew as well as we how the success of the rebellion depended on the Danes: once this chance was gone, we might never rid ourselves of the usurpers.

One day in early September, Rahere came to find me. I was preparing to ride to the minster, having urgent business with Thurstan who was beginning to question the volumes of beer his monks were having to brew to keep camp and abbey supplied but the Fen-man's obvious discomfiture stayed me. Some of Harald's men were splicing rope nearby. Rahere tilted his head meaningfully and we walked out of camp and up the hill where we could not be overheard.

'They're making ready to leave,' Rahere said bluntly. '"Raven's heart and weasel's fealty": isn't that what they say of their kind? They've been dealing secretly with the Bastard this past month. Face it, Hereward: there's no force coming from the north and they know it. They'll be gone ere Michaelmas.'

I glanced down at the score or more warships beached on the mudflats and an iron fist seemed to close about my heart. 'What proof is there?'

Even as I spoke, certain memories fell into place: the self-conscious silence that overcame some groups of Sweyn's men when one of us passed; discrepancies in supplies brought to the Isle and what reached the stores, a myriad little things which on their own were hardly worthy of note but taken together pointed to conspiracy. As I stared at the camp, folk going about their business as usual while some of my men played a group of Danes at the rough stick and ball game they had brought from Ireland, I considered what measures we could take to keep them here whilst punishing Sweyn's treachery.

'We could burn their ships,' Rahere said softly. 'But even with the newcomers we barely outnumber them and they are all hard-handed fighters.'

His tone was calm, matter-of-fact, his expression resigned, and reason overtook my anger. I let out a short, harsh breath of laughter.

'Aye, and invite the Bastard in to dance on our corpses? Sink the ships and we have two thousand Vikings on our hands, eager to rend us apart and the abbey also, for whatever gold is still there. Ach!' I cursed and shook my head ruefully. 'A fine fool they must think me, to willingly hand them the treasure of Borough! No doubt the Bastard'll let them keep it: he's hardly likely to let it fall into our keeping.'

The tall Fen-man nodded gravely. 'That I do not know. But I think you rede the situation aright.'

Martin, ever prudent, advised caution when I told him the news. There were many women and children in camp and if the Danes were antagonized, ample opportunity for hostage-taking or worse: none of us wanted a massacre when only our enemies could benefit from it. Thus I resolved to say nothing to the other Fen-wolves until a peaceful resolution had been agreed.

I took Martin when I went to see the King and his sons. A royal booth had been constructed for them near the centre of the camp but though it was richly appointed, with hangings taken from churches; ornate chests and carven oak chairs, I noticed little gold. The figures of the saints seemed oddly out-of-place, misappropriated as they were from holy sanctuary to raider's lair. Some stared down sadly while others, St. Peter among them, looked vengeful. But Sweyn, Harald and Cnut were oblivious to the painted eyes. Their attention was all on a roast suckling pig which a slave had just set on the ground before them.

'It's more than a year since my sons and their men saw their homes,' Sweyn pointed out reasonably when I asked if there was any truth in rumours of their defection. 'Any longer and their wives will look to other men for pleasure and their children will not know them. Since Easter we've been kicking our heels waiting for the fighting we were promised and nothing's happened. You cannot blame us if your leaders turn out to be white-livered cowards. We gave fealty in return for gold: it was up to them to use it.'

Arguing with Vikings has been likened to hunting foxes with a boar-spear. I clenched my teeth and forced patience on myself.

'Moreover,' Sweyn bent to pull off one of the piglet's legs, 'we are not minded to spend another winter in this Godforsaken country. If we have to starve, we may as well do it with our own kin.'

'Then will you give back the supplies that are on your ships?' I could not wholly conceal my anger and Martin shook his head, almost imperceptibly, in warning.

'Alas,' the Danish King spread his hands in a gesture of sorrow, before tearing a strip of meat from the leg he held and chewing it with relish. 'We shall have hostages – guests – with us and the sea-road is perilous and grows more so with each passing day. You would not have it said that Prior Athelwold and his companions, who have pledged to guard the holy relics we carry, perished because the grasping hand of Hereward snatched back the food apportioned for their sustenance?'

At this, Snorri, the Royal Skald, who sat in a corner to observe proceedings, chuckled appreciatively. Beside me, Martin stiffened and muttered under his breath. Amused by our discomfiture, Cnut grinned and licked his greasy knife. 'Careful, father: in another moment, he'll demand we hand back the treasure. Maybe we'd best leave ere these English fighters grow angry.'

'It was I who led that raid and my men were first to the Minster,' I said tightly. 'If you wish to challenge me, Cnut, I will not disappoint you. Half the gold of Borough is ours by right.'

'If that were the case, you would have it by my command.' As the tension in the booth increased, so the King's apparent nonchalance had faded. 'Yet while the contribution of you and your men cannot be denied, that treasure is the price King William paid for our departure. He is an arrogant and cold-hearted bastard but one with an eye for a bargain. The gold of Borough is ours.'

'Really?' I was hamstrung by the fact of their possession of the gold, their numbers, and they knew it. Yet there was still uneasiness in Sweyn's manner: he would not meet my eyes. 'Was that all? It seems to me he overpaid if your leaving was all he got in return.'

'Not quite all.' Harald, who up till then had watched with the calmness of one who knows his position is inviolable, sat up in his chair and looked at me with the concentration of a cat at a mouse-hole. 'The matter of certain hostages was agreed also. The castellans of York are to be freed and we promised them safe passage to Norwich.'

It took all the self-control gained over a lifetime's fighting to contain my fury at that moment, to keep my face still.

'That agreement was made without my knowledge or consent.' My voice was low, little more than a growl, but the words came clear enough. 'Gilbert de Ghent is my sworn enemy: he has insulted me and my kin.' Sensing their interest kindled by my passion, I put it in terms they would understand best: 'There is blood-feud between us. Let me meet him in single combat, here, according to ancient law. To let him walk free is a slight to my honour. Let us meet and the kites and crows will have the loser.'

Dauntless in war, Sweyn was yet a shrewd man and a skilled negotiator.

'Could I grant your wish, I would,' he said, then sighed and shook his head regretfully. 'If we had drawn swords together in open fight, no Norman bastard could have withstood us. But I have already reneged on one agreement with William and it is needful that he learns to trust me for the future. I shall offer you recompense, though it may be small comfort. Shall we say half the store of grain and mead aboard my ships?'

I glanced helplessly at Martin, knowing I was beaten and he gave a half-rueful, half-sympathetic smile and bowed his head.

'You leave me no choice,' I told Sweyn and as he nodded, turned the whole thing into a bitter jest. 'Next time I'll know how to deal with jackdaws come in the guise of ravens.'

'Do not forget: your prior will come with us, to ensure the bones of your saints are treated with respect and properly housed.' Neither Sweyn nor his sons rose to my insult. 'And we also bear these Normans no great good-will. You and your cause will be in our thoughts and prayers. Should you one day renounce this fight, you and your men will be welcome at my court.'

Doubtless in courtesy I should have thanked him, but the words stuck in my throat. Instead I inclined my head in bare acknowledgement, turned on my heel and left.

'At least we know now where we stand,' said Martin.

By the time the Danes left, a week later, I was resigned to their treachery though I did not forgive their possession of the gold. True to his word in one instance, Sweyn ordered half the stolen supplies to be returned. The sheer volume of grain, salted meat, mead and honey that had been secreted away was astounding and became the cause of renewed conflict between my men and his. Nothing worse than flesh wounds resulted but eventually Acer and I had to enforce discipline with a heavy hand. Thereafter the Fen-wolves treated the Vikings with disdain, saying their standard should be a magpie or jackdaw (somehow my parting words to Sweyn had become common knowledge), and their pride in themselves, which had taken a sore battering since the loss of the treasure, was restored a little.

It was a cool, blustery day with the wind from the west when Sweyn's ships set sail. Siward Beorn, who had avoided me since the Danish King's treachery was revealed, came shame-faced to ask leave to stay. It was to him that care of the hostages had been entrusted and his task also to make sure they reached Norwich unharmed. Emaciated, hairy and stinking, Gilbert de Ghent and William Malet sat in their chains and watched with the rest of us as the great ships left, their broad sails billowing in the gusts, the oars dipping in perfect unison to speed them on their way. Gulls wheeled overhead, their white wings gleaming in the fitful sunshine and their aching calls echoed the emptiness we felt as the sails diminished between the grey-brown line of the marshes and the vault of sky. All our hopes for a lasting victory went with those ships and without gold to lure them, there was no surety that the Danes would ever return to aid us. We were alone, isolated on the Isle as I had always feared, our stronghold become a potential trap. And yet as the sails were at last swallowed by the horizon, it was not despair that gripped me but a hardening of resolve. And looking at the faces of my men, I saw that for them it was the same.

Siward Beorn took his charges to Norwich next day with a band of twenty of his Northumbrians. The hostages were dunked in the river to rid them of the worst of the filth and vermin, then clad in the clothes of Normans slain in our raids. Gilbert de Ghent glared at me as I and my men went to bid Siward farewell but beneath his hate I detected fear. Guessing that without the protection of the Danes, the two must have spent an uneasy night in camp, I laughed in their faces and told them that next time we met they would die. Although released from their bonds, they were left unarmed and two quiet palfreys found for them while Siward Beorn and his men were mounted on the finest of the captured *destriers*. From the expressions of the hostages as they were helped into the saddle, the point was not lost on them but they were both too weak to handle warhorses in any case.

'I shall watch for your return,' I told Siward. 'You may have surety of safe passage while the hostages are in your keeping but it is a long road from Norwich. Trust no-one.'

He grinned and nodded as if I were a scolding parent, then called to his men and they cantered across the slope, heading for the ferry which would carry them to Stuntney and the tidal causeway east. Martin and I watched until they were lost to view, then went to join the others in the mead-hall. Already the wind had more than a breath of winter in it and we did not need speech to know that a harsh and bitter time lay ahead.

To keep from brooding on the uncertainty of our situation, I led the Fen-wolves to meet Siward Beorn. It was well that I did so for, as I suspected, the Normans had no intention of letting him return. They had pursued him almost from Norwich, their intention to drive him into an ambush at the very edge of the Fenland where William de Warenne held a fiefdom. Mens' shouts and a horse's whinny alerted us but by chance, Siward Beorn and his men were on the same side of a deep watercourse as us, while the Normans had waited on the wrong bank. As usual when stalking in the fens, we were on foot and armed with bows: the first De Warenne knew of our presence was a hail of arrows. The Northumbrians were no less surprised by our unexpected appearance; they spurred their horses forward while the frustrated Normans shouted abuse and hurled their lances, all of which fell into the clear, still water. Seeing me, William de Warenne yelled that when he caught me he would stretch my neck from the nearest tree as befitted a felon; I replied that once we were within sword's reach he would have no reason to be glad, and discharged an arrow which took him square on the chest and, had it pierced his mailcoat, must have killed him outright. As it was, it knocked him from his saddle and he writhed helplessly on the ground, winded by the force of the blow. His men bore him quickly out of arrow-range, our jeers following until they were lost to view.

We returned triumphantly to the Isle and feasted in the abbey until dawn. Athelwold and most of his monks had gone with Sweyn while a few sought refuge in Ramsay. It transpired that these had managed to steal away St. Oswald's arm, one of Borough's most prized relics, ere the Danes sailed. The reliquary in which the sacred bones had been housed remained with the Vikings but, Thurstan told me, an even finer one would be wrought once the saint had given us lasting victory.

My disquiet at the monks' duplicity was tempered by amusement at Sweyn's expense and respect for the Prior who, it seemed, had spirited the bones away under the King's very nose. Leofric the Deacon was among the few of Borough's monks that stayed at Ely and hearing we had no priest in camp, he offered his services. I agreed reluctantly but he proved loyal and was a skilled fighter though like many churchmen he refused to carry any weapon save a cudgel or mace, the spilling of blood being forbidden them.

Our lives settled once again to a strange existence of labour in the fields and raiding. There was still a steady trickle of incomers, many of whom had been with Eadric the Wild in the west and were thus seasoned fighters, but realizing after the Danes' defection how vulnerable we were to treachery, I made all my men, Fen-wolves included, pledge allegiance to me and our cause on the tomb of St. Etheldreda. Grey-eyed and dark-haired as she was portrayed in the great hanging that adorned her chapel, the saint reminded me sharply of Turfrida. The same calm sagacity lay in her smooth features and whenever I looked upon that image, a deep longing took hold of me.

Those of my messengers that survived the journey north returned at the start of November with no good tidings. The ravaging of their country had so disheartened the Northumbrians that they were loth to fight openly for fear of further retribution. Famine was his main enemy now, Waltheof's message ran, that and the coming winter. When next I heard of him, he was back at the Bastard's court, being promised the hand of one of the royal nieces as my nephew, Edwin, had been before.

From the atheling, the message was even vaguer, amounting to no more than an invitation to join him in Scotland. There was no hint of any plan of rebellion and while I tried to convince myself that maybe he was fearful of my messenger proving false or being captured, in my heart I suspected that he had revealed no strategy because he had none. Of my nephews no news had come all summer but as the autumn gales boomed across the marshes, they also turned up at court in London. I wondered cynically if they would be allowed to leave what was reputedly the greatest fortress in England or whether they had been lured south into a trap, like the hapless churchmen still languishing in prison cells after the Easter Council.

It was now, as the geese winged their way south once more, that I most missed Turfrida's steady counsel. Pride, and the knowledge that her stubbornness was equal to mine, prevented me going to Croyland and demanding audience with her: I could not countenance another encounter with Ulfkil like the last. Yet given the poorness of the harvest and the fact that the abbey's demesne lands had been divided into Norman fiefdoms as part of the Bastard's reorganisation of the monasteries, I sent provisions there at the same time as supplying the reed-cutters who still dwelt deep in the Fens as they had ever done.

Martin and Wuleric, who I sent with the supplies, returned with news that my wife and child were well but Turfrida would not speak with, much less join me until I had made peace with the King, though she would stay in England while hope remained that I would accede to her wishes. Hearing this I ground my teeth and, desperate for solitude, took Swallow and rode about the Isle until twilight. But what I most desired was not to be found there.

All Saints and All Souls, when superstitious folk put food and drink out for the spirits of the dead, passed and the weather worsened. Many needy folk struggled along the now flooded tracks to the Isle but only those able to fight were permitted to stay. Groups of starving women and children would trudge hopelessly back the way they had come, cursing the names of the abbot and myself for our hard-heartedness, and few of us could look them in the eye though we knew there was no choice if a fighting force was to be maintained on the Isle. (Some of those unfortunates had used their last reserves of strength to reach us and sank down and died before reaching the causeways. We collected their bodies and took them to the abbey for burial so at least they got to lie in consecrated ground, a rare privilege in those days).

At Christmas, the Bastard celebrated the further subjugation of England by holding a great feast over the twelve holy days. Whether Waltheof was there I do not know but rumour had both my nephews attending though by now anyone of English blood must have felt extremely uncomfortable at a Council where Norman power was deliberately vaunted. Maybe it was then that the two realized the fragility of their position for both had lived as *silvatici* between their oaths of fealty and it was clear enough by now that the Usurper was not a man who forgave easily.

On the Isle, the winter passed in the usual meld of cold and drudgery interspersed with rare joyous occasions. Aelgytha bore a son sired by her half-Welsh lover, Harald, and they decided to wed to avoid scandal (though in truth most folk were so glad to have food and shelter, only those of shrewish disposition cared whether a child was born in wedlock). They called the babe Toli and he was a big, lusty child doted on by Aelgytha's other children. By the time he was a month old, they were pulling him about on a wicker sledge, wrapped in so many layers of lamb and wolf-skin it was a wonder he was not smothered. Aye, compared with the misery of most folk that winter we lived like kings in the safety of our refuge. Elsewhere, only Normans and those who pandered to them were fat. Ordinary folk and the dispossessed, living like animals in the forests and hills, starved and died in their thousands as sickness spread and the bitter weather continued.

No doubt encouraged by their success in the north the previous year and the plunder gained from the systematic scouring of the abbeys, bands of Norman knights began to roam the countryside as soon as the roads were passable. The capture of rebels and punishment of those sympathetic to the rebel cause was their stated purpose and thus a new wave of terror spread across the land. Corpses hung from the trees outside many vills, not only of men but women and children who were the kin of dissenters and now, when they saw Norman bands ride past, serfs labouring in the fields or toiling in the mud to build more mounds for the hated castles, no longer stared or ran for cover but merely bowed their heads and continued working with the indifference of those who have lost all hope.

A castle had now been constructed at Cambridge. In mockery and defiance we built a small wooden fort on the ridge behind Aldreth. More a watchtower than defensive post, it stood stark and seemingly tall on the bare hill and was widely known as 'Hereward's Castle'. For those on guard over the causeway it provided some protection from the weather and a clear view over half the Isle as well as the marshes and was thus welcomed but to me its very existence was an ominous sign, verification of how we were isolated. I concealed my unease and our raids continued as before but increasingly we went out not as a mounted company, accoutred as knights, but by boat, lightly armed for swiftness.

I sent messages north again as soon as the sea-passage was safe but it was Easter before any replies came. Waltheof was at the Bastard's court for the customary gathering and Great Council; from Scotland the atheling sent nothing but his prayers and hopes than men would gather to our cause. Perhaps, having been the pawn of men like Stigand, Gospatrick and Waltheof for so long, Edgar had simply tired of empty promises and decided to stay under the protection of his brother-in-law, King Malcolm, where the Normans could not reach him.

It was just past Holy Sunday when the look-outs in the north of the Isle reported the approach of three warships from the Wide Sea. I doubt there was one amongst us who was not overtaken by wild hope that Sweyn and his sons had returned to aid us: we ran up the slope behind Cratendune to watch the ships come in. But although the vessels exhibited the clean, graceful lines and low draught of northern craftsmanship, the sails were furled and the oarsmen lacked the natural seamanship of the Vikings, men who seemed to take in the handling of boats and weapons with their mother's milk. We watched the leading ship falter when it reached the confluence of the Ouse and the narrow channel that led to our moorings then, as it continued on its way upriver, I saw a dark-haired figure lean disconsolately against the mast. He was slighter in build than most of the men surrounding him yet clearly in command. When the helmsman shouted a warning as the keel grazed an emerging mudbank (the tide was against them), and the man went forward to look ahead, I recognized my nephew, Morcar.

Rahere went swiftly in his reed punt to guide them and they beached on the flats beside the fishermen's cots. We had planks to lay across the mud and Morcar looked round with evident approval at the buildings, horse-pens and booths packed inside the palisade, the sprawl of the camp beyond, the herd of *destriers*, already glossy with the spring grass, grazing the slopes.

'Is Edwin here?' he asked after greeting and embracing me like a brother. 'No doubt he's stuffing his face in the abbey: it was a hard winter in West Mercia.'

'We've heard nothing of him,' I replied bluntly. 'Was he not at court for

Easter?'

If he detected the edge of bitterness in my voice, he did not remark it. A look of deep concern had overtaken his features and he bit at his knuckles like the nervous boy of old.

'He was coming by land,' he said, after a moment's thought. 'We heard the King meant to imprison us once he had proof of sedition – God knows, that wouldn't take long to find. We were fighting on the borders with the Welsh, then took to our own woods after Gruffydd was killed but Edwin still pretended to be a loyal supporter of the Usurper wherever the Normans were gullible enough.' He frowned and looked at his men, busy unloading the ships. 'There were some with him I mistrusted, Bretons who pledged allegiance not for honour but gold. A man who sells his sword for one price may be open to a higher offer, especially if it comes from the stronger side.'

'So we have found,' I told him ruefully and related the tale of the raid on Borough and Sweyn's defection. He listened sympathetically but with only half his mind. His eyes scanned the marshes and fields, the track across the hillside to the camp, as if expecting his brother to ride into view at any moment.

'The Danes may have deserted but you are not alone,' he said when I had finished. 'Edwin has two hundred with him and there are more besides. We sent word to Athelwine and others to rally here at Ely, aye, and the Atheling also: there's nothing to be gained by attacking York again. The Normans have made a desert of the north: our men would starve ere they encountered an enemy. Better to start the fight at Cambridge and Borough, then aim for Winchester and London, push the bastards south until they've nowhere to go but back across the sea.' He paused and surveyed the camp and harbour more critically. 'This is a good place. Does Turfrida like it? She and the children are safer here than at Bourne.'

Martin had joined us. He glanced warningly at Morcar but it was too late.

'She is not here,' I said. 'And Aedgifu died when I was away fighting in York. Turfrida wants me to make peace with the Bastard: she thinks our cause already lost.'

'Ah God.' Embarrassed, Morcar looked down and scraped his feet in the mud like an admonished child. 'Did she return to Flanders? I'm sorry, Hereward.'

'No fault of yours,' I said roughly. 'And she has more regard than to forsake me utterly. She is at Croyland. In any case, she should know I will never submit while there are men willing to follow me.'

An uncomfortable silence fell between us: I glanced towards the boats, wondering how many men Morcar had with him.

'Edwin was bringing gold,' Morcar said suddenly. 'When the Normans began taking thegns' deposits from the abbeys, we took ours and hid it elsewhere. But we thought it would be safe in Ely and it occurred to us that the Danes might return if we outbid the King. The abbey must guard treasure equal to Borough's if there's truth in the rumour that Stigand stored his gold here.'

'Thurstan will take more than the asking to give up what he has so far kept from Viking and Norman hands,' I replied. 'And I'm loth to raid the abbey unless there is no choice: we need their allegiance.'

Sensing that the conversation was heading towards a subject none of us on the Isle wanted to contemplate (though it was already causing me sleepless nights), namely the loyalty of the monks, Martin gestured towards the booth previously occupied by Sweyn.

'We're crowded but that place is free,' he said. 'It's fitting you should have it though you might have to share when your brother arrives. There are no other representatives of the Witan here.'

Morcar grimaced. 'There are few of us left and all have sworn fealty to the Usurper,' he said grimly. 'Look at Edwin: it took him long enough to see through the Bastard's lies. His eorldom restored and a royal wife – he was mad to believe it. And when he realized the truth – well, I've never seen him so angry or so hurt. He felt utterly betrayed: it was as if William was a brother, not an enemy.' Morcar hesitated and a strange, thwarted look settled on his lean features. 'Maybe it's true that the Bastard's in league with the Horned One. He has the stature of a Norse hero and fiery hair to match his ruthlessness but his eyes are like stones. A cold man and uncompromising: I saw what he did in the north. And yet he has the power to beguile and persuade men to his will such as I have never known before. Waltheof, Edwin, the atheling, all have fallen under his spell at some time and even when the truth dawns, such men begin to doubt themselves and question all they do as if it's impossible that William meant to trick them.'

I made the old sign against evil, fingers spread, caught Martin doing the same and grinned ashamedly. 'The Bastard won't find us so pliable to his will, should he ever come here. He's a man like any other: when struck, he'll bleed.'

'No-one ever gets close enough,' Morcar said. 'He believes no-one can wound or slay him with such force, no-one ever does. Maybe God protects him.'

'More likely the Devil,' I growled. 'Has he not set wergild of a hind higher than a man's?'

Martin shivered and crossed himself. 'Don't let that sort of talk spread amongst the men. The odds are stacked enough.'

'Aye.' I clapped Morcar, who still seemed uneasy, on the shoulder. 'Come on, we have food and drink fit for a king's table. Let's have it ere the Bastard comes to claim it.'

We feasted that night to welcome the new arrivals, all of whom looked in dire need of a good meal and ale. More than three hundred had come, some of whom had survived the carnage at Fulford Gate though most were disaffected thegns and sokemen. Their arms were mixed and a few who lacked decent mail we promised to equip, there being no lack of captured weapons and gear on the Isle. A few women and children had also come (though most had been left behind to fend for themselves): these had worked for their places on the crowded ships, cooking, mending and making clothes, even fletching arrows. All these we accommodated where the Danes had been before and their presence heartened us. Nonetheless, I made them take the same oath as the rest, swearing fealty on St. Etheldreda's tomb. These were Morcar's men, not mine but he seemed happy for them to swear undying enmity towards the Normans, to accept me as war-leader, and the rule of the Witan though in truth such a body no longer existed.

The days passed, the air was full of larksong, the bawling of new lambs, the clash of weapons from the training field but there was no news of Edwin. Bishop Athelwine and a host of supporters arrived a week after Morcar and were welcomed with mixed joy and trepidation by the monks of Ely. With so eminent a seditionary now ensconced at the abbey, Thurstan could not longer pretend that circumstances had forced him to co-operate with the rebels and outlaws on the Isle.

Rumours began to circulate that Edwin was dead, that he had been ambushed and his whole force massacred by Norman knights; that he had been treacherously slain by his own men; that he had been tide-trapped on a mudbank and drowned. Morcar steadfastly denied there could be any truth in such wild tales: the brothers were well accustomed to using false information to cover their movements or entrap enemies, but as days became weeks and still Edwin did not appear or send word, he could no longer conceal his disquiet.

It was Rahere and his scouting parties of those most skilled in fen-craft, sent to scour the wide expanse of marshland from end to end, who noticed birds of prey and carrion-eaters spiralling over the same area day after day. When they went to investigate, his men found a swathe of trampled ground on a remote river bank and came back to fetch me and Morcar. As our boats floated down river on the tide a bittern boomed close by and I shivered, remembering Toli's tale of the warhorns of the dead.

We beached the craft at the river's edge, noting deeply incised prints of men and horses in the black mud, and Acer set off along a trampled swathe through the sedge while the rest of us searched the bank. The big man grunted and pulled at something that had been trodden into the wet ground. It came free with a sucking sound: a sword-hilt, the blade broken a foot from the cross-piece. Morcar snatched it from him, studied it a moment, then handed it to me. It was of fine workmanship, the pommel decorated with gold inlay and bright enamels. The leather bindings were dark-stained with years of use, sweat and blood ingrained.

'It looks like my brother's,' Morcar said wearily. He half-drew his own sword so that we could compare them. 'They were a pair, a gift from our father, wrought in Flanders.' He hesitated, stared across the marshes with the studied self-containment of sudden grief. 'The blades – we thought they were flawless – he must be dead.'

None of us replied but resumed our search though there was little to be told from the ground save that many mounted men had been there. Then Rahere who had, as usual, gone off alone, returned. He stood silent, watching us but there was something compelling in the intentness of his gaze.

'This way,' was all he said and led us through what appeared to be an impenetrable bank of sedge (the reeds simply sprang back behind anyone passing through), to a narrow tongue of land surrounded on three sides by water which had become a killing ground.

Had the air not been so still, we must have found the place by the stench. Maybe three score bodies lay there, stripped and mutilated: many had been decapitated. Flies buzzed and rose in clouds as we stepped among the dead. The ground was pocked with hoofmarks; many of the corpses had been trampled. I bent to inspect a body lying face down, pulled it over, recoiled at the maggots seething in the torn, rotting flesh. Spiralling bracelets of tattooing around the wrists, elbows and thighs identified the man as a northerner. Many of the dead bore such.

'This was the core of Edwin's force,' Morcar said with an effort. 'Some of these men had been with us since we were of an age to bear arms. Wulfnoth ' - he crouched beside the body I had just overturned, grimaced at the gaping throat and belly, the mangled genitalia – 'he fought his way out of the ditch at Fulford; his kin were slain when the Normans took revenge for York.' He bowed his head, muttered unintelligibly under his breath, then rose. 'We must at least give them a decent burial.'

It took most of the rest of that day to dig a long trench in which we laid the dead, placing their broken weapons beside them as a mark of honour. But though we scoured every reed-bed and mudbank for half a mile roundabout, Rahere poling his punt where men could not tread, of Edwin himself we found no further sign. Mired and stinking, we stamped on the grave so that no bird or animal could disturb it and Morcar bent to push his brother's sword into the ground so that it stood upright like a cross.

'God grant we take your blood-price thrice over,' he said and then he stripped the gold rings from his fingers, dug a small pit and buried them there as gift and promise to the dead.

We stood a moment in silent communion and made our way back to the boats. None of us spoke much until we reached the Isle. That a massacre could happen so close and undetected had shaken us all. Only later in the Great Hall of the abbey, after Athelwine had said a Mass and praised the fallen, did we begin to piece together what had happened and the full truth was only revealed two days later when Rahere brought a snivelling, cringing wretch into camp, a boy of barely fifteen summers who, the Fen-man told me with grim satisfaction, had been paid to guide Edwin into an ambush.

I sent Erik to fetch Morcar while the lad, who said his name was Ivar, sank to the ground and began to weep. He was shaking, so great was the fear upon him and when Morcar arrived with a deliberate show of ceremony, clutched my knees begging for mercy.

'Speak truthfully and your life may be spared,' I told him, 'but if you lie or we're not satisfied with your tale, Morcar shall have you, to do with as he wills. And if you die at his hands, there will be no redress for are you not of Edda's kin?'

The lad moaned and began to gabble about a stolen boat, how his father had cursed outlaws and Normans alike for the ill-fortune come upon him, but he fell silent when Morcar stood looking down at him. My nephew's face, always lean, was gaunt and pale, his eyes red-rimmed and sunken: he felt his brother's loss keenly. He met my gaze with a brief smile of anticipation then crouched beside the boy, whipping his dagger from its sheath in the same movement.

'You will tell me who paid you, how my brother and his men died, why you betrayed us. If you do not answer to my liking, I will cut off your fingers, then your toes and if I'm still not satisfied, I'll start on the parts that matter.'

He spoke with a cold self-control more menacing than rage and the boy squirmed and whimpered. Morcar watched him for a moment, rose to his feet and waited, turning the dagger slowly in his hands. 'Speak!'

In his terror, Ivar had peed himself: the pungent stink of urine mingled with the smells of peat and wood-smoke from the forge and cooking fires, the familiar odour of many men crowded together (by now most of the Fen-wolves had gathered to see what was happening). At last, exasperated, Morcar caught hold the boy's shoulders and dragged him upright. 'Begin, else you'll lose your thumbs!'

Realizing he had nothing to gain by silence, Ivar shrugged free of Morcar's grip and knelt straight-backed though his head was bowed to his chest.

'He said he would burn all the Fenland vills to the ground, hang the men, rape the women and sell them as whores,' he said. 'And we believed him: why should we not? He said he wanted a guide to lead friends of his to a secret meeting-place where a ship would come to take them away. He promised gold and that our vills would be safe. No-one wanted to do it but then they set fire to Bolli's hut and we knew we had no choice.'

I felt a tightening about my brow, as if an iron band were closing there. 'So who is it the Fen-folk fear more than me?' I asked harshly.

He raised his head and looked about with the frantic gaze of a trapped wild animal then, seeing there was no escape, became calm, mouth set in a stubborn line. For the space of maybe five heartbeats we waited. I nodded to Acer who stood nearby. 'Hold him still.'

Pinioned as effectively as if bound, the boy moaned then shrieked as Morcar grasped his right hand and pressed the point of his dagger into the knuckle of the thumb, ready to prise the bones apart.

'Ivo Taillebois! It was Ivo Taillebois!' Ivar sobbed and gasped but neither Morcar nor Acer relaxed their grip. 'Please! I didn't know they meant to kill them!'

'Did you know who you were to betray?' Morcar's voice was a low hiss. 'How was my brother so easily fooled?'

'There were men in his force, Normans, I was told to contact,' the boy moaned. 'He trusted them and somehow they knew who I was. They told him I would lead the way to a secret hythe deep in the marshes where there were boats to take them to Hereward's Camp. Edwin questioned me but I thought of my mother and sisters and the lies came easily to my tongue. I swear I didn't know they were going to their deaths. It was only by chance I escaped with my own life for I think the Normans meant to slay me also.'

'Aye, dead men tell no tales,' Acer growled. 'And have you seen the gold they promised, gold stained with the blood of your own eorl's kin?'

Ivar did not reply or try to withdraw his hand: he merely shuddered and shook his head. Morcar, the muscles of his face rigid so that the cheekbones stood out, twisted the dagger a little and the boy yelped.

'Tell us the full tale, whelp, or die!'

In stumbling, barely coherent sentences, the boy related the events of ten days before. Having led the way into the river loop (known ever afterwards as 'Eorl's Bend'), Ivar had stood irresolute while Edwin, his suspicions aroused by the lack of hythe and boats, demanded what was going on. But even as he moved to lay hands on the boy, the Normans and traitors in his force drew weapons and fell upon their comrades with such unexpected ferocity that many died before realizing what was happening. The mules bearing the eorl's baggage were swiftly led away and as the core of Edwin's force began to fight back, one of the Bretons blew a hunting horn, a pre-arranged signal that brought two score Norman knights charging from the cover of the sedge. After that, Ivar said, it was a massacre. Terrified by the noise and blood, he ran and hid in the reeds to watch as the renegades stripped the dead and dying, then hacked at the bodies, hurling the pieces into the river and mires which lay nearby. Edwin was one of the last to die and his corpse had been quartered and thrown into the bog where, like the others, it had sunk without a trace. But it was then, with the eorl dead, that the attackers seemed ill-at-ease and instead of disposing of all the bodies, they gathered their booty and left, the horsemen sending their mounts plunging through the reed-beds while the rest followed as quickly as they could, blood-splattered and bent under the weight of plundered mail and weapons.

'What of the gold?' Morcar asked savagely.

'I don't know!' The boy, who had grown calm as he told his tale, looked, panic-stricken, from Morcar to me. 'For God's sake – I never saw any of it! Please!'

He pleaded desperately for mercy but my nephew's face was mask-like, hard and unreadable. With a movement so swift none of us saw it, he severed the boy's thumb. Blood spurted: Ivar stared horror-struck at the stump.

'The truth,' Morcar said grimly, catching the boy's other hand and placing the bloodied dagger point in the hinge of the thumb knuckle as before. 'And be quick, ere I lose patience.'

Torture is not something I have ever enjoyed. The helplessness of the victims brings back memories I have long striven to forget. As the lad writhed and wept, I pitied but felt no urge to aid him, craven coward and traitor that he was. His other thumb and all the fingers of his right hand he lost ere Morcar believed there was no more to be had from him and then my nephew walked away in disgust, saying that the life of one so wretched was not worth the taking. I had Acer take Ivar to the forge for his wounds to be seared (his screams could be heard across half the Isle), and thence to the abbey. Once it was certain he would live, Rahere ferried him to his own kin, dumping him on a mudbank near their reed and peat hovels, naked, hands and feet bound, his head shaved and a noose around his neck so that the Gyrwas would understand how traitors were dealt with on the Isle.

A strange mood of expectancy fell upon us after that. We were restless without knowing why, as horses and dogs become nervous, sensing an approaching storm before the first clouds appear on the horizon. Such fortifications as we thought necessary were already built; we organised tourneys to keep the men in fighting mettle, gathered supplies, waited to see what the Bastard would do next.

The active core of the rebellion was now gathered on the Isle. All those disaffected with the lack of resolve demonstrated by Waltheof, Gospatrick and the rest had joined us. Most travelled by the sea-road from the Humber or Scotland but some made the perilous journey through the closely guarded wasteland of the north. Many of Siward Beorn's men came, those left behind when he had joined Sweyn's force and he rewarded their fealty with gifts of weapons and gold. He winked when I asked him the source of the latter and I let it go. If he had filched some of Borough's treasure after the raid, I did not want to know of it.

It was some of these men, doughty fighters all, who warned us of mass movements of Norman knights. Up till then, most of William's force had been deployed in Yorkshire and Northumbria, tightening their grip on that land from the chain of castles which now guarded the borders. Now, with the north subjugated, they were moving south. Most ominous of all was news that the Bastard himself was at Northampton, his stated purpose to set up a base at Cambridge though what he intended there, no-one knew.

We were apt to dismiss such tales at first, for with the departure of the Danes and continuing faintheartedness of the atheling, the Bastard must have realized the uprising was effectively hamstrung. But as Martin pointed out patiently when Morcar, Siward Beorn, Thurstan, Athelwine and I sat in council one evening, the King trusted Sweyn even less than we and once rebellion broke out from Ely, he would be hard put to stop its momentum, if we had support.

'Let him attack the Isle,' Siward said recklessly after a protracted and thoughtful silence. 'He'll never take it, not with the fighting men we have.' He raised his wine cup to the churchmen. 'I've heard you are not averse to hard hand-strokes. You'll join us, eh? If your monks fight as well as they brew ale and pray, we can't lose!'

'Moreover,' Morcar said slowly, 'once it's seen that the bastards can be beaten, the atheling's force may be tempted to join us, if not Sweyn's. And if Malcolm of Scotland came with him, the balance would tip in our favour.'

I fingered the silver chasing round the rim of my cup, drained the sour wine at a gulp.

'Don't fool yourself,' I said bluntly. 'Four years we've waited for Edgar and each time he's run away with his tail between his legs. As for Sweyn, he'll wait awhile ere he makes another move against the Normans. Best plan as if we're on our own.'

Morcar frowned. The manner of Edwin's death had affected him deeply. He had become morose, blaming himself though it was not of his doing.

'How long - ?' he began at last but I caught his eye and shook my head slightly and he said no more. As the evening progressed, Thurstan had grown noticeably more ill-at-ease. For us (and the outlawed Bishop Athelwine), the choice was simple: to leave the Isle or fight on and die, if necessary, in its defence but rebellion had been forced on him and his monks and they would, if the uprising failed, have to account for their actions not only to the King but to Archbishop Lanfranc, who was now head of their church.

'This is our land,' I said deliberately. 'Whatever the legality of the Atheling's claim, it is we who must rout the usurpers. And according to our law, it is the Witan that chooses the king, not right of conquest.'

'The Witan?' Siward Beorn looked pityingly at me, then spat on the flagstone floor, ignoring the abbot's disapproving glance. 'We'll have to elect a new one then: what's left of the old is more spineless now than in 1066. Killing Normans: that's all we have to do and, it must be said, we're good at it. When we're rid of them, that's when to think about who rules and if I've anything to do with it, it won't be the gutless whelp hiding behind King Malcolm's throne.'

'If we can beat whatever force is mustering against us, break out and unite all those still willing to fight, that's the best we can hope for,' Morcar said grimly. 'But if we have to die here, let's make an ending worthy of remembrance. That will be a kind of victory in itself.'

Silence fell. These words seemed ill-omened though they were but stark statement of the truth. Then Siward grinned and thumped the table with his fist with such force, the cups and trenchers jumped. Spilled wine glistened in the torchlight like blood.

'I've spat often enough in the face of death not to fear it,' he said. 'I only pray the Bastard dares show his face. I'd like to take him with me if I can.'

To this sentiment, at least, we agreed whole-heartedly, all save Thurstan who began tracing patterns in the spilled wine, his expression one of profound resignation.

5. The Siege of Ely

The sheep had been shorn and hay-cutting was in progress when the alarm sounded from Aldreth. Morcar, Siward Beorn and I rode at once to the watchtower where a great crowd had gathered. From the top of the wooden platform a dark mass could be seen moving from the south. Like a shadow it over-ran the low ridge between Cottenham and Willingham, then crept inevitably along the causeway. Yet even as it stretched towards Belsar's Hill there was still no sign of its ending, as if an inexhaustible supply of men and horses were springing from the earth itself. It was a blustery day: lance points, helmets, mail and harness glinted in fitful sunshine.

'He's brought his whole army!' Erik, as usual, was at my side; there was awe and incredulity in his voice. 'There can't be a Norman left in all the south!'

'Then be proud, lad.' Acer, who had come from the north of the Isle to report on ship sightings, clapped the lad on the shoulder so that he staggered. 'The Bastard fears what might spring from our defiance. If the Vikings return or a force comes from the north, he'll be hard-pressed and he knows it. He's come to destroy the uprising before it gains momentum.'

'He'll be hard-pressed to defeat us anyway.' I looked towards Belsar's Hill where the garrison led by Thorald had already lit a signal fire to tell us they were ready. 'There are men here worth a hundred spears apiece and had he twice his force, they could not take the Isle while we defend it. He can throw what he likes at us. This is not York, nor will we run away. Here he'll discover what happens when he meets men who do not fear him!'

'Aye.' Acer grinned. 'So far he's met no real resistance since Hastings. Now we'll see his true mettle.'

We had long planned for this moment. Belsar's Hill, halfway along the causeway between the river and the mainland, could not be held but we intended to delay our enemies there and make the wide stretch of marshland on its flanks a place for Normans to fear. To this end we had constructed withy hides and peat bulwarks in the reed beds, none of which were visible from the causeway or Belsar's Hill. Most of Thorald's men, along with Rahere's were already hidden in the marsh; the rest, still in the hill-fort, made a great show of defiance from the palisade as the Norman vanguard advanced but not a single arrow was fired until the first knights were within easy range of the gate.

After York, I had trained my men to aim at the unprotected horses rather than their riders since a well-made hauberk may be arrow-proof. The causeway was so narrow and the edges so treacherous, there was barely room for three horsemen to ride abreast. As the first came within range,

Thorald gave our wolf's howl and a hail of arrows and javelins poured not only from the shelter of the palisade but from the reed-beds adjacent to the causeway. Pain-maddened *destriers* squealed and tried to turn; some plunged straight off the embankment into the mire; others reared and crashed down, their thrashing hooves causing as much death and injury as our arrows: the screams of men and horses rent the air. The whole column was thrown into confusion but there was no room for retreat. Instead there was a desperate heaving of the dead and wounded into the bogs to clear the way for a ram, an oak trunk slung on a cradle drawn by a team of oxen. As they began to batter the gates (which had not been built to withstand such an onslaught), Thorald and his men abandoned Belsar's Hill and joined the attack from the sides.

When, having run out of arrows, the bowmen returned, I praised their efforts which had seen at least forty knights killed outright and many others injured. The numbers of *destriers* slain or maimed no-one had counted. Not one of our men had been hurt save a lad from Witham who had been struck in the shoulder by a carelessly aimed arrow. The vanguard of the enemy had now overrun the hillfort and was advancing towards Aldreth but at the other end, more were still setting out.

If any of my men felt apprehension as the full might of the Normans became clear, none betrayed it. Nearly everyone on the Isle, fighters, cottars and monks, had congregated around the watchtower to see what the Bastard planned for us. We yelled our scorn as the first knights to reach the river tried to force their mounts into the fast-flowing water. The horses became bogged in the soft mud and one fell while the others managed to turn and regain firmer ground by a series of ungainly, plunging leaps which all but unseated their riders. The trapped horse drowned swiftly while its hapless rider was hauled out and lay retching on the bank. Had he been without help, he would have shared his *destrier's* fate and I heard Rahere grunt in satisfaction. Weighed down by mail, our enemies were easy prey once in the water.

In his arrogance, the Bastard had assumed that the river could be forded. In dry summers it was just possible to cross at neap tides (though the current and deep mud made the venture perilous), but otherwise a ferry carried travellers from the end of the causeway to Aldreth, following a winding channel which drained one of the broad meres on our side of the river. In the past there had been another causeway along the strip of marsh between the meres to the river but only a few rotten stubs marked its course. We had, of course, long since taken possession of the ferry: anyone wanting to enter or leave the Isle by that route could do so only with our aid.

As more knights crowded down onto the ferryman's hard, milling about uncertainly as they wondered what to do, I left the tower and took Swallow from Wuleric who was waiting below. She quivered as I swung into the saddle and a *destrier's* harsh neigh sounded from across the river. Siward Beorn, Acer and Morcar had followed me. I wheeled the mare and drew Brain-biter. 'Come on, let's show the Bastard who he has to fight!'

We galloped downslope to a point where we could clearly see our enemies and they us across the fen and river. The wind carried their voices as they talked together. We shouted our defiance, trying to goad them into crossing but they merely paused a moment to stare, then seeing we were no threat, resumed their debate. It was a scene that was to be repeated many times over the next few days for instead of dividing their force and attacking from several directions at once, they concentrated on Aldreth, driving piles into the river bank while a great store of timbers and hides, along with bundles of reeds and straw (enough materials to build a vill the size of Bourne), were brought along the causeway. As they began to lash all these together, stuffing the hides with reeds and straw, we harassed them from our side of the river until they built screens of withies to protect themselves from our arrows as they worked. Eventually we realized they were building a kind of floating bridge but the depth of the channel and the difficulty of working in mud which swallowed men thigh-deep as soon as they stepped away from the root-bound banks, forced them to give up the attempt to drive more piles into the river to stabilise the structure.

'As much use as an iron boat,' was Rahere's comment when he saw what they were doing. 'Don't worry: they'll drown before they set foot on the Isle. This is our land, our river, and it will protect us. You'll see.'

His confidence did much to reassure those who had begun to watch the Norman engineering with trepidation. Belsar's Hill and the distant ridge between Willingham and Cottenham were crowded with tents and shelters and more wagons crawled along the road from Cambridge. Every day, strings of *destriers* had to be led back and forth to good grazing. The squires that tended them must have looked at our green hills with envy.

At Thurstan's suggestion, we made the great wall hanging of Saint Etheldreda into our standard. All the folk of Ely cheered when they saw it. It gave the Usurper pause when he came to inspect the works: as it spread out in the wind, he reined in his stallion, a powerful bay which must have stood sixteen hands, to look. His hair flamed in the sunlight, a great sword hung at his side; he sat his horse with careless pride, as if the animal were but an extension of his indomitable will.

At the sight of him, our enemy personified, a strange silence fell upon us. He was beyond arrow-shot and knew it: his gaze raked us over and I shuddered. Hate, pure as ice, immutable as stone, made my skin prickle. To my right I heard the abbot (who now wore a fine mail hauberk beneath his robe), mutter a prayer.

'Ach now, are we children to be tongue-tied by terror?' Siward Beorn drew his sword, the gold-twined hilt and pommel glittering in the sunshine. 'Hear this, Norman bastards!' he shouted. 'You're made of blood and bone like us and we'll prove it if you set foot upon this Isle. Your flesh will feed the eels and your widows will be our whores. Come across if you dare, and meet death!'

His enthusiasm was infectious. We drew our own weapons and waved them in defiance, then Acer said grimly, 'Aye, let him know the wolf-pack is waiting,' put his hands to his mouth and gave the howl which all Norman usurpers in the Fenland had learned to dread. If the Bastard and his knights had missed Siward's words, they heard our paean as all the Fen-wolves on the hill and hidden in the marshes gave voice. Wild and defiant, the cry rang out across the river and fens and many on the causeway and at Belsar's Hill paused and turned to see whence it came and what it might signify.

There was a moment, a heart-beat's length of utter silence. Not a bird called, nor a horse neigh nor any dog howl. The Bastard and his escort stared up at us; his *destrier* pawed the ground as if eager to charge. Then, as one, they wheeled their horses and trotted back towards their camp, our jeers following.

Despite our efforts, work on the floating bridge did not stop though we mocked and harried the labourers day and night. It became a popular pastime for Isle folk to come to Aldreth and alternately deride and threaten those on the other side of the river, while for skilled archers it was a kind of game to punt through the cover of the marshes and shoot whenever they were exposed. But the dead and wounded were quickly replaced and the work continued.

The ungainly construction was maybe two-thirds complete when we discovered that the main waterways to the north and east of the Isle were being guarded. Outi had set out for the Wellestream where we had fish and bird nets set, when his boat was hailed by a vessel of the broad-bowed type used on the coast. Thinking the fishermen wanted to trade, Outi and his men sailed closer, then the sun flashed on a blade and they realized that the boat, though crewed by Saxons, was full of Norman fighters.

It was through their superior local knowledge that Outi's band escaped, lowering their sail and rowing or poling their way through narrow inlets and shallow channels where the larger vessel could not follow. But whilst on their return they were full of their adventure, having fired on the enemy from the cover of the reeds and seen two of the boatmen and one Norman struck, when I took Outi aside and spoke to him alone, he said that was not the only fishing craft they had seen which neither set nets nor made for any landing place but rather plied back and forth across the same stretch of water, as if waiting.

After that, it was no surprise when Rahere reported boats on every major waterway in the whole of the fenland. These were not warships but fishing and trading vessels requisitioned from every harbour for miles around. Their purpose was clear: to place a cordon around the Isle.

'The net's closing,' Thurstan remarked gloomily when I called a war-council to discuss this development. 'They're stopping the gaps and then they'll strike, like a cat at a mouse-hole.'

'These mice may have a bigger bite than the bastards've bargained for,' Siward replied. 'And we've supplies enough to last another winter while they rot their arses off squatting in the mud.'

'Moreover, they do not know this country as we do.' I glanced towards Rahere. 'We'll harry them until they come to fear every splash in the water and those who aid them will burn. I am in no mind to despair.'

'Nor I.' Siward and Morcar spoke as one, they raised their wine-cups and drained them at a gulp. The rest of us followed but I noticed that Thurstan and Athelwine seemed reluctant, ill-at-ease. Neither met my gaze as I pledged and enjoined them to look forward to the coming fight so thinking them afraid, I told them that as we were sworn to keep Etheldreda's sanctuary from Norman ravaging, so she would surely help and protect us, her monks in particular, who had served her so long and faithfully.

'It was not on a whim that I had my men swear fealty on her tomb,' I said. 'And it was a blessed thought that inspired Thurstan to use her image as our banner. We will not lose this fight while we are true to our oaths.'

At this, abbot and bishop smiled and joined in the drinking. The blood flowed hot within us as Siward began to chant the Saga of Harald Hardrada, which he had learned from Snorri, Sweyn's skald, and I thought no more upon the churchmen's reticence.

By the time the Normans were ready to attack, we were well prepared. The evening preceding the assault, we watched through pelting rain as they pushed the result of their labour into the river and moored it. Siward Beorn was for crossing after nightfall and cutting it loose but Rahere argued against this, the construction being so long that it would most likely lodge across the flow, blocking the river passage and perhaps settling in a more stable position than any our enemies could devise. 'Also,' he said, 'is it not our purpose to kill the bastards? Let them try: we'll make them pay dearly for the crossing. You'll see.'

Such was his certainty, no-one doubted him. Though some were wary of the taciturn Fen-man, all respected his knowledge of water and marshland. In the darkness before dawn I positioned our best marksmen on the reed platforms and behind the peat bulwarks in the marshes between the river and the firm ground of the Isle. The main part of our force I held back on the ridge behind Aldreth.

As a wan light spread over the meres and low hills that morning, the Normans must have believed themselves unopposed. Cattle and sheep grazed the slopes near the watchtower and a herd boy watched with apparent indifference as the Norman camp stirred and seethed, but there was no other activity to be seen on our side of the river.

I lay on my belly at the top of the ridge, Morcar, Siward Beorn and Martin beside me. It was a dank, dismal morning with drizzle veiling the hills to the south. Emerging mudflats gleamed in the grey light and the flat line of the marshland merged into the weeping sky. To our eyes, the frenzied activity of our enemies seemed like the scurrying of ants. We watched with a strange detachment as they began the operation of spanning the river, though the reason for their hurry was clear. Unless they finished before the tide turned, the whole enterprise was doomed.

Perhaps the Bastard believed even the river would obey his will: he had not the innate wisdom of Cnut. Before the tide had sunk to its lowest, boats began to tow the long line of stuffed hides, timbers and reed-bundles out. Men armed with long poles to guide and steady their progress sat at intervals along its length but they had reckoned without the strength of the current. Before they reached the opposite bank, the middle section was bowed downstream despite the efforts of those upon it to keep it straight.

I had warned the bowmen hidden in the marshes to hold their fire until the main force was in range and somehow they restrained themselves though the men now struggling to haul and drive the front of the structure (which the Normans called a *ponton*), onto the muddy bank made certain targets and were without mail or weapons. Stout poles were driven into the mud and peat and ropes looped round and fastened to hold the structure. Then the cunning of the Norman engineers was revealed, for once the *ponton* was secure, they used it to guide other sections across the river, with which to span the treacherous marshes and so reach the Isle.

'Now they'll learn!' Rahere had made his way up from the riverside. 'Tide's turned and they've nothing to give them a firm foothold. No Norman will cross that thing alive, believe me.'

His words were quickly borne out as the men attempting to haul the water-logged hides and reed-bundles over the mud became stuck. From the other side of the river their comrades mocked them but someone restored order and more men were sent to help, scrambling along the *ponton* with difficulty. The structure was beginning to buckle as the water rose.

Gradually the ungainly mass, a crudely articulated snake of bound timbers and stuffed hides, was extended to the very shore of the Isle though in the doing of it we saw two men lost in the bog, the peaty water closing over their heads ere their comrades could pull them out. Their cries for help, piercing and desperate, made us shudder. There was no one amongst the Fen-wolves who had not at some time felt the sodden peat quake beneath his feet, seen a ripple run across the surface and drawn back onto safer ground or stood frozen, counting off the heartbeats as the earth settled, praying that this time he would not be swallowed by the ever-hungry mire.

On the other side of the river, the knights filling the causeway all the way back to Belsar's Hill, stirred restlessly, waiting for their path to be clear.

As the end of the structure was made fast to an ancient alder tree at the very edge of the marsh, the horsemen at the front jostled to be first across. A gust of wind ruffled the surface of the river and the sections of the *ponton* heaved and tossed. Beside me, Rahere muttered under his breath: a prayer or incantation it seemed; Siward Beorn let out a breath of mirthless laughter.

We discovered afterwards that the Usurper had promised all Ely's treasure to the man who first reached the abbey. Otherwise the chaotic nature of their onset made no sense. No horse, not even *destriers* trained to board boats, would step foot on the unstable timbers at the far end of the *ponton* and their fear turned to panic as those on foot tried to push past. I saw one knight, an eminent man from the richness of his gear, fall from his plunging stallion and disappear, trampled underfoot by eager men and frantic horses.

Those who managed to rush onto the *ponton* were carried halfway across the river by impetus alone. Then, as the whole structure moved violently, throwing many to their knees and some into the water, they hesitated, for the sections ahead were beginning to twist and buckle. Yet they had no choice but to go on. Lusting after the gold and renown awaiting them on the other side, the knights still on land shoved and fought to step onto the jostling rafts even as those who had already fallen and clung desperately to the ropes and timbers ahead of them, cried for aid.

I doubt there was one amongst those who tried to make that crossing who was not wearing mailcoat and swordbelt: even the poorest mercenary in the Bastard's force had had ample chance to pillage during the years of oppression. Now, as the dead weight of iron dragged them under the swirling water, they most likely cursed the luck by which they had come by it, the lure of riches and fame which had brought them to such an end. Then, ere the first of the enemy came within spear-cast of the alder tree, Rahere gripped my arm and pointed to the opposite side of the river where, presumably in a effort to save those clinging to the *ponton*, many had entered the marshy tracts to either side of the ferryman's hard.

We who knew the Fenland understood the significance of the waves which propagated through the ground, betrayed by an ominous swaying of the reeds. Moorhens and Little Bitterns concealed deep in the reed-beds heeded the warning and broke cover, their startled cries adding to the bewilderment of men who stood rooted as land they had thought solid began to shudder like a horse trying to dislodge a fly. Some, panicking, started to run back to the causeway and that movement proved their undoing for the ground liquefied and they found themselves floundering. They sank as they struggled to free themselves and those that tried to aid them themselves became trapped. But their cries failed to daunt the fighters still crowding the causeway all the way back to Belsar's Hill. These continued to press forward and many who had fallen in the river and clung desperately to the *ponton* were swept away by the current as the timbers bucked and heaved under the weight of men still forcing their way across.

To see enemies die in battle is one thing: to watch them drown in bottomless mire brought a creeping horror upon us. Then, his motley brown and green clothing rendering him all but invisible against the reeds and sedge, Erik crept to the alder tree. Rahere let out a long, slow breath as the lad sawed at the thick hide ropes and when they fell free, slipped back into the reed-cover. Moments later, the pull of the current and the weight of those struggling to advance along it, caused the *ponton* to bow and pull away from the Isle. The unfortunates who had laboured to drag the sections across the mire and then waited for the onset, tried desperately to hold it but they were dragged into the fen. As the free end reached open water, the whole structure tipped, throwing the knights packed onto it into the river and marsh and it was then that our men loosed their arrows.

What the Bastard thought as hundreds of his knights (and by their eagerness and gear, the best), struggled and died in such desperate straits I can only guess: we saw neither hide nor hair of him that day. Compared with the numbers that drowned, our arrows took few but they added to the confusion as men shouted in vain for aid, thrashed and clawed at each other in their efforts to keep afloat, struggled in mire which devoured them inexorably before the appalled gaze of watching comrades. The sections of the *ponton* separated. Some sank under the weight of the men who had hauled themselves on top while others overturned again, taking those who clung on with them. Of all that had ventured onto the structure, less than a score reached safety and of those, only one managed to crawl to firm ground on our side of the marsh. Wuleric, who was leading a band of bowmen, immediately took him prisoner.

'God spare us such an end,' Martin muttered, with a quick glance at Rahere. The Fen-man's gaunt face was unreadable but his hands were clenched. I wondered how often he himself had narrowly escaped the maw of the hidden mires and peat-hags despite his skill.

'By their own pride and arrogance are they doomed.' Thurstan's expression betrayed unutterable relief: if the Normans had over-run the Isle he would have had to answer for his compliance with rebels. Athelwine, the lines of his face scored deep by tension, gave a brief smile, wan as winter sunlight.

'Be sure that the Almighty does not overlook the merest ill-deed,' he said. 'Who knows what evils these men have done? We should heed the lesson of their fate and seek to atone for the wrongs balanced against our own souls ere we also come to death.'

His keen grey eyes sought mine as he spoke and though I returned his gaze steadily enough, his words resonated. It was the raid on Borough he meant but the guilt he had stirred into wakefulness was rooted at my very core. Martin, perhaps sensing our growing tension, suddenly exclaimed aloud and pointed downhill where a knot of men was making its way up the slope. In their midst plodded a Norman prisoner. He was clad still in hauberk and coif and his swordbelt remained about his waist but the scabbard was empty.

'When I come to death, I shall be ready to account for my deeds,' I told the churchmen savagely. 'Until then, I have more pressing things to deal with. Has God not made me what I am?'

I was turning as these words left my lips and had just time to register the flicker of recognition in the abbot's eyes; for an instant I wondered if he knew more of my past than I had guessed or wanted. But then Siward Beorn, who like many of Norse ancestry clung to pagan beliefs at heart and had scant regard for the Church, took my arm and set his back to them. 'Come on, Hereward: let's make this Norman bastard squeal!'

Though he would never know it, Athelwine's speech had affected me more than I cared to admit even to myself, reminding me that though a landless outlaw, I was no common brigand but the son of Eorl Leofric, rightful thegn of Bourne.

'This man will be treated with courtesy, as a welcome guest,' I commanded when the prisoner was brought triumphantly before me and forced to kneel. 'And if he proves honourable, he will be set free to bring news of the Isle to his King. If not, he shall remain captive.'

Though I did not recall seeing him before, the knight, Dada by name, was obviously a man of some renown for when I helped him to his feet, his bearing was proud and he acknowledged me not as Hereward the Outlaw but *miles* Hereward. His hauberk, beneath the stinking slime, was of fine make, his sword-belt richly decorated in the Continental style. I greeted him in his own tongue, then switched to English (courtesy only extending so far). Knowing how many on the Isle were itching to avenge Edwin and his men, I ordered him into the care of Bishop Athelwine and decreed that anyone who insulted or abused him would answer directly to me. He walked away between the churchmen looking pale and bemused after I had promised to see him that evening when we feasted in the Great Hall. No doubt he had expected different treatment: to be ransomed at best, tortured or hanged at worst.

By now, the pieces of the doomed *ponton* had come to lodge against the mudflats; were sunk midstream or had floated away, no doubt to be viewed with curiosity and no little bewilderment by fishermen, women washing clothes on the river banks and folk tending beasts in the water meadows as they floated past. Drowned men had also beached on a sandbar in the closest bend of the river but I guessed many more would emerge at low tide, being weighed down by their hauberks. Of the unfortunates swallowed by the mire and fens there was no sign. Perhaps, in some distant time hence, a peat-cutter would strike the rusty remains of their iron-ring mailcoats, maybe even glimpse their faces, leathery skin drawn back over spongy bone, hair leached to pale red tufts. (In my early days as leader of the Fen-wolves,

Rahere had once shown us such a corpse buried in the peat, to warn us of the fate awaiting those who trod unwarily in the Fen country.) The survivors plodded wearily back along the causeway to Belsar's Hill, shoulders sagging; carts came to collect the recoverable dead and those wounded by our arrows.

'They'll think twice before trying that again,' Rahere remarked. There was not a trace of pity in his voice, only the satisfaction of one whose predictions have proved true. He gave a slight nod, winked and strode down the slope to praise and relieve the bowmen still concealed in the marsh. A heron, disturbed by his approach, launched itself into the air with ungainly wing-strokes, veered towards Belsar's Hill, then wheeled and flew directly overhead. I watched it with a vague sense of misgiving then turned and followed the others to where the horses and our main force were waiting on the crest of the ridge. If the bird's flight was an ill-omen, then it had been meant for the Normans first, I told myself and thought no more of it.

We feasted that night to celebrate our success but also because I wanted Dada to report what he saw to the Bastard, that our enemies might be in no doubt as to our surfeit of supplies on the Isle, or our strength. To this end I took him, with Morcar and Athelwine as witnesses, to swear on St. Etheldreda's tomb that he would speak only the truth of what he saw and experienced whilst in our care, in return for which I assured him safe conduct from the Isle within a few days. That done, we made certain he ate and drank only of the best and the abbot and bishop, as well as many of the monks, told him that they also were sworn to the rebellion. Dazzled by the splendour of gold utensils and fine tablecloths, plied with wine, his platter heaped with meats, fish and fruit of all kinds, Dada praised the valour of our resistance, decried the cruelties perpetrated on the innocent by Norman arrogance and swore that even in the courts of Europe he had never been better fed or entertained, though he wondered that so many fighting men could be content without women. At that, Siward Beorn laughed and thumped the table, saying that Dada was a man after his own heart and tomorrow he would be permitted to visit the camp at Cratendune where there were whores to suit all tastes.

True to our word, we ferried Dada back across the river after a few days in which he rode with us all about the Isle. We made no secret of the size of our force but the number and kinds of boats in our possession we were careful to conceal. And the extent to which we had fortified the slopes and marshes around Aldreth we also kept from him.

His sword having been lost in the marsh, we gave Dada a parting present of a fine weapon of Norse craftsmanship from our store and if he detected irony in such a gift, he did not remark it but thanked us courteously. To Wuleric, who had hauled him to safety at no little risk to himself, we gave the honour of escorting him blindfold to a hythe about half a mile upstream of Aldreth and there, beyond sight or sound of our enemies, he was ferried across and guided onto a winding path which would bring him safely to his comrades. Long after, I heard that he had fulfilled all our expectations, extolling to the Bastard the bounty of the Isle and warning of the determination and fighting skills of its defenders. William de Warenne and Ivo Taillebois accused him of having been beguiled by the cunning of common brigands but the Usurper apparently accepted Dada's tale and it may be that much of what followed was due to our pride, our eagerness to display our strength, our belief that the Isle could not be taken while we defended it. The Bastard was not a man to tolerate a direct challenge to his authority: he had come to contain rebellion; he would stay to destroy it.

At first, the Normans gave little sign of their intent. Two days after Dada's return, what remained of their main force began to file back the way they had come, a dark column of men and horses winding up the slopes to the Cambridge Road. They left a large garrison at Belsar's Hill after strengthening the gates and building a watchtower which was, significantly, sited on the northern side of the fort. The Bastard himself and his commanders were first to leave, their banners flying in the breeze, the horses restive, no doubt sensing the frustration of their riders.

Had there been any strategic advantage in doing so, we would have re-taken Belsar's Hill but it was on the wrong side of the river and could only be supplied and reinforced from the causeway. Also, having thwarted the first attempt on the Isle without the loss of a single comrade, I was in no mind to throw lives away to little purpose. The numbers arrayed against us had brought stark realization of the truth: we were cut off from all aid unless help should arrive unlooked-for from the Atheling or Danes. We watched our enemies depart with an odd sense of foreboding, knowing that when they returned they would be better prepared.

More ominous than the occupation of Belsar's Hill, was the effectiveness of the cordon placed around the Isle. Each navigable waterway now had its guard and enemy watchers were set on every upstanding piece of land, be it only a root-bound hillock on the edge of the smallest mere. At Reach and on the Isle of Wisbech at the northern end of the Wide Sea, forts of wood and turf were built and heavily garrisoned, supplied from the castles at Lincoln and Norwich.

To such as Rahere, to whom the Fens were embedded in his blood and soul, the penetration of an enemy so far was an outrage; that many of the Gyrwas were collaborating in the watch and search for rebels, a bitter affront. To punish the latter, we Fen-wolves crept through the marshes under the very noses of our enemies and burned to the ground any settlement known to harbour traitors. We went lightly armed on these raids and slew only those that resisted: these were our own people after all, but sometimes, when a woman, her face bruised and smoke-besmirched, cursed us, saying we were no better than the usurpers, I was ashamed though they should have known better than to betray their own kind and their true lord.

There is no room for pity in war.

Our lives, as so often since the invasion, settled to a kind of uneasy routine. We watched the garrison on Belsar's Hill as closely as they watched us but with the sea-road all but cut off, the success of the harvest took on a new and urgent significance: we could no longer rely on merchant and supply ships getting through. To keep men from brooding, hard labour in the fields worked almost as well as raids yet as weeks passed and no help came nor was there any sign of enemy movement, our restlessness grew. Though I and the other leaders never admitted it, we knew in our hearts how effectively we were trapped.

Harvest began and still we could glean nothing of the Bastard's plan save that he had not given up. We knew where he was: at Brandon to the east where he amused himself hunting and hawking across the lands of my enemies, Ivo Taillebois, William Malet, De Warenne, Gilbert de Ghent. After the disaster at Aldreth, his force had not been dismissed but was split between Cambridge and Norwich where the castles had been extended and the populace groaned under the burden of having to feed and house so many. He was waiting, that much was obvious, but our ignorance compounded our frustration and as the weeks passed, the resolve of some of the monks and those fighters who had lately joined us began to falter.

It was now that exasperation at Turfrida's stubbornness turned to a longing I could no longer deny. It was not sex I missed (there were willing women and girls enough in Cratendune), but her steadfastness and wisdom; her faith in me which, until I had gone to York, had never wavered; the trust we had shared through the years, unconditional and, (or so I had believed), inviolable; the touch of a loving hand.

'Go to her,' was Martin's advice when I broached the subject as we rode to the north of the Isle to check on the rye. 'Perhaps, seeing you, she will relent. And is it not time that little Godgifu should see her father again? Before long she'll have forgotten who you are.'

He must have known even as he spoke that my pride precluded such a course. His expression did not change as I wrenched Swallow's head up with a savage hand and turned her towards the east. It was a blustery August day. Water glittered between the reeds; in the distance a flight of oyster-catchers burst from the mudbank where they had been feeding as a reed punt nosed its way into the channel.

'Turfrida knows where I am. It is for her to make the first move, since she wronged me,' I said roughly. 'And I warned you never to interfere if you value your life.'

'Aye.' Martin wheeled his horse, a powerful grey *destrier*, to come alongside and Swallow flattened her ears in threat. 'But you asked my advice. And I cannot rest easy and watch those I love wilfully destroy themselves. Have you forgotten that you have a son also?'

That fact I could neither ignore nor deny. It was gouged into my mind like a wound which is both a mark of honour and a source of pain. I had been ready to launch Swallow into her long-striding gallop in an attempt to outrun Martin, the voice of conscience, and my own thoughts. Instead, detecting an odd reticence in my friend's manner, I checked the mare, held my face still, asked levelly, 'What have you heard?' while my heart lurched in my chest and a light sweat sheeted my skin.

'Ymma is less than a day's ride away,' he replied reluctantly. 'There was a slave Toli freed: Osfrith is his name. He is an old man now but he took her and the child into his care when her own kin were dispossessed. They are on one of William Malet's estates near Brandon.'

'How long have you known?'

He looked uncomfortable, turned his gaze across the marshes to the distant line of the sea. 'A while. I was afraid you'd throw your life away on a needless errand. You know the Bastard and his commanders are lodged close by.'

'Then I will make sure the errand is not needless.'

That is the true reason I went alone into the very heart of the enemies' lands in East Anglia. By this time, of course, a price equal to an eorl's wergild had been set on my head: the irony of this was not lost on me or my followers. To Martin's consternation I left Brain-biter in his keeping and took the guise of a potter we had lately discovered skulking round the abbey. (Suspecting him of spying, we bound him hand and foot and left him on a conspicuous mudbank to lure would-be rescuers into arrow-range. Maybe he was innocent or the Normans grown wary because none came ere the tide turned and he drowned.) I daubed clay on my hair and clothes, slung his pots, which were of rough Stamford ware, across Swallow's back, and set off at first light. Rahere ferried the mare and I across the river to Stuntney and though he was taciturn as usual, the mocking light had left his eyes and he watched regretfully as I led Swallow through the peaty water to where a path was marked by withy wands.

The few that knew of my venture, which was ostensibly to discover the Bastard's plan, were dismayed though none save Martin tried to dissuade me lest I think them faint-hearted. I left Acer in command of the Fen-wolves; Siward Beorn in my place as war-leader of the Isle. With Morcar I did not speak. Since discovering the truth of his brother's death he had grown bitter, venting his anger and frustration on his men until the usual dislike of fighters for an unfair commander had turned to a darker resentment – they obeyed, but sullenly - and I sensed trouble brewing. Glancing back as the path bent, I saw figures watching from the other side of the river: Acer's unmistakeable bulk; Wuleric; young Erik who had looked stricken when I told him where I was going; Martin. Maybe they believed this was the last they would see of me, a ragged figure leading a scrawny nag, and at that thought a kind of reckless joy swept through my blood like a draught of mead. It was that sense of luck every fighter knows, the certainty that this day it is your enemy's guard that will open, his sword that will break, his arrow that will fly astray, his javelin that will go wide of the mark.

Afterwards the gleemen made much of the fact that I journeyed to the very manor where the Bastard had set up court and escaped with my life but Norman arrogance saved me from any great danger. What affected me most that day was the sight of a child, a toddler clad in a rough homespun smock, who crouched in the doorway of a tumbledown hovel far from any vill. It was a bleak place surrounded by willows on the edge of the Fenland; a little plot of vegetables and a patch of rye lay to the side of the hut but all else had turned to a waste of tussock, bramble and nettles: piles of charred timbers marked where other cots might once have stood. An aged, raw-boned cow raised her head and lowed mournfully and the boy pulled himself to his feet. Beneath a tangled mass of straw-pale hair, a pair of odd-coloured eyes, one grey, one blue, stared with an intentness that smote my heart.

'Hereward!' I froze as a woman came to the doorway. Her tunic was patched and faded, her frame spare but her pale hair was wound about her head like a coronet. No doubt the sound of hooves had alarmed her for this was a little-used path. She stared a moment, eyes fixed not on me but Swallow, and a puzzled, half-hopeful, half-fearful expression fleeted across her features. Then she shook her head as if to dispel a lingering doubt, swept the child into her arms, turned on her heel and went inside. I remained as I was, gazing blankly at the shutting door before realization came to me, sharp and bitter as a spearthrust. It was not me she had called but our son.

Often I have thought back to that moment and wondered what might have happened had I knocked on the door; whether realizing who I was, she would have reacted with love or hate: there was too much between us for it to end in indifference. Seeing her, I had felt no desire but rather resentment that it should have been she who had borne me a son and not Turfrida, my helpmeet. And yet that was not what turned me back to the muddy path, but simply that face to face I did not know what I should say to her. She must have heard how Turfrida had renounced me; deep in my heart I feared her scorn. And though she looked careworn and thin, the boy was sturdy enough. Whatever Osfrith might be, it seemed he was not averse to providing for another man's son though doubtless he believed it was the grandchild of his benefactor he was rearing.

(Afterwards, when I told Martin of this encounter, he was philosophical, pointing out that Ymma also had obligations, not least to Eadric's memory. And, when the Normans had been defeated, he added wryly, there was no reason why I should not fulfil my promise to act as mentor and teacher to the lad: as he grew up, he would discern the truth for himself. Yet if we failed, I need feel no regret at leaving them alone for in defeat I would have nothing better to offer than what they already had, and perhaps only exile.

At that I smiled grimly, remembering how I had met my wife as a landless outcast seeking fortune and renown in a foreign land. Seeing Ymma had made my longing for Turfrida all the keener.)

The mare and I plodded on along the path and the sere marshland and boggy pasture gave way to drier sloping ground, rich tillage though many of the fields seemed neglected. I noticed that much of the woodland was despoiled, trees hacked down and sawn without regard as to their type or age. Deep ruts marked where some of the lumber had already been hauled away towards the Cambridge road.

Laymakers tell it that I gleaned the truth of the Bastard's strategy from a pair of witches but I encountered no-one more uncanny than a wizened crone clad in filthy rags who offered to rede my fortune in return for a silver coin.

"'The length of my life and the day of my death were fated long ago,'" I quoted, not unkindly, and gave her a piece of bread from my pack, for she looked in dire need.

She took the food with a kind of proud diffidence, saying quietly, 'Nonetheless be careful, lad, lest your tongue betray the fighter beneath the potter's guise,' and with that she shuffled away to where a couple of bundles, all her worldly possessions, lay beneath a tree. I nodded in acknowledgement and continued on my way with a strange feeling of disquiet sensing that she, like Edda and Rahere, was one whose life resonated to different rhythms than the rest of us, embedded in the turn of the seasons, the cycle of life and death which turns all flesh to grass. So long had Gyrwas lived in this land that it defined them and they, over uncounted generations, had shaped it.

It was mid-afternoon when I reached the road from Norwich to Cambridge. It was crowded with ox-wagons laden with timber and stones, rounded flint pebbles from the beaches and gravel spits of the Norfolk coast. All were travelling west and they were in a hurry. Many of the beasts' flanks dripped blood from the goad and the drovers shouted at their teams and at each other. None gave me a second glance. I kept my head down and led Swallow on the verge but I noted each load and my mind raced, wondering to where and for what purpose these materials were being transported with such haste.

In this manner I came at last to Brandon where the old thegn's hall had been replaced by a great building of flint and rammed chalk. Two palisades of sharpened stakes divided the inner court from the outer which contained stables and storehouses. The serf's hovels were crowded outside. The cottars were thin and dressed in rags and none gave me more than a cursory glance. They seemed cowed, all defiance long since bludgeoned out of them.

Bare earth surrounded the outer defences. All the trees had been felled save a great elm on the approach to the main gate. From one of its lower branches three corpses hung, the oldest no more than a skeleton held together by sinews and scraps of skin, the most recent still a feasting ground for crows. A putrid stench filled the air and Swallow snorted in disgust and tossed her head. I stroked her neck and spoke gently to her and she settled but in truth I was eager as she to leave that dismal place and it was only the thought of why I had come that kept me from turning back.

The gates stood open but the guards lounging on the watch-platforms called down, demanding my name and purpose. Before I could answer, the thunder of many hooves sounded from behind. Swallow jibbed and pulled and as I steadied her I saw a band of fifteen horsemen trotting along the track. They were armed for hunting, not fighting, and I could not see the Bastard among them but the stern features of De Warenne and the hawk nose of Ivo Taillebois I noted and loosened the dagger hidden beneath my cloak, determined that if I was to die, I would take at least one of them with me. But full of the day's sport, they saw nothing suspicious in a ragged potter and his broken-down mare, only an object for scorn. Swallow, who had swung round to face the strange horses with bared teeth and flattened ears, was blocking the way and as I moved to lead her hurriedly into the courtyard, a spear-butt prodded hard between my shoulders. Only my fighter's agility saved me from sprawling beneath the leading *destrier's* hooves but forcing down the urge to whip out my dagger and strike, I cringed and kept my head bowed, whining, 'Fine pots, my lord. I have the best ware from Stamford to offer your graciousness.'

The stallion moved forward until its breath was hot and moist against my neck. Though I did not look up, I felt the rider's eyes rake me over and kept a firm grip of Swallow's reins.

'They might do for the pigs and serfs.' His contempt was like the touch of a white-hot flame. 'Very well, you may go to the kitchen to ply your trade. Move!'

I hoped never to repeat the experience as I shuffled across the yard, surrounded by Norman horsemen who took every opportunity to jostle and barge their mounts into me while Swallow snatched at the reins and tried to lash out, the pots clinking on her back. All the while, the knights insulted me and every Saxon in their own tongue, assuming I could not understand and the blood rose to my face as I struggled to contain my anger.

Stableboys came to take the horses but ignored Swallow who I tied in a corner where soiled straw from the stables was piled in a great heap. As I lifted the pots from the mare's back, I noted the position of the guards, the structure and height of the outer palisade. From inside it was climbable but the drop to the ditch was more than I wanted to risk unless it was a matter or life or death.

'What are you waiting for, doomsday?' A young man, thin and pale with his hair cut roughly to ape the Norman style, regarded me insolently from a distance of a few paces. 'We sent one of your kind away a week ago. Your pots had better hold water or you'll get a worse hiding than he did. Follow me.'

The kitchen was a huge, low building, full of steam and the stench of boiling fat. The heat was overpowering. There was no light except what fell through the door and the glare from the cooking fires but through the fug I saw that the place was crowded with women bustling over pots and iron cauldrons, men beating hunks of raw meat, girls plucking fowls and cleaning fish.

'Well?' As I waited for my senses to adjust to the noise and gloom, my guide poked me rudely in the chest. 'A strange peddler who forgets to cry his wares!'

'I have no need: the quality of my pots is widely known,' I replied. 'Is there a master or mistress of this place?'

'What name should I give?'

There was a knowing look in his eye that I mistrusted and I bent to untie the pots. 'Ulf of Stamford. If they have not heard of me, it is to their discredit.'

He fetched a man tall as Acer and twice the girth but his bulk was fat, not muscle. His eyes, sunk in corpulent folds made my stomach clench and I wondered why until I remembered Brand, my uncle: the same lazy malice glinted from under the heavy lids. From his shaven chin and short hair I had guessed him to be a Norman but his accent betrayed his local origin and my instinctive dislike turned to loathing. Rather than speak, I handed him the first pot, a thick, roughly glazed dish, standard ware from Stamford.

'A trough for pig-swill,' was his comment. 'How many of you time-wasters must I deal with ere the guards learn their duty? Only last week one came with pots as badly made as these. Get out!'

I protested the quality of my goods while the cook balanced the dish on his forefinger to demonstrate its unevenness. When it did not tip, he tilted his hand deliberately and it crashed onto the stone floor. I held out my right hand, palm uppermost. 'For that, at least, you must pay.'

There was an edge of menace to my tone I had not intended and the cook's gaze sharpened. 'Oh yes? And who will make me? You? Go on, try. I could do with a laugh. It's been all work and no play since the King arrived.'

'Sir, sir - your brother is here!' The intervention was timely: I had already seen implements which would serve as weapons. The cook took a step back, not in deference to me but to make room for the newcomer. In doing so he contrived to kick over one of the stacks of pots: they slid to the floor but did not break. The youth had retreated to a corner but his eyes gleamed in the firelight as he looked on. I glanced at the stranger and the shock of recognition must have been as clear on my face as it was on his.

Oswin the leatherworker had clearly prospered under Norman rule. His clothes were of foreign cut and fine cloth, his cloak fastened with a gold and enamelled pin of rare quality. But the costly apparel could not disguise the grossness of the man. His flesh shone greasily as he reached out to grasp the cook's arm.

'This is no potter but Hereward the Outlaw! Call the guard before he cuts our throats!'

Everyone in the kitchen stopped to stare for there was no mistaking his alarm but the faces of most expressed amusement rather than dismay. The cook gave a great guffaw and slapped his kinsman on the shoulder.

'For a moment there you had me worried! Come on, look at the man: he's of no stature or countenance to wield a weapon. Give him a sword and see whose foot he chops off first: his or yours!'

'For God's sake, listen to me!' I crouched to gather the fallen pots, keeping my face hidden whilst noting with satisfaction the rising panic in Oswin's voice. 'I spoke with him in Borough, years ago before the Normans came. He was clad in mail and rode a fine charger but I swear on my life it was the same man. The exiled son of old Eorl Leofric, thegn of Laughton before he was outlawed by the King. Fourteen knights he slew single-handed, De Warenne's brother among them, and stuck their heads over the gates of Bourne. You' - he pointed a trembling finger at the youth in the corner who had put a hand across his mouth to hide his laughter – 'Go for the guard and tell them to bring fetters!'

'Ah now,' I made my tone aggrieved. 'This is an injustice when that brigand robbed me of my donkey, a bag of coin and my choicest wares but a week ago. I'd like to get my hands on him myself!'

'Still . . .' There was growing doubt in the cook's face. 'Maybe we should take him up to the Hall. There are men there who know the outlaw. Let them decide. If they're in the mood there'll be good sport even if he is but a simple potter.'

The youth slipped out and the noise and bustle of the kitchen resumed though Oswin's eyes were fixed upon me as if I were a manifestation of the Devil. The cook handed him a skin of mead and the leatherworker drank deeply but sweat beaded his skin and he did not speak. His reticence was countered by his brother's volubility: he and his cronies began to taunt and insult me, presumably hoping that I would be provoked into betraying myself. But I kept my eyes lowered and my shoulders hunched and my dullness soon bored my tormentors. They began to talk across me, regretting their eagerness to take the matter of my identity to their overlords since no man of mettle would endure such abuse without defending his honour.

It was not long before their messenger returned. He jerked his thumb at me and grinned at the others. 'He's to go up to the Hall. There's a heavy price on his head if he's the man you think. And there are plenty there who'll know.'

I wiped my nose with my fingers and got clumsily to my feet, bent to pick up the pots.

'Ah no, leave them here. It's your pretty face they want to see, not this rubbish.'

After the stifling fug of the kitchen, the open air was cool and refreshing. I looked round as if confused as to where to go though in reality I was noting where the guards stood. The doors of the Great Hall, which formed the whole ground floor of the main building, stood open. I shuffled in between the two brothers, the thin youth following closely on my heels. All were eager to claim the reward if it proved I was indeed the famous outlaw.

Most of the hunting party was gathered there, talking animatedly about the day's sport but I was careful to keep my eyes downcast. Thus I heard rather than saw someone approach.

'What do you want?' The voice was one I recognized. I raised my head reluctantly but kept my eyes averted. De Warenne said nothing but I felt the force of his gaze, pulled my shoulders in and whined, 'I've done nothing wrong, lord, only come to sell my pots and they laid hands on me.'

The Norman was taller than me; his smell of sweat and horses sharp in my nostrils. He stared a moment longer then began to berate my captors in a torrent of abuse of which I doubt they understood half. They shuffled their feet and looked increasingly uncomfortable as the tirade continued. De Warenne finished by shouting in exasperation, 'What kind of fools are you that you mistake a beggar with clay in his hair for an outlaw chief? And why would the commander of Ely come here, alone, at such a time? He'll be watching Cottenham and the causeway, shitting himself as we build our way across. If you bother me again, you'll join your countrymen hanging outside the gates!' And with that, he spat disgustedly on the ground, turned on his heel and strode to join his comrades who were watching with undisguised amusement.

It is a mark of the small-minded that when made to look stupid themselves, they vent their frustration on those they perceive to be weaker. Oswin, his fears assuaged by De Warenne's certainty, clapped a hand onto my shoulder and pushed me back across the yard. The cook, frowning, strode at my right and I sensed the youth close behind.

'How then will I be compensated for your accusations and the broken pot?' I asked once the reek of the kitchen had engulfed us. 'Two pieces of silver and I'll say no more of it and be on my way. I'm late already: my kinsfolk at Norwich will think some ill has befallen me.'

'I beg your forgiveness.' With exaggerated care, the cook delved in a corner, brought out a jar stoppered with beeswax and opened it with his knife. 'Here's a tipple to put spine even into a clay-boned potter. Sit and drink with us, man: if we're not enemies, why not pledge friendship – of a kind.'

A look passed between the brothers that I could not mistake: the gloating anticipation of bullies who have their victim helpless and cornered. Oswin suddenly grasped my hair from behind but I was no helpless peddler.

I jabbed my elbow into his fat-cushioned midriff and he doubled up with a wheezing groan and crashed onto the piled pots, scattering shards in all directions. Some of the women screamed as I dived for the door while the cook lunged for me, missed, and tripped over his prostrate brother.

I crossed the inner court and entered the outer without hindrance. When Oswin stumbled out and called for help no-one heeded him – maybe drunkenness and brawling were nothing new around the kitchen. To my relief, the main gates were still open, perhaps awaiting stragglers from the hunt but as I approached Swallow, she whickered nervously. I crept forward to untie her.

There was a blur of movement yet I was faster. Before he could cry out my hand was at his throat and I shoved him against the stable wall. His long knife clattered to the ground as I pressed the point of my dagger beneath his chin.

How the youth from the kitchen had got there before me I do not know but his dark eyes watched me with contempt.

'I have no wish to kill you but if you draw breath to shout, you die,' I told him, and relaxed my grip a little.

'You may have fooled them but I know who and what you are,' he whispered and suddenly I knew why the sight of him had made me uneasy. I had seen him before, in the abbey courtyard at Borough when we brought Abbot Leofric home. 'Hereward the Exile, Eorl Leofric's son, Brand's favourite. Even as he lay dying, he boasted of how you feared him, the mighty outlaw no more than a monk's boy.'

Had his words been different, still his sneering tone would have sealed his fate. I thrust on my dagger, felt the blade pierce through the roof of his mouth into the brain. He jerked like a stuck pig and slid down the wall to the ground and I prodded him with my foot to make sure he would not move again, then turned and leapt astride Swallow, urged her straight from a standstill to flying gallop. She swerved to avoid two guards who, alerted at last by the movement in the corner of the yard and the clatter of hooves, were running to investigate, then we were through the gate and away, charging down the road in the deepening twilight. After a while came sounds of pursuit, drumming hoofbeats, angry and perplexed shouts, but by then the mare and I were heading for the marshes on a little-used path, and they dared not venture off the road at night.

The Normans were easily eluded; the ghosts of my past it seemed I could not escape.

My return to the Isle was greeted with great relief and no little wonder: many had believed I would be captured if not slain. I had Wuleric tend Swallow and called a war council straightway. Martin, being privy to the real purpose of my foray, watched me with a kind of brotherly concern but he knew better than to ask outright whether I had found Ymma. The fact I had come back alone told its own tale.

Siward Beorn was dismissive when he heard of the Norman plan to build another causeway at Aldreth (thus I had interpreted De Warenne's speech), but Morcar, Acer and the churchmen were more circumspect.

'One might have supposed the King would wait till next year, given what happened last time,' Thurstan remarked. 'While we are under our saint's protection, he will never gain the Isle. I wonder at his persistence.'

'The bastard never gives up,' Acer growled, laying a fist scarred as an ancient tree root on the table to emphasise his words. 'Look at York. All we can hope for is to hold out through winter and pray that the Sweyn or the Atheling get off their arses and come to aid us in the spring.'

So blunt an appraisal of our situation seemed to discomfit the churchmen. They looked meaningfully at one another though in truth our position had not changed since the last attempt on the Isle. An uncomfortable silence fell.

'Ely will not fall while we defend it,' I said firmly. 'We have yet the means to thwart him. Whatever he plans to build, wood burns and stones sink. He will never step foot on the Isle.'

Thus the council ended and I doubled the watch on all the surrounding waterways and marshes, sending men to stalk those who sought to spy on us. But we did not have to wait long before the Bastard betrayed his intent by marching his whole force back to Belsar's Hill and the ridge behind. Once again, the green slopes seemed to sprout man, horses and tents like mushrooms. Though it was noticeable that they were less than before, it was still a mighty host and beneath our bravado as our bowmen harried them from both sides of the causeway, our trepidation grew.

Once the camps were established, ox-teams dragged great timbers to the river's edge and a great pounding and hammering began as these were fitted together to make siege engines. But *trebouchants* need firm footings and I reassured my men, who were much alarmed as the massive frames were erected, that there was nothing to fear since as they were fired, the machines would sink into the soft ground. I told them also that we were well out of range but I had the turf ramparts at Aldreth strengthened lest the engines be moved to our side of the river.

Whoever was in command of our enemies (perhaps the Bastard himself, though we did not see him), had a cunning understanding of siegecraft. No attempt was made to fire bolt or stone at us yet the threat preyed on the minds of many, the monks not least. Rahere and Acer were undaunted but some of the younger Fen-wolves were afraid, realizing at last what the more experienced had understood straightway: that this time the Normans would not leave until they had achieved their objective or were beaten. To restore their confidence, it was these, Thorald, Wuleric, Erik and the like, I chose to accompany me when the chance came to strike back, along with any others eager for the adventure. They looked at me dumbfounded when I told them to dress as fishermen and leave all weapons behind save the knives and short bows the Fen-folk bore, but I made sure each boat carried a large firepot stoked to last through the day.

There was nothing to distinguish our craft or appearance from any of the others commandeered locally for the task, thus we sailed straight to Cottenham and spent the day ferrying timbers to both sides of the river opposite Aldreth, watched with some amusement by our comrades on the Isle. The Norman overseers did not understand our language nor deign to address those they considered slaves, thus we had much sport misinterpreting orders given by a Saxon crony or sullenly refusing to move at all. But while the spirits of my comrades lifted as our enemies cursed and spluttered in futile rage, the sheer volume of materials gathered there dismayed me: enough timber to build my father's hall at Bourne ten times over, pebbles and gravel to fill a hundred labouring ox-wagons. And even with an unwilling workforce, these were being transported at an ominous rate. Within five days I guessed all would be on the river banks, leaving only the marsh between the invaders and ourselves.

Often I have maintained that a man makes his own luck, but that evening time and tide played into our hands. As the sun sank, the tide began to ebb. We lingered after the real fisherfolk had gone home and set fires in the woodpiles so that by the time we reached the first bend, they would be well ablaze. Our ships were loaded: we set sail as the first wisps of smoke wisped from the base of the stacks and so swiftly did the current run we had time to do the same at the other end, the great river bearing us safely to Cratendune where we unloaded our cargoes of timber with great satisfaction.

We celebrated that night at the makeshift camp that had grown, inevitably, around Hereward's Castle. The burning stacks of timber at the river's edge shone like beacons in the darkness. By their flaring light we saw men scurrying like ants to contain the fires. We sang and challenged each other to feats while they worked on through the night though what they were doing, once the stacks had burned to heaps of glowing embers, we could not tell. Through the mead's haze I noticed again that the churchmen seemed subdued, detached from the reckless mood that had hold on the rest of us, but I put it down to their piety.

Dawn revealed what had occupied our enemies all night. As we caroused, they had set up protective barriers to shelter the works on both sides of the river. These were much the same as we had erected to conceal and protect our bowmen, made for the most part of woven withies and reeds, simple but effective. In addition they had posted heavily armed guards not only on land but in boats stationed up and down-stream of Aldreth.

'They're determined, I'll say that for them,' was Acer's grim comment when he, Siward Beorn and I went to appraise this new development. Our efforts the day before had not stopped other boats bringing materials from Cottenham. Stone does not burn and it seemed to us that there was a new urgency to the work as they unloaded the pebbles and spread them thickly to make firm patches on the soft ground, a focused purpose that boded ill. The reason became clear later that day when a group of horsemen came to survey the work. Even before we recognized him by his stature and the magnificence of his stallion and gear, we knew the Bastard must be there from the reverential demeanour of overseers and labourers alike. He rode his *destrier* hock deep into the swirling river and stared at us, a knot of horsemen watching from the slopes opposite. His mount began to paw the water with an iron-shod forefoot and he reined it in and forced it to back onto dry land but his eyes did not leave us. Even across the wide expanse of marsh I felt the force of that glance as if we stood within sword's reach and rode Swallow a little closer to demonstrate that we were undaunted. Then, to my right, I heard Siward let out a breath of admiration. 'So that's what they're up to!'

Their failure on the previous attempt had, it seemed, taught the Normans much. From the cover of the screens they slid great rafts of lashed timbers into the river. The first of these were held steady by men with poles while piles were driven into the river bed on both sides. Once one was stabilised, the next would be moved past it and the process repeated. Within a few hours, the river was spanned and the rafts tied loosely to one another. The piles (which from a distance looked no thicker than large poles but comprised, as we discovered later, tree trucks thicker then a man's two hands could span), held the rafts in place while its flexible construction allowed the *ponton* to move with the tide.

'Clever bastards.' Acer grimaced and spat. 'What now, Hereward?'

'They have still to cross the marsh.' I stared down, trying to conceal my disquiet. 'We're not finished yet.'

Of all the times of waiting we had been forced to endure since the invasion, the next week was the most frustrating. So heavy was the guard set around the *ponton* and all that section of the river, we could only watch as they built footings for two more siege engines on our side of the river and then, once the machines had been raised, began construction of a causeway across the marsh. This time they used the pebbles brought with so much effort from the coast to stabilise the ground (though sometimes these were swallowed by the mire), and then laid timbers across, wide enough for two horsemen to ride abreast.

At the same time, Rahere reported the gathering of a ship-force in the Wide Sea which, though insignificant by compare with the number of ships brought by Sweyn, made me wonder if the Bastard planned a two-pronged attack. To prevent easy landfall near the abbey and at Cratendune, I had the hythes and moorings destroyed and most of our craft moved to secret locations all about the Isle.

(When Thurstan complained at the loss of his harbour, I reminded him that if the Normans set foot on the Isle, he would have to account for his actions and those of his monks, many of whom were now valued fighters amongst our force. At that he was chastened and agreed that a ship-borne attack should not be over-looked, then offered some of his novices as look-outs to free experienced fighters from that duty, a service I accepted gladly.)

That afternoon, Gamal Longbow, Rahere and I led small groups of bowmen into the marshes on our side of the river. We crossed the meres adjacent to the works using the slim reed punts that were now our main means of transport since they could be used in the narrowest waterway and were all but invisible in the reedbeds. Keeping to the cover of the sedge, we slipped under the very noses of those sitting nervously on the siege-engines (which as yet served as watchtowers: none had been fired), who made easy targets. But the causeway itself, which now extended halfway across the marsh, was so heavily guarded as to be almost unassailable. We shot as many of the look-outs as we could see and made the workers cower in alarm as our arrows rained upon them but the work was only delayed, not stopped, and we left before their cross-bowmen and archers could pin us down.

Siward Beorn and Morcar, who had been watching from Hereward's Castle, rode to meet us as we pulled the punts onto dry land. They waited while I praised the marksmanship of the men (all of whom had returned unscathed), and sent them back to camp, then Morcar said starkly, 'Another two days and the Isle will be over-run. Maybe it would be prudent to submit now, before we are forced to it.'

I stared at him, dumbfounded, while anger, cold and clear as the blast of a north wind, swept through me, then glanced at Siward whose face remained impassive.

'Are you mad?' The words escaped ere I could stop them; the fair-haired giant grinned and I realized he was there not to support my nephew but for his own amusement. 'Have you forgotten how Edwin died?'

Morcar's face tightened. 'No,' he said slowly. 'But I was at Fulford Gate. I do not want to see such slaughter again. This time no-one will come to aid us.'

I was still, listening to the lap of wavelets against the muddy edge of the mere, the rustle of reeds in the breeze, the ceaseless shouting of our enemies in their foreign tongue, the thud of mallets. From high above came the piercing call of a bird of prey and I looked up to see a marsh harrier gliding overhead. It was a moment before I realized the significance of its flight.

'We need no such aid,' I said. 'War council at first light: make sure all the group leaders and churchmen are there. It is not yet time for despair.'

Next morning it was clear even from the faces of such stalwarts as Acer and Siward Beorn that the relentless approach of our enemies and their number was having its effect. The men were quiet and few met my eyes as I strode into the Great Hall and took my place between the bishop and Morcar. Yet though the usual banter and boasting were missing and the atmosphere of dread was almost palpable, there was no word of complaint, nor did any urge me to submit or flee. They had lived by the sword long enough to know that one day their luck would run out and, having faced death, did not fear it, only the manner by which it came to them.

I looked long upon them: Rahere, Acer, Gamal, Siward the Red, those I had known since boyhood, and the new additions to the Fen-wolves like Wuleric and Thorald, who already led their own bands, and pride swelled within me at their steadfastness. When I explained my plan, they listened incredulously at first but then a dawning hope sprang in their faces. They glanced at one another and grinned in anticipation.

Only the churchmen seemed dismayed. Morcar clapped me on the shoulder and begged forgiveness for his earlier doubt. I gave it willingly on condition that he kept his men ready, along with Thorald's, to repel any ship-borne attack on Cratendune and the abbey. He left the hall with Athelwine and the abbot and I thought nothing of it though Martin watched their departure with an odd expression of disapproval as if he sensed trouble, like a dog made uneasy by approaching thunder.

The rest of that day and the next, the Normans must have thought us already defeated for we made no forays against them and kept our preparations secret though the imminence of their attack was clear. By evening on the second day, the causeway across the marsh was within arrowshot of Aldreth and I had all our best bowmen waiting behind the turf bulwarks in case of night attack. It had been a still day and the sky was clear but as darkness fell, a slight breeze rustled the reeds. It came from the northwest.

By dawn we were ready though to anyone looking from the other side of the river, the slopes of the Isle appeared empty. The tide was low and the wheep of oystercatchers flocking to the mudbanks to feed sounded loud across the marshes; a heron flapped lazily overhead. From Belsar's Hill to the river, the ancient causeway was packed with iron-clad men and restive horses. The sounds of their voices and the *destrier's* neighs were clear above the lapping of water and the sough of the wind through the reeds.

We watched as the last section of the causeway across the marsh was set in place and secured to the alder trees on the bank. Then the whole mass of waiting men and horses began to seethe. As the sun slipped over the horizon, turning the meres and the surface of the river to fiery gold, an eerie quiet fell. I, who had been on the attacking side in many sieges, knew how the men across the water felt looking at the apparently deserted hillsides and marsh: the silent menace; how at the last minute they would fidget to ease the discomfort of a kinked coif-ring or tighten their sword-belt, occupying their minds with little things to keep thoughts of death and wounds at bay.

A score of knights rode onto the *ponton* and crossed to the firm ground on our side, drawing rein between the gaunt frames of the siege engines, which now, at last, went into action. To our satisfaction most of the rocks and iron bolts fell short of our defences and splashed harmlessly into the marsh. Indeed, they were more of a hazard to the new causeway and it seemed the engineers swiftly realized this, for after the first few volleys, the firing stopped.

Waiting on the ridge where our main force was concealed, I rubbed my palms on the grass, expecting an immediate rush onto the Isle. But the knights who had crossed the river had not yet set out along the causeway and those behind them shifted restlessly, the horses stamping and lunging at each other in frustration, making the sections of the *ponton* heave alarmingly.

'What's going on?' Acer spoke for all of us: we were eager for their advance so that we could spring our trap. There was a stir amid the crowd on their side of the river and the ranks parted to let an old woman through. At first we assumed she was a prisoner and wondered what new atrocity the Normans had devised but though she was accompanied by two knights, it seemed they were an escort rather than guard for she walked free and many of those on the *ponton* shrank from touching the foul tatters in which she was draped.

We watched amazed as her companions (one of whom I recognized with a stab of hatred as Ivo Taillebois), helped the crone mount the wooden frame of the closest of the siege engines to the Isle. She clung to the very top, her rags and filthy hanks of hair flying about her in the mounting breeze, seeming more like some bird of ill-omen, raven or crow, than a woman as she gesticulated wildly towards us. The wind carried her words away but those hidden in the marsh told us later how she screamed curses and imprecations, calling down all manner of doom upon the king's enemies, condemning our souls to unending torment and our flesh to the wolves and kites.

That the Bastard should be reduced to calling on the services of a witch to prepare the way for his assault seemed a mark of desperation. In response, I had our banner raised above the ridge. The painted colours were bright and clear as jewels, our Saint's face serene, and a murmur arose from the men behind who knew she would keep them safe from any curse. And then a great shout of laughter and derision burst from them as the hag turned her back and lifted her skirts to reveal her scrawny buttocks, howling like a mad dog as she did so.

Thrice she made that obscene gesture and it seemed that this was the signal for action because the Normans on the *ponton* jostled and pressed forward while those that had already crossed forced their *destriers* onto the causeway. The beasts were unwilling, no doubt feeling the peaty ground shudder beneath the beams, and some tried to turn or leap into the marsh.

Glancing back across the river, I saw that the Bastard had at last dared to show his face. He and a knot of other horsemen were waiting at the foot of one of the *trebouchants* on the other side of the river, no doubt intending to cross when their main force was on the Isle.

Never had our paean sounded with such passion as then. As the first of the horsemen came within three lengths of the end of the causeway, I sprang up and stood beneath our banner and the wolf's howl swelled within me, resonating through every fibre of my being. Only Gamal and Rahere's men hidden in the marshes on either side of the causeway did not give voice. Their contribution was a hail of arrows, boulters and javelins which threw the vanguard of the assault into chaos.

The causeway was only wide enough for two horsemen to ride abreast and I had instilled in my men that once the *destriers* were felled, we were fighting on equal terms. Thus the bowmen aimed mainly at the horses while Wuleric's band rose from behind the turf rampart at the base of the slope and attacked those who had emplaced the last section of the causeway and then remained on guard, waiting for their comrades to overtake them. Outnumbered and dismayed by the screaming tangle of men and stricken horses which blocked the way back across the marsh, these fought bravely but they were lightly armed and swiftly overcome.

Smoke was already wisping from where Rahere's band was concealed on the margins of Ewell Fen; now more men, bearing pails of pitch, bundles of reeds and flaring torches, ran from cover of our defences onto the causeway, dodging past Wuleric's fighters. The fuel was thrown across the causeway, pitch was flung on top and then the whole was set ablaze. Fanned by the northwesterly, the flames leapt high, forming a wall of fire no man or horse could cross. This done, the skirmishers drew their weapons and ran back to help Wuleric's men. Soon no Norman remained alive on our side of the flaming barrier.

Three of the siege engines had resumed firing but the witch clung still to the fourth, her shrill screams audible even above the squeals of dying men and horses, the growing roar of fire. Though adjustments had been made so that some of the stones and bolts reached our outer defences, these were more an inconvenience than a real threat. As the fires set at intervals in the marsh took hold, the engines stopped. Those manning them had seen their danger more swiftly than their comrades on the causeway itself, but there was no escape. They joined those trapped between the spreading fire and the mass of men and horses behind, unable to go forward or back, confused by the smoke and flames which swept to engulf them with terrifying speed.

From the ridge, the scene was like something from a nightmare. Sheets of fire swirled across the causeway, setting the manes and tails of the horses alight. Wreathed in flame, they tried to bolt back the way they had come, trampling any in their path, or else plunged into the marsh where they sank instantly amid a welter of flame, setting the reeds on the eastern side alight. Their screams rent the air and the cries of men added to the cacophony for so cunningly had the fires been set that both ends of the causeway were now impassable and there was no escape for those trapped upon it: they burned or, leaping into the mire, were drowned. The witch shrieked horribly as her thin rags caught alight, and fell: I did not see her again. Soon the great engines toppled under the weight of those who tried to climb desperately beyond reach of the flames and we yelled in triumph as each of them crashed down though the roar of the fire overwhelmed all sounds save the piercing screams of its victims.

The chaos had spread to the *ponton* and beyond. A seething mass of panic-stricken men and horses was trying to escape towards Belsar's Hill but there was not enough room for them on the causeway or the firm ground made for the siege engines. Many were struggling in the mire while others floundered in the river itself. Our arrows and javelins took a great toll amongst these for such was the confusion no-one heeded the slim reed punts that suddenly appeared from the cover of the sedge. Rahere told me many of the enemy cried out to him for help ere he stopped their mouths forever. The ships meant to guard the river were now engaged in picking up survivors though this was a hazardous operation. Our fighters threw fire into them wherever they could and the peat itself had begun to burn, exploding in great gouts of flame which sent lumps of flaming turf and embers high into the air, spreading the fire to the other side of the river. As the great reed banks lining the old causeway began to blaze, the remaining ships were forced to leave.

The Bastard and his favoured knights were still beside the river, each of their horses held by men on foot to prevent them bolting. No arrow or javelin had touched any of that group but as the first of the burning Norman ships turned over and sank, I saw Gamal Longbow creep through the reeds towards them. Acer had also seen. He gripped my arm as our comrade bent his bow, then the Bastard toppled from his horse and a great cry rose from all the men gathered on the ridge. Acer and I embraced in triumph and would have danced for joy save that Gamal still had to return.

So dismayed was the enemy by the fall of their leader, there was no answering volley. We watched, exulting, as he was borne in his shield towards the safety of Belsar's Hill but though our bowmen continued to harry them, he was not struck again and our excitement was curbed when we thought to see him lift his arm and wave his fist.

'That bastard can't be so easily killed,' said Acer grimly. 'I'll wager he takes no lasting hurt from this.'

We watched anxiously as Gamal and Rahere withdrew, skirting the marsh where fire was now the main hazard and making landfall west of Aldreth. Between the meres was a blackened, smoking waste, fire flaring wherever the wind fanned the smouldering peat. In places the causeway itself was burning; elsewhere the timbers had sunk deep into the mire or stuck up at crazy angles, tilted by the weight of the remains of men and horses which lay in grotesque, twisted heaps all along its length. Men still clung to one of the fallen engines but they did not move: the heat of the fire had fused them to the frame. From somewhere an agonized screaming sounded though whether it came from man or beast was impossible to tell.

By now the *ponton* was deserted save for the dead which lay thick upon it, men who had perished beneath the feet of their panicking comrades in the crush to escape the flames. The survivors trudged wearily towards Belsar's Hill, seemingly heedless of the fires which threatened the camp itself; some simply sat down a little way beyond bowshot of the river and rested their head on their knees in exhaustion or despair. Smoke momentarily veiled the carnage but even on the ridge there was no escaping the reek of burnt flesh nor the cries and moans for help that still came from those trapped in the mires though the screaming had, mercifully, ceased.

Gamal and Rahere's bands had joined those now gathered by the alders at our end of the causeway and we rode down to praise and thank them. Our meeting was a joyful one though so close to the marsh the stench of the burning was enough to turn the stomach. Amid the celebration, Gamal was quiet; he stood a little apart, leaning on his bow as he stared bitterly through the smoke-reek towards Belsar's Hill.

'The arrow was all but spent,' he said when I complimented his marksmanship. 'I could have got closer: no-one would have noticed. The bastard'll try again – he'll never give up!'

There was a note of desperation in his voice, unwelcome as it was unexpected. When I tried to reassure him, he smiled ruefully and shook his head.

'Does a wounded boar lie down and wait for the cleaver?' he asked and then, ashamed, added quickly, 'But whatever happens, we're with you, Hereward. If you think we can hold out here, we'll stay.'

By late afternoon, most of the fires were out, including those which had burned all the way to Belsar's Hill, but the peat could not be extinguished. Threads of smoke marked where it smouldered and wind gusts made it flare though there was little left in the marsh to burn. Morcar sent a message that the Norman ships had remained in the Wide Sea; the lad who brought it stared in horror at the scene before him and I heard him swallow hard as a breath of wind brought the thick reek of fire and death to our nostrils.

Even as he rode swiftly back with our news of the Normans' defeat and the King's wound, there was a stir along the distant causeway and we heard shouting from Belsar's Hill. This was no note of mourning but rather joyful acclamation and we guessed the Bastard had shown himself to his men, to prove that he was still alive. Yet while this must have enforced their belief in his invincibility, that very afternoon the Norman force withdrew, not even pausing to collect and bury their dead.

We watched in amazement as the long line of men, horses and ox-wagons trailed back along the causeway and up the slopes towards the Cambridge road, leaving only a small garrison at Belsar's Hill. Although hundreds had perished that day they were still a host, crawling over the hills like a swarm of devouring ants. The sun was westering by the time the last of them was lost to view and lingering smoke turned the sky red so that all the meres and waterways seemed to be filled with blood.

Working by the flare of the burning peat, we laboured hard that night, wrecking the *ponton* and destroying all that remained of the causeway across the marsh. The corpses we heaved into the river, our faces muffled against the stench of scorched and burned hair and flesh: some resembled figures hacked from burnt wood more than men. We made no attempt to salvage mail or weapons (the former, in most cases, was welded to the charred flesh), having in any case no lack of either. Some of the carcases sank straightway but others floated for a while like grotesque swimmers from a dreadful dream until the current and the darkness swallowed them.

The *ponton* had been well constructed but it is always easier to destroy than build and the men who had waited all day on the ridge were eager for action. When two Norman guard-ships ventured close we shot fire-arrows into them and they turned sharply and rowed away, followed by our jeers. Soon the timbers of the *ponton* were floating with the corpses to the sea and our refuge was truly an Isle again.

'This day will be long remembered.' Siward Beorn brought me a horn of ale which I drained almost at one draught: my throat was parched, my mouth tainted with the reek of the fires. We had returned to the camp on the ridge to find the men deep in celebration. Two hogs were roasting and Wuleric was playing his pipe to accompany the revelry. Even Morcar was laughing as some of Rahere's men re-enacted their stalk through the marsh and the Normans' horror at finding themselves under attack. Only the churchmen were missing and at that realization a cool finger seemed to press against the nape of my neck. Glancing up to where our banner was set proudly on the watchtower, I read warning in the Saint's steady gaze and shivered for it came like an echo of the past, some recollection half-stirred to life but not quite to remembrance.

'Hereward – what's your reckoning?' Acer and Harald were laying bets as to when the Bastard would attack again. 'Will he show his face here before winter or wait until another witch tells him what to do?'

I went to join them and in the flow of beer and mead, the boasting and feat-challenging, my misgivings faded, seemed no more substantial than the ghost-lights which sometimes flicker in the fens. Yet it would not be long before memory of that warning came to haunt me.

6. Betrayal

Days after the conflagration, peat still smouldered between Aldreth and the river, flaring unexpectedly until the whole marsh was reduced to a black waste of ash and filthy water, fouled by the rotting corpses of men and horses. Of the *ponton* nothing remained but a few broken piles sticking out of the water. Morcar had *destrier's* heads nailed to these as a warning to enemies but it sickened me to look at them, remembering Tiw's fate. The carrion birds took full advantage of my nephew's gesture: soon nothing remained but bare skulls save where the carcases were so burned that the skin and flesh had shrunk and dried into a nightmarish parody of what a horse should be, not worth the picking.

The Bastard was not so distempered by this new disaster as to relax the cordon around the Isle. The guard-boats lost at Aldreth were swiftly replaced and it became almost impossible to travel unseen across the marshes save by moving under cover of darkness. On Belsar's Hill, the garrison seemed content to stay within the safety of the palisade and watch us as we watched them, with vigilant and unceasing hostility.

It had been our hope that once news spread of our success, help would come from Denmark or Scotland. The key to the rebellion lay in momentum: our victories should have been used to inspire and incite insurrection across the whole of the south. But as days passed and no messages came, we realized no aid was coming.

'Sweyn's playing a waiting game and the atheling's a spineless sycophant,' Siward Beorn said bluntly when we sat in council three weeks after the Norman retreat. 'He'll be licking his brother-in-law's arse for an eorldom in Scotland and if Gospatrick and Marleswein let him alone, that's where he'll stay. No doubt Waltheof's planning to regain power in what's left of the north but while he has the Bastard's ear, he'll not move against him until he's sure of support. We could have a long wait before us.'

Heavy silence followed. Most of the harvest was gathered but a period of heavy rain had followed the burning and much of the rye, which formed the Fenlander's staple, was blighted: it would be a hard winter. Looking round the table, I read grim resolution from the faces of Siward Beorn, Acer and Morcar but Thurstan and Athelwine exchanged self-conscious, almost furtive glances. Then the abbot cleared his throat.

'Perhaps the time has come for prudence,' he said, speaking with a careful deliberation which made me suspect he had long prepared this speech. 'There is no doubting the valour by which the Isle has been defended, nor that the King is much angered by his failures. But winter approaches and we must consider the future. Thus far our cause has been just and fortune has favoured us: our Lord ever defends the righteous. Yet now we are cut off from all hope of help, with no sign of support from former allies. It may be that the poor harvest is a sign the tide has turned against us. Should we not then consider the actions of King Sweyn and Eorl Waltheof and, like them, submit with honour? The King has lost enough men attempting to take the Isle to understand the value of such an offer. Morcar,' - he appealed to my nephew with upturned palms - 'you have experienced his clemency more than once. Do you not agree?'

Morcar looked more uncomfortable than I had ever seen him. His eyes skewed away from the churchman's and he bit savagely at his thumbnail.

'I am not war leader here,' he said at last and the breath hissed between Thurstan's teeth as if he had expected a different answer. 'But it cannot be denied that our refuge has become a trap. Eventually, if no aid comes, the Isle will fall. Yet we can hold out for a long time while the will remains to fight. And William fears what we might do: why else should he have sent his whole force against us?' He looked at me as if for encouragement, took a deep breath and added firmly, 'I do not think we should submit until there is no other choice but certain death.'

I sat with my hands flat on the smooth surface of the table, and waited. The churchmen exchanged glances then Thurstan shifted in his seat. His face was beaded with sweat but his voice was steady, as if he were discussing a point of theology rather than condemning comrades to the doubtful mercy of the enemy.

'You, my lord,' he inclined his head towards Morcar, 'will best understand that there are degrees and means of concession we can negotiate. If we offer peace now, from a position of power, the King will be more lenient than if we wait until need drives us to beg mercy. Now is the time for reason. This fight cannot be won by force of arms.'

'What is this, Berkhamstead again?' Siward muttered while Acer turned his head and spat, then grinned his defiance. But through my anger I sensed behind the abbot's fair words a resolve stern as my own. When I stared at him, his face blanched but he did not lower his gaze.

'The King treats those who offer fealty in good faith with honour.' Athelwine looked piously at the standard of our saint. 'We would do well to consider what will happen if we continue to defy him. Why not be content with the victory we have? Thurstan is right: let us meet him as equals, not supplicants.'

I glanced at Morcar but he was staring intently at his hands, as if he wished himself far away. Siward Beorn's mouth worked but evidently he did not trust himself to speak. His hands, laid on the table before him, were clenched so hard the scarred knuckles stood out white. The silence stretched like a pulled bowstring – one heartbeat, two – I thought of the sack of Bourne, the desolation of York, little Aedgifu's grave in the woods, and got abruptly to my feet.

'I will hear no more of this!' My gaze swept startled faces: even Siward could not withstand it. 'We will not submit. Let those who would have peace with the Bastard leave now. The Isle will not fall while there are men who will follow me.'

As I strode out with Siward and Acer at my heels, I registered shock on Thurstan's face yet the Bishop's betrayed the same kind of fulfilled expectancy I had seen on Stigand's at the fateful council in London after the fall of Harold Godwineson. But I dismissed it as nothing more than the contempt some churchmen hold for those who risk their lives in war, and thus unworthy of further consideration.

After that, relations between the abbey and our camps were strained. Though neither Thurstan nor Athelwine dared refuse us supplies from the abbey stores, we no longer feasted together in the Great Hall. Word had spread quickly of the churchmen's wavering and the monks among our force were subjected to much abuse which added to the atmosphere of distrust and resulted in many of them deserting. Yet even the youngest and least experienced among my fighters understood that without the abbey's support, life on the Isle would become very difficult. We could survive for a while by raiding but if the Fen-folk turned against us, we would not last long.

I was in no mood to apologise to Thurstan or Athelwine for my roughness but Morcar begged me to speak with the men ere rancour became bloodshed. This I did grudgingly after Leofric the Deacon, who was often in Cratendune, was set upon and beaten senseless. The culprits were reprimanded and put on guard duty in the marshes at Aldreth (unpopular because of the stench from the rotting corpses). Leofric watched me intently, his eyes mere slits in his bruised and bloodied face but when I asked what he wanted, he looked abashed, mumbled some excuse and limped away.

'Poor lad wants to be a hero but he's afraid of breaking his vows,' Acer remarked. 'Pity: he's a good eye with the bow. If he's got any backbone, this dithering of the abbot should make up his mind. Easier for him if he gets rid of that monk's robe.'

Over the next few days I noticed Leofric always at the margins of wherever I happened to be but whenever I caught his eye, he looked away as if afraid. Siward Beorn joked that he was infatuated with me: the giant northerner knew nothing of my past so I let it go. Martin, however, watched the deacon with a jealous eye and Erik pointedly ignored him, even refusing to pass him the wine at our evening meal. Leofric took no more notice of their hostility than a duck of rain yet still he dogged my footsteps until in exasperation I assigned him to Wuleric's band who were keeping watch on the waterways east of the Isle.

Soon I had more to occupy my mind than a young man's adulation. News came that the main part of our enemy's force had retreated to

Cambridge while the Bastard recovered from his arrow-wound but so tight had the cordon become that our spies were finding it difficult to reach us. Every fisherman was now stopped and questioned and the Gyrwas spoke of beatings, rapes and burnings in any vill whose inhabitants were suspected of collaboration. We heard that William Malet was among the knights that had perished in the fire at Aldreth and those from the north rejoiced at his demise but I could not help feeling that a chance had been lost when it transpired that both Ivo Taillebois and De Warenne had escaped unscathed. There were rumours also that the Bastard intended to divide the lands and possessions of Ely Abbey among his followers but we dismissed these as scare-mongering lies, intended to further strain the loyalties of the churchmen.

Many locals, caught between fear of Norman intimidation and reprisals from us should they be coerced into helping our enemies, chose to leave that autumn, a decision abetted by failure of the rye. Some headed further east into Anglia, others had no choice but to take to the Brunneswald or seek shelter with kin deeper in Mercia. One day Martin took me aside and told me that Ymma had moved to the coast of Suffolk where a kinsman of Osfrith's still held a few acres. They had taken the child with them and left no message. It seemed she wished to leave the past behind.

It was early evening. I stared emptily across the darkling marshes to where the line of the sea shone silver. That a single brief glimpse should be the first and last I might see of my son, that Ymma should have estranged herself so completely, I could scarcely believe.

'Hereward.' I do not know how long I stood there in silence: it seemed to me I could feel the earth reel beneath my feet. But there was a note of urgency in my friend and servant's tone that brought me back to myself. I dragged my gaze from the horizon to his face, a pale wedge in the twilight.

'There is something else.' He hesitated and when he spoke again, his voice was barely audible. 'Thurstan and one other have left the Isle and I do not think they have yet returned. Some say they took a great part of the abbey's gold with them.'

'When was this?' All thoughts of Ymma and our child were wiped from my mind as I struggled to remember when I had last seen the abbot. 'Who knew? Why was I not told at once?'

'Siward challenged the bishop this morning when Thurstan did not appear,' Martin replied unhappily. 'Athelwine said the abbot had gone to one of the reed-cutter's vills where someone was dying. We thought no more of it until Leofric ran to Cratendune with news that half Stigand's gold is missing. It was pure chance he'd been asked to fetch a chalice from the vaults. It may be that Sweyn stole it months ago only Leofric swears it was there last week.'

I was silent, recalling the furtive glances that had often passed between the churchmen of late while my guts turned cold at the idea of treachery.

'Ach, surely they would not dare!' Martin's words matched my thoughts so exactly, they startled me. He grasped my arm. 'After all this time? Maybe Leofric is trying to gain favour with such a story: it's common knowledge you're no great lover of the Church.'

We stared at each other as the implications of betrayal sank in, then I pulled away and began to run back to camp. 'We must have the truth!'

Leofric, when he was brought before me, was proudly defiant. Under the none-too-friendly eyes of Martin and Siward Beorn; the open hostility of Erik who, jealous of his role as armour-bearer, stood at my shoulder, he told his tale with a clarity and succinctness that left us in no doubt that this was the truth as he perceived it.

I did not question him too hard, saving my ire for the abbot and bishop themselves. Neither deigned to meet us when we went to the abbey that same evening (perhaps Thurstan was still away), and this refusal only fuelled our doubt. We spent a sleepless night arguing over what to do if they withdrew their support completely.

When we returned to the abbey next morning, we were greeted with a fulsome good-will that deepened our suspicion. To my surprise, Morcar was there: I had thought him with his men, guarding the northern islet of March. Thurstan and Athelwine professed outrage when I accused them of dealing with our enemies. They maintained that not a single coin was missing from the abbey's hoard and implied that Leofric was the one unworthy of trust. After all, Thurstan argued, did not his lies prove his intent to cause trouble between the abbey and our men?

So persuasive was he that Siward Beorn grunted and apologised but I had experienced the perfidy of monks too often to be so easily swayed.

'Will you renew your oath of fealty on Etheldreda's tomb?' I asked and the two exchanged uncomfortable glances and hesitated before assenting.

'We've been stuck here too long,' Acer remarked as we made our way back to Cratendune. 'Put too many pigs in a pen and they start to fight. We'd better break out before we're at each other's throats.'

'With the way the harvest's gone, we'll be starving by All Souls if we don't get supplies,' said Martin drily. 'Perhaps we should submit: then we'd be feasting at the Bastard's table come Yule.'

'When iron floats,' I retorted and cuffed him so hard, he staggered.

An uneasy peace prevailed on the Isle after that. Leofric, affronted by our apparent dismissal of his tale, was seen no more about the camp. With the meagre harvest complete, we fighters joined in the labour of threshing and winnowing, picking apples and grapes, preparing fish and eels for smoking. This year no-one grumbled at the drudgery of these tasks for there was already rumour of famine in the north and it was as yet only early autumn. To keep the men from becoming stale and disheartened, we amused ourselves by harrying the Norman guard-ships, especially those patrolling the Ouse west of Ely which had no egress to open water save the meres watched by our bowmen. Such was their fear of fire after the disaster at Aldreth, the mere threat gained us two fine vessels. The fighters on board were treated with more mercy than they would have afforded us: instead of slaying them we stripped them naked, broke their hands so that they would never wield a weapon again and set them loose in the trackless marshes to find their own way to safety. No doubt some drowned and for days afterwards we heard strange cries echo across the fens but we felt no pity.

Throughout this time the Normans on Belsar's Hill made no attempt to harass us. Their presence curbed our activities and with that they seemed content. It became a game amongst our youngest fighters, eager to prove themselves, to try and lure the enemy outside their palisade. I put a stop to this after two of our lads were struck by cross-bow bolts: we could not afford to waste lives. After that we stayed on our side of the river and they theirs and though we saw messengers and supplies pass to and fro along the causeway, the size of the garrison remained the same and we feared no attack from that direction.

Of what the Bastard planned as his wound healed and he hunted deer on the edge of the Brunneswald we heard nothing. No force was reported mustering anywhere in the region and Gilbert de Ghent and Ivo Taillebois had returned to their estates. Yet remembering how swiftly the insurgency at York had been countered, I did not underestimate the Usurper's prowess as a war leader and was careful not to be lulled into complacency. However, when he made his move, it was from a wholly unexpected quarter. Force having failed to gain him the Isle, he resorted to guile.

While its treasures could not match the gold accumulated at Borough, Ely Abbey was rich in land, most of which lay beyond the Isle and comprised some of the best tillage in East Anglia. Soon after Michaelmas, the Bastard issued a decree granting the abbey's holdings as fiefdoms to those that had served him against the rebellions in the north and on the Isle. The monks, by their continuing sedition, had put themselves outside the law and therefore forfeited their rights to land. Henceforth they would be treated as rebels and could expect no redress.

This message was brought by a monk from Cambridge who, drunk with his own importance, did not wait to reach the abbey but gabbled his tidings to anyone who would listen. Gamal, who had ferried the man across, was first to hear. Realizing the significance of this development, he ran straightway to find me.

'Aye, but we have no proof,' Siward Beorn said reasonably when I voiced my fear that the churchmen might now try to negotiate their own terms of submission. He and Acer had received the news with grim resignation but Morcar stood tense and silent. 'Though it's true the loss of their lands may outweigh their fear of us. Yet what choices do we have other than to seek another refuge or take abbot, bishop and monks hostage?'

'And turn all the Fen-folk against us?' Acer snarled. 'Might as well cut our throats now or else go to the Bastard first and beg his mercy on bended knee. Na – our worthy abbot is playing a close game and all we can do is watch and wait. But let us make certain that not a monk sets foot outside the abbey without we know of it.'

We doubled our guard on Aldreth and the abbey. Pilgrims brave enough to face the Normans at Belsar's Hill were still allowed along the causeway and though we could not stop those who came and went in God's name, we questioned them before allowing them to pass onto the Isle. I told my men to hold anyone well-fed or with a fighter's mien but none such was apprehended and as days passed, we began to believe the abbot's assertion that as a man of peace he would accept the loss of Ely's lands as a temporary inconvenience until, with our victory, all would be restored.

Around the fifth anniversary of the disaster at Hastings we noticed an increase in the number of Norman ships on the major waterways surrounding the Isle. At the same time, the garrison at Belsar's Hill was strengthened. We could only watch as men marched into the fort and none doubted that this boded ill. I had the captured ships loaded with provisions and arms so that, if necessary, we could take our fight to the water. Only the Fen-wolves knew of this and I swore them to secrecy for there were not enough boats to carry all the rebel force. But with so many crowded together, it was inevitable that rumours spread and tensions grew within the camps, fuelled by continuing animosity between fighters and monks.

It was in an attempt to ease this disquiet that I led a force of nearly three-score to the abbey's demesne farm at Marham. This was Thurstan's suggestion, to take the tithes due to St. Etheldreda ere the Normans stole them but I had a personal interest: it was rumoured that the estate was to be granted to my old enemy, William de Warenne. To catch the tide, we set off at dawn in small fishing boats. Mist hung low over the marshes that morning and we slipped past the enemy guard-ships like eels through an open sluice-gate and made our way along the narrow channels towards the mainland with no fear of pursuit.

This part of the Fenland was unfamiliar to me and it took most of the morning to find a safe passage through the marshes from our landing place. When we reached the farm, we found it deserted save for a few women and children who ran and hid at our approach and a naked half-wit who screamed obscenities, then fell down in a fit and lay as if dead. As we broke into the granary and began to shovel the grain into sacks, an aged monk shuffled over and stood watching in silence until Wuleric, discomfited by his steady gaze, asked roughly what he wanted.

'I came to offer absolution to those who will soon face God's judgement,' was the enigmatic reply and when Wuleric shrugged and turned away, the old man shook his head regretfully and muttered to himself, though whether in benediction or anger I could not tell.

Thurstan had promised that we would find several fine mules to help bear the tithes back to the boats but though we searched every building, there was no sign of any beast of burden. One of Siward Beorn's men suggested we should catch as many serfs as we could find and use them instead but this I would not allow: there was bad blood enough between us and the abbey without abusing their bondsmen. So we were forced to carry the sacks ourselves and what should have been less than half a day's journey took twice as long, in part because someone, for amusement or from malice, had moved the withy wands with which we had marked the way back to the boats and we became lost.

By nightfall we had reached the edge of one of the great meres which join to form the Wide Sea and there we were forced to camp, having no wish to risk struggling through the marshes in the dark. It was a long and uncomfortable night for we had no means of making fire and the biters swarmed. For food each man had to be content with as many handfuls of raw grain as he could stomach and thirst kept us awake for the mere was brackish. Though Wuleric fetched a helmet-full from a fresh pool, he had to go far to find it and it was only enough for a lucky few.

I woke from an uneasy slumber to find Martin sitting beside me, alert and still as a stag which hears the hounds far away. It was not yet dawn but his figure was clearly outlined against the starlit sky and something in the tense set of his head, maybe a prescience of danger, made me sit up. 'What is it?'

'Listen.' I strained my ears and there, on the edge of hearing, beyond the unceasing lap of water, the scream of some small creature caught by a night-time hunter, was a low rumble, like distant, continuous thunder. As I listened, an iron hand seemed to squeeze my bowels and the pounding of my heart drowned the sound I was trying to hear until I shook my head in frustration.

'It's been going on for some time,' Martin said quietly. 'And I thought I heard horses neighing. But the water plays tricks on your ears.'

As he spoke, there sounded a faint but furious barking, barely audible but unmistakeable. I thought of the many dogs that had attached themselves to our camps, animals which while of mixed breed and origins, rarely made a sound save when fighting each other, and the fear which had stirred upon my waking crystallised to a dreadful certainty.

'The Isle!' I sprang to my feet and scanned the horizon. Ely was a black hulk to the south; a faint lightening of the eastern sky heralded the approach of dawn. A bright point of flame suddenly sprang to life between ridgeline and sky: the warning beacon set on the hill behind Cratendune.

'Cunning bastards!' I glanced at our makeshift camp where tired men lay about like hounds after a long hunt, their heads pillowed on sacks of grain, the getting of which, I now realized, must have been a ploy to ensure my absence. 'If this is the monks' doing, they will pay dearly for their treachery.'

Men were stirring all around. Seeing the red flare of the beacon, many exclaimed aloud in dismay for all had kin and friends on the Isle. I breathed deeply, forcing calm on myself, knowing we could do nothing until daylight. In a low voice, Martin said, 'Do not forget, Hereward, the Normans are our enemies, not the abbey.'

The dark seemed endless that morning and we had still to find our boats. We checked our weapons but we had gone lightly armed and many of the men were without mail for speedy travelling across the marshes. Gradually the translucence in the east turned to a pearly dawn and we set off, abandoning the grain with no more thought than one casts aside a broken shield-strap. As the light strengthened, the beacon on the ridge faded but behind it a great cloud of smoke billowed into the sky and we increased our pace until the breath sobbed in our throats, knowing that its source must be the settlement at Ely or our camp at Cratendune.

It seemed an eternity before we came to the creek where the boats were moored but the sun had only just slipped above the horizon. Guessing that to attempt a landing on the east side of the Isle or at Aldreth would be to walk straight into the arms of the enemy, we were forced to take a roundabout route, crossing the Wide Sea and slipping into West Fen by winding, little-used channels. Though it was a clear morning with a light wind from the west, the waterways were ominously empty. We landed in a secluded, sedge-rimmed inlet and all seemed peaceful: sheep grazed on the slope rising away from us and the bubbling song of skylarks sounded from high above. But the smoke sullying the sky from the other side of the ridge told a different tale.

My anger had turned to a battle-focus so clear it was as if some outside force guided me. I was calm and cold and had left fear behind with the night. I sent Erik, who was the best runner among us, up the hill to see what was happening.

The men were restless as we waited for his return. They sat honing weapons whose edges already gleamed bright in the sunlight and talked and joked with the dark humour that affects those who know they may soon face death. At last the lad appeared, moving warily downslope as if fearful of being spotted. Then Martin grasped my arm and pointed, not at Erik but another figure riding towards us at full gallop, leading a horse on either side and with another following at a few lengths. From her easy gait and lean frame I recognized the laggard as Swallow but who the rider was I could not tell until he came within spearthrow. It was Leofric the Deacon and he had abandoned his monk's robe for a fighter's hauberk. How he had harnessed and induced the mare to follow, I could not begin to guess, nor was there time to ask. Maybe it was simply that at least once that day fortune favoured us.

'Hereward – thank God!' He reined in his horse (the smallest of the captured *destriers*), and swung down from the saddle. 'I was afraid I'd never find you. The King and all his army are on the Isle: they've been crossing since before dawn. Some waited for low tide and pushed rafts across the river at Aldreth then laid bundles of reed over the marsh to make a crossing, while more came by ship and landed at Cratendune and opposite Stuntney. The abbot came out to meet them, along with Athelwine and all the monks. They've been planning this for weeks: I tried to warn you!'

His face was pale and taut, his eyes fixed on mine.

'What of those at Hereward's Castle?' A fist seemed to press against my throat as I thought of my comrades trapped and leaderless. 'Did any escape?'

'The Bishop held a great feast last night.' He almost choked on the words: he was, after all, betraying his lord and mentor. 'Morcar and Siward Beorn went, along with most of their men. Athelwine said that with you away there was no shame in them leaving their posts, that it was time to mend the rift between abbey and fighters and no danger threatened now it was past Michaelmas. But Acer believed him no more than you would have done and he doubled the force at Aldreth, thinking it strange that Thurstan should arrange such a feast with you away. And Rahere's people had brought word of a ship force gathering at Wisbech. We thought they might be on their way to the Humber but it seems they were waiting for the tide and guides to take them through the Fens.'

'Is Acer still at Aldreth?' I was thinking that once the watchtower was surrounded, those inside would have had no choice but to submit or die. To my relief, Leofric shook his head.

'The Normans were a long time crossing the marsh and they lit their way with torches: when we saw their number, we knew we could not win. So we left the fort and harried them with arrows and javelins from the dark. Then when they reached the Isle, Acer had the beacon lit so that you would know we were under attack. After that he went to defend Cratendune. He told me to find you.'

'You did well.' In my heart I thanked and praised the old Fen-wolf for his good sense though the smoke still billowing from the other side of the ridge boded ill. 'And it was good thinking to bring horses. Is there any news of Rahere?'

'I haven't seen him.' A chastened look overtook the young man's eager expression. 'Should I go and look?'

'No.' I was sharply aware that Erik had returned. He stood panting, watching his rival with an unfriendly eye. 'Rahere can look after himself. Erik: what news from the ridge?'

The boy looked strained and sick but he gathered himself together with a visible effort. 'Cratendune is burning: the Normans have surrounded it and a great host of them is gathered outside the abbey. But the ridge is free of them - they must have thought their ships would keep us away. The King himself is there: I saw him.'

A murmur arose from those crowded close to hear the news, a ripple of apprehension generated by the unconscious note of awe in Erik's voice.

'So the Bastard's come for the kill,' Wuleric muttered. 'Well, he'll pay thrice-over for every drop of our blood.'

'No – you don't understand!' Leofric's face was anguished. 'He was invited! Bishop Athelwine and Thurstan have been negotiating terms for weeks, even before the abbey lost its lands. That was only part of it: the King proving he was not to be trifled with. Gold they gave him and promised peaceful submission of the Isle in return for their lives and property. It was all planned!'

The breath hissed between my teeth. 'How long have you known?'

'My lord!' His gaze darted from face to face like that of a trapped animal. 'Did he not speak with you? He told me he would three days ago.'

'What?' I grasped his shoulders, my fingers pressing to the bone. 'Who was this?'

'Morcar.' He licked his lips and his scrawny frame quivered beneath my hands. 'Please – he swore he'd tell you!'

I let him go and turned abruptly lest my face display my feelings. That my nephew could betray us was beyond my comprehension: the knowledge jarred like a sword-blow. The men were silent. It took no great wit to understand that the Isle was lost but none dared speak for fear of my wrath.

'We will leave but first I will be revenged upon our betrayers,' I said. 'We shall burn the abbey to the ground and all those inside, traitors to their oaths, kin and faith. Let none say after that Hereward slunk away like a beaten cur.'

I caught Swallow's reins and was about to swing into the saddle when a hand on my shoulder stayed me.

'No, wait!' To my astonishment it was Leofric, his thin, earnest face set in an expression of reckless determination. So fervent was his gaze, I did not strike him away as was my first impulse, but hesitated.

'Well?'

'Do not burn the abbey,' he pleaded. 'You cannot win against the King and all his men. Go now, while you have the chance. No-one will think less of you if you live to fight another day.'

I pulled away, mounted, ordered him to hand his *destrier* to Wuleric. 'To the ridge!'

Only berserkers, who fight more like wild beasts than men, knowing neither fear nor pain until they are hacked down, would have been undaunted by the sight that met us when we scaled the hill. Smoke billowed across the fields between the burning camp at Cratendune and the abbey but it could not hide the vast host which milled and seethed across the slopes like a dark tide. Nearly all the Bastard's force must have been there; ships and boats of all kinds were beached on the flats between the wrecked hythes and the moorings opposite Stuntney, and even as we watched, more

Normans marched along the track from Aldreth. It was gratifying to note that some of these were wounded, a few being carried in their shields, but had all our force been gathered together we would have been outnumbered five to one and what was left of us was scattered all across the Isle.

Patience may be as much a mark of a leader as daring. As Swallow shifted uneasily beneath me, smelling the smoke and hearing the sounds of fighting which on this side of the ridge came clearly to our ears, I realized the hopelessness of charging down the slope to join the fray. Three-score men, however doughty, would be absorbed by that host easily as stones sink into mire: there would be no returning and nothing gained. Wuleric's *destrier* moved forward and he reined it in savagely, his eyes fixed not on the scene below but my face, awaiting the signal. I backed Swallow off the ridge-line, gave my orders. Many who had left their families in Cratendune hesitated but they knew the odds as well as I and obeyed without question. Suddenly the weapons in their hands and my commands had become their only certainties save death which is every man's end.

Risky though it was, I split my band. Two groups of ten I sent to Downham and Haddenham, not to engage the enemy but to muster stragglers and then abandon the Isle using the boats long hidden in the marshes. Twenty I sent back to guard the craft we had come in, to await survivors from Cratendune, and if none came by late afternoon, to leave the Isle. However many of us were left after this disaster, without boats we were finished. The captured ships we had equipped with stores, including spare mail and arms, were moored in a secret place between Wicham and the islet of Coveney: it was my purpose to take them to an island in the Wide Sea we had often used as a staging post and there await the others before deciding what to do next.

Even as the first two bands departed, moving swiftly in the cover of the hedges and copses, a great shout arose from below. I dismounted, crept forward with the others to see what was happening and was not alone in groaning aloud. Cratendune had fallen.

With most of the camp burning, this outcome was inevitable but that knowledge did nothing to lessen our frustration and shame as we watched the Normans surrounding the gates move back to accommodate those that spilled out. Men, women and children, the unscathed supporting the wounded, they formed a great crowd though there were fewer fighters than I had expected. They stood uncertainly within the ring of our enemies, most of the men casting down their weapons, the children clinging to their mothers. The jeers and taunts of the victors rose above the roar of flames as the Normans swarmed through the camp, setting fire to anything not yet aflame within the broken palisade.

Though I tried to ignore the agonized whispers of those around me as they searched for kin and comrades in that sorry throng, I strained my eyes no less than any of them. No-one in camp was unknown to me and many had been friends since boyhood: Aelgytha, Acer, Siward the Red foremost among them.

'Ah no!' Erik's voice was laden with the fierceness verging on despair. Following his gaze I saw Acer singled out and dragged from the crowd. He was obviously wounded because when the Normans let go, he fell. He struggled to rise but had barely got to his knees when they booted him savagely to the ground. He did not resist as they wrested off his swordbelt and hauberk.

'We must leave.' Martin's calmness saved us because at that moment anger and despair overwhelmed me like a wave. Had he not spoken, that fey mood might have driven us to destruction, throwing ourselves upon our enemies like the ravening beasts that were our name-sakes, lusting after blood and death. His voice brought me back to myself. I saw the expectant faces of my comrades who looked to me for hope and leadership and my madness was stayed. I glanced one last time at the wreck of our camp, the mass of prisoners who were already being sorted, the women and children herded together like cattle, the men made to strip naked and sit in line.

'We can do no good here.' I mounted Swallow and set off across the slope. The hill cut off all sight and sound of our defeat. The men were silent as they followed and the grazing sheep took no more notice of us than of cloud shadows fleeting over the grass.

The Normans had not discovered the captured ships but we had to fight to reach them because the Bastard had chosen Witchford as his base. The main fighting force being engaged at Cratendune, it was those guarding the baggage train and setting up picket lines and tents we encountered. We were heavily outnumbered but these were their weakest fighters, the young and inexperienced or else veterans slowed by age and old wounds, and many tried to flee, shocked by the suddenness and ferocity of our attack. We slew without mercy and fired as many of the tents and wagons as we could, then left as swiftly as we had arrived, our arrows making sure that none dared pursue us. Three score at least we left dead and the cries of the wounded came as music to our ears for all of us escaped unscathed. Wuleric, inspired maybe by the thought of his sister in Norman hands again, fought like one possessed: when his horse was brought down he leapt clear and felled its slayer with a single sword-blow.

Once clear of the camp and watchful eyes, we veered into the marshes on the southern edge of Hale Fen. Soon the sounds of confusion from behind were lost beneath the suck of hooves and feet in the wet ground and the rustle of sedge which stood so tall we could see no more than a few feet in any direction save the narrow path ahead. The mingled stench of blood, sweat and smoke was cleansed from our nostrils by the cold rooty smells of water and peat.

'Thank God!' A shadow rose from the depths of a low alder clump.

Gamal Longbow unnotched the arrow which I realized must have been aimed at me and a grin of pure relief lightened his face. 'We feared you were dead. The abbey was barred against us when we went for help: we knew then the monks had betrayed us. Rahere went to watch for you at Downham in case you'd missed the beacon. What's happened at Cratendune?'

I told him all we had seen and heard as briefly as possible and while I spoke his men crept in from all around, treading softly on the springy ground until they reached the safety of the trees. They had been sent by Acer to guard the ships after the taking of Aldreth.

'We brought down two score of the bastards ere they set foot on the Isle,' Gamal said when I had finished. 'But the darkness hampered us more than them in the marsh: their torches made them easy targets but we could only move slowly for fear of the fen. By daylight hundreds had crossed and it was clear we could not hold them. Acer left us to delay them as long as we could while he took his men to Cratendune. He guessed you'd make your way here if you could and told us to guard the ships to the last man.' He hesitated and looked at me askance. 'Did we do right? Maybe we should have joined him.'

'It would have made no difference.' I reached out, gripped his shoulder in a brief gesture of reassurance. 'The Normans were too many. Do not berate yourself: we need you here.'

Martin, who had been moving among the men to see how many were there, came back looking worried. 'The tide will soon be on the turn, Hereward. Should we leave now or wait? And what of the horses?'

We had two *destriers* with us still but it was Swallow he meant. Each of the ships could carry three-score men with ease but we had no hoist or ramp with which to load animals. The eyes of all the men were on me as I went to the mare. After my escape from Brandon, she was famous even among my enemies. I imagined her in their hands, beaten or starved into submission or death, and knew what I must do. She turned her head and nudged my shoulder as I unharnessed her.

'No Norman will boast of getting Hereward's horse,' I said. 'We leave now: there's a clear trail behind for anyone to follow and we cannot risk being trapped here at low tide. Slaughter the *destriers*, throw their harness into the mere and get the ships ready to sail. Go!'

'The ships are ready now,' Gamal said, looking at me with a kind of wonder. Martin bent to pick up Swallow's harness and I nodded my thanks, grasped the mare's long mane and led her a little further into the trackless marsh.

It is the burden of all war leaders that they fail their comrades from time to time through ill-luck or circumstance but in all my years of fighting I had never knowingly betrayed a friend. Swallow followed me trustingly and stood still as stone even when I slipped my dagger from its sheath, rubbing the broad place between her eyes with the palm of my left hand while the fingers felt for her poll. I struck with all my strength and jumped clear as her legs folded: she dropped without a sound. To make sure, I cut her throat and then she shuddered as if to dislodge a fly, the breath hissed from her cloven windpipe and blood spread in a wide pool about my feet.

From the ships came the creak of wood as the men boarded; a *destrier* squealed: someone had struck clumsily. It was time to leave but I paused to stroke Swallow's neck in acknowledgement and farewell. In all the years we had been together (longer than I had known Turfrida), she had never failed me.

We sailed unhindered into the Wide Sea. No Norman ships were there for they had all gone to join in the sack of Ely. Seabirds wheeled above, thinking us fishermen, and their aching cries echoed our pain. Behind us the green hills of the Isle were still overshadowed by a cloud of smoke but there was no other sign of the terror being enacted there. The men leant panting on the oars and we lowered the sails lest they be spotted from afar and let the boats drift, thinking of kin and comrades left behind.

How long we rested there on the glittering water I do not remember: time enough to bind our wounds and slake our thirst from the water-skins stored in the boats. The sun was westering when Wuleric, who had been staring aimlessly northwards where the distant line of an ancient embankment marked the boundary between beach and marsh, said, 'There is a punt approaching.'

His face was haggard with grief and exhaustion. I put a hand on his shoulder in an attempt to comfort him and my gaze followed his pointing finger but it was some time before I descried the slim craft and its steersman against the rippling surface of the mere. It was Rahere and his eyes, bright in his gaunt, weather-beaten face, scanned both ships carefully before he waved.

'We've camped on the Isle of Alders,' he said when his craft came alongside. 'All my band escaped and more stragglers have been seen: I have men bringing them in. Where are Acer and the rest?'

I gave a brief account of what we had witnessed and the tall Fen-man grimaced but made no comment. From one of those behind came a stifled sob and a gasp. They were my men: it was for me to keep them from despair.

'It won't be long before the bastards begin the hunt: they must have realized by now that we've slipped though their fingers,' I said with an effort, my voice harsh and dry, devoid of emotion. 'We'll join you, Rahere, but tonight we attack. We'll keep them guessing, harry them like a wolf-pack and we will not submit even when the last drop of our blood is spent!'

A murmur of assent rose from men too weary to shout; Gamal strung and stretched his bow to send an arrow flying towards the Isle in defiance; Rahere grinned his wolf's grin and gave a low, fierce laugh that boded ill for our enemies. And then we bent again to the oars and sent the boats speeding to the northeast.

The Isle of Alders was where a thicket of alders and willow had bound the peat and mud into a carr upstanding from the chain of meres known as the Wide Sea. Less than an acre in area, it seemed crowded even before we landed. Rahere's men, along with those I had sent to Haddenham were camped there but when I asked, no-one had heard anything of the ten that had gone to Downham under the leadership of Aelgytha's husband, Harald. We set a watch then ate a meagre meal of smoked fish and barley while the sun set in a sky streaked like blood and fire mingled. But as twilight gathered, no more fugitives arrived, nor was there any sign of enemy ships.

From frustration, grief and anger, few were minded to sleep that night. When I asked for volunteers to return to Ely with me nearly all came forward but I chose fifteen from those, like me, who had seen little real fighting that day. We slipped away into the darkness and headed back the way we had come for it was my hope we would find fugitives from Cratendune gathered where we had left the fishing boats that morning (a lifetime ago it seemed). But when we reached the place, having moored some distance away and stolen along a path known only to the Fen-wolves, we found a great fire blazing nearby and a score of Normans lounging beside it. There was no sign of any of our comrades. If they had gone there they must have been captured, slain or crept elsewhere to hide.

When we were certain there was no-one in that place but enemies, we surrounded them as best we could and attacked. The combination of our war-cries and arrows, which slew many before they realized what was happening, struck terror into them and instead of defending themselves, all but six turned and fled into the darkness. So panic-stricken were they that some ran straight into the marsh where Rahere, whose eyes were keen as an owl's in the night, shot them with ease.

Their wounded we slew outright save one who appeared to be their leader and those that fled we did not pursue, leaving them to spread the news that there was still a rebel force active in the Fens. The leader I questioned while my men stripped the dead of gear and weapons and hamstrung the *destriers* tethered to a nearby tree. There was little to be got from the prisoner, for an arrow had sunk deep into his chest. I slit his throat, bent his sword and flung it into the fen. Then we threw all their possessions into the fire and left as swiftly and silently as we had come.

Two more raids we conducted ere dawn, striking at March and crossing the Ouse to burn a vill on the lands of Gilbert de Ghent. The cottars we spared for they had done us no harm but the flames leapt high and must have been clearly visible from the slope between Cratendune and Ely, a sign of hope to the captives, a signal of defiance to our enemies. By first light we were safe back on the Isle of Alders, the ships moored in a tiny inlet invisible to prying eyes, and there we lay on the damp ground (which seemed soft as a feather mattress to our spent limbs), and let the black tide of exhaustion take us.

For two days the Wide Sea remained free of enemy ships but the shores of Ely were closely guarded and we did not venture there, preferring to strike as far afield as tide and the hours of darkness allowed. Thus we knew nothing of what was happening on the Isle save that the Bastard and his force were still there.

It was on the second day that we discovered how our enemies had revenged themselves but news came first from a wholly unexpected quarter. We had just returned from a night foray into William Malet's estate to the east when from the midst of one of the reed-beds surrounding the islet came a flurry of grunts and curses, not unlike the worrying of hounds as they close over their quarry. Martin and I motioned the others to wait while we went to investigate. No sooner had we splashed our way along the trail when Gamal and Wuleric appeared, dragging a figure attired as a monk between them.

'Here's another filthy rat of a churchman!' Wuleric snarled, thrusting hard so that the monk fell sprawling at our feet. 'A spy no doubt. We'll show him how we treat renegades and traitors. He'll be glad to meet his maker by the time we're finished.'

'No, by the grace of God, please listen!' Even as Wuleric reached to grab the hood of his robe, the monk, who was little more than a youth, struggled to his knees in the morass and stretched out his hands in supplication. 'I'm from Croyland. Ulfkil sent me to find Hereward. I have news for him concerning his wife.'

'Liar!' Wuleric whipped his dagger from his belt and put it to the young man's throat. 'What kind of fools do you take us for? That Turfrida claimed sanctuary at Croyland is widely known: you seek to gain our trust so that you can betray us!'

'No – I swear by Saint Guthlac's blood!' The monk neither flinched nor tried to resist as Wuleric pressed a knee into his back. 'I must speak with Hereward alone!'

'I am not minded to put overmuch faith in the oaths of monks,' I broke in grimly. The man's back was bent like a bow but his eyes remained fixed on mine. I jerked my head at Wuleric who let go so suddenly that the monk fell forward onto his hands and knees. 'Let him speak. Then we'll judge if he's a traitor.'

'The message was for you, lord.' The monk knelt upright and though the front of his robe was soaked, his hands and arms dripping with muddy slime, his calm assurance was like a shield. I sensed that here was one, like Ulfkil, whose faith, while simple, was yet inviolable.

'Do I not stand before you?' I kept my voice stern and cold though my bowels crawled with apprehension. 'These are my comrades: you may speak freely before them.'

He hesitated and a faint smile curved his lips. Martin shifted uneasily at my side, the peaty ooze bubbling beneath his feet while Wuleric and Gamal averted their gaze.

'Let all know then,' the monk's voice was suddenly clear and ringing, 'that the lady Turfrida renounces Hereward unless he submits to the King in good faith, swearing lifelong fealty within three days. After that time she will become the bride of Christ and no man's wife. That is the message.'

The breath had stilled in my throat as his words unfolded. Then Wuleric let out a choking sound which might have been a half-stifled chuckle. A flush of shame mantled my face: Brain-biter sprang to my hand. The monk's gaze did not waver as I swung the sword but a weight dragged at my arm. Martin clung there.

'Hereward – no! To slay a monk is God-cursed!'

I thrust him aside, sending him sprawling into the marsh but the momentum of my anger was checked. I rested my sword-point on the ground, saying harshly, 'You say this message comes from my wife but I hear only the speech of my enemies who wish me to submit because they cannot win by fighting. Did she send no token as surety of your good faith?'

For the first time the monk seemed ill-at-ease. He lowered his gaze and swallowed hard. Wuleric's eyes narrowed and his hand went meaningfully to his dagger, then the monk looked up and cleared his throat.

'She bade you remember your daughters, the one already lost and the other, who believes herself fatherless.'

I stared at him and a howl seemed to gather deep within me, of loss, regret and guilt mingled. And then a dreadful cry pierced the stillness, a keening wail which echoed what I felt so exactly that at first I thought it had come incontinently from my own lips. My comrades looked all around in confusion, then, as one, we turned and sped towards it, those with weapons still sheathed drawing them as they ran.

Rahere, his face oddly twisted as if he were fighting the urge to weep or vomit, was on his way to fetch us. He stopped in his tracks then turned and led us to where the rest of the Fen-wolves were gathered on a muddy bank beneath spreading alders. A murmur arose from them like that which accompanies news of some calamitous and wholly unexpected event but at our approach they fell silent and drew aside to let us through.

All that we had suffered since the fall of Harold Godwineson could not prepare us for what we found. Three small craft were drawn up on the mud, two fishing boats barely fit to float and a crude raft of bound logs, all roped together. They were crowded with our comrades. The oarsmen in the first boat looked like living corpses, their faces masked with blood from their empty eye-sockets; those in the second were unable to row because their hands had been cut off: they must have shouted guidance to the blinded. The raft was piled with naked and mutilated bodies, some of which still moved and cried. So covered in blood were these, we thought at first they had been flayed.

We got them ashore and I ordered Rahere to tow the boats out and sink them. It was due to his vigilance that our comrades were saved for they had been drifting seawards when he spotted the craft and went to investigate. Those from the first two boats we gave water and tended as best we could (the stumps of the dismembered had been seared, so most would live), but there was little we could do for the rest, many of whom had been wounded in the fight for Cratendune before falling into Norman hands. Some begged for a quick sword-stroke to end their suffering, others were beyond speech or comprehension. These shuddered, whimpered and gasped their way towards death like mindless beasts despite the efforts of Leofric the Deacon and the monk from Croyland to comfort them.

Torn between shock, outrage and pity, I think few gave thought as to why our comrades should have been treated with such cruelty but to me the message was clear. The fate of Morcar and Siward Beorn I did not know but I guessed they had been imprisoned; it was the ordinary fighters that had been punished most severely. The Bastard knew that without support from the common folk, the rebellion could not last: he wanted to ensure that fear would prevent them rising again. And, too, he wished to avenge the humiliations he had suffered in his attempts to take the Isle by force.

'Hereward.' Martin, the front of his tunic slick with blood, took hold my sleeve. 'Acer is here.'

In the welter of blood, nameless filth and barely living flesh on the raft, I had not recognized my second-in-command, doughtiest fighter of us all and hardiest to withstand pain. He lay curled on the ground and the stench which hung about him made the gorge rise in my throat because among his other wounds he had been stabbed in the groin and the blade must have pierced his bowels. Perhaps because he had led the defence of Cratendune, the Normans had singled him out for special treatment: his hands, feet and genitals had been cut off and one eye gouged out. The other was tightly closed. I prayed he was beyond consciousness of pain, wondered at his strength. His flesh was bled to the colour of marble, his wrist stumps pressed into the clotted mess at the base of his belly. The rasp of his breath was all the sound he made.

'They left him one eye so he could see how the rest of us were rewarded.' Siward the Red was propped against an alder trunk. He could barely speak but there was no mistaking his bitterness and revulsion. Both his hands had been severed halfway between wrist and elbow and his eyes were brilliant with fever. He waved in a gesture of helplessness and disgust then, seeing his stumps, blackened and swollen from the searing, fell abruptly silent.

'Dear God.' I knelt beside Acer, put one hand on his shoulder. He quivered then went rigid. A mewling sound escaped him; his breath harshened. I thought of how Aedgifu had loved him, how we of the Fen-wolves all owed our lives to his dauntless valour at one time or another, how I had betrayed him at the last by failing to come to his aid. I talked to him in the hope he would know he was among friends, held him while he died. 'True friend and brave heart, forgive me,' I whispered. 'Be at peace.' Then I bent to kiss his brow and sat back on my heels, overcome with weariness.

After a moment Siward called me over.

'It was the priests and Morcar,' he whispered hoarsely. 'We saw nothing of them until they came from the abbey under Norman escort. They told us to submit, then we'd be treated justly and set free. Acer was down and we were fighting to prevent the bastards rushing in from the river. But soon most of the camp was on fire and folk were screaming to be let out before we all burned. A few of the northerners managed to climb over the palisade but they were hacked down straightway, cut to pieces: none of us wanted to die like that, for nothing. So we opened the gates in good faith and poured out, carrying the wounded as best we could. Morcar, Athelwine and Thurstan were safe back inside the abbey by then but the Bastard was there, gloating.' He paused and shuddered. 'We were tired and confused, parched with thirst, surrounded and heavily outnumbered: the choice was between submission and death. So we threw down our weapons and gave ourselves up, though had we known what they planned for us maybe more would have chosen a fighter's end.'

He grimaced and looked away towards the dark hulk of the Isle. 'He knows what he's about, the Bastard, I'll say that for him. All day and night they kept us there, naked and without food or water. Some bled their lives away and their flesh grew cold against ours. And we heard the screams of our women from the Norman camp. Next morning they gathered all the folk of Ely and the survivors from Cratendune to bear witness as we were led before the Bastard and our punishment was decreed: imprisonment for Morcar and Siward Beorn, blindings and maimings for the rest. They dealt with Acer first. I think they wanted to make him beg for mercy but he laughed when they gouged out his eye and after that he made no sound other than cursing them. How he lived through it, I don't know. Siward Beorn had been brought in fetters to watch: his men and Morcar's were marched from the abbey and given the choice between swearing fealty to the King and sharing our fate. Once it was clear they'd all join the Bastard, the Normans began on the rest of us.'

Again he paused and I held a waterskin to his lips. When he had finished drinking, he moved his arm as if to wipe his mouth with the back of his hand, stopped and swore softly. 'Sometimes it feels as if it's still there,' he explained. 'God, we thought they'd hear our screams in Borough. The axe-blows, they were nothing, but the searing! And those who were blinded: some had their eyes put out with a red-hot blade but there was one knight, of Ghent I think, who used his thumbs and left their eyeballs hanging on their cheeks until it amused him to pluck them off.' He hesitated and swallowed hard. 'If you manage to avenge any of us Hereward, do it on that man.'

I did not answer at once and he leant forward a little, his haggard face set as if hewn from wood, his eyes blazing. 'You're not going to submit?'

It was part question, part accusation and his vehemence startled me: with part of my mind I was wondering how to deal with so many who would never fight again. I thought of Turfrida's ill-timed message, toyed for an instant with the idea of submission, of leaving for Flanders and living there with my family in peace. But I felt the fervour of Siward's gaze like the touch of a blade against my breast. If nothing else, the Normans had made my path clear before me.

'We fight on.' I looked round the islet, at my comrades, the maimed and the whole, knew I was right to keep faith with them. Turfrida had made her choice, now I made mine. With my dagger I cut a lock of my hair, twisted it into a rough cord, then returned to Acer's body and tied it round his neck. Siward and the others who lay nearby watched this in amazement but they must have assumed it was meant as homage to the dead and none made any comment.

Often I have been forced to decisions no man has the right to make, sometimes condemning men to certain death for contingency's sake: such is the burden of war leaders. Yet none was so hard as that moment when I told those men reduced from hard-handed fighters to cripples that they would be taken to Thorney and Croyland abbeys and left to make what lives they could there or with whatever kin were willing to accept them.

They took the news quietly, without protest and their calm acceptance of their fate shamed me. I could not meet the eyes of the dismembered, still less look upon the raw sockets of the blind, and went to join Martin, Gamal and Rahere who stood listening discretely at the edge of the trees.

'We must transport them without delay,' I said roughly. 'Before long, enemy ships will enter the Wide Sea and we have not enough boats to bear us all. Use the warships. Martin, take one to Croyland; Wuleric, you go to Thorney. Meanwhile Rahere and I will attack the Isle to draw the bastards' attention.'

They looked startled but did not argue: shock and grief made them malleable. But before the boat left for Croyland, bearing the dead as well as half the maimed, I pulled Martin aside and told him that Turfrida must be informed of Acer's death.

'Is there any other message?' he asked carefully.

'Acer was a dear friend, beloved by Aedgifu not least,' I replied. 'Have Turfrida tend his body and she will find her answer there, though not the one she seeks. She should know why I cannot submit. Maybe now she will relent.'

He knew better than to argue but I stalked away ere he could open his mouth and concentrated on honing my weapons as the ships left.

Rahere and I had barely returned from our raids and the sky was pale with pre-dawn twilight when we were beset. The two points of light where we had fired buildings at March and Wimblington (where the enemy had a look-out set), were still flickering when more bright points appeared, clustered together at first, then spreading out smoothly to form a line. At first we could not understand how this was done, or what the lights signified for the line extended beyond the limits of the main Isle and the smaller humps of land which lay between us. Then, as dawn turned the meres to silver, we realized they marked ships, fanning out to cover the whole span of the Wide Sea.

'What now?' Rahere asked grimly. In the faint light he looked like an old man, the lines of his face scored deep by grief and weariness, his eyes sunken and red-rimmed; no doubt I appeared much the same. Martin, always pale, looked like a ghost as he made his way over, having returned to the Isle of Alders ere nightfall.

'If we lose the ships, we're done for.' I glanced northwards where the network of fens and narrow waterways extended far beyond Wisbech. 'Rahere, take half the men and both ships deep into the marshes: you know the channels better than anyone. The rest stay here with me. There are enough smaller craft to bear us all at a pinch. Go!'

The tall Fen-man looked searchingly at me and half-opened his mouth as if to argue, then thought better of it and went to rouse men still sunk in the black sleep of exhaustion. They groaned and stretched, then reached resignedly for their weapons but not one complained or hesitated. A new mood of grim resolution had hold of them since yesterday.

'We'll lie low but if any Norman sets foot here, they'll wish themselves back in Rouen,' I told those that remained when Rahere had gone. 'And while we keep them occupied to the fore, I want the best boatmen among you to slip among their ships and fire them. Then we'll leave them to enjoy this place alone.'

Our luck was not wholly spent: all fell out more or less as I planned. I had, in any case, no wish to die in defence of a muddy alder knoll though according to Siward, the Bastard had ordered me taken alive. The Isle of Alders made an obvious hiding place but loth to break their line, the Norman ships did not converge to surround us but remained strung out. One ship only beached on the muddy shore and while we engaged those on board, slaying them all, our boatmen attacked the others with fire-arrows, then slipped between them and sped across open water to the cover of the sedge where the war-ships could not follow. Such confusion resulted that we escaped with ease but once the fires were out, instead of turning about and sailing back the way they had come, the enemy ships dropped anchor and settled down to wait.

The days that followed were the most uncomfortable I had known in all my years of fighting. Like a stoat latched onto a hare, our enemies would not give up and though in the evenings and at dawn we took our chances and attacked, then slipped away to the safety of the reeds and wooded islets, we were pushed inexorably towards Wisbech where the Normans were turning the timber fort into a massive *donjon*. Cut off from supplies, we quickly ran out of arrows, food, clean water and beer to drink. Autumn gales brought driving rain. Soaked to the skin most of the time because we could not risk lighting a fire, and weakened by hunger, men succumbed easily to fevers, chills and fluxes.

Yet in the end, a storm was our salvation. This time the wind came from the north, bringing with it the noise of the sea, a continuous roaring like that of some wild beast. Sheltered from its main force by a thick tangle of reeds and alder, we watched as the normally calm surface of the Wide Sea became churned and flecked with foam and waves drove the Norman ships backwards, dragging their anchors as they went. The largest of their vessels, an ungainly merchant-ship, capsized and we lost no time in speeding out to dispatch those who bobbed helplessly in the water or clung to the upturned hull. None of their comrades attempted to aid them or could not, thus we took our chance and made our way west, hugging the reedbeds where possible until the familiar outline of Croyland appeared through the shifting veils of rain and we nosed our craft into the winding river that flows past the abbey.

Martin was in my boat. I felt his gaze upon me as the familiar green banks and mottled walls slid past but he did not speak. There was a great patch of raw earth in the graveyard but we had already bidden farewell to our fallen comrades: they had no more need of us. It was the living who occupied my mind: Turfrida and the daughter I hardly knew, less than an arrowshot away on the other side of the thick clinch wall.

'We will find no comfort here,' I said when Wuleric asked tentatively if we should stop. 'And I for one have had enough of the hospitality of monks!'

It was a poor and bitter jest but it struck home. A few grunted appreciatively and Thorald spat over the side. But I dared not meet Martin's eyes and a mixture of shame and remorse seemed to press upon the nape of my neck like a heavy hand as the abbey fell behind and the sedge rose high to either side.

We did not leave the river until nightfall. Weary and hungry as we were, I could not risk blundering into a band of Norman knights for I suspected the Bastard would be patrolling the land as diligently as the waterways. Twilight came early. We hid the boats in a tangle of willow carr, covering them as best we could with branches and brambles, then made our way stealthily to where the edge of the Brunneswald loomed like a black cliff though the rain and gathering darkness.

The months we had lived in the forest served us well. We found the way to our old camp without difficulty though the roar of the gale and creaking of branches overhead was enough to disconcert any woodsy. No other reason than a craving for the familiar drove me. I plodded in the lead until a red glow between the trees warned us of habitation.

The brightness of the fires dazzled us at first and I had the men fan out and draw their weapons lest enemies be encamped there. But as we crept to the edge of the clearing and saw the familiar humpies and homely squalor, we knew we were safe. We sheathed our swords and I shouted a greeting then stepped into the light, hands open and outstretched so they would know we meant no harm.

They stared suspiciously at first, women, children and men, all hollow-faced and clad in rags, but where they realized who we were, their initial hostility turned to joy. As news of our arrival spread through the camp, folk spilled from their shelters heedless of the rain and wind and gathered around us. While some went to slaughter a pig in celebration, others collected all the food they could find and we ate ravenously while excited chatter drowned out the noise of the gale. There were faces I recognized: cottars from Bourne too old and set in their ways either to bear Norman rule or join us on the Isle. Ade the Crone and Oda Crook-back were but two. As we told our tale they listened as untravelled folk hear stories of distant lands, with a childlike wonder and concentration, as if these things had happened to people and places remote from their own lives though many had had kin and friends at Cratendune. But later that night, when the crowd had dispersed after feasting on charred pig-meat, a few came to ask after the missing and we comforted them as best we could and told them to go to Thorney and Croyland lest their loved ones be among the maimed.

To a hunted man, the chance to sleep in safety comes rarely and, like my companions, I slept long past dawn, our full bellies mitigating the discomfort of the wet ground. Daylight revealed how our camp had grown into a permanent settlement. Brush shelters had been extended into substantial huts and there was even a wattle church where, Ade told me proudly, one of Ulfkil's monks came on holy days to pray and bestow blessings. Several acres of forest had been cleared to make the little plots which are the pride of every diligent cottar and the pigs which wallowed in the middens and rooted for beech mast looked fat. Maybe sixty people, a third of them children, lived there, the crone said, and so far no Norman had harassed them, perhaps, she cackled, because they feared outlaws. But then her bright, beady eyes became hooded as she asked how long we intended staying and though her voice did not change, her meaning was plain. They had known peace in the forest: with our presence, all that would change. They could not support a force of fighting men and we were too many to live by foraging without being noticed.

'Do not fear: we'll stay only until all my men are gathered,' I reassured her. 'And we shall repay your kindness with coin against the day some

Norman comes demanding geld. Let their greed be rewarded with their gold.'

We rested there for several days while the sick regained their strength and more fugitives crept in from the Isle. These included Outi and most of Harald's band. The latter had seen fierce fighting at Downham and escaped only through the valour of their leader who covered their retreat single-handed, slaying one knight with his shield before being speared in the back by two horsemen at once. I praised the dead as was his due but my thoughts were with Aelgytha, who had lost two husbands to the usurpers. Any Norman who had attempted to master her after the fall of Cratendune would have had his hands full.

It was Outi, able to blend amongst any folk despite (or perhaps because of), his lack of a hand, who brought news of what had happened at Ely after the despatch of our comrades. Untrue to his promises as ever, the Bastard had had Morcar and Siward Beorn led away in chains to imprisonment in Normandy while Bishop Athelwine was confined in the abbey at Abingdon. Most of Ely's store of gold was taken as recompense for the monks' collusion in the rebellion and a knight's fee of forty imposed. It was also decreed that the abbey's lands already confiscated would not be returned: thus was Thurstan's treachery rewarded. It was said, Outi reported with grim satisfaction, that when the Bastard entered the abbey after dealing with the prisoners, the monks were gathered in the Great Hall to eat. By the time they were aware of his presence (he had gone to pray in the minster), he had left in high wrath. After that, he ordered them to Witchford to hear his demands. In fear and shame they grovelled before him and begged mercy but his patience was at an end and he would not negotiate.

A murmur arose from the crowd gathered round to hear the tale and Outi stroked the stump of his wrist self-consciously. The rash youth had grown into a modest man though his escape from the Isle in the guise of a pilgrim was no mean feat.

'It was easy to leave,' he added, 'because they have built a causeway across the marsh and bridged the river at Aldreth. The monks are bound to maintain the crossing: Ely is no longer an island. But there is more.' He hesitated and licked his lips. 'The Bastard has returned to Cambridge but word is, he's called on the fyrd of nine shires to muster there. When they're ready, he's sworn to hunt us down, even if it takes all winter. They looked for us everywhere on the Isle. Not a cot went unsearched and many were destroyed. He's out to finish us, Hereward.'

In the silence that followed, a child's wail rose from one of the huts and a woman sang to comfort it: these sounds reminded me of all we had lost.

'Then let any man of faint heart leave now,' I said. 'For we shall use these woods as we have used the marshes, to lead our enemies such a dance they will curse the day they landed on these shores. It will take time for the fyrd to muster: let us use these days to prepare. Then we'll leave this place ere the bastards find and destroy it.' I paused and sniffed the air, sweet with the scents of wood-smoke and leaf-mould, noted the trees already turning red and gold. 'Winter approaches: few of our countrymen will have stomach for this fight. And come spring we shall know what to do!'

I spoke these last words with a conviction I did not feel but only those closest to me would, I hoped, realize their emptiness. Acer was dead; Rahere somewhere deep in the fens, eschewing the forest as was his custom; Siward the Red languishing at Croyland. Martin gave me a dark, brooding look but I knew he would not voice his doubts before the others. The rest dispersed for there were arrows and bowstrings to be made, and children were recruited to help gather rounded flints for slingstones and balters. We were an outlaw band again and must rely on such weapons as fortune brought to hand. Then Martin jerked his head towards the high ground at the back of the camp and I followed him, albeit reluctantly.

He did not stop until we reached the clump of hollies which Turfrida and I had once made our home. A ring of stones still marked the hearth but ferns had sprouted all about and the roofs of the shelters were caved and rot-blackened. Remembering the last time I had stood there, the stricken faces that had greeted me on my return from York, I was angry with him for bringing me here to remind me of my guilt.

'I am leaving.' His voice was so low, I barely caught the words; his eyes were unnaturally bright, his face strained. 'I have told you before: I will not stay and watch you slain or captured to no purpose, nor take that news to Turfrida. This fight is over, only you will not see it. Hatred has blinded you, Hereward, even to those that love you most. The choice now is between exile and submission.'

I stared at him in disbelief and he returned my gaze.

'You cannot!' There was a cold griping in my guts, unknown since as a child I overheard my parents deciding my future as an oblate: a feeling I barely recognized as fear. 'Where would you go - a known outlaw without home or kin? Or is it your purpose to betray us?'

His thin face twisted in a look of such pain I instantly regretted these words but they could not be unsaid.

'In all the years I have followed you, I have never been untrue,' he replied quietly. 'But I will not stand by and watch your demise. Lands, home, a child and now your wife and second daughter you have sacrificed to this cause: is that not enough? Must you throw away your life and those of your men also? There is nothing to be gained by any of it, not any more. Why do you not see it?'

'Traitor!' All that I could not express in words nor dared admit to myself exploded in anger, all-consuming and unstoppable. Had I reached for my sword or dagger he would have died then but we were standing so close, I needed to step backwards in order to draw Brain-biter. Instead, I grasped his throat and began to shake him as I squeezed, like a dog worrying a rat.

He did not resist but he gripped my arms, and that saved him. As his face blackened and he sagged, I seemed to see myself from the outside, mad, possessed, in the act of slaying a beloved friend, and I let go in shame and horror as if the touch of his flesh had burnt me. He fell onto his hands and knees, retching and gasping.

The great trees stood in silent witness as I knelt beside him.

'I do not release you from my service,' I said, when his breathing had steadied, then added desperately, 'Martin, stay. I need every man who can bear a weapon. You owe me fealty!'

He sat back on his heels, wiping his mouth and looked at me. There was no anger or accusation in his glance, only a tender and profound compassion which shook me to the core.

'Since the day I found you stranded on a mudflat I have loved you,' he said. His voice was harsh and cracked. He coughed but his eyes did not leave mine. 'Yet if you fight on and wish to keep me here, then you will have to bind me. I would die rather than betray you. That is fealty, Hereward.'

'A dog would not desert its master thus in his hour of need,' I muttered. 'And you have seen how the Bastard keeps his promises. You know me better, Lightfoot. How can I submit, then look Siward the Red or Aelgytha in the eye?'

'The rebellion has failed,' he answered flatly. 'You know it in your heart as well as I. It is stubborn pride which keeps you here. The only hope of beating the Normans is with Sweyn of Denmark or Malcolm of Scotland. Many of the men would follow you to join them. Or else return to exile, if not to Flanders then to Byzantium. There is much honour and renown to be won in the Varangian Guard by hard-handed fighters. If you stay here, you will die like a trapped wolf.'

At these words a memory stirred unbidden in my mind: matted white fur, curved yellow claws and teeth, the twisted bars of an iron cage and a length of broken chain, the bleeding hulk of the Fairy Bear. To dispel it, I shook my head and said savagely, 'That is the counsel my enemies would give me if they could. And I have never been afraid to die in battle. But I thought you would be with me to the end.'

Shame overtook him: his head drooped and I thought he would relent. But then he gave a shuddering sigh and lurched to his feet where he stood swaying unsteadily, his face bone-white. My fingers had left great purple-black bruises around his neck but he did not touch them as a beaten woman might have done. His hands hung like a dullard's.

'This is the end,' he said with difficulty, then turned abruptly and limped away, not back into camp but deeper into the wood. I watched until his figure was lost in the darkness between the trees, certain that he would be back by nightfall to beg pardon for his lack of faith. But twilight came and the women called us for the evening meal and he did not return.

7. The King's Peace

Martin's absence went largely unremarked save by his rivals, Erik and Leofric, who now dogged my heels like a pair of bickering curs. No doubt the men thought I had sent my most trusted companion on some errand: they were used to furtive comings and goings. Soon, in any case, they had more pressing matters to occupy their minds for our spies reported the mustering of a massive force at Cambridge. Rather than risk the discovery and destruction of the woodland camp, we moved westwards.

The Brunneswald was still one of the greatest forests in England at that time though it was fragmented by roads and the work of woodsmen. Since the coming of the usurpers, great swathes had been felled without replanting and thus turned to waste. Even after the losses at Ely, we numbered a force of over eight score fighting men and many had their women and children with them. So many could not pass unnoticed through any other type of country and the woods could provide all we needed save food, thus I resolved to pass the winter in the very heart of the forest, which was deep in Mercia.

Such a strategy had worked from the camp near Bourne when we had only the garrison at Borough and local knights to contend with but now there was a force of thousands set against us. Lest they think us daunted by their determination to find and finish us, we raided far afield and lured our enemies into ambushes, using the forest to our advantage as we had used the Fens. As always, it was the ordinary folk that suffered most, for while we slew only Normans or suspected collaborators, we burned as we went and their cots were not spared. Yet such was their hatred of the usurpers, many joined us and we welcomed them. There were few days when we did not have men wounded or sick and yet at least three bands of raiders needed to go out, to gain supplies and spread terror among our enemies, most of all to keep them guessing as to where we were.

Though our success fired the enthusiasm of those like Wuleric and Thorald, young men just realizing their full strength, I felt weary at last, a heaviness of the spirit rather than any physical ill. It was late autumn: looking up at the stars through half-bare branches, I dreaded the onset of winter when mere survival would become a hardship. And in the tedious hours of darkness, on watch or lying in unwanted wakefulness, I brooded on Martin's parting words.

A war-lord is rarely alone but it was companionship I craved, non-judgemental and unconditional, neither that of fighters who looked to me for leadership, nor the half-fearful sycophancy of camp-followers be they healers, gleemen or whores. Sometimes, when the mood was on me, I took a woman to my bed but such encounters only exacerbated the pain that nagged like a rotting tooth, a gnawing emptiness no amount of sex or bloodshed could fill. And yet a man must live as best he can while God gives him breath. Our fight continued and, as when I was a boy, anger and hatred kept me from despair and my resolve from faltering; aye and the pride which enables a warrior to endure beyond the wit and strength of ordinary men, that most of all sustained me.

We raided deep into Northamptonshire and Leicestershire in those first weeks, ravaging estates that had once been my father's. But as winter gathered we were pressed back eastwards for instead of disbanding once the foul weather began, the force set against us was strengthened by Turold's knights from Borough. Ivo Taillebois and Gilbert de Ghent had joined them.

The Bastard had gone south as was his custom at that time of year but it seemed his orders were for the campaign to continue until we were slain or taken. Gradually, sections of the Brunneswald were closed to us. Mounted patrols guarded every main road and wooden stockades were built at junctions to act as staging and rallying points, supplementing the castles which were being built on every large estate, supplied by the strongholds at Wisbech, Cambridge, Northampton and Leicester.

By the middle of November we had been pushed back to the camp near Bourne and though the folk there could not refuse us, and we paid generously for their hospitality, it was inevitable that one day we would be discovered and over-run. The force set against us still numbered several thousands and we barely three hundred. It seemed that our best course was to attack our enemies directly, to slay or take hostage their leaders. Once their Norman commanders were overcome I guessed that the levy, forced into service, would most likely desert.

Some of those that had recently joined us (including a group of Franks on whom I had imposed heavy oaths of fealty, distrusting their motives), looked dismayed when I gave my orders but the Fen-wolves grinned at each other and Gamal gave voice to our war-howl which echoed eerily between the dripping trees. He it was upon whom all our lives depended for his archers, sling and balter-men I stationed in and about the trees at the very edge of the forest where I planned to feign retreat, drawing our enemies into range and thence attacking again from the cover of the woods.

The main Norman camp was sited maybe half a mile from the Brunneswald and there was no palisade set about it: in their arrogance they had not considered defence. The tents, shelters and picket lines straggled over an area of nearly forty acres and had been set more with shelter from the weather in mind than enemy attack. Only in the centre, where the standards of Ivo Taillebois and Turold had been raised, was there any order. A rough thorn barrier had been constructed around lines of tents but less than four score men could have been camped within.

It being needful that the enemy force stayed together if my strategy was to work, we attacked at dawn. After weeks of rain and gales the morning was bright and clear but the ground was sodden still and that was to our advantage for even in full war-gear we were lightly armed compared with Norman knights and could move more swiftly, both on horseback and on foot.

The camp was barely astir when our wolf-howls rang out from the woods; barely had their guards scrambled into position when Wuleric and a picked band of thirty horsemen charged from cover, keeping just beyond arrow-shot as they circled the entire camp and galloped back to join us. Their purpose was to startle and provoke the enemy rather than inflict damage. As the poorly armed serfs of the levy jostled to form a shieldwall under the angry yells of Ivo Taillebois, and grooms ran to harness *destriers*, Wuleric's band turned and charged again, this time breaking straight through, slaughtering many of the hapless fyrd before wheeling and speeding back to the forest.

Many times this pattern was repeated, bands of our horsemen emerging from different areas of the wood while the shieldwall waited for us to engage: always our riders retreated after killing a few of their foot-fighters. Once the Norman knights were mounted, they followed eagerly, believing these small groups of horsemen to comprise all the force set against them but as they came under the shadow of the trees a hail of arrows and stones rained down upon them, felling and wounding many and turning their stallions, warhorses though they were, frantic with fear and pain until they too were brought down, legs tangled in balter-thongs.

After the first few feints, our enemies became cautious, loth to pursue us under the forest eaves and we frustrated them with little loss to ourselves. Then I saw Ivo Taillebois and Turold, their mailcoats shining silver in the sunlight, signal their standard-bearers and knew that this time they intended to unleash their whole force and crush us by sheer weight of numbers.

This was the moment I had planned for. As Wuleric drew his horsemen towards the woods and the enemy line advanced, I with three score men on one side and Thorald leading an equal number on the other, came in from the flanks, cutting them off from the camp. So swift and unexpected was our onslaught and so fierce that we caught their leaders, who had remained to direct the battle from behind, and took them prisoner, killing the horses beneath them and stripping them of weapons, helms and coifs before they had time to gather their senses.

This should have been my moment of greatest triumph yet as I forced my enemies to their knees and saw their faces, filthy with sweat yet undaunted, I felt no joy. I leant panting on my sword and looked all around, at the camp where grooms, cooks and other servants were rushing about in confusion or already fleeing across the fields, then towards the forest where my comrades were slowly falling back but fighting every inch of the way because they knew that if the Normans looked round and realized what was happening, we were doomed.

Turold, his grey eyes cold and fearless, was watching me with a strange mixture of expectation and contempt. No doubt he thought I would slay him. But meeting his steady gaze I realized that the deaths of these men would change nothing: the Bastard had no lack of knights as ruthless to replace them, though likely enough we would not be alive to see it. If the Norman force turned, I knew that Thorald's men and mine would be overwhelmed and the rest of the Fen-wolves, bound by oath and pride, would likely perish in their attempts to reach us.

A silver-chased hunting horn hung from the warrior-monk's sword-belt. Its note had sounded clear above the noise of fighting to signal the onset. I lifted it from his hip with Brain-biter's point and he looked down to see what I was doing.

'If you wish to live, call off your men.'

My voice was low, harsh with thirst and merciless. He hesitated and his left hand strayed to an ornate gold crucifix at his breast. Memory jolted me at the sight of it. Abbot Leofric had worn it, then Brand. I lunged forward and ripped it from his neck with such force, the gold loop attaching it to the heavy chain snapped. 'Do it!'

He obeyed then, lifting the horn to his lips and giving three short blasts which caused his knights to disengage immediately. Seeing their masters dismayed, the men of the fyrd threw down their weapons and some ran away. I sent Erik, who had been at my shoulder throughout the day, to tell Gamal and Wuleric that the fight was over and we had the victory. A great shout arose from all my men when that news reached them and they cheered as Thorald and I led the prisoners, blindfolded and with their hands bound behind their backs, through the ranks of stunned and exhausted Norman knights into the forest.

Along with Turold and Ivo Taillebois we captured the sheriffs of Lincoln, Huntingdon and Warwick, who had brought levies by direct command of the Bastard. All these we held hostage for their lives were surety of our safety though so disheartened were their men by the ease of our victory, if we had slain the captives I doubt any would have had the will to rejoin the fight. Indeed Outi, who remained behind to check there was no pursuit, reported that most of the fyrd dispersed that evening, leaving only the core of the Norman force to tend their wounded and the many dead scattered between camp and forest. These were thickest under the trees but less than a score of our men lay among the slain.

In the gathering darkness it seemed to take an age to reach our camp for we were all bone-weary. While relatively few of us had been killed, most bore wounds and some had to be carried on rough litters, being too gravely hurt to ride. Stars glittered between the tracery of winter-bare branches when at last we saw the glow of cooking fires; sensing feed and rest ahead, the horses quickened pace.

We gave the prisoners water and bound them firmly to trees: after their treatment of our comrades at Cratendune, we were not inclined to kindness. Realizing we would not slay him, Ivo Taillebois began to rave, shouting that my men would soon swing at a rope's end while I would be blinded and dismembered before being put to death. He spoke in his own tongue so few of my comrades understood but I swiftly tired of his abuse and gagged him so tightly he could hardly breathe. By contrast Turold sat quietly, fingering the links of the chain about his neck like a rosary though if he was praying I doubt it was for God's mercy towards us but rather the chance of revenge.

The men were already celebrating but my heart and desire were far away. My sword-arm had been wounded by a tall Breton who had fought hard and long before I bested him and though the slash had not caused lasting damage, it had bled freely and the arm was swollen. Wuleric tended it but while Martin had always used a fine bone needle he kept especially to stitch wounds, (he had a trick of greasing the thread so that it would pull out easily once the flesh had knitted), the former stable-lad was using an awl meant for mending harness and a thread pulled from someone's cloak and I had to grit my teeth as he pulled the edges of the wound together.

'You know who gave you this?' he asked cheerfully, tying a rough bandage over his handiwork. 'Thorald saw that fight: he reckons it was Ogier the Breton, erstwhile Lord of Bourne. Did you kill him?'

I shrugged. 'He didn't get up but he may have been stunned. I wasn't in the mood to wait and see. No doubt we'll hear soon enough.'

'Aye.' He sat back on his heels and in the ruddy glow of the fires, his expression was thoughtful. 'Hereward: what happens when we hand back the hostages?'

He meant no disrespect nor to convey doubt; while I was undisputed leader of the Fen-wolves, free speech, aye, and criticism where it was due, was one of our strengths, the reason we had held together for so long, bound not only by our oath of fealty but by that special comradeship that develops between brothers-in-arms. And yet I hesitated long before replying because, in truth, I did not know. We had won a great victory against all the odds, a victory that gave us bargaining power, and instead of triumph or joy I felt a kind of terror because suddenly I was uncertain of my purpose.

'I have not yet decided our terms,' I said at last. 'But the lives of Abbot Turold and Ivo Taillebois I shall not sell cheaply: there are too many scores to settle. Why, what is it, Wuleric? Are you tired of fighting?'

'I don't know.' He gave a faint smile and it was as if a mask had dropped to reveal the young man, barely more than a youth, beneath the scarred and weatherbeaten outlaw's face. 'Only look at us, Hereward: most of the oldest and doughtiest Fen-wolves are dead or maimed like Acer and Siward, and there are less of us each time we meet the enemy. Don't mistake me – we'll follow you to the end. Only it seems to me the Bastard will just send men against us until we're finished, and what will we have achieved?'

A leader has a responsibility to all his men not to expend their lives needlessly; it was this that had weighed upon my mind since leaving the Isle. Wuleric's artless candour was like the voice of my own conscience. I knew in my heart that with this victory, in which we had put a force mustered from nine shires to shame, we had the chance to make peace on our own terms: to continue fighting would, in the end, prove futile. And yet such was my bitterness as I thought this that I swung my head from side to side like a wounded beast and ground my teeth. It was only Wuleric's look of dismay that saved me from despair.

'Go and join the others. Whatever happens, today we have won a victory that will be long remembered,' I told him and he grinned and scrambled away with obvious relief to where the drinking and boasting had begun in earnest, close to where the prisoners lay.

After visiting the wounded and joining in the revelry for a while, I stole away to a little hollow, soft and springy with fallen leaves. There I wrapped myself in my cloak and lay down, desperate for some sign that would tell me what to do. The stars wheeled overhead, the fires burned to heaps of glowing embers and the raucous singing and bragging turned to a more reflective mood as weariness and mead took hold. Someone began 'The Battle of Maldon' and the slow, sonorous music seemed to echo deep within the very core of me. I felt the blood pulse thick and hot through my veins and let its flow carry my mind far away while my body seemed to sink as if the earth had opened to receive me in my grave.

'Hereward – wake up!'

The voice penetrated a stupor insidious and clinging as mire. With an effort I opened my eyes and the bright daylight seemed to stab deep into my brain. Erik was leaning over me, his face drawn and anxious.

'The King's envoy is here. You'd better see him: he and his escort are growing impatient.'

'What do you mean?' I levered myself up onto one elbow. My very bones ached and my head reeled as I moved. Realizing that I was not where I had lain down but stretched on a bed of hay and cloaks under a lean-to of sticks and hides, I sat up abruptly, gasping as the half-scabbed gash in my right arm stretched.

'It's two days since the battle,' he answered tiredly. 'We feared you would die. Ade has been tending you while Leofric' a sneer crept into his tone, 'prayed. I'll go and tell the others you're awake.'

He left me and I sank back, wondering at my weakness, angry at having succumbed so utterly to the wound-fever that I could remember little since dismissing Wuleric save a wild confusion of blood-drenched, burning dreams. And lying there, staring out at the men stirring about the camp, hearing a horse whinny, the slow deliberate strokes of someone honing a blade, sorrow settled upon me. So heavy was it, it seemed to press me into the bed like a huge and suffocating hand. A strong wind was blowing, stripping the last leaves from the branches tossing overhead; the cawing of rooks filled the air and their black shapes soared and wheeled against the flying clouds.

Our fight was over. I knew it with a clear and bitter certainty and though I groaned with disappointment, the reality of it could not be changed. I had no right to expend the lives of my comrades to no purpose: it was my duty now to negotiate terms while possession of hostages gave us power. And yet beneath my certainty lurked doubt. The Bastard had proved faithless before. Once the captives were handed over, there was no surety his side would keep the agreement.

'Thank God!' Leofric's voice, fervent and relieved, broke the run of my thoughts. He dropped to his knees in front of the shelter and began to pray. Looking at his pale, earnest face, I felt a flicker of contempt but, with an effort, forced patience on myself. I felt old and tired, longed for someone with whom I could share my doubts and fears: the down-to-earth counsel of Acer the Hard; the sympathy of Martin Lightfoot; the sagacity of Turfrida, my helpmeet, and it was no comfort that these last were estranged by my own stubbornness.

Ade, after scolding the others for disturbing my sleep, put a drinking horn to my lips and the taste of the infusion brought the lingering remnants of fever-dreams crowding into my waking mind. I pushed them aside and felt my thoughts steady as the draught took effect though the sorrow that had lodged at my very core remained. To make peace with the Bastard would not only be a betrayal of comrades like Siward the Red, to whom I had promised vengeance, but a denial of the very purpose that had seen so many friends slain, lost me my wife and children and my lands: the shame of it would linger long. And yet I knew I had no other choice but death, not only for me but all my men and they, at least, deserved the best I could gain them.

My comrades greeted me with joy when I went to meet the Bastard's emissaries later that day though the hostages, now free to look about them, glared as I passed. No doubt Turold had prayed hard for my death. As befitted a leader and last free heir of Eorl Leofric, I went clad in full war-gear save coif and helm. The weight of the mail threatened to drag me to my knees and I was hard put not to stagger as I crossed the camp to the tent put aside for the negotiations. It was, I noted with satisfaction, well beyond hearing of the hostages.

The envoys, sent directly from the King's court, were richly dressed but unarmed save for the daggers at their belts, smooth-shaven with cropped hair and guarded eyes. They stared coolly as I entered with Gamal and Wuleric at my shoulders. Erik waited unobtrusively by the door-flaps as befitted a squire. (Once Martin would have stood there and afterwards we would have discussed every detail of the meeting, thrashing out the ramifications into the early hours. Rarely have I felt so alone as then for fighting was my skill, subtle wordplay his. Yet there was no-one to blame for his absence but myself).

It was not my intention to do anything but hear the enemy's demands that day. The Normans could barely conceal their disappointment when I walked out after they had made a bald statement offering me and five comrades free passage into exile in return for all the hostages.

'Your King would sell his men cheaply,' was my only comment. 'I will state my terms tomorrow. Do they know what price their master puts on their heads?'

No doubt they had thought me a common brigand who would be glad to escape with his life: so taken aback were they by this response (I had done them the courtesy of speaking their language though they had not deigned to use mine), they did not protest until I had left the tent. Their voices sounded like the chatter of starlings. Erik made some comment and Gamal chuckled but I was in no mood for laughter. My head ached, my wounded arm throbbed from having forced it through the sleeve of my hauberk, my bones seemed to jar at every step but physical pain was easy to endure compared with the choices that lay before me. In an attempt to delay the final moment of decision, I called a full war council and sent Leofric to find Rahere for he was the eldest of the Fen-wolves though he had ever shunned the responsibility of leadership save of his own close-knit band. But he replied that he would abide by my ruling though he would not leave the Fens for any man.

In the end the negotiations lasted several days though any urgency to conclude them came not from our side but the Normans who had been ordered to find a swift resolution ere news of their humiliation sparked rebellion elsewhere. In return for the hostages and the promise of my formal submission to the King at Christmas, a substantial sum of gold, the return of land and remission of our outlawry was agreed. And I swore henceforth to be a man of peace, enacting or inciting no act of war or disloyalty to the Bastard and his officers: such was their demand. Though no written accord was made, they had brought the gold with them and that I accepted as surety of their pledge. Until the court gathered at Christmas, we would be permitted to live peacefully in the Brunneswald, unmolested by any Norman, and safe passage was assured to London where, in exchange for my oath of fealty, a writ would grant me fiefdom of Laughton and Bourne and freedom for my followers. That was the agreement, made before God in the name of the King and it was not sworn lightly or willingly on my part but because it was the best I could do for me and my men. The true price was higher than any Norman could have understood.

When all was over, we escorted hostages and envoys to the edge of the forest. The sheriffs and Ivo Taillebois seemed glad to have escaped unscathed but Turold shot me a glance of pure hate as he passed. Abbot and monk though he was, his nature was foremost a fighter's and I had shamed him: only the King's decree would force him to peace. For myself, I felt only an immense weariness as I rode back to camp with the others. Turold's resentment had not gone unnoticed and behind me I heard Wuleric, Thorald and Erik laying bets on the number of days we would be let alone. They knew as well as I that the first drop of Norman blood spilt would break the agreement, whatever the provocation.

It was but a month to Christmas and it was my hope that if we could reach court without hindrance the agreement would be secure for the Bastard had kept faith with Eadric the Wild and his kind who, having sworn fealty, had gone on to serve him. Some of those who had lately joined us dispersed to find or make trouble elsewhere once they realized I would not tolerate the slaying of any man, Saxon or Norman, nor the forcing of women for their amusement. But the remaining Fen-wolves stayed, most having, in any case, no other homes to go to until I came into my own again. And though we spent our time hunting or, when the weather was foul, sitting round the fire drinking and telling tales, we did not relax our guard. The force gathered to destroy us had been disbanded but Turold's knights were stationed at Borough and we heard that Ivo Taillebois and his men were also staying there though none knew their purpose.

'They're waiting their chance,' Wuleric said one morning as we bent over the foot of a lame horse. 'I'll wager it's the gold that lures them as much as the thought of revenge. They'll trap us into killing someone, then strike. With both forces together, they outnumber us now.'

I straightened and rubbed my arm. The wound was healing slowly and at times it itched unbearably. Wuleric let go the hoof and the horse turned its head to nuzzle his shoulder. Watching, I felt a pang of regret that I had no son like him, clear-headed and strong, compassionate yet hardy. The former stable-boy had grown into one of the most trusty and skilled fighters among us.

'Then we'll thwart their hopes and keep peace whatever happens,' I replied. 'As for the gold, that will soon be where even Turold cannot reach it. This is our chance to regain some of what the usurpers took from us: I do not mean to squander it.'

'Aye, maybe come spring we'll see the lambing at Bourne.' He grinned. 'And the girls'll be eyeing up prospective husbands at the Easter feast.' He stopped abruptly and a haunted look overtook his features. I guessed he was thinking of his sister of whom nothing had been heard since the fall of Cratendune. 'God curse them: they've ruined it all.'

'No, not all.' The conversation I had had with Toli soon after my return from exile sprang unbidden to my mind, when the Normans had seemed but a vague threat and we had talked of the Fen-folk. 'And we have not been defeated: we have negotiated a peace. We shall endure, Wuleric, believe me. There are some things the bastards cannot change and men's hearts and minds are among them.'

He stared at me uncomprehendingly and I gave a short laugh, embarrassed at having revealed too much. 'Ach, who knows: all we can do is live from day to day and make the best of it we can.'

'If they let us,' he said darkly. 'You've heard what they're calling the Bastard now? "The Conqueror." It's as if we never existed.'

A few days after this conversation, I went at last to Croyland. It was my secret wish to be reconciled with Turfrida now that her main condition had been fulfilled (albeit more through circumstance than will), but my stated purpose was to give half the ransom gold to our maimed comrades. A war leader and thegn has an obligation to those in his service yet the usual gifts of rings and weapons were of no use to the limbless or blind. And knowledge of how the gold had been gained would, I hoped, in some way compensate for the bitterness they must feel at my submission.

Not wishing to leave the camp unguarded, I took an escort of twenty and we went fully armed though our helms and shields were slung on our backs. Five of us were mounted on *destriers* with the gold packed in our saddlebags: thirty marks, equalling the amount demanded of Borough to recompense the Bastard for Brand's insult. (It had given me great satisfaction to quote this precedent during the negotiations for Turold's release). The wind blowing fitfully from the north-east bore the scent of snow and the men marched briskly. Soon the huddle of abbey buildings appeared above the bleak expanse of dying sedge and flint-coloured water. The wooden bridge rang hollow beneath our horses' hooves.

The gates in the high clinch wall were shut and we were kept waiting until Ulfkil could be found: it was a new rule that none could enter without his direct approval. The wind chilled our sweat-soaked undershirts and we blew dripping noses into our fingers or on mud-caked cloaks and cursed all churchmen while the horses tried to turn their hindquarters into the rising gale.

Without warning the gates creaked open. The abbot stood there, robes billowing in the wind. I dismounted stiffly and bowed my head in acknowledgement. In response, he exposed a long-fingered, bony hand just long enough to make the sign of the Cross before tucking it once more in his sleeve.

'We heard you have made peace,' he said, standing aside to let us pass. 'God be thanked. You are welcome, you and your men.'

My first duty was to our maimed comrades. Many of those taken to Thorney had moved to Croyland. Perhaps in each other's company they felt at ease, free from the pity of their countrymen and Norman scorn. Though they were well-housed in former stables, sickness and hunger had taken their toll, aye and the despair that affects a man reduced from the fullness of his strength to a cripple. Twelve had died since reaching the abbey. They flocked round when they realized who was there and in the expressions of my companions I saw my own pity and sorrow reflected, for our comrades were all thin and pale and their blundering movements shamed us. Though they welcomed us and some wept at the gift which would see them fed and sheltered for many years, I read disappointment and a kind of mute accusation in their faces.

Siward the Red, his stumps bound in filthy rags, was the only one who dared voice what perhaps they all felt but in fealty were bound to leave unspoken. He drew me aside, his lean face hard and blazing, to hiss, 'Have your wits turned, Hereward, to submit? You think they'll let you live in peace? For us it's finished but for you it will never end until you or your enemies are dead.' He raised his stumps, thrust them towards my face. 'This is what I got for trusting the Bastard. If you want to live, leave now while you have the chance.'

I had thought he was angry because I had reneged on my promise to avenge him and all the others tortured and mutilated at Cratendune. His earnestness shook me to the core.

'Turold and Ivo Taillebois were at my mercy and I spared their lives,' I said. 'They know that debt is worth more than gold. And,' I lowered my voice lest others overhear, 'there are few of us left now: we number barely six score. They would have hunted us like wolves until we were all slain. This way we live to fight again if Sweyn returns or the Atheling and Malcolm of Scotland finally get off their arses and move south.'

He shook his head.

'The Normans will not rest until they have broken every man, woman and child in this land,' he answered bitterly. 'But I will pray for you since that is all I have power to do. May God and all his saints and martyrs protect and spare you such an end as ours.'

He spoke without self-pity yet there was desperation in his tone. I grasped his shoulders and rocked him unresisting back and forth, working out my own frustration, whispering fiercely, 'Do not lose hope!' But recalling this afterwards, I could not tell which of us I had been trying hardest to convince.

My companions and I all knew that it was only by the contrivance of Thurstan and Athelwine (and perhaps Morcar), that we had not been trapped at Cratendune and shared our comrades' fate. Guilt made us awkward and we did not linger. As we made our way back to the courtyard where the horses were waiting, I seethed with resentment at having to betray those who had paid so heavy a price for following me. It was not until I had my foot in the stirrup, the reins gathered in my hand, that I remembered my secret purpose.

Throwing the reins to Erik, who stared after in astonishment, I strode towards the Great Hall. The abbot was just inside, presumably on his way to bid us farewell. When I wrenched open the door he stepped back involuntarily. I forced past him and the door slammed behind, sending smoke billowing from the hearth.

'Where is Turfrida?'

He regarded me steadily. There was a knowing, wary glint in his eye. It sent a thrill of fear through me that she was dead or gone. My hand went to my sword-hilt and my muscles tightened: it was a struggle to keep control.

'You could at least frame your demand in courtesy, as befits an eorl's son,' he replied calmly. 'But there is no-one called thus in this abbey save a small child who has taken her mother's name lest she forget whence she came. Your former wife is now the bride of Christ and has renounced all men, even her one-time husband. Go, Hereward, and be sure that she will pray for you.'

'I have done as she wished and made peace with my enemies,' I said, forcing out the words against an invisible hand that seemed to have tightened round my throat. 'What more must I do: crawl on my belly before them and lick their boots?'

He looked at me with a kind of stern compassion, the long-suffering patience of a kindly father admonishing a wilful child.

'Had you submitted when she asked, how many who are now dead or maimed would be alive and whole; how many widows would still have husbands, and children fathers?' He shook his head slightly. 'Were you not forced into this agreement by contingency rather than your own wish?'

Trammelled by an argument I could not counter, I simply stared. My perplexity must have been written clear upon my features because after a moment he gave a wry, almost pitying, smile.

'There is nothing for you here,' he said firmly. 'Leave now, ere you come to harm.'

I was an armed fighter, he a defenceless monk but I could no more have drawn sword upon him in that moment than sprout wings to fly: he had the better of me and knew it. I felt again the humiliation of utter helplessness I had known as a boy in the clutches of Brand and his cronies, and cold sweat bathed me.

'Go, Hereward.' His tone was gentle but commanding. 'Turfrida will not see you.'

'She is my wife!' My voice was low and harsh with a pain I was barely conscious of but which sapped my strength like a mortal wound.

'Not any more.' Ulfkil moved to the door and opened it a little, letting in a stream of raw air and the cold, rooty smell of fen. 'We reap what we sow and sometimes the harvest is bitter.' He paused, his hand on the latch and an odd, guarded look fleeted across his features. 'There was one message she entrusted to me lest you come here. She bids you remember your promise to Eadric, since Ymma has given you what she could not.'

With that he pulled open the door and I stumbled outside, senses reeling as if I had been bludgeoned. The curious glances of my waiting comrades brought me back to myself but I knew nothing would ease the ache of loss and longing that swelled within me, the rage aimed not at Turfrida but against myself. From behind, the abbot called a blessing but I did not look round. Instead I snatched my horse's reins from Erik, swung into the saddle and heeled the beast savagely away, wishing destruction on all the world, with me at its centre.

In the days that followed I rued Martin's absence most. Apart from Turfrida, he was the only one to whom I could have opened my heart. There was a rumour he had been seen at Bourne but I dismissed it as the gossip of those who envied him. As ever when my purpose was thwarted or uncertain, I grew silent and morose and would stalk alone deep into the forest or to the edge of the Fenland though I avoided places where Croyland abbey was visible. Erik and Leofric shadowed me about the camp despite my orders to the contrary but beyond its bounds my woodcraft was better than theirs. Being young they lacked patience and I would simply wait behind some tree or in a tangle of fern until they became bored and wandered back. Then I would creep from my hiding place, ashamed and resentful at being forced to act like a skulking child.

When I returned at nightfall, often soaked to the skin, exhausted and shivering, they fussed over me like old women and I did my best not to lose my temper with them. They, like the others, attributed my foul mood to the formal submission which loomed ahead like a dark cloud. We would start south within a few days so as to be sure of reaching London by Christmas.

In truth, despite my unwillingness to go, the preparations for the journey came as welcome relief from the mire of uncertainty in which I floundered. Only the faith of my comrades kept me from sinking into despair, that and the hope that my enemies would keep their word, that my lands would be restored to me and I could live in peace at Bourne. At times I even contemplated raising my son there but remembering my last sight of Ymma, I shied from the idea. I could not think of her without recalling Eadric's head stuck above his own gates; hearing her voice, husky with just-sated lust, saying 'Since you first came to our Hall, it has been you I wanted', and the memory of that first betrayal, of Eadric, Turfrida, myself, was like poison in my blood.

The day before I and a picked retinue of twenty were due to leave, Outi sought me out. It was a miserable afternoon. Gusts of sleety rain made the branches creak overhead while underfoot the camp was a morass of trampled muck. I was sitting alone, brooding as I fed a sullen fire with damp twigs, when he splashed his way towards me. He was so bundled in rags against the cold and wet, his face was hardly visible.

'I've just come from Borough.' He squatted beside the fire and pushed back his head coverings. 'Ivo Taillebois and his knights are still there. Word is, he and Turold have sworn vengeance against you. I don't know what they're planning but something's afoot: you can feel it all over the burgh. I don't like it, Hereward. I'm sure they mean to trap you.'

I snapped a green ash twig between my fingers, cast it into the fire and shrugged.

'They are bound to the agreement as am I and they fear the Bastard more: their power depends upon his good-will,' I said. 'We shall ride openly upon the road and if they attack, we shall defend ourselves as is any man's right. We are fugitives no longer but under the King's protection. They will not risk his wrath, knowing how he treats renegades. I do not fear them.'

Outi smiled grimly. 'Aye, I thought you would say as much. But if you must go, be watchful. Should you reach London alive, they will seek some way to have you slain or imprisoned. Their men talk as if you were already dead.'

'Then I will be careful,' I told him. 'But I will no longer keep to forest or fen like a fugitive. Under the agreement we are free men, or as free as any can be under Norman rule. And remember, this is not a defeat but a parley.'

He looked through the dripping trees into some indefinable distance where I could not reach him.

'Go and find something to eat and take some rest,' I said at last, to break the silence that stretched between us. 'You've done well, Outi. And don't worry: my enemies have ever found me a hard man to kill.'

'God grant your luck does not run out then,' he muttered then rose and trudged away, head bent against the sleet.

It was snowing when we left next day: it drifted silently between bare branches in big, soft flakes which did not lie long. The horses stood hunched miserably as we harnessed them. Beneath their thick winter coats their ribs stood out starkly and their flanks were sunken; we had to put pads under the saddles to make them fit. At least we had enough beasts for us all to ride and Wuleric assured me that if we kept to an easy pace and looked after them, they would get us to London. That, in the end, was all that mattered.

We left without ceremony. Those remaining behind watched in silence as we rode away. The news from Borough had spread swiftly and I do not think there was a man among them who doubted we were riding into a trap. I left Thorald with instructions to keep the camp well guarded and, if we did not return, to split the remaining gold between the Fen-wolves and disperse ere our enemies attacked. He accepted these orders without arguing but afterwards would not meet my eyes, as folk avoid the gaze of a man condemned to death.

We had reached the junction between the winding deer path we had followed from camp and Ermine Street, the line of which slashed straight as a spearshaft through the Brunneswald, when my horse shied and staggered, almost unseating me. Cursing, I shortened the reins, angry with myself because I had not been concentrating on the way, then, seeing what had startled it, pulled up so hard it shook its head in protest.

Head and shoulders mantled in snow, two figures stepped away from the trunk of the ancient oak against which they had been sheltering. The first was Rahere (he was clad in his usual leather clothes despite the cold). Seeing that I recognized him, he stopped and nodded in greeting but he did not speak as the other, who was heavily cloaked, made his way to my stallion's shoulder. Snow swirled between us: when it cleared the figure had pushed back his hood and I saw with a jolt of surprise that it was Martin. From somewhere in the darkness of the woods a horse whinnied but otherwise there was no sound but the soft whisper of settling snow all around. Martin's face, always pale, had the pallor of bone; his eyes were sunk in dark hollows as if he had not slept for days.

'Ogier the Breton and more than forty knights are waiting in ambush at the next cross-roads,' he said. 'Turold and Ivo Taillebois told him that if you reached London, the King would grant you Bourne. Not that he needed much persuading. This way they get rid of you without breaking the agreement. When you do not arrive, the King will know only that you failed to keep your word and then they will hunt down the rest of us until none are left.'

Snow had begun to lie thickly on the ground, forming a blanket across the uneven surface of the road. I looked away from Martin's thin, earnest face, unable to bear the fervour of his gaze, then asked slowly, 'How do you know this?'

'Ogier is an ignorant bully, like most of the Bastard's force,' he replied and his tone was both defensive and defiant. 'I offered him my services as scribe and interpreter. He speaks no word of English and accepted gladly, seeing in me both servant and a new source of amusement.' He hesitated and licked his lips before adding quietly, 'He is a man with cruel taste in entertainment and the nights are long this time of year. He was unwilling to let me go, else I would have come sooner.'

Rahere, his gaunt face unreadable, leant forward and spat while Martin took a deep breath and grasped my horse's bridle so that I could not ride away. 'Hereward – this time you must listen!'

'What were you thinking of?' I spoke with more feeling than I had intended, appalled that my closest friend should have so abased himself. 'I thought you far away.'

'Where would I go?' He gave a wry smile. 'It was in my mind that a spy in Ogier's household might prove useful. It is nearly all Normans and strangers at Bourne now: the few that knew me kept silent.' He paused and looked into the trees where a dark shape shifted slightly. 'And I thought also that if the King kept his word and ceded the estate to you, it would be as well to have a friend there in case of treachery.'

After the violence of our parting, his loyalty smote my heart. Lost for words, I followed his gaze, saw the movement was that of a tethered horse made restless by the presence of others. 'Yours?'

'It is now.' His voice was oddly flat. 'I took it as payment for services rendered. I am not returning to Bourne.'

'Then come with us.' It was part order, part invitation and afraid he would refuse, I looked for Rahere, intending to speak with him while Martin made his choice. But where the tall Fen-man had stood were only footprints, a trail leading into the darkness of the forest, filling rapidly with snow. For an instant I wondered if he had really been there at all, so swift and complete was his disappearance.

'Where are you going?' Martin spoke, I think, more from hope than any real belief I had changed my mind: he knew me too well. Yet still he voiced the question and I felt a rush of affection for him, lifelong friend and servant, who had risked all to give me this warning and was now, I was sure, ready to ride with me to whatever fate awaited us.

'We go to London by the swiftest way,' I replied. 'I have never run from any challenge, even one that comes through treachery. Yet I would be glad of your company.'

For a moment he was utterly motionless, considering. From behind I heard Erik's disgruntled mutter and a horse pawed the ground. Then Martin let go my stallion's bridle.

'My place is with you,' he said simply. 'If only to take news of your death to those that love you still.' And with that he turned and went to fetch his horse.

By the time we set off, Martin's news had, of course, reached all twenty and it is a measure of their loyalty and trust in me that not one faltered. Aye, and it was largely for their sakes that I bade Gamal Longbow and two other skilled archers to skirt round on foot, so as to come upon the ambush from the sides. I suspected that Rahere might have thought likewise so told them to use the signals long employed by the Fen-wolves to keep track of one another on the hunt, whether the quarry was beast or man. They slipped off their mounts (which we took in our midst, there being nothing suspicious in bringing spare beasts on such a journey), and within moments had disappeared into the wood while we urged our horses on. The flakes were coming more thickly now and the snow was already fetlock deep on the verges while on the road hidden ruts made the going almost impossible.

A strange calm descended, perhaps partly due to the snow which laid its silence on us all. No-one spoke. There was only the suck and splosh of our horses' hooves in the mud, a snort or curse when an animal slipped or pecked, the dull clink of harness and bits. We rode hunched over our pommels against the weather, felt the breath condense clammily on our beards, let the reins hang loose through numbed fingers and, as the horses plodded stoically on, wondered if Martin was mistaken or the Normans had tired of waiting and were even now drinking and boasting beside a blazing fire in my father's hall.

The snow and delay had disoriented us. When we came to the great oak at the cross-roads marking the edge of Barholm Hundred, they were waiting. They were heavily cloaked against the cold and wet, their *destriers* fat and glossy beside our half-starved mounts. Their breath and that of their horses streamed out in great plumes: they loomed like giants in the mirk. As I rode forward, pulling my horse to a stumbling halt a spearthrow from where the Breton waited beneath the spreading branches, more horsemen closed in from the side-roads and the woods behind. I counted swiftly: they numbered fifty-two. Some bore maces and I knew them for Turold's men, warrior monks bound to slay without spilling blood. Once we were surrounded, they drew rein and a few mocked us. Though their speech was all in French, the tone needed no interpretation. My men had instinctively drawn together. I growled: 'Wait: remember what rests on peace' and tried to ignore the insults which grew more personal as we maintained our silence.

I do not know what Ogier had expected. Perhaps he thought the mere blocking of our way would goad us into action. Steel gleamed from beneath his hood; from either side of his nose-guard his eyes appraised us with a mixture of contempt and disbelief.

'I am waiting for my road to be free,' I said at last, in my own tongue. I had had enough of pandering to Norman ignorance and was resolved that from now on no word of French would pass my lips.

He looked puzzled for a moment then spurred his stallion so that it bounded forward. After a couple of strides he reined it in so brutally that it half-reared and bloody froth dripped from its mouth.

'You have something of mine in your possession.' He jerked his thumb at Martin who, although unarmed save for his long dagger, rode in his usual place at my side. 'A horse-thief and, it seems, a spy also. Hand him back so that we can hang him.'

'He is neither bondsman nor vassal though he has long been in my service,' I replied. 'And he took the horse in part payment for the abuse he suffered under your roof. He owes you nothing.'

Ogier stared while a lanky youth, his beardless face pinched with cold beneath a cape of marten-skins, drew rein alongside and murmured in his ear. When he understood what had been said, the Breton let out a great guffaw.

'As you took the ransom of Scaldemariland after Baldwin's death?' he sneered. 'And what service does he give you that you value him so highly? But maybe with you he plays the master: that would be more in keeping with what I've heard.'

A look of anguish settled on Martin's face; he opened his mouth as if to speak but at a stern glance from me, shut it again and bent his head. Snow swirled and the Normans chuckled together but my men kept their silence though I sensed their anger grow with each passing moment.

'I am travelling to London under the King's protection,' I said grimly. 'By what right do you seek to stay me? We have offered you no challenge or insult. Let us pass.'

He laughed. 'You think the Conqueror cares if you reach his court alive? The outlaw who has constantly mocked and harassed him, who has cost us thousands of lives? If I bring him your head in my game bag, he will thank me.'

'Abbot Turold pledged peace between us, along with Ivo Taillebois and the other hostages,' I replied. 'That was an oath made before God, in the King's name and witnessed by his men. I have no desire to fight you nor will it serve any purpose. Let us pass.'

These words took some time to translate (I wondered what the interpreter might be adding), and for a moment Ogier looked uncertain. Then one of his knights, a Warwick man by his accent, shouted, 'Well if he won't fight for his honour or his fancy-piece, how about we set to anyway? The sooner the job's done, the sooner we get back to the pig-sty his father built and the whores we got at Cratendune!'

Before Ogier could react, his men urged their horses forward while I felt the eyes of mine fixed upon me, awaiting my word. They had already formed a tight circle, spears facing outwards but the Norman lances were longer: it would be a bitter and bloody fight but it would not last long. My horse shifted uneasily beneath me. I prayed with all my heart that Gamal and Rahere had not been intercepted, held up my hand. 'Wait!'

So commanding was my tone that the Normans pulled up and looked round as if uncertain who had spoken. The Warwick man began to speak again but this time Ogier, perhaps sensing his authority slipping, shouted for silence.

'My bowmen surround you,' I said, speaking slowly and clearly more for the benefit of my own men than our enemies. 'At the first blow against us they will bring down your horses and then we'll slaughter you like pigs. But I say again: I have not asked for this fight. Let us pass and I swear no-one will ever hear of this encounter.'

Dismay fleeted across the Breton's features as his gaze swept the surrounding woods and fields, all veiled by falling snow. 'I see nothing. It is a brigand's trick. If you have archers here, prove it!'

I looked him in the eye, sensed his doubt. The *destriers* jostled together and the knights lowered their lances. Ogier glanced uneasily into the swirling snow.

'What are we waiting for?' The Warwick man urged his horse forward. He was a thick-set lout who sat his stallion like a sack of meal but it was as if the iron helm and Norman hauberk had imparted some of his masters' arrogance. When Ogier did not answer, he spat at me and made an obscene gesture. 'Don't you realize it's over, you and your lot? We'll piss on your corpses and come spring we'll do the same to the rabble in Scotland. You're finished!'

I disdained to look at him but saw Ogier's features harden, knew that to save face he would order the attack. The touch of snow was like a cool caress as I tipped back my head and gave our wolf's howl, willing the hidden bowmen to understand.

To make few seem many is a skill learned by all successful raiders and the Fen-wolves were masters of the craft. We had been together a long time: they guessed my mind and answered straightaway. The Normans looked about in confusion as the paean rose first from one direction then another, heart-rending, defiant, promising death.

I unsheathed Brain-biter with slow deliberation and rested the sword on the front of my saddle as the cry, haunting and terrible, faded into the muffling snow-quiet. Ogier and his knights stared at me. Even the Warwickshire loudmouth seemed disconcerted.

'I have been forced to live as a hunted man these past years: did you think I would walk blindly into so crude a trap?' I asked. 'You will gain nothing by fighting us but death. And when the King returns the lands usurped from me still I will not fight you, a mere bought butcher, for what is mine by right.'

I caught a glimpse of starting eyes beneath Ogier's iron helm as I tugged my horse round and rode straight towards the line of horsemen that blocked the road south. Without orders, his knights gave way and I urged my mount to a trot. My men followed closely, spears held ready.

'Go then!' Ogier's voice was laden with scorn. 'Then I can boast of how the renowned Hereward, last hope of a cowardly and craven people, ran away with his tail between his legs to crawl before his sworn enemies: one cringing cur amid a whining pack. Now you have no monk's skirt to hide behind, you are not so brave, wolf's-head. Why, even your wife has abandoned you from shame!'

'Liar!' The other insults I had borne with patience but this I could not ignore. Unwittingly he had struck at the doubt which lurked at the very heart of me, the feeling that to submit was, after all, an admission of defeat more complete and humiliating than the fall of Cratendune, a failure that could never been redressed, that meant all our efforts had been in vain and the suffering of friends like Acer and Siward, needless. I wrenched my horse round and forced it back against the mass of my own riders who were bunched close behind.

'Very well, you shall have your fight.' My voice was harsh with barely contained fury. 'You against me, Ogier, one on one, no others. And whatever the outcome, the King will never hear of it. What say you?'

Martin had somehow managed to turn his horse alongside mine. He reached out to stay me then, seeing my face, withdrew his hand. I registered his stricken expression but paid it no more heed than his agonized whisper: 'Hereward, no! Have you forgotten what's at stake?' My knees bumped against those of my comrades who, in confusion and dismay were also trying to turn. I shoved horses' heads and quarters aside until at last there was clear space before me. Ogier was waiting, he and his horse still as a statue while his men withdrew to give us room. His eyes were narrowed and suspicious but as I drew rein, he inclined his head slightly in acknowledgement.

'Agreed.' There was grudging respect in his tone. 'One on one and your men will be permitted to carry your corpse to the midden unhindered.'

'As your curs may gather your remains for the fattening of your swine.' An exchange of insults was usual, almost ritualised, before single combat: as we spoke, we were each surveying the ground. A man on foot has no chance against a man on horseback I had told my fighters often enough but on this treacherous, part snow-covered, patch of churned mud and slush the reverse was true: I had no wish to end my life trapped beneath a struggling horse. I balanced my sword across my thighs as I put on coif and helm, then dismounted. After a moment's consideration, Ogier came to the same conclusion, clambering off his *destrier* and handing its reins to the Warwick man. Martin, in silence, unslung the shield from my back and freed me of my heavy cloak, ignoring the snide comments of those Normans who had seen him at Bourne. Disapproval was evident in his every movement but he knew me too well to attempt dissuasion. When he had finished, he stepped back to join the others, many of whom had also dismounted. They had withdrawn to leave a clear area maybe a spearthrow in diameter of which they defined one half, our enemies the other. None of the Normans had dismounted and their horses, facing into the snow which was now being driven by a rising wind, tossed their heads and shifted restlessly. Even as I tested the ground with my feet and brought shield and sword to fighting readiness, I felt their menace.

Ogier had kept his sword sheathed and taken a great spiked mace from one of Turold's men. He was taller than I and had the longer reach. I knew his purpose clearly as if it were my own: to strike me to my knees and then finish with a crushing back-blow to the face. As he stood hefting the weapon and muttering obscenities designed to goad me into rash attack, I circled him warily, trying to get him facing into the snow, my feet sliding in the morass. Used to fighting from horseback or commanding from behind his men, Ogier followed my movements with careful concentration. Our breath smoked in the chill air; the men had fallen silent, awaiting the onset.

Before his knights, Ogier had more to lose than me: the Fen-wolves knew my method of fighting so well, they understood why I waited. With an incoherent yell, he launched himself forward, swinging his mace and bringing it down in a blow that would have felled an ox. But I twisted away and the mace struck the ground with a force that sent up a great splash of slush, and stuck there.

Ogier had stepped forward with the momentum of the blow and was forced to half-turn to tug the weapon free. As he did so, I brought Brain-biter down between his neck and shoulder. Any ordinary man would have dropped to his knees under such a blow but the Breton was tougher than most. He stumbled but did not fall and as I sprang after, slipping in the mud, he spun round. I had no choice but to parry his mace with my sword.

At the shock of our weapons meeting, a searing pain shot through my right arm: for a terrible instant I thought the bone had shattered. But my hand still gripped Brain-biter's hilt. Gritting my teeth, I whirled the sword two-handed over my head, crying aloud as I brought it down upon Ogier, who off-balance from the momentum of his strike, had slipped and was struggling to recover. Somehow he brought his mace up again and this time, as iron and steel crashed together, my sword snapped and I stumbled to my knees with the force I had put into the blow. It was like taking a step and finding that what looked like solid earth was, in fact, a void.

A great cheer rose from Ogier's men. Brain-biter's blade had broken a hands-breadth from the cross-piece. It was useless even as a dagger. In that moment time seemed to slow: I knew I was closer to death than I had ever been. And I felt no fear but rather bitterness that after all it should end like this, dying at a usurper's hands because I had been untrue to myself and those who followed me. Then, as so often in my life, anger saved me: the self-hatred kindled by Brand's cruelty long ago fanned to a consuming fire. As Ogier, who had paused to savour his triumph, looked towards my comrades and began to laugh, I lunged to my feet.

My back was towards my men. I heard their agonized shouts as, half-blinded by snow, I looked for another weapon. Then the Breton was upon me, so suddenly that I had no time to scramble away from the falling mace, could only drop the useless hilt and meet the blow with my shield, bracing it with both hands, hoping it would not split. It held, more because Ogier slipped as he struck than any intrinsic strength in the leather-cased oak, and so the blow was a glancing one. The weight of the weapon slewed him round and he staggered like a drunkard.

This was my chance. I leapt after him, pulling my arm from the shield-straps and, with all the strength I could muster, brought the iron-rimmed shield edge down on his neck. Under the force of that blow he pitched forward. The mace dropped to the ground and he fell sprawling, then lay still. His head was twisted sideways and chain-mail of his coif had been driven into his flesh but though his eyes were closed, he was still alive. His fingers clutched and opened feebly. He groaned.

The raw air seared my lungs as I picked up his mace and threw it beyond his reach. My right hand was slippery with blood from where my half-healed wound had burst open. I bent to wipe it on his surcoat, then unsheathed his sword. It was a fine weapon, damascene-bladed with runes marked on cross-piece and pommel. Some Viking must have carved them, perhaps a man who had served alongside Harald Hardrada in the Varangian

Guard, homesick for the wild North amid the splendours of Byzantium. I wondered if it was the same man's corpse Acer had plundered, remembered my friend's joy in the sword, knew that if I could slay Ogier thrice-over it would not bring Acer back or Cole One-Hand or the countless others who had suffered at the Breton's hands. My men were shouting for the death-blow while Ogier's had fallen silent, but the hatred that filled me could not be so easily appeased.

'One day I will hang you from the gates of Bourne.' My voice shook with loathing. Ogier was struggling to rise, hampered by the clag and the weight of his mail. I booted him in the side to keep him down, spat upon him, and, as he writhed and moaned, turned to rejoin my men.

Next moment, a blow from behind drove me to my knees. The jar of the impact numbed my right shoulder and arm; the sword dropped from my grasp. Shocked and half-stunned, I could not move. Horses loomed, there was a flurry, a squeal and a spray of blood, then hands grasped me and pulled me away. I snatched up the sword with my left hand. The air was full of angry shouting, the suck and splosh of hooves, the howling of wolves. In the confusion, I had just time to realize that it was Martin who had pulled me to safety through a pool of bloody slush, that two Normans lay there: Ogier and another whose slashed throat gaped like a second mouth, then I was bundled onto my horse and we were galloping back along the road, the horses pecking and sliding, clods of mud and snow flying from their hooves. Dazed from the blow which, had I not been turning, would have struck me on the head, I clung onto the sword and my stallion's mane with my left hand as best I could and prayed that neither horse nor I would fall.

That lurching, stumbling ride was like something from a nightmare. Waves of sickness swept over me and I could not tell whether the blots whirling before my eyes were snowflakes or the blindness that comes before a man loses his senses. Many times I felt myself sway in the saddle and it was only Martin's hand and voice that kept me there. But at last we were off the road and the stillness of the forest enclosed us. The others dismounted to rest and breathe the horses and an eerie calm descended. Great clouds of steam rose from beasts and men alike; rooks cawed, their black shapes stark against the snow-laden branches and lowering sky; my men walked in silence, heads bowed. Martin, who had been at my side all along, led my horse and his but, like the rest, he did not speak.

That there was no pursuit was due entirely to the skills of Gamal Longbow and Rahere who, with the other bowmen, kept our enemies pinned down. The wolf-howls had been theirs, intended to stop the Normans following for fear of being shot from behind: lest the reality of the threat be doubted, they felled three *destriers* in the first moments of our retreat. After that, the knights formed a defensive circle around the fallen who were lifted onto hurdles to be carried back to Bourne. When the bowmen returned at nightfall, they were still arguing over whose arrow had struck the Warwick renegade's mount in the eye, bringing it crashing down with him trapped beneath, but sensing the mood in camp they soon quietened.

'So much for peace then,' said Rahere when we gathered round a blazing fire that evening. We had feasted on a sheep supposedly lost in the snow on Bourne lands but the celebration was forced for no-one underestimated the significance of what had happened. The blizzard had stopped but every-so-often we all started when a branch snapped or lumps of snow crashed to the ground. All those that followed me were there save Gamal and his band who, after eating, had taken it upon themselves to keep watch. ('Whatever you decide, we're with you,' he had told me. 'Therefore there's no need for us to debate the issue.')

Now, as I sat on a fallen log covered with deerskins, watching my men, the eldest dour, the younger animated by a mood of reckless defiance, I felt immeasurably weary. My head pounded and my right arm and shoulder ached (the feeling had still not fully returned to my fingers), while the re-bound wound throbbed and itched, yet my mind was clear. As the mead passed round and those who had been there began to relate (and embellish), the tale of my fight with Ogier and their part in the retreat, my thoughts returned to another night of drinking and boasting: the eve of our journey south to join Harold Godwineson's force, the greatest ever mustered on English soil, the might that would rout the Normans and end that threat forever. Such hope we had had, buoyed by our victory at Stamford Bridge, knowing our King matchless in leadership and valour but since then we had lost everything save our resolve and the pride which keeps a man fighting on when all else has failed.

I waited for a lull in the talk and, painfully, unsheathed my sword. The long, finely-honed blade glittered in the firelight as if wrought from flame and all eyes turned towards me. An expectant hush fell as I held the weapon up for a moment then set the point on the ground between my feet, my hands resting on the pommel.

'As Rahere has said, we now know what kind of peace we can expect from the Normans,' I told them grimly. 'Whatever agreement we make with the Bastard, the likes of Ivo Taillebois and Turold will not rest until I, at least, am imprisoned or dead. We have gold to pay weregild for the slain man ten times over but our enemies will argue that by the spilling of Norman blood we are outlawed and they will hunt us down.' I paused, looked at the circle of faces, some eager, most weary but all hanging on my every word, and took a deep breath before continuing, 'Therefore it is in my mind to go north, to join King Malcolm and the Atheling in Scotland. It seems the Bastard has designs on that land also and there lies the only chance of mustering a force great enough to fight and drive the Normans back. If we stay here, we shall find no peace, nor can we fight an open war. The time of the Fen-wolves is over.'

Stunned silence followed this speech. The men looked askance at one another and some shook their heads resignedly. Then Martin, who had been standing quietly in the shadows, stepped into the circle. He pushed back his hood and his face was stark in the flickering light, his eyes unreadable.

'It was I slew the man,' he said. 'Maybe if I went before the King and submitted to his judgement, he would still honour the agreement. I was not even here when the oath was sworn.'

'How long do you think before Ogier or another of Turold's cronies sticks an arrow in Hereward's back, even if he is granted a pardon and land?' Wuleric asked scornfully. 'Do you want to live the rest of your life looking over your shoulder lest some enemy is there? Na — we learned their intent today and it's a dead wolf that having escaped the trap once, puts his head in a second time. Did you not learn enough of Ogier at Bourne to know what kind of men these are? They do not understand the meaning of honour.'

Martin's face twisted, whether from anger or hurt I could not tell, but his gaze was locked with mine.

'Martin, without your intervention I would be dead,' I said. 'And we did not choose that fight. Yet Wuleric is right. We may have lived like wolves but I've no wish to die like one.'

A murmur of bitter laughter ran round the assembly but in the faces now turned mostly to the fire, I read a kind of grim acknowledgement. They were fighting men, pragmatists: they understood well enough what threats we faced.

'Then when should we leave, and how?' Martin's head was uplifted. Suddenly he seemed surer of himself than at any time since going to the Isle. Erik and Leofric, who had ever snickered and exchanged jealous comments behind his back, watched him with grudging respect. He had pulled down and slain my assailant while they stared in shocked disbelief, and they felt their failure like a wound.

'Even with Rahere to guide us, I doubt we can slip our ships unnoticed past the castle at Wisbech and even the Vikings do not venture on the sea-road this time of year,' I replied. 'Therefore we shall go by land and we will leave while most Normans of note are at court, say in three days. I do not think Ogier's men will attack us here or they would have already done so. But,' I rose to my feet to give my words greater emphasis, 'I claim no right of command over any of you. You have all fulfilled your oaths and upon those who wish to stay there is no dishonour. The ransom gold we still possess will be split between all who were at that fight and that will be my last act as war leader until we set out upon the road.' I paused, then added, 'And if any believe me a poor gift-giver after all we have endured, blame Norman greed and Viking treachery!'

'If you think we were fighting for gold, you must have lost your wits along with Brain-biter!' Outi called. 'Like it or not, we're coming with you.' He hesitated, grinned wildly. 'After all, what have we to lose?'

'You'll likely never see homes or kin again,' I warned, overwhelmed by their steadfastness, the eager mood that had overtaken young and old alike. 'I can promise nothing but hardship and fighting, and our enemies have not changed.'

'It'll be like old times then.' Thorald leant forward and spat into the fire. 'Anything's better than rotting here while the Normans destroy the little that's left of our world. No, we've no choice really.' He paused and looked at me intently, suddenly serious. 'They never meant to keep that agreement, did they?'

'It was a fool's hope,' I replied evasively, 'aye, and fools are rarely rewarded. Perhaps if the King had been there, they would have been forced to it. But I do not think the Normans want peace until every one of our people is under their yoke, nor will they rest until they have achieved it.'

'That will never happen,' Wuleric broke in fiercely. 'Not while I live, or any who remembers what it was like before. God curse the bastards!'

'Listen.' With that uncanny ability he possessed to move unseen, so that his figure seemed almost to materialize from the leaping shadows cast by the flames, Rahere stepped into the circle. His face in that lurid light was like something hewn from wood, its lines harsh and uncompromising; his eyes gleamed like polished stones. 'The time of the Normans will end as have those of the Vikings, the Angles and Saxons, the Romans and the Celts before them. My people, the Gyrwas, the folk of the marsh, have endured the invaders as a withy bends in the flood tide and though each time we may have changed a little, we are still here. We remember the deeds of our fathers and their fathers and their fathers before them, beyond memory into legend. Homes may burn and men may die but only when the tales of their lives, told in their own tongue, are lost forever are a people wholly defeated.'

An astonished silence followed this speech: few had heard the usually taciturn Fen-man speak for so long or with such passion. And he, sensing this, gave a wry, strangely self-conscious smile wholly unlike his customary wolf's grin, and stepped back into the crowd.

'Out of field, out of fen, out of forest we rose - '

The words came low at first, half-chanted in the rhythm of a saga: the voice was Thorald's. He did not move from where he sat cross-legged close to the fire but as the flow of the poem took hold, he raised his head and stared into the glowing core as if to draw inspiration from it:

' - putting fear behind us. Foe fled before us:
hard-handed death-dealers, wolf-howling warriors,
fierce in fealty; our swords glittered in the sunlight.
By the sea-road from the south the usurpers came:
iron-clad, cold-hearted: none could withstand them.
Darkness fell, raven gorged, blood soaked the land;
former friends forsook us: we stood alone.
Grimly we fought them, the cruel-handed Normans,

rivers ran with gore, fire ravaged fen
till churchmen betrayed us, craven-hearted cowards:
camp burned; kindred died; captives were maimed;
ships bore us to safety: bitter was that fate.
The knights of nine shires by our cunning defeated,
offered false peace, masked treachery with gold;
sent mace-wielding renegades, men without honour,
to trap and slay us when we rode to keep faith.
Not for nothing did wolf's howl sound then:
arrows' flight stayed them while we slipped away.
Steadfast, undaunted, hardy in hatred,
to fight on in another land, another day.'

As he finished, Thorald's gaze swept the circle, his expression one of half-defiant expectancy. Yet though the composition was crude and the metre rough (he might even have been making it up as he spoke), it struck a chord in all of us. A murmur of appreciation arose as at the conclusion of one of the ancient lays told by a skilled gleeman.

'Aye, that's the kind of thing I mean,' said Rahere after a long silence. 'Well done, lad. "Cattle die, kindred die; all men are mortal. But there is one thing that never dies: the fame we leave behind."' He paused, then added sardonically, 'Don't forget to put some names in next time, eh?'

There was a faint ripple of laughter but it was respectful, without envy or malice. A reflective mood settled as each remembered the fallen and all that had been lost since the invasion yet it was no maudlin humour. The self-belief that rests with a fighter's pride; the trust existing between comrades who hold each other's lives precious as their own, fierce and intimate in its way as that between lovers, these had been re-kindled beneath the snow-laden branches and looking at the lean war-weathered faces around me, I knew they would not easily be extinguished. Aye, that night my faith also was renewed: with such men alongside me, I could not give up. Faint-heartedness ill becomes a fighter who can still stand and wield a weapon, whatever the odds against him.

In the morning a more sombre mood lay on the camp but if anyone's resolve had faltered during the night, none dared admit it before his comrades. The wind had swung to the west, bringing a thaw and scudding grey clouds: melting slush soaked everything as we prepared for the journey.

I had slept fitfully, my arm and shoulder aching, made restless by dreams of the sack of Bourne and the attack on the reed-cutter's settlement; guilt-ridden at how I was abandoning Turfrida and Godgifu; reneging on my promise to Eadric, leaving Ymma and my son unprotected. I was checking the horses when Martin (who had been watching me with grave concern), wandered over.

'They need rest.' He put a hand on the neck of the stocky grey he had taken from Ogier. 'It was hard work for them yesterday.'

'The roads will force us to easy stages, at least at first,' I replied, frowning at a deep cut where a *destrier* had over-reached. Now the decision was made, I was filled with a strange urgency and from the bustle about the camp, it seemed that most of the men felt likewise. 'We need pack-beasts more than war-horses: we can lead them at the start.'

'Aye.' He looked searchingly at me. 'What about Turfrida, and the children?'

I bent to lift the hurt animal's foot so that my hair fell forward to hide my face. 'I have no wife and Godgifu will be safe enough where she is. As for the other: Ymma already has a guardian it seems.'

He waited until I was forced to let the hoof go and straighten.

'I have known you a long time,' he said. 'When you are in the north, you will rue your hardness. Leave someone here to watch over them, who can help tend the maimed at Croyland. And Rahere also will guard them from Norman guile, Godgifu especially. Young girls do not stay children forever.'

'Rahere?' Martin's eyes held mine steadily but there was something in them, a kind of barely veiled hurt that warned me not to probe too deep. 'That was his farewell then, last night?'

'Aye.' He gave a faint, guarded smile. 'And he bade me tell you that while he lives, the time of the Fen-wolves is not quite over. I think the Normans will go warily in the marshes for the next few years.'

There was a note of regret in his tone he could not conceal and he glanced away like one overcome by sudden grief. I put a hand on his shoulder. 'Martin – you could stay. Is that what you meant?'

'Ach no, I've already made that choice.' He pulled away and stood looking at me with an expression that somehow conveyed both sorrow and amusement. 'But did you never wonder what I was doing so deep in the fenland all those years ago? I was strong for my age and tall but I could never have carried you all the way to Laughton unaided.'

With that he turned on his heel and strode away, leaving me astounded that he had never spoken of it before. Only long after did I realize how even then he sought to protect me, knowing what I had suffered at my uncle's hands. I thought of him as steadfast friend and loyal servant: what he desired I could not have given nor would he have asked, knowing my nature. And yet as I watched him exchange words with Outi, his demeanour easy as usual, I wondered at his devotion, unconditional and unrewarded save by the love that grows between those who have been comrades since childhood. Maybe, after so long, he had learned to be satisfied with that alone. The faithful hound is true even to an unjust master.

In the end I chose Leofric to stay behind, not only for Martin's sake but because he could assimilate himself easily into the life of the abbey. He looked at me like one condemned to death as I gave him his orders but when I added sternly that he was being entrusted with the care of those most dear to me and would answer for the well-being of our maimed comrades, he realized this was no light or demeaning duty. It was not long before he was boasting to Thorald and Erik of how he had been especially chosen for the task.

The following dawn, five days before Christmas, we left. Leofric stood watching as the long line of fighters passed, some leading scrawny horses loaded with supplies and weapons, their women and children trudging behind as was the custom, many bent under packs bulky as those borne by the beasts. So used were they to a fugitive life, these made no complaint: endurance was etched into their gaunt and weather-beaten faces. To come through the day without harm, ending it with food, shelter and their man alive beside them was all they asked.

'God grant no Norman crony spies us,' Martin remarked as we came to where the path reached the edge of the forest on a high ridge east of Ermine Street. 'There are many castles between here and Scotland.'

'Not the way we shall take.' It was a clear, still morning though a distant line of cloud presaged rain from the south. 'And we are a fighting force of more than a hundred. If they see us they will have little choice but to let us pass. The fyrd of nine shires could not beat us: if we keep to the woods and wild hills, we shall be safe enough.'

I was speaking with only half my mind, my eyes on the great expanse of fenland which spread to the south and east, becoming lost at last in a grey haze which veiled the low hills of Norfolk and the Isle of Ely. Water glittered between winter-darkened stands of sedge; the castle at Wisbech stood like a jagged tooth along the curved line of the great embankment built by the Romans to keep out the sea. Somewhere in that world of marsh, reedbeds and winding waterways nestled Croyland. I thought of Turfrida and wondered whether she also was stayed at that moment by a sudden yearning for all that had been and now was lost forever. But no man can change the past, nor should he dwell upon it until a time comes when nothing else remains to him. I eased the shield-strap across my shoulder and set my face to the north.

Epilogue: Note appended to the manuscript by Leofric the Deacon.

It has long been my intent to collect all the acts of famous Englishmen from ancient times to today, for the edification of readers and, in these days of Norman rule, to preserve something of those deeds in our own language lest our history be forgotten. Of these men, the most renowned is Hereward, son of Eorl Leofric, my leader and our hope in the troubled times following the fall of Harold Godwineson, whose fate after leaving this district was unknown save for rumour and speculation. (Hearing that a man of the same name was living peacefully in Warwickshire, I went there but was disappointed). Therefore, following the death of his wife, Turfrida, I took it upon myself, with the abbot's blessing, to seek out my former lord, both to give him the sad tidings and to write down his tale in full.

Of the hardships I endured there is no need to tell: the man I sought proved elusive as when he was an outlaw, though not through his design. After many months, by perseverance and the grace of God, I discovered him imprisoned, not here in England but at a castle in the heart of Normandy. (The name of which I swore to keep secret, else I should have been refused entry and my long endeavour would have come to naught)

It was with great reluctance that I was permitted to see the prisoner but the name of Turold carries weight in that land and at last I was escorted to a dark and noisome hole where he lay fettered. That this was the right man, I was sure since his guards grumbled that in all the years he has been in their care, no action of theirs has induced him to speak a word of French though it is clear he understands it well. And remembering a vow he made when he was my war-leader, I knew I had reached the end of my search.

He did not know me and, truth to tell, nor would I have recognized him if outward appearance were the only clue to a man's nature. Long confinement in darkness and solitude has been a sore trial to one so bold and vigorous in action and decision: he was grievously diminished in body and, it seemed at first, in mind, so that I wondered if my mission was doomed to failure after all. Yet praying for guidance to Jesu, saviour and healer of us all, I spoke gently in our tongue and then he stirred and looked around like one waking from a dark dream. When I told him of his wife's death, he turned his face to the wall and was silent so long I was afraid but I reminded him we are all mortal and, with God's mercy, they would one day be re-united. And then he revived, muttering words that Rahere had spoken long ago in the Brunneswald, and agreed to tell his tale.

Of his early years however, his exile as a youth; the slaying of the Fairy Bear which earned him the enmity of his godfather; his exploits in foreign lands where he learned his skill in arms and renown as a leader, he would not speak, saying the latter had been recorded by his patrons and it was not for those deeds that he wished to be remembered in his own land. Nor did he tell willingly of the events following his departure from our region, and became sullen and angry when I pressed him. Eventually I learned that he and his men reached Edinburgh in March 1072 after an arduous journey in which many were lost to cold, sickness and the mishaps which may befall any traveller. (Not least among these was the loss of his servant, Martin Lightfoot, killed when his horse stumbled and threw him.) The remainder were, he said, welcomed with joy and surprise by King Malcolm and his brother-in-law, Edgar Atheling. Nor were Hereward's hopes in vain for they planned to muster a great force in the spring and strike deep into England.

That this plan was foiled by the Norman invasion of Scotland; that no blow was struck yet Malcolm agreed to be King William's vassal, sealing the pledge with the giving of eminent hostages, is chronicled elsewhere. But that Hereward was among these is not so widely known, his presence perhaps being eclipsed by the main prize, the atheling, who has since been seen at the King's court in Rouen. As for those who followed Hereward so faithfully, I have as yet discovered nothing certain. Maybe some went into exile, perhaps to join the Varangian guard like many renowned Englishmen. But others may have returned secretly to the district of Bourne. Indeed, it is a mark of how the King feared Hereward that after a year's imprisonment in England, he was moved to Normandy where there was little chance of his friends coming to his aid.

It is my hope therefore that this account, gathered over many days and set down as he told it, will help assure Hereward's place among the great. Had fate decreed otherwise he would now be among the highest in the land; if others had shared his resolve and foresight at the beginning, our fight against William of Normandy might have ended differently. But all is as God wills and we must make the best of it we can.

Written at Croyland Abbey in the year of our Lord 1084.

S. Pitt's family roots are in Ely and her mother, like Hereward, had odd-coloured eyes. This coincidence led to a life-long interest in Hereward, the Fens and their turbulent history. Readers who have enjoyed *Fen-wolf* may also be interested in her other historical fiction related to the region: *Cromwell's Promise* and *Four Wonders*, both set during the English Civil War.

Also by S. Pitt:

The Boy who found Salt

The Cove

Korunah's Gift

Trouwerner

Find out more at:

www.spittbooks.com